DATE DUE

5\7			
MAY 15 2014			
JUL 2 2 2014			
AUG 2 0 2014			
OCT 6 2014			
APR 0 7 2015			
SEP 1 5 2017			

Demco, Inc. 38-293

UNDER
A SILENT
MOON

A NOVEL

ELIZABETH
HAYNES

HARPER

www.harpercollins.com

For Samantha Bowles, who made this book so much better

HarperCollins books may be purchased for educational, business, or sales promotional use. For information, e-mail the Special Markets Department at SPsales@harpercollins.com.

This book is a work of fiction. The characters, incidents, and dialogue are drawn from the author's imagination and are not to be construed as real. Any resemblance to actual events or persons, living or dead, is entirely coincidental.

The illustrations in the appendix are courtesy of International Business Machines Corporation, © 2012 International Business Machines Corporation.

Originally published in a slightly different form in Great Britain in 2013 by Little, Brown.

FIRST U.S. EDITION PUBLISHED 2014

Designed by Fritz Metsch

Library of Congress Cataloging-in-Publication Data

Haynes, Elizabeth, [date]
Under a silent moon / Elizabeth Haynes.
pages cm
ISBN 978-0-06-227602-5 (hardback)
1. Women detectives—Fiction. 2. Murder—Investigation—Fiction.
3. Young women—Crimes against—Fiction. 4. Psychological fiction.
I. Title.
PR6108.A9677U53 2014
823'.92—dc23   2013026038

14 15 16 17 18   OV/RRD   10 9 8 7 6 5 4 3 2 1

Author's Note

In addition to the fictional case documents found in the text, charts produced by the Major Crime analyst for the Op Nettle investigation, created using IBM's Analyst's Notebook software, are available in an appendix at the end of the book. Additional documents can also be viewed online at www.op-nettle.info.

Although this book is intended to simulate an authentic murder investigation, all characters, locations, and situations are fictional.

MEMO FROM DETECTIVE CHIEF SUPERINTENDENT GORDON
BUCHANAN, BRIARSTONE POLICE

Officers currently engaged in the investigation into the murder of
Polly LEUCHARS (Op NETTLE) are as follows:

Detective Chief Inspector Louisa (Lou) SMITH—Senior
Investigating Officer
Detective Inspector Andy HAMILTON
Detective Sergeant Samantha (Sam) HOLLANDS

Investigating Officers and specified investigative roles:
Detective Constable Alastair (Ali) WHITMORE
Detective Constable Leslie (Les) FINNEGAN
Detective Constable Ronald (Ron) MITCHELL
Detective Constable Jane PHELPS—Exhibits & Disclosure
Officer
Detective Constable Miranda GREGSON—Family Liaison
Officer (FLO) deployed to the MAITLAND family
Detective Constable Barry HOLLOWAY—Incident Room
Reader-Receiver

Civilians attached to the investigation and their roles:
Jason MERCER—Analyst
Mandy JOHNSON—HOLMES Data Inputter

Op Nettle Interview Strategy Planning/ Persons of Interest
1. Hermitage Farm residents and employees:
Polly LEUCHARS—deceased, subject of Op Nettle
Nigel MAITLAND—farm owner
Felicity MAITLAND—manager of the stables at Hermitage Farm
Flora MAITLAND—their daughter, lives in Briarstone
Connor PETRIE—groom/farmhand, casual employee
2. Hayselden Barn residents/relatives:
Brian FLETCHER-NORMAN
Barbara FLETCHER-NORMAN (deceased)
Taryn LEWIS—daughter of Brian, lives in Briarstone
Chris LEWIS—Taryn's husband

09:41

DISPATCH LOG 1101-0132

- CALLER STATES SHE HAS FOUND HER FRIEND COVERED IN BLOOD NOT MOVING NOT BREATHING
- AMBULANCE ALREADY DISPATCHED—REF 01-914
- CALLER IS FELICITY MAITLAND, HERMITAGE FARM, CEMETERY LANE MORDEN—OCCUPATION FARM OWNER
- INJURED PARTY IDENTIFIED AS POLLY LUCAS, FAMILY FRIEND OF CALLER
- CALLER HYSTERICAL, TRYING TO GET LOCATION FROM HER
- ADDRESS YONDER COTTAGE CEMETERY LANE MORDEN VILLAGE
- LOCATION GIVEN AS OUTSIDE VILLAGE ON ROAD TO BRIARSTONE, PAST THE LEMON TREE PUB ON THE RIGHT-HAND SIDE
- SP CORRECTION POLLY LEUCHARS DOB 28/12/1984 AGED 27
- PATROLS AL23 AL11 AVAILABLE DISPATCHED
- DUTY INSPECTOR NOTED, WILL ATTEND

10:52

In years to come, Flora would remember this as the day of Before and After.

Before, she had been working on the canvas that had troubled her for nearly three months. She had reworked it so many times, had stared at it, loved it and hated it, often at the same time. On that Thursday it had gone well. The blue was right, finally, and while she had the sun slanting in even strips from the skylight overhead, she traced the lines with her brush delicately as though she were touching the softest human skin and not canvas.

The phone rang and at first she ignored it. When the answering machine kicked in, the caller rang off and then her mobile buzzed on the windowsill behind her. The caller display showed her father's mobile. She ignored it as she usually did. He was not someone she really wanted to talk to, after all.

Seconds later, the phone rang again. He wasn't going to give up.

"Dad? What is it? I'm working—"

That was the moment. And then it was After, and nothing was ever the same again.

11:08

Thursday had barely started and it was already proving to be a challenge for Lou Smith. Just after ten the call had come in from the boss, Detective Superintendent Buchanan. Area had called in a suspicious death and requested Major Crime's attendance. A month after her promotion, she was the DCI on duty, and it was her turn to lead the investigation.

"Probably nothing," Buchanan had said. "You can hand it back to Area if it looks like the boyfriend's done it, okay? Keep me updated."

Her heart was thudding as she'd disconnected the call. *Please, God, don't let me screw it up.*

Lou reached for the grubby *A–Z* on the shelf in the main office; it'd be a darn sight quicker than logging on to the mapping software. She couldn't remember ever having to go to Morden, which meant it was probably posh. The paramedics had turned up first and declared life well and truly extinct, waited for the patrols, and then buggered off on another call.

The patrols had done what they were supposed to do—look for the offender (no sign), manage the witnesses (only one so far, the woman who'd called it in), and preserve the scene (shut the door and stand outside). The Area DI had turned up shortly afterward, and it hadn't been more than ten minutes before he'd called the Major Crime superintendent. Which meant that this was clearly a murder, probably not domestic.

"Nasty," the DI said cheerfully when Lou got to Yonder Cottage. "Your first one, isn't it, ma'am? Good luck."

"Cheers."

Lou recognized him. He'd been one of the trainers when she'd been a probationer, which made the "ma'am" feel rather awkward.

"Where have you got to?" she asked.

"They've started the house-to-house," he responded. "Nothing so far. The woman who found her is in the kitchen up at the farmhouse with the family liaison. Mrs. Felicity Maitland. She owns the farm with her husband, Nigel—Nigel Maitland?"

The last two words were phrased as a question, implying that Lou should recognize the name. She did.

Maitland had associates who were known to be involved in organized crime in Briarstone and London. He'd been brought in for questioning on several occasions for different reasons; each time he'd given a "no comment" interview, or one where he stuck to one-word answers, in the company of his very expensive solicitor. Each time he had been polite, cooperative, as far as it went, and utterly unhelpful. Each time he had been released without charge. Circumstantial evidence, including his mobile phone number appearing on the itemized phone bill of three men who were eventually charged with armed robbery and conspiracy, had never amounted to enough to justify an arrest. Nevertheless, the links were there and officers in a number of departments were watching and waiting for him to make a mistake. In the meantime, Nigel went about his legitimate day job, running his farm and maintaining his expensive golf club membership, the horses, the Mercedes and the Land Rover and the Porsche convertible, and stayed one step ahead.

"Mrs. Maitland's in charge of the stables, leaves all the rest of it to her husband," the Area DI said. "The victim worked for them as a groom, lived here in the cottage rent free. I gather she was a family friend."

"Any word on an offender?"

"Nothing, so far. Apparently the victim lived on her own."

"What happened?"

"She's at the bottom of the stairs. Massive head trauma."

"Not a fall?"

"Definitely not a fall."

"Weapon?"

"Nothing obvious. CSI are on the way, apparently."

Yonder Cottage was a square, brick-built house separated from the main road by an overgrown hedge and an expanse of gravel, upon which a dark blue Nissan was parked. The scene tape stretched from the hedge to a birch tree; outside of this a roughly tarmacked driveway led up to a series of barns and outbuildings. Beyond this, apparently, was the main house of Hermitage Farm.

"Right," Lou said, more to herself than to anyone else, "let's get started."

Her phone was ringing. The cavalry was on the way.

To: DCI 10023 Louisa SMITH
From: DSupt 9143 Gordon BUCHANAN
Date: Thursday 1 November 2012
Subject: Op Nettle—Polly Leuchars

Louisa,
Hope the MIR is coming together. Ops Planning have given us the name Op Nettle for the murder of Polly Leuchars. Let me know if you need any further help.
Gordon

To: Central Analytical Team
From: DCI 10023 Louisa SMITH
Date: Thursday 1 November 2012
Subject: Op Nettle—analytical requirement

Could someone please contact me asap about providing an analyst for the Major Incident Room of Op Nettle. I have a full MIR team with the exception of an analyst and I have failed to reach anyone by phone.

DCI Louisa Smith
Major Crime

11:29

Julia Dobson, fifty-eight years old and current Ladies' Golf Champion at the Morden Golf and Country Club, pulled the heavy velvet curtain slightly to one side and peered out. From where she stood in the bay window of Lentonbury Manor—which was not actually a manor house, in much the same way as Seaview Cottage, a few yards further toward the village, did not actually have a sea view—she could see some distance up Cemetery Lane toward the entrance to Hermitage Farm on the left, and Hayselden Barn on the right.

"That makes three," she mused. "Good lord, what on earth is going on?"

Ralph, her husband, murmured in reply from behind his copy of the *Financial Times*, delivered by the newsagent's van an hour ago. They didn't have a paperboy anymore. The last one had nearly been run over by a tractor, and his mother had insisted he went and got a Saturday job at the greengrocer's instead.

"Ralph, you're not listening," she said peevishly.

"Three, you said," and then a moment later he shook his paper and looked up. "Three *what?*"

"Police cars, Ralph. Three police cars in the lane. The first one had the siren going. You must have heard it! I wonder what's going on?"

He put the paper down and joined her at the window, mug of coffee in one hand, in time to observe an ambulance driving at high speed down the lane. It turned into the driveway of Hayselden Barn, which was just within sight before the road bent sharply to the left. A police car rounded the bend from the opposite direction and followed the ambulance into the driveway.

"Barbara must have had one of her turns," Julia murmured.

"*Turns?*" he snorted. "That's a new word for it."

Julia set her lips into a thin line. "Well, there's only one way to find out." Without further ado, she retrieved the phone handset and dialed the number for Hermitage Farm.

12:45

Taryn stared at her screen, trying to catch the reflection of the activity that was going on in her boss's office, behind her and to her left.

"They're talking," Ellen said. She was sitting at the desk opposite and had a commanding view.

"Have they all sat down?" Taryn asked.

"No. Reg is sitting behind his desk, but the two police are just standing there. Oh, hold on, here we go . . ."

Taryn heard the office door open and couldn't help turning round to look. Reg was heading in her direction. The two police officers were still in the office. One was a woman, which indicated that whoever they were here to see was about to receive some bad news.

"Taryn, would you step into my office, please?" Reg said, giving her a look that should have been empathetic but was somehow the wrong side of slimy. He scuttled off in the direction of the kitchen. Maybe they'd told him to go and make a cup of tea—*first time for everything,* Taryn thought.

She entered the office and shut the door firmly behind her.

"Mrs. Lewis?" The male officer rose and introduced himself and his partner, but the names flew by her. "Would you like to take a seat?"

They sat too, and she wanted to say: Tell me now, tell me straightaway. But the words wouldn't come.

"We're here about your parents, Mrs. Lewis. I'm afraid it's bad news."

"My parents?" That was a word she hadn't heard used with any degree of accuracy since she was eleven years old.

"Mr. and Mrs. Fletcher-Norman—"

"Barbara Fletcher-Norman isn't my mother."

This clearly was news to the young police officer; he seemed to momentarily lose his thread.

"I'm sorry," Taryn said, "please go on."

"I—er—your father, Mr. Brian Fletcher-Norman, is in hospital, and I'm afraid he's seriously ill. Your stepmother, Mrs. Barbara Fletcher-Norman, was found dead earlier today. I'm very sorry."

Taryn looked at her hands. "Oh. I see. Thank you."

Now it was the female officer's turn. "Is there anyone we can contact to be with you? I understand this must be difficult for you."

"No. Thank you."

They seemed to be waiting for her to say something more, so she looked at them, in turn, and said, "Can I get back to work now?"

The officers exchanged glances.

Taryn felt sorry for them. "I don't get on with my father," she said patiently. "I haven't seen him for . . . a long time. Thank you for your kindness, but really, I'm fine."

She stood and the officers got to their feet in unison. At the door she stopped and turned. "Do you need me to do anything?"

The policewoman shook her head. "Not at the moment, Mrs. Lewis. But if you did decide to go and visit your father, he is in intensive care at Briarstone General."

"Thank you."

Taryn slid back into her seat just as Reg slopped a coffee onto her desk. I don't drink coffee, she thought, but Reg had never offered to make her a drink before so how would he know? She was trying to think when she had last been at the Barn. Maybe April? It had been the argument about the bike, and instead of making the effort to put things right she had left it, and then continued to leave it. It was the longest they'd gone without speaking.

"Well?" Ellen said, eyes eager. "What was all that about?"

"Oh. My father's in hospital, that's all."

"That's all? Goodness, are you all right? Shouldn't you take the rest of the day off?"

"No." She took a swig of the coffee despite herself, because it was there, and because her throat was horribly dry. "I haven't seen him for ages. We don't get along. So, really, I'm fine. And I'm sure he will be too."

Ellen had no reply to this, so she left it, although she did continue giving Taryn the occasional odd look over the top of her screen.

Despite her desire to get on with things, it was quite hard to concentrate after that. Only half an hour later did she remember what they'd said about Barbara. Had they really said she was dead?

13:02

Louisa sat on the edge of a table, her mobile pressed to her ear. All around her was chaos and next to her a telecom engineer plugged in a phone, which rang immediately. One of the DCs picked it up.

"Incident Room. She's on the phone, I'm afraid. Can I help? Who? Okay, what's your number there? Hold on; let me find a piece of paper. Right. Okay, I'll get her to call you."

It was amazing how quickly the room was coming together.

The first desk set up had been the reader-receiver's. Barry Holloway was there, monitoring everything coming into the room. Initial witness statements, intelligence reports, transcripts of calls from the public; nothing came in without first going through Barry. He checked everything, gave it an audit log number, decided how urgent it was and who should get it next.

Who should get it next was still up in the air. Desks were being pushed together, people arriving minutes after being assigned to the operation.

On a whiteboard behind her, Louisa had written a notice in foot-high black letters:

OP NETTLE

BRIEFING 1600HRS.

She checked her watch, wondering if it was out of line to task one of the DCs with going to the canteen, when finally there was a voice on the other end of the line.

"Senior analysts."

"Ah, so there *is* someone alive in there?"

"Yes, there is." The man's voice was decidedly chilly, and with an unexpected accent—American or Canadian? "Can I help you?"

"This is DCI Lou Smith. I'm waiting in the MIR for Op Nettle in the hope that we might get an analyst."

There was a pause.

"I'm sorry. Bear with me."

He didn't sound sorry. He sounded pissed off. There was a longer pause.

"Les?" Lou said, putting a hand over the mouthpiece. "Can you save my life and go and get me a double espresso? And a Kit Kat. Cheers."

Then, in her ear: "I'm afraid there's no one available today—they're all out."

What the fuck? Lou took a deep breath. "This is a murder investigation. What do you mean, there's no one available? There must be sixty bloody analysts, and I only want one!"

"Actually, since the reorganization there are in fact only thirty-two analysts and they are all assigned to other duties. I'm the only senior here, and—"

"What's your name?"

"Jason Mercer."

"Jason, *please*, find me someone in time for the briefing at four, and someone else who's prepared to do the late shift."

A heavy sigh. "For sure."

Definitely Canadian, Lou decided.

13:15

After.

Flora had spoken to her father and at the time she'd been calm, almost serene. She'd asked the right questions: When? How? And then she had put down the brush that was still in her hand, stared at the canvas that she knew already she would now never complete, and left.

When she drove past Yonder Cottage there were police cars blocking the drive, an ambulance on the gravel outside the house. The PC who was standing beside the fluttering tape in his fluorescent jacket regarded her closely.

She went on to the next turn, the main entrance to the farm. She drove up the driveway, which, at the top, curved round through the yard and back down toward the cottage. She parked outside the farm-house.

Flora's mother, Felicity Maitland, was sliding into comfortable oblivion. Nigel Maitland had poured her a tumbler of brandy in the hope of calming her down before she made it into a full-on panic attack.

Following her call to the police, Felicity had been looked after by the ambulance crew, and the police had taken an initial statement from her at the cottage. Then she'd been walked back to the farmhouse by someone in a uniform.

Now, hours later, Felicity was still in a state, vacillating between shuddering sobs and unnatural, staring stillness.

"It was so utterly horrible," she said now. "Blood all over the walls, everywhere! The whole place will have to be redecorated, and we only did it last summer."

There were times Flora wanted to slap her mother, hard. She went to make toast for everyone, not least to soak up the brandy. The plain-clothes police officer who'd been assigned to them was leaning against the breakfast bar, fiddling with her mobile phone.

"Would you like me to do that?" she asked, when Flora came in.

"No, it's fine, thanks. Do you want some tea?"

And at that moment Felicity's voice rose again in a wail: "Oh God! Who's going to do the horses?"

"I'll do them," said Nigel.

"Oh God! I'll have to put an advert in the paper, then it will be in-terviews! I can't bear it, I can't!"

"What about Connor, Dad?" Flora shouted. "I thought he was sup-posed to be a groom?"

Nigel didn't reply. Other than the phone call, he had not spoken directly to Flora.

"He can't be trusted," Felicity wailed. "Polly said he was always slacking off. I don't know why you insist on having him here, Nigel, he's more trouble than he's worth, and—"

"Oh for God's sake!" Flora called sharply. "I'll do the bloody horses."

The toaster popped up and Flora applied herself to the task of buttering, slicing into halves. Tea. Must make the tea. What had the police officer said to her offer, yes or no? She couldn't remember. She would make one anyway, not wanting to ask again, aware of the way the woman was watching her. Pretending to be here to help, but they were being watched, that was the truth of it. And right now the policewoman was watching *her*.

Flora could remember the exact moment of the exact day when she fell in love with Polly Leuchars. It was on the fifteenth of December, almost a year ago. Half past ten in the morning and Polly was sitting at the kitchen table in the farmhouse, her long blond hair pulled back in a tight ponytail, wearing a sweater, jeans, and thick socks. Her boots were on the mat.

"Where's my mum?" Flora asked, wondering who this was.

"Are you Flora? My, you've grown up since I last saw you," the person said, with a beautiful smile. "I'm Polly. You probably don't remember me. I've come to work."

It turned out that Felicity had known Polly was coming but had neglected to tell anyone else. Polly was the daughter of Cassandra Leuchars, an old school friend of Felicity's. Polly needed a job for a year or so before she went traveling. And when she was reminded, Flora remembered her from years ago, from family holidays when Cassandra had been abroad and had left Polly with them.

She was twenty-six, and the most beautiful thing Flora had ever seen. It was hard to believe that the thin, quiet blond girl who lurked on the fringes of her childhood memories could have turned into this lithe, confident, always-smiling young woman.

Who on earth would want to hurt Poll? Who could do it?

15:37

Nearly time for the briefing. Lou had asked Barry Holloway to do most of the talking for the first one. Not, strictly speaking, the way it was usually done, but to his credit he didn't argue or ask her to explain. She wanted to watch the room, keep an eye on them all, see their reactions—gauge from it who she could use, who she would need to keep an eye on.

The room was almost ready—it had previously been the central ticketing office, but they'd been moved to the new Traffic Unit two weeks ago. Fortunately, as it turned out, because the room usually reserved for MIRs was already in use. There had been three armed robberies in the space of a month, a bank manager and a member of the public shot dead, and the investigation for that was well under way.

In a way this room was better, Lou realized; the area briefing room was right next door, which meant they could use it without having to lug all the equipment back and forth, and the canteen was just up the corridor. The only downside was that the only windows looked out onto a brick wall. And the nearest custody suite was a few miles away in Briarstone nick, which wasn't ideal, but no one asked anyone who was ever actually affected by these management decisions what they thought.

A knock on the door of her goldfish-bowl office, which was right in the corner; Mandy, one of the HOLMES inputters. "More for you," she said, handing over another pile of papers to add to the collection.

"Thanks. How's it looking out there?"

"Well," Mandy said, with a discreet cough, "were you expecting DI Hamilton?"

"Oh shit." Lou felt the blood drain from her cheeks. "What's he doing here? I asked for Rob Jefferson."

"Apparently DI Jefferson's done his back in. Sorry. Thought you should know."

Lou pulled herself together and managed a smile. "Thanks. All the photos ready?"

Mandy nodded, and left her to it.

Fucking Andy Hamilton—that was all she needed. Another knock at the door, and Lou looked up to see Andy's bulky frame filling the glass window. She took a deep breath and beckoned him in.

"Guv," Andy acknowledged, giving her his best charming smile.

She regarded him steadily. He'd put on weight since she'd last seen him, but he was still attractive, that dark hair and dark, neatly trimmed goatee. Eyes that were wicked, that suggested imminent misbehavior.

"Andy. How are you?"

"Great, thanks. You're looking . . . well." His eyes had managed to travel from her new shoes, up her legs, to her face, within a fraction of a second.

She gave him a smile so tight it pinched. "We've got a briefing in twenty minutes. Have you got a desk?"

"I'll find one. It's going to be great working with you again, Lou." He was disarmingly relaxed. Not fair.

"How's Karen? And the kids?"

Andy's expression tensed, but only slightly. "They're all fine."

"Is Leah sleeping through yet?"

"Not quite. We have the odd good night here and there."

"This is going to be a tough case, Andy. If you're finding it difficult fitting it around home, I want to know about it, okay? I can't have you not with us a hundred percent on this."

"You know me, Boss. Loads of energy and up for anything." He finished with his cheekiest grin, and a wink.

Lou felt something twist inside her. She looked up at him. "Strictly work, Andy, okay?"

"Sure thing." And he was gone.

But he had always had trouble taking no for an answer.

15:40

Flora pulled her cold Wellington boots on over her thick socks in the mudroom at the back door.

"Can I come with you?" the policewoman asked, appearing in the doorway.

"Sure," Flora said, her tone unnaturally bright. "You'll need boots. Here, try these."

The woman slipped off her shoes and pulled Felicity's old boots up over the cuffs of her smart gray trousers. "They'll do," she said.

"What's your name?" Flora asked, giving in at last.

"Miranda Gregson," came the reply.

As soon as she heard the name Flora remembered it. "Of course. Sorry."

"That's okay. It's a difficult time."

She gave Miranda one of her father's jackets to wear and they set off toward the stables. It was already starting to get dark, a wind blustering and swirling around the farm buildings, tugging at their clothes.

"I used to go riding when I was younger," Miranda said. "I helped out at some stables on weekends. Loved it."

Flora didn't answer. Given a choice, she would much prefer to work with this woman over Connor Petrie. Nigel had phoned him twenty minutes ago and told him to get his arse down to the stables. He'd been somewhere else, clearly, even though he was supposed to be working.

Petrie, leaning against the horsebox, gave them a wave as they approached. "Who's this, then?"

"This is one of the police officers," Flora said quickly. "Miranda."

"You here about Polly?" he asked. "Boss told me. Lots of blood everywhere, right?"

"Shut up!" Flora snapped at him. "Have some bloody respect. You're here to work."

"I'm the family liaison officer," Miranda said, her tone even. "Here to help, if I can." She offered her hand, and after some shuffling and wiping, Connor gave it a brief shake.

Oh God, this was no good. The ugly little bastard was going to have her crying in a minute. She had come out here to try and take her mind off the subject of Polly's death, lose herself in mindless physical activity. She walked away from them to the hayloft. Connor could talk to the police all he wanted, she wouldn't be there to listen. Didn't care anymore, in any case.

MG11 WITNESS STATEMENT	
Section 1—Witness Details	
NAME:	Felicity Jane Elizabeth MAITLAND
DOB (if under 18; if over 18 state "Over 18")	Over 18

ADDRESS:	Hermitage Farm	OCCUPATION:	Farm manager/housewife
	Cemetery Lane		
	Morden		
	Briarstone		

Section 2—Investigating Officer

DATE:	Thursday 1 November
OIC:	DS 10194 Samantha HOLLANDS

Section 3—Text of Statement

My name is Felicity Maitland and I own and run Hermitage Farm, together with my husband Nigel. My main role is running the stables. We have five horses, three of which are liveries, the remaining two belong to us.

Polly Leuchars is a family friend and has been working with us since December last year, looking after the horses. As part of the arrangement we allowed Polly to live at Yonder Cottage, which is part of the farm estate. She was expected to be working with us for another few months, after which she was planning on going abroad. I do not know where to.

On Wednesday 31 October Polly came to work as normal. She asked if she could go into town at lunchtime, and I agreed. She offered to do some shopping for me as well. She left in her car at about 12.30. I did not see her again until 3, when I saw her riding out in the top field.

I saw her return a couple of hours later through my kitchen window and I went to the stables to talk to her. She said she had been unable to get the things I wanted. I was very disappointed, as I could have gone into town myself if she had told me sooner. We had a bit of an argument about it. She left without finishing off the work in the stables, claiming she had a headache. The last time I saw her alive was around 5.30.

The next morning Polly was due to start work at 7 but at about 9 I noticed that the horses weren't out in the back field, so I went down to see what was happening. Polly wasn't there. The horses were quite agitated as they usually have breakfast by 8. I fed them and let them out into the field. After that I went to Yonder Cottage to see where she was. By the time I got there it was probably gone 9.30.

I noticed Polly's car was in its usual place and the back door to the cottage, which we use as the main entrance since it is nearer the road, was wide open. It opens into the kitchen and I could see blood there. I called out several times but there was no response. I was very frightened. I went to go through to the stairs. The door to the hallway was not completely shut, but I needed to push it open in order to go through.

I could see a body on the floor, right by the door, and a lot of blood everywhere. I almost fell over the body, which I recognized as that of Polly Leuchars by the color of her hair and her build.

I went back into the kitchen and used the phone there to dial 999.

I did not notice if anything was missing from the house and I do not know why anyone would want to kill Polly.

Section 4—Signatures

WITNESS: (Felicity Maitland)   OIC: (S Hollands DS 10194)

15:57

"Right, let's have some hush, please," Lou said, hoping her voice sounded more commanding than she felt. The briefing room was packed. Andy Hamilton was sitting right at the front; next to him was Barry Holloway. Her detective sergeant, Sam Hollands, was right at the back, her mouth set in a determined line. Lou knew she would probably never have so many people at a briefing again; by the time the first week was over, she would start to lose people to other duties and would have to beg, borrow, or steal to get them back. If, heaven forbid, the case was to drag on into months, she would end up with only a couple of the people here now.

She needed a quick arrest.

A few moments before her mobile had rung. The display said it was the superintendent, probably calling for a prebriefing update, or maybe to wish her luck with it. Whatever it was, she would have to ring him afterward. Being late for the briefing would not be a promising start.

She was quietly relieved at how quickly silence had descended on the room. She wasn't going to get too many chances to find her place at the head of this team.

"For those of you I've not met, I am DCI Louisa Smith. I'm going to give you some background, and then I'll hand over to Barry, who will get us all up to speed on where we are now. Firstly, let me say that if you have any problems here I want you to feel you can come and see me or call me at any time. We all need a swift result with this one. And, as you're aware, this is a murder inquiry, and anything you hear

in this briefing may be of a sensitive nature, so please keep it to yourselves." The standard warning.

Clicking the down arrow on her laptop, the first slide:

OP NETTLE
Murder of Polly LEUCHARS

With a picture of Polly herself, taken earlier in the year; it was a
poignant photograph because she looked so young, so alive, beautiful,
in a fresh, carefree sort of way, with long white-blond hair and tanned
skin from spending the summer outdoors.

"This morning at just after nine-forty, Polly Leuchars's body was
found by her employer at her home, Yonder Cottage, Cemetery Lane,
Morden. Polly worked as a groom at Hermitage Farm and lived in the
cottage because she was a family friend of the Maitlands, who, as we
all know, own and run Hermitage Farm."

A few murmurs.

"Polly was on the floor in the downstairs hallway and had been severely beaten. She was wearing pajamas and her bed had been slept in.
Early estimates from the pathologist put the time of death as between
midnight and four, although this needs to be confirmed."

Lou looked at the sea of faces. She still had their undivided attention
and some of the late shift were busy making notes. "Right. Over to
you, Barry. For those of you who don't know, Barry Holloway is our
reader-receiver."

"Guv."

Lou stepped to one side of the projection screen, watching the
room.

Barry fiddled with the laptop. "Anyone not happy with scene photos, look away now, folks. Otherwise I'll warn you when we get to the
really grim ones."

The first slide came up, a picture of the kitchen of Yonder Cottage.
Blood on the floor, on the work surfaces.

"Good news and bad news so far. The good news: we've probably
got forensics all over the place. Nothing confirmed until we get the CSI

report back, but for now spatter marks indicate the main attack took place downstairs in the hallway. No sign of forced entry but apparently the back door wasn't routinely locked. No sign of the murder weapon, and we're waiting for confirmation of what that could be. Something solid and heavy, in any case."

The slides clicked over to the stairs. "We've got some good shoe marks, and a smeared handprint. Likelihood of fingerprints is pretty good. Brace yourselves for the next few, if you're squeamish."

Next slide, the hallway, stairway to the rear. Body in situ.

Click. Close-up on what remained of Polly Leuchars. She was face-down, one arm up near her head, the other by her side, one knee brought up, wearing cotton pajamas, patches of pink still visible in all the dark brown and red; flashes of still-blond hair; white bone showing through.

Click. The side of Polly's face, swollen purple skin in the places where you could actually see the skin. What could have been bruising under a still perfect shell-like ear.

Someone in the room let out a long breath; otherwise there was silence.

"As you can see, this is a nasty one. There's not a lot of Polly's head left. We had to get initial identification from the Maitlands via some jewelry, although Felicity Maitland assumed it was Polly from her size and her hair. Extensive blood loss here, here, and over here."

Lou looked across at the faces earnestly taking in the bloody scene on display and trying not to show emotion. They'd all seen stuff like this before, but it didn't mean they were unaffected by it.

"Postmortem hopefully tomorrow. We'll have to wait until then for the first thoughts. Guv."

"Thanks, Barry." Lou resumed her place and flipped on to the next slide. "This is where we are now. We have an initial witness statement from Felicity Maitland. Sam's been in touch with Miranda Gregson, who is our FLO. She's been with the family all afternoon. How are they, Sam?"

Sam Hollands, stockily built with a sweep of heavy blond hair, spoke up from the back. "Felicity Maitland is in a bad way and her husband keeps feeding her alcohol, which isn't helping. Flora, their daughter, has been looking after everyone, not saying much. She's got a flat in Briarstone."

"What about Polly's parents?"

"The mother, Cassandra Leuchars, died a few years ago. I asked about Polly's father but nobody seems to know who that is."

A hand went up at the back. "Ma'am?"

"Yes?" Lou didn't know this one. A brown-haired chap, older.

"DC Ron Mitchell. We just had reports come in of another body being found this morning, might be linked to this—did you get that already?"

Lou hated to be wrong-footed, especially in a briefing. "Thanks, Ron, could you enlighten us, please?"

"I got a report from Briarstone nick. They've been dealing with a suspected suicide, complicated by the husband of the deceased keeling over with a heart attack when a patrol went round to break the news. Dog walker saw a car had gone over the quarry cliff at Ambleside, called it in. Initial patrol and paramedics went down via the access track. Too ropey for cars, unfortunately, so they got down there on foot. After that it took a while to get the rescue team to get some climbing gear down there. Anyway, there's a woman's body in the driver's seat of the car. Bit of a mess. The car's a silver Corsa, late model. Registration in the name of a Mrs. Barbara Fletcher-Norman, address Hayselden Barn, Cemetery Lane, Morden—right across the road from Hermitage Farm."

That got everyone's attention.

"What happened with the husband?" Lou said.

"They got to the address and the old man was getting out of the shower. Said he thought his wife had gone out early, that he got back from work late last night and went to bed, assumed she was out with friends. So he hadn't seen her since yesterday morning when he left for work."

"Right," said Lou, not sure where this was heading.

"Well, then it gets interesting." Ron, loving the attention, flipped over the pages of his notebook with a flourish. "They went into the kitchen with him, and there's what looks like blood in there. Not all over the place, but the kitchen's a mess, and there's blood on a tea towel by the sink. Husband seems dead shocked by this. Claims he never went into the kitchen last night or this morning. Pretty soon he starts having trouble breathing, then all of a sudden he goes gray and collapses. They called for Eden District Ambulance Trust and did CPR in the meantime but it was a few minutes before the ambulance got there. I think it was the one that had been up at the cottage."

Lou looked across the faces for someone reliable and unfortunately alighted on Andy Hamilton. The call from Buchanan must have been about this. What were the chances? Two bodies from adjacent properties, on the same morning, in a tiny place like Morden? They *had* to be linked.

"Andy, they'll probably open a second case for this, even though it might be part of our job. Can you find out who's in charge and see if you can take it on? We won't be able to get a search team or CSI in there but we need to make sure the Barn is sealed off until we can treat it as a scene. We don't know it's linked, but I think for now we should assume it is."

"Ma'am." Andy smiled warmly, clearly pleased with himself for landing a juicy job.

"Ron, anything else?"

"Briarstone ran a next-of-kin check through the old boy's work and the only name they came up with was a Mrs. Taryn Lewis, daughter of Brian Fletcher-Norman, the husband. Turns out she's not spoken to her father for months. That's about where we've got to."

"Where is this place in relation to our cottage, exactly?"

"A hundred yards or so away, no more."

"Right." Lou digested the information, working out the best step forward with it. "Thanks, Ron. How's Mr. Fletcher-Norman doing, do we know?"

"He's in intensive care in Briarstone General. Not looking too bright. Be lucky to get an interview anytime soon."

"And what about the body in the car?"

"Waiting for PM."

"Thanks, Ron. I'll leave that one with you."

Ron was slightly red in the face. Lou guessed it had been a good few years since he'd been able to play a trump card in an initial briefing. "Barry? Back to you. How's the intel looking?"

Barry Holloway was the most experienced member of her team as far as Major Crime was concerned. He'd been the reader in more MIRs than she could count.

"Thanks. Right. Pin your ears back, chaps. We've got a witness who thinks he saw a car going over the cliff last night. That came in on the box while you were talking, ma'am. And something from Crimestoppers. An anonymous caller saying Polly Leuchars was having an affair with someone in the village. Another Crimestoppers call suggesting we might want to look closer at the Fletcher-Normans— well, we're ahead of the game on that one. Mrs. Maitland says that Polly went on a shopping trip to Briarstone yesterday lunchtime, was gone three hours or so. We'll get CCTV, see if we can track her movements. I had a look on ANPR for Polly's plates—no results unfortunately, but then the back road into Briarstone isn't covered unless the mobile camera unit happens to be there. We've got a sighting of Polly in the Lemon Tree last night. She left before closing time, so we'll need to interview the regulars, see who she was meeting. And two reports of a car revving and driving away at speed during the night not far from the cottage. We'll get more tomorrow morning after the press conference."

"Right." Lou had almost forgotten that she was going to be broadcast to the nation tomorrow morning and felt a lurch of nausea at the prospect. It would be nice to be able to go to the press conference with a firm picture of what had happened to their victim.

"Can we see what the latest is on Nigel Maitland?"

"Already checked that," Barry said. "Nothing recent. I've got a source tasking in."

"What about the house-to-house?"

"Jane Phelps is organizing that; she's still out there with Les. I spoke to her before we came in, and it's all village gossip so far, no dramas. She said she'd ring in when they're done. Patrols did most of it this morning before we got there, anyway. She's going round again to make sure."

"Thanks. Well, that's about it for now. Any questions?"

Murmurs, everyone itching to get on with it.

"Right. Next briefing tomorrow morning, eight sharp. I'm talking to the press at nine, so let's see if we can stay ahead of them. Okay. Let's go."

A moment of quiet, and then the shuffling of chairs, rustling of papers, laughter, voices. A few handshakes, people who'd been off working other areas and found themselves back on the team together.

Lou let out a long, slow breath, dealt with the few people who came up to her afterward with comments, suggestions, or ideas that they hadn't felt brave enough to pipe up with in the briefing.

Then there was only one person left, someone she didn't know, leaning casually against the back wall, arms crossed, giving her his complete and undivided attention. He had dark hair, broad shoulders, and—most disconcerting of all—a black eye.

"Can I help you?" she asked, wondering with a snap of fear if someone had been in the briefing who shouldn't have been.

"I'm Jason Mercer."

She'd forgotten the name but there was no mistaking that accent. Shit! Had she been really rude to him on the phone earlier? A warm flush spreading across her cheeks, she decided there was only one way to play this: pretend it never happened.

"Hi. Did you have any luck finding me an analyst?" she asked, shaking his hand. His was warm, his grip firm. He looked her in the eye, held her gaze. The dark bruise, a smudge across the bridge of his nose, made the green of his eyes more striking.

"Yes and no—I'm afraid you've got *me*."

"Well, thank you. I'm glad you're here. Did you get everything you needed from the briefing?"

"I think so. Presumably you want a network, timeline, that sort of thing?"

"Yes, please."

"What about the phones?"

"Jane Phelps is going to be the exhibits officer. When she's back later I'll get a list of them for you. She's already put the applications in for the records of all of the phones we have. We didn't find Polly's phone at the cottage, unfortunately, but we've got the number from the Maitlands."

She led him out of the briefing room, stopping at Barry Holloway's desk to introduce them. But they had worked together on a case before and shook hands briefly.

"We've got you a desk sorted out and the workstations all loaded and ready to go," Barry said.

"Can you brief me tomorrow morning?" Lou asked. "Before the press conference?"

Jason looked her straight in the eye once again. "Sure. I'll see what I can do."

Turning away, walking back to her poky little office, Lou wondered why her heart was pounding and her skin felt as if it were on fire.

16:10

When Flora got back, Miranda Gregson and Petrie were nowhere to be found. She began mucking out the stables, managing to hold herself together as long as she didn't think about Polly doing this and now never doing it again. She kept her eyes on the wet straw and horseshit, shoveling it into the wheelbarrow and then over to the heap.

"Flora!"

Flora groaned. He was back. Connor-bloody-Petrie.

"Where have you been?" she said, not looking up until his green Wellingtons appeared in her line of vision, directly in her way.

He was standing with his hands in his pockets, looking casual and jolly as if he owned the stables and felt the need to supervise his own personal shit shoveler. "I was giving that nice police lady a tour of the farm," he said. "None of you lot bothered to do that, did you?"

"Where is she now?"

"Back in the kitchen."

"You're in the way," she said.

He didn't move, but his weasel smile dropped from his face, making him look decidedly nasty—which he was. But as well as being an evil bastard, he was also a foot shorter than Flora and she wasn't afraid of him.

"What you doin' here, anyway? You don't even live here."

She put down the fork and leaned on it. "What does it look like I'm doing?"

"Looks like you're taking your time about it, if you ask me," he said.

"I'm not," she said. "And you should be doing this. It *is* your job. Grab the barrow and give me a hand."

"Not me. Your dad's got important stuff for me to do today."

"What important stuff?"

He tapped the side of his pointed nose conspiratorially. "None of your business, Flora. You keep mucking out like a good girl and I'll come back later and check you done it right."

That was it. Enough.

She dropped the fork. It clattered and bounced off the concrete yard, but Flora didn't even hear the noise because by that time Petrie was facedown in the muck, Flora's knee in his back. She had him by the scruff of his too big, hand-me-down waxed jacket that made him feel so self-important. He was shouting as best he could, calling out: "No, no! Lemme up! You stupid bi-bi-bitch!"

"Flora! Let him up."

She took her knee off his back and turned to see her father in the yard.

"Nige!" Petrie was shouting, wiping his face and pulling bits of straw and manure from the front of his jacket. "You see what she did? Did ya see? Bitch!"

He made a move toward Flora, but Nigel stepped forward and Petrie backed off immediately.

"You're fine, Connor," he said, calmly. "Go and wash your hands and face."

Petrie complied, looking daggers at Flora as he made his way round the yard toward the offices at the end. "Fuckin' cow," he muttered.

"Feel better?" Nigel asked, when Petrie was out of the way.

"He's a piece of crap. Why do you bother with him? He doesn't want to work, he's a lazy little bastard."

"I know. But he has his uses."

"Polly hated him," Flora said, and then stopped short.

"Polly tolerated him," Nigel said.

A single tear fell, taking her by surprise. She turned back to the stables, wiping her face angrily. She wasn't going to cry in front of him, that was for sure.

"Come on, Flora. Let's go and have a drink. All right?"

"I need to get this done," she said. "Nobody else is going to do it, are they?"

He stood for a moment watching her, haunting her peripheral vision, and then he turned and left her to it.

One more stable to do, and then she could go and walk. Clear her head.

17:54

Over the course of the afternoon, police came and went at Hermitage Farm. Flora finished at the stables and left Connor to bring the horses in. It was dark by that time, so she gave up on the walk and stayed in the kitchen, making endless cups of tea.

Felicity sat holding court as various neighbors came to call and talk about the trauma. Miranda Gregson loitered, making detailed notes of all the visitors, who they were, where they lived, taking contact phone numbers should the police wish to ask them further questions.

At a quarter to six the one Flora remembered as Sam came back again. She had an air of kindness about her, patient with Felicity despite all the dithering and rambling.

When the madness had isolated itself into the room that held her mother, Flora slipped upstairs to the bathroom and tried to phone Taryn. She wanted to tell her about Polly, but also that it seemed something was going on at the Barn too. None of the police officers had said anything, but there had been an ambulance and police cars over there since late morning. Maybe Polly had been the victim of a burglary or robbery that went wrong and the same thing had happened over at the Barn?

It was pointless to speculate. Taryn's phone number went unanswered, and her mobile phone was switched off.

"Flora? Flora?" shouted her mother. "Flora? They want to take our fingerprints—and our DNA!"

She returned to the kitchen, heart thudding.

"It's fine," said Sam, gently. It was as if she could tell that Flora was feeling the loss more than the rest of them. "It's routine. We expect *your* prints to be in the cottage; it's the ones we don't expect to find that we're interested in. We need to take yours for elimination purposes."

And there, on the table, an ink pad, a roller, sheets of paper, plastic sealable bags. Her mother at the sink, already scrubbing at her fingertips with the Fairy Liquid and a pan scourer.

Nigel came in as Sam was explaining the process to Flora: fingerprints, then cheek swabs for the DNA.

"You can forget about taking mine for now; I want to speak to my solicitor first," her father said and went to the office to make a phone call. By the time he came back Flora was washing her hands.

"I'd like it to be noted that I'm cooperating fully," he said to Sam.

"I'm happy to note that."

Flora watched her father as he allowed the officer to manipulate his fingers, one by one, against the ink pad. He must be hating this, hating having them here. He was hiding it well, though, and it was something she had always grudgingly admired—the more difficult the circumstances, the more he turned on the charm, the easy, relaxed confidence.

And the oddest thing: Flora, with nothing at all to hide, felt nervy and guilty and afraid, while Nigel, with the most to fear, was as relaxed and confident as she'd ever seen him.

MG11 WITNESS STATEMENT	
Section 1—Witness Details	
NAME:	Richard John HARRISON
DOB (if under 18; if over 18 state "Over 18") Over 18	

| ADDRESS: | 35 Priory Acre
Morden
Briarstone | OCCUPATION: Retired | |

Section 2—Investigating Officer

| DATE: | Thursday 1 November |
| OIC: | DC 8745 Alastair WHITMORE |

Section 3—Text of Statement

I am a retired accountant and I live in the village of Morden. On the morning of Thursday 1 November I was walking my Jack Russell, Lima, on the Downs outside the village. Our usual walk takes us across the fields to the old quarry at Ambleside, skirting round the top of the quarry, and then back home.

I left home at around 6.30. It was still quite dark but by the time we reached the quarry it was fairly light. I estimate that we were there no later than seven.

When we reached Ambleside quarry Lima ran off into the bushes, barking. I believed she was chasing a rabbit and I followed her because I didn't want her to go over the edge of the quarry. When I cleared the bushes I noticed that there was a car lying on its roof at the foot of the cliff on the far side of the quarry. I believe this is directly under where the car park is situated.

I could not see what make of car it was, except that it was silver in color. I do not believe the car had been there yesterday when we took our walk as I would have noticed it.

I called out in case someone was trapped in the car, shouting that I was going to get help.

I walked back to the path where I found Lima waiting for me. I attached her lead and walked quickly home, where I phoned for the police and an ambulance.

Section 4—Signatures

WITNESS: (R Harrison)   OIC: (A Whitmore)

20:39

It was heading toward nine, and Lou was reaching the point where nothing more could be usefully done until the morning. She would grab a takeaway on the way home—her stomach was growling and she realized she hadn't eaten anything since the Kit Kat she'd had in the morning.

"I thought you said the witness saw the car go over the cliff?" she asked Ron when the statement came back.

"Sorry, ma'am, it was third-hand info by the time I got it. We know it definitely happened overnight, though. The countryside warden says it wasn't there at six the night before. PM on the body should tell us more."

"Do we have any idea when that's going to be?"

"I've asked for it to be prioritized and linked it to Op Nettle. Might have it by the morning if we're lucky. They recovered the body and the car."

Back in her office, she braced herself to phone Andy Hamilton's mobile. Went through the motions of looking it up on the Force Directory, even though she knew it off by heart.

"Andy, it's me," she said when he answered.

"Yeah," he said.

Of course. He knew her number as well as she knew his. God, this was so awkward; she was glad she'd managed to push him aside to the other body. With a bit of luck, the two cases would be completely unrelated and she could get another DI in.

Could she ever be that lucky? Of course not.

"Area are desperate to get rid of this one, Boss. They've been on to Mr. Buchanan, claiming it's definitely linked to Hermitage Farm. I think we're going to have to take it."

Shit! *Shit!* She'd completely forgotten to phone the superintendent back. She would have to do it the minute she got off the phone.

"Have they got any actual evidence linking it?"

"Witness statements to say that Brian Fletcher-Norman was having an affair with Polly Leuchars. Witness statements going on about how unstable Barbara—that's our body in the quarry—was, how she was jealous, an alcoholic."

"Evidence, Andy? Rather than village gossip?"

"Nothing yet. I reckon Barbara went over to confront Polly about her affair with Brian, got riled up enough to kill her, then went back to the Barn. Washed her hands, was overcome with remorse, drove drunk to the quarry, and went over. Accidentally on purpose."

"Thanks for that, Sherlock."

"You're welcome."

"If you know anything more by tomorrow morning, come to the briefing?"

"Wouldn't miss it."

Every little thing felt like flirting where Hamilton was concerned. Did he do it to everyone, or just to Lou? And how did you stamp your authority on the working relationship when there was this sort of history between you? Two months ago she'd been a DI, and his ranking equal. When it had happened, she'd been his sergeant. Her swift rise to DCI was all to do with her grim determination to get her head down and concentrate on work rather than let herself be distracted by men, or one man in particular—Andy Hamilton.

Sooner or later she was going to have to have a chat with him. It wasn't going to be pleasant, but it had to be better than this.

She dialed the number for Mr. Buchanan's secretary. No answer, of course, not at this time of night. She tried the mobile, and got the answering service.

"Sir, Lou Smith. Sorry I didn't get back to you earlier. I'm guessing you were calling about the second case in Morden. I've sent Andy Hamilton over to establish links, if there are any. Hope this is okay. If you need me, the mobile's on, otherwise I'll brief you tomorrow first thing. Thanks. Bye."

With luck, Buchanan wouldn't phone back tonight.

The next person on the list was Jane Phelps, who had finally made it back to the office. Lou had worked with Jane before, had confidence in her.

"How's the house-to-house?"

Jane waved a small pile of papers. "All done for now. Area had covered most of it before we got there. Lots of people seem to be away on holiday—it's that sort of place, weekenders and well-off families. And I tell you what, some of these women who sit at home all day planning lunch parties—it feels like all they want to do is gossip about their neighbors. You wouldn't believe some of the things they've come up with."

"I think I know what you're going to say, but carry on, I like a good goss."

"Well . . ." Jane rifled through the pages, handwritten at this stage. "Mrs. Newbury at Willow Cottage, she seems to think Polly was having an affair with Nigel Maitland. Apparently he's the reason she came here to work."

Lou raised her eyebrows.

"Marjorie Baker from Esperance Villa—honestly, I'm not making it up—seems to think it was Brian Fletcher-Norman that Polly was seeing. Saw Brian coming out of Yonder Cottage once late at night when she went round there to deliver a Christian Aid leaflet or something."

Just as Hamilton had said: Polly Leuchars and the man from the Barn across the road. But Nigel Maitland as well?

"Have we got anything we can actually use?"

"The next house along, toward the pub, is Rowe House. Occupant's a Mr. Wright, a weekender from London. He's staying for the week with his two children because of it being half term. Says he was woken up at two fifteen by the noise of a car driving along the lane at speed. Didn't look out of his window, went back to sleep."

"Okay. Let's get a proper statement from him. Remind me, where does that lane end up if you follow it in that direction?"

"Takes you to the crossroads, then straight over would be toward Briarstone. The other way would be out toward Baysbury."

"Any ANPR cameras on that road?"

"Afraid not."

"Too much to hope for, I guess."

"It's really quiet, that area. I've been looking at the crime data—hardly anything goes on down there. Most of the traffic seems to be related to the farm."

"I need to get a nice map," Lou said absently, wondering whether the analyst had gone home already.

21:04

Drifting in and out of consciousness was at times a delicious and a devastating thing, Brian thought. You saw faces, not knowing if they were real or imagined, a thought came and then it was gone, voices came and went . . .

"Have we located any next of kin?"

"Police found a daughter, we are waiting for more from them."

Music . . . light and dark . . . pain . . .

Taryn. Where was Taryn? Suzanne . . . Polly . . . ?

And darkness.

21:05

Andy Hamilton pulled out of the hospital car park and headed through the rain toward home, wondering if there was any chance Karen would have cooked something for him, or if he should stop and get a kebab. He could have phoned her, of course, but that would risk waking Leah, who might, with a bit of luck, have gone off to sleep. He'd sent a text an hour ago, letting Karen know that he was going to be a bit late. No reply had been forthcoming.

In the end his car seemed to pull in of its own accord to the parade of shops where the Attila Kebab House and Pizzeria's bright lights beckoned, and a few minutes later he was back in the car, a steaming polystyrene carton warming his thighs. He picked at bits of grilled chicken, wiping them in the chili sauce that dribbled out of the edges of the pita, thinking about Detective Chief Inspector Louisa Smith.

It wasn't the first time he'd seen her since it happened, but it was the first time they'd worked together. Was it awkward? Not for him. She was looking even better these days, or was it this new brisk air of authority about her that made her even more of an exciting challenge?

I'd go there again, he thought.

Outside the off-license a little crowd of the usual halfwits had gathered, and he kept a contemplative eye on them while he crammed the pita in. They were here all the time. Patrols got bored with coming out here night after night, sending them on their way, getting all the verbal abuse that went with it, only to be called out again by the shop-keeper an hour later because they were back, throwing stones and beer cans around and shouting obscenities. It was putting off her regular customers, Mrs. Kumar complained. It was bad for business.

Neighborhood was supposed to be putting together a dispersal zone. In the meantime, the local arseholes sat on Mrs. Kumar's storage unit, spat great gobs of phlegm at the pavement, and shouted incomprehensible twaddle at each other and at passersby.

If they did something really bad, he'd have to get out of the car, kebab or no kebab.

He watched one of them, a skinny lad with a shaved head, wearing a vest—a *vest*, for crying out loud, it was November—push one of the girls on the shoulder, hard enough to knock her off her perch on the metal barrier. She kept to her feet but immediately turned to square up to him, her fist brought back behind her ear.

"Oh, no," Andy groaned, "don't be a muppet."

The skinhead in the vest, one of the Petrie family, judging by the extensive monobrow and weaselly chin, was laughing at the girl, pointing. Her mate, squeezed into too-tight white jeans with some appropriate word sequinned across the arse, shouted back at him, wobbled her head and waved her hands, ghetto style, and for some reason, that seemed to be more of a legitimate challenge because the halfwit backed off then, hands up in mock surrender.

Two minutes later the skinhead was snogging the face off the girl who'd nearly punched him and Andy had finished his kebab.

21:53

There was no one in the Intel Unit. The late-shift officers were all out on a job, and Lou went back to her desk and sent an email to the Source Handling Unit to try and hurry up the latest on Nigel Maitland, copying her email to Ali Whitmore.

It would be a bonus, Lou thought, if she could be the one to nail Maitland, the smarmy bastard. She had met him once, and charming and handsome as he was—hair graying at the temples, light-blue eyes with plenty going on behind them, a warm smile—she'd been wary of him. And it might have been a whopping great coincidence that this young woman, who may or may not have been having sex with her employer and "family friend" who was not quite twice her age, ended up with her skull smashed to pieces on Nigel Maitland's property: or it might just be the mistake that would finally see him brought down.

The MIR was still active, but there weren't many people left. Behind some screens and a long table supporting fax machine, scanner, color printer, and black-and-white printer, Jason Mercer was still hard at work. There was something about him that was making her feel . . . odd. Yet he wasn't especially good-looking, although he was tall and probably had a good body underneath his meticulously ironed shirt. He held himself with an easy confidence, as though he were here for fun, yet at the same time he was clearly very focused on what he was doing. And he had agreed to work on her team even when he obviously hadn't wanted to.

"Hello," said Lou, smiling as he started. "Sorry—didn't mean to make you jump."

He leaned back in his chair and stretched his arms above his head. "I hadn't noticed it getting dark." He checked his watch. "My God!"

"What time did you get to work this morning?" Lou found herself perched on the edge of the desk opposite, tugging at her skirt.

"Half past seven. Oh, well." He gave her a smile. "I daresay your day has been at least as long and twice as stressful. Are you going home?"

Lou nodded. "The mortuary first, to see if there's any update or if they need anything from us. After that, home. I need sleep, otherwise I won't be able to function at all tomorrow. How are you getting on?"

"Fine so far," Jason said. "Do you want me to brief you now, or can you wait for the morning?"

"Tomorrow will be fine. I will have to find some way to contain my excitement until then. By the way, what happened to your eye?"

It must have been a corker when it was still swollen but now it was a purplish smudge under his right eye with a tiny cut on the bridge of his nose. She'd been dying to ask ever since she'd first laid eyes on him at the briefing.

"I play hockey," he said. And then added, as he must have had to do every single time someone asked, which was probably several times a day: "Ice hockey."

"Ah," Lou replied, as if that explained everything.

"Did you find out about the phones?" he asked.

Shit. "Sorry. I saw Jane briefly but we were talking about the house-to-house. Have you checked the coms folder on the computer?"

"Still empty."

"I'll give her a call, hold on." Lou headed back to her office to grab the mobile but he called her back.

"Don't worry, it can wait till morning. I don't especially want to start on it at this time of night, anyway."

He stood up and stretched, pulling his jacket off the back of his chair.

22:12

The reception desk at Briarstone General Hospital was empty, the flower kiosk shut, the only activity was around the vending machines but Lou knew where she was going. The public mortuary.

She rang the bell on the door that was tucked away, its only identification the simple word MORTUARY. After an age, an assistant appeared. She recognized Lou but still checked her warrant card before letting her in.

"Dr. Francis has just finished. You're lucky to catch her."

Adele Francis was in the staff room, changing out of her scrubs and wellies into a smart skirt and high heels.

"Hi, Adele," Lou said. "Sorry, I don't want to keep you. I know it's been a long day. I wanted to check if you've got everything you need."

Adele did look tired, but she managed a smile. "Yes, thanks. You can walk me to the car park if you like and we can talk on the way. I've got a date with a bottle of wine and I'm late already."

They went out a door marked FIRE EXIT ONLY which was a shortcut out to the fresh air.

"Not bad going, two bodies already. How's your first MIR?"

"Okay so far, I think. And the second body isn't officially mine yet."

"Well, I'm not convinced the two are linked by anything more than location. You're going to have to wait for the blood results to confirm it."

"Anything you can tell me that might help? I've got the press conference tomorrow morning."

"Polly Leuchars died of head injuries, multiple trauma with a blunt instrument, plenty of force needed, very aggressive. Someone had had a go at strangling her first. Bruises around the neck, possibly enough to render her unconscious. She was still alive when the head injuries occurred."

"Time of death?"

"I'd say between midnight and two, no later. There was some evidence of older injuries which may be worth considering in your investigation."

Lou stopped. "Older injuries?"

"Healing bruises, mainly. Some around the wrists, barely visible unless you've got the best sort of light."

"So she'd been restrained?"

"Possibly. Not recently, but within the last week or two. She was a horsewoman, wasn't she?"

"She worked as a groom, yes."

Adele considered this. "I saw similar bruises around the wrists and lower arms of a child once. She'd been thrown at a gymkhana. Had wound the reins around her wrists. So don't go jumping to any premature conclusions, Chief Inspector."

"I'll try not to," Lou said, then added: "What about Mrs. Fletcher-Norman?"

"Yes, that one was interesting. I only got her late this afternoon. Do you happen to know if she was wearing her seat belt when she was found?"

"I'll ask. We're waiting on the CSI photographs."

"I did phone earlier; someone was going to call me back. Never mind. I'll do the PM tomorrow and let you have the report as soon as I can."

"Thank you."

They had stopped beside a silver BMW, parked in a designated bay in the staff zone, the one reserved for consultants and senior management.

"Enjoy your wine—I think I might pick some up myself."

Lou paused at the main entrance, then on a whim walked all the way back to the Intensive Care Unit. She showed her warrant card, said she was here to check on Mr. Fletcher-Norman's progress. She waited for twenty minutes while they found someone who was prepared to commit to an update, even a vague one.

Still unconscious. Nothing further.

That's it, she thought. I'm going home.

23:14

After work, Taryn had phoned the hospital to check if her father was still alive. They'd suggested she should come in, that he was still in a critical state but might respond to her voice. Fat chance of that, she thought, but after speaking to her husband, Chris, she had gone in anyway.

She was surprised at how old he looked without his glasses on, his eyes closed, and tubes and monitors everywhere. He was wearing one of those hospital gowns and his skin was pink, the hair on his head was white and tufty, not neatly groomed. He looked frail and vulnerable, not like him at all. From this position she could see there were marks like yellowing bruises on the top of his right arm. Maybe he got them when they were trying to keep his heart going—wasn't it supposed to be really brutal? Or maybe Barbara had been beating him up; Taryn wouldn't have put it past her.

The last time she'd seen him had been at the Barn. He had been complaining about the bike she'd bought him last Christmas. It wasn't right for his needs, apparently, even though it had been the one he had chosen from some enthusiasts' magazine, and she had gone round to look at it.

Barbara had opened the door to her.

"Oh. It's you. Well, you'd better come in."

Her father was in his armchair, reading the *Telegraph*, paisley-patterned feet up on the footstool.

"Good heavens," he'd said, peering at her. "What the hell is that thing you're wearing?"

"It's a poncho, Dad. I've come about the bike."

"It makes your legs look enormous," he said. "You'd be better off with a long coat."

She'd taken a deep breath in, and repeated slowly: "I've come about the bike."

"It's outside, next to the garage," he said. "You'll have to take it back."

"What's the matter with it?"

"Gears keep slipping," he said from behind the newspaper.

"What? What do you mean?"

He lowered the newspaper slowly and looked at her over the tops of his reading glasses. "It's a road bike, Taryn."

She remembered the feeling bubbling up inside her, the frustration and the misery of being spoken to like that. How long would she have to put up with it? "I know what it is. It's the one you asked for. The one you picked out of the magazine!"

"I don't want a road bike, I don't enjoy cycling on the roads. If I wanted to cycle on the roads I would have asked for a road bike, wouldn't I? I can't ride that thing through the countryside. It's not suitable. It's not appropriate."

His voice rose over the course of the outburst until he was on the verge of shouting, his face flushed to a deep crimson.

She stared at him for a moment, counting to ten. Then fifteen. Then she looked away, defeated. "All right. I'll see if I can trade it in for a different one."

Her father shook the creases out of the newspaper. The matter was closed, resolved to his satisfaction, for the time being at least. He always won. If he didn't win, he would carry on and on until he could claim the victory in another way.

She'd gone out to the garage and looked at the bike, leaning miserably against the wall with the front wheel turned out at an odd angle, as though it had been casually tossed aside and had slumped down under the weight of its own inadequacies.

It had started to rain by then and she was wondering whether she could fit the bike in if she put the seats down in the car, when Barbara came to the back door with a bag full of bottles for the recycling bin.

"I'll see you, then," Taryn had said, with an attempt at a cheerful wave.

"What? You're not coming back, are you?"

"No. I just meant—never mind."

Head down against the rain, she'd gone round to the front as the back door slammed shut. She spent a good twenty minutes trying to fit the bike into the car, scraping the skin on her ankle with a pedal, getting grease on her hands and her new wool poncho and the fabric of the backseat, blinded by tears and hating herself for bothering with them; the pair of them, they were as bad as each other. Hateful people!

The next day she had taken the bike back to the shop where she'd bought it, at considerable expense since it wasn't the cheapest. And despite his protests that it didn't meet his needs, he had chosen this one specifically, which made it all the more frustrating.

"He says the gears keep slipping," she'd said.

They took the bike back to examine it and then phoned Taryn at work to tell her the good news. The gears were fine.

When she went back to the shop she asked if there was any way she could exchange it for a mountain bike. The manager showed her round the mountain bike selection and told her he would give her a trade-in value for the road bike. Less than half what she'd paid, and the mountain bikes were much more expensive.

She had wheeled the bike out of the shop and spent another twenty minutes fighting to get it back into her car. Subsequently she chose a Friday lunchtime, when she could be reasonably certain that Barbara would be playing tennis and her father would be at his office, and dumped the bike round the back of the barn. Then put a note through the letterbox, explaining that she couldn't exchange it, she had tried, and if he wanted to buy himself a mountain bike that was up to him. She had signed it simply "T," no niceties. And that had been it.

But she'd been working up to seeing him again, working up to contacting him, knowing that the immovable boundary of Christmas was approaching and that someone would have to break the silence and say something about letting bygones be bygones, blood being thicker than water, the wrong time of year to be holding grudges, all of that old nonsense that would still be directed at her as though she were the guilty party.

And now Barbara was dead, and her father was breathing through a machine. She tried to feel sorry. She even tried to feel happy, but that didn't work either. She couldn't seem to feel anything apart from tired.

What she had wanted to hear was that he was dead. It was bad of her, very bad, to wish something like that, but it didn't stop her wishing. And if he was going to die, she wanted it to happen soon so she wouldn't have to keep going back, day after day. She wanted it to be over with.

Day Two
Friday 2 November 2012

00:52

Flora was in a bar in town, numbing everything from her lips to her heart with alcohol and loud music. At some point she would walk back to the studio, sleep there. Not the flat. It was too full of Polly's presence, the ghost of her.

Flora could have stayed at the farm; her mother had specifically asked.

"What if I need you, Flora?"

"Need me for what, exactly?" It was like speaking to a petulant child. When she'd been at the wine, their roles were often reversed.

"But what about the horses?"

"The horses are fine. Dad's here, and that Petrie idiot, if you need him."

"But Flora . . . Polly . . ."

More tears. It wouldn't have been so bad if the tears had been for Polly, but they were selfish ones: Felicity was cross that her life had been thrown upside down, that her home had been invaded by police, that Polly had gone and got herself killed and made such a mess in the cottage. And the only way to deal with it was to make it all about herself.

Her mother was pathetic, frustrating, but her father was worse. There was a calmness about him that felt dangerous. The more pressure he felt, the more relaxed he seemed, and today, when they had been taking his fingerprints, police in his house, he had been almost casual. Flora knew how his moods worked, how his temper built, masked by the composure, until a point of no return had been reached. Then his fury was explosive.

Flora left the farm without saying goodbye. They were all busy, anyway.

She'd been approached in the bar several times, propositioned, turned them away. The last one, a bloke twice her size who had also consumed more than his fair share of alcohol, got aggressive when she turned him down, called her a "frigid fucking bitch." The door staff ejected him, and then came back and asked her to leave too. She'd had enough anyway by then.

The studio was echoing in silence, the only sound the buzzing inside her own head. She curled up on the old sofa, pulled a dust sheet over herself, and sobbed until sleep took her.

05:30

The alarm rang at five thirty, too early, still deeply dark. Lou pressed the snooze button and allowed herself another few minutes. She would feel better after she had been in the shower. As soon as the alarm rang again she got out of bed. If she was late today she would never live it down.

Her mobile was charging downstairs, and already there were two missed calls. One from Andy Hamilton's mobile, late last night, and one from the office. Nothing on voice mail, so nothing urgent.

Her mind was starting to race ahead. Results from the initial inquiries would be pouring in to the MIR today. Once she had finished the press conference and the results were aired, broadcast, printed, and published, even more would come in. Of course, a lot of it would be worse than useless—the cranks, the would-be investigators, the psychics, the people who only wanted to be helpful, and somewhere, in among it all, would be the crucial bits of information that would lead them to the person who took Polly's life.

Briefly she wondered about the Fletcher-Normans. Of course it could be something straightforward, with no connection to the Polly Leuchars murder other than a horrible coincidence of time and location. But it felt like an uneasy tangle of events. The forensics would help to sort out one case from the other, and Jason's reports, once they started to come through. She was lucky to have him; not any old analyst, since they were in such short supply, but one of the seniors. Unhelpful as he'd been during that initial phone call, it was clear that he knew what he was doing, and he was committed enough to the investigation to put in the hours. They weren't all like that.

Hope I get to keep him, Lou thought.

07:14

From somewhere far away, Flora could hear her phone ringing. In her dreams she kept answering it, only for there to be no one on the other end.

"Polly?" She woke herself up saying the name out loud, then, as she realized that her mobile was ringing, it stopped.

Moments later it rang again.

"What." Her voice sounded like it was a long way off, even to her.

"Flora. It's me. Are you okay?"

Taryn, at last! Her best friend, the only person who would understand the devastation . . .

"Oh, Tabby . . ." Tears started. Only moments since she'd opened her eyes and everything was there despite the headache thumping inside her skull. Polly was dead, Polly was dead . . .

"Flora? What's the matter? I know about Dad, if that's what you were calling about. The police came round to work yesterday. I got your messages and—"

"Polly's dead."

"Polly? What? Flora, how?"

Flora took a moment, a few deep breaths to steady herself, prepare her voice. "She was murdered, Tabs. Someone hit her on the head. The night before last. They don't know who. I've been trying to ring you, but there were so many people at the farm, and Mum's gone mental, of course."

Shocked silence, then: "Barbara's dead too!"

"What? How? And what's happened to your dad?"

"I don't know about Barbara, I didn't wait for them to tell me. I suppose it was a car crash or something. Dad had a heart attack. He's in the hospital—they said he's critical but they don't know him, do they? He's a tough old sod . . ." Her voice trailed off. And then: "I didn't realize. Poor, poor Flora, I'm so sorry about Polly."

"There's been nobody I can talk to about it. Mum—well, you know what she's like. And she found her—Polly, I mean. Oh, Tabs, I missed you so much yesterday."

"Where are you? Do you want me to come round now?"

Flora ran a hand through her hair. "No, I've got to go back to the farm. Maybe—could I come round to yours later? I can't go back to the flat, and I certainly don't want to stay with *them*. Would you mind? And what about Chris?"

"Chris won't mind at all. Have you still got the spare key?"

"Yes." She had moved in for a fortnight in the summer, when Chris and Taryn had gone to France on holiday, to water the plants, keep an eye on things.

"Well, come round whenever you like. I'll make the spare bed up later. And, Flora, it will be all right, okay? Everything will work out."

No, it won't, Flora thought. How can it be? Nothing could ever be all right again. But what she managed to say was, "Okay. Thanks."

"Deep breaths, Flora. Yeah? You have to get through this bit. This is the difficult part."

"At least you haven't said I told you so."

"What do you mean?"

"You always said she would break my heart . . ."

There was a pause. The tears were blinding Flora, pouring down her cheeks. She rubbed them away with the back of her hand, sniffed.

"I didn't mean like this," Taryn said quietly.

"You never really liked her, did you?"

"You know why that was," Taryn said, with emphasis.

"She wasn't flirting with Chris," Flora said, remembering Taryn's housewarming dinner party.

"She absolutely bloody was. She flirted with *everyone*, Flora, you know she did."

"That's—that's simply how she was."

"She wasn't good enough for you. There. I've said it."

Flora couldn't speak. It was too much. She hated herself for the high-pitched wail that she couldn't hold in anymore.

"Oh, Flora, I'm sorry. But you know what she was like; you deserve to be treated better than that. She was beautiful, but you deserve someone who is going to put *you* first, someone who is going to love you properly. I'd rather be honest with you—and I know she hurt you. It wasn't fair."

After a moment she got control of herself again. "Yes," she said. Not meaning it.

"Will you be okay?"

"Yeah, sure."

"I'll see you later? And you can ring me anytime."

She said goodbye and rang off, just in time for the tears to overwhelm her again.

07:52

The Op Nettle MIR was buzzing, full of people, and it wasn't even eight.

The press packet for the briefing was the first item on Lou's agenda. The media officer had started preparing it yesterday, had obtained photographs of Polly Leuchars and her car, written up a statement. First thing this morning the color copiers on the command floor would be churning it out for the press conference.

Back in the Incident Room, the first bit of news from forensics was a pile of fingerprint idents.

"Right, what have we got?" Lou asked, flipping through the pages. Jason was peering over her shoulder. He had on some very subtle aftershave. God, what was the matter with her? It wasn't as though she needed any distractions.

The first three pages were fingerprints taken from Yonder Cottage. Fingerprints identified were those of Polly Leuchars (all over the house), Felicity Maitland (downstairs only, including the downstairs bathroom), Flora Maitland (all over the house). Several other sets, some recent. And three clear prints made in blood, indicating someone present in the house when Polly was already dead or dying.

"Oh, crap!" Lou said, reading the final sentence again.

Prints in blood belong to Mrs. Barbara Fletcher-Norman (print idents taken from cadaver). Others unidentified.

"Well, at least we know it's definitely connected," Lou said.

A few pages further on, mention of shoe marks, badly smudged, at Yonder Cottage, a small size, indicating a child or a woman.

A few pages further on, fingerprints taken from inside Polly Leuchars's car, which had been parked, locked, in the driveway to the cottage.

"Prints belonging to the victim, Nigel Maitland, and three unidentified sets. That's a bit odd, don't you think?"

"Is it?" Jason replied.

"Well, how many different sets do you think would be in your car?"

Jason thought for a moment, his skin flushing. "Well, quite a few. I had the car fixed a couple of weeks ago. Could have been several mechanics working on it, right?"

"Hmm, fair point, I guess." Lou made a note; someone would have to check the car's service history, get a list of people who were insured to drive it. "Wonder why Nigel's prints are in there? He has better cars to drive than hers."

"Maybe it was in the way and he moved it."

"Maybe." Next report, forwarded from Andy Hamilton—the prints from inside the kitchen of the Fletcher-Normans: two sets, his and hers. No others.

"We need Brian to wake up," Lou said.

"The phone data is coming through," Jason said. "I need to start work on that."

"Will it take long?"

"You're a hard taskmaster."

When she looked up he was giving her a smile. Cheeky.

"Damn right I am. You'd better get busy before I start thinking up penalties for slacking."

07:57

Detective Superintendent Gordon Buchanan had descended like the Lord Almighty from the command floor to attend Lou's second briefing.

A small man, he made up for his lack of stature with a personality that demanded full attention, rewarded it with hearty good wishes, and punished the lack of it with a merciless bellowing that put the fear of God into all those unfortunate enough to find themselves on the receiving end. Lou had worked for him on a previous case, had been lucky enough to spot something that should have been glaringly obvious but which everyone else had missed. She took it to her colleagues first, who were grateful that she'd not taken the matter straight to Buchanan himself. They'd worked through the case, but somehow Buchanan had got wind of what had happened and had had a soft spot for her ever since. He valued hard work and bright intelligence, and she was there ready to dish out both in spades.

In addition, she wasn't half-bad-looking either, and as everyone knew, Gordon Buchanan liked his ladies.

He sat at the front, facing the room, a reminder that there would be hell on a stick if anyone made any unfortunate cock-up, and that if things went well there might be future glory for whoever made the vital breakthrough that helped bring Polly Leuchars's killer to justice.

Lou was supposed to have offered some sort of prebriefing briefing for him, but she had been too busy. As she strode into the room ahead of everyone else she mouthed an apology. Buchanan pointedly looked at his watch as though things were running behind schedule and he was a very busy man, but Lou was on time and she knew it. Her priority was the investigation, in any case, not sucking up to the boss.

"Sir," she said, "thanks for coming. I appreciate it."

"Not at all," he said, melting. For someone with such a lot of front, he was very easily buttered up. "How's it going?"

"Rather well, I think," Lou said, "but it's very early days."

"Thanks for your voice mail last night. I'm afraid you're going to get the other case too, by the look of it. However, I've managed to get you a couple more DCs, for now."

Andy Hamilton was sitting behind Buchanan, chatting happily to Ali Whitmore, one of the DCs who'd been working on the Fletcher-Norman case yesterday. Who was the other one?

Lou had a PowerPoint presentation that Jason had knocked together for her with bullet points which had already emerged from the investigation.

"Right, thanks, everyone, let's get on with it," she said.

First slide, the Op Nettle title slide.

"Okay, we've got the initial pathology report back which tells us that Polly was killed between midnight and two, no later than that. Priority for me is to trace her exact movements on the evening before she died. Andy, can you give us an update on the Fletcher-Normans?"

Andy coughed to make sure he had everyone's full attention. "Right. Well, I understand we're working on the possibility of the cases being linked. If you weren't here yesterday, come and see me and I can give you an update after the briefing. To summarize: Barbara Fletcher-Norman was found around the same time as Polly. She was in her car at the bottom of Ambleside Quarry. We're still waiting on the full PM report, which should be later today. Patrol reported that when they went to give the death message to Brian Fletcher-Norman, there was blood in the kitchen of Hayselden Barn, as if someone had washed their hands in the sink. The Barn's been sealed since then, but until now we've not had the powers to go in. However, the CSI report from Yonder Cottage shows Barbara Fletcher-Norman's bloody fingerprints in the kitchen and the hallway. She was in the cottage when Polly was dead or dying, and so we have a suspect, albeit a dead one."

There was a little murmur from the people in the room.

"Thanks," Lou said. "Les, did you get back to Dr. Francis about the seat belt?"

Les peered round Andy Hamilton. "Yeah. She had half fallen out of it when she was hanging upside down, but it was in place. I'm off back to the hospital in a minute for the rest of the PM."

"When can we get CSI into the Barn—do we know?"

"Later today. Simon Hughes is going to be the senior."

Lou had all but forgotten that Buchanan was there; this was one of her favorite bits of the job, bringing everything together, prioritizing, making sure that things got done and nothing was left out.

"Okay. Our priority for today is to find out what the connection was between Polly Leuchars and the Fletcher-Normans. How's Miranda getting on with the Maitlands—anyone know?"

Jane Phelps said, "She's still there. There seems to be plenty of people paying visits to the farm. Nigel Maitland claims he was out all day, came home late, last saw Polly a few days ago. He won't say anything else without his solicitor."

"And the daughter?"

"She seems to be the most sensible one in the house, shame she doesn't live there."

Lou thought for a moment. "We should talk to her properly, I think. Get to know her a bit." She looked around for a suitable person, aware that allocating tasks was something she should trust to her sergeant— old habits were dying hard. "Andy, can you take that for me?"

He looked up in surprise. Did he think he'd done his bit?

"I've got meetings—I was going to brief the CSIs, sort out the Fletcher-Normans."

He was trying it on, Lou thought. She took a deep breath. "Nevertheless, since you're going to be across the road from the farm most of the day, I'd appreciate it if you'd take a moment to talk to Flora."

"Jane's going to be at the farm all day."

An embarrassed hush descended on the briefing room and for a moment they all faded into the background, even Buchanan, until it was just her and Andy, facing each other. It reminded her of the last confrontation they'd had, when she'd been in tears and he'd been tender, gentle with her, pleading. She hadn't backed down then, either.

There was a cough and Ali Whitmore raised a hand. "Ma'am, I'd like to take that one, if I can? I've worked on Nigel Maitland before, so I might be able to bring something to that line of inquiry . . . if it would help?"

Andy kept up the hard stare but didn't say anything else. It was tempting to push him to take the job but he'd been thrown a lifeline by Whitmore. Really, that had been embarrassing and unprofessional. He should have known better, and the room was charged with excitement now, as if they'd all enjoyed the little argument.

"That would be really helpful, Ali, thank you. Which brings us neatly on to intel," Lou said briskly. "Barry—anything useful?"

"We should be getting some stuff in this morning. One thing that did stand out for me, though, is that on the list of the farm employees is one Mr. Connor Petrie. He's showing as a casual farmhand-slash-groom. Been there since March."

"Connor Petrie?" Lou echoed.

"One of the younger Petries. Son of Gavin Petrie and Emma Payswick, charming couple that they are."

Lou smiled. "Well, at least this one seems to have a job. But, Ali, can you find out how Mr. Petrie came to be employed by Nigel Maitland? That seems like an odd combination. You might need to put in a request for more intel. Anyone else interesting on the list, Barry?"

He shook his head. "They've got a cleaner for the farmhouse, comes twice a week, various people who work with Nigel on the farm side of it, mostly casuals, but nobody jumps out. We're working our way through them."

She had one eye on the clock—half an hour to go until she was in front of the press.

"Jane, how are we doing with the phones?"

"We don't have Polly's phone—wasn't in the cottage—but we've got Felicity's and Nigel's, although from the casual way he handed it over I would imagine it's clean. I don't know about the ones from the Barn, though."

"Andy?"

He looked pissed off. "I'll get back to you on that one. Leave it with me."

"I will," Lou said. "I want billings and cellsite for both their mobiles. Landline billing too."

"I've already applied for billings from the farm," Jane said.

"Thanks, Jane. Can you make sure Jason's down as the appointed analyst?"

"I've done that."

"Great. Where are we up to? I'm conscious of the time, so any urgent questions?"

She scanned the room, looking for hands, for confusion in the faces, and her eyes stopped when she got to Jason. He was looking right back at her, attentive, interested. That was a good sign, at least.

08:21

BT151—Message left on 01596 652144

Hello, this is a message for Mrs. Taryn Lewis from Sister Roberts of the Lionel Gibbins Ward, Briarstone General Hospital to let you know that your father has regained consciousness. Could you call me, please, on 921000, extension 9142. Thank you.

PRESS RELEASE

Statement prepared by Eleanor Baker, Media Officer for Eden Police, Briarstone Police Station

Briarstone Police are appealing for witnesses following the murder of Polly Leuchars in the early hours of 1 November. Polly was a regular at the Lemon Tree public house in Morden and had visited the pub on the evening of 31 October, Halloween. Police would urgently like to speak to anyone who saw Polly in the pub that evening, or who may have any other information that might help the investigation.

"We're trying to build up an accurate picture of Polly's last day," said Detective Chief Inspector Louisa Smith, leading the investigation. "In particular, we don't know who Polly was meeting. Was it you? If so, I urge you to come forward now so that you can be eliminated from our inquiries."

Twenty-seven-year-old Polly Leuchars was found at her home, Yonder Cottage, Cemetery Lane, Morden, on the morning of

1 November. She had been brutally assaulted and was pronounced dead at the scene.

Anyone with any information is asked to contact the Incident Room directly on 01596 555612. Alternatively, you can call Crimestoppers anonymously on 0800 555 111.

- END-

08:58

"Andy," Lou said.

He was disappearing out of the briefing room, quicker to his feet than any of the others. He froze when he heard his name.

"My office."

She went back to the MIR next door, hoping he was following but determined not to look back at the arrogant piece of shit.

He came in behind her and closed the door. He didn't move to sit and she didn't request it. Instead they stood facing each other, the space in the small office made still smaller by his bulk. Even though she was wearing heels, he towered over her.

She waited for a moment, composing herself and wondering how on earth she was going to do this, and at the same time as being angry with him—*furious*—she realized that this was the closest they'd been since everything had happened and she could feel the warmth from his body, and her body was reacting to it in spite of herself.

"I'm sorry," he said, unprompted. "It was unprofessional."

"Yes," she said. "It was."

He started to say something else, then stopped.

"What?" she said. "Say it."

"You should have known Ali Whitmore would have wanted to take that side of it. He did the last job on Maitland when he was in intel."

"I'm not bloody psychic!"

"Well, it all worked out for the best, then, didn't it?"

"I don't want you playing games like that again. I don't do pissing contests."

In spite of her fury, Andy smirked. Damn the man! How was it possible to hate him so much and still find him attractive?

His shoulders had relaxed and he leaned forward slightly. "It wasn't that long ago that we were proper friends, Lou . . ."

She didn't need reminding of it. "Is that what you call it? Felt more like betrayal than friendship."

"I didn't mean that. I just meant—sometimes I forget you're in charge. And I'm sorry."

"It doesn't matter what rank I am, what rank you are," Lou said. "We're here to do a job, aren't we?"

"Sure."

She waited for more, half-expecting him to bring up the one big subject that they were both ignoring, but he remained silent.

"I think we should leave it there. Now are you doing the press briefing with me, or are you too busy?" She smiled, to soften the sarcasm, and to her relief he took a deep breath and smiled back.

Opening the door of her office, the silence in the main room despite the number of people crowded into it made her realize that they'd probably all been watching through the glass, straining to hear.

She took five minutes in the ladies' to apply some lipstick and run a brush through her hair. Her cheeks were pink, her eyes staring back at her, challenging her to admit to the crushing weight of self-doubt that she was feeling. Why this case? Why not something nice and straightforward, like every other Major Crime job that had turned up in the last few months?

You asked for it, her reflection suggested insolently.

The main conference room at Police Headquarters was full: lots of cameras being set up at the back, press of varying types chatting happily together as if they were all best friends.

Lou had had media training as part of the three-week Senior Investigating Officer's program. They'd staged a press conference at which various police staff pretended to be members of the press, asking the most awful questions they could, with some sort of internal competition to see who could be the one to "break" the poor trainee. They'd got the police photographer in with his big camera to flash away while they were talking. Part of the test was to see if you could remember to set the ground rules for the press conference before it started—no flash photography until the end, all mobile phones turned off, no questions until the end of the briefing. If you failed to do this, you'd have mobile phones going off left, right, and center; flashing in your eyes the whole time; questions fired at you from the back of the room with no warning. You'd lose control of the room, lose your thread, lose your marbles.

"Good morning, ladies and gentlemen," Lou said in a voice that sounded more confident than she felt. "Thank you all for coming. My name is Detective Chief Inspector Louisa Smith and I am the officer in charge of this investigation. Before we begin, can I ask you please to turn all your mobile phones off? Thank you. There will be time for photographs at the end of the press conference, so I would ask you to refrain from flash photography until then. I would like to introduce my colleague Detective Inspector Andy Hamilton—I will run through a brief summary of the pertinent points of the investigation, and then DI Hamilton and I will be happy to take your questions. We will also be issuing you with a press pack at the end of the briefing which contains photographs that can be used in your reports, together with a written statement. There are also telephone numbers for the Incident Room, which I would be grateful if you could make public for the benefit of those people who may have information for us so they can contact us directly. Thank you."

She moved to the chart stand on one side of the table where she and Andy were sitting and flipped over the top sheet to reveal a photograph of Polly Leuchars, happy, smiling, blond hair blowing away from her tanned face. How fortunate it was for the investigation that the murder of good-looking people always received more press attention than the murder of the unlovely. Lou had worked on the killing of a middle-aged prostitute and drug addict, back in the days when she was a new DC at the Met. They'd held a series of press conferences, and after the first one almost nobody came. None of their readers would be likely to know anything that would help anyway, one arrogant old hack had told her, as though they moved in certain circles and remained untainted by the detritus of life that floated past.

"We are currently investigating the brutal murder of a young woman," Lou began, turning to face her audience and standing in front of the table behind which Andy sat. She knew it was much harder to be intimidated by your surroundings when you were standing up with no barrier between you and your audience.

"Polly Leuchars was twenty-seven years old, and was working as a groom at Hermitage Farm in Morden to earn some money to go traveling. In the early hours of Thursday, the first of November, Polly was violently assaulted in the hallway of her home, Yonder Cottage, which is part of the Hermitage Farm estate on Cemetery Lane. We are anxious to get a clearer picture of the events of Wednesday, thirty-first October, particularly in the evening, and we would like to appeal to anyone who has any information concerning where Polly might have been, and who she may have spoken to, on the day before she died. If anyone saw Polly's vehicle, which is a blue Nissan Micra, I would ask them please to come forward and speak to a member of the investigation team as soon as possible."

There was silence as Lou scanned the journalists, some watching her intently, some busy scribbling notes.

"I would like to emphasize that we are dealing with the murder of a popular young woman who had her whole life ahead of her. Her family and friends are needlessly dealing with her loss, and our feelings and thoughts are with all of them at this tragic time. If anyone has any information that might help us find out who was responsible for this crime, I would ask them to come forward and contact us as soon as they can."

Lou paused. Then, "Thank you for your attention. Are there any questions?" While she waited for them to decide which was their most pressing question, she took her seat next to Andy. They'd agreed to take it in turns answering, and the media officer was in charge now.

"Yes—lady in the pink top."

Hers wasn't the first hand to go up, but Lou knew that this particular journalist had been promised the first question because of a recent favorable article she'd written regarding the Force's response to antisocial behavior.

"Alison Hargreaves, *Eden Evening Standard*. DCI Smith, can you tell us anything about the death of Mrs. Barbara Fletcher-Norman? Are the two deaths connected?"

Lou felt her cheeks flush.

"Thank you," she said, "we are not connecting the two incidents at this time. Next question."

There was a sudden buzz as all the other journalists started wondering who the hell Mrs. Barbara Fletcher-Norman was.

"Do you have any suspects at this stage?" This was from the local BBC Radio reporter.

Andy answered. "At this key early stage of the investigation, we are keeping an open mind about who the perpetrator of the crime was."

"Roger Phillips, *Daily Mail*. Any idea of a motive at this stage?"

Good question, thought Lou, and Andy was going to deal with this one too.

"Again, we are keeping an open mind. We cannot rule out the possibility that the victim woke in the night to find a burglary in progress."

"Were there signs of a break-in?" Roger Phillips again.

"Next question," Lou put in. She was only being fair—there were several other people with their hands up and she didn't want the inquiry to be pushed in one direction, especially not at this early stage.

"What about forensics? Have you got any fingerprints, stuff like that?" This one was from Lucy Arbuthnot, from the local ITV news network.

"Several sets of fingerprints have been identified at Polly's home address. We are in the process of eliminating them as we speak. If anyone visited Polly in the days before her death, we would be grateful if they would come forward so we can eliminate them from our investigations." Lou was ready for something made of chocolate. It felt like the longest day of her life, and she was only a tiny bit of the way through it.

"This is a question for Ms. Smith. Can I ask about your personal qualifications to lead a murder inquiry?" It was Roger Phillips, revenge for her failing to answer the break-in question.

Both Andy and Ellie, the media officer, looked like they were going to try and fight in her corner, but she silenced them with a look.

"Thank you for that question," she said with a wide smile that made it look as if she meant it. "I have been a police officer for fifteen years, the last eight of them spent working on major crime investigations. Although this is the first time I have led a murder inquiry, I have worked on several murder investigations, both with Eden Police and the Metropolitan Police. I am proud to be running this case with a highly professional, highly trained team behind me and I am confident that we will bring Polly Leuchars's killer to justice very soon."

Ellie stepped in, despite more hands being raised. "Ladies and gentlemen, thank you for your time. I have the press packs here . . ."

Andy and Lou posed behind the desk for a couple of photographs and did a couple of TV and radio interviews outside the front of the main building, saying the same things over and over again for the benefit of viewers and listeners on the BBC, Sky News, Five Live, Eden County FM, and ITV local news. They would be lucky if they would get one or two lines out on air, so better make them good ones.

As soon as it was all over, Lou whispered to Andy, "I really need a drink."

"Coffee, or something stronger?"

"Ideally coffee, followed by something stronger, but I guess I'll have to settle for coffee."

As they walked to the rear of the building to get access to the staff canteen, Andy said, "I thought you did really well."

"Thank you," she said, still wary of him. "So did you. Thank you for being there."

Lou paid for three coffees and a Kit Kat for herself, a bacon sandwich for Andy, and then they walked back down to the MIR.

"One thing's for sure," she said as she pushed open the heavy fire door, balancing her paper coffee cup on the back of her Kit Kat, "we need to get to the bottom of the whole Fletcher-Norman thing before they do."

If Andy thought he was going to accompany her into her office for more cozy chat, he was mistaken. "Jason," Lou said, passing his desk, "can I borrow you for a sec?"

He ran a hand through his hair. "Sure."

Andy called after her, "I'm going to go and catch up with Flora Maitland, Boss. Okay? I'll be on the mobile if you want me."

Thank God for that.

"I got you a coffee," Lou said as Jason shut the door.

"Thanks," he said.

"How's the timeline?"

"It's okay. There's more coming in all the time, should be a lot more by the end of today, thanks to the press conference. I'll make sure it's up to date before I go tonight. Do you want me in tomorrow?"

"No," she said. "You deserve a weekend and I need to hang on to my overtime budget."

"I don't mind."

"Have you got nice things planned?"

Oh, subtle, she thought to herself, feeling her cheeks warming. What the hell was she doing? Wasn't it awkward enough with Andy Hamilton?

"Nope. I'd rather be in here getting on with it."

Well, that was honest—give him credit for that.

"Really?"

"Sure. There's a ton of stuff to do—I don't really want to spend the whole of Monday catching up. I can take it as hours instead of over-time, anyway."

"Well, thanks. See how you get on today and I'll leave it up to you, Jason. You know I'm really grateful for your help." Lou slipped the lid off her coffee and emptied a sachet of sugar into it.

"Are you having briefings over the weekend?"

"Depends on what comes in. We'll have one this evening when the shift changes, then maybe an informal catch-up when we need one, until Monday."

"Well, if you need my input you know where I am."

"Thank you," she said.

"No problem. Been a while since I worked a major incident."

"What do you make of the whole Fletcher-Norman connection?"

"I'm trying not to get stuck on it. You realize that Polly is turning into quite something, don't you?"

"In what way?"

"Well, if any of the gossip is to be believed, she was having or had an affair with just about everyone in the village, male *and* female."

"Really? God, the press are going to love this. Do you think it's simply gossip? Jealous wives, that sort of thing?"

"Might be, if there weren't such a lot of it. We've heard from a couple of her ex-boyfriends—there are intelligence reports and two statements already—and both of them were unceremoniously dumped after she refused to stop sleeping with other people."

Lou sighed, taking a swig of coffee. "This makes the whole motive question rather interesting, at least," she said. "I almost wish it were a simple burglary."

"Nothing's ever that simple," he answered softly. "You know that."

MG11 WITNESS STATEMENT	
Section 1—Witness Details	
NAME:	Simon Andrew DODDS
DOB (if under 18; if over 18 state "Over 18")	Over 18
ADDRESS: 18 Oak Rise Brownhills Lewisham LONDON SE15	**OCCUPATION:** Sales Manager
Section 2—Investigating Officer	
DATE:	Friday 2 November

OIC:	DC 13512 Jane PHELPS

Section 3—Text of Statement

My name is Simon Dodds and I live and work in London. I heard from a friend who lives in Briarstone that Polly Leuchars had been murdered.

Approximately two years ago I had a relationship with Polly Leuchars. She had joined the company I worked for at the time, SVA Consultants Ltd, as a receptionist. A few weeks later I asked her out and she accepted. I thought she was a fantastic girl and I enjoyed being with her a lot.

A few months into our relationship she told me about someone else she was seeing. She said it very casually, as if it was no big thing, but I was upset. She was surprised at my reaction and explained that she was not into monogamy and I could not expect her to be faithful.

I was very upset by the whole business, although I was in love with her and could not end the relationship. I asked her about the other person she was seeing and she admitted that she was seeing more than one person, and that one of them was a woman. I asked her to stop seeing them and she told me she could not, and that it was better if we ended our relationship.

I tried to win her back but she was adamant, and the next day she handed in her resignation. I never saw Polly after that, although I have often thought about her. She was a hugely charismatic person and was very attractive. I am sorry Polly is dead, and I have no idea who killed her, although I do feel her lifestyle was unusual and may have contributed somehow to her death.

Section 4—Signatures

WITNESS: (Simon Dodds)   OIC: (J. L. Phelps)

10:04

The worst thing was the smell. That was how he knew he was in hospital. His throat was sore from the tubes that were down it, his skin felt dirty, clammy, and he could smell himself. He couldn't speak because of the tubes, but his eyes were open now. And there was that bloody nurse, the loud one. He remembered her voice from somewhere. Somewhere he'd been that was dark.

"Brian? Are you all right there, Brian? Are you in any pain?"

Irish, of course. They all were. That, or Malay. And the doctors would all be Indian. All the good British nurses were earning a fortune in the Middle East. Where the hell was Barbara? Off playing bloody tennis or something. Never there when you needed her.

Why did they bloody keep asking him questions? How the hell did they expect him to answer when he had a mouthful of plastic tubing?

He raised a hand feebly to his mouth and the nurse slapped it down.

"Ah, no, Brian. Mustn't touch. We'll see about getting those taken out later, if you're up to it. Doctor will be around shortly."

It was easier with his eyes closed, after all. The light was too bright, too loud. But in the darkness bad things waited for him. Something had happened—he couldn't quite grasp it—an accident? Had he been in an accident? He could see Barbara, and . . . was that blood? He felt sick, the same way he'd felt when he'd hit his head on that bloody door frame at the golf club. He must have had a head injury, or something.

And her? Of course, she would have no idea that he was in hospital. A tear slid unbidden and silent from the corner of Brian's eye. *I wish I could tell her*, he thought. *I wish she were here.*

11:50

Andy Hamilton considered himself to be easygoing and positive, but today was trying his patience almost to the breaking point.

First off, Leah had chucked up all over his last remaining clean, ironed shirt, and Karen had laughed when he'd asked if she had any idea where his clean shirts were. He'd had to drag one out of the washing basket and iron it while Karen got Ben's breakfast. And then he'd had to watch both of the kids while Karen had a shower.

Consequently he was nearly late for the briefing and wasn't giving it his full attention until he realized Lou had started picking on him.

He felt like he was being deliberately shown up in front of the others. Of course, the sensible way to handle it would have been to agree and then have it out with her later on. But he wasn't sensible, was he? He was an idiot, clearly, because he enjoyed picking verbal fights with people, especially women he fancied. He'd sorted it out anyway, told

Ali he'd take on Flora to keep the boss sweet. Ali had looked disappointed, but he had said nothing.

Waiting at the lights on Forsyth Road, he closed his eyes slowly and pressed the flat of his palms onto the edge of the steering wheel.

Still fancied her, despite all the shit she'd given him last year. Maybe that made it worse, in fact, and in that moment he knew it to be true. He was more turned on by her anger than he'd ever been by her flirtation. What sort of a man did that make him?

Fourteen Waterside Gardens turned out to be a smart Victorian villa in the nicer end of Briarstone. Steps led up to two front doors, side by side, each with a neat sign indicating flat one and flat two. The doorbell to flat one had a small typed label that read MARTIN. Flat two had nothing to indicate who might live there.

He tried flat two first and couldn't hear any sound from within to indicate whether the bell actually worked. There was no reply.

The upstairs flat was in darkness—no sign of the red Fiesta on the graveled area passing for a front garden, only a sleek black Mercedes.

Giving up on flat two, he tried the bell for flat one. This one he heard ringing from somewhere within. Through the frosted glass door he saw lights on toward the back of the house and after a long while a middle-aged woman wearing a navy-blue nurse's uniform answered the door. She was holding a coat and a bag, as though she was on her way out. He saw the uniform first, the fob watch above the curve of her breast, the way the dark cotton fitted close around her body, and then he raised his eyes to take in her attractive face, the short, ash-blond hair, the ice-blue eyes. He produced his best smile.

"Sorry to trouble you," he said, holding out his warrant card. "Detective Inspector Andy Hamilton, Eden Police. I'm looking for Flora Maitland, from the flat upstairs. Any idea where she might be?"

"None at all," the woman said in a voice that would freeze vodka. She'd taken Andy's wallet so that she could get a better look at the photo; when she'd examined it to her satisfaction she handed it back.

Andy watched as she pulled on her coat. Red gloves were pulled briskly onto her slender hands. As she shut the front door behind her he had a sudden mental picture of her snapping on a pair of surgical gloves and smiled to himself.

"Is she in some sort of trouble?" the woman asked.

"No. Just need to ask her something. If she comes back, could you ask her to call me, please?" He pressed his business card into her gloved hand.

"Of course," she said, looking at him curiously. "Although I'm unlikely to see her. She comes and goes at odd times, as do I." She pressed her key fob and the central locking system of the Merc clunked invitingly.

He turned to go, wondering how she could afford it on a nurse's salary, but her voice, low, called him back: "Inspector Hamilton?"

She waited until he was standing in front of her again, so he had plenty of time to appraise her. As well as the appeal of the uniform, she was very attractive; her eyes, although they were cold and an unnerving pale blue, were bright and focused on him. He felt the hairs stand up on his arms.

"She has a studio. I'm not sure of the address, but she's probably there."

"A studio?"

"She's an artist. A very talented one."

"Thank you, Mrs. . . . ?"

But she was already heading for the car, her back to him. He had been dismissed. Charming, he thought. Bet she was a winner with the patients.

He went back to his own car, spent some moments jabbing with his massive fingertips at the screen of his nonwork-issue iPhone, trying to persuade it to Google "Flora Maitland Artist."

Proves my point exactly, he was thinking. That woman had been cold to the point of rudeness and now all he could think about was what she might be like in bed. He'd always had a bit of a thing for nurses.

The signal here was crap, and the phone wasn't going to cooperate. Quicker to go back to Hermitage Farm and ask the Maitlands. Flora was probably there, anyway.

MG11 WITNESS STATEMENT

Section 1—Witness Details

NAME: Anthony MORTIMER

DOB (if under 18; if over 18 state "Over 18") | Over 18

ADDRESS: Newbury House
Bedlam Lane
Baysbury
Briarstone

OCCUPATION: Corporate Lawyer

Section 2—Investigating Officer

DATE: Friday 2 November

OIC: DC 13512 Jane PHELPS

Section 3—Text of Statement

Polly Leuchars was my girlfriend before she moved to Morden. She had been living with me at my home in Baysbury, Newbury House, from January 2010 until December 2011. We met through mutual friends at a New Year's dinner party in Briarstone. Polly was living in a bedsit in the city at the time. I fell in love with her almost immediately. She was honest with me from the start and explained that she wanted an open relationship. This suited me because I have had partners in the past who have been very possessive; I thought Polly would be different, and she was.

Polly and I became involved with the swinging scene in London and we attended a couple of parties together where we both had sex with other people. We also met up with another couple a few times and had sex. Polly was very liberated and incredibly attractive. Because of this I felt I had met my life partner and I asked her to marry me in November last year.

She was upset by this and turned me down. I tried to explain that I was happy with our lifestyle but she didn't want to listen. We had a long discussion about it and we were both rather upset. In the morning she was gone. She left a note to say she had gone to stay with some friends and that our relationship was over.

I saw her about a week later when she returned to the house to collect her possessions. I tried once again to ask her to stay, but she refused. She seemed very happy and relaxed, I presumed by this she had met someone else, although she didn't say she had.

I saw Polly again in Briarstone a few times this year, but on neither occasion did I speak to her. The last time I saw her was in May or June. She was walking through the precinct near where I work with another girl.

I am now involved in another relationship.

I was very upset to read about Polly's death in the newspaper and I do not know who may have killed her.

Section 4—Signatures

WITNESS: (A J R Mortimer)   OIC: (J. L. Phelps)

12:40

Miranda Gregson answered the door to the farmhouse.

"Are they up to seeing me?" Andy asked. "Don't suppose Flora's put in an appearance?"

"She was here earlier. Left about half an hour ago."

"Bloody typical, that is. Just my luck."

Felicity Maitland was having coffee in the kitchen with two other women. They were huddled around a cafetière and three bone china mugs, looking to Andy's eyes rather like Macbeth's three witches, no doubt discussing the case and solving it all by themselves.

"Mrs. Maitland, sorry to trouble you again."

"Oh! It's you, Inspector Hamilton. No trouble at all. Would you like some coffee?" Felicity Maitland had taken a shine to him, not something he was unused to. Under normal circumstances he would have declined the offer, but he felt that this conversation might be valuable. "I'd love a coffee, thank you."

Sitting down, he was aware of the subtle changes in the body language and posture of the three ladies: stomachs pulled in a little, sitting up a little straighter, turning oh so slightly so that all three of them were facing him.

"Have you met Marjorie and Elsa, Inspector?"

"I'm afraid I haven't had the pleasure . . ." He knew how to turn on the charm and he enjoyed all the attention, even if there was part of this flirting that slightly turned his stomach.

"Marjorie Baker, my bridge partner, and Elsa Lewington-Davies, ladies' captain of the Seniors Tennis."

They cooed up at him. Wasn't Marjorie the old trout who had suggested Brian Fletcher-Norman was having an affair with Polly?

"It must be a very difficult life for you, Inspector. Do you get much time off?"

"Please, call me Andy. Yes, one sugar, thank you." He was wondering how quickly he could steer the conversation around to a point where he might learn something useful. "It's not so bad. There are quiet periods as well as busy ones. But of course you get to meet some lovely people." Smiling round at present company.

"And some nasty ones too, no doubt," Marjorie Baker added. She was pushing seventy but still looked after herself: unnaturally blond hair that was being allowed to meld gently with the gray; a complexion that had seen the benefit of many expensive treatments over the years. Makeup that was subtle and did justice to her age as well as her fading beauty.

"Have you made much progress? We all think it's a simply dreadful thing to happen, and in Morden of all places! Shocking, really." This last from Elsa. She was younger, dressed more casually, looking like she was fighting to stay in touch with the next generation.

"We're still working on several lines of inquiry," he said noncommittally, but allowing a lingering look to pass between him and all three of his companions.

"And, may I ask," Marjorie said with a slight cough, "would the Fletcher-Normans be one of those lines?"

Andy smiled at her, as though in deference to her sharp mind. "I really shouldn't," he said conspiratorially, "but, yes, we have been investigating recent events at the Barn in case they might be linked to the murder."

"I knew it!" Marjorie said triumphantly. "He's a dreadful man, that Brian Fletcher-Norman, I've always thought so."

"Rubbish," interjected Elsa. "You used to fancy the pants off him."

"Nevertheless," Marjorie continued, "I saw him coming out of

Yonder Cottage late that night. And when I knocked at the door, there was poor Polly in her bathrobe. He took advantage of an impressionable young girl, there's no doubt about it. He probably killed her when she started to see sense."

"Marjorie, really!" Felicity was looking slightly uncomfortable because Andy was there. "I'm sure Inspector—I mean—Andy, doesn't want to hear about our theories."

"On the contrary. You ladies know more about this village than I'll ever know. Something you've seen, something seemingly minor, might be the key that cracks this case. Tell me, what was Mrs. Fletcher-Norman like?"

They paused, and the replies, when they came, were a little too measured for Andy's liking.

"She was a reasonable bridge player," said Marjorie.

"Her tennis wasn't bad either. Especially after she had those lessons," Elsa added.

"I thought her common," said Felicity, and got an admonishing look from the other two. "Well, she was! Even though she tried hard to act like the Lady of the Manor. Remember that dinner party we had, not long after Polly arrived? She was perfectly beastly when she'd had a few glasses of wine and poor Brian had to take her home, saying she wasn't herself. Don't you remember, Elsa? You were there. Marjorie, I rather think you were in Spain—or was it Jamaica?"

Andy's phone rang at that moment. He mouthed "Excuse me" to the women and went outside.

"DI Hamilton."

"Andy, it's me," Lou said. "Can you talk?"

"Yes, it's fine."

"The hospital phoned. Brian Fletcher-Norman is awake and they say we can talk to him briefly. I'm sending Sam down with Ali Whitmore because everyone else is busy. Thought you should know."

"Sounds good to me," he said. "I'm at the farm."

"How are you getting on with Flora?"

"Haven't managed to track her down yet."

"Well, you don't need to worry about the phones for Hayselden

Barn. Jane's got all the numbers, and she's put the billing application in already. For now, you're down as the officer in the case."

"Right."

The call ended. Was she deliberately trying to make him look like he didn't know what he was doing? Because it felt exactly like that. He was a DI, for fuck's sake; he'd been a DI when she was still a probationer. What was she trying to prove?

He went back to the kitchen. Whatever it was they'd been talking about, they all stopped when he came in and turned and looked at him. Felicity was looking very pink. He took a deep breath.

"You all keep yourselves very fit," he offered as an opening gambit. "Did Polly play tennis?"

Elsa made a noise. "I don't believe she did."

"She kept fit in other ways," said Marjorie, meaningfully.

Felicity cleared her throat. "She was very busy at the stables most of the time. When she had time off, I think she went to the pub, or she was off out with friends."

"Anyone in particular?" Andy asked.

"Oh, Lord knows. She didn't tell me anything."

"What about Connor Petrie, was she friends with him?"

"You all seem very interested in the Petrie boy, don't you?" Felicity said sharply. "Why's that, I wonder?"

Andy leaned back in his chair. "Well, they must have spent a lot of time together at the stables. I thought they might have been friends."

"She was perfectly pleasant with him, but I wouldn't have said they were friends. He followed her around like a little puppy until she gave him something to do. I remember her telling Flora about it."

"What about Flora—was she friends with Polly?"

"I suppose so, they went out into town occasionally, although not for a while. Flora's been spending more time at the studio recently." She gave a strange, high-pitched sort of laugh. "Actually, I was starting to think she was avoiding me."

"Why would she do that?" Marjorie asked, before Andy had a chance to.

"I have no idea. She used to stay over at the farm all the time in the summer, every day. I asked her why she'd gone back to her flat and she said she was busy with her painting. But I don't know."

Andy saw a glance pass between Elsa and Marjorie and wondered what it was they weren't saying. He decided to risk stirring things up, see what might float to the surface.

"Mrs. Newbury at Willow Cottage. Is she someone you know?"

Felicity straightened in her chair. "That old witch," she said. "You don't want to pay any attention to her."

"She's a nasty old gossip," Elsa said. "Her husband ran off with one of the partners at his firm two years ago and she couldn't deal with it."

Andy made a note. They were watching him like hawks now.

"She was very pretty, wasn't she?" Andy coaxed. "Polly, that is. I'm surprised she was single."

There was a silence, then eventually Elsa said, "Well, *I* liked her. She was fresh and bright and always seemed to be happy." She bit her lip and continued: "I'm sorry for her, sorry she's gone. She was a nice girl, despite everything . . ."

"Despite what?" Andy asked, unable to help himself.

But after Elsa's glowing recommendation, none of them seemed willing to elaborate on this. They had all fallen quiet, and Andy thought he had probably reached the limits of their sociable conversation. The rest of it was up to Miranda Gregson, who had tactfully left him alone to do his thing.

"Mrs. Maitland, thank you very much for the coffee, but I'm afraid I must leave you. It's been lovely to meet you all."

They cooed their goodbyes and Felicity rose to show him out. "You simply must call me Felicity—all my friends do."

Andy treated her to his best smile. "Felicity, I did want to ask one thing. I've been trying to get in touch with Flora but I keep missing her. Any ideas where she might be?"

"Oh," Felicity said, her voice quavering as it tended to do when people demanded something of her. "I'm not really sure. She might be at the studio."

"Where's that?"

"On the road to Briarstone, just past the fire station. There's a few industrial units, her studio is on the upper floor, above the printing shop. I'm afraid I'm not sure of the actual address."

"Don't worry," Andy said, soothingly, hiding his rising impatience. "Do you have a mobile number I could catch her on?"

13:21

Flora wasn't in her studio. She was sitting in the car outside, looking up at the big windows, thinking of the canvas in there and wondering if she'd ever be able to look at it again.

Crying again, of course. How long would it take before she could think of Polly and not cry? It wasn't even as if they'd been together when it happened. It had finished months ago. But that didn't stop the hurt, didn't make it any less, didn't make any bloody difference.

The canvas was huge, swirls of green and gold, flashes of navy, dots of bright red.

It was an abstract, and it was based on the memories of what had happened in the top field at Hermitage Farm. The field where, on that hot spring day when the world had seemed so suddenly full of prom- ise, Polly had kissed Flora for the first time. And then, when Flora had looked at her in amazement and kissed her back, Polly had pushed her gently into the shade of the trees, the buttons being undone one by one while Polly met her gaze and smiled at her surprise.

Flora had been breathless, stunned, unprepared for how she would feel the moment Polly's cool hand slipped over her burning skin. She didn't wear a bra—nothing worth putting inside one—so when Polly's fingers met her bare nipples they reacted instantly.

The taste of Polly, the coldness of the lemonade they'd shared, the smell of the hot, baked earth, the horses on Polly's clothes, her own sunburned skin, the salt of her sweat on Polly's fingers, the softness, the incredible softness of her mouth . . .

And she had lain back, the ground hard beneath her shoulders, breathing hard while Polly's hand inside her jeans brought her to orgasm, looking up at the pattern made by the sunshine through the leaves on the trees, such a bright, bright green, and somewhere nearby a blackbird sang a song of uplifting joy while Flora writhed, clutching Polly's wrist with one hand, the other buried in that thick blond hair.

That was what she had been trying to paint.

It had been a way of dealing with the way things had finished between them at the end of August. She had stayed away from the farm, avoided Polly as much as she could. And it had hurt that Polly hadn't really pursued her, hadn't asked her why, had seemingly carried on with her life as though nothing had happened. Finishing the painting had been like a catharsis, and Flora had believed that when it was completed she would have what they called closure.

But this was different. How could she ever finish it, when Polly had been taken from her? How could she ever even look at it again?

No point staying here—she wasn't going to be able to paint today. She turned the key in the ignition and drove back out toward the town.

13:25

"Slumming it a bit, aren't we, Sarge?" Ali Whitmore said with a smile on his face, as Sam Hollands crossed the car park toward him.

"What's that?" she said, not hearing him—or maybe pretending not to.

"Interviewing with me."

"Boss clearly thinks you can't manage on your own. How are you getting on?"

Ali dropped his voice, although there was nobody near enough to hear them. "Bits and pieces coming in on Maitland; still the same stuff he was up for when I was working on him—you know, all the trafficking, the links to the McDonnells. We had a couple of arrests and convictions—drivers, dealers. None of the big nobs, though. Whatever we did, Nigel Maitland came up clean. Felt like he'd been tipped off, it was that obvious, but we couldn't get any further with it."

"Happens a lot," Sam said. "Karma says one of these days we'll get to put him away."

"Yeah," Ali said. "Fingers crossed for this job, then. I can't wait to see that smarmy bastard locked up."

The Intensive Care Unit nurse looked them up and down appraisingly, as though she could sense them bringing germs into her domain. They were shown to the antibacterial hand gel, and she watched them closely as they rubbed the stuff into their hands.

"He only woke up this morning," she said, "and had the tubes removed a couple of hours ago, so he's still very tired and out of sorts. I don't want you upsetting him if you can help it."

"Is he aware that his wife is dead?" Ali asked.

"Yes, but I'm not sure how much you'll be able to get out of him, so don't expect miracles."

"How is he, physically?"

"He's fine, for now. We take things one day at a time with heart attacks. And his was particularly nasty—you should be grateful he's here at all."

More grateful than you could possibly realize, thought Sam.

Brian Fletcher-Norman was propped up at an angle of about forty-five degrees, connected to various machines. His eyes were closed and monitors attached to the wires coming out from underneath his blue hospital gown kept reassuringly steady beats. Sam looked at the gray chest hair at the neck of the gown and wondered idly how much it would hurt when they took off the sticky pads. Maybe they'd shaved those bits underneath . . .

"Mr. Fletcher-Norman? Brian?"

The eyes opened and swiveled round to Sam's face. He managed a smile, although he was pale.

"I'm Detective Sergeant Sam Hollands, and this is my colleague Detective Constable Alastair Whitmore." She took Brian's hand, resting on the white sheet that reached up to his waist, half shook it and half gave it a gentle squeeze. "I wonder if we could take up a few moments of your time."

"As you can tell," said Brian, "I'm not exactly busy." His voice was a little hoarse, but otherwise strong and with a resonance that was curiously attractive.

"I wish we were meeting under other circumstances, Mr. Fletcher-Norman. I'm very sorry about the death of your wife."

His gaze fixed at some point in the middle distance. "You must call me Brian."

"Thank you. How are you feeling, Brian?"

He gave a little shrug. "Quite tired . . . Do you know any more about what happened to my wife?"

"That's why we're here, I'm afraid. Can you tell us a bit more about that day? About what happened?"

Brian cleared his throat weakly. "I said goodbye to her in the morning as usual. Well, she was still in bed asleep when I left. I don't—don't remember much about the evening. I got home late. Barbara—she's often out in the evenings, playing bridge or tennis, or at dinner parties or whatnot."

He paused for a moment, brows furrowed.

"I've been trying to remember. I sat in the living room, drank a whiskey. Read some papers from work. Then I went up and had a bath, went to bed."

"So you didn't see Barbara in the evening?"

A long, long pause. For a moment Sam wondered if he was drifting off to sleep.

Then he sighed. "I don't remember. It's very hazy. I wasn't feeling well."

"And in the morning?"

"I didn't set the alarm because Wednesday isn't one of my working days. I woke up some time after nine, had a shower. I was going down the stairs when I heard the door knock, and it was the—the police officers."

"So you didn't go into the kitchen at all?"

"I don't think so. No. I didn't."

Sam took his hand again, gave it a little squeeze. There had been a little tremor in his voice, his eyes filling slightly. He was a handsome man, despite his circumstances, and still looked strong, fit. No wonder Polly had been attracted to him—if that rumor was true.

"Brian, I'm not sure if you're aware of this, but Polly Leuchars was murdered in the early hours of Wednesday morning."

She'd kept hold of his hand, knowing that his reaction to this news was fairly crucial. The monitor tracking his heartbeat noticeably speeded up. He was looking at Sam again, eyes wide.

"Polly? What—what on earth happened?"

"She was attacked at Yonder Cottage. Brian, I am so sorry about this, but you realize there is a question I have to ask you." Sam's voice was gentle. "Is there any reason why Barbara might have wanted to harm Polly?"

The eyes closed. There was a long pause. Sam was desperate for him to say something, as she could sense the approach of the nurse and knew she did not have long.

"Brian?"

"Barbara was a very jealous woman. Polly and I were friends. She'd given me riding lessons at the stables in the summer. We had—we had some arguments about it, so I gave them up. But I never thought . . ."

His hand gave Sam's a little squeeze.

As expected, the nurse's footsteps squeaked across the lino toward them. "Now, Brian, are you feeling all right?" She started fussing around the monitors, checking things.

"Quite well, thank you."

"Just a few more minutes, then," she said, with a strong warning look toward Sam before she headed back to the nurses' station.

"Barbara was suffering from depression," Brian continued without any prompting. "Had it for ages, finally got some drugs from the doctors a few months ago."

"Do you think she had been drinking that night?" Sam asked.

"Probably. She drank most nights."

"Okay." Sam took Brian's hand in both of hers and held it for a moment. "Thank you for your time, Brian. I understand this must be very difficult for you."

He gave her a weak smile.

"Is there anyone we can contact for you? A friend, a neighbor?"

Brian shook his head sadly. "You could try my daughter, but I doubt she'll come."

Sam wanted to ask him about that, too, but the nurse was back again. "I'll show you out, Officers," she said, in a voice that invited no argument.

At the door, she asked, "What about his daughter? Have you spoken to her?"

Ali said, "We spoke to her briefly; we'll go back to her now Mr. Fletcher-Norman is awake."

"See if you can persuade her to come. He needs somebody, and this would be a good time for a reconciliation."

"Is he likely to make a full recovery?" Sam asked.

"You'll need to speak to the doctors, but he isn't out of the woods yet by any means."

"Please do call us if he remembers anything, won't you? Please?" Sam asked, handing her a business card.

Then Sam was marching down the corridor, heels sounding loudly, Ali having trouble keeping up. "I hate hospitals," she said passionately. "I'll see you at the station later," she said, without even looking back.

14:12

Flora's studio bore little resemblance to Felicity's description, the building being a converted mill rather than a purpose-built industrial unit—and the office downstairs was a management consultancy, not a printer. A nice place to work, Andy thought, admiring the landscaped lawns and flower beds around the building. The door which led directly to the stairs and the upper floor had a handwritten sign taped to the inside of the glass which said "No junk mail thanks." There was a buzzer, which also had a handwritten note: F MAITLAND STUDIO.

F Maitland was not there. The buzzer remained unanswered, and the parking space reserved for the studio was empty. The office downstairs was also locked.

Andy Hamilton sat in the car and dialed the mobile number he had been given for Flora Maitland. It rang several times and went to an answering machine. He thought about leaving a message but decided against it. Waited for a few moments and dialed again. This time it was answered.

"Hello?"

"Is that Flora Maitland?"

"Yes. Who is this, please?"

"Detective Inspector Andy Hamilton. I'm working on the Polly Leuchars murder investigation."

There was silence on the other end.

"I'm sorry about Polly. She was a friend of yours, wasn't she?" He had an instinct that being official wasn't going to get him anywhere with Flora, so he decided to try sympathy instead.

"Yes," came a small voice.

"Flora, I wondered if I could meet up with you today? I need to get more of an idea about what Polly was like, who her friends were, what she liked to do. I get the feeling you would be the best person to help me out with that."

A longer pause.

"Are you in Briarstone? I could meet you for a coffee, if you like?"

"I guess so," Flora said.

Like pulling teeth. "How about if I meet you in the Caffè Nero on the corner by the old post office? About three? How does that sound?"

"Okay."

"Flora? You won't stand me up, will you?"

He thought he could almost detect the hint of a smile in her reply: "No, I'll be there."

He was on the outskirts of Briarstone now, joining the back of the queue to the town center car parks. He wondered what sort of day Lou was having, whether she was making progress and whether she would bother to keep him updated. He still had a lot of ground to make up with her, he knew, but despite her best efforts to persuade him to the contrary, he could not quite believe that everything between them was over. She had been one of the best shags of his life. She hadn't been the first of his trips "over the side," as his colleagues put it, and she probably wouldn't be the last. He didn't think of it as cheating. There had been no real emotional connection with any of his sexual partners. The one who had come closest, however briefly, was Lou, so it was probably a good thing that it had ended when it did.

He remembered the moment Lou had found out that he wasn't single, the fury in her eyes. She had made him promise that he was going to come clean with his wife and tell her he'd had a fling, ask for her forgiveness, otherwise she would do it herself. He believed her.

"Why?" he'd said. "If it's all over between us, Lou, why do I have to tell her? She'll . . . she'll be devastated." He'd been about to say "She'll kill me," which was nearer the truth, but he realized Lou would probably have been even more adamant if she knew that would be the reaction.

There were tears in Lou's dark eyes but her voice was cold. "You have to tell her, Andy, because you have to start learning that there are consequences to your behavior. And if she knows about this, then it's much less likely that you'll feel inclined to try and resurrect things with me. Do you understand?"

The following morning he told her that he'd confessed to Karen.

"How did she take it?"

As if you care, he'd thought, but he'd answered: "She was pretty upset. She's gone to stay with her mother for a few days, taken Ben with her."

She'd seemed satisfied, which was a relief, because it was all a complete fabrication. In reality he would no more have confessed to Karen than he would take up a vow of celibacy. Karen might only be five foot one, but she had a fearsome temper on her and he was genuinely scared of her reaction. Besides, Karen was fine just as she was. She had no need to know; as long as Andy had no intention of actually leaving her for someone else, why trouble her with information that was only going to hurt them both?

Of course, Lou had been partly right; he still had this feeling like they had unfinished business. He thought of her sometimes, late at night, when Karen was asleep, her back to him.

07194 141544 To 07484 322159
02/11/12 14:16

Police want to interview me later. Can u be there with me? 3pm in town. Call if u get chance. F Xx

14:19

The MIR was quiet when Lou got back from an update meeting with Buchanan. He'd bid for additional resources on her behalf at the tactical meeting, and she now had a tiny overtime budget. And even more pressure for a quick result.

She thought the office was empty but Jason was there, focused on his computer screen. From her office, sitting at her desk, she could glance to the side of her screen and see him in profile: good cheekbones, a strong jawline and a straight nose, short, dark hair that would have been curly if he'd let it grow. He moved abruptly and she looked quickly back to her own screen, feigning fascination with it as he tapped on the door frame.

"Hi!" she said brightly.

"I wondered if you'd like a coffee?" he said.

She stared at him for a moment, as if he were a figment of her hormonal brain.

"I've got a better idea," she said. "Would you like to see the scenes? I think it helps to see where everything is."

"Sure, that would be great." He gave her a smile then, and it lit up his face.

14:52

"We can go to Reg's office," Taryn said. "He's not here today. What do they want to see you about, Flora, do you know?"

Flora shook her head. She looked rough, Taryn thought, her hair unwashed, dark circles under her eyes. "They haven't interviewed me yet. The guy that wants to meet me—he said he thought I could give them some more information about the sort of person Polly was."

Taryn almost laughed at this. "Never a truer word, huh? You know her better than almost anyone. If only they realized."

"What on earth am I going to say to him, Tabs?"

"You answer his questions as truthfully as you can. You don't have to tell him you had a relationship unless he asks you. And if he does ask you, tell him the truth."

"The truth?"

"Flora, you don't have anything to be ashamed of." She put her hand on Flora's knee, squeezed it reassuringly. "You fell in love, that's all. And Polly loved you back, in her own way. What's wrong with that? You're less likely to be the one who killed her than someone who didn't love her, after all, aren't you?"

"Did she, Tabs? Did she love me back?"

"Of course she did."

"They'll suspect me, then, won't they? After all it's usually the victim's partner. They just don't know who the victim's partner was yet."

Taryn bit her lip to stop herself saying it out loud. *You weren't her partner.* "I thought it was all over between you two."

Flora was rubbing the palm of her hand over her jeans, over and over again, as though her skin was itching. "It was. I mean, we weren't together. But she wasn't with anyone else. I was the last one. The last proper relationship she had."

Taryn let the words "proper relationship" hang in the air between them like a tattered piece of tinsel.

"Are you sure? You hadn't seen her for ages."

"I saw her a couple of weeks ago, only briefly. I went to the farm to see Mum. You know I'd been avoiding them. Polly saw me as I was leaving. She wanted to talk but I—well, I didn't want to listen. I was too scared of falling for her again."

"What did she say?"

Flora shrugged and said nothing.

Taryn tried again. "How did she seem?"

"She was happy. As always. Happy and bouncy and completely at ease with life."

The very opposite of the Flora who now sat opposite Taryn, in fact.

Taryn found herself wondering how this policeman would react when he realized who she was. Would he be the same one who had been here yesterday, the one who had broken the news? Well, there was no need to explain anything. She was only going to be there in support of her friend. She didn't have to say anything, did she?

MG11 WITNESS STATEMENT

Section 1—Witness Details

NAME:	Ivan ROLLINSON

DOB (if under 18; if over 18 state "Over 18")	Over 18

ADDRESS:	The Lemon Tree Cemetery Lane Morden Briarstone	**OCCUPATION:** Publican

Section 2—Investigating Officer

DATE:	Friday 2 November
OIC:	DS 10194 Samantha HOLLANDS

Section 3—Text of Statement

I am the landlord of The Lemon Tree public house, which is situated on Cemetery Lane in Morden, about half a mile away from Hermitage Farm.

Polly Leuchars was known to me as she visited the pub regularly, probably once or twice a week at least. She met friends in the bar, and she was well known to the other regulars too.

On Wednesday 31 October I recall Polly came into the bar at around 8.30. She ordered a vodka and Coke and sat with it at one of the tables to the rear of the bar area. I did think she would be meeting someone because she was sitting alone, and because she was wearing smart clothing. She was usually more casually dressed. She had black trousers on with a white blouse, and she was wearing makeup. Unless she was meeting a friend, Polly usually stayed at the bar and chatted either with me or with Frances Kember, our barmaid.

At 9 Polly was still on her own and came back to the bar for another drink. I joked that it looked like she'd been stood up, and she replied, "Seems that way, Ivan" or something of that nature. She did not look very happy.

Much later on, I'm not sure of the exact time, I saw Polly outside the pub talking on her mobile phone. You need to go outside as there isn't much of a signal. I didn't hear her speak. I was putting some rubbish out into the bins and when she saw me she ended the call and went back inside.

Soon afterwards I noticed she had gone. I think it must have been between 11.30 and 11.45 that she left. I did not see her again after that.

<table>
<tr><td colspan="2">Section 4—Signatures</td></tr>
<tr><td></td><td></td></tr>
<tr><td>WITNESS: (Ivan Rollinson)</td><td>OIC: (S Hollands DS 10194)</td></tr>
</table>

15:00

"That's got to be him," Taryn said. "He looks like a policeman."

"How do you know what a policeman looks like?" Flora countered, eyeing the man in a suit who had come into the coffee shop and was looking around.

"He's on his own, and he's looking for someone. And it's not exactly busy in here. He's looking for a girl on her own; he's not expecting there to be two of us. It must be him."

Flora got up and crossed to where Andy Hamilton was standing. "Hello," she said. "Are you—I mean, are you looking for me?"

"Flora?" He held out his hand. "I thought you'd be on your own."

"I was meeting a friend. I hope you don't mind."

"That's fine. I'll grab a coffee and I'll be with you in a sec. Can I get you anything?"

He seemed all right, Flora thought, as she went back to sit with Taryn. "It's him. He's getting a coffee."

"He looks like a rugby player," said Taryn, and Flora smiled. Tabs had always had a bit of a thing for well-built men, and this one was certainly well built, and at least six foot tall. He had kind eyes, too. Flora felt a little bit better. But thank goodness Tabs was here.

"Detective Inspector Andy Hamilton," he said when he got to the table, holding out his hand to Tabs. "Your name is?"

"Taryn Lewis," she said.

His expression told Flora that he'd not made the connection.

"I hope you don't mind," Taryn said. "I thought Flora could do with a bit of moral support."

"No, no, that's fine. As long as *you're* happy?" This to Flora, who nodded.

"I'm going to take a few notes, if you don't mind," Andy said, pulling his notebook out. "Right. How about you tell me a bit about Polly. What was she like?"

Flora hesitated, biting back the tears that were ready to fall at the sound of that name. She cleared her throat. "She—she was full of life. She was clever, witty, always smiling. Always happy."

Flora fell silent, remembering.

"Did you know her too?" Andy asked Taryn, as though to give Flora a moment to collect her thoughts.

"I met her a couple of times. As Flora said, she was very bubbly and fun to be with."

"Was she seeing anyone, that you know of?"

Both girls looked at each other.

"She saw lots of people," Flora said slowly. "Nobody serious. Not that I knew of, anyway."

"Anyone recently? Or maybe she *spoke* of someone in particular?"

Taryn stepped in. "She didn't talk about who she was seeing, ever. She was always discreet. But you can guarantee there was at least one person. More likely two or three."

Andy, furiously scribbling, looked up. "You mean she slept around?"

Flora made a little sound, like a sigh, but cross. "No, she didn't sleep around. She had friends and she usually ended up having sex with them, that's all. She was always honest about it. But she had lots of partners. It's not a crime, is it?"

"Not at all. But maybe someone she was seeing didn't like it."

He took a swig of his coffee, grimaced, added two sachets of sugar, and stirred; all the while they watched him intently, not speaking.

"Flora, do you know the Fletcher-Normans? They live at the converted barn across the way."

"I know where they live," Flora snapped back. Taryn let out a nervous cough. This was getting into awkward territory. "Yes, I know them."

Before Andy could ask his next question, Tabby was standing. "Excuse me," she said. "I'm going to the ladies'."

Flora watched her go, understanding completely why she wanted to leave the table, and yet desperate for her to stay. "Sorry, were you going to ask me . . . ?"

"Yes. I wondered whether the Fletcher-Normans also knew Polly?"

"Everyone knew Polly. It's a small village, Inspector. And one with a very active social life. Whenever Mum had one of her dinner parties, she included Polly. Polly played some golf at the golf club, sometimes drank in the golf club bar with my father and his cronies. Polly used to use the gym at the country club and half the village is in there most days."

"And the Fletcher-Normans?"

Flora's brow furrowed. "I think Brian Fletcher-Norman came for riding lessons. I was living in Briarstone by then and not around much. But I remember Polly saying that he was fawning all over her."

"Did she mind?"

Flora snorted. "Polly *never* minded that sort of thing. She thrived on attention."

"Do you think she had an affair with him?"

She wouldn't meet his eyes. "Probably."

"And Mrs. Fletcher-Norman?"

"I don't think she was Polly's type."

The policeman looked startled. "I meant, did she know Polly too? Can you remember seeing them together at any stage?"

Flora managed a smile. "I'm sorry, I knew what you meant. It was a little joke. I don't remember Barbara and Polly specifically. But Barbara was always at Mum's parties. They both were. Barbara used to get a bit loud when she'd had a few drinks, and we always tried to make sure she didn't have too many. I believe Brian used to get her to drive whenever they went anywhere that was driving distance, so I think coming to the farm was Barbara's chance to get let off the leash, as it were."

He smiled, and then he put in the blinder. "And you, Flora?"

"Me?"

"You and Polly were friends?"

Flora blushed, stared at him. Tears were in her eyes before she could help them. Damn the man. "Bit more than that," she said, in a very small voice. Two fat tears fell into her lap; she rubbed at her eyes furiously.

"I'm sorry," he said, his voice as gentle as he could get it. He put a hand to her knee. She didn't brush it off. "I'm really sorry. This must be very difficult for you."

"Yes," she said again.

"So you were in a relationship?"

"Yes. I suppose you could call it that."

"Had you been together long?"

"We weren't really 'together' as such. She was with other people. It's—it's the way she was. It was very difficult to deal with. But I was in love with her. I hadn't seen her for a while. Since late August. I went back to my flat in Briarstone and I was busy with work. I only saw her once or twice since then. So it was all over, really."

"Right."

Although Flora strained to look, she could not decipher what he'd written.

"Was that why you moved out of the farm?"

Flora swallowed. "Partly. I had some arguments with my dad. He wanted me to get involved in the farm more. Help out with the business. I—I didn't want to do that."

"What about Polly? What did she think?"

That brought a smile to Flora's lips. "She thought I should tell him to shove the farm up his arse. She thought everyone should follow their dreams. Not let anyone tie them down."

"But you didn't see her, after you moved out?"

"She was—she was involved with other people. I just couldn't deal with that anymore. So I let things come to an end. There wasn't any argument, nothing like that."

"Did you speak to her on the phone?"

"Sometimes. We kept in touch. Like friends, you know. But that was all."

"So . . ." he said, flipping back through his notebook, "you moved into the flat in Waterside Gardens?"

"I've actually had the flat there for years. I stayed at the farm a lot when I was with Polly, but after we . . . after it ended, I avoided coming to the farm and stayed in Briarstone instead."

"And you have a studio?"

"Yes."

"I've never met an artist," he said.

I'm not surprised, Flora thought. He didn't look like he had much appreciation for the aesthetic.

"You said Polly was involved with other people, when you moved out. Can you tell me who?"

"I didn't want to know."

"But you must have had an idea, Flora."

He waited again. Let him wait. He would hear about Polly from everyone else in the village, let them gossip about Polly—she wasn't going to.

They were still staring each other down when Taryn came back. She cast a glance at Flora and saw the expression on her face.

"I told him about me and Polly," she said.

15:14

They'd driven for almost three miles before he spoke.

"Are you okay?"

She was watching the road with a fixed expression, eyes forward. The weather was closing in and it was almost dark. Rain spattered on the windscreen and reflected on her face as they waited at traffic lights.

"Louisa?"

"Hmm? Sorry, I was miles away." She turned to look at him and for a moment could not look away.

"I asked if you're okay. You seem a little distracted?"

She managed a smile that didn't quite go up to her eyes. "It was something somebody said earlier, I can't even remember what. But it's making me think about other things."

There was a long pause as the traffic lights changed to green. The queue of traffic, however, did not move. They were waiting to join the long ranks of the commuters on their way home.

"I'm sorry," she said at last, "this was probably a bad idea. Bad timing, anyway."

"I can think of worse places to be."

She laughed. "Are you sure?"

"So," he said resignedly, "if we're going to be stuck in traffic for an hour, you can tell me all about what's really bothering you."

Another pause while she decided whether she really wanted to go there or not. After all, she had nobody else to talk to. Jason was as good a bet as any.

"Parental responsibility."

"Ah."

"Nobody is ever good enough for their parents, I find. Do you get on with yours?"

"Sure. I talk to them all the time. It's difficult being so far away sometimes."

"Are they in . . ." she thought for a moment and then risked it: "Canada?"

He smiled at her. "Yeah. You know, you wouldn't believe the number of people who assume I'm American."

"Really? But the accent's completely different," she said, glad that she'd made the right guess.

"I think so. But most Brits seem to get them easily confused."

"How come you're here?"

He hesitated, looking out of the window. "Kind of a long story," he said. "I've been here six years already."

He hadn't actually answered the question but she let it go. "Do you have brothers and sisters?"

"One brother, older. He lives over here too, works in IT. You?"

"I have a sister and a brother. My sister is happily producing babies. My brother is bumming around Europe at the age of twenty-nine, having never held a job down longer than four months. And they are both utterly wonderful in the eyes of my parents, whereas I am always sadly lacking. I've never been able to work it out."

"Maybe their expectations of you are higher?"

"You're probably right, but how is that fair? No matter what I do, they always make me feel like a failure."

"At least it keeps you striving."

She laughed. "Are you trying to make me feel better, Jason? Because it's not working."

"You're probably too tough on yourself. I've no doubt they must be really proud of you and what you've achieved. But you're always pushing yourself to achieve more, and I'm sure that drive is in you, rather than in them."

He had a point, of course. "I think my mother will be happy when I'm married with two-point-four children, and my father will be happy when I've done that *and* got to chief constable."

"Save that for next year."

She looked at him, smiling because already she felt better, and the eye contact between them went on until the traffic began to move and someone beeped behind her.

"So what about you? Don't you feel under pressure to start having kids?" It was the sort of flirting that you could almost get away with when you got to your mid-thirties.

"I've fallen behind the field with that one," he answered. "I guess I've been single a bit too long."

She waited, knowing that if he really did want to participate in this particular conversation, more would come along.

The traffic ground to a halt again. The rain was coming down so fast now the wipers were having trouble keeping up. There was a tension in the air that had nothing do with the storm. Lou felt the warmth of the air, almost thought she could feel him breathing. She felt his eyes on her face again and turned to look.

"Can I ask you something personal?" Jason said then.

"Go on." She turned her gaze back to the road ahead.

"You and Andy Hamilton—is there something going on?"

"Shit. That *is* personal."

"Sorry."

"Why do you ask?"

He shrugged. "Just curious."

Lou sighed, wanting to be honest but also not wanting to rake over what she still thought of as something sordid. "Yes, there was something going on, but there definitely isn't anymore. And that's something I'd like to keep quiet, if possible. How's that?"

"So you're not seeing him anymore?"

"No. He neglected to tell me he was married, I found out by accident, and that was that."

Jason nodded slowly. "Figures."

For a moment she couldn't speak.

"Look, I'm sorry," he said. "I wasn't going to mention it. And you know I won't say anything, right? This is between you and me."

"I'm sorry that you're seeing me in a really unprofessional light here. I did everything I could to do the right thing . . ."

"I can see that," he said. "I'm sorry if I embarrassed you."

"You didn't," she lied. She thought she had detected a note of amusement in his voice.

"Good. Is this the place?"

Hardly realizing it, Lou had driven all the way to Morden and they were pulling up on the driveway of Yonder Cottage. There wasn't a lot of room; two cars and a CSI van were already squeezed onto the gravel. Polly's car had gone for forensic examination.

They got out of the car. The rain had stopped, and the sun was trying to force its way through the breaking clouds.

"This is Yonder Cottage," Lou said, although he could have seen that for himself by the slate sign hanging on the wall. "There are two entrances to the farm—you can go further up this driveway, which goes through a farmyard with barns and outbuildings, then curves round to the left, and eventually you get to the farmhouse itself. There's another drive about a hundred yards further down the road which also goes to the farmhouse."

High heels sinking into the gravel, picking her way between the puddles, Lou led the way up the road to a five-bar gate on the opposite side. This time a handsome oak sign with gold lettering proclaimed it to be Hayselden Barn. From the road the driveway stretched between manicured lawn and flower beds up to a vast horse chestnut tree, and beyond it a black-timbered former barn.

"There you go," she said. "Not far, is it?"

He shaded his eyes against the sunshine. Lou was only aware that she was gazing at him like a teenager when he turned his head toward her and smiled.

"They must be seriously loaded," he said. "All of them. What does Fletcher-Norman do for a living?"

"Some sort of executive, shipping I think. Although he's supposed to be semiretired."

They walked back to Yonder Cottage. The road was quiet and Lou could hear birds singing. She unlocked the car but stood for a moment, looking from the cottage up the driveway toward the outbuildings. Somewhere a horse neighed. From the map, you'd imagine that there would be a view of the cottage from the upper floors of the farmhouse, but there were several big trees obscuring the line of sight.

"You want to go someplace else?" he asked.

She was lost in thought, hardly heard him. Then her phone rang and she pulled it out of her jacket pocket. She recognized the number on the display, stared at it for a moment. She wasn't ready to talk to Hamilton. If it was important, he would leave her a voice mail.

"I think we'd better get back to the office," she said.

There was silence between them for the rest of the journey. To try and distract herself, she turned on the radio to catch the local news headlines, but she wasn't listening to it. Their earlier conversation was going round and round in her head. His easy confidence had taken her by surprise, the relaxed way he'd asked her questions that were so personal. And now she was suddenly uncomfortable in a different way, not knowing what to do with herself, believing that he could see right through her and that it was all a game to him.

A game that she already knew she was going to lose.

15:17

This time Taryn saw her coming, escorted to the sales floor by the receptionist, who looked far too excited for this to be a regular visitor. With Reg away, there was no intermediary. They approached Taryn's desk.

"Taryn, this lady is here to see you," said Juliet, and scooted back off to reception.

Taryn stood up uncertainly. This one was younger, on her own, dressed in a smart linen suit with short, honey-blond hair and green eyes behind rectangular-framed glasses. "My name is Detective Sergeant Sam Hollands. I'm working on the Polly Leuchars murder investigation. I wondered if I might have a word with you? Somewhere private?"

As she showed Sam Hollands into Reg's office, Taryn was partly worried that she was going to get told off for failing to tell Andy Hamilton who she was, and partly worried about what on earth Polly's death had to do with her.

"Thanks," Sam said as Taryn indicated Reg's small conference table. "It's not bad in here, is it? I can imagine worse offices to work in. I gather my colleagues came to tell you the news about your father and his wife. I am sorry you had to hear about it under such circumstances."

Taryn gave a tiny shrug. "As I explained to your colleagues, I am not really in contact with my father, so the news was probably less upsetting to me than they were anticipating."

"So I gather. Have you been to visit your father at all?"

"Yes. I went last night. He was still unconscious."

"You know he's come round now?"

"The hospital left me a message. I might go back after work, if I get a chance."

"I think he might appreciate that."

Taryn made a noise, and Sam Hollands tried a different tack. "Are you aware of the circumstances of Mrs. Fletcher-Norman's death?"

Taryn shook her head. She wanted to say, *Actually, I'm not especially interested in that, either,* but a part of her somewhere was certainly curious. "Car crash?"

"Mrs. Fletcher-Norman was found in her car at the bottom of Ambleside Quarry. We're trying to establish whether there might have been any connection between her death and the murder of Polly Leuchars."

"She was found at the bottom of a quarry? You mean she drove off the edge and killed herself?"

"It's possible."

"How strange."

"Why?"

"I can't think of anyone less likely to commit suicide than Barbara."

"What do you mean?"

Taryn thought about Barbara being mean, vindictive, and rude; thought of her voice getting louder when she'd had a drink. "I guess she was always a bit flaky. But I never realized she was unhappy. You said you're linking her suicide to Polly's death? Does that mean you think she killed Polly?"

"We can't rule anything out yet, but it's one of the lines of inquiry."

Taryn took a deep breath. She had a sudden mental picture of the bruises she had seen on her father's arm last night. "I didn't think she was prone to violence. Has my father said anything?"

"About what?"

"About—oh, maybe she was violent at home, or something. You don't simply turn psycho and kill people overnight, do you? Even if you have a reason."

"Not usually. You know, your father may tell you things that he wouldn't feel comfortable telling the police."

Taryn gave a short laugh. "Have you met my father?"

"I saw him earlier."

"Well, then. He tells you what he wants you to hear. That goes for you as well as me."

"I realize things are—difficult between you. Can I ask how that came about?"

Taryn was useless at fibbing, even when she was doing it with good intentions; she would blush, fluster, get things muddled up. The safest thing to do would be not to answer.

So she took a deep breath, tried to be calm. "It's nothing in particular. He left my mother when I was quite small. Ever since then I've been a bit of an inconvenience to him. Having to see me was always a chore. It was hurtful. But it's only in the last few years that I can't seem to put up with it anymore. He's not used to people standing up to him; he doesn't like it. So these days we steer clear of each other."

"And Barbara?"

"She was a complete bitch. I know I shouldn't speak ill of her after she's died in a horrible way, but she was. She was always hostile toward me, which is bad enough when you're an adult; when you're a small child it's very difficult to deal with."

"I can imagine," Sam said. "I'm sorry."

Taryn was taken aback by the sympathy, more so because she could tell that Sam Hollands meant it. "Are you?"

"Of course. You can't choose your family, can you? And you can't really escape it, not when you're too young to be able to speak up for yourself."

"No. Exactly."

"Can you remember when you last visited them?"

"Months ago. I can't remember exactly. April, sometime. That was the last time I saw him until last night in the hospital."

"Did you speak to them on the phone in that time?"

"No. The last time I went to the Barn, with the bike, they weren't in and I left a note."

"The bike?"

Taryn sighed. It sounded so stupid, this. "He'd taken up cycling, for some reason. I got him a bike for Christmas. It wasn't right. Long story."

There was a pause. Taryn wondered if she was supposed to say anything else. Then Sam smiled at her and produced a business card. "I've taken up enough of your time. Will you give me a call if you think of anything that might help us?"

"I don't think there's anything I *can* help with," Taryn said quickly. "I only met Polly once or twice."

"But your father might mention something to you that would be helpful. After all, they were right across the road from Polly. Who knows what they might have seen, or heard."

"Surely he would tell you that himself."

"Nevertheless. You never know if you might need to talk," she said. Her voice was calm, soothing. Taryn wondered at the woman's patience.

"Thank you," she said at last, giving in. "You've been really kind."

She watched Sam Hollands heading back toward reception and thought about the other police officer, the great hulking rugby player, and she knew which one of the two she preferred.

16:05

The MIR was busy when they got back. Jane Phelps collared Jason as soon as he got through the door, and when Lou logged on to the workstation she saw that she had received a hundred and fifty new emails.

She left her door open to listen to the buzz from the room, trying to catch up on all the stuff that had come in, and as a result Andy Hamilton thought it was okay to walk straight into her office and sit down. She deliberately ignored him until he gave a discreet cough.

"Have you got an update for me?" Lou asked, still looking at the screen. Deleting emails.

He looked surprised when she finally managed to look at him.

"Everything okay?" Andy asked.

"Everything's fine. What have I missed?"

"We've had intel back on Maitland. Only the same stuff we had last year about him and the McDonnells doing people trafficking. Special Branch were looking at it, but they've got other stuff on their plates right now. Mandy says there should be some more later this evening, she's putting it all on HOLMES."

"Good—it's something, anyway. Would be excellent if we could get another phone number for Maitland."

"Speaking of whom, I met up with Flora. She's pretty done in by Polly's death. Seems she had a relationship with her earlier this year. She said it ended in the summer when she moved out of the farm."

"What do you think?"

"I think there's more to it than she was telling me, but whether she bumped her off I couldn't say."

Lou realized he was jumpy, excitable, beyond what might have been caused by her bad mood. "What else?"

"The PM is done with Mrs. Fletcher-Norman."

"And?"

He smiled. "Multiple head wounds. Multiple trauma. Excess blood alcohol, consistent with her being rat-arsed. And some of the blood she was covered in wasn't actually hers."

07484 322159 to 07194 141544
02/11/12 1732hrs

Going to go to hosp see dad. Not sure what time will be back. Hope OK T xxx

17:45

He saw her before she saw him, stopping at the nurses' station and waiting patiently for them to pay attention to her. She'd put on weight, of course. Impatience nearly made him call out to her but, really, what was the point. Everything just felt too exhausting. She would find him eventually, and if she'd just turn her head slightly she would see him anyway. Like a sensible person would do. He despaired of her.

And at that moment she looked round and, very briefly, there was the happy, girlish smile of recognition before she put the mask back on.

"Hello."

She approached the bed but did not kiss him. Did not touch him at first, then after a moment or two took his hand in hers.

"Taryn. I'm glad you've come. Thank you."

"How are you feeling?"

He gave a light cough. His throat was still dry from all the tubes. "I'm fine. I don't know how long they're planning to keep me here, though."

He wanted her to say something about Barbara but knew she wouldn't. She wasn't one to hold with convention, his daughter. "How are you? How is Chris?"

Taryn's husband had only been to the Barn once. Likable enough—heating engineer, or something like that. For a while Taryn had tried to organize meetings; she had invited Brian and Barbara to dinner in that godforsaken terraced box they lived in, tiny rooms and flatpack furniture, until they'd made it clear that they had other things to do. Chris, the husband, was as disinterested in their lives as they were in his. They had zero to talk about, and on those rare meetings it had been nothing short of awkward.

Taryn had married him quietly in the register office a couple of years ago, which suited Barbara, who hadn't been at all happy at the prospect of them having to pay for a big bash. He'd slipped Taryn some money toward the honeymoon. Where had they gone? Cornwall. That was it, Cornwall, in October. Of all places. They'd had to save up, apparently.

"Chris is fine. I'm fine. Is there anything you need me to do?"

His eyes closed, just for a moment, in concentration. "Yes, lots of things. Can you go and see if the house is all right? I don't trust the police to set the burglar alarm and lock up properly. Sister Nolan, the Irish one? She's got some of my things somewhere. The door keys, car keys. Can you go inside, make sure it's all in order? Check the post, that sort of thing?"

"If I get time. I'm busy at work. Do you need me to bring you any-thing? Clothes?" Her tone was flat.

A voice came from behind, loud and Irish. "He needs clean paja-mas, a towel, a flannel, toothbrush, all of those things. With a bit of luck he will be on the ward before Monday, and we can't have him there without him being nice and clean. You should also find him a set of clothes, it would be good to get him up and dressed before too long. Okay now? I have the keys for you."

For a moment Brian and his daughter locked eyes, years of things unsaid passing between them. Then she turned and walked away.

5X5X5 INTELLIGENCE REPORT

From:	Karen ASLETT—Source Coordinator
To:	DCI Louisa SMITH
Subject:	Nigel MAITLAND
Date:	02/11/12

Grading B / 2 / 4

Nigel MAITLAND is currently involved in money-laundering enterprises using off-shore accounts.

5X5X5 INTELLIGENCE REPORT

From:	Karen ASLETT—Source Coordinator
To:	DCI Louisa SMITH
Subject:	Nigel MAITLAND
Date:	02/11/12

Grading B / 2 / 4

Nigel MAITLAND was responsible for a recent shipment of illegal immigrants. They traveled into the country via Dover aboard a Lithuanian-registered lorry. The shipment was due to travel to London but was diverted elsewhere following a tip-off.

5X5X5 INTELLIGENCE REPORT

From:	Karen ASLETT—Source Coordinator
To:	DCI Louisa SMITH
Subject:	Nigel MAITLAND—Harry McDONNELL—Lewis McDONNELL
Date:	02/11/12

Grading B / 2 / 4

Harry McDONNELL and Lewis McDONNELL are working with Nigel MAITLAND to operate a people-smuggling enterprise. The younger females are forced to work in a brothel in London, and are threatened with violence. The males are put to work on farms in the north of England until they have paid their transportation costs.

5X5X5 INTELLIGENCE REPORT

From:	Karen ASLETT—Source Coordinator
To:	DCI Louisa SMITH
Subject:	Nigel MAITLAND—Harry McDONNELL—Lewis McDONNELL
Date:	02/11/12

Grading B / 2 / 4

The McDONNELL brothers and Nigel MAITLAND are still bringing illegals through Dover. MAITLAND organizes legitimate shipment of goods to and from the continent via his farming business. One in five of the lorries is carrying immigrants. They are housed in a special container between the lorry cab and the refrigeration unit.

5X5X5 INTELLIGENCE REPORT

From:	Karen ASLETT—Source Coordinator
To:	DCI Louisa SMITH
Subject:	Nigel MAITLAND—Harry McDONNELL—Lewis McDONNELL
Date:	02/11/12

Grading B / 2 / 4

It is believed that the recent shipment of illegal immigrants that Nigel MAITLAND and the McDONNELL brothers arranged via Dover ended up in the Briarstone area following some problem at the original drop-off location. Lewis McDONNELL was not happy about this and it is likely that MAITLAND will get into some trouble over it as the brothers see it as his mistake.

From 07122 912712 to 07194 141544
02/11/12 1742hrs

We need to talk. Can you come to office later? Dad

17:50

Since returning to the MIR, Lou had barely stopped for breath.

The blood found on Barbara Fletcher-Norman's clothing had been taken to the lab by Les Finnegan personally for further analysis on the premium level of service, which cost the taxpayer a small fortune but would likely steer the investigation one way or the other. With a bit of luck the results would be back in a few hours.

Buchanan had called her in for a meeting with the assistant chief constable which had been brief, and surprisingly jolly. They both seemed convinced that the blood was going to be Polly Leuchars's and were therefore happy with her blowing a large chunk of the operation's budget on the lab work. It was going to be a quick result after all, they joked, even if they didn't have an arrest. And with a bit of luck, this would disrupt Nigel Maitland's criminal enterprises for a while. Who knows, he might even let something slip over the interview process, something that could unravel things for Special Branch.

Buchanan hadn't even asked her about the details of Barbara's postmortem report, for which she was grateful. She hadn't had a chance to read the report properly, and for the rest of the meeting she waited to be caught out with a question that would show up this oversight.

But there were no dramatic revelations about the way Barbara had met her death. As Andy had said, multiple injuries consistent with being inside the car as it fell. Adele Francis had asked her about the seat belt, and reference was made to that point, something Andy hadn't mentioned: " . . . broken ribs consistent with pressure from the seat belt during impact." She read through the report in detail, looking for other things that Andy might have missed. There had been multiple injuries, but death had most likely been caused by an open skull fracture on the side of the head. Lou looked at the pictures. The side of Barbara's head was concave, most likely from the car's door frame, which had been pushed inwards on the quarry floor. She looked at the pale skin of the woman's face, crisscrossed with rivulets of blood which had dried to a black lacy pattern that was almost beautiful. Her eyes were closed, her expression almost serene. Sometimes the faces of the dead registered traces of the expression consistent with the manner of death—fear, pain—but not in this case. Lou wondered if it had something to do with the amount of alcohol in her system. Had she parked at the top of the quarry, left the handbrake off, and passed out, and had the car then rolled over the edge?

No easy solution would emerge from the postmortem, in any case.

On her desk was Jason's first report on the phone analysis he was working on, as well as the timeline of events, the network associations, and the intelligence. She flicked through it, looking blindly at tables and paragraphs until she got to the end. He'd done a summary. Fantastic.

Preliminary Phone Analysis on Numbers Ending:

774—attributed to Felicity MAITLAND

712—attributed to Nigel MAITLAND

544—attributed to Flora MAITLAND

920—attributed to Polly LEUCHARS (note: the handset is still missing)

SUMMARY OF FINDINGS

774 (Felicity MAITLAND)
- call traffic during the day, little in the evenings
- little contact with the number ending 920 (Polly LEUCHARS)—final contact with this number was on 31/10/12 at 11:15hrs

712 (Nigel MAITLAND)
- little call traffic on this number
- all contacts are with numbers attributed to family members
- only additional numbers dialed/contacts are landlines and open source research shows these to be local businesses connected with farming
- should be considered that this is likely not MAITLAND's only phone

544 (Flora MAITLAND)
- regular, frequent contact with number ending 920 (Polly LEUCHARS) until 27 August 2012
- regular contact with 07484 322159, which is attributed via HOLMES to Mrs. Taryn LEWIS (daughter of Brian FLETCHER-NORMAN)

920 (Polly LEUCHARS)
- contacts with phones attributed to Flora MAITLAND, Felicity MAITLAND, but notably not that attributed to Nigel MAITLAND. As his employee, and given intelligence that he was in a relationship with Polly LEUCHARS, again this may indicate that he has at least one other number in regular use.
- cellsite activity shows the phone traveled from Morden to Briarstone between 12.30pm and 3pm on 31/10/12, consistent with reports of shopping trip mentioned in statement of Felicity MAITLAND
- there were two outgoing calls made to 07484 919987 (unattributed number) at 22.15 and 22.20. Cellsite for both calls was in Morden. (Possible that one of these calls was

that observed by Ivan ROLLINSON at the Lemon Tree).
At 22.58hrs there was a further unanswered call to the
same number, but the cellsite location for this contact was
Briarstone.

- at 23.49 an incoming call was received from the same
  unattributed number, 07484 919987, with a duration of 3
  minutes 42 seconds. Cellsite location was Morden. (This
  may indicate that Polly LEUCHARS received the call
  when she was back at Yonder Cottage and was therefore
  alive at 23:49.)

Morden 719643 (Yonder Cottage Landline)

- this line was used only once in the entire billing period.
  The only call registered was at 23.43 on 31/10/12—an
  outgoing call to 07484 854498 (unattributed)—duration
  of 23 seconds.

RECOMMENDATIONS

- billings/cellsite data to be obtained for 07484 919987 and
  07484 854498 to enable attribution
- interview Flora MAITLAND / Taryn LEWIS to determine nature of their association
- identify other phone(s) for Nigel MAITLAND

When Lou looked up from Jason's report, he was standing in the
doorway, hands in his pockets, watching her.

"This is good stuff," she said.

"I've got something else," he said.

"Have a seat. I'm on the last page."

He sat and waited for her to finish, and when she got to the end he
was tapping an inaudible rhythm with his fingers on his right knee.
Lou looked at him expectantly.

"I've been looking at Polly's cellsite data some more, comparing it
with the maps, trying to trace her movements on the last day."

"And?"

"You saw from the data that the phone traveled from Morden to Briarstone around eleven, and then was back in Morden just before midnight, right?"

"Yes."

"Well, the cellsite in Briarstone ends up at Forsyth Road."

She thought for one horrible moment he was going to wait for her to make the connection, the way her geography teacher used to stare at her expectantly, demanding an answer that she was unequipped to provide, but thankfully Jason didn't seem to want to play that particular game.

"Forsyth Road is the nearest cellsite phone mast to Waterside Gardens."

This time she knew what he was getting at before he could say it. "Where Flora lives."

"Exactly."

Lou stood, looked past Jason out to the main office, and the person she most wanted to see had just walked through the door. "Sam!" she called, and beckoned her over.

Jason stood up as Sam came in, offered her the seat. Sam looked at him with amusement in her eyes. "No, you're all right," she said. "I can manage."

They all stood in the tiny office while Jason repeated what he'd just said about the cellsite.

"What do you think?"

"It's not enough to arrest her," Sam said. "But we can bring her in and take a statement, at least."

"I agree it's a bit feeble," Lou said. "If we can bolster it up, it would be very good. And if we could get a search warrant for the farm—who knows what else we might get from that."

"We still need to find the murder weapon," said Sam. "Chances are it hasn't gone far from the cottage. And we still haven't found Polly's phone handset, either."

"I want Nigel's dirty phone," Lou said. "This is the best chance we've got."

"What about that other call, the one made from the landline? Any ideas?"

"I've already emailed Jane about it," said Jason. "Hopefully we'll get a result from the checks. In the meantime, at least we might get something from the search of Flora's place."

"Right," Sam said. "Well, I can try for a Section Eight search warrant, at least. Let's hope I don't get Boris."

She went back out into the main office to start putting the warrant request together.

"You want me to give her a hand?" Jason asked.

"Everything you've got, thank you."

"One question—who's Boris?"

Lou smiled. "Your friendly local magistrate, Jan Bryant. Also known as Battleaxe Bryant. Never raises a smile, never looks pleased to see you, under any circumstances. And to keep us all amused, she wears her hair like Boris Johnson."

18:05

Taryn had phoned Chris when she got back to her car, sitting in the hospital car park with the fan heater on, trying to get the windscreen to clear.

"Flora's been here," he said. "She's gone off to see her father. Said she'd be back later. Are you on the way home?"

"I'm going to stop off in Morden. He needs some things."

"You want me to meet you there?"

She thought about it, just for a moment. "No. I'm probably better off doing it alone. Thanks, though."

Twenty minutes later she was pulling into the driveway of Hayselden Barn. Morden, being a village, wasn't particularly well lit, but here, out in the sticks, it was black as black could be. When she parked and turned the lights off, the world outside disappeared. For a moment she sat listening to the wind bend and stretch the horse chestnut tree which towered over her, wishing she could have just gone home and forgotten about everything. The door key was on a silver key ring with car keys, what looked like a locker key, and one for something else, a padlock maybe?

She took a deep breath and stepped out into the blackness. Almost instantly a bright light came on and Taryn almost jumped out of her skin. Of course. A security light, triggered by a sensor of some kind. She headed for the front door and opened it. As she did so, she wondered what she would do if the alarm actually went off, but fortunately there was no sound at all from inside. Everywhere was in darkness. She found light switches by groping along the wall, knocking something off the hall table and treading all over the post on the floor in front of her.

Taryn gathered up the envelopes and shuffled them into a pile. One letter, addressed to Barbara. Handwritten. It was so unbelievable. One day she'd been living her life, as normal, and then she left this house and never returned. Here were letters she would never get to open, bills she would not pay, laundry in the basket she no longer had to bother with.

For a moment Taryn stood in the hallway, listening to the silence broken only by the ticking of the enormous grandfather clock. How strange it was to be in this house on her own. She had never lived here, never even spent a night here, and yet the place was furnished with antiques she remembered from her gran's house, all the pictures and ornaments and dark wood she had grown up knowing so well. A glass-fronted mahogany bookcase under the stairs held her grandmother's collection of dolls from around the world, old and faded. As a child she had been allowed to take them out and look at them, had given each of them a name and treated them with such reverence and care when all she had wanted to do was set up tea parties and hunting expeditions into the wild corners of the garden. They had probably never been taken out of the case since then.

She was wasting time. Upstairs, then—into the bedroom at the far end of the long hallway that stretched the length of the barn. It was neat and tidy in here, but the bed was unmade. On the back of the bedroom door she found a bathrobe. She draped it over one arm and had a look in the chest of drawers for something that looked like pajamas. Underwear, socks, trousers, a shirt—God, this was a hideous task. There was a leather holdall in the top of the wardrobe. She pulled it down and inside was a black leather dopp kit containing various male-smelling things, a toothbrush, toothpaste. The bathrobe went into the bag, along with a handful of pants and socks, a pair of khaki trousers and a polo shirt, a pair of worn-looking brogues in the bottom of the wardrobe that he probably never wore. She gave up on the pajamas. Perhaps he didn't wear them.

Going back out into the bland, beige-colored hallway, Taryn was struck by the transition from the maleness of the room she had just left. There was nothing feminine about it, nothing at all. And at the other end of the hallway, she could see through an open door into another bedroom. Curious now, she dropped the bag at the top of the stairs and carried on, pushing open the door at the other end and reaching along the wall until she found a light switch.

This must be Barbara's room. How strange, that they had separate rooms! And yet, why wouldn't they? When you had five bedrooms to choose from, and visitors only infrequently, why not spread out a bit more? This room was in a curious amount of disarray, the wardrobe doors open, revealing clothes draped over hangers and in piles on the floor. The bed was made, but a large rectangular indentation was on the plain white duvet as though someone had been packing a heavy case and had only just removed it.

She turned off the light and took the bag back downstairs. On a whim, she took the envelope addressed to Barbara Fletcher-Norman, Hayselden Barn, Morden, away with her. Barbara was never going to read it, so Taryn decided she should read it instead. It might help her understand this woman after all, might help her get some answers about why she had always been so unkind.

30 October 2013

Dearest Bunny,

I hope this letter finds you well and happy? I must admit the tone of your last worried me a little. I understand that what you feel for Liam at the moment surpasses what you feel for Brian, but you have to try and keep things discreet for the time being or else you might end up with nothing. Goodness knows we all know what Brian's like when he's cornered! Do you remember that time in Rome when you told him we all wanted to leave early? He was just unbearable.

Darling girl, don't do anything rash—I know Liam has been

putting pressure on you to leave, but really, there's no need. I'm sure he can wait just a little while longer, until you are sorted out financially and ready to make your move. You never know, if Brian is seeing the stable girl as you suspect then he might be happy with the arrangement!

All is well here. Andrew is finding the commute very hard again—I am trying to persuade him to try for more part-time hours, but it's a big ask. We will see what they say. I live in fear of the hospital calling to say he has had another heart attack.

All for now, Bunny, dear, write soon and we will talk at the weekend,

Love from your
Lorna
X

5X5X5 INTELLIGENCE REPORT

From:	Karen ASLETT—Source Coordinator
To:	DCI Louisa SMITH
Subject:	Nigel MAITLAND—Connor PETRIE—Harry McDONNELL
Date:	02/11/12

Grading B / 2 / 4

Connor PETRIE has been working at Hermitage Farm for a few months as a groom. Nigel MAITLAND gave him a job as a favor to Harry McDONNELL, whose wife is Emma PAYSWICK's (Connor's mother) best friend.

5X5X5 INTELLIGENCE REPORT

From:	Karen ASLETT—Source Coordinator
To:	DCI Louisa SMITH
Subject:	Nigel MAITLAND—Connor PETRIE—Harry McDONNELL
Date:	02/11/12

> **Grading** B / 2 / 4
>
> Connor PETRIE has been working at Hermitage Farm for a few months as a groom.
>
> Nigel MAITLAND also has PETRIE doing other small jobs for him in relation to the criminal association with the McDONNELL brothers. This includes running messages between MAITLAND and the McDONNELLs, as PETRIE sees them at home.

18:18

By the time Flora got back to Hermitage Farm, it was almost dark. The halogen lamps that lit up the main farmyard showed the yard was glossy in the way that meant it was turning to ice. It would be slick as a skating rink tonight.

She drove through the yard and up into the secluded turning circle in front of the farmhouse. Most of the lights appeared to be on inside.

The kitchen was warm and steamed up from whatever had been in the Aga for the past few hours; Felicity was sitting at the dining table with one of her cronies, an empty bottle of wine and a half-full one on the table between them. Her mother's cheeks were red, as were her eyes.

"Hello, Mum," Flora said, bending to kiss the fiery cheek.

"Flora, dear. Check the roast for me, would you? Of course, I never knew what to think"—this last directed at the elderly woman in the pink tracksuit seated across the table.

"Well, she was always a bit of an unknown quantity, for all you knew her mother," said the visitor, and Flora knew that they were talking about Polly. She opened the Aga door and inspected the meat. It looked decidedly pink. Taking a pair of oven gloves, she moved the joint up to the hotter part of the oven.

The woman's voice dropped to a coarse whisper: "Of course, you know that she swung both ways, don't you?"

"Swung both ways?" echoed Felicity, aghast.

Flora would have smiled if the situation hadn't been quite so grim.

"You mean she—she liked *gels*?"

Flora stood, and of course the visitor looked from her to Felicity and back again. Her short hair, inevitable jeans and T-shirt, lack of makeup, and lack of a boyfriend had not gone unremarked upon in the village. Although not yet within Felicity's earshot.

"Where's Dad, Mum?"

Felicity looked up, her eyes unfocused. "Hmm? Oh. In the garage, I think."

Outside, the wind had picked up again. A sleety drizzle had started and Flora pulled her jacket around her chest, folding her arms to keep the wind from blowing it open again. Right around the side of the house, a former barn was used as a garage housing Nigel Maitland's collection of vehicles. When he wasn't in the farm office, or visiting "associates" in London, he was most likely to be found here.

The side door to the barn was unlocked, the fluorescent lights bright within. At the far end of the barn, the old tack room had been converted into a second office—one that most of the "associates" were never invited to. If Felicity wanted him when he was in the garage, she usually phoned his mobile.

"Dad?" Flora called out from the doorway, knowing full well that he would have reacted when he heard the door open at the far end of the barn.

"In here," he called back. That was her permission to approach.

He had a laptop open on a desk that was cluttered with paperwork. She didn't look too closely, knew better than to be nosy where her father was concerned. It was one of the reasons why she was admitted where few others were.

The ladder to the hayloft, in the roof space above them, was down. Normally it was stowed away out of sight. In the loft, on a specially reinforced floor, was a second safe—a much larger one than the small safe holding paperwork and his wife's jewelry, which was to be found in the main house. Flora didn't know what it contained, didn't want to know, but for a brief moment she thought of Andy Hamilton and wondered what he would give to view what was inside.

Pictures of the family and various horses lined the walls, and a Pirelli calendar, two years out of date.

At the bottom of June—the page that never seemed to get turned over—was a scrawled list of names and phone numbers. One of the names on the list was "Flora," but the mobile number listed next to it wasn't hers. In fact, it was the combination to the safe. He'd told her that, one afternoon, out of the blue. He'd said that one day, if anything happened to him, she might need it. She had been surprised that he had trusted her with something as important as the contents of his safe, but thinking about it afterward Flora realized that he didn't have anyone else. Who could he tell? Not Felicity, who was flaky at her best and downright unstable at her worst. Certainly not Connor Petrie. Despite the amount of time he spent on the farm, Flora didn't trust him, and she suspected Nigel didn't either. What the hell he was doing working here at all was anyone's guess. Nigel must owe someone a bloody big favor, she thought.

Against one wall, next to an oil-filled radiator that was on full blast, was an old threadbare sofa. Nigel waved toward it. "Want something to drink?"

"No thanks. I'm not staying long."

A bottle of ten-year-old Benromach single-malt came out of the bottom of the filing cabinet, and a tumbler on Nigel's desk was half-filled. He drank from it as though preparing himself for something.

"So, Flora-Dora. What's new?"

She'd not been called that in years. What was that about? Suddenly overfriendly, trying to catch her off guard? He regarded her with those bright, electric-blue eyes. Polly had once told her that she'd thought he was wearing colored contact lenses. But they really were that color. Flora's were brown, like her mother's.

Flora wished she hadn't bothered coming. "Is there something specific you wanted to see me about? Because if there isn't, I'd rather go home."

Nigel drank some more, watched her, clearly deciding his next move. "Have the police interviewed you yet?"

She nodded.

"And?"

"And what? Do they think I killed Polly? Probably. I couldn't give a fuck anymore to be honest."

"You should have phoned me. I could have got Joe for you."

"I didn't think I needed a solicitor, thanks," Flora said. "Especially not that little turd."

Nigel fished through the papers on his desk and found a small box full of business cards. He rooted through it and handed one over to her. "Keep this handy. You never know. Whatever your opinion of him, he's good at his job."

Giovanni Lorenzo, known to his close friends as Joe, had been Nigel Maitland's solicitor for the last twenty years. Flora personally found him uncomfortably familiar and always thought he wore too much aftershave, which meant that in confined spaces, like interview rooms, people rarely wanted to keep him there for long.

"So have they got you pegged as a suspect?" Flora asked, although she already knew the answer. The police didn't bother with friendly chats with her father anymore—they would only interview him if they were ready with a caution, and enough evidence to back it up. Of course, Joe wasn't paid a fortune for nothing, and he'd always managed to get Nigel out of any sticky situation that he'd failed to avoid.

"If I'm a suspect, I'm in big trouble. It's all about the wording. To them, we're 'nominals.' Know what that means?"

Flora shook her head.

"We're in their system, in connection with this particular case. We're a number to them. The minute they start to refer to us as 'suspects' it means they're about to make an arrest, no more talking nicely—it all gets very official. So for the time being, let's be happy that we're nominals and not suspects. In any case, they're probably building up a nice meaty case against me. Trouble for them is, I didn't do it."

He poured another tumbler of whiskey.

"Where were you?" he said, his voice rough from the whiskey. "The night Polly died. Have you got an alibi?"

She thought back, trying to remember what she was doing. She remembered the next day clearly enough . . .

"It was Halloween night, wasn't it?" she said at last. "Mum phoned me up about six. I painted. Went to bed. Woke up, painted some more, and got your phone call. So—no alibi."

Nigel grimaced. "Me neither. At least not one that I'd be prepared to share with the fucking police."

"You were out, then?"

Nigel nodded. "With some friends. But they wouldn't thank me for mentioning their names, and in any case I was back here at midnight.

Crawled into bed about two. Your mother was snoring her head off, as usual. If I'd known I was going to need an alibi I'd have shaken her awake."

"Would they believe her as an alibi anyway?"

He snorted. "Probably not. She doesn't come across as entirely lucid at the best of times."

Flora raised a smile at this, just for a moment, and then remembered where she was and who she was talking to, and let it die on her lips. "Was there anything else?"

He looked sad for a moment, if that was even possible. "Flora," he said. "I know things have been . . . awkward. But I want you to know that if anything kicks off, I'm still your father—"

"What's going to kick off? What do you mean?"

"I don't mean anything in particular. I just think we should present a united front."

That was bloody typical, Flora thought. She felt the anger rise up to meet the misery she'd been feeling all day. But there was nothing she could say to him, of course, because he was entirely right. They were in this together, for better or worse—the Maitlands against the force of the law. Just as it had always been. Except this time she was right at the heart of it, instead of watching from the sidelines.

18:24

Andy Hamilton was waiting for Flora outside 14 Waterside Gardens, even though he knew she wasn't there. Doing as he was told, because Lou had asked him to keep an eye on Flora while they got the warrant together. Andy was pretty much convinced they were all barking up the wrong tree—it was going to turn out to be Barbara Fletcher-Norman, of course it was.

Phoning Lou for an update, no answer—no answer to the text he sent her, either. Not work, just checking she was okay. Mildly flirtatious. When he'd seen her in her office, the first day of the case, he had seen that same gleam in her eye and had thought that he was in with a chance. She still wanted him. She would fight it, but in the end he would win.

Now he wasn't so sure. Briefly he wondered if she had found someone else, and then quickly dismissed the idea. She was too busy here, didn't have time to meet anyone outside the job—and there was nobody else on this case that he could see her being interested in. Ali Whitmore? More likely to want to go home to his slippers than wind up in bed with an energetic girl like Lou. That weird American analyst? More keen to go home to his PC and fiddle with his webcam, probably. That left Sam Hollands. Andy smirked a little at the thought—that was something he'd pay to see. Pay even more to join in with.

If he didn't find Flora he might get another chat with the nurse he'd seen here yesterday, Flora's very attractive downstairs neighbor. She must be a nurse, he thought—they wore the navy-blue uniforms, didn't they? They were the ones in charge—and the thought of it was curiously arousing.

He frowned. There was something not quite right about 14 Waterside Gardens, and for a moment he couldn't quite place what it was. Flora's flat was in darkness, the curtains drawn, and downstairs . . . downstairs the front door to flat one was slightly ajar.

He got out of the car and walked up to the house, standing for a moment at the bottom of the steps, looking up to the front door. It wasn't open by much, just enough to tilt it slightly into shadow, which is what had attracted his attention.

He climbed the steps and stood listening. He should call it in. He should get backup. Maybe she'd been burgled—or maybe she was lying in a pool of blood in the hallway, like Polly.

He gave the door a little push, letting it swing soundlessly into the hall. He could see down a long corridor into a kitchen at the bottom. A light was on, but no sign of anyone inside.

"Police! Anyone in here?" he called. Alarm bells were ringing so loudly in his head he thought they must be audible halfway up the street, but still he stepped inside. This was wrong, all wrong. He kept telling himself that he had legitimate concerns for the welfare of the occupant, and yet he didn't want to call out again, didn't want her to know he was in here.

Holding his breath, he walked down the corridor into the kitchen. On the table a copy of today's *Eden Evening Standard* was open to page two, the continuation of an article about Polly's murder. There was a picture of Yonder Cottage with that PC—whatever his name was—standing gamely guarding the driveway.

He hadn't heard her, but suddenly she was behind him.

He spun round to see her standing close to him, those blue eyes regarding him. Beyond his surprise at how he had managed to find himself in this woman's kitchen came the sudden shot of desire. She wasn't wearing the uniform this time but somehow she looked even more sure of herself: a skirt, short, showing tanned, well-toned legs and sharp sandals with a killer heel. Her white shirt was open at the neck, showing cleavage.

"You took your time," she said.

Andy felt his skin color. "Sorry—what?"

She smiled at him, taking a step closer. "You've been sitting outside in that car for over half an hour. And you know as well as I do that Flora isn't home. Therefore you must be waiting for me. What do you want, then?"

He couldn't think of anything to say.

She put one hand on his chest, sliding under the fabric of his suit jacket and over his cotton shirt, her fingers pressing into the skin underneath. Her other hand joined in and she pushed the jacket off his shoulders, letting it fall onto the kitchen table.

She brought her face close to his, so that he could feel her breath on his cheek. He was about to take a step back, ask what the fuck she thought she was doing, when he felt her hand run down the front of his trousers, curving around the hardness of his erection. Her grip on him was strong, and deliberate. Jesus!

He stumbled back, knocking into the table, staring at her in shock.

"Next time, I expect more from you than this," she said.

"I'm—I'm sorry?" He had no idea why he was apologizing. What she'd done was pretty much sexual assault—even if he had been about to kiss her.

She laughed at his expression, turned at the kitchen door, and gave him an amused little smile. "Shut the door behind you on your way out, Inspector."

For a moment he stood there, dazed, wondering what the hell just happened. Then he retrieved his jacket from the table and did as he was told.

19:14

Flora was lying on Taryn's spare bed, scrunched up into a tight ball. Downstairs, Sky Sports was on and Chris was sitting in front of it. Tabby was at the hospital, still. Maybe if Flora was asleep by the time she got home, they wouldn't have to talk about it.

If only she could stop thinking, just for a moment, she might be able to sleep. Still, every thought led back to Polly.

That morning in August, the sun already hot although it was barely nine, the air smelling of ripe wheat from the field opposite, the sound of the tractor trundling up the lane. There was no car parked on the drive of Yonder Cottage. Sometimes there had been a car parked there; different cars. If there had been a car, Flora would have turned around quietly and driven away.

There was no car.

Just the sunlight, and the morning. By now Polly would have seen to the horses, would be back for a shower and breakfast. If Flora was lucky she would catch her in her bathrobe, hair damp from the shower, skin glowing, the bed still unmade . . .

The back door was unlocked the way it always was.

Flora didn't call out. She wanted to surprise her.

Only when she was halfway up the stairs did she hear it—laughter, gentle, light—Polly's voice. And another voice, low, one that made Flora's heart pound and the bile rise in her throat.

She couldn't stop herself then, although she already knew what she was going to see. She could hear the voices properly now, at the top of the stairs.

" . . . you're silly. You always were."

"Polly. Come here. Where are you going?"

"Nowhere. I'm staying—right—here . . ."

Flora pushed the door to the bedroom just enough to see her father lying splayed on Polly's bed, the single white sheet covering a leg, an ankle, and Polly completely naked, the masses of blond hair falling like a golden river over Nigel Maitland's lap. Polly was too occupied with the task in hand to see Flora turn, slowly, and go back the way she had come. But Nigel had met his daughter's eyes, briefly, before she had turned away.

She had gone back to the flat she rented in town, avoided the farm where she had been every single day. Polly had called, and sent texts. Flora had not responded. Her father had called, several times, and then turned up at the studio. She had not opened the door. Felicity was by far the most persistent. Flora returned her mother's calls and texts with brief, conciliatory responses. Nothing was wrong. She was busy working. It was all fine; she was just busy. Eventually her mother had sent her one of those ultimatum texts she was so good at, and Flora had reluctantly come back.

"What on earth's the matter with you?" Felicity had said, sitting in the garden with a cup of tea because the kitchen was too damned hot with the Aga on.

Flora had lost weight; all her clothes were hanging off her already thin frame. "Nothing, Mum. I've been busy working."

Felicity snorted. She'd never considered Flora's art as real work, even when the exhibition she'd had last year had netted several thousand pounds in sales.

"Is it a boy?"

"What?"

"Are you having problems with a boy?"

Flora stared at her, not sure whether to laugh or cry. "No, nothing like that. Where's . . . ?" Flora hesitated over the word, tried again: "Where's my father?"

"Daddy? In his office, I shouldn't wonder."

Flora considered. It was time. "Perhaps I'll drop in and say hello."

He wasn't in his office, he was behind the main barn, talking on his mobile phone the way he did when he didn't want to risk anyone in the house overhearing.

"Tell him I won't have it. It's the whole deal or nothing." Nigel Maitland saw his daughter approaching and tried to end the call as quickly as he could. "I don't give a fuck. *You* sort it out. It's what I'm paying you for."

He snapped the phone closed and stood a little straighter. "Flora."

"Dad."

They stood for a moment regarding each other. It was cool here, in the shade, no sound but the occasional neigh or snort from the horses in the field behind them.

"I remembered," Flora said at last.

For a moment Nigel hadn't a clue what she was talking about. "What?"

"Seeing you with Polly. It brought something back to me. Of course, when you're just eight you don't always understand things that you see. It's only afterward when you realize."

A glimmer of realization was starting to creep across his rugged features. "Oh. And what was it that you saw? When you were eight?"

"We were on holiday in Spain with Polly and her mum and lots of other people. I'd completely forgotten. I remembered you playing in the pool with Polly."

There was a pause while Flora remembered, and Nigel tried to remember the moment.

"You were . . . you were tickling her, and she was laughing. She must have only been fourteen. There was nobody else there. I was watching from the window. *And you were tickling her.*"

There was a long moment. Nigel looked at the floor. "But you know what she's like. She was like that even then. It wasn't about sex, not then. She was just so bright, so vivacious. She was—addictive."

Flora felt tears, fought them back. "Have you been sleeping with her all these years?"

Nigel gave a short laugh. "No! God, no." He took a step toward Flora, who took a step back. "Flora! There was nothing between Polly and me until about a month ago. I promise you."

She couldn't stop it now. A sob, a gasp—and he stepped forward as if to embrace her. At the same moment she took a step back, shaking her head. Something had broken.

He was staring at her, unmoving, his jaw clenching. "I won't see her again," he said.

"It doesn't matter," she sobbed. "You do whatever you like. I don't care!"

And the tears fell, then and now, in the privacy of Tabby's spare room. And what she had been unable to say to him then: the true hurt, the ultimate betrayal lay not in the fact that the woman she loved was unfaithful, she already knew that; nor that her father had been intimate with Polly for longer than she herself had, probably—despite his denials—long before it was right or appropriate for him to do so, even putting aside the fact that he was a married man. No, the pain that tore her apart came from that secret, terrible knowledge in her own heart that, as an eight-year-old girl, she had seen the secret moment between her father and Polly and had been burned raw with the acid of jealousy. She had been envious of them! How stupid, how foolish she had been.

Later, walking back past the barn at the top of the drive, she had seen Polly getting out of her car at Yonder Cottage. Always at a rough angle, wheels turned, as though she'd just tossed the car to one side instead of actually parking it. Polly had seen her and waved.

Flora had continued walking. Then she heard Polly call out, and when she looked round again she was running up toward her.

"Flora! Flora, wait for me!"

She stopped and waited, heart thudding, pounding in her chest. She didn't feel ready for this, so soon after her father. Polly was wearing tight jeans, a clinging T-shirt, her hair tied back in a messy bun. She was breathless when she reached Flora.

"Where have you been?" she asked. "I've been trying to call you."

Flora tried out several possible responses in her head, eventually settling on: "At the flat."

"Why didn't you answer your phone? Have you been avoiding me?"

How could she not know? "You—and him. My father."

"Oh, that!"

She said it cheerfully, dismissively, as if it was such a trivial thing. "But, Flora, you know I see lots of people. You've always known. I've never kept it a secret from you. And I thought you were okay with it!"

"Not him. Not with my dad."

"Oh, Flora. My lovely girl . . ." She had put out a hand toward her, and Flora shrank back.

She was already walking away when Polly said, "I'm not seeing him anymore, Flora. I've stopped all that now. There's someone else, someone important . . ."

"I don't want to know," Flora said, over her shoulder. "It's nothing to do with me."

"Don't be like that, please, Flora!"

Flora got to the car, stopped and waited, took a deep breath. "Why are you doing this?" she asked quietly, not even sure if she was talking to Polly or to herself.

Polly had caught up with her, her eyes bright. "Everything's changed. My whole life has changed."

"What are you talking about?" Flora turned to look at her, moved round to the driver's door, keeping the car between her and Polly as if she needed it for protection.

"I'm sorry," Polly said, at last. "I'm sorry if I hurt you. I didn't mean to."

They stared at each other. Flora couldn't think of anything to say. Polly was looking radiant, beautiful, even more than normal. And she was smiling, a wistful smile that could have been genuine, sorrowful for how things had turned out, or maybe it was just pity. Eventually, wanting a way to bring this to an end, Flora said, "Thank you."

Then she opened the car door and got in, shutting the door and, at last, breathing out in a long, gasping breath.

20:11

The hospital car park was a lot quieter than it had been earlier. Taryn found a space near the entrance and didn't get a pay-and-display ticket, despite the sign saying that charges applied twenty-four hours. Bollocks to that, she thought. If she got a ticket, that meant she was really here. And she couldn't see that there would be any security staff looking for ticket flouts at this time of night. They were all tucked up in their cabin, watching *EastEnders* and drinking tea.

The ICU was quiet, too, although a few of the beds had visitors. Not many of the patients were conscious. At first Taryn thought her father was asleep, too, but when she approached the bed he opened his eyes and turned to look at her, a halfhearted smile on his lips. The machines beside him beeped quietly. They had been turned down so people could sleep—those that weren't unconscious, at any rate.

"Taryn," he said, with a cough. "I didn't think you'd be back to-night."

"I can't come tomorrow," she said. "I have a visitor. Maybe not the day after. So I thought I'd bring this stuff."

"Thank you."

She stared at him for a few moments, then dropped the leather holdall by the bed. There was nothing on the cabinet next to him, no flowers or cards. Taryn wondered vaguely if any of his friends knew he was in here. Did he have friends?

"Is the house okay?"

Taryn gave a tiny shrug. "Looked fine to me. I locked the door."

His eyes closed slowly. Taryn thought his breathing sounded a bit funny. She wondered if he was asleep and turned to leave, but he raised his hand as if to touch her. She was too far away from the bed, though.

"Taryn," he said, whispered. She had to come closer to hear him.

I don't want to hear this, she thought. Whatever it is, I know this isn't going to be something I am going to want to hear.

"I need you to do something for me." He coughed again, a low rumble from inside his chest.

"What?"

"I need you to phone someone. Just to tell her what's happened, and where I am."

"Who?"

"Her name is Suzanne. I don't know her number offhand; it's in my mobile. The number is listed as 'Manchester office' in the address book."

Taryn raised her eyes to the ceiling. "Who is she, this Suzanne?"

"Will you do it? Will you phone her? My mobile should be in my briefcase, it will be in the office at home."

"Who is she?"

Brian gave a deep sigh, turned away for a moment. Taryn thought there might be a tear in the corner of his eye.

"Don't tell me you were cheating on Barbara, Dad? Wasn't she good enough for you in the end?" This confrontation felt good, and yet bad at the same time. What was this? Was she starting to feel sympathy for him, this tired old man, lying here all alone with no one to care for him? Nobody left? Where were all his golfing friends? Bridge partners? Mistresses galore, going back through the years like a line of Tiller Girls, all legs and tits and sarcasm?

"She was going to leave me," Brian said, with a small voice. "She was having an affair with her tennis coach. She was planning to go to Ireland with him."

"So you thought you'd beat her to it?"

"Suzanne is different. It's not what you think. She—she's special. Will you phone her?"

"What about Polly, Dad?"

"What about her?"

"Did you have an affair with her, too?"

Brian managed to raise a smile at this. "Of course. Didn't everyone?"

Her heart grew colder toward him again. The poor girl was dead. She might have broken hearts everywhere she went, but someone had taken her life from her in a brutal way. And taken Polly away from Flora, who deserved better.

"What happened with Polly, Dad?"

"Tabby, please. I am so tired. Will you call Suzanne for me?"

"Tell me about Polly."

Brian sighed. "If I tell you, will you call Suzanne?"

"Yes."

He looked away for a moment, remembering. "Polly came on to me at one of Felicity's dinner parties. Not long after she moved into the cottage. I'd taken Barbara home—she'd had a few drinks too many—and as soon as I came back, Polly sat next to me and, well, she flirted. Made me feel good. That was the start of it."

"Barbara found out?"

"She was suspicious, but she could never prove anything."

"She might have followed you, or something."

He shrugged, as if it didn't matter anymore. "I didn't see her for long."

"So why did you stop?"

Taryn wondered if it was her own curiosity leading her to ask these questions, or whether Sam Hollands had put the idea into her head.

"She introduced me to Suzanne."

"The woman you want me to phone? She was a friend of Polly's?" Brian nodded.

"Like I said," Taryn said, her voice cool, "I've got a visitor. I don't know if I'll get back to the house again this week. If I get a chance, I'll find your phone and let Suzanne know."

Brian's eyes closed, and his breathing deepened. That was her cue to leave. She had had enough, anyway.

20:12

Les Finnegan took the call on his mobile and by the expression on his face and his frantic hand signals to those that were left in the office, everyone stopped what they were doing and waited in silence for him to finish. Lou got up from her desk and stood in the doorway.

"Right. Thanks. Yeah, I'll wait for the details, thanks. Bye."

He looked around, a big grin spreading on his face. "Blood results back. The DNA on Barbara Fletcher-Norman's clothes is definitely Polly's."

Some of them cheered. Jason was smiling and suddenly everyone was talking at once.

Lou went back into the office to ring Buchanan, and when she came out again they all had their coats on and were waiting for her.

"King Bill, is it?" she asked, somewhat redundantly. "I'll catch up with you."

She spent another half an hour working her way through emails, writing a brief report for Buchanan that he could take into the chief officers' briefing tomorrow morning.

She tried Sam's mobile, but it went to voice mail. Sam had called to say Boris had put up a bit of a struggle and then caved in, possibly due to the fact that she was having a dinner party that evening and was making a soufflé.

Flora Maitland or Barbara Fletcher-Norman . . . The stronger evidence pointed to Barbara, who was dead and could not therefore be arrested and interviewed. But whatever the reason that Polly's phone had been used in the immediate vicinity of her former lover's home address just before she had been murdered, it wouldn't hurt to ask her about it. And have a good old rummage through the farm while they were about it.

Sam arrived a few minutes later and looked crestfallen when she came into the MIR and found only Lou in attendance.

"Oh, let me guess," she said. "King Bill?"

"Sam, I've just had a thought—did you specify all the outbuildings on the warrant?"

Sam grinned and waved the piece of paper. "All properties on the land pertaining to Hermitage Farm, Morden," she said with triumph.

Definitely cause for celebration. "First thing tomorrow, we'll bring her in."

"Do we know where she is?"

"Mr. Hamilton's in charge of keeping tabs on her. Shall we go and have a little drink, Sam?"

She logged out of the system and told Sam to go on ahead while she took a copy of her report upstairs to the management corridor and slotted it into Mr. Buchanan's pigeonhole. After that, she went to the ladies' and stared at her reflection, criticizing her hair and her tired face and the state of the makeup she'd applied in the morning. If it hadn't been for Sam, she might not have bothered going to the pub after all, but it wouldn't hurt to show her face across the road. If they were to get a quick result, it warranted a drink or two. And if this *was* a blind alley, then it would serve as a consolation.

20:14

Andy was tired. He'd called in to the MIR to report back to Lou and found they'd all buggered off. A note in Les Finnegan's handwriting on his desk read "King Bill."

One of the phones was ringing. It was an outside line and he wanted to ignore it, wanted desperately to pretend he wasn't here so that he could fuck off to the pub with the rest of them, start the weekend, even if it was going to be a working one.

In the end, his conscience got the better of him and he answered it.

"Incident Room, Andy Hamilton speaking."

"Can I speak to Detective Sergeant Sam Hollands, please?"

The voice on the other end was familiar. Andy searched through the catalogue of people it could be—someone he'd met recently, someone he'd liked.

"DS Hollands has left, I'm afraid. Can I help? Take a message?"

There was a long pause. "No, I'll ring tomorrow."

"Who's speaking, please?"

"My name is Taryn Lewis."

The link clicked into place between the voice and the curvy blond who'd been at the café earlier in the day. Taryn—Tabby. Bugger.

"Mrs. Lewis. You didn't explain who you were when we met earlier."

"You didn't ask."

"Are you sure there's nothing else I can help with?"

"Tell Sam Hollands to call me as soon as possible, would you?"

It could wait. It could all wait. Apart from one thing: "Mrs. Lewis, there was something else I needed to ask Flora. She's not answering her phone and she doesn't seem to be at home. You don't happen to know where she is?"

"She's staying at my house. I didn't think she should be alone at the moment, until she's had a bit of time . . . you know."

Bingo. "I understand. She's going through an incredibly difficult thing."

"Exactly. And she can't go to the farm, of course."

"She's lucky to have such a good friend," Andy said. I should be on some therapy talk show, he thought. He could spout bollocks when the situation demanded it.

"Thank you," Taryn said. "Do you want me to ask her to call you?"

"It's fine. I'll catch up with her tomorrow. As long as she's okay," he said. As long as she's not planning to leave the country or disappear, is what he meant.

When she rang off, Andy sighed with relief. The day was ending favorably, and he had earned the right to finish off with a pint or two with the lads. With a bit of luck, Louisa might be in there too. With a lot of luck, she might be ever so slightly pissed already and therefore less immune to his charms.

20:19

Brian's eyes closed. Talking to Taryn about Suzanne and Polly had brought back all the memories of how tangled his romantic life had become. He'd had many affairs over the years, had lost count somewhere along the line of all the one-night stands he'd had, the expensive prostitutes paid for by clients overseas, the women he'd met in bars, hotels, the women he'd met socially and seen regularly: Emma, a sports therapist at the gym; Andrea, the wife of one of his colleagues, hungry for some danger; Sheila Newton, Barbara's friend who'd wanted to set Barbara up with her corpulent stockbroker husband, Derek, and try and engineer a foursome—that had brought that particular liaison to an abrupt end as Brian couldn't imagine anything less sensual or appealing. And then there was Christine, Barbara's bridge partner. He'd had her on more than one occasion.

The first time he'd cheated on Jean, Taryn's mother, it had been difficult and shameful, and he swore he would never do it again. But the second time it was easier. The third time, it was with Barbara, and she hooked him good and proper. When he married Barbara, he promised briefly that he would mend his ways. That lasted three months, until one of the stewardesses on a transatlantic flight slipped him her New York phone number.

Infidelity was only an issue if you let it be. He was happy to come home to Barbara, happy to share his life with her, happy to have an attractive woman on his arm at parties, even if she did fail to behave herself after her third gin.

And then, just when everything was simple, there was Polly to complicate things.

She had curled up beside him on the sofa in Felicity's conservatory at one of those interminable drinks parties, put her hand on his knee and laughed, throwing her head back and baring her throat. She told him she liked sex, a lot, couldn't get enough of it. She liked people. And she was so young, so *alive*.

Later, walking back to the Barn, the silent moon lighting the way, he had heard a low whistle behind him. Polly had followed him out. She was running across the pavement with no shoes on, her short sequinned dress swishing against her naked thighs. She threw her arms around his neck and kissed him, giggling softly.

He brought her into the garden and, in full view of the house, he pulled her dress above her head. Underneath, she was naked, her skin silver in the moonlight. Aside from the noises they made themselves, everything was silence. She pulled at his trousers to get at what she wanted, and from then on it was a mad tangle of limbs—the smell of the grass, the thought of the grass stains on his clothes; even if he took them off now it would be too late . . . She climbed on top of him, her hair around her like a cloud. He looked up into the night sky, at the moon watching them without comment, and laughed, not believing the madness of it. He knew Barbara would be asleep, snoring off the effects of several too many, but still, the dare of it, the challenge of fucking this beautiful girl, twentysomething, full of life and energy and the bold confidence of her own sensuality, overwhelmed him completely. Who cared if anyone saw? He would never live like this again, never.

He wasn't naïve.

He knew Polly's type, although he'd never met anyone really like her. She was what they used to call a nymphomaniac, needy for sex in the same way that many women were needy for emotion. She had sex as often as possible. She got depressed if she went without it for more than a few days. She cared about the people she slept with, some of them at least. But that was as far as it went—Polly could no more be faithful to someone than she could fly to the moon.

He also knew, because she told him, proudly and excitedly, that she had been involved with the swinging scene when she had lived in London; that she still met up with some of the people she had played with from time to time. He remembered lying in Polly's bed, upstairs at Yonder Cottage while Barbara was drinking tea at Hermitage Farm with Felicity. He loved the whole danger of Polly. She was dangerous and intriguing. She was lying next to him, her hands idly playing with him, teasing. She was telling him about this woman who was nearly as insatiable as she was.

"Her name is Suzanne," Polly said, and a wistful look came over her face that Brian had never seen before. "I met her when I was traveling, but she's here, living in Briarstone now. She is so amazing! One of these powerful women, you know? All about power."

"What sort of power?"

"Control. I didn't think it was my thing, but there's something about the way she does it. She makes me feel scared, and safe, all at the same time."

"Can't be good, feeling scared, surely?" he murmured.

Polly laughed. "It gives me the most incredible high the way she does it. I've never had orgasms like that, Brian. You wouldn't believe how it feels—it's like flying. She's my idol. My goddess." Her eyes went back to his face. "Want to meet her?"

"Yes," said Brian, before he had time to think about it.

"Did you ever do a threesome, Brian? Fancy it with me and Suzanne?"

He had done a threesome, years ago. Well, of a sort. In a hotel room in Bangkok. One of his clients had paid for a show—two girls licking and fingering each other enthusiastically. Once he'd given up watching and joined in, they'd left each other alone and concentrated on pleasuring him. They weren't really into it—it was all just acting—but enjoyable for that, mind you, if not exactly real.

A few weeks later, Barbara away visiting her friend in Norfolk, he had gone with Polly to a flat in town to meet Suzanne.

To say the woman was charismatic was an understatement. She was animated, confident like Polly, but witty and intelligent, even intellectual. And completely insatiable. They had dinner, wine, and then fucked the night away, all three of them. He flagged long before Polly and Suzanne did. Polly had been right, there was something dangerous and yet addictive about relinquishing control to another person. And when the other two finally fell asleep, he knew that something had changed. He wanted to see Suzanne again. More than that. He had never thought for one minute a woman would come along who would be sensational enough to make him want to leave Barbara, with all the hassle and financial costs that would incur. But as he slipped in and out of consciousness, his thoughts strayed to how on earth he would persuade Barbara to leave him without it costing him an arm and a leg.

And now, as Brian felt himself drifting toward sleep, he smiled. He'd done it. He belonged to Suzanne, now, in every sense. And Barbara was gone.

20:22

The pub was noisy and warm, the windows steamed up from the beery breath of a hundred or so patrons, fifty percent of them job from one department or other. When they'd shut the subsidized bar at the station two years ago, the landlord of the King William had suddenly found his takings up by nearly a hundred percent. He'd lost a few of his old regulars, the ones who didn't fancy sharing their pint with the likes of the local CID and who had used the nickname "Old Bill" for the pub, rather than the King Bill—but the huge leap in profits more than compensated for it.

You couldn't miss Andy Hamilton in a crowd, Lou thought. He was a head taller than anyone else, propping up the bar with Les Finnegan and some of the others. She almost ducked back out of the door when she realized Jason wasn't there, but by that time Hamilton had beckoned her over. "Here she is, look," she heard him saying to someone else.

"What are you having?" Ali Whitmore was at the bar, most of a round of drinks lined up in front of him.

"Just a Coke, please, Ali."

Hamilton made her a space on the bar stool next to his, gave her a warm smile. The others were all laughing and joking, the tensions of the case forgotten. She realized she had forgiven him, because suddenly the anger she'd felt this afternoon wasn't there anymore.

"You look great," he said, quietly, leaning toward her so the rest of them didn't hear.

She smiled. "I feel like shit."

He laughed. "In that case, I'd like to see you on a good day. Guess who I just spoke to?"

"Who?"

"Taryn Lewis. Brian Fletcher-Norman's daughter. She rang to speak to Sam."

"And?"

"She didn't want to leave a message. Just that I recognized the voice, is all. She was with Flora this afternoon when I met her in the coffee shop. Didn't tell me who she was."

"What's she like?"

Hamilton hesitated and she knew that he was thinking about how she looked rather than what sort of a personality she had. "She was all right, I thought" is what he said. Eventually. "Anyway, Flora is staying at her house so she's all tucked up safe and sound, and we can pull her in first thing tomorrow. I told Sam to call her back, anyway."

His eyes looked tired, and Lou wondered how he was sleeping. He'd once told her that he never slept a full night, needed tablets to catch up on sleep during the day when he was on nights.

"Just like old times, huh?" he said, raising his glass and only just stopping short of giving her a wink.

She pulled a face at him. "Yeah."

Across the bar, she saw Jason coming out of the gents' and making his way through the bodies back toward the table. He met her eyes and gave her a smile.

Andy had edged closer, having followed her gaze across the pub. "We should go to the Palace of India," he said. "I fancy a curry. Don't you? Fancy a curry?"

A year ago they were in the Palace of India celebrating the end of the case. The drug dealer they'd been targeting for months had been arrested; the search teams had seized eight kilos of heroin and nearly a quarter of a million pounds in cash. The interview teams, led by Lou, had managed to get not only a confession of sorts, but evidence links to other organized-crime gangs across the county and the whole team had headed into town, drinking from one place to another, Andy flirting with her as he had done through the case, both of them not letting it get any further because they were both too busy, too focused, to let something get in the way. Now that was gone.

In the Palace of India Andy sat next to her, his thigh pressed against hers, the smell of his aftershave, faint after a long day, driving her mad. While everyone was too drunk, too loud to notice, he slipped his hand under the table and between her knees, sliding her skirt up her thighs, stroking her skin. Lamely she pushed him away, once. Then everyone was going, heading off to a club or something. He'd hung back, the others hurrying ahead to get in the queue. He pulled her into a doorway, pressed her tight against the glass door, his body pressed against hers. She pushed her hands inside his jacket, feeling the warmth of him, while his mouth invaded hers. She felt the pressure of him through the fabric of his jeans, his hand up her skirt at the back, on the verge of pulling aside her underwear until she noticed over his shoulder that they were about to fuck in full view of a restaurant full of people.

Instead of turning left toward the nightclub, they turned right to the taxi rank, took a cab back to her house. He left at half past three, when she was just falling asleep. Kissed her goodbye so tenderly she barely felt it, only the smile that went with it.

"No thanks," she said now. "You guys go ahead. I've gone right off curry."

Finishing the last of her drink, she gave him a cool smile. "Night everyone. Thanks for the drink, Ali. See you tomorrow." As a parting shot she palmed Ali forty quid to get a round or two in, then went out into the cold to find her car.

The wind was tugging at the corners of her coat while she fished in her bag for her keys. She didn't hear the footsteps behind her until a second before she wheeled round, and there he was, right behind her. He grabbed her arm to steady her.

"Jesus, Andy. Don't sneak up on me like that."

He leaned forward a little, pinning her against the car. "Don't go," he said, his face close to hers. "I wanted to spend a bit of time with you. Like the old days."

"Andy," she said sharply. "We're in the bloody station car park. Right under the CCTV. Get off me."

His hand was around her waist, strong and firm. He fitted against her exactly, his whole body warm and solid and safe. She felt her heart give, just a little bit. Then she felt the unmistakable hardness of his erection and the feeling passed in a sudden, nauseating rush.

"Inspector, get the fuck off me. *Now.*"

He moved quickly, almost stumbling back. "I'm sorry," he said. "Sorry. Don't know what came over me."

Lou looked at him, his face shadowed in the half-light from the arc lights by the exit.

"I'm telling you," she said, her voice soft, carried away on the wind, "it's not going to happen. If you pull a stunt like that again I'll put in a complaint."

His expression changed, grew cold. "You wouldn't do that to me, Lou. Would you?"

"You seem to be having trouble getting the message. I'm telling you again, it's not going to happen. Can we just call an end to it now—please?"

He attempted a smile. "Sure. I'm sorry. I just—well. You're beautiful, and I won't stop wanting you. That's all."

"You're *married*," she said, with an air of finality, opened the car door and got in. He stood there for a few moments, then he turned away.

Lou exhaled, rested her head against the window, trying with long deep breaths to stay focused. As she felt herself calming, the car parked two spaces away from her beeped and flashed its indicators. She watched as a familiar figure crossed the car park in front of her and she took a sharp breath in.

He stopped when he saw her sitting there. He even chanced a smile and a wave but then he hesitated, changed direction, and walked instead over to her car.

Shit. Not now, not right this minute.

He was right by her window. She looked straight ahead, thought too late about rooting in her bag and bringing out her phone so she could pretend she was taking an urgent call.

What the hell, there was no point pretending, was there? Not when all she wanted to do was go somewhere Hamilton wasn't, get drunk, and spend the night with someone who was not, just for a change, married to someone else.

By the time she glanced up at her window he'd gone, and at that precise moment the passenger door of her car opened and Jason Mercer climbed in beside her.

21:55

"What's wrong?" he asked her.

She laughed at this, and even to her own ears it sounded forced. "Nothing, everything's fine."

And then his hand was on her shoulder and he was pulling her across into his arms and holding her tightly. The warmth of his body, through the thin cotton of his shirt, against her hot cheek; the smell of him, his masculine warmth, so good that she realized she was taking deep breaths on purpose.

"It's okay," he said. "It's all right. I've got you."

And for a moment it was all right, and then it was completely not all right and she pulled away from him.

"Oh God. I'm sorry. What am I thinking?"

For a moment she couldn't look at him, and then she did and she was lost in the way he was looking back at her. *I don't want to do this. I don't want to make these stupid mistakes all over again.*

He broke off the eye contact and looked straight ahead, out of the windscreen at the cars and the darkness and the rain spitting on the windscreen. He cleared his throat.

"So, I'm going to go get in my car," he said. "You're welcome to follow me, if you like. I'll cook you dinner and we can get drunk together and you can tell me all about what's happened to you and why you're unhappy."

She made a sound as if to say something—thanks, but no—you're kind—I'm your SIO, it's not appropriate—I can't—

But he wasn't quite finished.

"Or you can drive home on your own and I won't mention it again. Does that sound okay?"

She nodded dumbly. Christ, what on earth was she doing? He was giving her the option to walk away from this horribly embarrassing encounter and yet she already knew what she was going to do.

He opened the door.

"Jason," she said.

He looked back at her.

"Are you sure about this?"

He smiled as if that was a reply and shut the door. She started the engine immediately, thinking that she was going to drive away now, right now, before he even got back to his car and she would have to exit through the barriers behind him, thinking that if she did it quick enough he would have got the message properly and there would be no more flirting, no more lingering looks, no more intense silences.

And then he was reversing out of the parking space and her chance for that particular dramatic gesture had gone.

She waited for a moment and then turned on the lights and the windscreen wipers and eased the car out. His car went through the barrier and waited at the junction while she swiped her pass. Then he indicated left.

After just the briefest hesitation, she followed him.

22:12

Jason parked on the driveway of a house about two miles across town, and Lou pulled up to the curb outside. He was waiting for her in the doorway. He took her hand to lead her inside, and then didn't let go of it. She stood in the darkness of his hall, the door still open behind her, looking at him. He pushed the door closed, slowly, purposefully, with one hand, without taking his eyes off her.

His hand threaded through her hair and pulled her close to him and then he kissed her. Oh, it felt good. Like a huge sense of release.

She kicked off her shoes and that felt good too, even though she didn't quite make it up to his shoulder without her heels. He took her through to his living room, turned on a table lamp next to the sofa, kissed her again.

There was a pile of laundry folded on the sofa, newspapers and a cereal bowl and a mug on the coffee table.

"Sorry," he said, "wasn't expecting . . . this."

"It's a nice room," she said, to make him feel better.

He put the laundry on the other chair and pulled her down onto the sofa with him. There was no debate about it, no hesitation. It was a this-needs-to-happen-now moment; his arms pulled her close against him, one of his hands at the small of her back, one in her hair.

As they kissed, his hands moved over her body, exploring her. Lou thought distractedly how it was good precisely because he didn't just get his hands straight up her skirt or into her blouse—he was getting to know her body, all of it, even the parts most men tended to miss: the back of her neck, her throat, the insides of her elbows, the small of her back. She pressed her fingertips into the muscles on his chest, feeling the beating of his heart as he breathed into her hair, ran her fingers down the back of his head, feeling his short hair.

Her phone bleeped loudly to signify an incoming message. She ignored it but a second later he pulled his head back and said, "You need to get that?"

"No," she said. And then her stomach gurgled loudly and they both laughed.

He extricated himself and sat up. His shirt had become untucked at the back and she pushed her fingers up inside, over his warm skin.

"I should get us some food," he said, looking down at her.

"I'm not hungry, really," she said.

"You should still eat. I haven't seen you eat anything except Kit Kats."

"I think it counts as one of my five a day, or at least the orange ones do."

He went to the kitchen that was separated from the living room by a breakfast bar, turned on the lights. The text was from Hamilton. Just a single word: *Sorry.*

She watched him moving around his kitchen, cutting slices of whole wheat bread that looked homemade, then bringing out lettuce, radishes, olives, and cucumber from the fridge and chopping and mixing.

"Tell me how come you're in the U.K.," she asked again.

He stopped for a moment, looked at her. That blue-eyed gaze again, so intense. "It's a long story," he said.

"I'm interested."

He got a plastic container out of the fridge, and, when he pulled the lid off the tub, a waft of garlic and lime and chile came out of it.

"So I was working in Toronto and I got talking to a girl in the U.K. online," he said. "I came over here and kinda stayed put."

Lou waited for him to continue, expecting there to be more. He took chicken out of its marinade and added it to a wok that started up an immediate fragrant sizzle.

"I thought you said it was a long story," she said.

"Felt like it at the time."

"What happened to her?"

If she'd stopped to think about it she would probably have changed the subject, because he was looking increasingly uncomfortable. But that was the trouble with being a police officer. You started off with the little things and sooner or later there was a nugget of information that was too interesting to ignore, and you dug and dug at it until what you eventually found was the great big mine of information that lay buried beneath. It was addictive—and easy to lose sight of the fine line between professional curiosity and tactless intrusiveness.

"She wasn't serious about it." He was looking at her again, his hands spread on the breakfast bar, facing her.

"That's a shame."

"Yeah, well. Doesn't matter now. I'm over it, a long time ago."

He turned back to the stove, flipping the pieces of chicken with a pair of tongs, then adding them to the two plates that already had salad on them. The smell was wonderful. He got two forks out of a drawer, a bottle of red wine from a rack under the breakfast bar, two glasses from the cupboard. He opened the wine and poured it. The discussion about his love life was clearly at an end.

"Let's eat, hey?"

5X5X5 INTELLIGENCE REPORT

From:	Crimestoppers
To:	DCI Louisa SMITH
Subject:	OP NETTLE—Polly LEUCHARS
Date:	02/11/12

Grading E/5/1

Call from MOP [Member of the Public] to Crimestoppers at 2153hrs on 03/11/12 regarding Op Nettle.

Caller reports seeing Polly LEUCHARS on the night of 31/10/12 in a small dark blue car. The car was parked halfway into the driveway of one of the houses on Cemetery Lane with the rear end of the car sticking out into the road. Caller had to swerve to avoid it.

Caller states he parked up in the lay-by just ahead of the driveway and walked back to the car to remonstrate with the driver. Driver described as young woman, aged late twenties, long blond hair. Woman was in a distressed state and was arguing with a man who was in the passenger seat of the vehicle. Caller states he decided to leave it and went back to his own car and drove home.

Time of sighting of car was approximately 2325hrs as he states the news was on ITV when he got home shortly afterwards.

Caller saw press briefing regarding the murder earlier today and felt he should report this sighting.

No description of male seen in vehicle.

Caller wishes to remain anonymous.

23:58

I shouldn't fall asleep here, Lou thought. But it was a battle she was losing—already her eyes were closed. She was lying on the sofa with Jason, both of them still fully dressed, if a little disheveled. His breath was heavy and deep against her hair, and if it hadn't been for his fingers still gently stroking her shoulder, she would have thought he'd dozed off.

Dinner had been great, the bottle of wine was great, and she'd managed to restrain herself from inappropriate conversation, like quizzing him about previous relationships. In fact, back on the long, deep sofa that seemed just the right size and shape for two people to lie face-to-face, when he'd touched her hair and then whispered "You're beautiful" in her ear, she even forgot that she wanted to ask him about ice hockey and didn't they wear some sort of face protection these days?

And now it seemed much too late to mention it, and the most important thing seemed to be remembering not to fall asleep here—and then it was too late for that, after all.

Day Three
Saturday 3 November 2012

08:50

The briefing room was busy, despite it being Saturday: full of people talking at the top of their lungs. Jason was logging on to the computer, preparing the slides that would take everybody through the main points.

Lou sneaked in at the back. She felt flushed, like the first day back at school, waiting to see the boy you fancied.

She'd left his house at six, having woken up chilly and with an ache in her shoulder. At some point in the night he'd covered them both with a fleece blanket, but it had half-fallen off the sofa. He was still fast asleep, still fully clothed. When she moved, he stirred and woke.

"Hey," he said sleepily.

"Morning. I should go."

"In a minute." He moved and stretched, pulled her tighter against him. "We should have gone to bed, you know."

"I shouldn't have fallen asleep."

She eased herself out of his embrace and went to find her shoes. "I might see you a bit later, then? Only if you don't have anything else planned . . ."

"You kidding? I'll be there for the briefing."

He was not only there, he was looking smart and refreshed and fully in control. By contrast, she felt half-awake and, despite her shower and change of clothes, hopelessly crumpled.

This is ridiculous, she thought, checking out the room to see who was there, who was ready to go. No sign of Andy. He'd better turn up in time for the start of the briefing or she'd have him.

Sam Hollands approached her. "Ma'am. How are you today?"

"I'm fine, thanks, Sam. How are things with you?"

Sam smiled. "Going well, I think. I spoke to Taryn Lewis last night. She went to see her father in the hospital and quite a lot of info came out of it. Seems Brian was seeing Polly after all."

"Really?"

"Polly introduced Brian to swinging, through a woman called Suzanne. Yesterday Brian asked Taryn to phone this Suzanne to ask her to come and see him in the hospital."

"Do we know any more about her?"

Sam shook her head. "CSIs are due to start work on the Barn this morning, now we've identified Barbara as a suspect. Search teams are going in first. We know where Brian's phone is, thanks to Taryn, so we'll get started on it as soon as we've got it in an evidence bag."

Lou made her way through the tangle of chairs and gave Jason a brief smile.

"Right, let's have some hush," Lou called, got everyone's attention. "Just a few things to bring you up to date. As most of you know by now, today's priority is to get a statement from Flora Maitland. Sam's managed to secure a Section Eight warrant for Flora's flat and for the farm, so we'll have another briefing this afternoon once we know what we've got from that. Sam, who's going to bring Flora in?"

"I'm going to go with Les," Sam said. "Miranda Gregson is lined up to do the interview but she's not coming in till later, though. Dentist."

"Right, thanks, Sam. And as for Flora, we haven't got enough to nick her, but at least if we bring her on board we can get her account down on paper. Any questions so far?"

Nothing other than rapt attention.

At the back of the room, the door opened and Andy Hamilton came in. He stepped over toes, jackets, and bags, muttering apologies, found a seat.

"Sorry," he whispered.

She gave him a look, but didn't reply.

Lou ran through the events of the previous few days, up to the discovery of Polly's body and on to the discovery in Ambleside Quarry.

Confirmation now that Polly's blood had been found on Barbara Fletcher-Norman's clothing, as well as forensics from Yonder Cottage, meant that she was officially a suspect in Polly's murder. The sighting of the car on Cemetery Lane provoked some murmurs—not all of them had seen the information report.

Lou was nearly done. "Now, I know it all looks very much like Barbara was responsible, but we still need to evidence it. By the end of today I want to know who that man in the car was, what that argument was about. Can we sort out another press release?"

Sam nodded. "I'll see if I can get the witness to come forward—see if he can ID anyone."

"Thanks. I want to sort out Polly's relationships, I want to know exactly who was sleeping with whom and when—and did any of them get jealous? We need to follow up everything that came in yesterday, even if it sounds trivial. I know we've finished the house-to-house but half term's over with now, people who were on holiday will be coming back, so we need to go back and check all the houses we missed. When that's done, I need someone to get Barbara Fletcher-Norman's medical notes. See if she was as unstable as Brian's trying to make us think. Andy, I'd like you to liaise with CSI at the Barn today. Anything useful that comes out of that, you can follow up, okay? Right. Thanks everyone. Next briefing this afternoon."

The room cleared quickly and noisily, Andy Hamilton waiting at the back for her. Lou saw the way he was looking at her.

"How are you today?" she asked Jason.

"Fine," he said. "Could have done with a bit more sleep."

"Ah. The case going round and round in your head, was it?"

"Something like that."

She smiled at him. "I'll catch up with you later." Then, as an afterthought: "I nearly forgot. Sam Hollands has got some info from Taryn Lewis—make sure you get her to tell you about it before she disappears."

By the time she turned away from Jason, Andy had gone. Lou made a mental note to talk to him at some point during the day, knowing at the same time that she would put it off.

09:05

When Sam Hollands arrived with a ginger-haired man whose name Taryn instantly forgot, Flora had been sitting at the kitchen table, eating toast. Chris had left the house early, going with his dad to watch Spurs at home to Wigan.

"We need a witness statement," Sam said.

"Why can't she do that here?" Taryn wanted to know.

"It would be very helpful," the man said. He was standing in the doorway, arms folded, in his long wool coat. His light-reactive glasses were taking their time to adjust to being inside the house and as a result he looked like he was trying to be Sam Hollands's enforcer.

"You could have told me about this when I spoke to you last night," Taryn said crossly.

Sam gave her an apologetic smile but turned her attention back to Flora. "We're not treating you as a suspect at this time, Flora. It's just easier at the station. Less distracting."

Flora clearly didn't want to make a fuss. She looked shattered, as though she'd not slept at all. She went with them, leaving the half-eaten piece of toast behind.

After they'd gone, Taryn wondered whether to phone Felicity, or Nigel. And then she remembered that she had agreed to phone that Suzanne, her father's whatever she was—fancy woman?

Reluctant as she was to fall into that passive-aggressive trap of being at his beck and call, and feeling that even her best efforts would always go unacknowledged, the lure of disobedience was feeble compared to the tug of guilt she felt inside. It wouldn't take long, then she would go to the police station and wait for Flora.

She drove out of Briarstone and on to Morden. As she rounded the bend on Cemetery Lane she could see that the driveway to the farm was blocked with police cars, three of them this time, and a van.

She carried on to the Barn and parked. It felt like her world had suddenly shifted on its axis and left her off-balance. Everything felt wrong. What did they want with Flora, when it was so obviously Barbara who had killed Polly? Who else could it have been?

Hayselden Barn was silent, but warm. The heating must have come on. In fact, it felt stuffy inside; Taryn spent a few moments opening windows to let in the fresh air. More post had arrived, along with another letter for Barbara, and one that looked like it might be a bank statement.

Upstairs in Brian's study she found his open briefcase, the mobile phone lying on some files. She picked it up and examined it. It was turned off. She wondered if the battery had died, and pressed the on button fully expecting no response, but it lit up brightly.

It took a moment to work through the menu options until she found "Contacts" and there, under "Manchester office," was a mobile phone number.

Taryn found a pen and wrote the number down on her hand. As she did so, the phone vibrated and beeped in her hand and she nearly dropped it in shock.

It wasn't a call, though, it was a text. Three of them.

09:10

07252 583720 "B MOB" to 07252 583200
31/10/12 2229hrs

youfucking bastard, i hate you i hate you i hae you youll b sorry

07484 919987 "Manchester Office" to 07252 583200
01/11/12 0105hrs

Did you get home safe and sound? Let me know.

07484 919987 "Manchester Office" to 07252 583200
02/11/12 0950hrs

Hope you slept well. I'm looking forward to seeing you soon.

09:11

For a moment Taryn sat at her father's desk, in her father's house, and contemplated how strange a turn events seemed to be taking. Just a few days ago she was living in blissful ignorance of her father's doings, and now, it seemed, she knew more about him than she would ever hope to know about another living soul.

Before she could chicken out of it, she dialed "Manchester office" and waited, breathless, wondering what she would hear from the other end of the phone.

"Hello?"

"Is that Suzanne?" Taryn said, her voice trembling slightly in spite of herself.

"Who is this, please?"

"My name is Taryn Lewis. I'm Brian's daughter."

"Oh. I see. How can I help you?"

She was certainly cool, this Suzanne, Taryn thought. She'd given nothing away, absolutely nothing. Almost as if she were expecting someone else to be phoning her using Brian's mobile.

"Brian is in the hospital in Briarstone. He had a heart attack on Thursday morning. He asked me to call you and let you know."

On the other end of the line Taryn could hear voices—an office?

"Thank you for letting me know."

And, abruptly, the phone was cut off.

She took her own mobile out of her back pocket, scrolled through to find Sam Hollands's number, and dialed. But the call never connected; at that moment a loud banging came from the front door, along with the doorbell chiming.

She opened the door to a whole team of police officers wearing black boiler suits. She didn't know who was more surprised.

REPORT

To:	Op Nettle
From:	DC 13512 Jane PHELPS
Date:	Saturday 3 November 2012
Subject:	Medical Disclosure—Summary

Details of Barbara FLETCHER-NORMAN's medical records received from GP Dr. Thomas SUTCLIFFE at the Village Surgery, Morden.

Mrs. FLETCHER-NORMAN had been suffering from depression and insomnia diagnosed in March 2012. She had been prescribed various antidepressant medication, antianxiety medication, and sedatives and had been taking these sporadically (according to prescription collection data) since. Additionally she was prescribed hormone replacement therapy (HRT).

> On 19 September 2012 Mrs. FLETCHER-NORMAN was admitted to Briarstone General Hospital following an overdose of medication combined with excess alcohol. She admitted this was a suicide attempt and she was discharged two days later. She was offered counseling but declined. Since then she had been taking her medication regularly.

09:45

The wind continued to howl, and now, as if to make the whole day worse, occasional showers of sleet and hail began to fall, driven horizontally into the faces of the shoppers in the town center.

Brian Fletcher-Norman was oblivious to the weather. Following the ward round by the ICU consultant, a man Brian had met once on a golf course, it seemed Brian was well enough to be transferred to the Coronary Care Unit. Most of the monitors had been removed; just his IV drip remained so they could continue to pump him full of "clotbusters," as Sister Nolan affectionately termed them, and a wire attached to his finger that was monitoring his oxygen levels. Last night they had been at ninety percent, and this morning they hadn't fallen below ninety-eight percent since he'd been woken, which had been at six thirty.

He didn't suppose being on the ward was going to be any more pleasant than being in the ICU; in fact, it would probably be much worse, but at least it would offer a change of scene. And moving to the ward was a step closer to going home.

Plenty of time for thinking about things, sitting here, waiting for those brainless porters to come and wheel his bed away to the ward. Surely they must want to clear the space for some other poor bastard?

How long would it be before he would be back at the golf club? Would he have to sort out Barbara's funeral first? Surely nobody would say anything if he put in a couple of rounds, something to take his mind off things.

After all, it had been undoubtedly the worst week of his whole life.

As he settled into the warm coziness of a true bout of self-pity, he was interrupted by a porter, helpfully wearing a name badge which proclaimed him to be RON, who roughly took hold of the gurney.

"You all right there, mate?" Ron asked cheerily. "Where to? CCU? Right-o."

Passing the nurses' station, Brian's load was added to by Sister Nolan, who dumped his notes, files, and charts on the bed, then gave his arm an affectionate pat. "Good luck," she said softly, as Ron wheeled the bed through the ward doors.

Good luck? Brian thought. Am I going to need it for the CCU? Or does she just think I'm going to die after all?

10:02

Buchanan had kept her waiting, of course, but she'd expected that. It was a control thing. He liked her to be sitting down in his office, trying not to nose around the room, trying not to fidget, so that she would have to stand when he entered, like a schoolgirl in the headmaster's office.

"Good morning, sir," she'd said as he finally blustered in, standing up while holding on to all the loose bits of paper she'd been scanning, waiting for his appearance.

"Ah—how's it going? Progress?"

"As you know, we're in the process of getting a statement from Flora Maitland. Meanwhile, we've got search teams all over Hermitage Farm, so with a bit of luck we'll find something we can put to her in interview. For the time being, we need to establish her movements on the night Polly died, since the cellsite data from Polly's mobile seems to indicate that she visited Flora at home that night."

"What about the—er—suicide?"

Barbara Fletcher-Norman: the only person Lou could legitimately identify as a suspect, and she was lying on a big metal tray in Adele Francis's mortuary.

"We've got several strong lines of inquiry. Her husband, Brian, is looking promising—at least for further information. He told his daughter that he was having an affair with Polly Leuchars. And we have forensics linking Mrs. Fletcher-Norman to the murder scene."

"Hmm." Buchanan was reclining slightly in his big leather chair, which dwarfed him. "So you think the wife killed Polly out of jealousy and then went to the quarry to commit suicide?"

"That does seem the most likely explanation at the moment."

There was a pause. Buchanan was skimming through his emails. Come on, Lou thought. Some of us have work to do.

"What do you think?" he asked.

Lou hesitated. Although she trusted her instincts, she never liked to share them with other people until she had good solid evidence to back it up.

"I think there's a lot more to it than that. And we still need to establish whether Nigel Maitland has anything to do with it."

Another pause. Something he'd read on his PC was making him chuckle.

"Sir? Was there anything else?"

He gave a short cough and returned his attention to her. "No, no. Just checking how things are going. Got everything you need? Resources?"

"For now, we're managing. As long as I don't start losing staff to other ops."

"I'll hold them off as long as I can."

Of course, he was still doing her favors and making sure she knew it, Lou thought as she hurried back to the MIR. It didn't feel right, the way he oversaw her investigation and granted her things she needed to run it as though he was her Lord and Master granting her largesse. At some point she was sure he would start asking for some sort of favor in return. She'd heard from Sarah Singer, a DCI who'd gone to the Met last year, that Buchanan had taken more than his fair share of credit for her investigations when they'd got a good result.

The MIR felt warm and more than a little stuffy by the time she finally made it, two coffees and a Kit Kat from the vending machine balanced on top of her stack of paperwork.

Jason was on the phone when she passed his desk. She gave him a smile, indicated the second coffee with a nod of her head, and he nodded back. She went on into her office and sat down.

Already on her desk was another pile of information reports, witness statements, and charts. Jason was working on a new network chart indicating the various people involved in the case and their relationships to each other.

She looked up at the knock on the door, felt her heart lift slightly as she gave him a wave to come in. He didn't waste time with a greeting.

"I've got some news. Well, three things."

"Go on," Lou said, although he hadn't paused.

"Firstly, Jane got the medical history for Barbara Fletcher-Norman. Suicide attempt in September, not a serious one, but she was on antidepressants when she died."

"Well," Lou said, "that puts a different slant on things."

"Secondly, Mandy just took a call from the hospital. Brian's been transferred to a regular ward."

"And the third thing?"

"Not such good news. The search team went into Hayselden Barn this morning. Taryn Lewis was there, playing with her dad's mobile phone."

"Shit! I thought the Barn was supposed to be sealed off."

"Brian gave her a key, asked her to check the post. Nobody thought about that one."

"What's happened to the phone?"

"The search team bagged it and took it straight to Computer Crime for download. Let's hope they haven't got too much of a backlog."

"Where's the DI?" asked Lou.

"He went out after the briefing," Jason said.

"Thanks, Jason. The coffee and the Kit Kat's for you," she said.

Something was going on with Hamilton. He had always been a bit of a risk taker, it was one of the things she'd liked about him, but that—whatever it was—last night in the car park, that was something completely different. It was like he'd crossed the line into reckless. And she had crossed a line, too: from being still attracted to him, despite his behavior, into a nagging concern for his welfare. He had been a little drunk. Maybe that explained it, but it still felt like something was wrong.

10:17

For a moment she stood waiting at the access door to the ICU, looking through the glass, past the posters encouraging healthy living, avoiding drunk driving, and advertising self-help groups, to where the bed Brian had previously occupied was being made by two health care assistants.

Taryn hadn't rung the bell yet, to gain access.

Maybe he had died in the night. She considered how this made her feel, searched for something, but found nothing. She turned to go.

There was to be no escape, though. Sister Nolan was coming toward her, wearing a thick wool coat buttoned up to the neck.

"Ah, you'll be disappointed now if you're looking for your dad," she said, her voice loud in the quiet corridor. "He's been moved down to Stuart Ward. Ground floor. Much better this morning, he was. All right?"

Taryn tried to arrange her face into an expression of gratitude and relief. Back on the main corridor, which connected the different wings of the hospital, the traffic was unrelenting, porters pushing people on beds, relatives carrying magazines and Sainsbury's carrier bags. Further down, past the maternity wards, mothers-to-be going for walks to try and encourage labor, leaning against the wall every so often as another contraction hit. Oh yes, whatever you were here for was done entirely in public these days.

At last Taryn located Stuart Ward. It was far from peaceful, a world away from the ICU, with a constant flow of people coming and going. The nurses' station was unoccupied, so Taryn consulted a huge whiteboard that listed everyone on the ward—who their consultant was, and what they were in for. Everything from "appendix" to "hip replacement"—and there he was: Brian Fletcher-Norman, Bay 3, coronary.

He looked so miserable that Taryn felt a curious rush of both pity and joyous revenge.

"Tabby. Good to see you." He was still wearing that hospital gown, she noted, one of those ones that opens at the back so everyone can see your arse if you need to go somewhere. Good job I didn't find any pajamas, she thought. But then she noted the bathrobe she'd brought last night, slung over the chair next to the bed. She moved it and sat down.

"They moved you, then," she began.

"Ah, that's my daughter. Mistress of the Bleeding Obvious."

She pressed her lips together tightly.

He must have seen her expression and remembered that he needed her, because he said quietly, "Sorry. Been a tough morning."

"Right," she said.

He was twisted awkwardly in the bed, trying to turn to see her. It would have been better for her to sit on the edge of his bed, but she didn't want to get any closer to him.

"Did you get hold of her?" he asked quickly.

In the bed to Taryn's left, an old man was fast asleep, snoring like an elderly pig, wheezing and rasping. The curtain was pulled slightly across, but she took a quick peek behind it. The man's mouth had fallen open, revealing pale gums. On the lap trolley next to the bed, a plate of congealing shepherd's pie lay untouched. As she watched, a fly buzzed past and settled on it.

"Taryn. Did you phone her?" His voice had a sharp edge to it.

The more he spoke to her like that, the less inclined she was to be helpful. "Nice here, isn't it, Dad? I thought you were better off upstairs, myself."

"They were going to put me in the coronary care ward, but they didn't have enough beds. This is the 'leftovers' ward. Fucking unbelievable."

"Mmm. I expect you'll be glad to go home, won't you?"

Brian stared straight ahead at the curtains around the opposite bed. If they'd been opened, Brian might have had a chance to see a bit of window. "Apparently they want to keep me in for a bit."

"Jolly good thing, too," Taryn said brightly.

He shot her an evil look. "How do you work that one out?"

"Well, at least the police will go easy on you while you're in here."

He looked away again, concentrating on the curtains. "What do the police have to do with anything? And keep your voice down."

Taryn relaxed a bit more, leaning back into the armchair. Although the bay was bright enough, there was a distinct smell of something—urine, probably. A bag of it was hanging below the curtain, attached to the bed next door. "I should imagine they're just desperate to talk to you. Your lover and your wife, both dead on the same night? Good Lord."

"For your information," he growled, his cheeks reddening, "they've already seen me. They know I had nothing to do with Polly's death, for Christ's sake."

"But you didn't tell them Polly was your lover, did you?"

Slow realization crossed his face. "You told them?"

She shrugged, wondering if he could tell just how much she was loving every minute of this conversation.

He was so angry he couldn't look at her anymore, but his cheeks were pale now. "Did you phone her?" he asked again, quietly.

"Yes, I did."

"What did she say?"

"Nothing much. I just told her where you were, and she said thanks. That's all."

"Did you bring the phone with you?"

"No, I didn't."

"Why not?"

"Well, firstly, you didn't ask for it. And secondly, the police took it and put it into an evidence bag."

"What?"

"They turned up at the Barn while I was there. They've got a search warrant. Or something. I didn't really look. After all, it's not my house, is it?"

The snoring stopped abruptly. Taryn waited for it to resume. A minute passed, during which she'd been wondering if she should go and find someone, but then the bed creaked and it resumed as a low, throaty rumble.

"Polly's death," Taryn said.

"What?"

"You said you had nothing to do with Polly's death. Does that mean you had something to do with Barbara's?"

"Are you stupid? Of course I didn't. She killed herself, didn't she? Isn't it obvious?"

Taryn stood up to go, buttoned up her jacket, fished around inside her bag for her car keys. She'd had entirely enough of being called stupid.

"Are you going? What about—look, Taryn, can't you go and buy me some pajamas? From M&S?"

Her heart was as cold as her voice, when it came. "I don't think I'll have the time."

On the way out, thinking about how she could make Flora feel better, Taryn just missed the striking woman who was making her way to the Stuart Ward. They passed in the corridor, each entirely unaware of the other, Suzanne having never been shown a picture of Taryn, and Taryn having no knowledge of what her father's lover looked like.

11:37

"Stop," said Ali, pulling out of the police station car park into the traffic. "Tell me that again, bit by bit."

Jane Phelps had started off the conversation by passing on the news from Sam Hollands about Brian's daughter, and Ali had been only half listening. Now, though, something Jane said had dragged him back to full awareness.

A rustle of Jane's notebook as she consulted what she'd scribbled earlier, the phone receiver tucked behind her ear. "Taryn Lewis said her father had told her that he had been Polly's lover, but wasn't anymore. And that he had a new lover, a woman called Suzanne. He asked Taryn to phone her to tell her about his heart attack. No mention of whether she also had to tell her about poor old Barbara, but there you go."

"Good Lord," Ali muttered. "It's all going on in Morden, isn't it? So that's why she was at the Barn this morning, phoning this Suzanne?"

Jane shrugged. "I guess so."

Silence fell for a moment while Ali waited at the traffic lights. "How do you want to play this?"

"By ear. He should be on the mend if they've moved him to a regular ward, so I think he's up for a few more robust questions. But we really need to get him on his own, so it depends how private the ward is."

Not nearly private enough, was Ali's first thought when they found their way to Stuart Ward. The curtains around Brian's bed were partly drawn, so it was only when Jane pulled them slightly aside that she got a view of Brian's bare back as he sat on the edge of the bed, his feet dangling a few inches above the polished vinyl floor. He looked around sharply. "What the—?"

Jane apologized but held her ground. "Sorry to intrude, sir. How are you feeling?"

Brian sat back on the bed and Jane pulled the thin sheet and blanket over his legs, giving off the professional air of someone who has seen it all before.

"We're police officers, Brian, as you might have gathered. My name is Detective Constable Jane Phelps, and my colleague there is Detective Constable Alastair Whitmore. Hope you don't mind if we have a chat with you?"

"Not at all," he replied, although he looked far from comfortable.

"How are you feeling?" she asked, keeping her voice low.

He cleared his throat. "I was feeling much better, but I just had a visit from my daughter. She really is a piece of work."

"In what way?"

"She's gloating at my predicament. We don't get on, and she's refused to get me any pajamas, which is why you find me in this state. And, to cap it all, I understand she's told you that I was romantically involved with Polly Leuchars!"

Brian was clearly upset. Ali diffused the situation by changing the subject: "You don't mind if we take some notes while we talk?"

A brief hesitation. "No, I suppose not. It's all lies, what she told you."

"Are you comfortable talking here, Brian? I'm sure the nurses might be able to arrange something more private."

Brian considered this for a moment. "No, no, this is fine. As long as you're not going to shout about it all."

Jane gave him a sweet smile. "May I?" And without waiting for a definite response, she perched on the edge of the high-backed chair by the head of the bed.

"Why don't you tell me about Polly, Brian? When did you first meet?"

"I went to the stables for horse riding lessons. Nigel Maitland and I played golf together and we've been to dinner at the farm a few times. He suggested I should have some riding lessons to keep fit, get me out into the fresh air."

Jane sat completely still, trying to maintain eye contact, letting the vacuous sweet smile remain on her lips, listening to what she could already tell was a complete load of bollocks. "And did you have lessons with Polly?"

"A couple. I didn't know her name then. She was at a dinner party we went to at the farm a few weeks later."

"You had lessons with her and you didn't know her name?"

"No—yes. I mean, she told me her name, but I didn't really pay attention."

"And did you carry on with the lessons for a while?"

"I had a couple, as I say. Then we were away on holiday, and I was busy at work, and it sort of tailed off. I can't say it was really my thing. I'm too old to be starting things like that."

Jane made a little sound to suggest that she considered him far from decrepit, managing to get him to raise a slightly suggestive grin in response. He leaned toward her a little.

"I do believe she was a bit of a naughty girl, though. I heard a rumor that she was seeing a married man in the village, but I can assure you it wasn't I."

"Come on, Brian. You must have a good idea—who do you think it could have been? Nigel Maitland?"

Brian tapped the side of his nose conspiratorially. "I'm saying no more," he said.

Jane leaned back in the chair, satisfied. He was lying through his teeth about Polly, of course.

"What about Barbara? What did she think?"

Brian's face flushed a little. He took too long over his answer. "My wife was a jealous woman. She was always ready to believe rumors in that respect."

"She believed you were having an affair?"

He let out a sigh, raised his eyes to the ceiling as he spoke. "Someone made a comment about Polly and a married man, she put two and two together and made eighteen, the way she always did."

"You argued about it?"

"More than once."

"Was your relationship ever a violent one, Brian?"

"No!" His answer was quick, his voice raised. Then he added: "At least, never on my part."

Jane leaned forward again a little to make sure she didn't miss anything. Ali, scribbling furiously in his notebook the whole time, had barely looked up.

"What do you mean?" Jane asked.

"Barbara was always—er—physical when she had had a drink. She would lash out at me sometimes. Never hurt me, of course, but she would get tongue-tied, slur, and then she would resort to slaps, pushing me away, that sort of thing."

"And how did you respond?"

"I would walk away."

Brian's eyes met hers, unfaltering this time. He'd been lying about Polly, but he was telling the truth about the arguments. Whether he was lying to protect his reputation, his integrity, or to distance himself from Polly's murder, the outcome would be the same. Lying to the police was never a good idea.

"We understand that your wife had been diagnosed with depression, anxiety. That must have been quite tough on you."

"Oh, it was. She tried to kill herself a couple of months back, you know. Not seriously. Just enough to make it bloody awkward for me when I had some important meetings coming up at work."

"How was she recently?"

"All right on some days, bad on others, especially when she'd had a drink."

"Did she ever drive when she'd had a drink?"

"If she needed to get somewhere. Most of the time, though, she got drunk at home."

Jane sat back again. "Thank you, Brian. Have they said how long it will be before you can go home?"

He breathed out in a long sigh, visibly relaxed. Jane wondered what it was he'd been expecting her to ask.

"It can't be soon enough as far as I'm concerned. This place is appalling."

Jane gave him a reassuring smile, remembering the irony that his wife was actually lying in a cold storage compartment not a million miles away, and he'd not mentioned the loss of her at all, or shown any concern for the violent way she'd apparently chosen to die.

"Will your daughter be coming back to see you?"

Brian shrugged. "Who knows? I wouldn't be surprised if she comes back to have another gloat."

Jane stood, raised the strap of her handbag over one shoulder. Ali took the signal and stood too. Jane took hold of Brian's hand and gave it a friendly squeeze.

"Don't listen to her," Brian said, his voice a low whisper once again. "She's just making things difficult for me, that's all."

"Your daughter?" Jane asked.

Brian nodded.

"We will need to interview her again," Jane said reassuringly, "but I promise I'll bear in mind what you've said."

With that they said their goodbyes and left. On the way back to the car, Ali phoned Sam Hollands to report on their progress and see if they had another tasking.

"Head back to the Incident Room for now, guys," Sam told them. "I'm on my way to the quarry with the DCI. Les Finnegan says they've found something that might be the murder weapon."

"In the quarry?" said Jane into the hands-free kit. "What is it?"

"No idea. Les is being all secretive, canny old git. It's like he lives for moments like this. I'll let you know later, okay?"

13:52

Being on Stuart Ward was not unlike being in Piccadilly Circus at rush hour, Brian thought to himself. First of all, there had been the initial confusion about where he was to go: the porter had taken him to the cardiac ward, where he was left by himself, reclining on his bed in a draughty corridor for half an hour before another porter had turned up and wheeled him along to the far less attractive Stuart Ward. Then there was the ordeal that was Taryn's visit. He'd been harboring hopes that she might have got over whatever foolish tantrum it was that had caused her to go off in a huff, but obviously that was not the case.

After Taryn, Suzanne. Oh, he'd felt so much better, seeing her beautiful face looking for him—hearing her voice was the best tonic he'd had in days. Then, of course, the conversation that needed to be had. What was to be done? He wished someone would take it all away from him, leave him be to concentrate on getting better. Instead he found he was once again working to a detailed, precise set of instructions.

And then, minutes after Suzanne had left, just as he was gearing himself up to head off to the bathroom for the first time, the two police officers had turned up for one of their friendly chats. He'd had to think quickly, worrying less about what it was he needed to say and concentrating instead on what he absolutely shouldn't. When he spoke to them again he would make sure it was on his own terms.

Now, though, the ward was quieting down. Official visiting time was a few hours away, and it was entirely likely that he wouldn't have any visitors at all. He could just relax, close his eyes, and think about how he was going to recover.

Date: Saturday 3 November 2012
Officer: DC 13521 FINNEGAN
To: DCI Louisa SMITH / Op Nettle MIR
Re: Taryn LEWIS / Op NETTLE
CC: Computer Crime Unit CCU

Visited Mrs. Lewis at home at 1415hrs today. She confirms she has visited her father in hospital three times now but has no intention of visiting him again. She is quite scathing in her opinions of him.

She confirmed that her father told her that he HAD been in a sexual relationship with Polly LEUCHARS (Op Nettle). There was no indication when this affair had begun or ended, although it seems that her father has recently been involved with another female, known to Mrs. LEWIS only as "SUZANNE." Brian Fletcher-Norman asked Mrs. LEWIS to telephone this Suzanne and ask her to visit him in the hospital, which she duly did. Mrs. LEWIS used Mr. FLETCHER-NORMAN's mobile to do this, which she handed over to officers at Hayselden Barn this morning.

I would respectfully request that a contact number for "SUZANNE" should be obtained from this phone as a matter of urgency and subscriber check completed.

13:52

In Briarstone Police Station, Flora sat in what she couldn't possibly know was the most comfortable of all the interview rooms. When difficult interviews needed to be conducted with traumatized people, this was the room they used. It had a window, albeit too high up to see out of unless you stood on tiptoe; carpet that was stained here and there with various spillages, but nevertheless it was carpet. The chairs were the sort you might find in an office reception waiting area, low and padded, with a coffee table in the middle and a further table against the wall upon which was the obligatory recording device.

She had been sitting huddled on one of the chairs, waiting for Andy Hamilton to get back from wherever it was he'd gone. He'd explained that they were performing a search of her flat, and the farm, and that they were looking for Polly's mobile phone. Flora had looked at him as though he were slightly mad. Why would she have Polly's phone? Andy had told her they had a search warrant, but for all of their sakes it would be much easier if she were to give him the keys to her flat and save them having to break in.

She handed them over without a word, and now she was sitting here, waiting for them to come back.

They'd asked her if she wanted a lawyer, offered to provide one if she didn't have one of her own, like a solicitor was a handy gadget you carried around in your pocket. She had said no automatically but now she was starting to wonder whether it would be worth calling the number on the card her father had given her. She went over the same arguments in her head: she didn't need a solicitor, because she hadn't done anything wrong. She should get one anyway, because she was her father's daughter and who knew what the police would try to pin on her, even if only to get at Nigel? Joe Lorenzo was phenomenally expensive, and if he wasn't needed, then she would have wasted a lot of money, and Nigel would know she'd been giving them a statement. Until she knew what it was they wanted, then she was better off playing it by ear.

The door opened abruptly and her thoughts were interrupted by the arrival of Detective Inspector Andy Hamilton. He seemed mountainous to her, huddled as she was into her chair, her knees tucked up under her chin. A few moments later the door opened and Miranda Gregson came in. She gave Flora a smile. That was encouraging, at least.

"Sorry to keep you waiting," Hamilton said, although he didn't sound very sorry, and he wasn't smiling. "I'd just like to remind you that you're under caution, but you haven't been arrested at this stage, and you're free to go whenever you choose to. We asked you if you wanted a solicitor present while we speak to you, and you declined. If you change your mind at any time, we can get a solicitor for you."

"I understand. I don't want a solicitor, not at the moment, anyway."

Miranda spoke next. "When we spoke to you yesterday, you told us that you'd been in a relationship with Polly Leuchars. Can you tell us how that came about?"

Flora looked from one of them to the other. They wanted to know? Right, then. That wasn't something she needed Joe Lorenzo for. Flora tilted her chin, just slightly, and assumed an air of quiet defiance.

15:25

Les Finnegan was waiting for them in the car park, leaning against the bonnet of an elderly BMW, smoking, looking for all the world like an extra from *The Sweeney*.

"Ma'am," he acknowledged when Lou got out of the car; "Sarge," to Sam Hollands.

"Hold on a sec, Les. Won't be a minute," Lou said. She beckoned Sam round the back of her car. "Just stand there, Sam. I'm going to get my jeans on."

She opened the boot of the Laguna. The first thing out was a piece of old carpet, about a meter square, which she flopped down on the gravel of the car park and then stood on to remove her shoes. Fishing around in the boot, she found a carrier bag containing a pair of jeans, muddy at the bottom, and some trainers. Sam stood with her back to the DCI, giving Les Finnegan a look, while behind her Lou wriggled into the jeans under her skirt, which she then unzipped and stepped deftly out of. A pair of trainer socks over her stockinged feet, and then the trainers. From another bag she pulled out a new pair of latex gloves, which she pushed into the pocket of her jacket. Lastly she picked up the square of carpet, shook it down, and threw it back in the boot.

The wind was strong and cold as they walked toward Les, the sky gray and menacing above them. It was still early afternoon, but it was already getting dark.

Les gave her a yellow smile. "They're about finished down there, to be honest. Just thought it might be worth a visit."

As he spoke, three members of the party came into view, climbing up the slope. One of them was a CSI, the other two members of the Tac Team—but they were all dressed in white protective suits. Les introduced Paul Harper, the CSI.

"We found it further down the slope, toward the bottom of the hill. Half buried in the sand. You can track it back up to where it landed—it must have been thrown a fair old way."

He held up a plastic evidence bag containing what looked like a black orb of some kind. Gray sand clung to half of it. The way it was pulling down the plastic of the bag, it looked heavy.

"It's a shot put," Les said helpfully.

Paul added, "There's a stand for it on the small table in the hallway, with a little plaque. Apparently Felicity Maitland was a county champion when she was at school."

"The hallway . . . ?" Lou asked.

"Yonder Cottage. I think it was a repository for all the ornaments Mrs. M didn't want to keep at the farm."

Lou took the bag from Paul. It was heavy. And the sand clinging to the side of the shot put—"Is it blood under there?"

"Yes, ma'am. We've got a sample—been biked over to the labs already. Hair, too."

"Prints?"

"'Fraid not."

Lou turned to Paul Harper again. "So where was it, in relation to the car?"

Paul pointed vaguely over the edge of the cliff, the wind making the white suit flap against his arm. "About fifty yards further on. Although it was thrown from up here—it didn't fall out of the car."

"You're sure about that?"

"I'll take some proper measurements and check it all, but yes, I'm sure. We're going to have a look at analyzing the trajectory to see if we can work out where it was thrown from."

"You want to show me?"

The Tac Team officers exchanged a glance which said, actually, no we don't, but Paul Harper gave a nod and took Lou back toward the edge of the slope. "Wait for me, Sam," Lou called over her shoulder. "I won't be long."

There was a steep path running around the edge of the quarry, and they followed this, a sheer drop to their left. Lou watched her feet, choosing her way carefully. When Paul Harper stopped in front of her, she nearly ran into his back. He indicated the quarry floor, small flags marking the place where the car had been found. Other markers indicated the path of the vehicle through the undergrowth, the locations of bits and pieces that had fallen off the car on the way down.

"You can see it best from here. If we go all the way down you won't get a sense of the perspective," he told her. Just to the right of them, at the very bottom of the quarry, a small red flag flapped from within a patch of nettles. "That was where we found the ball. Right down there."

Lou tried to get a feel for whether the weapon could have fallen out of the vehicle on the way down, but since it had gone so much further it seemed somehow doubtful. "Did it roll far?"

Paul nodded. "There's a definite track. That's why I want to trace it back properly, but it's going to take a while to do it with all the foliage, and the light's starting to go. We'll get back onto it first thing."

Climbing back up to the edge of the quarry, gingerly picking her way through the nettles and scrub, Lou stood for a moment, feeling the wind trying to free her hair from the ponytail, whipping it round her cheeks. Sam was waiting, shivering, at the top.

"Dreadful place to choose to end it all," Sam said, her voice all but lost in the gale.

To: DCI Smith

From: Mrs. Lorna Newman

Message: Please phone regarding Barbara Fletcher-Norman.

MG11 WITNESS STATEMENT		
Section 1—Witness Details		
NAME:	Flora MAITLAND	
DOB (if under 18; if over 18 state "Over 18")		Over 18
ADDRESS: Flat 2 14 Waterside Gardens Briarstone	**OCCUPATION:** Artist	
Section 2—Investigating Officer		
DATE:	Saturday 3 November	
OIC:	DC Miranda GREGSON	
Section 3—Text of Statement		

My mobile phone number is 07194 141544, it has been my number for the past two years and it is the only mobile phone number I use.

I have known Polly LEUCHARS for a number of years as she was a family friend. In December 2011 Polly started working as a groom at Hermitage Farm, which is owned by my family. I helped out in the stables often and we became very close. Around April 2012 our relationship became more serious, although I knew Polly was not monogamous and was involved with other people at the same time. She was the only person I was involved with. I believe she would have told me who else she was seeing if I had asked, but I did not want to know.

Our relationship came to an end around the end of August when I realized I wanted our relationship to be exclusive, and Polly was not prepared to continue on this basis. We did not argue but I moved back to my flat in Briarstone, partly because I wanted to be on my own for a while. Polly tried to contact me by phone a few times but after a while this stopped.

I last saw Polly when I visited the farm at the end of September or beginning of October. I spoke to her briefly in the yard and we parted on good terms. Polly told me she had found someone special she wanted to be with, but I did not ask who this was. I said goodbye to her and went straight home. This was the last time I saw Polly and I had no further contact with her either by email, phone, or in person after that.

On 31 October 2012 I spent the day painting in my studio. I do not remember what time I went to sleep. I slept in the studio and carried on working the next morning until my father telephoned me to tell me that Polly had been found dead.

I do not know of any reason why someone would want to harm Polly and I do not know who might have killed her.

Section 4—Signatures

WITNESS: (F Maitland)   OIC: (M Gregson DC 9323)

16:20

Even though she was under caution, and therefore free to leave at any moment, Flora agreed to help the police with their inquiries until late afternoon. They'd written down all their questions and all her answers to them, had got her to sign several times to say that she agreed with what they'd written. Then she had written out her statement and signed it.

All the searches were complete. Flora's flat had revealed nothing of any interest; Polly's phone was still unaccounted for. Now that the shot put had turned up at the quarry, the investigation had once again veered off in the direction of Barbara Fletcher-Norman. The opportunity to search the farm and all its outbuildings had been thoroughly exploited.

Unfortunately, nothing had come to light there, either. Nigel's solicitor had been called as soon as the team turned up. He observed every part of the process and commented on everything. Their warrant was in relation to Flora Maitland, who did not work at the farm and did not even live there anymore. He tried his best to argue that there was no justification for the police to remove anything pertaining to farm business, including computers, files, or paperwork. With the warrant they could have taken whatever they wanted—computers, files, the lot. But in the event, Nigel's offices, including the second office at the far end of the barn housing his 4×4 and his Mercedes and the Porsche convertible, had yielded nothing they could use. In the loft above the office, a large safe stood empty, its door open. Whatever had been in there had been moved.

The frustration in the MIR, when Lou returned to it after a visit to the farm to discuss progress with the search coordinator, was evident.

"He must have been tipped off," Les Finnegan was saying. "That's all there is to it."

"Well, at least you got him to give a statement," Ali said. "That's bloody impressive, if nothing else."

"It was hardly worth bothering," Les muttered.

Hamilton came in at that moment, interrupting the debate.

"Andy," Lou said. "How are you getting on with Flora?"

He leaned back on the edge of Sam's desk, unbuttoning his jacket. "Well, the good news is she never called that wanker of a solicitor."

"He was busy with us at the farm," Ali said gloomily.

"That's the good news? Did we get anything useful out of her at all?"

Andy sighed. "She claims the last time she saw Polly was weeks before she died, and that was at the farm. Flora said she hadn't been near the farm since then."

"What about the phone?"

Jason said, "We still don't have a subscriber for that number that Polly was calling."

"Why not? Have we chased it up?"

"They've been having computer problems at the service provider. No subscriber checks are going through—I chased it up an hour ago."

That was typical, Lou thought. "Well, how long's it going to take—do they know?"

"They said they would update me, but I'll ring them back if they haven't got back to me in an hour."

"I don't think it'll help," Andy said. "So she was visiting someone in Briarstone on the night she died. That's not so surprising, is it, given what we know about her? She went for a fuck somewhere, came home, and in the meantime the mad old woman from across the road had decided to confront her. Got herself covered in blood, pissed up, drove to the quarry full of remorse, and there you go. Over the edge. Job done."

"Incredible," Sam muttered.

"I'm talking about evidence," he said. "You've got the weapon, the blood, the motive for it, everything. I think we should stop wasting resources on the Maitlands and concentrate on Barbara and Brian. I wouldn't be surprised if it was Brian that Polly was meeting that night. She met up with him somewhere in Briarstone—away from the farm and the Barn—for a quick shag. Barbara caught them out somehow and saw red."

He might not be putting it in the nicest of terms, Lou thought, but he had a point.

"So Flora was seeing Polly," Sam said. "But so was half the village, including Brian. We don't know who else she was involved with, do we?"

There was a momentary silence.

Lou sighed. "I think we need to bear in mind that it's still really early days," she said. "We've found out a lot already, and yes, it would be nice to have an arrest, but we have some good strong leads and plenty to keep us busy, right?"

Everyone looked as tired as she felt.

MG11 WITNESS STATEMENT	
Section 1—Witness Details	
NAME:	Nigel MAITLAND
DOB (if under 18; if over 18 state "Over 18"):	Over 18
ADDRESS: Hermitage Farm Cemetery Lane Morden	**OCCUPATION:** Farm owner

Section 2—Investigating Officer

DATE:	Saturday 3 November
OIC:	DC 8244 Les FINNEGAN

Section 3—Text of Statement

Polly LEUCHARS was employed by my wife, Felicity MAITLAND, to assist at the stables, which are part of the farm business. I saw Polly infrequently and I cannot remember the last time I saw her. I do not know of anyone who might have wanted to harm her.

Section 4—Signatures

WITNESS: (N R Maitland)   OIC: (L Finnegan DC 8244)

17:40

Lou had been running through the intelligence and comparing it with Jason's latest charts and timelines, which he'd left on her desk. They went from the last sightings of Polly in the days before her death, right up to the discovery of the possible murder weapon in the quarry. Adele Francis had already been shown the shot put and agreed that it was "likely."

Of course, if the shot put *was* the murder weapon, then pretty much everything was still pointing to Barbara Fletcher-Norman as the offender. Tomorrow she would get Jane and Ali to pay another visit to Brian and try to get more out of him about the fatal night. She made a mental note to put in a medical disclosure form to Brian's doctors—it wouldn't do to put pressure on him when his health was so fragile. The last thing the case needed was another death.

She thought Jason had gone home, long ago—or gone over to the King William with the rest of them—until a gentle knock on the door frame made her jump.

He looked tired, the black eye was yellowing a bit around the edges.

"Hey," he said.

"Hey, yourself. Come in."

"I was hoping for some results from the download of Brian's phone," he said, sitting down, "but they won't have anything until Monday at least. They've got a backlog, apparently."

"They've always got a backlog," she said a tad sourly.

"It would have been a whole lot easier to just check the phone before we handed it over to the CCU."

Lou smiled. "Unfortunately, we have to comply with RIPA. Can't have anyone accusing us of tampering with evidence, can we? I know it feels like we've been doing this for weeks, but really we're only into the second day."

"Two days, huh?" he said. "You're right. Feels longer."

"Are you finished?" she asked. "You should get home. You've done a brilliant job and I'm really grateful. And it's Sunday tomorrow, so you are definitely taking the day off."

He smiled at her. "I guess I should stop hanging round here late at night. I'm looking way too keen."

Lou looked up in surprise. "Keen? You mean on me?"

He looked back into the empty office behind him. "Yeah, keen on you. Nobody else here right now."

"Oh."

"You're really sexy when you blush, Lou."

She tried a stern look. "Jason. This isn't happening here, okay?"

"Sure. Just—you know. Whenever. You want me to make you some dinner?"

God, how tempting, how very tempting to just go home with him again. And maybe, this time, stay the whole night and not on the sofa either.

"I'd like to . . ."

"I can hear a 'but' coming on."

"I'd like to. But I can't do this. Not at the moment. I need to focus on this case, and I'm spending too much time distracted, thinking about other things . . ."

" . . . like what we could be doing if we went back to my place?"

Lou looked at him for a long moment, drinking him in while there was nobody else watching. He matched her gaze and the longer she looked, the more tempting it was.

"You know Hamilton is a huge asshole, right?"

"What brought that on?"

"It's just the way he speaks to people. Arrogant piece of shit."

"He gets the job done, Jason," Lou said, wondering where this was coming from.

"He'd do it much better if he could stop showing off all the time."

Lou sighed. "Unfortunately he's still my DI. Much as I wish he wasn't sometimes."

"Right. Just know that we're not all shits like that, huh? And when this case is over, or when it quiets down, or when you just need a bit of moral support, I'll be here waiting for you. For whatever it is you want, or you need."

21:44

Flora was thinking about lying in Polly's bed in Yonder Cottage, the late-summer heat drifting lazily in through the open window with the scent of the farm and the white lilies in a vase on the windowsill, naked, too hot for covers. She was gazing at Polly, the almost unbearable beauty of her.

"Flora, don't look at me like that," she said, smiling.

"Like what?"

Serious, all of a sudden. "Don't fall in love with me, Flora. I'll break your heart if you do."

Of course, it was too late. Flora only found out what she meant a month later.

I can't stand it, she thought. I miss her too much.

She heard Tabby coming in, heard the door bang. Heard her muffled conversation with Chris, the kettle going on, mugs clinking in the kitchen.

"She's upstairs. Been there since you phoned."

" . . . try to talk to her?"

"I don't know . . . thought she was asleep."

All those text messages between Polly's phone and hers. They were always texting, even when Flora was working at the farm and Polly at the stables. It was like a secret between them, a delicious secret that nobody else could be involved in. At the stables, once, Connor, who had a crush on Polly like everyone else did, was mucking out while Polly brushed Elki's coat and Flora kept interrupting her with messages:

You look so sexy when you bend over

And she'd laughed and Connor had demanded to know what she was laughing at, and that had made her laugh harder, shaking her head so her blond ponytail swished from side to side like Elki's tail.

And the replies Polly sent, late into the night, all of them saved on Flora's phone:

You are all mine. Later. Wear your red shirt. P x

This weekend I am planning to not get dressed at all. Shall we go to the Lemon Tree naked? What will yr mum say?? P x

Well, the police had her phone now. They would have seen all those messages, everything that had been private between them. Would they tell Felicity?

Polly was always teasing Flora about coming out. It was time, she said, for Flora to come clean to the world, release herself from the chains of parental expectation. For a while Flora thought this was because Polly wanted to be able to go out in public as partners and lov-ers, not just as friends. But in reality, of course, it was neither here nor there to Polly whether Flora came out as gay or stayed firmly in her little closet, because from her point of view there wasn't a relationship. The word simply wasn't in Polly's vocabulary. After all these weeks of agonizing over what went wrong, Flora realized that it was simply because there was nothing Polly found more depressing than people who weren't true to themselves. She'd phrased it exactly like that once, when they'd been talking about Felicity, whose inhibitions were more of the social-class variety.

I wish I could talk to her, thought Flora. Just once more. I just want to tell her I love her, that I miss her, that I don't care that she didn't love me back. I just want to let her know I'm still here and I will always love her . . .

The weekend after that first afternoon in the top field, Flora had taken Polly out for the evening to meet some of her friends. They had drunk too much, giggled like schoolgirls, and when the last of the friends disappeared off home, Polly had pushed Flora gently but insistently against a wall and kissed her hard. Flora had responded, at first uncertainly, and then with a force that surprised her. Polly's hand cupped her firmly between her legs, while all Flora could think of was how soft her mouth was, how sweet her taste.

They'd stumbled their way back to Flora's flat.

"Is this where you live?" Polly asked, astonishment on her face, as Flora felt through her pockets for the key.

"Yes, why?"

Polly's face opened into a big, beaming smile. "No reason. It's lovely, that's all."

Inside, Polly took Flora by the hand and led her straight to the bed-room, as if she had been in the flat before, as if she knew exactly where everything was. And there she had stripped Flora gently, of her clothes first, and then her inhibitions, and held her as the tears finally came, hours, hours later, when the sky was turning gray.

I never knew, she thought. All those years, I never knew it could feel like that. My heart and soul, so complete. So happy.

22:40

Andy Hamilton's crap day had not been improved any by the transition into evening. Quietly sinking the last of his pint, he wondered whether Karen was in bed yet and whether he really should have phoned her—he checked his watch—about three hours ago.

"Time to go home, gents," the barman said, to Andy and some other poor souls who should also have made their way out a long time ago.

The rest of the squad had gone looking for a curry house at least an hour ago. He'd stayed, claiming he just wanted to finish this one off and then he was heading home, but the truth was he didn't want to. He wanted to be with Lou. Not forever, just for one more night.

He wasn't used to not getting his own way where women were concerned. Every time Lou kicked up a fight he felt a twinge of humiliation—and wanted her all the more. If she would just give in, let him fuck her one more time, he would be able to get her out of his system.

Twice in the last few days he'd felt rejected by women he fancied: Lou last night, and that blond nurse. Although that wasn't so much a rejection as a tease. What made it worse was that he knew that if he went home to Karen now, four hours after the end of his shift, reeking of beer, he wouldn't get much of a welcome there, either.

Still, beggars couldn't be choosers. He tipped the dregs of his last pint down his throat and made his way outside.

The night air was brisk and he debated going to fetch his car and taking a chance on the five miles between here and his house, but even with his judgment clouded by alcohol he knew it was a risk too far. He wandered off in the direction of the high street, got lucky with a taxi driver who knew him heading back toward the rank.

"All right, Andy?" Geoff said, as Andy collapsed into the backseat. "Big night out, was it?"

"Something like that," Andy said. "I'm getting too old for these things."

All the lights were off in the house. That was a bad sign. Andy walked up the driveway, tried his key in the lock. He couldn't work out for a while why the door wouldn't open, then he realized it was deadbolted and he didn't have a key for that one.

He banged on the door with his fist and a light went on somewhere across the street. Then he saw a piece of paper thumbtacked to the doorframe. He ripped it off and took it over to the streetlight so he could read it.

TOOK KIDS GONE TO SARAH'S.

Why had she bloody double-locked the door? She knew he didn't have that key. He groaned, slowly, and lifted his head to see Geoff's cab coming toward him. He'd been to the end of the road to turn the car around. Seeing his fare standing forlorn by the side of the road, the cabbie stopped, wound down his window.

"Locked out, are you? Need a ride somewhere?"

"Waterside Gardens," Andy said, almost without thinking, and climbed back into the warm cab out of the drizzle that had developed in the cold, misty night.

22:40

Flora had managed to eat some of Taryn's spaghetti Bolognese. It tasted great, the first proper meal she'd had in days.

"I still say you need to go and see your father," Taryn said.

"He can wait. If they'd found anything at the farm, we'd all know about it by now."

"Even so! They had you in custody, Flora."

"It was a caution, that's all. Helping them with their inquiries. And if they had anything on me, they would have arrested me, wouldn't they?"

After they'd finished eating, Flora went to help Taryn with the washing up.

"I need to go home," Flora said. "I've got no clothes, Tabs, and I'll be all right tonight. Thank you for letting me stay. You've been such a good mate. But, honestly, I need to go home. And I feel so much better, you know that."

Taryn shot her a wry grin. "I know my Bolognese is good, but I didn't realize it could mend broken hearts."

Having consumed three glasses of wine with dinner, Flora caught a cab back to her flat an hour or so later. She let the cab drop her off at the end of the road, then walked the hundred yards up Forsyth Road to the small cul-de-sac where the flats were. She hesitated when she got to the end of the garden wall separating the small car park from the road and saw a figure standing on the top step. In the faint orange glow from the streetlight she recognized that hulking great police officer, Andy Hamilton. Flora was indignant. Surely he wasn't going to try and talk to her at this time of night? She was about to turn back when, to her astonishment, the door to the ground-floor flat opened and, without any sound that she could hear, Hamilton was admitted.

She waited for a moment, holding her breath, looked at her watch: it was nearly eleven.

Then, as fast as she could, she ran across the gravel on tiptoe to her own front door, slid the key in the lock, opened the door, and shut it quietly behind her. At first, no sound came through the wall separating her hallway from the one of the ground-floor flat; she stood there for several minutes in the dark, the dark staircase leading up to her flat in front of her, standing on a small pile of post and junk mail, listening. She even pressed her ear to the wall; then she heard just two words. The inspector's voice, low, quite close: "Can I . . . ?"

No reply, but then footsteps, heading toward the back.

And then silence.

23:15

It had been inexcusably late when Andy appeared at 14 Waterside Gardens, that much was clear. By the time the taxi dropped him off for the second time since leaving the pub, the cold air had sobered him up enough to realize that what he was about to do was pretty serious. He'd misbehaved in the past, but every time it had happened had been with someone he knew well. This was uncharted territory.

In his wallet was the packet of three he'd bought, against the odds, in the machine in the gents' toilet of the King Bill last night. His objective then had been Lou, but now his needs were different. And after all, he thought, his mind wandering back to the encounter on Friday morning, he was nothing if not obedient. She expected more from him, that's what she'd said. And that's exactly what he intended to give her.

He'd stood for a moment outside, the air chill and damp, his breath in clouds around him, contemplating his choices. If she didn't answer, he'd head for the Travel Inn.

He didn't want to end up in the Travel Inn. He wanted a bed, but also a warm body to share it with. He'd been thinking about Lou, how her body felt, for so many hours today that it seemed the height of cruelty to be denied it. Now, though, there was another option: that tight arse, those breasts, small but firm, and that smart mouth. To be taken in hand by the good nurse, told what to do, relieved of all responsibility for himself and his actions.

He knocked quietly, although there were no lights on in Flora's flat, and her car wasn't outside. He assumed she was staying at Taryn Lewis's house in town. After a moment the door opened, and before he could say anything she was already standing aside to let him in, shutting the door behind him with a soft click.

To his great delight she was wearing the uniform, although her feet were bare, neat, tanned feet with toenails painted pink. She was looking at him inquiringly.

"Can I . . . ?" he said. Further words failed him. He must stink of alcohol.

Without saying a word, she led him down the hallway, opening a door halfway down. The bedroom was dark, and quiet, and cool. He looked at the bed and suddenly he was exhausted.

He undressed while she was somewhere else in the flat, crawled naked between the cool white sheets, and, listening to the sounds of her running water, the television in another room, and absolutely not intending to let himself doze off, instantly fell asleep.

What seemed like hours later he half woke and realized he was not in his bed at home, and the woman who was next to him was not Karen. It was not Lou, either.

He reached out a hand and touched naked skin. She stirred, turned toward him, and he folded his arm around her waist and drew her to him. Her body was warm, her skin soft. To his surprise he felt her hand close over his penis. It hardened quickly, and it didn't take long before he was wide awake.

A few moments later she pushed him firmly onto his back and sat astride him, her shape just visible from the small amount of light coming through the blinds. She put a condom on him expertly while he lay between her thighs, wondering whether he was dreaming.

As she lowered herself onto him, her head fell back and he heard her gasp. She put both of her hands flat onto his chest, pressing into him with all her weight. Light as she was, it was hard to breathe. But oh, this felt good. He was holding her waist, lifting her and pushing her back, trying to take some of her weight off his rib cage and moving faster, when she suddenly smacked him with the flat of her hand. "Listen to me. Do not come. Do not. You do *exactly* what I tell you to do."

This was more of a turn-on than anything, and in order to obey he had to almost throw her off him. For a moment he lay on his back, wondering if he could hold off when he was so close.

Then she threaded her fingers through his hair and without warning pulled him roughly around to face her. Her breath in his ear was loud, and fast. "Fuck me with your mouth," she said. She pushed his head down, down her body. While he licked her, she encouraged the pressure by digging fingernails into his shoulder. The pain was intense, and erotic.

"Stop. Stop." Her voice was quiet, calm. Not angry. He raised his head, trying to see her in the darkness.

"Lie on your back," she said.

He moved back up the bed and lay back. The pillows were whipped away from under his head. She sat astride him again, but this time higher up, over his face. She pulled at his shoulders and tucked her calves behind them, kneeling over him, tantalizingly out of reach. His hands were on her buttocks, trying to pull her down to him, moaning softly. And as she lowered herself onto him, one of the pillows was pulled over his forehead, covering his eyes, denying him the pleasure of the view. For a crazy moment he thought she was going to smother him. But as hard as it was pressed over the upper part of his face, his nose and mouth were clear.

"Can you hear me?" she asked. Her voice was quiet, but clear. He could imagine her barking orders at the junior nurses, expecting an immediate and compliant response.

"Yes, Nurse," he said, unable to help himself. Smiling.

"This is what's going to happen. I am going to sit down, and I expect you to try your hardest to make me come."

"Yes, please."

"Don't interrupt me. I expect you to make me come. You will find it hard to breathe while you're doing it. Do you understand?"

"Sorry. Yes. I mean—"

"I will be in control of when you can take a breath. You will need to trust me. Do you understand?"

"Yes," he said.

"Raise your right hand straight up if you want to stop. Do it now, to show me you understand."

He raised his hand obediently into the air, left it there for a second, and then reached forward blindly until he found her skin, her bare arm, the muscles on it flexed and holding the pillow tightly over his face.

"Good. Are you ready?"

He answered with a sound. He was absolutely ready. And then he felt her against his mouth, and nose, and he kissed and nuzzled and licked as best he could while his heart thumped; she was pressing into him, moving very gently, and there was no way he could have taken a breath. At first it was fun, if a little strange. Then it became intense, urgent; his lungs began to burn and just at the moment he thought he was going to have to push her off him, she lifted herself away from his face. He gasped in a fresh lungful of hot, damp air that smelled like sex. Another long breath in and she was back against his face again, and this time his tongue worked faster against her, and as well as the fear that she would not get up in time for him to breathe, he felt something else—a thrill, a buzz, a surge of vast erotic delight that rose and swelled within him. Oh, this was good, this was so good . . .

Sooner this time, she raised herself, and, muffled by the pillow, he heard her make a sound that might have been one of pleasure. Barely time, then, to heave a breath in and she was on him again. He felt the panic building together with the desperate need to do this right, to get her to come quickly so that he would be allowed his own satisfaction—but even more so to please her, to impress her. He blocked out the voice in the back of his head that was becoming shrill—*Fuck, she is going to kill me like this*—and his brain was bursting with stars and lights, his pulse pounding in his ears, the slick wetness of her skin sliding against his face. Sensation surged through his whole body like a drug, like pure energy.

When everything started to spin, he began to raise his hand feebly; and at that moment she tensed, the muscles of her legs closing around his shoulders with a grip that was painful. He held on for another few seconds while he floated inside himself, observing his lack of oxygen in a way that was now almost calm, that almost made him want to laugh. Who needed air, after all, when this was what lay beyond it?

She lifted herself away from him. The air surged painfully back into his lungs in a long, noisy, uncontrollable rasp that was followed by a choking cough. His throat was raw with it. Another breath, another. The stars were colliding behind his eyelids. She untangled her legs from his shoulders and moved away. The pressure on the pillow lightened, and he could have moved it off his face, but his arms didn't work.

Andy had managed perhaps three or four recovery breaths before her hand closed over his erection.

"Hold your breath," she said.

I can't, I can't do it, he thought, at the same moment knowing he wanted to. He reached out blindly and caught her other hand, pulled it up to his mouth and nose and pressed it against his wet face. And after a moment of her denying him breath again, the stars were back, the panic died away at the same moment as the floating sensation returned, and this time the stars were brighter and denser and he felt like he could almost reach out and touch them. And his body sang with it, every part of him burning. He didn't even know what she was doing anymore.

The stars began to fade and a darkness approached, sidling up to him like sleep. She took her hand away from his face and for a moment nothing happened. Space. Then she slapped him, hard, across the cheek, and he heaved a breath in. With it came sudden panic, his eyes wide open. She had stopped everything.

"Please," he gasped.

"Take some breaths. You need to be fully conscious."

When he could speak, he said again: "Please." Not even knowing what it was that he wanted.

"As this is clearly your first time, I will permit it."

Permit it?

"There are rules. Do you understand? Say yes if you understand."

"Yes," he coughed. His limbs, his body—everything was liquid. He could barely move.

"You do not touch me unless I tell you to do so. You ask for permission before you come. As you will be silenced, you will have to gain permission from me now."

"Please, can I—"

"Please, *may* you what?"

"I need to come—*please.*"

"I am going to restrict your breathing again. Remember you can raise your hand. Do it now to show you are in agreement."

He lifted his hand. It was like dragging a weight from the surface of the bed, his fingers feebly curled.

"Very well. Let's see what you've got."

This time it was the pillow, over his face, held down with one of her hands. Her grip was so strong, both on the pillow and on his cock. It wasn't going to take long, and, although it was difficult, he could get shallow breaths through the fabric. There was more panic this time, less bliss, until the moment when he came. It almost took him by surprise. He felt the orgasm in the whole of his body at once, a jerk that pushed him physically off the mattress and crackled through his nerves and muscles and sinews like an electric current. His head was spinning. The sensation of it lasted longer than he had ever, ever experienced. Minutes, hours maybe. He was soaring. The pressure on his face did not let up.

And then, after the thudding in his ears, silence.

Day Four
Sunday 4 November 2012

08:10

Lou woke up and before she opened her eyes she had a headache. It was dark except for the bright light coming from the digital alarm clock beside the bed, and looking at it felt like looking into the sun.

Time to get up.

Downstairs, her mobile phone bleeped intermittently, signaling that a message had come through. Lou groaned. It shouldn't be legal to have to be awake this early on a Sunday morning. Unfortunately that was one of the hazards of working incident rooms, particularly this early in an investigation.

She showered in the dark, not daring to put the light on, but when she got out of the shower her head had eased a bit. By the light of the orange streetlamp outside, she found a blister pack of paracetamol, popped two and swallowed them, cupping her hand under the tap to get enough water to wash them down.

Downstairs the kitchen light felt unnaturally bright, the tiled floor freezing under her stockinged feet. In her living room she fished around for her phone.

The message was from Ali Whitmore, timed just after seven:

Did you see msg re: Lorna? Really useful. Call when you get chance.

She dialed. "Ali? It's me. Who's Lorna?"

REPORT

Re:	Lorna Paulette NEWMAN DOB 18/02/1962 of 11 Downsview Road, Winterham, Norwich
Sunday 4 November	
From:	DC 9952 Ron MITCHELL
To:	Op NETTLE

Phone call received from Mrs. Lorna NEWMAN. Mrs. NEWMAN claims that Barbara FLETCHER-NORMAN has been a close friend of hers for a number of years. She last spoke to Barbara by telephone on the night of 31 October at about 2100hrs.

Mrs. NEWMAN states that Barbara FLETCHER-NORMAN had been having an affair with her tennis coach named as a Mr. Liam O'TOOLE and was planning to leave her husband for him. However it seems that the tennis coach had apparently run away with some of Barbara's money and this was the cause of Mrs. FLETCHER-NORMAN's upset that evening.

Mrs. NEWMAN claims to have in her possession a number of letters written to her by Mrs. FLETCHER-NORMAN and believes the letters provide some insight into the state of mind of the deceased.

R Mitchell

08:52

Flora's eyes opened and for a moment she wondered where she was. The last time she'd slept here was less than a week ago but already it felt like a lifetime. So much had happened, so many changes, her life no longer felt like her own.

Polly was dead.

She tested the thought, rolling it around in her head, realizing that it was somehow less panic-inducing than it had been even yesterday.

Her watch told her it was nearly nine. Surprised at how well she'd slept, she suddenly recalled the peculiar events of last night. It seemed unreal, dreamlike, in the bright sunlight that filled the room. Had that really been him? Surely it could have been anyone. She often had visitors, the woman downstairs.

Since Flora had moved in a couple of years ago, she'd seen her downstairs neighbor a few times but they had never exchanged more than the occasional polite "hello." Flora had seen her in the small courtyard garden at the back from her bedroom window. She was much older than Flora, but still beautiful, with a good body, fit. Flora had often wondered if she went to a gym somewhere.

Pulling on a pair of tracksuit bottoms and a hooded top, she padded down to the kitchen to put the kettle on. And then she reached for the phone.

It was the answering machine—probably too early for Taryn or Chris to be awake on a Sunday. "Tabs, it's me. Give me a call later on if you can. I saw the strangest thing last night—still can't quite believe it. I'll come over and pick up my car this afternoon if that's okay. Oh, and thanks again for everything. See you later."

09:02

Finally, after weeks of cold, gray days, wind and rain driving the last reluctant leaves from the trees, Sunday had burst into bright, cold sunshine. The light streamed in through the blinds, over the white duvet, up to the closed eyes and sleep-crumpled face of Andy Hamilton. It disturbed him, but instead of opening his eyes straightaway he turned his head, glancing across the bed to see if it was empty. Determining that it was, and that he was alone, he pulled the other pillow over his pounding head and plunged back into darkness again.

Oh God. What had all that been about? He had never had sex like that, never experienced a thrill like that before. He had been too drunk to refuse, of course, or too intoxicated to realize that being smothered by a woman he'd only just met was possibly not the cleverest thing to do. And yet—if he hadn't done it, hadn't allowed her to control him like that, he would never have known how it felt. He was twice her size and possibly twice as heavy, he could have thrown her to one side if he'd wanted to. And yet—and yet, she had controlled him utterly. At that crucial moment when he felt like he was flying, he could not have moved or spoken or asked for help if his life had depended on it.

You will have to trust me, she had said. He hadn't understood what she had meant, then, still pissed from the beers, thinking it was funny. Thinking he was going to get a shag and a warm bed to sleep in after all. She had even told him what she was planning to do, and the roaring in his ears must have drowned out the alarm bells that should have been ringing; but the drunk, the thrill seeker, the Andy who relished a challenge, particularly when a woman was involved, went with it.

He must have passed out last night. He knew this because she brought him round from it. He heard her talking to him, saying things like, "Open your eyes. Andy, look at me . . ." and the funniest thing of all was that he thought he was in hospital. She had that tone of voice that said "nurse" even more than the uniform did. He had opened his eyes and the room was still dark, but he could see her leaning over him. She did not look concerned.

She did not need to, after all: she was a nurse. She knew he was fine. Of course he could trust her—he was in the safest hands possible, wasn't he?

Half awake, he became aware of sounds. He moved, stretched, felt the soreness on his back. He opened his eyes to see her lithe, brown legs as she came back into the room. A steaming mug of coffee was placed on the bedside table beside him. He raised his head, his eyes traveling up her body, taking in the ironed uniform, the blond hair shiny and blow-dried, the makeup.

He reached out a hand toward her but she did not come closer. She sat on the chair in the corner of the room, facing him, crossed her legs elegantly. "How are you feeling?"

He thought carefully about his response. "Tired," he said.

She smiled. "That's to be expected."

Hard to know what to say that didn't sound idiotic. In the end, he settled on: "I've never done anything like that before."

"Yes, I could tell. But you liked it."

This time his response was instant. "Yes. I did."

Her smile changed from benevolent to faintly lascivious. "What we did was quite tame. There are plenty of other new experiences to try, if that's what you would like to do."

Andy grinned at her. "Will you teach me?"

Suzanne, for that was her name, stopped smiling then and said, "You'd better get up. You're going to be late, Inspector."

09:30

The briefing had the fewest number of officers in attendance since the investigation had begun. On the face of it, this wasn't surprising: many of the major crime specialists who had been temporarily deployed to the investigation worked regular office hours, leaving the weekends for the core team. If anything came up which required additional resources, Lou could bid for more bodies.

It felt like things were slowing down, as far as Polly's murder was concerned. Practically everyone who had the vaguest connection with the case had been interviewed at least once; the most promising of leads had already been followed up, paperwork was now churning through the Incident Room like a constantly flowing stream.

No Jason today. It was going to be a long slog of a day, even if she didn't spend all of it here. Looking on the bright side, it should be a hell of a lot easier to concentrate.

Altogether there were seven people in the room. Lou, near the front, legs neatly crossed at the knee, daybook and pen poised; Les Finnegan and Ron Mitchell; Sam, even though Lou was fairly sure she should have been off today; Barry Holloway was in, too—when was he due for a rest day? Lou scribbled a hasty note to remind herself to check. Paul Harper, the senior CSI, was there; and finally, late, Andy Hamilton had entered and sat at the back.

His hair was still damp as though he had only just fallen out of the shower, and out of the corner of her eye she observed that he looked even more disheveled than usual, but she kept her attention on Barry.

"The key focus for the investigation remains the Fletcher-Normans," he said. "Forensic evidence links Barbara Fletcher-Norman to the scene. We know she had a suicide attempt in September, and the medical disclosure indicates that she was still on medication. We now have further intel that Barbara was having a relationship with a man believed to be her tennis coach, which seemed to have ended on the day of Polly's murder. We should get more on that once the witness has been interviewed fully, but the indications are that on the night of Wednesday thirty-first, Barbara was extremely upset and had been drinking heavily."

A few murmurs. Lou glanced at Hamilton. He was scribbling notes, head down. She sighed, wishing, not for the first time, that Rob Jefferson's back had not chosen this particular time to fail him.

Lou caught Barry's eye and interrupted. "Ron and Sam are going to Norfolk today to interview Lorna Newman. We should be able to take all the letters that Barbara sent to her for the inquest."

Barry nodded.

"Paul?" Lou said. "Can you give us an update on forensics?"

Paul Harper cleared his throat. "So we now have three scenes that are being worked on." He indicated Jason's map, taped up to the whiteboard. "Yonder Cottage, Hayselden Barn, and the quarry. We are working at the quarry again today, trying to establish if the shot put that was found yesterday was thrown from the top of the quarry before the car went over, or if it fell out of the car as it went down."

Les Finnegan raised a hand.

Paul nodded to him.

"Are we definite on the shot put being the weapon yet?"

"No, but it's looking the most likely bet at the moment. Any other questions before we carry on?"

Silence in the room. There was a faint odor of stale beer, and Lou hoped it wasn't coming from the big man at the back.

"Okay," Paul continued. "So that's the quarry. We've finished at Yonder Cottage for now, awaiting results of blood tests and a few other things there. Hayselden Barn is still being worked on."

"Any results?"

"Bits and pieces. Yesterday Brian gave his key to his daughter and asked her to make a phone call from his mobile phone. So we've had some unexpected complications. We've managed to retrieve blood from the kitchen sink—likelihood is that it's Polly's. Should get that back today."

"Thanks, Paul. You'll let us know when you have any more?"

Paul Harper nodded. He looked relieved to be done.

Lou went on: "Sam spoke to Mrs. Lewis yesterday. Can you give us the update, Sam? I think some people might have missed it."

"Her father—Brian, that is—told her that he was no longer sleeping with Polly because she had introduced him to another woman. Brian asked Taryn to go and use his mobile to ring her, to let her know where he was. Mrs. Lewis kindly handed the phone over to us and it's being downloaded. Should be done later today. We're still waiting for the billings and the cellsite data on it, though. The service provider is still having computer problems, so we can't get the subscriber check done on that number Polly was calling the night she died."

"What about that other number, the one called by the landline in Yonder Cottage?" Lou asked.

"Unfortunately it's the same SP. We'll have to wait for that one, too."

Lou smiled at Barry again. "Nearly there. Just a few intel requirements remaining. We still need more on what happened at the Lemon Tree on the last day. Statement's gone out about that today."

Barry Holloway nodded his assent to this and added, "We've not had anything more about the car that was seen—that guy from Crimestoppers. We appealed for him to come forward again, but nothing so far."

"Shame," Lou said.

"If we're working on the theory that Barbara Fletcher-Norman was the killer, we need more information about that last night. Was she drinking at home? Did anyone else speak to her on the phone—we should get that from the landline billing, at least. And we need to locate this man she was supposed to be seeing, Liam O'Toole. See if he can corroborate the story put forward by Mrs. Newman in her first statement. That's about it for now. Just awaiting the results of the key interviews from today, really."

"Thanks, Barry. Right, then. We need to crack on today, folks," she said, standing and straightening her skirt. "Ron and Sam—you're going to see Mrs. Newman today. Try and get back as soon as you can, and give us a call if there's anything we can action straightaway. Les, we also need a check on CCTV. Keep you out of the cold wind today, eh? We've got another press conference booked for Monday, unless anything earth-shattering turns up over the weekend. Anyone got anything else they'd like to say?"

Quiet in the room, although chairs were squeaking and shuffling as everyone made ready to get out and get on with it. Barry was cleaning off the whiteboard.

Hamilton cleared his throat. "You got anything specific for me?"

Lou looked at him, mentally checking off her list of urgent tasks and wondering which of them she could bear to devolve to someone who looked like he'd had a particularly spectacular night on the town.

"You can find out what's happened to Brian's computer. How about that?"

"It's Sunday," he said.

"And?"

He didn't answer, just maintained the eye contact. They were on shaky ground again, Lou thought. "I know it won't take you very long. So maybe you could find out some more about Liam O'Toole. All right with that?"

"Yes, of course."

"Right, let's get on with it. Ron, Sam, can I see you both please—my office? Thanks everyone."

The room emptied quicker than water out of a drain.

For: DC Jane Phelps c/o DCI Smith Op Nettle
From: Brian FLETCHER-NORMAN
Tel: hosp
Message: Please call back. Has remembered further.

09:45

Lou picked up the message from her crowded desk as she went in, pocketed it. Ron Mitchell was waiting for Sam by the door, his coat already on. Sam was shutting down her workstation. Neither of them looked happy.

"I don't know why you two are looking so bloody grumpy," she said. "The sun's shining, it's a lovely day. Just right for a nice drive."

"A nice long drive," Ron said sadly.

"You never know," Lou said, "this might uncover something crucial. You two could be heroes."

"Yes, boss," Sam said. "It'll be great."

"And you might even finish early and then you can relax. Okay?" Lou regarded them both for a moment, knowing that sending her sergeant off to conduct an interview was not generally considered to be the best use of resources. But Sam had a knack with witnesses and suspects; she listened, and was intuitive, picking up on things that other interviewers missed. If she couldn't go up to Norfolk and meet Lorna Newman for herself, sending Sam was the next best thing. "You got a car sorted out?"

"Yes, we've got one of the Volvos booked."

"Okay. Call me later?"

"Yes, boss," Sam said, and they left.

When they had gone, Lou looked at the message again and dialed the number for Briarstone General Hospital, and asked for the Stuart Ward.

10:15

Flora was thinking about going back to the studio. Something about the sunshine had made her want to go back and look at that canvas, the one of Polly, even if she wasn't going to be able to complete it. She was just pulling on her leather jacket when there was a knock at the door.

Fearing it was Hamilton, she froze at the top of the stairwell, not making a sound.

A few moments later, another knock and an imperious voice suddenly through the letter box. "Flora? Let me in, for Christ's sake." It was her mother.

"Mum," said Flora, going down and opening the door.

"Where's your car?"

"I left it at Taryn's."

She could tell straightaway that Felicity was upset, given the outfit she was wearing: blue jeans, pink trainers, and her waxed jacket over the top of it, accessorized with a ridiculously large white designer handbag. Normally her mother took more care with her outfit, if she was planning to leave the farm.

"Aren't you going to let me in?"

"Sorry," Flora said, and stood aside as her mother marched on up the stairs. "I was just on my way out, actually."

Felicity ignored this and took a seat on one of the kitchen chairs, looking flustered.

"Are you all right, Mum?" Flora asked, laying a hand on Felicity's shoulder. For a moment she had a passing thought that her mother had come to confront her about her sexuality, a scene she had often imagined and long dreaded.

Felicity slipped the waxed jacket off her shoulders and Flora took it to hang up in the cupboard in the hallway. "It's your father," she said. "I'm worried about him."

"Worried?" Flora said, coming back into the room. "Why?"

"This business over Polly. He's been—different—ever since. Oh, I don't know. I can't understand it. You know the police were round? Searched the whole place. They had a warrant. Heaven alone knows what they were looking for."

"Some sort of evidence, I expect," Flora said.

"Oh, Flora, don't be flippant! Daddy was beside himself."

Flora doubted that. He would have descended into that level of Zen-like calm that was somehow even more terrifying than anger. "Did they find anything?"

"I don't think so. Daddy thinks they were on a fishing trip, whatever that means."

Flora was never quite sure if it was possible for Felicity to be that naïve, or whether an act she had carried on for so many years had become her natural state.

"He was always very close to Polly, even when she was a little girl," Felicity said, in a small voice. "I did wonder . . ."

"What?"

She shook her head. "No. No, you'll think I'm foolish."

"Go on, Mum. What did you wonder?"

Tears formed in the brown eyes and rolled down the cheeks. "I did wonder whether Polly—whether maybe Nigel had had an affair with Cass, years ago."

"With Polly's mum?" For a moment Flora didn't understand, then a wave of cold fear gripped her from the inside and held her tightly.

Silence. Felicity fished a tissue from the pocket of her jeans and wiped under her eyes.

"You—you think Polly might have been Dad's . . ." Flora's voice trailed off. She couldn't manage to say it.

"Oh, it's too silly. He'd never be unfaithful. But I couldn't see why he would be so different all of a sudden, and then I just got thinking—you know how it is. I had thought it before, to be honest. We used to see Cass and Polly quite often—you were very tiny—and Polly used to pull your hair when she thought nobody was looking. Daddy always seemed so pleased to see them. I thought that was so peculiar, he was never normally pleased to see anyone, you know how he is."

"Mum," Flora said, her voice barely under control.

"Of course, I always wondered where she got her coloring from. Cass had such dark hair, and there was Polly, blond, with those lovely blue eyes—"

"Mum!"

"Cass always seemed to have some man or other in tow, never the same one from one week to the next. I suppose that's where Polly got it from—you heard that she was having an affair with Brian Fletcher-Norman, didn't you? Julia told me. Whatever next? I ask myself. He's twice her age. Maybe that's what brought his heart attack on. You never know . . ."

"Mum!"

"Hmm?" Felicity paused.

"I'm sure that's not right," Flora said, with more conviction than she felt. "I'm sure Dad wouldn't . . . I mean, he would have told you, surely?"

Felicity had grown older in the last week, the lines on her face standing out more, her hair grayer at the roots, as though the horror of finding Polly's body had drained the color and the life out of her. "I don't know, Flora. I've been thinking it over for days."

"And Cass never said anything about Polly's father?"

"Never. Well, she led me to believe she'd been to a sperm bank. She said the time was right for her to have a baby, and all of a sudden she turned up one weekend and announced she was pregnant."

"Was Dad there, then?"

Felicity frowned. "No, he was away on one of his business trips and Cass and I had a girlie weekend, got quite drunk. Well, I did. Cass did manage to cut down a little."

"Dad would know, though. Wouldn't he? If—if he was? Surely Polly's mum would have told him?"

"Oh, I don't know, darling. She could be funny, Cass. One minute she was your best friend and then she'd take off and you'd not hear from her for months. I never knew what she was up to. And she loved having secrets."

Flora took a deep breath, laid her hand over Felicity's and gave it a squeeze. "Mum, I'm sure you're imagining it. Dad would never be able to keep something like that private. Have you asked him?"

"Of course not, don't be so utterly ridiculous! How do you recommend I bring that topic up? 'By the way, darling, is there a chance that the corpse in the cottage might be your love child?' But if it's not that, then what is it?" Felicity wailed plaintively.

"What is what? What do you mean?"

"If it's not something to do with Polly, then why is he acting so strangely?" Felicity looked at her daughter and stuck out her chin, demanding some sort of answer.

For a moment Flora was lost in thought, pondering why it was that, at so many points in her life, her mother would come up with a passing comment which devastated her so utterly—whether it was a mere mention of her school grades, or how she was expected to remain at the farm and work instead of wasting time on art, or how one or other of her cronies had remarked that Flora would never get on in life if she insisted on dressing like a hobo and never combing her hair.

Flora shrugged. "Maybe he's just worried about the business, or worried that the police will ask him too many questions about Polly's death."

Felicity's gaze became suddenly more penetrating. "Suspect him of the killing, you mean?"

"Maybe. You know how much the police love Dad."

Felicity shook her head impatiently. "Why haven't they been round to interview him, then? He's just as likely to be guilty as any of the rest of us. I mean, he had plenty of opportunity."

"I thought he went out. Somewhere in town with his friends?"

Felicity shook her head. "But that was earlier. He came home about eight, had told me not to make dinner, and then got all cross because it wasn't waiting for him. Told me I'd got the dates wrong. We had a bit of a row about it, even though I'd written it on the calendar. Seems silly now."

She looked at the table, running her thumbnail along a groove in the grain of the oak surface. "I *know* it was that day. I'd given Polly a telling-off about the shopping she'd promised to do for me in Briarstone. I told Daddy he should go and have a talk with her, and he did. He went down to the cottage. It was raining by then and he was gone for about an hour. I was about to go down and find out where the hell he was when he came back. Said Polly had made him cheese on toast."

She gave a small sound, half a laugh, half a sob.

Flora's heart had started beating faster. Something wasn't adding up. Why had he told her he was out? And he'd not mentioned going to the cottage. He'd not said he had been with Polly that night. Why would he lie, unless he was hiding something?

Flora put her hand over her mother's. "Mum, I've really got to go out now. Can we talk about this another time?"

"Hmm? Oh, of course darling. Sorry to hold you up. I just needed— someone to talk to, I guess. Thank you for being so understanding."

"That's all right, Mum." Flora got the waxed jacket for Felicity, then steered her gently toward the staircase.

"Flora dear, will you come over tonight and have dinner? Come and see if you think Daddy's any different. Will you?"

"I'll do my best," Flora said.

At the front door, Flora said goodbye quickly, shutting the door almost in her mother's face, not wishing to risk a meeting with Andy Hamilton, just in case he was still inside the flat downstairs.

11:12

It was nearing lunchtime by the time Lou made it to the hospital. She wasn't supposed to be interviewing people, but everyone else was out, and besides, she fancied having a look at Brian herself.

While she'd been parking the car a text message had come through on her job phone from Jason.

Hope u don't mind me texting work phone. This is my no in case u
need anything today. Not busy. Jason

It felt as if there was a coded message in there somewhere. She
thought about texting back straightaway, but there were more pressing things to attend to.

The hospital was busy with visitors—the WRVS shop buzzing with
people buying bottles of Lucozade, newspapers, and magazines. The
paracetamol she'd taken had finally started to kick in, although somewhere at the back of her head the headache lurked like a malevolent
creature, waiting for an excuse to take over once again.

PC Yvonne Sanders, casually dressed in jeans and a fleece, was waiting for her near the reception desk. "Ma'am," she said. "I'm sorry to be
dressed like this, I was on a plainclothes job today."

"Don't worry," Lou said. "I'm just glad I got hold of you. You got
your PNB handy?"

Yvonne patted her bag. Her pocket notebook, or PNB, was what
Lou needed more than anything else. If she was going to be talking to
Brian, she wanted a careful note of everything he said.

"You were there when he had the heart attack, weren't you?" Lou
asked, as they eased their way through the throng and headed up the
corridor toward Stuart Ward.

"Yes, ma'am."

"You did CPR on him?"

"Yes—well, we both did. Ian did a lot of it."

"Good job," Lou said. Short on officers, Lou had gone back through
the case files to find someone who had a vague bearing on the case and
who might actually be on duty—and had found Yvonne Sanders. Lou
hoped she was a fast writer.

"Er—anything you want me to do, apart from writing up?"

"I know it's a bit irregular, interviewing with a DCI," Lou said. "I'd
rather just get on and do it, though, while the ward's quiet. So I'll do
the talking, you take notes, and type up a statement for me back at the
nick, okay?"

"Of course."

So much for preparing the evidence for the coroner. At this rate she would still be working until midnight to get things ready. Under her breath she muttered a fervent prayer to whatever god was listening for this trip not to be a waste of time.

Eventually they found Brian Fletcher-Norman in the dayroom, sitting up in an armchair, watching television. He was sporting a smart-looking pair of burgundy pajamas, covered with a dark green terry cloth bathrobe and some matching slippers. On the dayroom door a sign had been taped: PRIVATE MEETING IN PROGRESS.

"Hello. Brian, isn't it?" Lou asked, offering him her hand.

"Yes."

"I'm DCI Louisa Smith. You've got me today, I'm afraid."

"A pleasure."

"You might remember my colleague, PC Yvonne Sanders?"

Brian shook Yvonne's hand but didn't make the connection.

"PC Sanders was there when you were taken ill. I believe she saved your life, Brian."

"Ah," he said. "Thank you, my dear."

Lou decided she could see the appeal. He might have been far too old for her, but he had a deep, resonant voice and a presence about him, even wearing pajamas and a bathrobe. Dark eyes in a tanned, surprisingly unlined face, and a good head of silver hair. He looked every inch the business executive.

She sat on a lower chair and pulled a low coffee table closer, treating him to a close-up view of the swell of her breasts under her black cashmere sweater. "You don't mind if Yvonne takes notes, do you, Brian? We can ask you to check through them when we're finished, and we can get a statement typed up for you. All right?"

"I'm sure it's fine, my dear. I don't need my solicitor or anything, do I?"

Lou pulled a face. "Lord, no. Not unless you're planning to confess to something." She gave him a smile and a wink, and watched him start to relax.

He used the remote control to turn off the television.

Lou glanced across at PC Sanders to make sure she was ready with her notebook and pen. Yvonne smiled back at her, keen.

"Now, when we spoke on the phone this morning you mentioned that you'd had some further recollections regarding the evening of your wife's death. Would you mind going over exactly what it is you recall?"

Brian paused for a moment. "Where shall I start?"

Lou gave him an encouraging smile. "Start from when you got home from work. Was Barbara there?"

Brian nodded. "Yes, she was upstairs. I didn't realize she was there at first. I assumed she must have been watching television because she didn't answer when I called."

"What time did you get home?"

He looked away before answering vaguely. "Eightish, maybe nine. I left town at gone seven, anyway."

He looked as if he was concentrating hard, trying to bring the memory back. He's a sly old goat, Lou thought. She was quite aware that he'd remembered all along. Was it because they'd had contact with Lorna Newman that he'd changed his story? Had she been in contact with Brian at the hospital?

"I poured myself a drink and sat down to read the paper. Barbara came downstairs much later. It must have been about eleven, twelve, and we had an argument."

"What was the argument about?"

Brian sighed deeply. "Much the same as usual. I was late home from work, and so she accused me of having an affair. She said I smelled of women's perfume; I said she smelled of gin. It got quite heated. She stormed off back upstairs; I heard her talking to somebody on the telephone, I don't know who."

"And why were you late home?"

Brian looked a little cross at this interruption. "Can't remember," he said vaguely. "It was work, nothing unusual."

"I understood you were semiretired—is there still a call for you to be working late? That seems a little unfair."

Brian shrugged. "Unfair or not, the work's there. And, to be honest, Barbara wasn't always that much fun to come home to. Miserable, most of the time."

Lou thought of Barbara's depression and recent attempt at suicide and suddenly felt rather sorry for her. "Sorry, I interrupted. Barbara was upstairs."

"Yes. I finished my drink and went into the kitchen to wash up the glass. I checked on the gin—we keep the bottles in a cupboard in the kitchen—and found it was nearly finished. That was a pretty bad sign."

"Did she drink every day?"

He shook his head. "Sometimes she'd go for several weeks without a drink. Those times were quite pleasant, really. I think they coincided with the times she was less depressed, less—low, I suppose you'd say. Also, I think she was aware that people thought she might be an alcoholic, and she was always trying to present everyone with evidence that she could manage without a drink, that she wasn't a slave to it." Brian looked Lou in the eye. "Her mother was an alcoholic, you know. Died of liver failure. And her father died of a heart attack at fifty, and he was also a man who liked a drink. So she was very aware of it."

"So, lately, had she been particularly depressed?"

Brian nodded again. "We've been having rows fairly often. Usually we only ever argued when Barbara had had a drink or two—she's too easygoing otherwise."

"Was there any particular reason for it, that you were aware of?"

Brian looked wary for a moment, then shrugged. "I can't think of anything in particular. In fact, I thought she'd been doing rather well. She'd been getting out more, playing golf with her friends. She'd started playing bridge again. Having tennis lessons three times a week at the country club—cost me an arm and a leg, that one, but she said she was determined to be fit by the summer."

Lou thought it unlikely that Brian was unaware of Barbara's infatuation with the tennis coach, but chose to let that one go. It could have been something as simple as it being a huge attack on his ego to admit that Barbara had chosen to go elsewhere. Doing it himself was no doubt just a bit of fun—for his wife to indulge was a different matter entirely.

She gave him an encouraging smile. "So, Barbara was upstairs and you were in the kitchen. Can you remember what happened next?"

"I went and had a bath. Fell asleep in the tub. I often do that if I'm late. Anyway, I've no idea what time it was when I got out again, but the water wasn't cold, so it can't have been hours. Barbara wasn't downstairs, so I assumed she'd gone to bed. The bedroom door was shut."

Lou watched him, eager for him to get on with the story, but waiting while he had a sip of water. Yvonne Sanders flexed her wrist.

"I went back downstairs to turn all the lights off and lock up. Then all of a sudden, Barbara came barreling into the hallway from the kitchen. I couldn't work out where she'd been, but I suppose she must have come in through the back door. She was hysterical, shouting and yelling about something. I told her to calm down and tell me what was wrong. She pushed me back and I fell back onto the stairs. She kept saying, 'It's done now, I've done it now, it's too late.' Something like that. Over and over."

" 'It's done now, I've done it now, it's too late'?" Lou repeated.

"Yes."

Yvonne was scribbling fast. Lou hoped she was getting every single word of this. He'd already changed his story once, they needed to make sure he could be pinned down somehow.

"What do you think she meant by that?"

Brian shrugged. "At the time, I hadn't a clue. She was pretty drunk, almost incoherent. Thinking about it now, of course, I'm wondering whether she'd been over the road to see Polly."

"Do you have any idea what time this was?"

He shook his head. "Well, after twelve, I think."

"Okay. So then what happened?"

"After she pushed me, I got up and went to bed. I told you, I don't put up with that sort of behavior. Everyone has a breaking point, and that's mine. I heard the door bang, but I thought that was her locking it—sometimes the front door doesn't lock properly until you've given it a good bang."

Something was being left out, Lou was sure of it. There was a tension in the air that hadn't been there just five minutes ago.

"Did you not notice any blood on her hands, her clothes?" she asked.

"No. It was dark in the hallway because I'd already turned the lights off."

"Before locking the front door?"

He shrugged, looked at her defiantly. "That's just my regular routine."

"So you went up to bed and you assumed she'd shut the front door and come up to bed herself?"

He nodded, seeming to relax again. "I didn't hear anything else. If she hadn't gone to bed she was probably passed out on the sofa. I was thinking I'd see her again the next morning, and she'd be right as rain."

"You sleep in separate rooms?"

"Yes. Have done for years."

"So when you woke up, you didn't notice anything unusual?"

He shook his head again. "I'd just got up when there was a knock at the door. I was already feeling a bit unwell. My chest hurt—I thought it was from where she'd pushed me. Then when the police officers came in—you," he said, smiling at Yvonne, "and the other chap—it was suddenly excruciating."

A pause. "Go on," she said.

"That's all I remember," he said with finality, sitting back in the chair and, to all intents and purposes, breathing a heavy sigh of relief.

Yvonne continued writing. Lou paused, to give Yvonne time to catch up and to give herself a moment to think. This version was a completely different story to the one he'd told immediately after the incident, before he'd had the heart attack. However poorly he was feeling, surely his memory wasn't affected at that point. And in hospital, just a few days ago, acting like the whole thing was a blur. Surely you'd remember such a dramatic confrontation with your wife?

She looked up at last. "Thank you, Brian. I know this must have been very difficult for you. I appreciate your efforts."

He gave her a wan smile, showing that he was prepared to battle through any adversity to make her happy. It just wasn't right, though. Bits of it probably were. There were undoubtedly bits missing. And other bits that were complete fabrication.

For a start, the amnesia thing. Lou had had dealings with amnesia when she'd worked a stint in Traffic Division; amnesia was an occasional side effect of head trauma. Retrograde amnesia, usually caused by injury or disease, resulted in a chunk of memory being lost. Usually this would return after a period of time as the injury healed, but the process would be gradual, with bits of memory reemerging as fragments until they could be placed in context, eventually forming a complete picture once again. Sudden, wholesale return of memory like the one Brian seemed to have experienced was, as far as Lou was aware, rare. Of course, he'd not actually had a head injury, although there had been a period of unconsciousness, which could also be a factor.

"It's great that your memory has come back," Lou said, with a bright smile designed to deflect any suspicion. "It's really helpful to us. Gives us a better picture of events."

Brian did not seem to be at all suspicious. "Do you think she did it? Killed Polly?"

"It's a bit too early to be coming to conclusions, Brian. But let's just say I think what you've told me today has moved things forward a great deal."

Lou gave the nod to Yvonne, who was flipping through the pages of her notebook. Lou made a display of gathering her jacket, distracting him. "Brian, does the name Lorna Newman mean anything to you?"

His face registered surprise, and Lou was about as certain as she could be that it was genuine. "Of course. She's a friend of Barbara's. A very old friend. They came to us in the summer—August, I think. Why do you ask?"

"She called the Incident Room. Saw the news about Barbara on the television, I believe. Just wanted to check with you that she is who she says she is."

Brian nodded with satisfaction. "Yes, she's a game old bird, Lorna. No nonsense. Always liked that in a woman."

So. His memory hadn't been jogged by any contact with Lorna. And he didn't view her contact with the police as any sort of threat. Did that mean he'd been telling the truth about that night, after all? Lou was confused. It wasn't that the whole story was wrong—more that there were some parts that were muddled, out of place.

Of course the usual way that stories like this were untangled was through repeated interviewing, going over the same questions, the same story again and again until things changed, or until things started to make sense. Or until new information came to light that changed the perspective on the investigation. It didn't mean he was somehow implicated in Polly's death. It didn't necessarily mean that he was lying.

At some point, of course, she would have to confront him about the affair with Polly. For the moment, though, she believed that he would just deny it further and accuse Taryn of lying to make him out to be a bad person. They needed some corroborative evidence, or at least firm proof that he'd lied about something else.

"Can I ask you to read through my notes," Yvonne said, "and sign each page to say you agree with what I've written? I'll type things up back at the office . . ."

Once he'd read through the notes and signed them, Lou held out her hand and found his handshake was now surprisingly warm, his grip firm. Overall, he had the appearance of a man for whom a great weight has been lifted from his shoulders.

"I'll be in touch if anything else comes to light, of course."

"Certainly. Thank you, Inspector."

As much as she dearly wanted to correct him, part of Lou held back. It might disrupt the balance of their relationship if he suddenly saw her as a senior rank, even if that was the case. And this despite the fact that she'd given him her business card, which clearly stated her rank. If he wanted to persist in addressing her as "Inspector," then there were other ways of tackling it.

"Call me Lou," she said. "After all, I've been rather cheekily calling you Brian."

"Lou," he said, testing the word, still holding the handshake, maintaining eye contact in a way that, in another place and time, might have been flirtatious.

She let him hold it until he relaxed his grip, and gave him another of her bright, slightly vacuous smiles. "Take care of yourself, Brian. Hope they let you home soon."

"Goodbye."

Lou juggled her bag and her coat, and together with Yvonne Sanders made her way back along the endless corridor to the front entrance, where they parted company.

"Thanks," Lou said. "Really appreciate your help."

"Anytime," Yvonne said, shaking Lou's hand. "I'll send the statement through as soon as it's done. If there's anything else you need, please give me a shout."

Lou drew in deep lungfuls of cold, clear air. The sun was about as high in the sky as it was likely to get, and still not a cloud to be seen. She hadn't realized until she was out in the grand space of the car park, cars circling slowly, competing for the next vacant space, just how stifled she'd felt in the dayroom of Stuart Ward.

12:16

Brian watched Lou's arse appraisingly as she walked to the door of the dayroom. Nice girl, he thought. Brighter than she pretended to be, just as he was brighter than she gave him credit for. She knew he hadn't told her the full story, and yet he felt like she'd believed him, which had been the key to it. Of course he remembered every single detail of what had happened that night, had gone over it a million times, lying here in the hospital.

From the pocket of his bathrobe he pulled out the mobile phone that Suzanne had slipped him when she'd visited. He turned it on, waited, then hit the speed dial that she'd programmed in.

"It's me. Yes, they've just been. A female inspector and another one who just took notes." He listened to her voice, relishing how she sounded, just a voice, a long way away, but next to him in the room.

"It all went well, I think. She didn't ask me anything I couldn't handle. No, nothing. Well, she asked if I noticed any blood. I said no, it was dark. It's all right," he said, trying for reassurance. "I'll be home soon, and then we can . . ."

He listened to her telling him what he had to do. Finally, he chanced his luck and asked: "When will you come in?"

Then, a pause. "I love you. Goodbye, my darling. See you soon."

12:19

Ron's phone rang when they were still some way away from Lorna Newman's house. He put his hand over the phone and mouthed "It's the boss" at Sam before pulling his notebook out of his inside jacket pocket, biting the top off a pen, and scribbling something down. "Right. Gotcha. Uh-huh."

He shut the phone with a snap. "Apparently Brian's memory has come back. Quite a lot, by all accounts."

Sam raised an eyebrow.

"Seems he remembers Barbara coming back into the house all hysterical, late that night. Then she disappeared off again and he went to bed."

"That's a bit odd."

He nodded. "Boss thinks he's not lying exactly, but not telling the full story either. She's going to have another go, maybe when he gets out of the hospital."

"She's not treating him as a suspect, then?"

"Nah. More likely it's her, isn't it?"

"You mean Barbara?"

He gave her a look which said of course fucking Barbara, but simply nodded. "You can't tell me she went and topped herself covered in Polly's blood because she was a bit depressed. She went over there to confront her husband's bit on the side, got the red mist on because she was half cut, and then took herself off over the quarry because of what she'd done."

Case closed, Sam thought to herself. He had a way of simplifying things that was by turns deadly accurate and horribly misplaced.

"What about if Brian did it—killed Polly—and Barbara saw him?"

"What—and then she topped herself?"

"No, he pushed her over the cliff. Might explain the heart attack. That level of stress."

He shook his head. "The woman was depressed, suicidal. You've got to stick with the evidence, Sarge, don't go off half-cocked with complicated theories. It's usually the most obvious explanation. Sometimes people just act funny, don't they?"

You got that right, Sam thought, putting her full concentration back to the road.

12:41

Lou parked in the station car park, pulled out her job phone and checked for messages—nothing—and then, on a whim, found her personal phone. It was turned off, as it often was, since nobody ever used it to phone her. She turned it on and sent a text to Jason's number.

> This is my pers number FYI. All good here. Hows your weekend going? Quiet without you. Lou

Almost immediately a reply bleeped.

> Hockey this morning. Bored now. Could meet 4 lunch . . . ? X

Lunch—what a great idea. And it gave her another idea. She sent a reply:

> Great. Meet you in the Lemon Tree? Soon as?

5X5X5 INTELLIGENCE REPORT

Date:	Sunday 4 November 2012
Officer:	PC 9921 EVANS
Re:	Op NETTLE

ECHR Grading: B / 1 / 1

Phone call received from Mr. Dean LONGFORD, DOB 27/01/87, address 15 Castle View, Briarstone.
Caller states he was the person who phoned Crimestoppers last week having seen two people arguing in a vehicle in Cemetery Lane on the night of the 31/10.

States he has seen the police appeal for him to come forward with further information, although he hasn't got anything further to add. Is willing to make a statement but is going on holiday next week.

In case the statement doesn't get taken, he gave the following details:

Small car, dark in color, like a Peugeot or a Fiesta size.

Parked in a lay-by or driveway entrance in Cemetery Lane, right before a sharp bend.

There was a lorry sticking out of a driveway on the opposite side so the inft had to slow down to pass—hence noticing the car.

Female with long fair hair in the driver's seat

Male figure (larger) in the passenger seat, no description

Couple appeared to be arguing, lots of finger-pointing etc.

Interior light was on but headlights off

Definitely Halloween night as Tuesday night is when the inft works in town

No idea what the time was exactly but inft left work at 2315hrs and arrived home around 2345hrs.

13:24

Number 11 Downsview Road was a smart bungalow, set back from a quiet road by a long, open driveway. The front lawn, along with all the others on the road, was neatly trimmed.

It was the sort of silence that indicated an elderly population, cars put away in garages reserved for that purpose, smells of dinner cooking from somewhere.

Ron and Sam parked against the curb opposite the house and got out. Sam resisted the urge to have a good stretch. It had been a long drive, the last part especially tedious.

The door was opened almost immediately.

"Mrs. Newman?" Ron asked of the woman who answered the door. Her dark hair was cut neatly in a bob, and gray eyes examined his warrant card closely.

"I'm Detective Constable Ron Mitchell. This is my colleague Detective Sergeant Sam Hollands."

"Come in," she said. Her voice was clear and steady. "I've got the kettle on."

She showed them into a large front room which was rather more modern than either of them had been expecting. Two huge leather sofas dominated the room, matching the cream which covered three of the walls. The fourth wall, mainly an archway into the dining room, was painted a color that might have been purple.

On one wall a handsome gas fire played pretty flames over realistic-looking bricks of coal. A low hiss from the gas flame could be heard above the noise of the kettle rattling into a boil from the kitchen.

Sam perched on the edge of one sofa. Ron sat next to her and sprawled backward into the leather, knees apart, displaying hairy white calves above the diamond-patterned gray socks and pale brown loafers.

Sam looked elsewhere.

Lorna Newman brought a tray through from the kitchen. A cheerful brown teapot, large enough for them all to have at least two cups, with three small mugs—Denby, Sam thought—a milk jug, and a sugar bowl. Matching.

"Thank you for seeing us, Mrs. Newman. I'm sure you must be busy."

"Oh, not really. Andrew's playing golf. My husband, that is. I do all of my chores in the mornings. Usually by now I would be either visiting friends or at the shop."

"The shop?"

"I volunteer at a charity shop in the town. Closed on Sundays, though."

"Mrs. Newman, I wanted to thank you for calling us," Sam said. "I'm sure you might be able to help us build up a clearer picture of what Barbara was like, which will be of great help to the inquiry."

"Which inquiry would that be?"

Sam looked up from her pad, where she had written the date and time but nothing else. "We need to gather evidence for the coroner's inquest into Mrs. Fletcher-Norman's death," she said. "The inquest is due to be held next week. That will determine the cause of death, so it's important we are able to present any evidence that might be relevant. Particularly if the evidence you have supports or refutes the theory that Mrs. Fletcher-Norman might have taken her own life."

Lorna nodded. Looking directly at Sam, she added: "But you are working on the murder case, aren't you? That Polly—what's her name?"

"Polly Leuchars," Ron said helpfully.

"Yes, Mrs. Newman," Sam said. "We're both working on that case. However, we also work on other unexplained deaths in the Briarstone area, one of which is that of Mrs. Fletcher-Norman."

"So you're not linking them, then?"

"We don't have any direct evidence to support a link."

Lorna was silent for a moment. "That's good. I'd hate to think of Barbara mixed up in all that. She was a good girl, you know. We've been friends for years."

"Can you tell me how you met?" Ron was having another go at conducting the interview.

"We were at school together. Kept in touch ever since, although there were long periods where we didn't write. Not for any bad reason."

"And you visited them recently, in Morden?"

"Beginning of August. Spent a week there."

"What was your impression of Mrs. Fletcher-Norman at that time? Did she seem in good spirits?"

Lorna hesitated before replying. "I think so. There were a few times—we went out for dinner, and she'd had a few drinks. Got a bit overexcited, I think. On the last night we were there, she and Brian had a stinking row. We had gone to bed and you could hear them shouting from downstairs."

"What was the argument about?"

She shook her head. "Couldn't tell you. Just a lot of shouting and banging. She didn't seem depressed, although I know she had been. The doctor had her on medication. She used to tell me about all the various pills she had to take."

"I gather she was hospitalized in September?" Ron said.

"Yes. She took an overdose. I think she had had a particularly difficult week with Brian."

"They argued often?"

She nodded. "Brian had had a number of affairs going back over the years, always with women he'd met through work, usually while overseas. Barbara tolerated those because she could pretend to herself that they weren't really happening. A friend of mine—Andrea—her husband used to work with Brian, years ago. Apparently they got up to all sorts when they were on their overseas trips."

Sam was scribbling furiously.

"She'd always been quite a jealous woman," Lorna said. "She was quite nasty to Brian's daughter, saw her as a threat, I believe."

"So when Brian semiretired . . . ?"

"Barbara believed he was having affairs closer to home. First of all it was some physiotherapist woman at the health club they belong to. That was just after they moved to Morden. Then it was all about the stable girl, Polly Leuchars."

"Mrs. Fletcher-Norman mentioned Polly in her letters to you?"

Lorna nodded. "Yes, and over the phone. At first it was just a suspicion, but Barbara has a way of latching on to an idea and going over it so many times in her head that it becomes the same thing as a truth. She said Brian was having an affair with Polly. Other women in the village had confirmed it to her."

"Did she confront Brian?"

"Yes. He denied it, of course. Even stopped having riding lessons to appease her. I felt quite sorry for him, really. I think going riding had been doing him some good."

"Do you know when it was that Barbara confronted her husband?"

"It was around the beginning of September. On the Monday before she was admitted to hospital she said he had denied it. She sounded very low about it. It was as though his denial made it worse—if he'd owned up to it, she might not have felt so bad. He'd admitted his foibles in the past, so it felt to Barbara as though he was really lying to her as well as cheating."

"You seem doubtful that he was having an affair?"

She thought about this, and nodded slowly. "I just can't see it somehow. I've seen pictures of that Polly on the television, what was she, twentysomething?"

"Twenty-seven," Ron said.

"And pretty, too. Forgive me for saying so, but Brian's not usually the sort to appeal to young girls. And I don't think he would be so foolish as to do it right under Barbara's nose like that. Far more likely he was seeing someone else and using Barbara's suspicions about Polly to cover up the real mischief."

For a moment the only sound was Sam's pen moving across the notebook. Ron seemed lost in thought.

"More tea?"

The mugs were duly topped up and Sam paid a visit to the bathroom. It was light and airy and she washed her hands with a purple soap that smelled of lavender, and dried them on a white fluffy towel. The bathroom was spotless. She wondered whether they employed a cleaner or whether Lorna did the housework herself.

Ron seemed to have found a way in. When she found her way back to the living room, both of them were chortling with laughter. She wondered what it was that had got him into Lorna's good books, but it seemed the joke wasn't going to be shared.

"Right," he said with a deep breath. "Where were we?"

Sam retrieved her notebook and flexed her right hand which had started to ache.

"You mentioned a phone conversation with Mrs. Fletcher-Norman on Monday last week. Did you phone her, or was it the other way round?"

"She called me," Lorna said. "It was about Liam O'Toole."

Ron said, "This was the man she was seeing? The tennis coach?"

"Yes. She'd written me a few letters about him, and the last one had indicated that they were planning to run away together. She'd been saving up money for years, money Brian knew nothing about. She called it her Rainy Day Fund."

"Do you have any idea how much money we're talking about?"

Lorna gave a little shrug. "Thousands. Every time Brian had an affair she used to get jewelry from him—keep her sweet, I suppose. She sold it all, as well as creaming money off the housekeeping allowance he gave her."

She took a drink of her tea, then went on. "I'd written a letter to

Barbara in which I'd asked her to be careful. I asked her if she knew everything about this Liam, whether she was certain he could be trusted. She phoned me to give me a telling off."

"You thought he was going to do a runner?"

She nodded. "It just always seemed too good to be true." She gave a rueful smile. "You must think me terribly critical of my friends to not see them as attractive to younger people. But I'm afraid the same thing applies. He was only about twenty-eight, I believe. Handsome, fit, reasonably intelligent. And yet he falls in love with a fifty-nine-year-old housewife? I don't think so."

Sam couldn't decide if Lorna was just a straightforward person who didn't believe in glossing over the issues, or if she was somehow slightly jealous of what Barbara had had. In either case, she looked defiant, as though challenging the officers to disagree.

"Mrs. Fletcher-Norman was angry with you, when she phoned?"

Lorna softened a little. "Not angry, exactly. She was just trying to persuade me that I was wrong about Liam. She was utterly convinced he was genuine. In fact, she said when they did make their escape, as she called it, she would bring him here for a visit so that I could see for myself."

"What did you make of that?"

"I told her she'd be welcome."

"So you parted on good terms?"

"Yes. Although I did post a letter to her on Wednesday morning to tell her not to rush into anything and obviously she hadn't got it by the time she rang me that night."

Ron nodded. "What time did she ring you on Wednesday?"

"It was about half past nine. I was just putting the dinner plates in the dishwasher. Andrew was watching some documentary on BBC Three. I had to take the phone upstairs because I couldn't hear what she was saying properly."

"She was incoherent?"

"She was drunk." She said it with an edge to her voice that suggested disapproval.

"When I eventually got her to make sense, it seemed that Liam had run off with all her money. She said she had given him access to her savings account so that he could get some money for a deposit on a flat. I don't know where. She'd gone to the bedsit he had in the village, an annex off one of the bigger houses. The place was cleared out. She had been trying his mobile, but it was turned off."

"What did you say?"

"Well, I certainly didn't say 'I told you so,' although perhaps I should have. I asked her where Brian was. She said he'd gone out with his fancy woman."

"'His fancy woman'?" Ron repeated.

"I assume she meant Polly Leuchars. I suggested she should phone him and ask him to come home. She was beside herself. I was concerned for her state of mind, particularly given her setback just over a month before. I thought she might try to harm herself."

"And what did she say?"

"She calmed down a bit when I mentioned Brian. Seemed to bring her back to her senses. She said she was going to phone him. I promised I would call her in the morning to see how she was, and then we said goodbye. By that time she seemed to have cheered up a bit. I thought she was going to be all right."

"How long had you been on the phone, roughly?"

"I'd say about twenty minutes or so. Afterward I tried to phone Brian's mobile, but it was engaged. I assumed Barbara had got hold of him."

"And the next thing you heard was the news?"

Lorna looked down at her lap. Her voice trembled slightly. "Yes. I couldn't believe it." She paused. "Well, no, that's not true. Of course I believed it, especially after our conversation on Wednesday. I just thought to myself, what a terrible business. I said as much to Andrew— what a terrible thing, to take one's own life."

Sam stopped writing for a moment. "I'm sorry, Mrs. Newman." Her voice was low, tender. "It must have been awful for you, losing such a dear friend in such dreadful circumstances."

Lorna gave her a weak smile. "Thank you, my dear. Yes, it was awful. You're kind."

Ron drank the last of his tea. He cleared his throat. "You mentioned the letters, Mrs. Newman?"

"Oh, of course. I'll get them." She stood, bustled off down the corridor.

"Get all that, Sarge?" Ron asked Sam.

"Yep."

They sat in silence until Lorna returned, carrying a thick brown A4 envelope. "I think this is all of them."

Ron took the package and looked inside. About twenty envelopes, opened. "Thank you. I need to evidence these and give you a receipt."

"Oh, are you taking them away?"

"I'm afraid I'll need to, Mrs. Newman. They will become property of the coroner until after the inquest, as evidence into Mrs. Fletcher-Norman's state of mind. Once the inquest is finished you can ask to have them returned to you."

She looked a little crestfallen. "I suppose that's all right."

They bagged the package in a clear plastic evidence wallet and Ron wrote out a receipt and handed it to Mrs. Newman.

"I need you to have a read of my notes, Mrs. Newman, if that's all right," Sam said gently. "If you agree that everything I've written is accurate, I'll ask you to sign my notebook. If there's anything in there you want me to amend, please say. Then I'll ask you to give me a written statement based on what you've told us. We need to have a bit in there to show that you've provided the letters as an exhibit for the coroner."

They spent a few minutes in silence, broken only by the sound of the notebook pages turning. From time to time, Lorna nodded. Ron went to the bathroom, and was gone for an inordinate amount of time. Sam hoped he wasn't snooping. Or at least, not in an obvious way.

"You have very neat writing, my dear," Lorna Newman said at last.

Sam laughed. "It's a struggle, writing that fast, and trying to keep it legible."

"I can imagine."

Taking the statement took a little longer. Once it was done, Lorna Newman offered them sandwiches to take with them for the journey, but they managed to refuse gracefully. Ron was desperate for a Mc-Donald's.

"You were gone a long time," Sam said, when they got back in the car.

"You thought I was having a poke round," he accused.

"I did wonder."

"I was having a dump. All right?"

"Well, I hope you opened a window."

"Bastard dreadnought couldn't fit round the U-bend. Had to beat it to death with the toilet brush, in the end."

Lorna Newman was watching them from the doorway. Ron gave her a wave.

"Well, what did you think?" he asked as they did up their seat belts.

"I think we need to get the telephone records from Hayselden Barn," Sam said. "So much of this case is going to come down to the phones. It's a good job we've got a good analyst."

"Just as long as he doesn't get distracted by the boss," Ron said with a smirk.

"What's that supposed to mean?"

"Oh, come on. You must have noticed. He can't keep his eyes off her. Completely besotted."

Sam considered it. "He'll have to join the queue, then, won't he?"

"Judging by the rest of her options, I'd say he's in with more of a shout than the rest of us."

"Give over. She's far too sensible. Especially . . ."

"Go on."

"No. It's nothing."

Ron was smiling at her now. It was his turn to drive, but even so he was glancing across at her, enjoying the way the conversation was heading. "You were going to say 'especially now she's learned her lesson,' weren't you? Talking about Mr. Hamilton?"

"It's gossip, Ron. Not very nice when it's about someone you get on well with. You driving, or dancing?"

He corrected the steering and brought the car back to the right side of the road, thankful it was clear ahead. "Les has got a book running. Her and the DI is fifty to one, the analyst only gets eight to one."

"And her abstaining for the duration of the case?"

"Two to one."

There was a brief silence. Then something else occurred to Sam. "What about me?"

This time Ron kept his eyes on the road ahead. "What d'you mean, Sarge?"

"Come on, Ron. What're my odds?"

It took him a while to pluck up the courage. "Last time I checked, twenty-five to one."

That was a consolation, at least—her odds were better than Hamilton's. One very small victory for the girls.

13:52

Lou spent a moment checking her face in the mirror on the sun visor. Her hair was a bit tangled, so she ran a brush through it, squirted a bit of her handbag-size bottle of deodorant under her top, ran her tongue over her teeth. She gave herself a stern look in the mirror.

There was no getting away from it. It was like an itch that wouldn't go away. Something in that kiss—the long, long kiss that had gone on for half an hour and had felt like thirty seconds. The way he'd touched her hair. Damn it. Would he turn out to be an utter shit like Hamilton?

With a deep breath in she put her hairbrush away and straightened her jacket. Time would tell.

Inside, a long bar ran along the back wall, with oak tables and benches interspersed with low sofas and coffee tables. Beside the roaring fire two high-backed fireside chairs stood as though guarding the warmth.

He was there already, at a small table, a pint of what looked like cola in front of him. He stood up when he saw her, and when she went over he kissed her cheek as though they were friends meeting up for lunch and they hadn't seen each other for ages. Which, perhaps, was a fair assessment of what they were actually doing.

"Hey," he said. "How are you?"

"I'm fine, thanks."

"Have a seat," he said. "I'll get you a drink. What would you like?"

"Just an orange juice. I'll get it."

"Go on," he said. "Pretend you're not my boss for a minute."

"All right, then. Thanks."

She watched him heading for the bar. Jeans, today, of course, and a blue hooded top with a stylized design on the back in white, formed out of two ice hockey players crossing sticks. Under it the words *Briarstone Jaguars*. She turned her attention to the menu: typical pub fare, but a few unusual offerings as well.

It looked as though the Sunday lunch rush was coming to an end. Not many tables free, but a lot of empty plates and people sitting back in their seats.

Jason brought her drink. "You decided?"

"I think the venison sausages," she said. "I'm intrigued."

He went back to the bar to order the food.

The barmaid had dark hair, short, with red streaks through it. Lou wondered if that was Frances Kember.

"I missed you last night," Jason said, sitting back down opposite her. "I don't think I can wait until the case settles down."

She felt her stomach do a little flip. She tried to smile, tried to make light of it. "Hmm. It's very distracting."

For a moment it was eye contact, nothing more, but the tension between them was electric. He smiled, a slow smile, stretched out a foot under the table and laid it against hers, just gentle pressure.

"I guess this isn't really the place, is it?"

"Not really."

"Later? Tonight?"

She hesitated. "I promised myself I wouldn't do this."

"Why not?"

"Last time I did this with someone from work it all went horribly wrong."

"Hamilton?"

She nodded, returned the pressure of the footsie game under the table.

"Sometimes you need a bit of time off, eh? What we're doing is important, but so is this."

"Let's see what the rest of today brings, okay? My head's buzzing with it at the moment. That's why I thought it would be good to get out of the office for a bit."

He looked up, past her head. She turned to see the barmaid bearing two platefuls of food. "Here you go," she said, putting the plates down on the table between them.

"Thanks," Lou said. "This looks great, thank you. Is Ivan around?"

"He was about to go to the cash-and-carry."

"Would you ask him if he can spare us a minute? That would be great." She handed over a business card.

"I'll send him out."

"Thank you."

When she had retreated into the back, Lou gave Jason a look. His foot was still pressed gently against her ankle. She liked it being there. Just having this contact with him made her feel good. Now, of course, she wondered what it would be like. Going to his house, late, straight from work—or would she go home first? Get changed? Or maybe he would come over to hers. She would have to tidy up a bit, change the sheets. The thought of what might follow was a delicious one.

"How was hockey?"

"Oh, good. We won."

"Did you score?" she said, and then instantly regretted it.

"Not yet," he said, and winked.

Christ.

"Sorry," he said. "I keep making you blush."

She was about to answer but caught sight of a man approaching them.

Ivan Rollinson was slender, with dark hair, an aquiline nose, and crystal-clear green eyes.

Lou introduced herself and Jason; they shook hands, and Ivan sat down with them. "I'm assuming you're the one in charge," he said. "I wondered if you'd come."

Lou gave him a smile. "Thank you for sparing us a minute." She pulled her notebook out of her bag. "I wanted to see if there might be anything else you might have recalled about Polly's visit on Halloween evening."

He shrugged. "I said everything to your officers who came here. She was waiting for someone. Then she left."

"You said she was dressed up that night," Lou said.

"Yes."

"Did she often come in here dressed up?"

He gave a sort of smirk. "Only when she was meeting women."

Lou looked up from her notebook. "She met people in here a lot, then? Women and men?"

He nodded. "She was in here once, twice a week. Tuesday night was the first time she didn't meet somebody here."

"Always different people?"

He shook his head. "Same ones. Maybe—eight, ten different people."

"Were these people you knew?"

"Some of them."

"Would you tell me their names?"

He didn't reply.

"Mr. Rollinson. It's vital that we make contact with all of Polly's friends. I'm quite sure nobody who was a friend to Polly would want to keep information from us. And I can assure you that none of them will know that the names came from you."

He considered this for a moment. Then: "Nigel—the man who owns the stables? She had a drink in here with him once or twice. They seemed to have a laugh, you know? As though they came from work. She was in her riding boots and jodhpurs. And Flora. She came in here a lot with Flora. At first she was in jeans. Then she was dressed up."

"She dressed up for Flora?"

"Like I say, only for the women."

"When was the last time she was in here with Flora?"

He shrugged. "More than two, three months."

"Anyone else?"

He gave a deep sigh, looked up again as though the answer might be printed on the ceiling. "An older man, with gray hair. He lives in the village, comes in here with his wife sometimes."

"You know his name?"

He shrugged again. "No. The last time with him was two months ago, maybe longer."

"Thank you. Mr. Rollinson, do you know who the last person was you saw Polly with regularly?"

"There was a younger man, maybe three, four times. She was here with him last week and the week before. And a woman a few times."

"Can you describe her?"

"Older—maybe forty, fifty? Fair hair. Very attractive, smart. Looked rich. But Polly always paid."

"And you didn't recognize her—didn't catch a name?"

He shook his head. "It was only twice, I think. In the last three weeks or so. I don't believe she lives in the village."

"And you haven't seen her since?"

"No."

"Or the younger man?"

He shook his head.

"Can you describe him?"

Rollinson was starting to look bored. "Young. He wore jeans, like he worked on the farm too. I thought he was another one from the stables."

Lou noted this down in her book. "Did you get the impression that any of these people were particularly special to Polly? As though one of them were a boyfriend, perhaps?"

"Or a girlfriend, you mean?" He smiled again. "No. It was like they were *all* her best friend. She used to laugh a lot, always seemed to be having a good time, but she never drank alcohol. I asked her once what was her secret, and she said she was high on life."

There was a pause. Rollinson seemed deep in thought, no doubt remembering Polly the way she was, all beauty and sparkle. "The woman—the fair woman? The last time I saw them here, I think they had a disagreement."

"When was this, can you remember?"

"Two weeks ago, more. Polly was in here and waited for her for about half an hour. She was chatting to Frances, the barmaid, and then to another one of the locals. They were playing darts and Polly was helping them keep score.

"The woman came in, and Polly left what she was doing without a word, and went to sit next to her. The woman hardly spoke, acted as though Polly was not there most of the time. And Polly was smiling at her, trying to get her to look. They had a few drinks, and then the woman got up and left, and Polly followed, a few steps behind."

"You thought they had had an argument?" Lou asked.

"Something like that. One minute Polly was happy and laughing and joking, the next she was looking at this woman as though begging her forgiveness for something."

"And the last night you saw her. Halloween. What time did she leave?"

"I told the other one. It was late—half past eleven. Something like that."

"On her own?"

"Yes."

"Thank you, Ivan."

He returned her smile, standing up. "You're welcome. Come again."

"We will," Lou said.

She was still thinking through Polly's various assignations at the Lemon Tree as she followed Jason out into the car park. The light felt unbearably bright after the cozy shadows of the interior and she felt in her bag for her sunglasses. No sign of them—they must be in the car. "Well, that was nice," she said.

"Yeah," he said, hands in his pockets.

"I'll see you tomorrow, then?"

"For sure." There was something in the way he said it that made Lou alert.

Behind them, two couples exited the pub, the women laughing about something. Lou moved closer to Jason, close enough to be able to whisper: "What's wrong?"

He didn't answer, watching as the doors slammed on a Land Rover and a BMW.

"Get in." Lou unlocked her car and went round to the driver's side of her car. When he climbed into the passenger side she turned in the seat so she was facing him. He was staring resolutely ahead at the hedge. She waited patiently.

"So," he began, "when you said we should meet for lunch—I was kind of hoping it would just be the two of us."

"I don't understand—it *was* just the two of us."

"Nah. That was you, me, and the job."

"I *am* on duty," she said, making an effort to keep her voice even.

"Still," he said. "Is this what it would be like?"

"Yes," she said. "If we're lucky. On some jobs I might not get to see you for days on end. You should get your head round that right now or else there's no point carrying on."

He looked at her then and for a moment she saw emotion in his eyes that she hadn't been expecting. Then it was gone. He shrugged, smiled, cupped her cheek, and kissed her. *That's better*, she thought, breathed in, moved closer to him so that he could kiss her again, harder this time and now she didn't care if anyone was in the car park watching. Another minute and she didn't care about the job, either.

From her bag, Lou's phone bleeped.

She was so lost in his kiss she barely noticed, but Jason pulled back. He looked into her eyes, stroking his fingers down her cheek, over her chin, down her throat, lightly caressing her skin until he got to the neckline of her sweater.

"Can I see you tonight?" he asked. "Please."

"I'll try my best." At least she was being honest—there was nothing Lou hated more than empty promises.

"You'd better get that," he said. "I'll see you later, Louisa."

He kissed her again, quickly, fiercely, and then opened the door and got out.

She pulled the phone out of her bag and looked. There was a text from Sam. They were on their way back from Norfolk. And a voice mail from Paul Harper, the CSI who had been at the quarry yesterday.

It was time to head back to the real world.

5X5X5 INTELLIGENCE REPORT

Date:	Sunday 4 November 2012
Officer:	PC 9921 EVANS
Re:	Op NETTLE—Liam O'TOOLE

ECHR Grading: B / 1 / 1

Database searches, employment records and Voters indicate the former tennis coach at the Morden Golf and Country Club was Mr. Liam James O'TOOLE DOB 1/5/1980.

Andrew HART, General Manager at the club, confirms Mr. O'TOOLE had been employed as a tennis coach at the club, from June until he left unexpectedly last week. He was expected to turn up for work on Thursday, but failed to put in an appearance. A letter of resignation was received on Friday morning, postmarked Briarstone. Letter has been seized for forensic examination, special property number CL/0004562/12.

Mr. HART confirmed that both Mr. and Mrs. FLETCHER-NORMAN were members of the club. Mr. FLETCHER-NORMAN regularly played golf. Mrs. FLETCHER-NORMAN had previously been an enthusiastic golf player, but in recent months had switched to playing tennis. She had been having tennis coaching sessions with Mr. O'TOOLE (at a cost of £45 per hour) twice or three times per week. Mrs. FLETCHER-NORMAN had a scheduled coaching session with Mr. O'TOOLE in the afternoon of Wednesday, 31 October, and this was the last appointment that day.

Mr. HART would not discuss rumors relating to the relationship between Mrs. FLETCHER-NORMAN and Mr. O'TOOLE. He did, however, say that Mr. O'TOOLE was particularly popular with female members of the club and he had received numerous complaints about his sudden and unexpected departure.

From: PSE Paul HARPER, Crime Scene Investigation Team
To: DCI Louisa SMITH / Op NETTLE MIR
Subject: Ambleside Quarry scene
Date: 4 November 2012
Grading A11

Full forensic report to follow.

Re: Shot put found at bottom of quarry, SP number CL/00003889/12

Forensic examination of scene suggests the shot put was thrown into the quarry after the vehicle containing the deceased Mrs. Fletcher-Norman went over the edge. This is indicated by an indentation in the sandy base of the quarry followed by a second length of indentation. The first indentation occurs about 20m from the car park level, on a small ledge.

Distance approx 2m out on a horizontal plane. Circular indentation in sandy soil, partially obscured by a plant growing to the left which has been squashed slightly. Smaller indentations around the area but NOT within the bowl-shape of the indentation suggest that the anomaly was caused after the period of heavy rain which took place on the night of 31 October. Bowl-shape of the indentation is consistent with the size and weight of the shot put being thrown from the car park area above, and is likely to be the first place the shot put came into contact with the quarry floor.

Second indentation occurs approximately 8m further down the slope and forms a track approximately 2m in length, through a patch of sand and light shingle, ending in a patch of scrub grass/weeds. Approximately 2m further from this in the direction of travel indicated by the track is the patch of gorse bushes/dense grass in which the shot put was found. This indentation is light and easily missed, indicating the force of travel of the object was much reduced and was effectively coming to rest.

Of interest is that the indentation CROSSES a larger indentation made by debris (namely the rear bumper) of Mrs. Fletcher-Norman's vehicle. This substantiates the premise that the shot put was thrown from the car park AFTER the vehicle had gone over the edge. Due to the lack of heavy rain since 31 October, I would suggest this occurred after 0100hrs on 1 November and before 0915hrs which is when the scene was identified and effectively sealed. Will require Met Office confirmation as to exactly when the rain stopped in the area, but from personal recollection I believe it was dry when I was driving to work that morning.

Scene photographs have been taken and recorded, submitted to the Incident Room under separate cover.

5X5X5 INTELLIGENCE REPORT

From:	PC David EMERSON, Tactical Ops
To:	Op NETTLE incident room
Subject:	Ambleside Quarry
Date:	4 November 2012

Grading: A/1/1

Searches continuing at Ambleside Quarry. A suitcase was located in undergrowth not far from the car park. Unclear how long it had been there. No identifying features but suitcase is full of clothes, including female underwear and a sponge bag containing toiletries. Suitcase looked to have been thrown into the undergrowth from the car park area.

CSI Paul HARPER in attendance, has removed same for forensic examination. SP number CL/0005682/12. PSE HARPER will submit further intel in due course.

5X5X5 INTELLIGENCE REPORT

From:	Karen ASLETT—Source Coordinator
To:	DCI Louisa SMITH
Subject:	Nigel MAITLAND
Date:	04/11/12

Grading B / 2 / 4

Nigel MAITLAND has been organizing regular shipments of illegal immigrants from Iraq/Kurdistan via Europe. On 31/10/12 a Lithuanian-registered lorry came through Dover. 14 illegals were concealed in a compartment between the cab and the main cargo area. These illegals were unloaded at MAITLAND's farm in Morden and transferred to a minibus.

MAITLAND prefers to conduct business off his regular premises but something went wrong with the shipment on this occasion.

From: CE Paul HARPER, Crime Scene Investigation Team
To: DCI Louisa SMITH / Op NETTLE MIR
Subject: Ambleside Quarry scene
Date: 4 November 2012
Grading A11

RE: SP number CL/0005682/12

Item received in labs yesterday. Good set of latent prints inside and outside case belonging to Mrs. Barbara FLETCHER-NORMAN (found deceased Ambleside Quarry 01/Nov/12). Interior may well reveal DNA.

Contents of suitcase include clothes (mainly size 12), shoes (size 5), underwear, toiletries, and makeup. No identification or anything else to indicate who it belongs to.

To confirm—handle of suitcase has NO prints, likely to have been wiped. Location of suitcase was well-sheltered within thick undergrowth, despite recent rain the outside was still quite dry so unlikely that prints were washed off, particularly as latents found on outside of case (consistent with lid being pushed down to close the case).

16:12

Andy Hamilton let himself in to the MIR to find it empty, the only light from the dwindling day outside making the untidy space and the mismatched desks look forlorn. He had just come back from a fruitless trip to the Computer Crime Unit in the hope of finding out if there was anything of interest on Brian Fletcher-Norman's laptop computer. There was nobody there.

Nobody in the MIR meant he didn't have to worry about accidentally giving something away, by smiling or looking like he'd got some action, or by looking overtired. In years past he would have ended up telling someone about it, maybe Ron, or more likely Les Finnegan, whose tastes ran to the distinctly perverse. He remembered one occasion—was it in the King Bill?—and everyone was pissed and having a laugh, right up to the moment when Les Finnegan started telling them about a warrant he'd been on where they'd found a fully equipped dungeon in the basement. They'd all been on warrants like that—Christ, these days it was unusual not to come across some sort of sex toy in the process of executing a search, but Les seemed to be particularly relishing the description of the room and what it had contained. Andy must have failed to express the right level of disinterest, because half an hour later he'd been calmly having a piss in the gents', when Les had taken the urinal next to his and told him more than he ever wanted to know about what went on in the dungeons of the rich and famous.

Andy wasn't going to tell *anyone* about Suzanne.

He made his way to the desk he'd been using, turned on the workstation. He had reports to write up, statements and other things to catch up on, leave to authorize, emails to delete.

His head was still spinning with it all.

Communications with Karen had been tentatively resumed. She had never locked him out before, and for no apparent misdeed: he had been busy at work, and neglectful, which was bad, but surely something that she should be used to by now? Locking him out was an extreme reaction, and by rights he should now have moral supremacy—she owed him an apology. She had making up to do.

This morning it had crossed his mind that something else might have prompted her to lock him out. He considered that she might have found out something about one of his previous misdeeds, but then the first text came:

Hope u OK. Where did u sleep x

He replied when he pulled in to get petrol:

Went to Johns. U OK?

No "x" to his reply. That would show that he was still offended, and hopefully lead to her trying a bit harder to make up. A few minutes later:

We need to talk. Try to get home on time tonite OK x

That was fair enough. And he needed something to stop him going back to Waterside Gardens. He felt like he'd had some kind of drug there, something that made him think about nothing else, want nothing else. He felt the pull of her like a physical bond.

He spent ten minutes deleting emails before he was distracted again. He looked at the clock on the computer—ten to five already. He could drive back to her place, spend an hour with her, and still get home to Karen and the kids at a reasonable time. After all, he didn't want it to look like he was dropping everything to get home to Karen because she'd told him to, did he? Especially after she'd locked him out. He needed to time it right—to prove to her that he was busy, that he was working on something really important, and that no matter what tantrums she felt like throwing, he had other demands on his time. But he wasn't a quitter. He wasn't going to give up on his marriage, on principle if nothing else—she was stuck with him, for better or worse.

18:17

Lou had never been one to talk about breakthroughs, but this Sunday, this incredibly long Sunday, had that breakthrough feeling about it.

Paul Harper, the CSI at the quarry, had spoken to her briefly on the phone and referred her to the report he'd emailed over. Apparently he was on his way to church.

Reading the report was like throwing a bucket of cold water over the investigation, Lou thought. If the shot put had gone over the edge of the quarry after the car, which is what Paul Harper seemed to be convinced of, then who the hell had thrown it? And why was Barbara's suitcase apparently hidden in some bushes at the top of the quarry and not in the boot of the car? Nothing was making sense.

And to top it all, just in case she'd thought about going to see Jason after all, he'd sent her a text:

> Hey beautiful. Forgot my brother was coming to visit. Wd still be great to see u wd love for u to meet him. X

Yeah. She had no desire to spend the evening listening to two Canadians talking about ice hockey.

In the end, desperation and the need to think things through led her to phone Hamilton's mobile.

"Hey, Boss." From the sounds of it, he was in the car.

"Are you on the way home?"

"Yeah. I spoke to the manager of the country club where the tennis coach worked. Nothing too interesting, although it matches up with what we got from O'Toole himself earlier. Did you see that?"

"I've been at the quarry."

"It's on an intel report. How's it going at the quarry, then?"

"Big development—it looks like the shot put went over the edge of the quarry after the car did."

She let this information sink in.

"So she didn't have it in the car with her? Ah, bollocks. Looks like my theory's blown."

"Someone wanted to use Barbara as a scapegoat for Polly's death, do you think?" Lou asked. "To draw attention away from themselves?"

"So who would do that? Brian? Why would he want to kill Polly? It doesn't strike me that he'd be that bothered about being black-mailed or something like that. Most of the village seemed to know he shagged her."

Another theory occurred to Lou right at that moment. "Or maybe someone really wanted to kill Barbara, and Polly's death simply gave them the opportunity they were looking for?"

"That would suggest Brian again," said Andy.

"Or the tennis coach, Liam O'Toole."

"He'd already got her money; I don't think he needed to kill her too."

"Did you get any more on him?"

"A fair bit, but most of it is still just more gossip. Half of the village thought he was God's gift, the rest of them seem to think he was a wanker. Benefit of hindsight, there, of course. But they all knew Barbara was carrying on with him. Which means Brian must have known too."

"Do we have any leads on where he might have gone?"

"His boss at the Golf and Country Club gave me some next-of-kin details for some woman in Ireland—they think it's his mother. Tried to call, no reply. I'll put it through the system in the morning. And I got his mobile number too, but it's disconnected."

Lou sighed. "This case is turning into one big tangled mess."

"We've got plenty of evidence. I'm sure it will become clear. You know we always get there in the end." His voice was soothing.

"What about Brian's computer?"

"I spoke to the guy who's on call. They expect to have some results tomorrow. He wouldn't give me anything else. He said we could hurry it along but we'd have to pay for it."

That was no surprise. "Oh, well, that's not bad; usually it takes weeks."

"Anything else you need me to do?"

"No," she said. "Go home, I'll see you bright and early tomorrow."

When she disconnected the call she put her head in her hands. There was nothing else she could do this evening and yet she didn't want to go home. She wanted to see Jason, despite how tired she was, despite the fact that his brother would be there. She could ask him to come round to hers—but that wouldn't work either. His brother would think she was rude. To put an end to the matter, she sent Jason a text:

Going home now. Enjoy your evening. See you tomorrow. x

Seconds later, her phone bleeped with a reply.

You OK? X

For crying out loud! It was late, and she was going to get chips on the way home. Every second was interrupting that process. One last text.

Yeah fine, tired now. See you tomorrow. X

When she got home, an hour later, a small bag of chips was nestling in her bag. She was starving. And the chips kept her from driving round to Jason's house. The thought of food, a soak in the bath, and an early night was all she could think about.

19:11

The studio was cold. Once the lights were on, Flora turned on the heating and put on the portable halogen heater to give the room an extra boost. She made a cup of instant coffee and, with the blanket from the sofa around her shoulders, studied her unfinished canvases.

The big one of Polly needed more work, but her mind was on other things.

She looked through the various canvases stacked against the wall, some of them long abandoned, some of them experiments, some of them useless—and yet she had learned at art college the benefits of never getting rid of anything, no matter how disastrous. Like drafts of a novel, her sketches and her failures plotted the path to whatever successes she enjoyed, which made them a part of the process.

There. Half stuck to a smaller canvas was a portrait she had done of her father. It was from long before Polly had arrived at the farm, not long after she'd got the studio, which meant she was probably a year out of college at most.

Nigel's blue eyes stared at her out of a roughly worked face—bold lines, dark colors. His features were angular, as they were in life, but this image, even more than the preparatory sketches and the other attempts, showed him as she knew him to be, with a vulnerability despite the coldness. Whatever it was that he did to earn his money, he did it not out of greed but out of a desire to succeed—in this as in everything else he tackled. She admired him for that, despite everything.

Maybe this was all because she had let him down. She was supposed to be a farmer's daughter, wasn't she? And since Felicity hadn't managed to produce a son and heir, she should have been learning the business, ready to take it over one day. But her heart had never been in it. When she told her parents that she had a place at art school, they had reacted much as she had expected them to: Nigel could barely speak to her for months afterward. Felicity found things to worry about while trying to be supportive and encouraging in her own limited way. If it had only been the farm, Flora might have given up her flat and done what had been expected of her. But it wasn't just the farm; it was the rest of it. The deals with those thugs he associated with. The drug imports that Felicity knew nothing about; the transportation of illegal workers from all over the world: people who'd traveled thousands of miles and ended up working in the shitholes of the U.K., with no rights and very little money.

Months after she had told them about her college place, Nigel had taken her into his office one afternoon and told her all about it. He brought everything out into the open: who he was working for, how he started off organizing the transport but then ended up taking over other parts of it, laundering some of the profits through the farm, handling cash and drugs and recruiting operatives because, at the end of the day, the rest of them were shit at it.

Flora told him she didn't want to know.

And in response he had offered her a deal: he would fund her college course, he would support her every step of the way, on the understanding that she would back him up when he needed it, and that one day she would be there to take things over. Manage the farm, do whatever else needed to be done. If she didn't want to get her hands dirty, that was fair enough—he would allow her that—but she had to know, in order not to fuck things up for him. If she knew what was going on, she would know when to look away. And that way, Nigel could keep the money coming in.

And so they had continued in this uneasy dance, Flora the artist, Nigel the farmer. As unlikely a father-daughter relationship as you could ever encounter, more alike than they would ever admit. If her art had not been so successful, who knew? She might well have got more involved with the farm, might have even helped him practically with some of the financial day-to-day stuff. But she was a success, and she could afford the studio, and while she could take commissions when things got a bit tight, most of the time she was comfortable and working on whatever she wanted to.

Then Polly arrived, and upset everything.

Now Flora looked into the blue, blue eyes and saw in them something she had never seen before. She took the canvas over to the one she had been working on, Polly's canvas, and put them side by side; and while Polly's was more abstract, there was the same blue in the shirt that was supposed to represent Polly, and the way her eyes looked first thing in the morning when she had been sleeping in Flora's arms and had looked up at her—*that* moment. And it was the same color. The *same*.

It meant nothing, of course. But Flora knew. And other things, things she had turned her mind away from: Nigel had told her he had been out late that night, had come home after midnight—but Felicity had said he had gone down to Yonder Cottage and Polly had made him cheese on toast. Flora had signed a statement at the police station declaring that she did not know the identity of any of Polly's other lovers. She had lied to them because he was her father and, even though she hated his guts right now, she still had that unswerving family loyalty that he didn't deserve.

But what if he had killed her? What if Nigel had been the one who had killed Polly?

06:45

From her desk, Lou saw Jason arrive. He was laughing and joking with Barry Holloway and Mandy before he'd even got his coat off. And then he looked over toward her office, and met her eyes, and smiled.

Already in his email inbox was a load more phone data, and the download of Brian's phone had finally come through from the CCU, and been sent to the analyst directly. Lou had received a copy of the email but the attachment wouldn't open. She was dying to know what it contained.

It definitely felt as though a turning point had been reached in the investigation. Beyond the interviews, the weeding out of the useful witnesses from those who claimed to have seen nothing, heard nothing, from those who claimed to have seen everything but clearly hadn't, there was a point in every investigation when a piece of information came in that felt different.

And this morning, there were several.

Right, she needed coffee before the briefing. Time to get going with it.

07:18

Jason had been sitting at his desk when the call came in. Barry Holloway took it, and even across three desks and half the room, Jason could see him sit up a little straighter.

"Right you are. Yes, all right, then. Ready now, is it?"

When he'd finished the call, he addressed the room. "We've got some CCTV of Polly from the town center. Who wants to go get it?"

There was only Les Finnegan, Jason, and Mandy in the room. Les stood and looked across to Jason. "Fancy coming along? Get some fresh air?"

The TV Unit was across the car park in a temporary building, pending their move to the refurbished Custody Suite along with Computer Crime. The cabin they were in was ridiculously unsuitable, freezing cold in winter and dangerously hot in summer. It was temporary, and yet they'd been in there nearly three years and all the other police stations had to rely on this unit for any downloads, leading to a huge backlog. Of course, being on site and being able to turn up and wait was a distinct advantage.

Inside, the unit hummed with servers, printers, and various recording devices. The council CCTV had sent over four disks with all the recordings from the town center CCTV cameras for 31 October and some poor sod in the TV unit had spent the last two days viewing everything between the hours of half past twelve and four, the times that Felicity Maitland had given for Polly's trip into town.

Josh Trent, the technical analyst, took them over to a desk in the far corner. "Grab a chair," he said.

The computer screen was frozen on a scene from the high street, shoppers stopped in their tracks in the pedestrian precinct. The time display showed 13:04:08, the date 31/10/2012.

"Ready?" said Josh, fingers poised over the keyboard. Jason and Les were both glued to the screen. With CCTV it was often a case of "blink and you miss it."

For a moment there was nothing, just people walking slowly up and down the high street, shopping bags bulging. From the right, a young female crossed and sat on a bench. Blond hair in a ponytail. Black coat. A few shopping bags, and a small tan-colored bag worn with the strap across her body.

"That's her?" Jason said, quietly.

Les nodded. "Hair's pretty recognizable. Is that it?"

Josh gave a self-satisfied look. "Keep watching."

The girl on the screen checked her watch. The time reference on the screen had clicked round to 13:06:12. After a moment she fished inside one of the carrier bags and brought out a bottle, dark-colored, a flash of a red label—Coke? She unscrewed it and swigged from the bottle, replaced the lid, and put it back inside the bag. She sat back, one leg crossed over the other.

13:07:43. "She's waiting for someone," Les said.

Polly stood up, stretched, leaving the bags behind her on the seat. She turned to face up the high street, her back to the camera. She had her hands on her hips. Checked her watch again. Turned, hair swinging over one shoulder.

"Watch this bit." Josh indicated the top left of the screen.

From there a young man appeared with a young woman, who was walking slightly in front. He was carrying half a dozen shopping bags. As they passed Polly, the man kept watching, turning his head to stare at her until with a smack he walked into a lamppost.

They all laughed, despite themselves.

13:09:10. Polly checked her watch again. Then she snatched up her bags and walked swiftly up the hill in the direction of the bus station and the arcade. They watched until she disappeared out of sight.

Les and Jason both looked at Josh. "That it?" Les said, obviously wondering why he'd bothered to leave his nice warm office for five minutes of watching a blond bird being stood up.

Josh looked smug again. "No, of course that's not it. Patience, lads, please."

Les started to look pissed off and Jason stifled a smile—Les was so easy to wind up.

A few keyboard strokes and a few mouse clicks, and a new file had loaded. This one was from inside the shopping center. Much busier here. Mums with buggies, elderly people dragging shopping trolleys behind them. At the top of the screen was the entrance to Marks and Spencer. The exit to the high street was just visible off to the right. The time stamp at the top read, disconcertingly, 14:22:27.

"The time's wrong on this one. The council CCTV unit confirmed they'd not got around to putting the clock back. Other than the hour it's right, though. So about one twenty. And here she comes." He stuck a finger, nail bitten to the quick, in the top left corner of the screen, and clicked the mouse.

From the top left, Polly appeared, half running. Her right hand was held up to her face. Same jacket, jeans, shopping bags in her left hand. She was heading to the high street entrance.

"She's on the phone," Les said.

"Right," Josh agreed. "Now she's going back out to the high street." After only a few seconds Polly had disappeared out of the right of the screen, her blond ponytail swinging behind her.

The screen froze again and they all breathed out, leaned back, and relaxed.

"She's going back to the bench?"

Josh nodded, his eyes shining. "This is so cool. How often do we get any usable CCTV? We're so bloody lucky all the cameras were pointing in the right direction. Although I'm afraid the next shot's a bit iffy. Can't have everything."

He loaded the third file, and once again the high street appeared. The sun had come out, the icy street was shining, and there was a disconcerting glare at the top of the screen from the sunlight. The starburst effect covered the top half of the screen, the bench where Polly had been waiting only just visible in the bottom corner.

"Ready?"

The camera clock imprint showed 13:26:52. A mouse click, and the dark shapes walking up and down the street started into life. Polly came down the street, running, facing the camera this time. It was not possible to make out her face, but somehow it seemed as though she would have been smiling. The phone was gone, the shopping bags still in her left hand, swinging against her leg. She dropped them on the bench, turned around a full three hundred and sixty degrees, then sat down on the bench.

"Here we go," Josh said quietly.

Polly jumped back up and ran to the left, throwing her arms around a figure that had appeared. They all leaned closer.

"I think it's a woman," said Jason. "She's not that much taller than Polly, look."

"Nah, that's a proper waxed jacket. Look at the shoulders. Got to be a male," said Les.

For a moment all that was visible was a bulk where Polly had folded her whole body around the figure. The blond head moved slightly.

"They're kissing," Josh said.

Les leaned closer. "What—like a snog?"

"It's a bloody long kiss, anyway," said Josh.

13:27:03. As they moved toward the bench the figure emerged from the flare of the sunshine. A dark jacket, red gloves, black shoes, black trousers underneath. That was about all you could see. The other figure pulled away abruptly, gripping Polly by the upper arms. Red gloves against the black of Polly's coat. Polly seemed to shake herself free.

Polly went to sit down on the bench, but the figure took her hand and pulled her up. Back to the camera.

"Whoever that is knows the camera's there," Jason said quietly.

Les looked up at him scornfully.

"I thought that too," said Josh.

The figure took Polly's left hand and pulled her away from the bench. Polly looked like she was struggling to keep up. The shopping was left on the bench. Right before they went out of the view of the screen, they saw a last swing of Polly's blond ponytail as she looked back toward her shopping bags—one arm extended out toward the bench. Then she was gone.

The footage kept running.

13:28:33. "She's left her bloody shopping behind," Les said.

People walked in and out of shot, some of them pausing to look at the shopping bags. The sun seemed to go behind a cloud, and the footage went momentarily dark while the camera adjusted, and then came back to normal. A better view this time, with the flare missing.

"I take it there's more?" Les grumbled, fidgeting in his seat.

"A bit. Hold on. Nearly there," Josh said.

13:29:11. Polly reappeared, standing near the bench, looking back over her shoulder in the direction from which she'd come. She raised a hand, once, and waved. Presumably to the person she'd been with, the person who seemed to be avoiding the CCTV.

Polly's hand went to her lips, and then back to a wave, blowing a kiss goodbye. She stood for a moment, watching. Then picked up her shopping bags and turned her back to the camera, heading up the high street once again.

They continued watching as the camera clock flashed to 13:30:48, then the screen went blank. For a moment they just sat there.

"That's it?" asked Les.

Josh nodded.

"That's fantastic," Jason said. There must have been a huge amount of work to get those three sections of footage. "The DCI is going to be thrilled, Josh. Good stuff."

Les shot him a look that said "arse licker" and went back to Josh. "Nothing else of the person she was with?"

"Nothing. The camera by the river is out of action," Josh was saying. "Camera one outside the Co-op was pointing in the other direction and the one at the other entrance to the center is fixed on the doorway of Carphone Warehouse following those burglaries. All the other ones that were working have been checked."

"What about the shopping bags? Any chance of identifying them?" Jason asked.

Josh shrugged. "There's one that looks silver, might be a Debenhams one. We checked there. Their CCTV operator is on holiday and he's the only one who knows how to work the system."

Les interjected. "We put out a message via Storenet last week, asking all town center shops to check their CCTV. I bet you none of them bothered."

Jason sighed. It was rare to get anything truly useful from CCTV, but to be fair to Josh, this was still a pretty good result. "Can we have the footage?"

Josh handed Les two disks in paper envelopes. "I made you two copies. Let me know if you need any more, but don't go overboard. Those things cost money."

Jason shook his hand. "Thanks, Josh. That's great."

Walking back across the car park, Les Finnegan puffing away on a cigarette, trying to walk slowly so he could have a precious few more moments' inhalation time, Jason considered the figure and mentally ticked off the list of people in the case.

"I'll be in in a minute," Les called after him, as he swiped his pass and dragged the door open. Jason didn't hear.

REPORT

To:	Op Nettle
From:	PSE Jason MERCER
Date:	Monday 5 November 2012
Subject:	Op Nettle CCTV /ANPR

Following the CCTV footage produced by the TV Unit showing a female who may be Polly LEUCHARS meeting up with an unidentified nominal in Briarstone town center, ANPR cameras searched for the relevant timeframe on 31/10/12 with the following result:

Briarstone Station NCP car park:

36 NRM—cherish plate registered to Nigel MAITLAND. Accessed car park at 1245hrs, exit marked up as 1402. Accompanying image shows male driver, vehicle Land Rover.

All others negative result for the indexes of vehicles known to the inquiry.

OP NETTLE BRIEFING—AGENDA

Monday 5 November 2012

Summary	DCI Smith
Analytical charts	PSE Mercer
CCTV	DC Finnegan
Nominals & Intel	DC Holloway
AOB and taskings	

07:52

Andy Hamilton had made an effort to come in early. He knew he was skating on thin ice all round, with Karen, with Lou, with everyone on the team. He was starting to be a liability.

He'd managed to reach some sort of a truce with Karen last night. A whole night without him had softened her temper; that, and the fact that he was home in time to help feed the kids, do bath time, and get them ready for bed. After that he'd run her a bath, put in lots of bubbles, lit a candle. While she soaked, he ordered them a takeaway, which was about as close as he ever came to the kitchen. She emerged, dressed in her toweling bathrobe, as the Chinese arrived at the front door.

After that, of course, she wasn't angry at all anymore. She told him they would have to have a "serious chat" about what his expectations of her were (more like *her* expectations of *him*, he thought, biting his tongue) and how long this could carry on before their marriage would fall apart. She didn't want to be another statistic, she said, another policeman's wife who'd had enough of coming second to whatever investigation it was that was the current big thing. They had the kids to consider.

He'd been contrite. Reached for her hand. He'd even teared up, and perhaps that had been the clincher. She had snuggled into his lap and he'd slipped his hand inside her robe. She told him he stank and should go and have a shower. It was good-natured and she was right. He'd had a shower that morning at Suzanne's flat, but of course she had no men's deodorant.

"Couldn't John have loaned you some deodorant?" she called up the stairs.

"He'd run out," he called back.

By the time he'd had his shower she was in bed, fast asleep. When he reached for her, she nudged him away, sleepily. He left her in peace. Bridges had been built; he could cross them another time.

"Right, everyone ready?"

Lou was at the front, ready to start the briefing. She looked good, as usual, dark blue trousers today, red suede high heels, a snug jacket that nipped in her waist over a plain white top, hair loose over her shoulders.

He was sitting near the front, freshly scrubbed and with an ironed white shirt, top button undone because his neck had grown and he couldn't actually do it up anymore, tie done up around it to conceal it.

She gave him a smile. Well, thank fuck he'd met with her approval today. He was sick of being in her bad books.

The briefing room was busier than yesterday; Ali Whitmore was back, Jane Phelps, Barry Holloway, and Ron Mitchell all in attendance. Lou had managed to rustle up a few uniformed PCs as well, which suggested something was kicking off.

"Okay, let's get on with it," Lou said. "Can we have some hush?"

The analyst looked nervous, Hamilton thought. Not for the first time he caught the glance he gave Lou and wondered if there was anything going on there. In his dreams, maybe. Lou didn't go for that geek type—she liked men with a bit more about them.

"We've had several crucial pieces of intel in the last twenty-four hours. It's all incorporated on the charts, which Jason's going to go through in a second, but first I've got a summary of the recent developments.

"Number one: Brian Fletcher-Norman recalls having an argument with his wife on the night of the murder of Polly Leuchars. He believes she went out some time after midnight and returned in a state of hysteria. He didn't realize why, believed she was drunk, left her and went to bed.

"Number two: We have some recent source intel on Nigel Maitland, suggesting that his latest venture is a people-smuggling operation which he is conducting with the McDonnell brothers. There is a 5x5x5 to indicate that a shipment was received at the farm on the night of thirty-first October. As we all know, Nigel prefers to keep his legitimate business well away from anything dodgy, so there must have been a special reason for this to take place at the farm, if the report is accurate.

"Number three: A friend of Mrs. Fletcher-Norman, Lorna Newman, confirms that Barbara was depressed before the murder. Mrs. Newman states she had a telephone conversation with Barbara at around nine thirty on thirty-first October. Barbara had just been badly let down by a man she had been conducting an affair with—more about that in a minute. When Mrs. Newman spoke to Barbara she described her as drunk and hysterical.

"Number four: Tac team has recovered a suitcase from bushes near the car park area of the quarry, which has Barbara Fletcher-Norman's fingerprints on it. It seems likely she had a suitcase packed ready to run away with O'Toole. The suitcase had been thrown into the undergrowth and fingerprints wiped from the handle.

"Number five: CSI suggests that the shot put, which we believe is the murder weapon for Polly Leuchars, was thrown over the edge of the quarry after the vehicle went over. Likely time frame for this is early Thursday morning. This means it's pretty much impossible that the shot put was in the car, and also that Barbara could not have thrown it into the quarry herself.

"Number six: According to Mrs. Newman, Mrs. Fletcher-Norman had been saving money in preparation for leaving her husband. The man she had been seeing seems to have absconded with this money on the day of Polly's murder, leaving Mrs. Fletcher-Norman particularly distressed. The man, Liam O'Toole, has not been seen since. Mrs. Newman estimates that the money amounts to several thousand pounds. We've been trying to trace O'Toole, but no luck so far."

She paused for breath. There were whispers of conversation in the room, but most of the group were giving her their direct attention. "Any questions so far? Right, then—Jason, can you take us through the charts?"

"For sure," he said. "Let's start with the timeline." A new image clicked on, a series of interconnected lines. One for Barbara now, one for Brian, and one for Polly.

"There are a few significant changes on here now that we've had more information from Brian and from Lorna Newman. Brian indicates that he heard Barbara making a phone call. We might assume this is the call she made to Lorna, but we will need phone records to check. The billing has come back, but only this morning and I haven't had a chance to work through it yet."

He indicated a highlighted area from ten until midnight. "Here's where we have a problem. Brian says he came home from working late between eight and nine in the evening and didn't go out again. He had a drink, read the paper, argued with his wife. Then he went and had a bath, fell asleep for a while, and then came downstairs to lock up. He says he bumped into Barbara, who had come in via the back door. Then he went back upstairs to bed."

He pressed a key on the laptop and Lorna Newman's information overlaid Brian's and Barbara's timelines.

"Mrs. Newman states that during her phone call with Barbara, which took place at about nine thirty, Barbara said that Brian was 'out somewhere with his fancy woman.' According to Brian's statement, he was sitting downstairs, reading the paper at the time."

"Hold on," Alastair Whitmore interrupted. "Maybe she simply didn't hear him come in?"

"I've been in the Barn," came a voice from the back. Jane Phelps. "You have to really bang that front door to make it shut. If he'd come in, she would have heard him. Definitely."

"He said he shouted up the stairs when he got home and she didn't answer," Lou interjected.

"Why would he lie about that?" said Andy.

"Because he was out with Polly?"

"She was at the Lemon Tree, remember? She was stood up."

"What time was she there until? Anyone know?"

Jason pointed at the timeline. "She left between eleven thirty and eleven forty-five, according to Ivan Rollinson."

A pause, then Lou said, "We've got a medical disclosure form in place now; waiting for the results on that. We're looking to give Brian a slightly more robust interview once the medics have given the go-ahead. I think there were some significant gaps in what he told me yesterday. Right. Thanks, Jason. What's next?"

"The second major issue we need to clear up is right over here . . ." He scrolled over to the far right of the timeline, indicated the early hours of Thursday morning. "The vehicle went over the cliff some time after the rain started, which was about nine on Wednesday thirty-first. The PM on Barbara Fletcher-Norman concurs with Brian's statement that she must have gone out again some time after midnight. The car was discovered by the witness at about seven thirty on Thursday morning. The scene was secured at about nine fifteen."

"Surely that means Barbara Fletcher-Norman couldn't have been Polly's killer?" Ali Whitmore said. "Surely that must rule her out?"

"It doesn't rule her out of the murder," Jane said. "It just rules her out of throwing the shot put over the edge, that's all."

"Why would someone else throw it over? Where the hell did she leave it?"

Jane shrugged. "She might have still done the killing. Maybe she had an accomplice."

"Or she left the shot put somewhere where it would implicate someone else?"

"Such as . . . ?"

"I don't know. Brian, maybe?"

Lou raised her hands. "Right, everyone. Let's try and keep this ordered, Jason needs to finish up. Then we can talk about it till the cows come home. Jane?" This last directed to Jane Phelps, who was muttering something to Ali Whitmore at the back.

"Sorry, ma'am," she said, and Lou gave Jason the nod to continue.

"Thanks," he said. "I'm almost done." He moved the timeline forward to the discovery of the suitcase thought to belong to Barbara Fletcher-Norman. "So—this suitcase. We need to get a positive identification that it belonged to Barbara, but the only person that can realistically do that is Brian. You might want to wait for that. If we assume for now that it is Barbara's, then we need to consider when it was packed, and where it came from. It's possible that she'd packed it that afternoon to go away with Liam O'Toole, and forgot it was there until she got to the quarry. Then, for whatever reason, she took it out of the boot and threw it into the bushes before she went over the edge—"

"Wiping her prints off the handle first," Jane interjected. "Sorry, ma'am."

"No," Jason said, "it's a valid point."

"There were gloves on the passenger seat," Lou said. "Red leather ladies' gloves. Maybe she was wearing them when she got to the quarry. Maybe her hands were cold. Maybe she used them when she threw the suitcase into the bushes, and then took them off before she went over the edge."

"That's a lot of maybes," someone said from the back.

"Of course, the biggest unanswered question is why she would take the suitcase out of the boot at all," Jason said. "But if she had gloves on, it's possible that any prints on the handle could have been obscured. So we still don't know whether she threw the case away. Let's not forget she was pretty intoxicated. She was also in a state of distress. Irrational behavior is pretty much a given, right before she committed suicide."

"I don't think she did," Jane said quietly. "I know she was depressed, having been let down so badly by Liam O'Toole. But I'm really not comfortable with the logistics of her driving all the way to the quarry, through the pouring rain, when she was that drunk. And then, for some reason, throwing the suitcase away before going over the edge. And then someone else getting rid of the shot put."

"You're saying it was an accident?" This from Barry Holloway.

"I'm saying someone pushed the car over."

"Is that possible?"

The debate was interrupted by Hamilton's mobile phone bringing the *Exorcist* theme loud and clear into the equation. "Sorry," he muttered, and headed for the door at the back. "DI Hamilton. Yes, hold on."

Meanwhile the room erupted with people interjecting on similar cases they'd experienced in the past, cases involving automatic cars and manual ones, the degree of the incline, the lack of a barrier or a fence between the car park and the edge of the quarry.

Lou raised her voice above the noise. "People, can we simply review the evidence for a moment? The *evidence*, not speculation. We know from forensics that Barbara Fletcher-Norman was inside Yonder Cottage when Polly was dead or dying from her wounds. We don't have any other identifiers for any other person around the time of death. So Barbara was definitely there. And the murder weapon ended up in the same place she did."

"Yeah," said Jason, "but *after* she was dead."

"Then we're looking for an accomplice?" Jane Phelps said.

"Hold on, Jane—we have evidence she was there, not evidence that she did it."

"Same thing," Jane muttered.

There was a pause.

"Right," Jason said. "I'm done."

"Thank you, Jason," Lou said. "Barry, can we look at nominals next? Les, we'll come on to the CCTV in a minute."

Mutters from the room.

"Right, then," Barry Holloway began. "I'm expecting a bit of discussion around these, along the lines of things we were talking about. Just to be clear, these are nominals we're interested in for the murder of Polly Leuchars. We're not talking about Barbara going over the edge of the quarry." He gave a nod to Jason, who obligingly clicked over to a new slide.

Nominals
1. Barbara Fletcher-Norman
2. Nigel Maitland
3. Brian Fletcher-Norman
4. Flora Maitland
5. Unknown Female (A)—"Suzanne"
6. Unknown Female (B)—CCTV image

"We have circumstantial evidence linking all of these people to the victim and the crime. Barbara, obviously. We have the forensic evidence linking her to the scene, and the murder weapon linked to the location of her death, even if it definitely wasn't her that threw it over the edge of the quarry. In addition, we have a pretty strong motive in that Barbara was convinced that Polly was having an affair with her husband. Despite her own marital infidelity, it seems from Lorna Newman's statement that she was more upset by this affair than by previous ones because of Polly's proximity to their home address.

"Secondly, Nigel Maitland. We have had intelligence that he had had an affair with Polly. We have forensic evidence that he had been upstairs in Yonder Cottage, but since he is the owner of the property and technically her landlord, we cannot assume anything from this. We have intel to suggest that Nigel's activities have moved closer to home recently, and in particular that he took delivery of some illegal immigrants at the farm on the night of thirty-first October. It's possible that Polly became mixed up in this, either as a witness or as a participant, and that she became dangerous to the criminal operation as a result. We know from an ANPR capture that Nigel Maitland's car was in town at the same time as Polly during that day, and we have CCTV footage showing Polly meeting someone—more on that in a minute. Seems possible this could be Nigel.

"Thirdly, Brian Fletcher-Norman. His daughter has confirmed that he told her he had had an affair with Polly, but he has denied this to us on two occasions. We have forensics linking him to the downstairs at Yonder Cottage, but again he may have had legitimate cause to visit the cottage as he took riding lessons with Polly. There is nothing to indicate the forensics there are recent. We have a witness statement suggesting that a woman matching Polly's description was in a small blue vehicle in a lay-by or driveway on Cemetery Lane at about eleven thirty on the evening of thirty-first October. Having examined the layout of the Lane, it seems that, realistically, this can only be the driveway of Hayselden Barn, as the witness describes it being near to a bend. It's possible that Polly had given Brian a lift home from somewhere, and that it was him she was arguing with. Polly's car was a dark blue Nissan Micra, which would fit the description of the vehicle seen by the witness. If it was Brian, then there is an indication that they knew each other rather better than he has described to us, and also that on the evening Polly was killed they had some sort of disagreement or argument."

"It could have been Nigel in the car," Ali said. "Don't forget we had his fingerprints in there."

"Yes," Jane said. "It could have been either of them—or someone else entirely."

"Hold on a sec," Lou said. "Ivan Rollinson at the Lemon Tree said Polly left the pub no earlier than eleven thirty."

There was an almost-audible groan from the group. "She's right," said Whitmore.

"We need to chase that up. Either one of them has the time wrong, or it's not Polly in the car. She can't be in two places at the same time. Sorry, Barry—carry on."

"Right. Well, that's about it for Brian. The only other thing to consider is the heart attack—it came on when the officers were telling him about his wife's body being found, but he said in the interview with the DCI that he was feeling bad when he woke up. It's worth considering whether he had had more of a stressful night than he led us to believe.

"Next—Flora Maitland. Another one who had a relationship with Polly. By all accounts she's been pretty distraught following Polly's death, but who knows how she really felt? She doesn't have any alibi for the relevant time; she could well have gone back to Yonder Cottage to confront Polly and ended up being a bit too physical with her."

"Where's the DI gone?" Lou asked suddenly. Hamilton hadn't returned since taking the call on his mobile. There was a general shaking of heads, and she tutted with annoyance. "Anyone else want to comment on Flora?"

Jane Phelps cleared her throat. "I don't think it's her, ma'am. I think she's in bits over Polly's death. When Sam was taking her prints at the farm, she said Flora was barely holding it together."

"That brings us to the woman Brian is supposed to be seeing, according to his daughter. She claims he told her he was having an affair with someone called Suzanne, who Polly had introduced him to. Suzanne had also had a relationship with Polly. Mrs. Lewis says she was asked by her father to contact this Suzanne and tell her that he was in the hospital, which she did. She knows nothing else about her."

"The number appears on Brian's phone as 'Manchester office,'" Jason said. "Has anyone checked to see whether she's someone he works with?"

"I did," Ron Mitchell said. "The company Brian works for is a global shipping company. They don't have an office in Manchester. Someone was going to contact their clients, subsidiaries, to check—I haven't chased them yet. I also checked that Brian was at work that day, as he said he was. The woman I spoke to agreed he left the London office at around six thirty on Wednesday; allowing for traffic, he would have been home around eight."

"Was Brian asked about this Suzanne when you saw him, ma'am?" Jane asked. She was taking notes.

Lou shook her head. "Didn't get around to that one. Didn't want to antagonize him, he's got a real downer on his daughter. Every time you mention her he goes on about what a liar she is."

"He's a charmer, isn't he?" Jane said.

"Yes, he is rather. Still, rest assured, it's on the list of things we need to know once we get the medical thumbs-up."

Hamilton opened the door and tried to get back to his seat quietly. The room was full and he had to climb over several pairs of knees to get there, muttering "Sorry" every time.

"Can we carry on now the DI's back?" Lou said.

"That's my bit done," Barry said. "Les has got the CCTV."

"Les?"

Les Finnegan turned his attention to the laptop. "Can someone kill the lights for me, please?"

The room was duly plunged into semidarkness. "Right, we've got three different files here so it's going to take a good few minutes if you want to see the lot, but I think it's important that you do."

The first file loaded and the image of the high street, the bench in the bottom right, filled the screen. Some of the detail was lost by projecting it to that size, but it was reasonably good quality.

There was complete silence as the first file ran. At the end of it, someone said, "Poor old Polly. She got stood up a lot that last day, didn't she?"

There was a ripple of laughter.

"Right," Les said, loading the second file, "watch closely, this one's really quick."

There was an audible leaning forward in chairs at the footage of Polly running through the shopping center, mobile phone clamped to her ear.

"That it?" said Hamilton.

"Nearly done. One more to see," Les said, loading the third file.

This time the silence lasted only a few seconds into the footage.

"Shame about that bloody glare."

"Can't see fuck all. Sorry, Boss."

"She's waiting for someone," came a voice from the back.

"Well, duh, of course she is."

"Wait for it," Les said.

The dark-clad figure appeared from the left and Polly rushed into that embrace. When they realized they were witnessing a kiss, there was a little uncomfortable shuffling and a low wolf whistle from the back of the room.

"Who *is* that?" Jane said.

"Not Felicity?"

"No, you muppet, that's a bloke. Look at the shoulders."

"It's Barbara. She had a jacket like that."

"Barbara's snogging Polly? I don't think so."

"It looks like Nigel Maitland to me," Ali Whitmore said. "Besides, I'd bet money he knows where all the CCTV cameras are in town."

"That's all," Finnegan said. "Shall we put the lights back up?"

The lights were turned on and everyone settled in their seats, blinking.

"I've got stills of the figure in the last file," Les said, "if you want to pass them round."

He handed a pile of prints to Hamilton, who sat for a moment perfectly still, holding them, looking at the picture.

"Recognize someone?" Lou said. "Andy?"

"Sorry, Boss," he said with a start. "Lost in thought for a minute there." He took the top sheet and passed the rest behind him to Ali.

"I've got the still on the Op Nettle briefing slide, so all the patrols can see it," Les said. "Someone is bound to recognize who it is sooner or later.

"Okay, everyone, settle down, please. We've still got the intel requirement to get through. Barry?"

Barry Holloway cleared his throat. He was starting to sound hoarse. "Intel requirement—firstly Brian Fletcher-Norman. We need to clarify his account. Suggest to him that he was out for at least part of the evening, see what comes back from that. Also need to challenge his denial of having an affair with Polly. We need to find additional intelligence to corroborate Mrs. Lewis's statement. I suggest that house-to-house is also completed for the entire route between Hayselden Barn and the quarry—not just for sightings of Barbara's car, I know that was completed.

"Secondly—and I know this is a tough one—we need to get more intel out of Nigel Maitland. We need to know what he was doing in town on the thirty-first. Did he see Polly while he was out? He might have seen her and recognized the woman she was with. You never know your luck."

"We'll need to get his solicitor on board," Lou said. "What's his name? That infernal little man with the aftershave . . ."

"Lorenzo," Hamilton obliged.

"That's it. Well, we'll give it a go."

"Thirdly, we need to press on with the identification of the person in the CCTV. Find out who it is and why Polly was meeting him or her."

He paused for a moment. Lou looked up. "Anything else?"

"I think someone needs to interview Taryn Lewis again," he went on. He was definitely losing his voice.

Lou gave him a warm smile. "Thank you, Barry. I know you worked really hard to get this all finished for this morning. I appreciate it."

She stood and faced the room again, left hand on her hip tucked under her jacket pocket. "Sam's on late turn today, so let's sort out some work for you lot to do, shall we?"

09:25

Hamilton left the briefing room, trying to catch Lou's attention. "Boss, can I have a word?" he asked, as she marched past behind Jason.

"I've got to go to a meeting with the superintendent—can it wait, Andy? About an hour or so, I think?"

He hesitated, then gave her a smile. "Sure. I'll catch up with you later." She breezed past.

He had been assigned to supervise the second round of house-to-house for the route from Hayselden Barn to the quarry. He had a team, including a whole bunch of probationers who were champing at the bit to get out there and do some "real" police work; so, realistically, it shouldn't take long if they could find anyone at home. He could think of more exciting things to do, he thought, heading out. Today had started off so well, waking up late to the noise of the children and the smell of breakfast cooking. And whatever the rest of the day brought, he couldn't be late home tonight. He'd promised Karen he'd take her and the kids to the Guy Fawkes Night display at the local fire station. Ben loved fireworks.

But on the passenger seat of the car, slightly out of his line of vision, was the grainy still shot taken from the CCTV. *Was* it her? It was something about the shape, the physique, that reminded him of her. And then there were those red gloves.

He shook his head, telling himself not to be ridiculous. It was because he couldn't get her out of his head, that was all. It was far more likely to be Nigel Maitland, or someone else entirely.

09:45

The Stuart Ward had taken on rather a desolate air for Brian. The bed directly across from him stood empty, its occupant having died yesterday. At least that one had gone quietly. Last night the man in the neighboring bed had also chosen to depart, but in a rather more spectacular fashion. Some heart monitor had alerted the nurses, who came at full tilt with their equipment. That, no doubt, was why they called it a crash trolley, since it had collided with Brian's bed on the way past, waking him up and giving him the fright of his life.

A lot of shouting, rushing people, consultants being summoned, together with the cloud-patterned curtains being hastily pulled and repulled around the bed, lest Brian should be in the least bit concerned about what might be happening behind them.

Whatever had caused his demise, the man was beyond recovery, and after a long, long while and, by the sounds of it, a great deal of effort, all the various doctors and nurses went their separate ways. The dead man was left there until the porters came to take him away in the early hours. When Brian woke the next morning, the bed opposite was clean and covered in freshly laundered sheets; the one next door was naked, down to its rubber mattress.

Get me the fuck out of here, Brian thought to himself, not for the first time deeply regretting not having spent a few extra pounds for the company health care insurance that would have placed him comfortably in a private hospital, away from all this degradation, despair, and death.

To add to it all, the weekend had been dreadful. Normal ward rounds didn't take place, and the food was even worse than it was during the week. His only consolation had been a visit from the registrar, who had looked at his notes, listened to his heart, and declared that in all likelihood he could be sent home on Tuesday or Wednesday.

"Really? That's great."

"Assuming, of course, you have sufficient care at home."

Brian was silent for a moment.

"Do you have someone at home who can look after you?"

"Yes," he said at last. "There's someone."

As soon as the registrar had gone, Brian had donned his bathrobe and taken himself off to the dayroom. It was an effort getting there; even walking just a few steps was physically exhausting. How could he cope at home on his own? He couldn't. He would need help. How handy, then, that he knew someone who happened to be an experienced private nurse?

In the dayroom he had managed to put in a quick call to Suzanne. As always, on the phone, she was brusque. There was no point indulging in idle talk. He told her about the registrar and listened to her response. It wasn't quite the solution he'd had in mind, but it would do for now. Agency nursing was going to cost a fair amount of money, but if it meant he could get out of this hellhole, then he would have to swallow the cost.

Suzanne would make arrangements for someone to take care of Brian as soon as he was discharged. Meanwhile she would maintain a discreet distance, despite his protestations that he needed her. She would have none of it.

Suzanne ended the call abruptly and Brian made his way back to bed.

For a fleeting moment, Brian had thought about Barbara. Had it hurt? he wondered. Or had she been almost anesthetized by the alcohol she had drunk?

He remembered her cold features, the mouth set in a hard line. "It's no use, Brian. I'm leaving you. I've found a man who can truly love me." Her words were slurred, her diction indistinct.

"Good Lord," Brian had said. "This must be some character. Well off, is he?"

She had shaken her head so fiercely that she had almost lost her balance. "We'll make do." Then she had laughed.

And now she was gone. She wasn't his problem anymore. She wasn't going to spend a penny more of the money he'd earned; it was all there for him to do with as he pleased.

10:02

Hamilton returned to his car, parked in the same lay-by that their Crimestoppers witness must have found himself parked on, the night that the blue car was spotted. Realistically, Hamilton had thought when he parked there, it must have been the driveway of Hayselden Barn that the vehicle had been sitting in; there was the lay-by, fifty yards further on. There wasn't another driveway within a mile in either direction that could have accommodated a parked car. Most of them had gates bang up to the road, or were not the sort of driveway you would just stop in. Here the gate was about ten yards from the road, leaving an entranceway suitable for a car to pull in temporarily.

It had to have been Polly in the car. But who was with her? Brian? Nigel?

The weather was definitely colder again, the wind biting his cheeks. He would have preferred to have been inside the office rather than out here on the house-to-house.

The probationers were keen, though, he'd give them that. And, to be fair, there weren't a huge number of houses between here and the quarry. It was mainly country roads, plenty of bends, a few open fields. The houses that were here were mainly large, set back from the road. If anyone had seen anything it would be a fucking miracle.

Inside the car, he shut the door, keeping the wind outside. From where he sat, he could see half into a drainage ditch that ran along the edge of the field bordering the garden of the Barn. A traffic cone, green with algae, was sticking out of it. A crisp packet fluttered, caught on something that looked like the wheel of a bike; then it was lifted by the breeze and was gone. He leaned forward in his seat, then got out of the car again and went round the front of it to the edge of the ditch.

It was a gent's road bike, half-submerged in the meter or so of water at the bottom of the ditch. Vegetation mostly concealed it, but Andy could tell it hadn't been there long. The bike wheel had mud and grass caught in the spokes, clumps of green that were wilting to a khaki color. He looked across to the barn, and back at the bike. The seeds of an idea were forming. Across from the lay-by a rough mud track led off along the other side of the ditch, forming a natural boundary edge to the field. A green sign, half lost in tangled foliage, proclaimed this to be a footpath. He wondered where it went.

He hunted in his glove box for the map book he carried with him and located the page that contained Cemetery Lane and half of Morden village. There was the track—a dotted line heading off into green space. He traced the line with his finger through a further field. At the edge it split off in two directions, one heading to the east and meeting up eventually with the Briarstone Road. The second track headed due west before splitting in various directions, finally running along the top of a dark-colored structure on the map marked up in small letters as "Quarry."

He looked up the track. What would that be like in the dark, on one of the windiest, rainiest nights of the year? And on a road bike?

He looked down at his shoes. "Fuck it," he muttered under his breath, and pulled his mobile from his jacket pocket.

"John. It's DI Hamilton. Can you take over for a bit? I need to go for a walk. Right. Yeah, I'll take the phone."

Back out into the cold air. He went through the boot of his car and found an anorak; it was thin but it might keep some of the wind out. He pulled it on over his head, locked the car, and set off up the track.

Away from the road, all noise was deadened and for the moment even the wind seemed to have dropped. He looked over the fence to his right, the structure of Hayselden Barn rising beyond it. By far the biggest thing other than the Barn for seemingly miles in any direction was a great horse chestnut tree, its branches bare, all the leaves blown away. The wind made it sway and dance like a living creature.

The path was muddy, as he'd expected, but it was cold enough for the ground to be hard underfoot and it was easy going to start with. At the end of the field he came to a stile, and another green FOOTPATH sign indicated the right-of-way continued into the field beyond.

He spotted the cows—a few dozen Friesians—across the other side of the field. Hamilton wasn't fond of cows, in the same way he wasn't fond of large dogs or any other unpredictable animals. But these seemed to be content to get on with their grazing, and he could see the path across the field would take him away from them.

Nevertheless, he crossed the field quickly, keeping an eye on the cows and not looking where he was going, until he sank almost up to his ankle in a fresh cow pat.

"Ah, fucking hell," he said loudly, wiping off as much of the shit on the grass as he could. He continued, this time keeping his eye on both the cows and the grass under his feet.

At the other side of the field the path disappeared into a hedgerow. He paused and looked back the way he had come. He had completely lost sight of the road now, but the roof of the Barn was within sight over the top of the hedge, in the distance. He estimated he had walked about half a mile. The clouds overhead were darkening and it looked like it might rain. He shivered. He hated this time of year.

Heading toward the hedgerow, he could make out a gap leading to a field beyond. He cursed his clothing, wishing he'd decided not to try and impress Lou with how smart he could look in a navy wool suit and had gone for jeans and heavy-duty boots instead. He could really do with something warm, like a fleece. And a woolen hat.

Never mind. At least the rainproof jacket he was wearing would keep the worst of the brambles away from his suit jacket. He squeezed through the gap in the hedge, fending off prickles and branches, and to his horror his clean shoe sank deep into a water-filled ditch. Now both shoes were ruined, both socks wet through.

At last he burst through the hedge and found himself at the bottom of a steep, grassy slope. He scrambled up it and found himself on a dyke, which seemed to go for miles in either direction. On the top of the dyke a well-worn path looked like a good place for walking dogs and bike riding.

That was a thought. He looked back down to the gap in the hedge. He doubted whether a bicycle could be squeezed through that gap, but then not everyone was his size. Could you do it all in the dark, though? It was hellishly dark around here at night. And with the rainy weather there would have been no moon, either.

He looked left and right, the dyke and the path stretching as far as the eye could see in either direction. He looked at his watch. He felt spots of rain. He remembered from the map book that the distance to the feature marked "Quarry" was at least three times the distance from the road to the junction where the path split in an easterly/westerly direction—presumably the place where he now stood.

He debated his options, then scrambled back down the bank and fought his way back through the hedge.

To his alarm, however, the other side of the hedge revealed a sudden gathering of large, inquisitive Friesians, seemingly waiting for the large odd man to return through the hole in the hedge.

Another change of plan, then. He fought his way through the hedge a third time and decided he would just have to go for a long walk.

He pulled his mobile out once again, hoping for a signal. "John? Hello? Yeah. It's DI Hamilton again . . . Can you hear me? . . . How about now? Ah, right. Listen, have you still got a car at the quarry? . . . Okay. Can you get them to stay there? I'm walking to the quarry now and I need a lift back. Okay?"

The signal finally died. He hoped it wasn't about to start pissing it down; that really would be the final straw.

10:19

Flora had had a productive day. For some reason, her mother's visit yesterday had sparked in her a new level of creativity. She had moved the large canvas of Polly to one side, and had started a new one, a portrait, but less abstract. It was Polly, of course. It was cornsilk and blue, mainly. And some red, the color of her heart.

She had fallen asleep in the studio at about three in the morning. All those hours she had worked, not eaten, barely drunk anything. By the time she felt the exhaustion hit her she had a headache and was covered in paint. She curled up on the old sofa, pulled the blanket over her, and fell asleep.

She'd woken this morning feeling nauseous with hunger. Without bothering to change or wash, she headed out to find something to eat. There was a greasy spoon on the corner—the owner was called Bob. He never batted an eyelid when Flora came in covered in paint.

"Good night, was it?" he asked when Flora opened the door.

Inside, it was warm and smelled of good coffee. She shrugged. "It was good in some ways, Bob. That's as much as I can hope for."

He gave her a lopsided grin. "What you having today, then?"

"Gutbuster. Coffee. Okay?"

"Five forty-five then." When she had handed over a five-pound note and a fifty-pence piece, he nodded toward the table by the window. "I'll bring it over."

Outside on the pavement people rushed to and fro.

She was avoiding him. Recognition of the fact slid into her consciousness now as easily as the denial which had preceded it. She would have to go and see him, talk to him, even if it was the last thing she wanted to do. There was no point waiting for the police to do it. They would carry on dragging their heels, leaving him to it, waiting for their evidence package or whatever it was they were doing. But something had happened that had changed her father. It wasn't just Polly's death, there was more to it. As though he knew something. As though he was guilty . . .

And what, then, could she do about it? She couldn't tell the police. They couldn't be trusted. And besides, all she had so far were her suspicions, the awareness that there had been some kind of shift in her father's demeanor. And who was better placed to find the truth than her? Nobody else could get as close to Nigel as she could. Somewhere there would be some kind of evidence.

Thinking about her father made her headache worse. The coffee arrived first, and she had nearly finished it by the time the vast oval plate arrived. Bacon, sausage, fried egg, fried bread, beans, black pudding, mushrooms, grilled tomato, and sautéed potatoes with two slices of buttered toast clinging precariously to the side.

She ate.

11:04

Lou had been providing Mr. Buchanan with his daily update, but now she was back in the Incident Room, complete with a tray of coffees and muffins from the canteen. Everyone was on the phone; everyone except for Jason, who was waiting in the doorway to her office, looking serious.

"What?"

"Phone stuff," he said. "I'm not done, but yeah, it's—interesting."

"Have a seat."

She had brought two of the coffees and two muffins in with her, and while he talked she pulled chunks off the side of hers and ate.

"So, Brian's mobile-phone download, to start with. One of the other analysts said this to me when I started doing phone work: ninety percent of text messages sent over the network are porn. I didn't believe it at the time, but hey."

Lou laughed. "Really? He's a right one, that Brian, isn't he?"

"This is serious stuff, Lou. Bondage and shit like that. There are about thirty images on there of him with a woman."

She stopped chewing. "Anyone we know?"

Jason shook his head. "She's quite particular about not showing her face, funnily enough. And there's more. Brian's billing. There are a whole lot of calls to a number ending 987, in and outgoing. Long calls and texts. This is the same number that was in contact with Polly's phone up to the night she died. This is the number she called when the cellsite shows the phone was in Forsyth Road. It's saved in Brian's phone as 'Manchester office.'"

"Suzanne?"

"Yeah. It's got to be her."

"What about Brian's cellsite?" Lou said.

"That's where it gets even more interesting. Assuming Brian was using his phone and hadn't given it to someone else, it hits cellsites all around Briarstone and Morden from the evening of the thirty-first into the early hours of the first. Most of the calls were back and forth between his number and the one we have for 'Manchester office.'"

"Briarstone?"

"I'm going to plot all the calls on a map, so we can see where he was at what time. There's one call near the quarry at"—he looked at the paper in his hand—"two thirty in the morning. Then the next one is at three, back in Morden. That's a long one, nearly twenty minutes, and it's the last contact."

Lou was staring at him, rapt. Brian's phone had been near the quarry, in the early hours. "Can you get all this in a brief report for me? I'll get everyone back here for four this afternoon for a briefing, okay?"

"Sure." He smiled at her. "So, you want to see some filthy pics now?"

"Of Brian? I think I'll pass. If you can get a still of the woman showing her face rather than anything else, that would be great."

13:11

Andy Hamilton was back in his car, heading toward Briarstone. He'd been home and had a shower, got changed, and gone straight back out again.

Bastard cows, bastard mud. His shoes were ruined and his suit had a bloody great rip in the seat. He'd rarely been this pissed off and now, to cap it all off, there was a voice mail and a text from Lou telling him to get his arse back to the office for a briefing at four.

At least the house had been empty when he'd got back. Karen was out, shopping probably, or at her sister's. It was a blessed relief, a rare moment of perfect peace.

His mobile rang and he pulled over into a side street to answer it. "Andy Hamilton."

"Yeah, this is Stacey from the CCU. You asked us to take a look at a laptop for Operation Nettle. Want the ref number?"

"No, I know the one you mean. Has it been analyzed?"

"We've still got some more to do on it, but I got a message to give you an update."

"Anything useful so far?"

"Lots of porn. Fetish stuff."

"What sort of fetish?"

"S and M mainly. Lots of amateur shots. I would think it's the machine's owner since most of the pictures feature this one man. Looks quite old, gray hair. Are you in the office? You can come and have a look if you're really desperate."

"I'm out at the moment. When I get back in later I'll come over."

"As long as it's before half two, I'm on earlies today and there's nobody else here."

Fucking typical. He rang off, promising to visit as soon as he could. Not that he was particularly interested in looking at pictures of Brian Fletcher-Norman getting jiggy.

There was something more urgent he needed to do. It had been playing on his mind all day, and he could not go back to the office until he'd sorted it out one way or another. The news that Brian was into S&M made a difference to it all, too.

She was unlikely to be there, he reasoned, after all it was the middle of the day, a Monday. She would be at work, whatever that was. But it was worth a try. At the shopping center he turned right, toward Waterside Gardens.

MG11 WITNESS STATEMENT	
Section 1—Witness Details	
NAME:	Samantha Jane BOWLES
DOB (if under 18; if over 18 state "Over 18")	Over 18
ADDRESS: Seaview Cottage Cemetery Lane Morden Briarstone	**OCCUPATION:** Smallholder
Section 2—Investigating Officer	
DATE:	Monday 5 November 2012
OIC:	PC 11625 BRIGHOUSE

Section 3—Text of Statement

My house is situated close to Hermitage Farm, approximately a hundred yards further along Cemetery Lane and on the opposite side of the road. From my kitchen window I can see both entrances to the farm clearly.

On the evening of Wednesday 31 October 2012 I was in my kitchen. At about eleven o'clock at night I saw a lorry in the driveway that leads to Yonder Cottage. I see lorries going in to the farm occasionally but they always use the other drive as it is much wider. It looked to me as though the lorry was stuck as it was parked with the rear of it still in the lane. I thought it was odd that the lorry was there at that time of night.

When I went back into the kitchen approximately twenty minutes later to turn off the lights, I noticed that the lorry had gone.

We went away the following day for a long weekend and I was unaware of the events at the Farm until today.

Section 4—Signatures

WITNESS: (Samantha BOWLES)   OIC: (M BRIGHOUSE PC 11625)

14:29

"You want tea?" Ron Mitchell asked.

"Yes, please," Jason replied.

"Yes, please," Sam piped up.

"Fancy a pint later?" Ali asked. "You too, Sarge," he said in Sam's direction.

"Depends," Sam replied. She'd come in early to catch up on things.

Ali and Jason exchanged glances. "Depends on who's going?" Jason asked.

"Something like that."

Whitmore grinned. "How about we don't mention we're going out?"

Sam looked up at last from her keyboard and treated them to a warm smile. When she smiled like that, her whole face lit up and she was suddenly beautiful. "You're on," she said.

Whitmore made them all a cup of tea and they went back to their respective desks for half an hour. Then Whitmore's phone made a chirping noise and he started chuckling.

"You're all right, Sam," he said. "Definitely up for that pint, then?"

"Why's that?" she asked, looking up again.

"The DI's managed to take himself off for a big adventure in the great outdoors. John Langton says he's trod in cow shit, fallen in a puddle, and literally gone through a hedge backward—then he had an argument with some cows and turned up at the quarry needing a ride back to his car."

Sam laughed louder and harder than Jason had ever heard her. Into this scene of merriment Lou walked in, looking tired and harassed after her second meeting of the day with the superintendent.

"What's the joke?" she asked.

Whitmore handed her the phone with the text that John Langton had sent him. She read it and a slow smile spread across her face, which turned into a laugh when she read the bit about the cows. Then she tried to look stern and failed. She met Jason's eyes.

"We're going out for a drink later. You coming?" he asked.

"Just us?"

"Just us."

"If we can get away," she said with a smile. "I think the first round is on me."

14:30

He kept the engine running for the heat, but even so he could see his breath in the cold, stale air of the car, which smelled of beer, cow shit, and rain. He watched the minutes tick past on the clock.

He wasn't even sure what he was going to say to her, how he could justify intruding on her once again. She was addictive, intoxicating, that was all there was to it. It wasn't that she was even beautiful, not in the same way Lou was, or Karen, for that matter. He was trying not to think too hard about what they'd done, about how it was so far beyond kinky as to be actually dangerous. And yet, the thrill of it was not only that of trying something new. It had been an unbelievable high. He wanted, *needed*, more.

That was it. He got out of the car, glancing casually up and down the road. Not a soul to be seen. He crossed the gravel and rang the doorbell for flat one.

He was half expecting her not to answer, even though there was a sleek black Merc parked on the gravel. But moments later the door opened and there she was.

She smiled when she saw him, looked up at him from under her lashes with an expression that someone who didn't know her might mistake as demure.

"Back so soon, Inspector?"

"I need to ask you something," he said. He'd intended to be firmer with her, use the voice of authority, use his size—something. But instead he found his resolve slipping.

She stood aside to let him in.

14:35

She called at the farmhouse first. The front door was unlocked but nobody was home. So much for security, Flora thought. She rang her mother's mobile.

"Yes, what is it? Flora?"

Flora could hear the wind, the intermittent noise of traffic. "Where are you, Mum?"

"Hacking with Marjorie. Is everything all right? Did you know the police were at the farm? They searched everywhere."

Flora realized that her mother had no idea she had been at the police station, giving them a statement, and decided it was not worth enlightening her. "We've been through this already, Mum. It's all just part of their inquiries."

"Where are you?"

"I'm at the farm. The front door's unlocked; I thought you were being more careful."

"There hardly seems any point locking it when the bloody police have been crawling all over everything. Honestly, I feel quite violated by it."

Flora tried a change of subject. "Do you know where Dad is?"

"Gone out somewhere, I think. I don't know, he never tells me bloody anything . . ."

There was no sign of Nigel's Land Rover in the yard, and heading up to the barn she could see all the other cars were in their spaces. The pickup truck Connor seemed to have adopted for his own use was missing.

The barn door had been locked but Flora knew where the spare key was. She also knew that the CCTV he had set up to record everyone who entered the barn was motion-sensitive, and sent an alarm text to his mobile unless you deactivated it as soon as you entered the doorway. She had memorized the code for it, but she had never had to use it before, so entering the number was nerve-racking. Why was she even doing this? What was she thinking?

She closed the door behind her and made for the office. It was empty, of course, but there was a presence there, nonetheless. The room was warm, the smell of alcohol, leather, the wax on her father's Barbour jacket, oil, mud. Wherever it was they'd gone, they had been in here quite recently.

Taking a quick look at Nigel's desk, she could tell immediately that the paperwork was for show. Not that he didn't have a legitimate farming business to run, but most of the paperwork was stored in the main office, the steel Portakabin beside the other barn. This was simply a carefully arranged display of farming crap that would fool anyone who might have managed to bypass all of Nigel's security.

The ladder to the roof space was raised, but she lowered it, careful not to make any noise, even though there was no one to hear.

It was dark up here. She found the switch, and the roof space was illuminated brightly by a single bulb hanging from the ceiling. Not taking any chances, she raised the ladder again, but already she could see there was a problem: the door of the safe was hanging open, and it was completely empty. And then she realized that the police must have been here. So had they removed everything? Or had Nigel managed to get it all out and hidden somewhere else?

Then she heard something, and quickly turned off the light. Sitting in silence in the dark loft space, the office below barely lit, listening, knowing that something was wrong but not able to determine what. Was it a car, from the lane?

Then another noise, outside somewhere. Voices. Looking down through the rungs of the raised ladder, she could see into the office. She heard the main door of the barn open and the bleep made by Nigel entering the disable code for the alarm.

"I still think he fucked up big-time, you can't get away with shit like that and he knows it."

That was her father's voice.

"You know I ain't sayin' that. You know I agree with you. It's one fuckup after another with him, right? But it's nothing we can't put right."

Then the two men—no, three—entered the office and she saw the tops of their heads. Nigel was the first, followed by a man she didn't recognize. Overweight, with a full head of curly graying hair. A dark-colored sweater, smelling—all the way up here—of beer and tobacco. Behind him, Connor Petrie.

"Want me to sort 'im out?" That was Petrie.

"You've done enough sorting out, haven't you?" Nigel said sharply. "Go home. I seem to remember giving you a job to do, remember?"

Suitably chastised, Petrie crossed his arms and left the office.

The second man lowered his voice. "You think it was him?"

Nigel didn't reply at first, then Flora heard a deep sigh. "You're not talking about the shipping, are you?"

"No. I'm talking about what happened on Wednesday night."

"Not here. All right?"

"Why not? Nobody here but us, right?"

"Still, don't want to talk about it. What's done is done. There's nothing we can do about it now except minimize the risk."

"I'm not calling it off, if that's what you mean. Got too much invested in this, Nige. Too much at stake."

"I'm saying they can wait."

"You're not that worried. If you was worried we wouldn't be having this conversation here, would we?"

Nigel laughed. "Bizarre as it sounds, this is still the safest place. At least I know the police aren't listening in. Can't trust anywhere else, right?"

"So what you want to do?"

"I think we should postpone for a week, maybe two."

"Fuck that! You serious?"

"It's too risky."

"It's fucking risky letting him down! The man's a complete psycho. You want to postpone, you can fucking be the one to break the news, all right?"

"He'll be fine. He can wait another couple of weeks. Besides, it'll be worth his while, won't it?"

There was a pause, then. Flora was starting to get a cramp in her leg. She heard the sound of the drawer opening, the chink as the bottle of whiskey was brought out, the twist of the bottle top.

"What about Petrie?"

"I don't know."

"You can't just leave him here. He's another liability. That kid's fucking not right in the head, if you get my drift."

"So would you be, if you'd seen what he's seen."

"Did he *see* it, though? Or did he *do* it?"

"Seriously. We are not talking about this. All right?"

There was a long pause, and then, finally, in a low voice, Nigel's companion said, "Whatever. I've got to go, anyway. I'll ring you about Friday, right?"

"I'll see you out."

Flora breathed out, a deep breath, as the two men went to the main part of the barn. There was a chance they'd both leave and not come back, but even so she stayed as still as she possibly could, listening to the door of the barn opening and closing, and, a few moments later, a car door banging and a diesel engine starting.

She moved her leg, stretched it out in front of her.

And nearly died when a voice from down below said: "Flora. I know you're up there."

REPORT

Re:	Liam O'TOOLE DOB 27/11/81 of No fixed abode
Monday 5 November	
From:	DC 8745 Alastair WHITMORE
To:	Op NETTLE

On Monday 5 November at approximately 1545hrs I took a call from a male claiming to be Liam O'TOOLE, formerly employed as a tennis coach at the Morden Golf and Country Club.

O'TOOLE claimed he was employed until Wednesday, 31 October 2012, when he handed in his resignation, stated this was due to issues with the management of the club, specifically their response to complaints he had made previously about harassment by some female clients which O'TOOLE felt had not been appropriately addressed.

O'TOOLE went on to say that Barbara Fletcher-Norman was one of his regular clients at the club. She had been having private tennis lessons for some months. O'TOOLE stated that he made efforts to keep the relationship strictly professional, however she made it clear she wanted to pursue a sexual relationship. He states he told her on several occasions he was not interested. He also heard rumors from other clients that he and Mrs. Fletcher-Norman were having an affair and he believed this rumor had originated from her.

As a result of this rumor, O'TOOLE was subject to a disciplinary meeting on 29 October, with the manager at the club, Mr. Andrew HART. Despite his claims that nothing was going on other than harassment toward him, O'TOOLE felt he was not believed and therefore decided to resign and leave the club immediately.

On 31 October a lesson had been scheduled with Mrs. Fletcher-Norman, after which O'TOOLE told her he had handed in his resignation and he was planning to leave the area. O'TOOLE stated she became very upset and even offered him money not to go, which he states he declined.

O'TOOLE claims he left the club at approximately 1500hrs on 31 October and traveled directly to his sister's house in Dublin, Republic of Ireland, arriving there in the late evening. On Monday 5 November O'TOOLE accessed his personal emails for the first time since arriving in Ireland, and he received an email from Gary STEVENS, a former colleague who works as a fitness instructor at the Morden Golf and Country Club. STEVENS informed O'TOOLE that the police had been looking for him in relation to the death of Mrs. Fletcher-Norman, hence the reason for his call.

A Whitmore

16:07

There was no sign of Hamilton. Lou knew he'd wanted to go home early today, but a job like this one was unpredictable, they all knew that. When something major broke, one needed to be there. She'd called his mobile, sent texts, even, as a last resort, phoned his home number just in case something had happened to his phone. There was no reply there, either. At that point, Lou was really pissed off.

"Does anyone know where the DI was going?" she shouted across the briefing room. They were late starting, and the atmosphere which had already been buzzing was rising to excited anticipation at the prospect of an arrest.

"Ma'am, I think he went home to get changed," Ali said. "John Langton said he was soaked."

"Well, I think we're going to have to start without him. Someone can update him later."

She was only half listening as Jason began to run through the phone work he'd done, the cellsite analysis showing that it was likely that Brian Fletcher-Norman had provided a completely fabricated list of events for the night of Polly's death.

They would have to prove that he'd been using the phone that night. But, realistically, who else would have been using it? He'd not reported it lost or stolen. He'd told Taryn Lewis where to find the phone in his home office, and she had handed it over to the search team who had turned up at the Barn. Was that going to be enough? Of course not. But Brian didn't need to know that, not yet anyway.

At least there had been some good news. Ali Whitmore had called in: he had been back to the Lemon Tree, and while waiting for his pint of cola had noticed that the clock on the wall was an hour out. When Ivan brought him his change, he'd asked him about it. They hadn't got around to putting the clock back, he'd said. It was a good two weeks since the end of British Summer Time—but, more to the point, when Ali asked him to confirm whether he could now be sure of the time Polly had left the pub on the night of the thirty-first, he became confused. Something about knowing what time to call last orders, and it had been "not too long" before that. But the crucial thing was that he wasn't sure. Which meant that the woman arguing with the man in the car could have been Polly after all.

"So, priorities," Barry Holloway was saying. "We're still waiting for a subscriber check for the number identified by Jason as attributed to Suzanne. With a bit of luck, it won't be too long. The computer problems at the service provider are fixed and they're now working their way through a backlog, apparently. In the meantime, we're looking at the Voters register for Briarstone, concentrating on the areas around the cellsite locations. We need to go back and ask all of Brian's associates who she might be, starting with his place of work. We need to find her," Barry said. "And as soon as Brian's discharged, we're going to nick him and take him to Briarstone custody suite, assuming they've got space. We need to make sure he doesn't get a chance to speak to his lady friend first."

16:25

"I thought you'd be at work" was the first, inane, thing he'd thought to say.

"I'm catching up on paperwork," she said. "And I am actually busy, so unless there's a good reason for you being here, I'd rather you called another time."

She was speaking to him as though Saturday night had never happened. As though he were here to try and sell her double glazing, or persuade her to change her gas supplier.

"I need to ask you some questions," he said.

"In an official capacity?" She had an amused smile on her face, unconcerned about his unexpected arrival. She took him into the living room and motioned for him to sit, then sat on the other end of the white leather sofa, tucking her feet underneath her.

"Not at this stage. Although I probably should . . . Shit, I don't know."

"Not a good sign, is it?"

He looked at her longingly, her presence affecting him. And it was pathetic, rotten that he felt so lost, so *scared*, in her company, as though she could hurt him, as though she could control him somehow, despite the fact that he was six foot three and seventeen stone of muscle and flab and he could probably have lifted her with one arm.

"You want to ask me about Brian, don't you?"

She looked so relaxed it was disarming.

"Yes. I want to ask you about Brian."

"How did you know about us?"

Well, you just told me, he wanted to say. But of course he couldn't. "Brian told us. In a roundabout kind of way."

She scoffed at this. "I doubt that very much, Inspector Hamilton. Brian knows better than that. It was probably that daughter of his, wasn't it?"

Andy didn't answer. If she told him something important it would be completely inadmissible. He should never have come back. The moment he realized she might be involved, he should have gone straight to Lou and told her everything and bloody hoped for the best. The longer he stayed, the more he put everything at risk. Not only his marriage or his role on this inquiry—he was risking the investigation, he was risking his whole career, he was risking the reputation of the force.

"Are you all right, Inspector?" she asked, her tone kind. "You've gone pale."

"I should go," he said.

"Are you worried about all this? You needn't be. Everything we say to each other, everything we do here, it's between *us*. You know that, don't you? We trust each other."

"We've only just met," he said weakly.

"Even so, you don't need to have any concern over my discretion. I expect the same thing from you. Whatever happens with your inquiry, our time here is between us alone."

He rested his head in both his hands, elbows supported on his knees, needing to get this right, needing to decide. He never bloody trusted anyone; it wasn't worth it. Rely on hard work and evidence.

"And, besides," she added, leaning forward and resting her hand lightly on his thigh, "I can help you."

"Help me? What do you mean?"

"I can steer you in the right direction. In terms of gathering evidence."

"Please don't say anything that means I've got to arrest you. If you're involved somehow, I don't want to know. Right?"

"Oh, don't worry. I'm not involved. But I can put you straight on a few things. I can be your—what do you call it?—grass. Your informant."

He raised his head then, feeling the beginnings of a sense of relief. She had given him a way out of the mess, an excuse. If anyone asked, she'd had information for him relating to the inquiry. And he had to protect his source at all costs, meaning he didn't have to tell anyone. There were procedures in place for dealing with things like this, of course. There was a whole unit dedicated to managing sources and protecting them. But this, a one-off information exchange in relation to a specific inquiry—he could manage it himself.

"I can't pay you," he said.

Suzanne laughed, threw back her head, exposing her throat. "I don't want payment! Is that what you thought?"

That was what sources were usually after, is what he'd wanted to say. "What *do* you want?"

Her answer, when it came, was simple. He hadn't understood what she meant but hadn't asked her to clarify. She clearly had her own agenda, and he would go along with it because now he had no choice. There was no other option for him but to agree.

"Compliance," she said.

16:52

It was dark outside. Felicity had sent a text to Nigel to tell him that she was going to the cinema with Elsa and Marjorie, and he could find himself some dinner.

He'd smiled at this as though it was funny. "Looks like we got let off the ordeal of your mother's cooking, Flora-Dora."

"Don't call me that," she said.

He was still smiling, which infuriated her even more. "So," he said. "To what do I owe the pleasure?"

For a moment she couldn't think of a suitable excuse for being in his private office.

"And, perhaps more importantly, what happened at the police station?"

"How did you know about that?"

He chose to reply to her question with another: "So what happened?"

"Nothing. They asked me lots of questions, I answered them, they let me go."

"What were they asking about?"

Flora looked away. "Polly, of course. I think they were looking for her phone. They kept asking me where it was."

"Did they arrest you?"

"No."

Nigel let out an audible breath. "Well, that's something."

Flora asked, "Who was that man with you?"

"Nobody you need to worry about, Flora. Unless you're suddenly going to start taking an interest in my business affairs, that is."

Then she thought of something else: "What happened on Wednesday night?"

"I don't know what you're talking about."

"That man that was here. He was talking about something that happened on Wednesday night. Was he talking about Polly?"

There was a momentary hesitation, as though he was carefully formulating his response. "This has nothing to do with Polly, I can assure you."

She didn't believe him. "Why did you tell me you were out until midnight when you actually came back at eight? Mum said you came home and went down to the cottage to see Polly. She said Polly made you cheese on toast."

He laughed then, a proper belly laugh. "She said that? How bloody typical of her."

"Are you saying she got it wrong?"

"Not at all. I had cheese on toast at the cottage. Then I came home. Your mother went to bed. I went out. I came back at midnight, as I said to you. Now, Flora, what's all this about?"

She didn't answer, her mind working over everything he'd said. Infuriatingly, he was right: the two differing stories she and her mother had been told did not actually contradict each other.

"You think I had something to do with Polly's death?"

"Did you?"

His face reddened, and the smile that had been playing on his lips disappeared in a moment. "Of course I didn't. How dare you even ask me that!"

"I don't know what to think," she said quietly. She wanted to remain angry with him but her fury lost some of its energy in the face of his anger.

"You *don't* think, Flora, that's the problem. You get these ideas in your head and you don't think them through properly. Did you say anything about me to the police?" He stood up, suddenly, and towered over her and she pulled back in her seat, alarmed.

"Of course not!"

"You only need to give them an idea, a hint, and they will fucking have me over. *You* know that, *they* know that. They will pin you down and fucking question you until you give them what they're looking for."

"I won't tell them anything!"

"You'd better fucking not!" He took a step back, ran his hand across his forehead and through his hair, and Flora took that opportunity to get out of his way.

She stood up, pushed past him, and ran out of the office. Behind her, she heard him shouting: "Get back here!"

Out in the fresh air, her heart racing, she ran back to her car, fumbled with the key, turned it in the ignition, and sped away, the tires kicking up a spray of gravel and skidding alarmingly until they found their grip. She braked, briefly, at the bottom of the driveway, praying he wasn't running after her and risking a quick glance in her rearview mirror to check. It was getting dark, but even so she could see the side of the barn and no sign of him. A car was coming up Cemetery Lane from her right and she waited for it to pass.

"Come on, come on!"

It dawdled past and in the moment that the road became clear there was a bang on the car's roof and, as she screamed in fright, the dark shape at the driver's-side window moved and the car door opened, letting in a sudden gust of cold air. She had time to hear him shout "Flora!" through the door before hitting the accelerator hard and lurching forward into the road. The car door swung outward as she turned, then slammed shut again as the car straightened.

She was whimpering, looking back in the rearview mirror, into the darkness. He would get the Land Rover. He would follow her.

Moments later she had to brake as she caught up with the dawdling car that she'd had to wait for. There was no room to overtake. Her heart still thudding, she realized that there was no car behind her. He would be there by now, if he was going to follow her.

Then her phone buzzed in her pocket with a text message. She pulled it out and glanced at the display. It was from him:

We will discuss this tomorrow. Think about what I said.

Okay, then. He was leaving her to think about things; this was good. She had some time. But not to think. She had thought enough, no matter what his opinion was. It was time for action. And she knew exactly what it was she needed to do.

17:42

She got up as soon as she was finished, leaving Hamilton lying there, splayed across the bed like a starfish, arms and legs numb and his head full of her, her scent, her taste, the sound of her voice.

He was exhausted, and at the same time more alive than he'd ever felt in his life before. The decision made, the moment for action passed, there was nothing else to do but allow his flesh to melt, to give in to it, to forget about the fear and simply accept that what was done was done, it was too late to go back. Too late to undo what had taken place. There was no point even thinking about it anymore.

"I can't believe we just did that," he said to the empty room.

He heard the noise of the shower in the bathroom, for a brief moment thought about getting up and joining her in there, but he doubted he had the strength to lift his head, let alone attempt a Round Two.

He lay still, dozing, until he heard the sound of his mobile phone bleeping from his trouser pocket. Where had he taken them off? He couldn't remember.

A few minutes later she was back, wearing a robe, silky. She sat on the edge of the bed and slipped it off her shoulders, lifting her hands to tease her hair back into some sort of a style. Her back was tanned, smooth, muscles beneath the skin. She kept herself very fit, that much was clear. How old was she? He had no clue, only that she must surely be older than him. Forty-five? Fifty? Suddenly he was dying to know, but even he knew such a question was unspeakably rude. He stretched out a hand and touched her back, his fingertips trailing across from her right shoulder to her left hip.

She half-turned, treating him to an indulgent smile.

"You need to go," she said.

"Not yet."

"Your phone hasn't stopped bleeping. They're probably thinking you've had an accident, or been kidnapped, or something."

"What time is it?"

"Nearly six."

He sat up, then, in a hurry. "You're kidding me!"

"Not at all. As I said, you need to go."

The thought of having to explain to Karen why he was late to take them to the fireworks was enough to get him upright. His clothes were scattered everywhere, his trousers in the bathroom, his jacket hanging over the chair, shirt and socks in the living room.

There was just one text from Lou:

Where r u? Call in. Urgent.

He sighed deeply, looking at it. Whatever she had done to him, this woman, it was complete. He knew he should have called Lou straight back, damn it, he knew he should have responded when he'd heard the phone bleeping. He took his job seriously. He loved being a police officer, for all the shitty hours and the lack of resources and the being sworn at and assaulted. He loved every second of it. Of making a difference. And in the space of two hours he'd gone from being a proud upholder of Her Majesty's Peace to being deeply ashamed of himself.

And there was no turning back. Not this time.

18:02

"Gotcha," said Barry Holloway. "Ma'am!"

Lou looked up.

"You want the good news or the bad news?" Barry asked, his eyes twinkling.

"Bad news?"

"The subscriber check on the number called by the landline—it's a pay-as-you-go, no subscriber registered."

"Well, that's no great shock. What's the good news?"

"It's that 'Manchester office' number."

And there it was in black and white—subscriber shown as Ms. Suzanne Martin, Flat 1, 14 Waterside Gardens. Jason was already opening the mapping software, looking for an aerial image of Waterside Gardens and plotting its location in comparison to the other scenes, overlaying the cellsite data from Brian's phone billing.

"That's weird," he said.

"What is?"

"I thought the address was familiar. It's where Flora lives."

"Flora lives with this woman?"

There was a pause. "No, Flora has flat two. This is flat one. But bizarre, don't you think?"

"Can't be a coincidence," Barry muttered. "At least it explains that cellsite. It must have been this Suzanne that Polly was visiting that night, not Flora."

The plan for an arrest phase was well under way. Sam Hollands had been put in charge of preparing the arrest package for Brian, in hopeful anticipation of having enough evidence to take before a magistrate and get a warrant. Jason had been busy summarizing, printing off charts, timelines, and spreadsheets in support of the package.

What they had so far wasn't enough, though, and Lou knew it.

"Trouble is," Lou said to Sam, "we don't dare risk Brian's health. And we definitely don't have enough evidence to arrest Suzanne with what we've got. If we arrest Brian, there's a risk that Suzanne will do a runner."

And Hamilton was missing. He still hadn't returned Lou's calls, and this time when she'd dialed his home number, a woman answered. She sounded pissed off, even more so when Lou told her who she was and what she wanted.

"No, he bloody isn't here! He should be, though, and it's bloody typical of him to be late again. If you find him first let me know!"

Two things hit Lou with a sudden, dramatic force, when she disconnected the call to Karen Hamilton. The first was that this was the woman that Lou had unwittingly wronged. When she had found out that Andy was married, the pain she felt had been as much for the woman she'd never met, didn't know, as for herself and the end of the relationship before it had even really begun. Lou didn't know anything about her, didn't want to know because she felt bad enough as it was, and yet she had still formed a mental picture of this woman, the strength of her, bringing up Andy's children while he was away working ridiculous shifts and putting himself in danger in the line of duty. She would be strong and yet resilient. Long-suffering. Patient. The Karen on the phone sounded less patient, more livid.

The second thing, with as much certainty as it was possible to have, was that something bad had happened to Hamilton and that, wherever he was, he was in deep shit.

"Barry," she said. "We need to put a trace on the DI's phone. I think he's in trouble. Do it now."

18:07

Back in his car, dressed, trying to calm down enough to decide what to do, Andy Hamilton stared at his phone and then looked up through the windscreen to the gravel driveway and the front door of flat one, 14 Waterside Gardens.

To start with, he sent a text to Karen's mobile, preferring that approach to calling her directly. Firstly, she wouldn't stop shouting at him, and he had other things to do. Secondly, he was afraid to.

Sorry, delayed at work. On way now. x

Message sent, he dialed Lou's mobile number. It connected almost immediately.

"Andy? Where the hell are you?"

"Sorry, ma'am," he said, with a note of forced cheerfulness. "Been in traffic, no mobile signal. What's up?"

In the background he heard her shouting something to Barry Holloway, and then she was back with him.

"You had no signal? It's been *hours*. Where were you?"

He was thinking on his feet, which at first was scary but then pretty quickly it became exhilarating. Maybe this was why the offenders spent so much of their time lying, often when they didn't even have to. It was almost fun. A rush.

"I was out near the quarry, took a wrong turn and came up against a tractor that had broke down. Been bloody directing traffic for the last God knows how long. Sorry. What have I missed?"

"As long as you're all right. I was getting worried."

"Were you?" he was surprised at the note of concern that had replaced the fury. "Really?"

She ignored his question. "So where are you now?"

"Outside the town center. Not far. Do I need to come in? Only I'm late taking the kids out to the fireworks."

"Your call, Andy. I don't think there's much you can do here, to be honest. We're putting an arrest package together for Brian Fletcher-Norman. Jason got the cellsite back and it looks like Brian was flitting back and forth between Briarstone and Morden on the night Polly was killed. In between long conversations with a woman who might have been the one Polly met up with at the shopping center."

"You've ID'd her, then?" he said, his heart sinking.

"Subscriber check goes down to Suzanne Martin. And get this: she lives in the flat downstairs from Flora."

Shit! Shit on a brick.

"Andy?"

"Yeah," he said, finding his voice. "So—where are you up to on the arrest packages?"

"We've got about enough to bring Brian in, assuming the hospital will let us. They're looking at discharging him tomorrow morning, so we're leaving him where he is tonight and we'll pick him up first thing. Sam's going to get the warrant. With a bit of luck he'll give us enough to arrest Suzanne. Anyway, you've got a rest day tomorrow, so I'll see you on Wednesday. Enjoy the fireworks, okay?"

He was being let off—he couldn't believe it!

"Thanks, Lou."

"Besides," she said, and he could hear the smile in her voice all the way across the slightly dodgy mobile line, "by the sounds of it you've probably had quite enough of farms for one day . . ."

5X5X5 INTELLIGENCE REPORT

Date:	Sunday 4 November 2012
Officer:	PSE Kelly FRANKS, Financial Investigation Officer, Fraud Unit
Re:	Op NETTLE—Liam O'TOOLE and Barbara FLETCHER-NORMAN

ECHR Grading: B / 1 / 1

Barbara FLETCHER-NORMAN, DOB 15/11/1953

Several bank accounts, including ISAs and stocks. One bank account of note is with the Eden Building Society and is in subject's maiden name of Barbara CROFT. This account received payments of various amounts, once or twice a month from the account opening in August 2009 until Wednesday 31 October when the account contained £22,941. At 11 on 31 October Mrs. FLETCHER-NORMAN attended the Briarstone branch of the Eden Building Society and withdrew £20,000 in cash. She required the manager's authorization to do so and as this is a large amount an SAR was raised (this needs to be followed up).

Liam O'TOOLE, DOB 27/11/1981

One current account into which regular wages payments from Morden Country Club Leisure Ltd were made. Overdraft facility of £800, which was used regularly. Occasional payments in of £100 and £200 over the course of the past 12 months.

No further accounts on record, although it should be considered that this subject is of Irish nationality and further authorization will be required for further inquiries into overseas bank accounts.

18:22

Flora had thought it might be difficult to find the house, but in the end it was so easy it was almost funny. She drove through the town center and into Tithe Wood, once Briarstone's largest social housing estate, the houses now mostly privately owned. From the light of the orange streetlights overhead Flora could see the confusing juxtaposition of front gardens containing neat lawns and borders, potted bay trees, and brick-paved driveways, alongside knee-high weeds, cars on bricks, and ancient sofas rotting in the rain.

A few moments after turning into Kensington Avenue, she saw it. Parked at an angle, two wheels on the mud that might once have been a grass verge, was the Mitsubishi L200 pickup that Connor Petrie was using.

Flora pulled in to the curb behind it. She got out of the car and looked at the houses. It wasn't hard to guess which one might be the Petrie residence. Various cars were parked haphazardly along the curb in front of the Mitsubishi, and the long, overgrown driveway was populated with a selection of other vehicles in various states of repair. On the scrubby patch of grass and mud in front of the house was a child's swing set that looked lethal, an empty pram on its side, a set of goalposts with no net, and a mattress.

A boy and a girl, teenagers, were coming out of the house as she approached. The door slammed behind them and a dog started barking.

"Hello," she said to them.

"Wotcher," said the boy, eyeing her suspiciously. "All right?"

"Is Connor in?" Worth the risk, she thought. Even though she was now convinced she was right, because the family resemblance was a remarkable one.

"Dunno."

They carried on past her. It was the confirmation she needed. She knocked on the frosted-glass panel of the front door, which rattled in its frame, no doubt loosened by the repeated slamming. The dog barking continued, and then she saw a figure approach. The door was opened by a woman wearing a vest top and a pair of tracksuit bottoms.

"Is Connor in?" Flora said again.

"Who's asking?"

"Flora Maitland," she said. "It's urgent."

The door shut in her face. She heard the woman shout: "Connor! Someone at the door for you."

Flora waited, glancing at the road behind her, expecting at any moment to see her father's car pulling up.

The door opened abruptly and there he was, in all his ferrety glory. "What you want?" He clearly hadn't forgiven her for pushing him into the manure pile.

"Dad sent me," she said, dropping her voice to an urgent whisper. "He's been arrested. He told me to come and get the stuff he gave you to look after."

It was the moment of greatest risk. She half-expected him to ask her what the fuck she was talking about; after all, would her father really have trusted this halfwit with the contents of the safe? But there had been such little time to dispose of it all, and there had been the moment in the space above the office when Nigel had told Connor to go home, reminded him that he had been given something to do.

It was nothing more than an educated guess. And her suspicions were confirmed when the expression on Connor's face changed from a scowl to a gawp. He was buying it. "You're joking," he said. "Fuck!"

"Yeah," Flora said. "He wants me to move it again, he thinks they might get a warrant to search your"—she broke off, trying to find the suitable word, settled on—"house."

"Wait," Connor said. "I should ring him, to check—"

"You can't do that," she said quickly. "The police have got his phone."

"Right, right. Course. Fuck! Wait. How do I know he sent you?"

"For crying out loud. He told me your address, right? How would I find you otherwise?"

He seemed reassured by this, then he frowned again. "Fuck. Nigel's been nicked, I can't believe it! What are we gonna do?"

"Look, they could be here in a minute. We need to get the stuff into my car."

"Where are you going to take it?"

"Safer for you if I don't say."

He hesitated. Flora could almost see the cogs whirring inside his skull as he tried to work out what else he should be doing. Then he seemed to reach a decision. "Wait here, yeah?"

The door slammed shut.

Flora breathed out. So far, so good. But she was in deep shit now. Nigel might phone Connor at any moment.

A few moments later, the door opened again, and Connor pushed a cardboard box toward her with his trainer. "You take that one. I've got the other one."

She picked up the box. It was heavy, the top flaps interleaved shut. Without hesitation she made her way back down the driveway. Back at the car, she put the box down on the pavement and unlocked the boot. Connor was behind her, looking up and down the road anxiously as though the police might appear at any moment. In Kensington Avenue they probably often did.

"Glad to be rid of it, to be honest," he said, sniffing. "Not the sort of stuff I like having under me bed. You know what's in there, right?"

"I don't want to know," Flora said, "so don't tell me. I'm just bloody doing as I'm told."

"Yeah. When's he gonna be out, do you know?"

"No idea. He said he'd contact you as soon as he can. He seems to think it's going to be okay as long as I can take care of this stuff."

He nodded excitedly. "Yeah, yeah. They ain't got nothing on him, other than what's in there. You bloody take care of it, right?"

"Don't worry," she said, taking the second box from him. This one was much lighter. She slammed the boot lid down and went to get in the driver's door.

"Wait a sec," he said.

"What?"

"Did he say anything about the phone?"

Shit. What does he mean? "The phone?" She had one hand on the open door, looked back over her shoulder at the road as a pair of headlights suddenly illuminated them both. She pulled the door in closer as the car passed.

"Does he want me to drop it, or what?"

For a moment Flora's mind was a terrifying blank. Then: "He didn't say anything, but then he only had a second, and I guess this was his priority. Did you have an agreement, then? To do something with the phone if he was arrested?"

"Yeah," Connor said. "He told me that if he got nicked I was to drop the phone and get another one."

Flora felt relief wash through her. "Yes, that's probably a good idea. Drop your phone. He'll come and find you when he's out. Just keep your head down for a bit."

"You won't want me over at the stables, then?"

"No. Don't worry about the stables. I'll sort that out."

"Fucking excellent!"

She got in the car and started it, tried to pull away smoothly, but the tension caused by her own mad behavior was making her jumpy. When she got to the end of Kensington Avenue and turned left, back toward the main road, she started to laugh. Her hands were gripping the steering wheel as though it were about to fly off. *What have I done? What the hell am I doing?*

19:25

"Your phone's been ringing," Chris said when Taryn came back down the stairs, bathrobe on over her pajamas, hair in a towel.

"Well, you could've answered it," she replied, rooting through her bag for the phone. She had had several glasses of wine in the bath, trying to relax, worrying about Flora. Her first thought was that something had happened, that Flora had been arrested again, but the missed calls—three of them—were all from an unknown mobile number.

There were no voice-mail messages. Irritated, she redialed. It was answered straightaway—and the voice on the other end, imperious, impatient, was a familiar one.

"Taryn," said her father. "They're going to discharge me tomorrow. Can you come first thing? I don't want to have to wait for those awful patient-transport volunteer people."

Her father must have borrowed a mobile phone from someone. She considered it for a moment, thinking about where Brian was planning to go. Would the police just let him back into the Barn? She didn't even have his key. Surely he wasn't imagining that he could come and stay with them? And she had to be at work by half past eight.

"Does it have to be first thing?" she asked. "I might be able to take an extended lunch break."

There was a pause on the other end of the line. Chris, on the sofa with his feet on the coffee table, was watching her face, mouthing *Don't let him give you any shit.* Brian didn't do compromise. It felt likely that he was working himself up into a rage and she contemplated what Reg might say if she phoned in to ask for the morning off, just as the answer came. "That would be really kind of you, Taryn. Thank you."

Well, that was unexpected. She raised her eyebrows for Chris's benefit. "Okay, then," she said. "I'll give you a call in the morning, shall I?"

"Thank you," he said again.

She couldn't resist the little dig. "Isn't your lovely lady friend available to come and pick you up?"

Another pause. "She has . . . other priorities," he said.

"Is she married?" Taryn asked.

"No, she's not married. That's not what I meant. It's—it's just not possible to ask her."

The wine she'd drunk was igniting her curiosity and giving voice to it: "Are you going to marry her, Dad? Now that Barbara's out of the picture?"

"No," he said after a moment, and there was an audible sigh. "No, I rather think not." His voice sounded so strange, so unlike his normal brusque tone that Taryn had to sit on the arm of the sofa.

"Have you had a falling-out?"

He chuckled slightly. "No, not that. I don't think I should get married again, you know. Wives are more trouble than they're worth. Don't you think so?"

"I'll have to ask Chris about that," she said, and winked at her husband who had glanced up on hearing his name mentioned.

"I think . . . I rather think Barbara was very unkind to you, Taryn," Brian said.

Taryn didn't reply, shocked to hear him say this.

"And I think I was, too. I'm very sorry for it."

"Dad—?"

"It takes something like this to make you realize, you know."

"Nearly dying, you mean?" she said and then instantly thought how tactless that sounded.

"Oh, I've nearly died before," he said, his tone light. "It's not as bad as you'd imagine."

"What do you mean?"

"A dicky ticker," he said. "And a woman that likes to kill people. Makes you put everything into perspective."

The wine she'd drunk was making the turn the conversation was taking seem more than surreal. She was about to ask him what he meant, but before she had the chance, he brought things to an abrupt end.

"Anyway, if you can get here tomorrow I'd really appreciate it. Very kind of you. You know my number now, in any case. See you tomorrow, I hope."

"All right, Dad. I'll ring you first thing."

"Good night, then."

"Bye, Dad."

Taryn sat for a moment, staring at the handset before reaching across to replace it.

"What was that all about?" Chris asked.

"He said she liked to kill people," Taryn said quietly.

"Who? Barbara? Doesn't surprise me in the slightest. We're all bloody better off without her."

21:42

Jason had barely paused for breath all day, and now Sam was back with the warrant for Brian's arrest; barely five minutes passed before the officers who'd stayed behind had their coats on, ready to go out to the King Bill.

Sam, the only one still on duty, was staying in the office to prepare the morning briefing for the arrest and interview team. Lou spent a moment debating what to do, stay or go. But then she saw Sam's face and realized that actually she preferred to get on with things on her own. Besides, Jason had already left with Ali and Jane.

"Don't stay past your hours, Sam," she said. "You've done enough."

"Ma'am. I was hoping I could swap shifts and do an early turn tomorrow?"

Lou looked at her. Sam already knew what the answer would be; she was just trying her luck. "I really appreciate what you've done, Sam. You've been brilliant. But you'll have to wait until your shift, all right? You need your rest the same as everyone else. And you never know, we might be able to bring Suzanne in, and I'll need you for that."

By the time Lou got to the King Bill, she had promised herself she was only going to buy a round, maybe two, and then make sure everyone buggered off home. They weren't celebrating, not yet, anyway. This was all about putting a barrier between the case and going home. It was a transitional phase, involving beer.

And at the bar, the crush of people from the team along with every other random punter, most of whom were job themselves, she found herself standing next to Jason, who was pressing against her like some frotteur on a crowded underground train. As she necked the bottle of beer someone had lined up ready for her, alongside Ali and Jane and Les Finnegan, who smelled as though he'd sneaked in a couple of whiskey chasers already, she felt Jason's hand on her waist. She looked round at him, his green eyes so close to hers, closer than they'd been since the night she'd spent tangled round him on his sofa.

"How *did* you get that black eye?" she asked with a smile.

"What?"

It was loud in here, music from some local band coming from the function room upstairs—and they sounded good, too—so she repeated her question, a little louder, a little closer to his ear.

"I got a stick in the face, of course."

"Don't you wear some sort of mask thing?"

"Yeah, on the ice. This was in the changing rooms."

Lou laughed because it was quite funny after half a beer and an improbably long working day, and he laughed too. "What, on purpose?"

"Maybe. Who knows."

"Someone from the other team?"

"Does it even matter?"

"I'm just interested."

But he didn't answer, distracted by Les Finnegan talking about the pornographic pictures of Brian and his lovely lady friend on the phone and what he could sell them for, if he had half a mind to get started in the granny porn market.

Lou felt for Jason's hand, gave it a squeeze, intending to let go. He held it.

21:53

Flora was sitting on the floor of the kitchen, a small windowless room at the back of the studio where she made cups of coffee and washed out her brushes. The main studio, a large room with big windows overlooking the car park at the front of the building, was in darkness. Her car had been moved round the back, behind the second warehouse, and it was partly concealed by two large Dumpsters full of cardboard for recycling. To the casual passerby, nobody was home.

She had shut the kitchen door before turning on any lights, boiled the kettle, turned on the radio with the sound low so that the thought of being here all on her own was not quite so scary.

Now, with her third mugful of black coffee in hand, she had almost reached the bottom of the first box.

The contents had been by turns eye-opening, confusing, and, frankly, terrifying.

Large brown envelopes containing bundles of cash, fifties in great wads, bound with elastic bands. There were files, too, in three thick lever arch folders. One marked "Leeds," one marked "Liverpool." The other with nothing on the spine at all. Inside the files were plastic sleeves, each one containing personal details, photocopies of passports, birth certificates, phone numbers, addresses from all over eastern Europe, North Africa, Asia. One plastic sleeve in the unmarked folder contained nothing but credit cards, new looking, all in different names.

Then there was a large carrier bag containing passports, lots of them, different sizes, different colors. Flora pulled one out at random. The picture was of a young girl, dark haired, aged about twelve. The date of birth on the passport would have put her at seventeen. The name on it—in a Cyrillic script and in roman letters too—Ekaterina Ioratova.

Flora pushed the passport back inside the bag.

Underneath the bag she'd seen something else. Something black, solid: a handgun, and next to it a cardboard box with ammunition.

She had been removing everything and laying it out on the floor, but when she got to the gun, she stopped. This had suddenly got crazier.

She got to her feet and turned her back on the boxes. This was no good. She had to think.

Whatever her father was doing—and she knew it had to be bad— unless it had something to do with Polly, she wasn't interested. And he had lied to her. Despite his clever explanation of the way he'd spent that Halloween evening, something about it didn't ring true.

They weren't seeing each other anymore, were they? So why would Nigel go and spend two hours with Polly in the cottage on the night she died?

The second box was still unopened. She sat down on the floor again, opened the box. Inside was a file which she recognized as relating to the farm business. Everything in it was a copy of a legitimate document that was filed in the stables office. So why had he given this to Connor to look after?

She lifted the file and underneath it was another carrier bag. A sudden chill ran through her as she understood. The file was Nigel's final line of defense. Whatever was in the bag, he'd used the file to disguise it, as though someone raking through the contents would somehow hesitate over the file and decide that this box was somehow unimportant.

Flora lifted the bag clear of the box. It was surprisingly light. She looked inside, at the same moment as her phone started buzzing on the work surface above her head. She reached up for it. Taryn.

Where are you? Everything OK? Just checking up on you T. xx

She sent a swift reply.

All fine. Will ring you later. Xx

She opened the bag and looked inside, and then tipped the contents out into her lap. And here was what she had been looking for. Another wad of cash, bound up with elastic bands, and a small, black mobile phone.

23:45

Karen was asleep, the kids were asleep, and he'd gone out to his car in his stocking feet, not wanting to make a sound. Driving away as quietly as he could. Back to Waterside Gardens.

Back to her.

She opened the door to him after what felt like an age. It had crossed his mind, waiting on her doorstep and hoping once again that Flora or anyone else for that matter wouldn't see him here and wonder what he was doing, that she might have someone else in her flat. She might have any number of people who called on her. Not just guys—family, friends maybe.

But she was alone. "It's very late," she said.

She didn't look especially pleased to see him and he was nervous about her reaction when he came inside.

"We need to talk," he said.

"That sounds ominous, Inspector," she said. She followed him into the living room, got a second glass out of the cabinet, and poured him some wine from the bottle she'd been drinking.

"My name's Andy," he said.

"I like calling you Inspector," she said with a smile. "I find it a turn-on, fucking a policeman. Especially one with a rank."

"Please," he said. "Don't tempt me, not now. This is important."

"I'm sorry," she said, making an apologetic moue. "Go on."

"You said you had information for me. Something that would help."

"I thought you'd forgotten all about that. I certainly managed to take your mind off it this afternoon, didn't I?"

She handed him the glass of wine and sat on the sofa, crossing her feet neatly at the ankle. "You might as well sit down," she said.

Andy started to get his phone ready to record what she had to say, but she picked it up off the table and turned it off.

"Can I at least take notes?" he asked.

"No."

He gave up, then. He had a feeling that it was all shit anyway. She was still playing with him, teasing him. Anything she told him would be on her terms and would likely be fabrication. "How about we start with you telling me how you met Brian," he said.

Suzanne gave him a slow smile. Her eye contact was direct. "We met through mutual friends, earlier this year."

"Mutual friends? Who?"

She drank some of her wine, watching him over the rim of her glass. When she had finished, she put the glass down on the table in front of her. "That's not relevant to our discussion."

"You and Brian—what was the nature of your relationship?"

"Very similar to the one I'm having with you."

"You were lovers?"

"He is my sub. Do you understand what that means?"

Andy took a big gulp of wine to try and help him swallow the facts she was offering him—or rather, the comparison of their brief association with what she had done with Brian Fletcher-Norman.

"You did that—that thing you did with me?" he asked. "You suffocated him?"

"The term for it is breathplay. Yes, that's one of the things we enjoy."

"So you're—forgive me, this is all new to me—you're in control of him? You tell him what to do?"

The smile faded from her lips. She smoothed her skirt, reached forward for her glass of wine. As she did so her blouse gaped and he saw the curve of her breasts, smooth, white. "You have to understand the nature of control. Brian is a very strong man, a very controlling man. In his career and at home he is completely dominant, focused, authoritative. In order to relax he likes to relinquish that need for decision making. But that doesn't mean I am taking control."

"What *does* it mean?"

"You remember I told you to indicate if you'd had enough by raising your hand?"

Andy remembered. The thought of it, even now, made him inexplicably aroused.

"Yes."

"You were in control, then, weren't you? All you had to do was signal that you wanted to stop. So, effectively you were telling me what to do."

Something she'd said had made him feel uneasy, but he couldn't think what it was. Her turning the conversation round to the things they'd done, the way she was sitting there, curled around herself, was distracting him from Brian. Then he had it.

"You said Brian was dominant at home as well as at work," he said. "What do you mean?"

The smile was back. "Exactly that. He's confident, arrogant, and utterly selfish. Why do you think his wife was planning to leave him? Why do you think his daughter hadn't spoken to him for months? He's ruthless and doesn't care for anyone but himself."

"His wife was planning to leave?" He knew this already, of course. But he wanted to hear her take on it; if she was telling the truth about this, it would be easier for him to assess if she was telling the truth about the rest of it.

"She was going to run off with her tennis coach, according to Brian. He wouldn't have stood for that, of course. Brian never tolerated anything that didn't happen under his terms."

"What do you mean?" he asked again.

She tipped the last of the wine into her mouth and swallowed, her eyes on him. "You want me to spell it out for you?"

"Yes," he said.

"Barbara was going to leave. Brian wasn't going to let her get away with it, with stealing his money and humiliating him, but he couldn't do anything to harm her, of course, could he? Because then he would have got the blame. He couldn't just do away with her. And he couldn't force her to stay, nor did he want her to. He loathed her by that stage."

Andy was feeling cold, all of a sudden. The chill of it was traveling through his body like an anesthetic, paralyzing him with horror, as he saw the facts of the case being revealed as though she were a conjuror dramatically pulling away a silk cloth.

"What did he do?" Andy asked, trying to keep his voice light.

"What do you think? He set her up. He made it look as though she had committed a violent murder because she was jealous of his relationship with the girl next door—which of course never happened—and then he pushed her car over the edge of the quarry as if she had been suddenly overcome with remorse. He's very clever, you know. He's been thinking this through for a long, long time. The only thing he didn't bank on was his own dicky ticker, the fact that his heart couldn't take all that running around in the middle of the night."

"Why are you telling me all this?" he asked, his mouth dry. The wine was all gone.

Suzanne smiled at him again, got to her feet. He looked up at her as she placed a hand on his shoulder. "Because I don't want anything more to do with him. If he can do that to his wife, control or not, I'd rather not be anywhere near him, Inspector."

He stood, towering over her, looking into her eyes. He wanted to kiss her but he was starting to understand that she had to make the first move. He didn't want to frighten her, especially given everything she'd told him. It had to be true. The most logical explanation of all—and sooner or later, now he knew where to look, there would be forensic evidence that would substantiate what she'd said.

"How do you know that's what happened?"

"He came here that night and told me what he was planning to do. I tried to talk him out of it but he had his mind set on it. He wanted her out of the way so he could be with me, and that poor girl was going to be the one who would pay the price for Barbara's mistake. I was afraid. It went beyond the boundaries of our association, and I told him that. But he went ahead and did it anyway. He knew I would never be brave enough to tell anyone."

"You just told me," Andy said, touching her cheek.

"I told you in confidence," she said. "And because I know you can do the right thing with this information, which will get a murderer locked up and therefore mean I am safe. Do you understand what I mean?"

"I can only use the information to look for evidence, Suzanne," he said. "Unless you're willing to make a statement and support a prosecution."

She looked away, clearly thinking about this. She took hold of his hand and squeezed it, like a little girl seeking comfort. "If you arrest him," she said, "and if I know he's definitely not going to be let out, I'll consider making a statement. Is that good enough?"

Hell, yes, Andy thought. This had gone from his worst nightmare to a dream ending to a case that had been heading down the toilet along with his marriage, his career, and his life. He could say he'd come here looking for Flora, which was true, that Suzanne had given him the intelligence in confidence and he'd been trying to persuade her to trust him, make a statement. He'd not wanted to share the information with the team because of the risk to her life if Brian found out she'd talked. Suzanne had all but told Andy that she was terrified of him. It could work. It could actually work.

Suzanne led him out of the living room into the bedroom, as though she had said everything that she needed to say and that now the time for talking was over; he would be able to comfort her, provide her with reassurance that Brian was gone and that she had no need to fear him anymore.

"I need to go," he said, without enthusiasm. "It's really late."

"Stay," she said, pulling him closer. "For a little while."

Moments after that he felt a swell of satisfaction that this clever, gorgeous, and sexually insatiable woman was now, with Brian out of the way, all his.

23:52

It was a mobile phone, just a mobile phone. It lay, black and inert, on her knee, until she picked it up and pressed the button to turn it on. It was a cheap handset with a keypad and a small display. For a moment she had thought it was Polly's phone, that this was what the police had been searching for, that Nigel had it and that must mean that he had killed her. But a glance told her it wasn't Polly's expensive smartphone at all. So whose phone was it?

She worked her way through the menus to find the list of contacts, hoping that would give her a clue as to who it might belong to, but that proved to be even more confusing. They were mainly initials: B, F, R, CR, J, and a few brief names and nicknames: Dev, Kel, Ken P, Dozer, Legs, Ian, Psych. She looked for "Polly" but the name wasn't there, not even a "P." Then she had a thought, started to type in Polly's number, and before she had got too far the predictive text suggested she might like to dial "Y." Polly's number, definitely, stored under a single letter, Y.

She tried the same thing with her own number and her mother's, but both drew a blank.

Flora left the contacts list alone and turned to the stored text messages. There weren't many; whoever owned this phone either didn't like texting or believed that deleting as you went along was a sensible policy.

There were no text messages sent to or received from "Y."

There was one text, received on Thursday from "Dev," with a mobile number and nothing else. Two texts on Friday from "J," and one just said *ring me*. The second was another mobile phone number. The third, and final, text message, received at 08:56 on Saturday morning, was from "F":

Coming to collect, be ready 20 mins

Nothing made sense, nothing! Flora could feel the frustration and anger rising inside her. All of this effort, all her subterfuge, and it was for nothing! Whoever had this phone had Polly's number, but that was no help at all.

She ran through the call history to see if that made any sense. On Wednesday there had been intermittent calls back and forth between "J" and "Dev" and "Psych," and then in the evening the contacts increased until the phone was in almost constant use. Flora scrolled through it, wondering why Wednesday, what was so special about it? Polly was still alive then, doing whatever it was she had been busy doing on Wednesday—and then she saw it.

One missed call, on Wednesday night, from a landline number she recognized—the number for Yonder Cottage.

Flora stared at the handset, thinking hard. Polly had called this phone on Wednesday night at 23:43. The next contact logged on the call history was to voice mail, ten minutes later. Flora selected "voice mail" and dialed.

A second later it connected. "Welcome to voice mail. You have no new messages. To listen to older messages, press one. To listen to—"

Flora interrupted the voice and pressed one on the keypad.

She held her breath and listened.

"Nigel? Don't you EVER do anything like that again, you hear me? I am fucking livid right now. What the hell were you thinking? I've told you I want nothing to do with any of this! How dare you put me in that situation? I can't believe it, you total fucking idiot. I'm this close to calling the bloody police on you, you complete TWAT."

23:54

I shouldn't be doing this, Lou thought.

He held the door open for her, held out his hand—as though she needed help!—and, in any case, she'd only let go of his hand briefly in order to open the door of the taxi.

He didn't bother to put lights on, didn't take her into the living room this time, didn't offer her food or put music on or even kiss her. He waited for her to kick off her shoes in the hallway and then he led her by the hand up the stairs to his bedroom at the front of the house. There was light coming in from outside, through the blinds, streetlight, enough for her to see him undoing the top buttons of his shirt, tugging it out of his trousers and then pulling it over the top of his head, ruffling his hair the wrong way. His face was in shadow. She couldn't see the expression on it, or his black eye for that matter, the injury she knew for a fact hadn't been caused by a hockey stick or else why would he be so evasive? There was more to it than that.

But she didn't care about that right now. *I need sleep*, her subconscious protested feebly, thinking about the arrests tomorrow and how she would need to be focused, ready to do a press conference if necessary, certainly ready to brief Buchanan, and probably the assistant chief constable too . . .

"Stop that," he said, quietly, running his fingers over the frown creasing her forehead.

"I shouldn't be here," she said.

"Shh."

Then the chink of his belt as he undid it, and as though that was some kind of signal, she realized that she was standing there like a complete lemon, mouth open, probably stopping just short of a drool. So she reached out a hand and found the bare skin of his chest. It was hot to the touch, the muscles under the skin solid, tense. He caught hold of her hand and brought it up to his mouth to kiss. Pulled her closer.

"Louisa," he said, and kissed her.

Oh, God, it felt so good to give in to it. She could no more have gone downstairs, called a cab on her mobile, than she could have walked over broken glass. It wasn't only sexual attraction, it was like this—this—*longing* to be with him.

She let him undress her. He did it almost reverently; and while his clothes had been discarded where they fell, he took each item of hers and folded it, leaving it on the chair at the end of the bed.

And, thinking that she needed to be sensible here, needed to take charge of the situation and point out that maybe they had half an hour, an hour at most and then she would have to go home so she could get some sleep, he took control of things and her body responded to him as though it was separate from her, with no intention of behaving sensibly at all . . .

In the early hours of the morning, as her breathing slowed again for what felt like the fourth or fifth time, he was stroking her arm with his eyes closed, as though he was sleeping, even though she knew he was wide awake because of the smile on his lips, she whispered to him: "Someone whacked you one, didn't they?"

"Hmm? What are you talking about?"

"Your eye. You got punched."

"Louisa, it doesn't matter. It really doesn't. You can sleep now, you know . . . unless you want more?"

"Why won't you tell me?"

"Because it doesn't matter. It's done with."

"Was it over a woman?"

He let her go abruptly, sat up in bed, and turned on the bedside light. She blinked at the sudden brightness, pulled at the sheet in order to cover herself.

"Hey," he said, tugging the sheet out of her grasp. "Don't do that. Let me see."

"Why did you turn the light on?"

"To get this over with. It's no big deal. I was in the locker room and one of the guys on the team was smack-talking another of the guys on the team. His wife has cancer. I got mad. I picked a fight with him. He clipped me in the face with a stick. And that is it, the full story. Are you happy now?"

"What the hell's smack-talking?"

"You know. Mouthing off."

He was absolutely telling the truth. "Why couldn't you tell me that before?"

"Because it's no big deal. We're buddies again now. They all think it's funny that I got a black eye from it. The only problem with it now is your personal insecurity."

"Not my insecurity. My professional curiosity."

He laughed, nodded. "Right. I believe you. Totally."

She found herself smiling.

"I really like you," he said. "I know it's only been a few days, but you don't need to feel insecure."

She leaned over and kissed him, and then got up from the bed and started to get dressed.

"Where are you going? Hey, come back to bed."

"I'm glad we've established that you like me," she teased. "I can go home now and get some sleep with what's left of the night."

Day Six
Tuesday 6 November 2012

08:47

Lou was in the canteen on the top floor at Briarstone Police Station with Jason, Ali Whitmore, and Jane Phelps. She'd ordered a full English breakfast for them all and they were keeping a close eye on the kitchen to make sure that there were no dangerous hygiene violations taking place. Unlike the canteen up the road at police headquarters, the Briarstone nick canteen was known to be a bit hit-and-miss. The kitchen was open plan, enabling the customers to watch their food being prepared from start to finish. This should have been reassuring, but unfortunately it wasn't.

Lou felt strangely relieved that Andy Hamilton was on a rest day. He was one less headache for her to deal with. Under normal circumstances she would have been grateful for every warm body she could get her hands on for the arrest phase of the operation, but keeping an eye on him was proving such hard work it was much better for everyone if he was out of the picture, for today at least.

It had all gone smoothly and, for a change, everyone seemed relaxed. Relieved.

Brian had been arrested as soon as he had been discharged. He had looked shocked, but had reserved his right to remain silent. He had spoken to his solicitor, who was waiting for him when he was brought into custody.

Brian's doctors had confirmed that, for now, he was fit to be interviewed. The force medical examiner had been briefed and the forensic nurse practitioner on duty in Briarstone nick had been asked to stay close at hand while the interviews took place.

Lou felt exhausted, not least because she'd had only four hours' sleep. Bits of the time she'd spent with Jason kept coming back to her and distracting her from the sudden flood of information that was pouring in to the MIR via Barry Holloway.

Later, she thought. *Tonight I'm going to ask him to stay at my house. And even if all we do is sleep, I want it to be with him there . . .*

"Ma'am?"

There was something about the tone of the voice from behind her shoulder, and the way Jane Phelps's smile had died on her face looking at the expression on Ron Mitchell's face as he approached Lou, that made her realize that this was not going to be good news.

"What is it, Ron?"

"Flora Maitland is downstairs. She's insisting she wants to talk to you."

08:52

Flora had been waiting for nearly an hour. The front office of the police station opened at eight, and she had been here since the doors had been unlocked. She had asked to speak to whoever was in charge of the investigation into the murder of Polly Leuchars.

The front office was an interesting place to sit. A man came in to report a stolen car. The woman on the counter ran through a series of questions, made notes, but the story kept changing: he'd last seen it on Sunday evening, then he corrected himself and admitted driving it to work yesterday. He'd left it parked outside his house, then he said it had been stolen from the car park where he worked. Flora could feel the woman's frustration building, and then she realized that the man was drunk. This early in the morning?

Eventually, the man went.

Flora asked, "How long will it take? Do you know?"

The woman had responded, "Sorry, love. No idea."

A woman came in to ask about some lost property, then another woman with a buggy and a toddler, asking whether her boyfriend was in custody again because he hadn't come home last night. A sign on the wall offered people the chance to discuss their query in a private room, but nobody seemed bothered by Flora's presence. She felt as though she were fading, becoming transparent. If she sat perfectly still, nobody would even be able to see her anymore.

At eight forty-five a man in a suit turned up. He was there for a meeting with someone from Crime Prevention. They made him sit and wait. He sat opposite Flora and stared at her in a way that made her feel uncomfortable. He was probably wondering what she was there for, and then she realized she probably didn't look too good.

"Will it be much longer, do you think?"

"I've rung them, they know you're here. I expect they're all busy at the moment."

She had barely slept, just dozed in the kitchen at the studio with the blanket around her shoulders. When it got light and nothing had happened, no phone calls, no texts, she tried to decide what to do. She wanted to phone her father, demand to know what he was doing, what Polly had meant by her frantic voice mail.

The last few days had been such a nightmare. First Polly's death, and then her father acting strangely. How could she not suspect him? And having listened to Polly's voice, tearful, furious, and terrified on that message, she was jumpy and afraid. She was imagining all sorts of things, her mind flitting from one possibility to the next. Why hadn't he used the gun, if he was going to kill her? Because he hadn't had it with him, of course. He had got her voice mail and had gone down to the cottage to confront her about it, whatever it was, and of course she hadn't made him cheese on toast, how ridiculous!—he had gone there to talk to her, and they'd had another row, and he'd hit her too hard and she had died. And after that he'd been covering his tracks, establishing an alibi with friends, or whatever it was he'd done. But no, that wasn't right either, was it? He'd been at the farm. He had told them he was at home, with Mum. And he was relying on Felicity to cover up for him, relying on her being vague and confused as she always was but nevertheless unflinching in her support of him.

Think, Flora, think. Her eyes kept moving from the front desk to the clock on the wall. Why were they taking so long? The longer they left it the more her resolve started to slip. This morning she had been certain of what she needed to do: go to the police and tell them she was ready to talk, as long as they were prepared to offer her some protection.

She had left the studio as it began to get properly light, looking around in case someone was waiting for her outside. Nobody there. She hurried to her car, checked it carefully. It seemed all right. Started okay. Before she did anything else, she had a very important task to complete: she drove to the farm, in through the driveway beside Yonder Cottage so that nobody in the farmhouse would know she was there. She left the car outside Polly's house and walked up to the stables, keeping an eye out all the way. Nobody was around, of course. Felicity would still be fast asleep.

The horses were surprised to see her but seemed quite happy to have an early breakfast. After they'd been fed she led them one by one to the paddock and turned them loose. They stood around looking dazed. That was fine. She wouldn't bother mucking out. Felicity probably wouldn't even check; she would see them out in the field and think—what? That Petrie had suddenly decided to do his job properly? Actually, knowing her mother, she probably wouldn't even care. Either way, by the time the horses needed to be brought in again, the day would have taken its course and nothing would be the same again anyway.

After the stables, there had been nothing else for it but to go to the police station. There was no point in going to her flat—that was a dangerous place now. Her father would be looking for her soon enough, and the flat would be the first place he would check. She couldn't risk going to Taryn's, either. It would be wrong of her to involve her friend now that the stakes had become so much higher.

"Do you think you could ring them again? I've been here ages," she asked.

"They're based over at HQ, could be a while yet. Sorry, love. Try to sit tight, I'm sure someone will be here before too long."

The longer she waited, the more uncertain she became. Every few minutes she checked her phone, even though it would vibrate for any incoming calls or texts. Since last night's text, Nigel had remained silent. This could mean one of two things: either he was carrying on with his daily business, blissfully unaware of her activities, or he had spoken to Connor Petrie, in which case she was in deep shit.

Yes, the police station was the only safe place at the moment, and as much as she didn't particularly like or trust the police, especially after they had brought her in for questioning, searched the flat, and accused her of murdering the only person she'd ever loved, they were definitely a better prospect than confronting her father.

And then her mobile phone vibrated in her pocket. She pulled it out and looked at the display: Taryn. And just at that moment the door to the side of the reception opened.

"Ms. Maitland?"

Flora looked up. The woman who had called her name was holding open a door next to the reception desk. "Would you like to come this way?"

Flora pressed the button to reject Taryn's call and sprang to her feet, wiping her hands down the front of her grubby, paint-stained jeans. "Thanks, yes." Her heart was bouncing around in her chest.

Focus. Think.

Above the swirling, panicky thoughts, Flora was acutely aware that what she was about to do amounted to a further act of betrayal and that from this point on there was no turning back.

The woman was young, slightly built, wearing a smart suit that made her look older than she probably was. Her long, dark, glossy hair must have taken a lot of effort to straighten every morning. Flora could never see the point of all that stuff.

She was led into a small, artificially lit room with a table and two chairs, a metal filing cabinet upon which sat a pile of dog-eared magazines, a box of tissues, and a plant that was so green it had to be made of plastic.

"Have a seat," the woman said.

Flora sat. The woman pulled the chair out from the desk and sat in the open space beside the table.

"My name is Detective Chief Inspector Louisa Smith. I'm leading the investigation into Polly Leuchars's murder and I understand you wanted to see me?"

"You're in charge?" Flora asked, surprised. She had a momentary vision of the brash, intimidating Detective Inspector Andy Hamilton and wondered how he could possibly be subordinate to this smiling, softly spoken woman.

"Yes, I am. How can I help?"

"Well, it's about my father," Flora began. This was the moment, she thought. After this, her choices would diminish. She hesitated, feeling panic and confusion and, in all of that, still this terrible aching in her heart because of Polly. And she was tired now, so tired. Despite the emotions, all she wanted to do was lie down on the floor of the room and sleep. And how could any of this possibly make sense?

"Your father—Nigel Maitland?"

Flora swallowed. She didn't want to cry in front of this woman but it looked like it might happen anyway. "I'm so scared," she said, her voice a whisper.

"Why are you scared, Flora?"

There was a long moment, a long, painful moment when she debated with herself about what to say next. And then, in a small voice, she said, "I'm scared of getting things wrong."

"You don't need to worry about that. If you have information for us, it's up to us to make sure we know what it means. So you see, you can't get things wrong, Flora."

Flora took a deep breath in. "He's been acting strangely since Polly's death. I think something happened that night, but I don't know what. I just know he's been odd. And he was having an—an affair with her. I supposed that's what it is."

"With whom? With Polly?"

"Yes. He said it ended months ago, but I don't know if that was true."

"In what way was he behaving strangely?"

Flora thought about this, and the confusion and the doubt seemed to lift a little. She couldn't tell them about the phone, or about Polly's voice-mail message, because to do so would be to admit to the boxes and their contents. She had hidden them under the kitchen sink at the studio, which wasn't the best hiding place, but at least they were out of sight. How could she tell them what she knew? How to start something like this? And, once started, how to stop?

There was a knock at the door behind Flora. She looked round as Lou Smith looked up. A man wearing a police uniform opened the door. "Ma'am. Sorry to interrupt."

"What is it, Noel?"

"Need a quick word, sorry."

Lou stood up. "Excuse me for one moment," she said and left the room.

Flora felt cold, chilled, and after all the panic, all the nervous tension, strangely calm.

Then the door opened and Lou came back in and sat down. "I think what we should do, Flora, is talk about this properly in an interview suite. I don't want you to worry; you're quite safe here with us. We just need to do things in a particular way to make sure we don't miss anything. Would you mind waiting for a while, until we can sort out a proper interview room?"

Flora shrugged. "I guess so."

"Can I get a cup of tea or coffee sorted out for you?"

"Coffee would be good. Thank you."

"I'll be back as soon as I can," she said, and then the door shut behind her and Flora was on her own again. She put her head onto her folded arms.

09:14

Bloody typical, to be called away right at that moment. Outside the interview room, she took PC Noel Brewster to one side. "Can you make sure Flora Maitland doesn't leave before I've had a chance to speak to her again? If she starts to look like she wants to go, will you come and find me?"

"Yes, ma'am," Noel replied.

"Promise?"

"Absolutely."

"And can you get her a coffee? Thanks."

Lou ran up the stairs to the office at the back of Briarstone Police Station that the team had been allocated while the interview was in progress. The MIR at Headquarters was only fifteen minutes' drive away, but even so, having everybody together, here, able to view the interview as it happened, by video link, was essential.

Only Jason had been left behind, to complete as many charts and reports as he could in the time they had left to interview Brian.

"Sam and Ron are in already, ma'am," Les said. "The solicitor didn't take long."

"Who is it?" Lou asked.

"Simon McGrath."

Could be worse, Lou thought. He wasn't a complete pain in the arse, but the chances were he was still going to have advised his client to answer "No comment" to every question put to him.

They all grouped as best they could around the monitor that provided a direct link to the interview room. They could see Brian sitting at a desk, a middle-aged man in a dark suit sitting next to him, the ceiling lights reflecting off the top of his bald head. A smaller, pop-up window in the bottom of the screen was feeding the image from the camera in the opposite corner of the room—Sam and Ron, getting themselves settled.

Sam went through the initial proceedings of the interview, setting up the recording, introducing everyone present, reminding Brian that he had been arrested and cautioned, and asking him if he understood everything.

The first few questions were straightforward, going over subjects that he had already quite happily discussed with them on previous occasions in the hospital.

"Can you tell us when you first met Polly Leuchars?"

To his credit, Simon McGrath was allowing Brian some freedom to answer the questions he felt comfortable with. The story was trotted out again: golf with Nigel Maitland, riding lessons.

The questions gradually moved around to Barbara. The answers, again, nothing they had not already heard. She was a jealous woman, prone to drinking too much and being aggressive.

And then, out of the blue: "She was having an affair with her tennis coach. His name was Liam O'Toole."

Neither Sam nor Ron showed any surprise at this, which was excellent. They had prepared well, they knew exactly what he had told them previously and this was the moment when they were venturing onto new territory.

"How did you know about this?" Sam asked.

"She told me," Brian said. His voice was low, sorrowful, as though the memory was painful, although his body language looked relaxed enough. "I'd had my suspicions, of course. She was spending a fortune on tennis lessons, and where she had been so bloody miserable before, she seemed to have perked up in the last few months."

"When did she tell you, Brian?"

"That last night. It was one of the vicious things she threw at me before she buggered off out."

Sam took her time, writing some notes. "Can you take us through the events of that evening again, Brian? Let's start with you getting home from work."

"I got home from work, and she started a row with me—"

"What time was it?"

"Between eight and nine."

He was sticking to the events as he had outlined them to Lou before, in the hospital. Sam knew this too. Lou found herself listening to the repeated story and tuning out; she kept thinking about Flora, in the interview room downstairs. She had looked exhausted and yet fidgety, as though she was on the verge of losing the plot. As soon as she had the opportunity, Lou was going to go down and check up on her, make sure she was all right.

Once Brian had told the story all the way up to the police knocking on his door the next morning, Sam tried a change of subject.

"Are you a keen cyclist, Brian?"

"I cycle occasionally to keep fit. I prefer golf."

"Where do you keep your bike?"

"Usually in the garage at home."

"And when did you last go for a cycle ride?"

"I don't know. Weeks ago. The weather has been bad."

"Is this your bike, Brian?"

The video screen showed Ron passing something across the table. Both Brian and Simon McGrath studied it closely.

"Looks like it. Hard to say."

"Why is it hard to say? It's quite a distinctive bike, isn't it?" Sam said. "An expensive one, too. Have another look."

There was a long pause, which included glances and a few private words being exchanged between Brian and his solicitor.

"I can't be sure," he said at last.

Sam looked as though she was going to ask again, but then Simon McGrath spoke: "My client has answered the question. I'd appreciate it if we could move on, and I'd like to remind you that we need to take regular breaks. Mr. Fletcher-Norman is still recovering from a serious illness."

They were clearly reaching the periphery of Brian's comfort zone. He was happy with his original story, that much was clear; now, every question they asked him would be thought about, discussed, and then quite possibly not answered. And they hadn't even mentioned his phone yet. It was going to be a long day.

09:25

"How are you feeling, Brian?" Sam asked, after she had reminded Brian of the caution and, for the benefit of the recording, identified everyone present.

"Tired," he had replied.

"We will try and keep things to the point, then, shall we?" said Ron.

"Let's talk about your phone, Brian," Sam began. "Can you take me through the calls you made on the night of thirty-first October?"

"I don't remember," he said.

"Can you confirm that this is your phone?"

Ron passed the evidence bag across the desk toward Brian and Simon McGrath.

Simon McGrath leaned across to his client and made some comment.

"It's a common type of phone," Brian said.

"Very well," said Sam. "It was given to us by your daughter, Mrs. Taryn Lewis. She said she found this phone in your office at Hayselden Barn, your home address. It has your fingerprints on it. The numbers saved in the address book generally have been identified as people known to be your associates, including a number saved as 'Office,' which, according to your company's website, is the main switchboard number for your workplace. There's also a number saved as 'B MOB,' which, according to a subscriber check, is registered to your wife, Barbara. Do I need to go on?"

Simon McGrath looked annoyed. "Was that an actual question, Sergeant Hollands?"

"All right," Brian said. "It's my phone."

Sam retained her calm, interested expression. "Very well. Can you confirm that you had this phone in your possession on the night of thirty-first October?"

Another consultation between Brian and his solicitor, this one longer. There seemed to be a disagreement between them. Sam was watching them closely.

"I don't remember," Brian answered at last.

"Your daughter said it was in your office. Is that where you left it?"

"Yes, it must have been."

"Did you make any calls on the night of the thirty-first?"

"I don't remember," Brian said again.

"Well, then, let me remind you. This phone made several calls during the evening, specifically to a number which is saved in the contacts as 'Manchester office.' Do you remember making those calls?"

"My client has already said he doesn't recall making the calls," McGrath said.

"I am just trying to help him out," Sam said. "Do you remember making any of those calls, Brian?"

"I don't remember."

"Can you tell me who 'Manchester office' is?" Sam asked.

"It's a work number. A client. I don't really know. I don't know why I rang them. I was feeling unwell."

"We've identified this number as belonging to a woman called Suzanne Martin, who lives in Briarstone. Does that help? Maybe you remember speaking to her on Wednesday night?"

Brian's face was coloring and he was looking increasingly uncomfortable. "Look, I've already said I don't remember."

Sam leaned back in her chair and took a deep breath. "Very well," she said. "Let's move on. We have evidence from the phone's service provider about the calls made by this phone on the night of the thirty-first, Brian. It's called cellsite data and it tells us where this phone handset was when it was in use. Do you understand what that means?"

Brian nodded.

"Could you answer yes or no, please," Ron said. "For the tape."

"Yes," Brian said. His voice was raised an octave. He cleared his throat. "Yes, I understand."

"The phone that you have identified as yours, and in your possession on the night of the thirty-first October to first November, made several calls to the number registered to Suzanne Martin. One of those calls, made at"—Sam checked her notes—"made at . . . half-past two in the morning, was in the vicinity of Ambleside Quarry. Can you confirm that you made that call, Brian?"

Brian's voice had gone.

"Could you speak up, please?" said Ron.

"I don't—I don't know."

"I suggest that my client needs a break, Sergeant," said McGrath.

"We've only just had a break, I'm sure he can manage another few minutes. Can't you, Brian?"

"I'd rather get this over with," he said.

"It would be very easy to wrap this all up if you could think carefully and remember what you were really up to that night, Brian. After the call made at the quarry, there's another call made to the same number at three in the morning. A long call, nineteen minutes and twenty-three seconds in duration. That call was made from Morden again. What about that one? Nearly twenty minutes, Brian. Do you remember making that call?"

There was a pause. Brian was staring at Sam across the desk. As she watched, a tear fell from his eye onto his sweater, absorbing into the navy cotton and spreading into a neat, dark circle.

"Brian? What was it you were discussing with Suzanne Martin?"

Still no response.

Sam, calm as ever, tried a different tactic. "I'd like to point out, Brian, that this morning you've claimed that you don't remember anything about the phone calls made that night, but I believe you're not telling the truth. You told us when you were interviewed before that your memory of the night had come back, that you remembered having an argument with your wife and then you went to have a bath and went to bed. And now you're claiming that you don't remember making phone calls in the early hours of the morning all around the county. That's going to look very bad. Do you understand?"

At last he cleared his throat and leaned forward in his chair. "All right," he said, "all right."

Simon McGrath started to speak but Brian raised his hand to wave him away. "There's no point, is there? It's all going to come out sooner or later, isn't it?"

Brian looked up again, right into Sam's eyes. She was struck with how afraid he appeared, his eyes desperate for help.

"I can't help you, Brian," she said, quietly, "unless you tell me the truth. Let's start from the beginning again, shall we?"

"I killed her," he said.

Sam's heart skipped a beat. She took a slow, deep breath in, not allowing the mask of calm to slip. "Who?"

"Barbara. My wife. I pushed her over the edge of the quarry. So what is it you want me to tell you?"

10:27

This was all taking too long. It wasn't just the traffic. Flora felt as though time itself had slowed and she was fighting against it. Fighting against everything, now.

Going to the police station had been a mistake. What did she expect them to do? What could she prove? Nothing. They wanted evidence. And what evidence could she give them? All the stuff in the boxes, there was no point in giving them that. Apart from the voice-mail message she had left on that phone, none of it had anything to do with Polly. And the message, by itself, proved nothing. They would take it and keep it on file and nothing would happen.

They were all scared of Nigel and Joe Lorenzo, the police. He was too difficult for them to touch. It made them reluctant to do anything, and as a result he kept getting away with it. He had been getting away with it for years.

Flora took a detour past the studio, to check that everything was as she had left it. Her intention had been only to check the car park, to look for the Land Rover or the Mitsubishi pickup, but once she was there and saw the car park was completely empty, she pulled in and turned off the engine.

Upstairs, the air was freezing cold. She glanced around the main studio, but nothing had been disturbed. The kitchen, too, was as she had left it this morning: her blanket in a pile on the floor, unwashed mugs in the sink, the radio on the counter. She pulled open the cupboard door, and inside were the two boxes.

She could take it with her.

She had thought this before. In fact, over the past few hours the thought had been there, persistently at the front of her mind, nagging, pestering. She could take the gun, threaten him with it. See if that did the trick.

A few minutes later, back out in the car, Flora was heading toward Morden again.

10:45

When Taryn had arrived at the police station she had been tense and tearful. Sam Hollands had phoned her at home, and when she heard the words "I'm calling about your father," her immediate thought had been that he'd suffered another heart attack and died. She barely registered what Sam said next, because her reaction to the thought of him dying had taken her completely by surprise. Despite how she'd felt, especially recently, being forced into being nice and kind and all the things she thought she was anyway, she had never thought for one moment she would feel this dramatic wrench of sorrow.

And then Taryn realized that Sam wasn't calling to tell her he was dead, after all, and she had to ask Sam to repeat what she had said.

Arrested.

Immediately she had so many questions: *Where? When? What do I need to do?* And all she could think was how Barbara had somehow engineered this, must have somehow set him up to take the blame. She had come directly, phoning Flora on the way, fretting and panicking and working herself up into a state because Flora wasn't answering, and everything was made worse because she couldn't find a parking space.

"Mrs. Lewis?"

Taryn looked to her right and saw a smartly dressed young woman holding open the door that led back toward the front counter.

"My name is Detective Chief Inspector Lou Smith," said the woman, offering her hand. Taryn shook it, confused. "Can I call you Taryn? I wonder if we could have a quick word? Let's go in here, shall we?"

They were in a small interview room, nothing in it but a desk and two chairs either side of it.

"Have a seat. I was hoping to talk to your friend Flora. She was here earlier but she left. I don't suppose you know where she is?"

Taryn reached into her bag for her phone, checked it. No missed calls, no texts. "I didn't know she was here. I tried to ring her, but she didn't answer. Is she all right?"

"I don't know. I have to say I'm quite concerned about her."

"Are you?" Taryn said.

"Before you arrived, she asked to see me. She seemed quite agitated. And yet when we had a few minutes to talk, she seemed uncertain and confused."

"I don't think she's been sleeping. She's been so upset, you know. About Polly."

"Understandable," Lou said. "I believe she and Polly were in a relationship for a time."

"Yes. She was devastated by what happened. I'm worried she's not coping."

"Taryn, I have some news about your father. We've just charged him with murder."

Taryn didn't answer for a moment. Unlike Flora, unlike her father, she had never felt any distrust of the police. In fact, she had rather liked that tall, chunky one who had met up with them in the café. Sam Hollands had been so kind to her, and now this woman, who seemed so genuine too. She couldn't think of anything to say.

"He'll be taken before the magistrate in the morning. We'll continue to interview him until then, but we will make sure he gets plenty of rest and the custody nurse will be keeping a close eye on him, so you don't need to worry."

Taryn cleared her throat. "Can I see him?"

"Maybe a bit later. It's all a bit hectic right now. I'll make sure we keep you updated."

"Thank you," Taryn said, as though Lou had offered her sympathies. She hadn't. Then another thing occurred to her: "Does he need anything?"

"I'll make sure someone asks him. He might like a suit to wear in the morning."

"Of course."

Lou smiled. "We're doing everything we can to minimize the stress of the situation, so try not to worry. But I'm afraid we're running an investigation into a very serious offense. We need to establish exactly what happened as quickly as possible."

"And you think my dad killed Polly?"

Lou's eyes flicked up to meet Taryn's. "What makes you say that?"

"You said he'd been arrested for murder . . ."

"He's been charged with the murder of Barbara Fletcher-Norman."

Taryn was confused again. "But I thought she killed herself? She drove herself over the edge of the quarry, didn't she?"

"There are still a lot of questions we're trying to answer."

Taryn said, "He said something really strange to me, on the phone. He called last night to tell me he was being discharged from the hospital today, he asked me to come and pick him up . . . and we were talking about Barbara, and he said, 'She liked to kill people.' I didn't know what he meant. I mean, I assumed he meant Polly, but even so . . . it was such a strange thing."

"You're sure he was talking about Barbara?"

Taryn didn't answer.

Lou Smith leaned forward in her chair. "Taryn. I think it's really, really important that I find Flora. Do you have any idea where she might have gone?"

11:14

It was only when she parked outside Yonder Cottage that Flora noticed her hands were shaking. She gripped the steering wheel tighter to see if that would help. Deep breaths. She needed to chill out. She needed to think.

But there was no time to think anymore.

She got out of the car and slammed the door behind her, setting off up the driveway. A moment later she was passing the stables. Behind them, in the paddock, Elki stood by the gate, chewing, watching her. The other horses were all out in the field with her, where she had left them this morning.

She carried on round the bend at the top of the driveway. Of course, she could have driven all the way up and parked outside the barn, but she needed a few moments—cold air on her face, the smell of the farm, a chance to get her bearings.

The door to the barn was open, the Land Rover parked outside. She walked in without hesitation, over to the office. Nigel was sitting inside, watching her approach through the glass panel in the door. He had a glass in his hand, whiskey already even though it wasn't even lunchtime. His face was florid.

Flora did not knock, just opened the door and went in.

"You might as well sit down," he said, after a moment.

She sat.

"You look worse than I thought you would," he said. "Where did you sleep?"

She shrugged. "I didn't sleep."

"Figures."

He offered her the bottle of whiskey and she took it, gulping it back in the hope that it would help, somehow give her the courage that she desperately needed.

"So," he said. "What is it you want, Flora? I'm guessing you're here because you want something."

"I want to know what happened," she said.

"It's not what you think," he said.

"Don't tell me what I think!" Her anger was swift, out of nowhere. She tried to calm it again with a big gulp of whiskey, fire going down her throat. "Just—just tell me the truth, if you can."

He took a deep breath in, his bright-blue eyes studying her. "Here's the deal, then. I will tell you everything that happened that night. You will then go and get the items you removed from Petrie's house last night and bring them back here. After that, we will decide how we can move on from this. Agreed?"

So he knew. Despite the pulse pounding in her head, the fear that this was all some sort of trick, Flora nodded. "Agreed."

"There was a delivery that night. Something went wrong and it turned up here at the farm instead of the place where the driver should have gone."

He didn't continue for a moment, looking across Flora's shoulder as though he was remembering it.

"A delivery of what? People?"

He didn't answer the question, but carried on as though he hadn't heard. "It was late, it was dark, I had them on my phone telling me to sort it out and I was getting angry because all of this should have been straightforward."

"Who's 'them'?"

"Friends of mine. Believe me, that's something you don't want to know."

He drank from his glass as though it were water. Flora passed him the bottle so he could refill his glass, and then accepted it back from him and drank some more, pretending she wasn't trying to match him gulp for gulp. If he wanted an anesthetic against this awful discussion, so did she.

"What's that got to do with Polly?"

"Polly had been out somewhere. The lorry was blocking the drive so she couldn't get in and she drove round the other way, to the farmhouse, and walked back down through the yard. She saw me and came over, asked me what was going on. I told her it was a feed delivery that had come in the wrong way."

He stopped and his eyes went up to the ceiling. Flora realized he was actually showing some emotion now. She knew how that felt: recalling Polly, remembering her alive. Every thought of her, walking, talking, breathing, smiling—it hurt like a blow to the face.

"She didn't believe a word of it," he said.

"I'm not surprised."

"I told her to go back to the cottage and stay there, told her to go to bed. But she was, I don't know, weird. She'd been crying and she was unsteady on her feet, as though she was drunk. And she was all dressed up. She looked . . . she looked . . ."

He put the glass down carefully, deliberately, on top of the papers on the desk and ran his hand across his face, through his hair.

"Then what happened?"

"She kept demanding to know what was going on. And I got the impression she didn't even really give a shit, she just wanted someone to shout at. She wanted an argument. And the driver, the driver of the lorry, he'd been making phone calls, I'd been making phone calls. And then the Petrie boy turned up with some others. I'd sent him off to get some help, meaning he should find somewhere else for the lorry to park up overnight and do the handover, and instead of doing that the stupid little fucker had gone and got half of his crazy family. And everyone was standing around arguing, and Polly was there, arguing too, even though it had nothing at all to do with her. I kept thinking the neighbors were going to hear, that Brian or that mad wife of his would hear and call the police."

A tear slid down Nigel's cheek, and the sight of it was somehow more alarming than anything she'd seen or heard today.

"I could have done something," he said. "I had no idea it would end up the way it did."

He rubbed the tear away, sniffed. "Anyway, in the end she'd had enough and she went back to the cottage. We managed to reverse the lorry out, went ahead with the rendezvous in a different location. It took hours, during which she phoned and left a message on my voice mail to have a go at me all over again. I tried to call back, but there was no answer so I assumed she must have gone to bed. I went back to the farmhouse. I hadn't realized Polly's car was still parked outside. The keys were inside, so I drove it round to the cottage. All the lights were off and I walked back round and went in the house."

He fell silent again.

The whiskey was making Flora's lips feel numb, and asking questions felt like a chore, like an effort.

"That's it?"

"Yes. Flora, I don't know for sure what happened to Polly."

"But you think it was one of the men who were here? One of your friends?"

"It's possible, although I don't know why. They're fucked in the head, half of them off their brains on gear of one sort or another. I don't think it was Petrie, unless one of his uncles told him to do it. He may be weird, but I don't think he could cope with that level of violence without giving himself away afterwards."

Flora thought about it. She thought about Petrie, the weaselly little shit, with his hands on Polly. Her brain was working better now. The alcohol, maybe. Gradually things were starting to make sense.

"You said . . . you said to that man, who was in here yesterday. You said that he'd seen something. You were talking about Petrie. You said, 'You'd be mental too, if you'd seen what he'd seen.' What was that all about?"

Nigel didn't answer. He was swilling whiskey round his mouth as if it were mouthwash before swallowing it in big gulps. His glass, once again, was empty. He reached for the bottle, refilled his glass, and put it back on the table between them.

"Dad? What did you mean?"

"Petrie was acting up the next day. Excitable. I thought it was just because he'd had a late night. Then, when all the police were here in the afternoon he told me he'd seen all the blood."

"*What?*"

"I asked him what he meant. He said he'd been in to see Polly, early. He used to pick her up on the way to the stables sometimes, did you know that? He said he'd gone in the back door and seen the blood. He said he'd been scared and had gone home for a few hours."

"Dad, why didn't you tell the police?"

"Oh, have a word with yourself, Flora. The kid knows way too much about the business. Think he'd just stick to what he's told to say?"

"So what did you do?"

"What do you think? I told him he'd imagined it and sent him home."

"He *imagined* it? Are you serious?"

Nigel laughed briefly. "I know. But it seemed to work. On Saturday I went round and had a long conversation with him and his dad, made our position clear. He's been all right since then."

There was another question she needed to ask, something that had been plaguing her for days.

"You know Mum thinks you're Polly's—"

"I know what your mother thinks. She's got this idea in her head that I had an affair with Cassandra Leuchars and Polly was the result. Right?"

Flora nodded.

"I don't know, is the honest answer. Cassandra told us all that Polly was conceived after she came back to the U.K., that she went and got herself pregnant thanks to some donor center, or whatever they call it. We didn't see her again for nearly three years because they went off to the States and I didn't think any more of it. Look, does it even matter?"

Her mouth dropped open. "Of course it fucking matters! Are you *mad?*"

"Flora," he said. "Don't raise your voice."

"You were screwing her, Dad, and I was in love with her. She could have been your daughter! She could have been my sister!"

He sighed, so calm, so matter-of-fact. "It's incredibly unlikely. I only slept with her mother once or twice, and believe me Cass Leuchars was sleeping with absolutely bloody everyone. And it's not as if I wasn't careful. Do you have any more questions, Flora, because this subject is now closed."

Flora gritted her teeth. He'd taken advantage of Polly, hadn't he? He might have told her that their relationship had been sexual only in the last few months, but why should she believe him? He might have been abusing her for years. They'd all taken advantage of her, hadn't they? All the people she'd gotten involved with. They'd all been pre-pared to take whatever Polly gave, because she was generous and kind and loving and she had so much love it was spilling out of her, love and pleasure and desire. And none of them had been there when Polly needed them. None of them.

Not even Flora.

"We had a deal, Flora." Nigel's voice was perfectly calm. "Now I expect you to go and get me those items. Come straight back here and there will be no more said about it. Understand?"

She stood up, unsteadily. She was clearly in no fit state to drive, but he let her go. The air outside the barn was colder, the breeze bringing her back to life again. It wasn't far to the studio. The chances were, she might pass only one or two cars on the way.

11:49

It was a relief, in the end.

They took Brian back to his cell and shut the door, locked it. It wasn't silent, it wasn't even quiet, he could hear shouting from some-where further down the corridor, the officers laughing and joking at the desk, but it was good to be alone for a moment.

He hadn't cried in years. He hadn't cried when Barbara died, he hadn't felt much need to cry with pain or self-pity when he'd been in the hospital, even though he'd felt plenty of both. But he cried in his cell. Shoulders shaking, tears squeezing from between tightly closed eyelids, face in his hands.

Just a few moments, that was enough. He pulled himself together quickly. *Can't go there, no point.*

The cell door opened again and they brought him food, pasta with some sort of sauce, a bread roll, a yogurt, and a paper cup of water.

"All right, Brian?" the custody officer asked him. "Want any magazines, anything like that?"

He shook his head, accepting the tray onto the plastic mattress next to him.

"Can I see my daughter?"

"I'll see if I can sort something out. But you're feeling all right? You don't need the nurse?"

The nurse—oh God, the nurse! He'd be perfectly happy if he never saw the woman again, heart attack or no heart attack.

The officer went away again. They'd already explained all the rules to him, what he could expect from them. He had been charged with the murder of his wife and he was to be taken to the Magistrate's Court tomorrow morning. There was no likelihood of bail. Seeing the magistrate was going to be amusing, Brian thought. He knew most of them; some of them he counted among his close friends.

The food remained untouched next to him. It smelled odd, synthetic. Even the water, when he got close to it, had a metallic odor that put him off.

In the end, he had decided it would be better all round if he told the truth about what he'd done. He was so tired, in any case, so fed up with the whole thing. He could not even blame it on a momentary lapse of judgment because there had been so many of them over the years, starting with the first time he was unfaithful to his first wife, to Jean, Taryn's mother. Because once you'd done it once, no point not doing it again, was there? If he'd remained faithful, he would never have misbehaved with Polly, he would never have met Suzanne, and when he'd argued with his wife and she had fallen, he would not have allowed himself to be persuaded that killing her instead of calling an ambulance was the best course of action.

Once the admission had been made, Simon McGrath, who had been almost jumping out of his seat, changed his stance toward damage limitation, told him exactly what he might expect and how he could still get off with a lighter sentence, particularly if there was evidence that he had been coerced into this course of action by his partner.

Tired of it, so tired. He listened to McGrath and nodded, and then went ahead and answered their questions anyway.

The woman who was doing most of the questioning, with the hint of a Brummie accent, did not give anything away. The man beside her straightened in his chair, flushed, and began to fidget as Brian explained what had happened, bit by bit. Every time they asked him a question in relation to Suzanne, that would have implicated her in any of it, he answered with a "no comment."

No comment, nothing to say about that. No comment . . .

He owed her nothing, but he felt safer to leave her out of it. Taking the blame for Barbara at least meant he didn't have to see Suzanne again, didn't have to confront her, feel the force of her disapproval.

It ended with more questions about Polly.

"I don't know anything about that," he'd said.

"Did you see Polly that night?"

"I don't remember."

"Brian," Sam Hollands had said. "Let's not start that again."

He waited for the question, looking at them both.

"We have fingerprints in Polly's car—on the steering wheel, the handbrake, and the gearstick, among other places—which have been identified as yours. So the evidence suggests that at some point recently you drove Polly's car. What can you tell us about that?"

He had had to provide his fingerprints, along with a cheek swab, a search, and the loss of the last vestiges of his dignity when he'd been brought in. He hadn't even thought about it.

He took his time answering, considered making up some story about helping her to park the car earlier in the week, but there was no point. He wanted to get it all over with. The trick of it was figuring out what to say without going into detail.

"I saw Polly in town. She was upset because she had arranged to meet a friend who had not turned up and I offered to drive her home, because I thought she might have been drinking. So I drove her home."

"Which friend?"

"She didn't say."

"Come on, Brian. You drove her some distance and she was upset, but she didn't say who had upset her?"

"I don't remember."

"Where did you meet her?"

"In town, somewhere. I don't remember."

Sam Hollands had paused then, checked her notes, taken her time with the next question. He took the opportunity to fill the pause, hoping that this would deflect her attention away from Suzanne.

"When we got back to Morden there was a lorry blocking the drive to Yonder Cottage, so I pulled in to the drive of the Barn, across the road, and got out of the car to see what was going on. Polly climbed into the driver's seat and drove up the road to go in the other drive, the one that leads to the farmhouse. That was the last I saw of her."

"What time was this, Brian?"

"I don't know. Late. Half-past eleven, maybe twelve."

"And what did you do then?"

"I went home and had a bath, as I said."

There were more questions about Polly. They explained to him about the shot put, suggesting he had taken it to the quarry and thrown it over. He had not. They explained that they believed it was possible he had killed Polly in order to frame Barbara for murder. He had done nothing of the kind.

Time passed. They were still having regular breaks, but now they took him back to his cell, leaving the nurse outside, for which he was grateful. She kept checking his blood pressure and that was about it.

When they charged him with Barbara's murder, it was a relief. Now he would get some peace, he would be able to rest.

He picked up the tray of food, which had long since grown cold, and moved it over to the floor beside the cell door. He moved like an old man because sitting in one position had made him stiff and his shoulder twinged when he bent down with the tray. Then he went back to the bed and lay down on his side. Everything was uncomfortable, but he was going to have to start learning to put up with it.

Soon he would get to see Taryn again, at least. The thought of that made him smile. The only thing he had left now was her.

12:14

Hamilton had had a queasy, off feeling all morning. This wasn't like him. Yes, he was a player. Yes, he liked flirting and misbehaving when the opportunity presented itself—but this was a whole new ball game. The situation, which had started with her telling him about Brian's calculated plan to get rid of his wife—which back then had seemed almost straightforward—was now beginning to feel uncomfortable. He was used to working as part of a team. This new policy of going it alone—which admittedly was brought about by his own failure to behave himself—was not sitting well.

Karen and the kids had gone round to visit her sister, and although he had promised to stay home and put some things in the loft, he found himself pacing the living room, trying to find the way to get himself out of the mess.

In the end, he dialed Lou's number, half-expecting to get her voice mail. But she answered.

"Andy?"

"Sorry to bother you, Boss," he said, keeping his tone light. "Just wondering how it went this morning."

He could hear the sound of her heels on a linoleum floor. That meant she was in a custody suite, probably Briarstone nick.

"All fine so far."

"Has he said anything?"

"We've just charged him. He's admitted to killing his wife—accidentally. Nothing about Polly."

"What about that woman he was seeing?"

"No comment to that. He's having a rest now while we get everything ready for the magistrate tomorrow morning."

This was the moment he should have told her what was going on. Not ideal to do it over the phone, but equally the longer he went on like this, the worse it would be once the suits at Professional Standards got hold of him.

"Is everything okay with you?" Lou asked. The faint echo had gone; she must have got herself into an office.

"Yeah, yeah. I think—I don't know—I might have a few answers."

"About what?"

"A—a few loose ends. It can wait until tomorrow morning." Brian would get charged no matter what. Nothing Andy told them now would affect the visit to the magistrate tomorrow anyway. Better to think everything through, plan how to tackle it. Make sure he had all the facts.

"Andy, I don't like being kept in the dark. You know that. If you want to talk to me about it—"

"No, no. Honestly, it's fine. I'll be in tomorrow, we can talk then."

And after he'd rung off, there had been nothing left to do but get into his car and drive across town. He parked outside 14 Waterside Gardens. And before he could talk himself out of it, he was knocking on her door.

Suzanne opened the door promptly, as if she'd been expecting him, and let him inside. She was dressed in smart black jeans, a beige cashmere sweater, simple gold earrings. As always, she looked calm.

"No uniform today?" he said, trying to sound jovial.

"It's my day off," she said. "I was half-expecting to see you, Inspector. I wanted to make sure I was appropriately dressed."

"I came to tell you Brian's been charged. He's admitted to dumping Barbara Fletcher-Norman in the quarry."

Suzanne looked up at him sharply. "Really? Good heavens."

"Don't worry. He refused to answer any questions relating to you."

That made her smile. "Good for him."

"There wasn't enough evidence to charge him with Polly's murder, though."

She seemed perfectly at ease with this idea. "Would you like a coffee?" she asked brightly. "It's a bit early for wine, I think."

"Coffee would be nice."

"Are you here for sex, Inspector Hamilton? Or are we just going to talk today?"

She was clearly amused by his expression. He should know her well enough by now to realize that she took delight in wrong-footing him.

"Well. I—er—I don't think I would turn it down. If it's on offer."

Suzanne laughed, ran her fingers through her hair. "Very well, then. Let's have coffee first, shall we?"

He followed her into the kitchen, where he leaned against the kitchen table and watched her as she busied herself with an expensive-looking coffee machine, retrieved two plain white cups from the cupboard, and added tablet sweetener to one of them. Just a couple of days ago she had felt him up in here, left him shocked and breathless. It felt like years ago.

He moved up behind her and placed a hand in the small of her back. She flinched slightly. Behind her, then, sliding his hands around her waist and holding her against him while the coffee machine made a loud churning noise and dribbled dark liquid into the two cups.

"Not yet," she said, removing his hands firmly and stepping to the side, turning to face him.

"Sorry," he said, unsure of what he was apologizing for. "I thought—"

"You may touch me only when given permission. That's one of the first things you're going to have to learn, if we are going to enjoy this regularly. Do you understand?"

"I'm not sure," he said. "I mean, don't get me wrong, I really enjoy the way you do things, but I've never tried this—whatever it is—before."

"Then I shall have to teach you. That's all part of the pleasure of it, learning what you enjoy. And the same goes for me. I have particularly enjoyed making you wait for it, seeing your face when you think I'm going to reject you. And then seeing your expression change when you realize what's coming. You give a lot away, did you know that?"

"It's all a game to you, isn't it?"

"Not at all. I am deadly serious about it."

Andy gave a short, ironic laugh. "Deadly. That's an interesting choice of word."

She smiled at him. "You're right. But this is all part of why I became a nurse. I've always enjoyed breathplay, but only within the boundaries of safety. I know what a high it gives you if you're being fucked just at the moment of losing consciousness. There is no orgasm on earth as powerful, unless you're using drugs, and that's something else entirely. But there is a risk—and at least with me you know you're safe. You're always in control, you can stop at any moment. And if you choose not to stop, and you lose consciousness, then you know I can resuscitate you if need be."

"That's very reassuring. Where is it you work?"

She stared at him, crossing her legs at the knee. The coffee machine had stopped whirring. "Milk and sugar?"

"Yes, please."

She pushed one of the cups and a sugar bowl toward him, getting a spoon out of the drawer. "Help yourself."

While he stirred in some sugar—two spoons, he had a feeling he was going to need the energy—she got a carton of milk out of the fridge and passed it over to him.

"I'm doing agency nursing at the moment," she said. "I was working overseas until two months ago."

"Whereabouts?"

"Oh, all over the world. I was in Dubai for most of this year."

"Sounds great. Why did you come back?"

Suzanne laughed. "Even sunshine gets boring after a while. Shall we go and sit down?"

She carried both cups into the living room, put them on the low table, and eased herself onto the sofa.

"I can't believe how calm you are," he said.

"I'm a good actress, Inspector Hamilton. You'll get to appreciate that when we have more time to play together."

Play? Such an odd word to use. There wasn't anything casual or recreational about it. What she did was focused, determined, meticulous.

"I wish you'd call me Andy."

"If I do that it will change the dynamic of the relationship," she said. "I like things the way they are."

He picked up the coffee and tasted it. One of those fancy ones, flavored with something—hazelnuts? Caramel? It wasn't bad, anyway. Maybe needed another sugar. He was aware of her eyes watching his movements closely, unblinking, and for a moment, despite how relaxed she appeared, he had the impression of being stalked by a big cat, relaxed, purring, waiting to pounce.

"How did your colleagues take the news about Brian?"

"I'm on a rest day today. So I haven't told them. It might be that I don't need to."

"That would be good for both of us, wouldn't it?"

"I need to ask you some more questions," he said. "There are still some things that don't make sense."

"Such as?"

Andy took a deep breath in. "Polly Leuchars. Her phone called your number the night she died."

"She was just phoning to see how I was. We were friends, of course."

"But she came over to see you. The cellsite showed the phone was in this area."

"She called me. If they ever ask me about it officially, I will tell them she was probably visiting Flora and that they should ask her, not me. Poor Flora. I would imagine she's taken it very badly."

"But she wasn't visiting Flora, was she?"

Suzanne smiled. "I'm so tired of all this, you know. I wish life could hurry up and get back to normal. It's wonderfully exciting, but really rather tiresome."

"What happened, Suzanne? You met Polly in town earlier that day, didn't you?"

She drank her coffee. "She wouldn't seem to get the message that things were over between us. I was with Brian and I couldn't deal with her, too. I'm quite monogamous, you know, Inspector. I only have enough attention for one sub at a time. And, besides, Polly was such hard work. She liked bondage in particular, you know, she liked to be restrained, and I find rope play an unnecessary chore. To do it properly, safely, takes a long time. Brian was turning out to be much more fun. So I told her quite plainly that she should move aside, but she kept on and on, phoning me, asking to meet, pretending it was to be simply as friends. So I met her in town and asked her to stop calling. She said she would if I would come for one last drink with her, in the Lemon Tree. I agreed, to get rid of her."

"But you didn't turn up?"

"Brian came over. We were busy." As if that explained everything.

"So she drove over to Briarstone to find you?"

"Walked in through the back door. It was unlocked. Honestly, Brian's face. I asked if she wanted to join in, but she simply stood there over the bed, sobbing as if she was unhinged. She was absolutely distraught. Brian and I didn't know what to do with her. In the end, I told Brian to put his bike in Polly's car and drive her home."

"He did that. They had an argument when they got to the Barn."

"Yes, he phoned to tell me. The first of his many calls that evening. Polly was trying to persuade him to leave me, so that I would go back to her."

"Then what happened?"

"You know the rest. Polly drove her car back across the road to the farm. Brian went home, but Barbara had seen him pull up in Polly's car and had assumed he'd been out shagging her. They had a lengthy argument about it, lots of shouting and yelling and long miserable silences. Quite funny, really, when you think about it. Then, eventually, she got all mad and went over to confront her."

"And Brian followed her? He killed Polly while Barbara was there?"

She didn't reply, finished off her coffee instead.

Hamilton could feel the pressure building behind his eyes, the beginnings of a sore throat. He was probably run-down, coming down with the flu. He felt overwhelmingly tired by the nightmarish situation that he had managed to get himself tangled up in and the knowledge that it would get worse, much worse, unless he stopped it now, called a halt to it.

"I can't see you, Suzanne, you know. I have to steer clear."

She laughed, quite casually. "Oh, I don't think so."

"It's for your own security more than mine. They'll realize there's something going on. The more time I spend here the more risky it is."

"There's no risk. Not if you do as you're told. I said the same thing to Brian."

He didn't answer straightaway, let his head rest heavily back on the sofa cushions. He almost missed it, that last comment, thrown in so casually. And yet there it was, and as exhausting as it was he would have to ask: "What do you mean, you said the same thing to Brian?"

"You're as bad as he was, Inspector Hamilton. When things start to get a little fragile in your personal lives you go to pieces. He rang me to ask me what he should do. And he would have been fine, except he just forgot the shot put. If it hadn't been for the shot put I wouldn't have even left the house that night."

Andy Hamilton felt the blood draining from his face and hands.

He dreamed of moments like this, of suspects who were intelligent and lucid and not actually psychotic on drugs telling him exactly, truthfully, what had happened when someone had been murdered. He dreamed of it happening in an incident room, the action being neatly recorded on DVD for generations of trainee detectives, and maybe a true-life TV show. He dreamed of a confession coming in response to one particularly pertinent, insightful observation, or a question he'd placed before the suspect that was so perfect they could not help but raise their hands a little in mock surrender, before uttering whatever the nonclichéd equivalent of "It's a fair cop, guv" was these days.

But this particular confession made everything much, much worse.

What he should do, of course, was arrest her right now. She'd made a confession to him. He should cuff her and take her down and book her in, because that was what he was trained to do, and to do anything else was to take him even further down the path that led away from his police pension and now, probably, toward some sort of serious misconduct charge and possibly even imprisonment. And yet he was so shattered, so tired, he doubted he could even manage to restrain her if he had to.

"Don't you want to hear about it?"

Not really, no was what he wanted to say. *No, what I want to do is run away and hide from my wreck of a life.* What he actually said was: "Go on, then."

She took a deep breath in, looked at the ceiling for inspiration. "Where to start? Well, Brian phoned me in a panic on Wednesday night. Barbara had gone over to Yonder Cottage to confront Polly, and when she came back she was hysterical and covered in blood. Brian was trying to calm her down, trying to get her to make sense, when she slipped over on something—I guess she was drunk, that's how she was most of the time—and she hit her head on the side of the kitchen worktop and passed out. That was when he phoned me."

"You said—last night—you told me that Brian had planned it all. He was setting her up."

"I think you misunderstood. He saw the opportunity to pass the blame on to Barbara."

"So if that's the case, why did he ring you? What was it he thought you could do?"

Suzanne smiled at him. "I'm surprised you even have to ask. What is it you all want, Inspector? All of you men who think you are brave and strong and manly, but in fact are completely clueless and helpless the moment you're confronted with a problem? He wanted me to sort it out for him."

"Why didn't he just call an ambulance?"

"Why indeed. I wondered that myself."

"Why didn't you tell him to call an ambulance, then?"

She didn't answer for a moment.

"Because I saw the opportunity it presented. For Brian, and for myself."

"The opportunity?"

"He had said himself. It was his idea. He was going to kill her somehow and make it look as though she committed suicide. Then she'd be out of the way and he'd be free to be with me."

"Is that what you wanted?"

Suzanne laughed out loud, tilting her head back. "Good grief. Of course not," she said. "I never thought for one minute he'd actually do it. He had no idea who had actually killed Polly, even though Barbara was raving about death and murder and blood everywhere. Brian thought she'd been in a fight, something like that. And now she'd hit her head, it made it all rather awkward. Brian knew she'd try to impli-cate him, try to get him to take the blame for it. It was so much easier to reverse the situation, to make her take responsibility for being per-manently drunk, and a nasty bitch as well."

"You spoke to him when it happened," Andy said. His stomach was churning in a way that made him wish the bathroom wasn't so far away, even though it was just across the hall from where he sat.

"He kept phoning me for advice. Honestly, it's like he couldn't man-age to make a single decision on his own. He put Barbara in her car and then he put his bike in the boot. He wanted me to meet him at the quarry and give him a lift home—as if I'd do that! I wanted to be nowhere near him, or her, or any of it. In the end I had to give him a bloody list of instructions of things to do, things not to forget. Put her seat belt on. Make sure you don't adjust her driving position in the car, even if it's difficult to drive it like that. Check the boot of the car before you push it over the edge. Take clean clothes with you to change into and get rid of the clothes you were wearing when you did it. Have a bath when you get home. Don't clean Polly's blood out of the kitchen. It was quite simple, really. Assume Barbara had done something horri-ble to poor Polly, let her take responsibility for it."

"And he rang you when he was done?"

"He told me he'd found the suitcase with her clothes in it in the boot of the car."

"Why couldn't Brian simply have phoned the police instead of kill-ing her? She would have ended up getting the blame anyway."

Suzanne looked at him as if he was dense. "She had a head wound. He'd pushed her against the side of the worktop and she was uncon-scious. I believe he also told me that she'd wet herself, which was a detail more than I really needed, but it served to tell me that she was quite badly hurt. We couldn't risk Brian being charged with her mur-der, or GBH, or whatever it would have been."

"I guess not." It was hard to focus. All this information—the thought of all this running around in the middle of the night, Brian cycling from Briarstone to Morden—no wonder they hadn't found his car on the ANPR when they'd looked. And the small nugget of consolation—

he'd been right about that bike. The one in the ditch, covered in mud and tufts of grass. Brian had cycled back from the quarry.

"It was all fine until Brian was on the way home. He phoned me, all out of breath because he was cycling through a field, and he said we should have got something more concrete to link Barbara to Polly, to be on the safe side."

"Why couldn't Brian sort that out when he got home?"

She sighed. "Because there was a limit to what I could trust Brian not to fuck up, Inspector. Pushing Barbara off a cliff edge was one thing, going into Polly's house when he didn't need to was something else entirely."

"So you did it yourself?"

"I did it myself."

"Polly was—dead?"

"Very much so."

"Weren't you worried about leaving forensic evidence?"

"Of course. I was quite careful, but you would have needed a reason to link me to the scene, and there wasn't much chance of that. Besides, I believed that once your lot had found Barbara covered in blood, then you'd stop looking for anyone else."

She smiled at him, completely calm. It dawned on him that she was mentally unstable, might actually be a complete psychopath, and she was telling him all of this because she knew he wasn't going to survive to share the story further.

A second later and he had dismissed the thought. He was a good judge of character, always had been, and he had a nose for trouble. He was always the first to spot the fight that was about to kick off, the disagreement that was going to escalate to the use of a weapon. He was famous for it. And she was telling him all this, the whole story, because she trusted him. She was afraid of Brian, wasn't she? *Brian* was the one who'd killed his wife. Suzanne had been terrified, had turned to Andy for protection, for advice. He couldn't go back on it now. There was no path back the way he had come, there was only the path ahead. His head spun, his stomach growled and churned.

"So you took the shot put?"

"I took a bag with me. It was quite obvious that it had been the weapon. It was lying right next to her head, covered in blood. I'm assuming they found it, by the way?"

He nodded, deliberately choosing not to add that they'd worked out quite quickly that it had been thrown from the top of the quarry after the car had gone over.

"So, you see, I don't really see that there's cause to worry. What can they prove? That Brian phoned me several times over the course of the evening."

"Is that what you're going to say in interview? Your solicitor will probably advise you to go no comment. Just so you know."

She considered this. "I'll worry about it when it happens. I'm good at thinking on my feet, you know."

Really? he thought. *I'd never have guessed.*

"What would happen if they knew what I've told you? And that you didn't share that information?"

"I'd get the sack. Lose my pension. Probably face criminal charges."

"Criminal charges, really? Goodness, how dramatic." She laughed again and her voice was light when she spoke. "It puts you in a very tight situation, doesn't it?"

"We trust each other. You've trusted me, and I trust you," he said. His voice sounded as if it came from a long way away, as though he were under water.

"And it's working fine so far, isn't it? So let's just carry on as we are."

That was clearly the end of the discussion. Andy was worried for a moment that he had made her angry, somehow, but there didn't seem to be much he could do about it.

She said to him, her voice low, "Aren't you going to finish your coffee? Or do you want me to make you another?"

12:15

The MIR was empty. A few minutes later Lou found Jason in the canteen, halfway through a sandwich. He waved at her, waited while she queued up to get a coffee and a Cornish pasty.

"Good to see you eating properly," he commented, when she sat down opposite him.

"I'll have a vegan stir-fry later, all right?"

"How's it going up the road?"

She lowered her voice, but there was nobody within earshot of them. "We charged Brian. He admitted pushing Barbara's car over the edge of the quarry. He came out with this long explanation of how she fell over and hit her head, and he thought he'd end up getting into trouble for it so he went to the effort of trying to make it look like she'd killed herself."

Jason nodded. "It's crazy enough to be true."

"Les contacted Adele Francis, who did the PM—she said that the open skull fracture could well have masked an earlier head injury. She's going to take another look. We should hear back by tomorrow."

"What about Polly?"

"He still claims Barbara must have done it, but he's wavering. In all honesty I don't think he knows what happened to her."

"And Suzanne Martin?" Jason asked.

"Interesting, but frustrating. He went 'no comment' every time her name came up."

"You think he's protecting her?"

"Quite possibly. I'm going to go over his interview now and see if there's anything in there we can use, but for now I think we should bring her in for questioning and see what she has to say for herself."

She bit the end off the pasty and blew the steam out of the interior of it.

"You're gonna enjoy that," he said.

"Absolutely."

"What kind of meat is it?"

"No idea. Could be anything."

He shook his head slowly. "It's not like there aren't some healthy choices up there."

She put the pasty down slowly and decided to change the subject before she got seriously pissed off with him. "I'm also worried about Flora."

"How come?"

"She was at the nick when it opened this morning, asking to see whoever was in charge. I went down, but she didn't seem that keen to talk. Then we had to start things off with Brian, and when I got back to the interview room Flora had gone."

"That could have been about anything," Jason said.

"You didn't see her—she looked like she was falling apart."

Jason considered this while Lou chewed.

"She seems to have taken Polly's death particularly hard," Jason said. "I don't think there's anything weird about that. Love does that to people."

He had finished his sandwich and was watching her eat with an intense interest that Lou found disconcerting. Eventually she put the pasty down, wiped her hands and mouth on the paper napkin. "Why are you so obsessed with what I'm eating?"

Jason had the grace to look a little embarrassed. "Well, you know. Your arteries. You kinda need them?"

She had finished, anyway. The rest of it didn't look nearly as appetizing.

"What are your plans for the rest of the day?" he asked.

Lou drank half of her coffee in one big gulp. "I need to go and see Mr. Buchanan. Get that out of the way as quick as I can. Then I'm going to take someone and go and look for Flora Maitland."

"Isn't Andy Hamilton supposed to be watching out for her?"

"It's his day off. Isn't that typical?"

12:25

"What if I told you it was me?"

Andy Hamilton was lying stretched out on Suzanne's bed, fully dressed, although she had undone his jeans, taken off his shoes. He was feeling queasy. Definitely coming down with something. And he felt so tired—exhausted. His eyes were closed and it felt like an overwhelming effort to open them.

He hadn't fully heard what she said, but registered it as somehow important. "What? What did you say?"

"I said, what if I told you it was me?"

"You said you'd always tell the truth, Suzanne," he said, his tone measured.

"And so I do," she said. "So I'll tell you. I killed her."

"We're talking about Polly?"

"Of course."

There was silence for a moment. He stared at her, trying to focus. So many things he needed to ask, and how to handle this? How to deal with it? And he could have been cleverer with his questions, but all he could manage to ask was: "What happened?"

"She was such a nuisance. I was fed up with it. After she turned up at the flat uninvited I was just so angry with her. I went in to the cottage, up to her bedroom. We talked for a little while. She wanted me to tie her up, I refused. She wanted me to choke her. I did that for a bit but then she got upset again, so I stopped. She was getting to be so difficult, so tiresome—she didn't know what she wanted. If I left things as they were I had no idea what she might do. I tried to leave, and she began screaming and flinging herself at me. We got down the stairs and she was holding on to me. I reached for something to get her to let go, and in the end I hit her with that shot put just to get her to shut up."

Hamilton felt sick. So casual. She was so fucking casual about it, it was terrifying.

"You must have been covered in blood" was all he could think to say.

"Yes, it was a little messy. I took a pair of Polly's jeans and one of her sweaters from the laundry basket in the kitchen. When I was getting changed I heard Barbara coming in. She was swaying and I could see she was going to get the fright of her life, but it was really rather funny to watch. She didn't even see me because I'd gone into the downstairs cloakroom. She ran out again a few moments after that."

"What did you do with your clothes?"

"I put them in a big brown paper bag and hid it in the middle of the pile of bonfire pallets they set alight in the park yesterday," she said. "I'd be surprised if there's anything left. Big effigy of the prime minister on top of it, I believe."

She had drugged him, somehow. The thought came to his awareness teasingly, hovering out of reach, and then, when he grasped at
it, the realization made his heart beat faster, made him start to panic.
There had been something in that coffee. Was it all part of her game,
her fetish?

He tried to focus, tried to put all his efforts into sitting up, getting
the hell out of here.

"It's all right," she said, soothingly. Her hand was on his chest, pushing him gently back. "You don't need to move. You don't need to worry
about a thing. I need to go out in a minute, and I want to make sure
you're safe while I'm gone."

"Where're you going?" he said. His voice was slurred, like he was
beyond drunk.

"It doesn't matter. I just have some errands to run. But I need you to
stay here and sleep, and then, when I get home, we can continue your
training if you like. I have so many delicious things to teach you."

"I need to go . . . to work. They'll come looking for me . . ."

She laughed. "No, it's your day off, remember? Your 'rest day.' So
you can rest here."

The tiredness was like a heavy blanket, covering his whole body.
Something over his face, too, something soft, the breath of something
brushing his cheek. Somehow it was too much effort to open his eyes.

He could feel something pulling, moving him about, his body inert.
There were noises, too, someone else breathing. He fought through
the glue in his brain, trying to think, trying to concentrate. Her. It was
her.

"I'd like to say I'm sorry," he heard her say. "I should be sorry,
shouldn't I?"

He tried to move a hand, lift the hand as she had told him to, if he
wanted it to stop. He wanted her to stop whatever she was doing, let
him rest, let him sleep.

"I'm running out of options," she said. "This is the only way left . . ."

He murmured.

"It's all right," she said, soothingly, her voice close to his ear. "I'll
take good care of you, Inspector Hamilton."

It would be so easy to sleep.

For a moment he drifted, warm and quiet and left alone, and everything was fine.

Minutes passed.

Something happened that made him aware again. The warmth had gone and there was a chill, a breeze moving over his skin. His face was hot, a sheen of sweat on his forehead. The air around his face was warm, damp. He could not move his limbs. Something about his breathing sounded odd, enclosed. He forced his eyes open and saw only a pale light, diffused, foggy, in an odd oval shape with darkness at the edges. Like looking down a tunnel. They said death was like this, didn't they? He needed to head toward the light if there was a tunnel, and the thought of it made him want to laugh. He tried experimentally to move but nothing worked. His chest so heavy that even breathing was hard work, so much hard work.

Easier to sleep. Easier to just let go.

12:25

The visit to Buchanan's office had been mercifully brief: the superintendent had gone for an emergency dental appointment. Lou left a message with the assistants that she would brief him whenever he was free, then raced back to the MIR, phoning Sam as she did so.

Of all the people to take with her, Sam Hollands was probably the one she should not have chosen. She was busy going over this morning's interview, checking things, preparing for the trip to the Magistrate's Court in the morning. But Sam was the one Lou trusted the most. And she was probably in desperate need for some fresh air.

A few minutes later, Sam was behind the wheel of a Ford Focus belonging to Area CID. All the Major Crime job cars seemed to be in use. Despite the rules about keeping cars clean inside and out—you were supposed to run a vehicle check before you got in one, for heaven's sake—this one looked like the inside of a high street litter bin on a Saturday morning. Crisp packets, takeaway bags, newspapers—all shoved into the backseat.

Lou opened a window slightly to get rid of the scent of burger and testosterone.

They went to the farm first, and nobody seemed to be home. The farmhouse was locked up, the offices all closed and empty. No sign of any cars. For a few minutes Lou looked down the drive back toward Yonder Cottage, the stables on her left.

"Where is everybody? Place is like a ghost town," Sam said.

"Do you know where Flora's studio is?"

"Not offhand."

Lou turned and headed back toward the car. "I'll look it up while you drive," she said. "It can't be far."

In the end, they never made it to the studio. They were heading through Briarstone when Les Finnegan phoned Lou's mobile.

"Ma'am. Where are you?"

"London Road, stuck in traffic. What's up?"

"I'm just ahead of you at an RTA. Cause of your traffic jam. Can you get here quick? It's Flora Maitland. You won't believe what she's got in her car."

Deploying the blue lights and siren scared the crap out of the young lad in the stationary car immediately in front of them, but to give him his due, he moved neatly onto the pavement and gradually a path through the traffic opened up ahead of them like parting waves.

It wasn't far. About half a mile further up the road Flora's car was embracing a lamppost. An ambulance was already on the scene, as was Eden Fire and Rescue Service, who were in the process of preparing to cut the roof of the car away to get to the driver.

Sam pulled the car to the side of the road, as far out of the way as she could. Two patrols were already on the scene, one of them managing traffic, the other collaring as many witnesses as they could get their hands on. And on the pavement, grinding a cigarette with the toe of his brown leather loafer, was Les Finnegan.

"Is she conscious, Les?" Lou said, as they got close to him.

"In and out," he said. "Hard to say how injured. She stinks of booze, though. I reckon she's paralytic."

Lou looked across to the remains of the car, but there were so many fluorescent jackets grouped around the driver's window she couldn't see who was inside.

"What were you saying about the car?"

"All over the backseat: files, passports, credit cards—and this." He held up a brown envelope and opened it enough so that Lou and Sam could see the contents.

"Jesus Christ!"

A black handgun, inside one of Les's handy clear plastic evidence bags.

"What the fuck are you doing with that?" Sam said. "Sorry, ma'am."

"Couldn't bloody leave it in there, could I? Not with that lot all over the car. Anyway, don't worry. I've put in a call to Firearms, they're coming to collect it."

"I need to talk to her," Lou said.

"They won't let you near," said Les.

But she was already crossing the road, opening her warrant card and holding it up for the fire and rescue team leader in his white helmet on the way past.

"Not a good idea to get close," he said. "Can you stand back?"

"I just need a minute," she said. "Less than that. Please—it's really important."

"We need to get her out. You'll have all the time you need after that."

Lou changed the tone of her voice from one of friendly camaraderie to one that permitted no further argument. "This is a police scene. We're just waiting for Firearms support, and I need to speak to the witness. I won't take long."

"Put this on, then," he said, offering her a spare helmet and a dust mask. "You don't want to be inhaling any glass shards. And try not to get in the way."

It was way too big and must have looked comical, but at least it gave her the authority to get in close to the smashed driver's window, next to a green-suited ambulance technician. Given the state of the car, Flora looked in reasonable shape. At some point she had vomited and the inside of the car smelled appalling; an oxygen mask was over her face, blood already drying on her cheek from a cut above her eye. A quick glance at the backseat confirmed what Les had told her.

The medics were trying to keep Flora awake, chatting about inane things while the rescue teams prepared the cutting gear.

"Flora, can you hear me?" Lou said. She lifted the dust mask from her face briefly so that Flora could see who it was.

She couldn't move her head or turn it because they'd already managed to get a neck brace around her. "It's you," she said, her voice muffled slightly through the plastic mask.

"Yes, it's me. Lou Smith. From earlier. I'm sorry we didn't get longer to talk."

"My dad. I have to get back."

"Flora, earlier today you wanted to tell me something. Do you remember?"

"No . . . it wasn't that. I was wrong after all."

"You can tell me now," Lou said. The medic who was right next to her shot her a look.

"Your—what's his name?—the big one . . ."

Lou had to think for a minute. "You mean Andy Hamilton?"

"That's it," she said. "Hamilton. I wish he'd leave me alone."

Lou smiled at her. "Shall I ask Sam to keep an eye on you instead?"

"Yeah, Sam. She's nice. I don't like the other one. He's downstairs all the time."

"You need to move away now." The fire and rescue officer had a hand on her upper arm, pulling her away.

"Downstairs? You mean waiting outside for you?"

"No," Flora said, her voice becoming indistinct. "The other flat."

"I'll come and see you as soon as you're in the hospital," Lou called. "Try not to worry."

Then she was taken back across the road, picking her way over bits of plastic from the smashed bollard and broken glass to where Sam was waiting. Les was sitting in the back of an unmarked van that had just arrived. Firearms, clearly, come to take charge of the weapon. Les would be briefing them so they could take over control of the scene.

"What did she say?" Sam asked. "Is she all right?"

"I think she'll make it. I hope so, anyway. Can you do me a favor? Make sure Les stays with the car and doesn't let that evidence out of his sight, whatever Firearms say. We'll need to start bagging it as soon as the roof comes off. Don't let Traffic take over or do anything until that's done, okay? Get one of the patrols to stay with Flora, especially if she's not too badly hurt after all. I can't risk losing her again."

"We're going to arrest her?" Sam asked.

"Soon as we can, yes, I'm afraid so."

"And Nigel Maitland?"

"I'll see if I can get the surveillance team on him until we've been through the stuff and got enough to arrest him. Christ knows we'll need plenty of time on the clock to argue the toss with that solicitor of his."

"Right."

As soon as Sam had gone out of earshot, Lou pulled her mobile phone from her jacket pocket and dialed Andy Hamilton's mobile number. "Come on," she said. "Answer, you piece of crap."

There was no reply. Lou swore gently, disconnected the call, and redialed the number she had called yesterday. This time, the call was answered.

"Hello?"

"Hi! Karen, it's Lou Smith."

"He's not here. No idea where he is."

"Oh."

"Went out this morning, hasn't come back. If you find him, tell him to get his arse back here, would you?"

When she had promised to do just that, Lou hung up and looked around for Sam. She was with Les Finnegan, standing by the back of the Firearms van.

"Sam!" she called, already heading back to the car. This time, she was going to drive.

Taryn Lewis had told her—she had actually fucking *told* her everything she needed to know. Her father had said, *"She likes to kill people."* Lou had thought Brian was talking about Flora Maitland—but he wasn't talking about Flora at all, or Barbara for that matter. He was talking about *her*. Suzanne.

She likes to kill people . . .

12:40

"What do you think?" Lou said.

They were parked on Waterside Gardens, across the road from number 14. A single car, a black Mercedes, was parked on the gravel driveway, and further down the road, clearly in their line of sight, was Andy Hamilton's people carrier.

"I don't know. He could be . . . I mean, it's his day off, right?"

Lou frowned. "She's a suspect, Sam. A bloody suspect. You really think he'd . . . ?"

Sam looked like she didn't want to say it, but went ahead anyway. "You know him better than me. What do you think?"

Lou sighed heavily. "I don't want to do this, I really don't. Everything about this feels bad."

"What do you want to do?"

This wasn't something they could train you for, as a senior investigating officer, but then no situation was like any other, was it? They trained you to think on your feet, make decisions and hope to God they were the right ones. And if you made the wrong decision, heaven help you. You weighed up the pros and cons and you did your best. The only thing you could do.

"Try his number again," Lou said.

"I just did. Still nothing."

"Okay. We need to get Tac Team down here, but we're going to go in, whatever happens. Let's hope to fuck he's in there interviewing her or something sensible like that."

Sam called it in and Lou kept her eyes on the house, the two doors side by side at the front; the one on the right would lead to Flora's first-floor flat, the other one to the ground-floor flat where Suzanne Martin lived.

"They're on their way," Sam said.

A moment later, the door on the left opened and Sam and Lou both sat up straight. The woman who came out—the woman on the CCTV, without a doubt—was in a hurry. She slammed the door and hurried over to the Merc, opening it and getting inside.

"Sam," Lou began, as the Merc's wheels sprayed gravel in an arc, turning fast in the driveway. "You follow her. Call backup."

As the Mercedes flew past, Lou got out of the car and ran across the road while Sam climbed across to the driver's seat, started the car, and moved off in pursuit.

Lou's heels crunched on the gravel as she hurried across to the house. Her mind raced through the possibilities of all the things that might confront her in this woman's flat. Not least the body of Andy Hamilton. The last thing she should do was go in there by herself.

The door had slammed fast, and would not open. She rang the doorbell, knocked on the door hard. Looked in through the letterbox. Nothing. The empty hallway stretched away toward the back of the house. A smell drifted to her. Coffee, she thought. And something else, something she could not identify.

"Andy?" she called through the letterbox.

Nothing. Not a sound. Halfway up the hallway was a door to the left, and on the floor by the door was a pile of clothes, crumpled into a heap. On top of the pile, a mobile phone. Lou reached for her own phone and speed-dialed Andy Hamilton's number—and the phone inside began to ring.

That was enough. Technically she needed a warrant to enter the premises. For her own safety she should wait for backup, for the proper equipment. But under these circumstances she could argue that there was a risk to life.

She went around the side of the building, looking for a back door. There was a wrought-iron gate at the side, which opened easily. And there, a second door, glass panels top and bottom. She tried it. Locked! Fuck it.

Lou went into the garden and, holding a piece of roof tile over a drain, there was a brick. That would do it. She went back to the door. "Andy!" she shouted. "I'm coming through the back door—stand back."

Then, one arm up, shielding her eyes, she hammered the brick at the glass.

It took two blows before the glass smashed on the tiled floor of the kitchen and over the step outside. The hole was big enough to put her arm through, and to her immense relief the key was in the door on the other side. She turned it and opened the door.

"Police!" she called. "Anyone in here?"

Nothing. From a long way off, she could hear a siren. Was it Sam's backup? She must have stopped the Merc . . . that was good.

She crossed the kitchen to the door at the far end. The hallway stretched up toward the front door. To her left, a door opened into the sitting room—empty. To her right, the pile of men's clothes and a closed door. *Deep breath and open.*

It took a second to register what she was seeing.

The man was stretched out on the bed, naked apart from leather straps around his ankles and wrists, which were attached to cords leading to the corners of the metal bed frame. But his head—the most bizarre thing of all—was encased in a wooden box, his neck disappearing into a padded hole at its base. On the top of the box was an oval-shaped hole, which should have revealed his face.

The whole box was wrapped in cling film.

A second later, she realized that he wasn't breathing.

"Andy!" She took hold of a wrist, felt for a pulse. His hand was swollen, bluish already. Kneeling on the bed she could make out his face through the cling film. He was blue. His eyes open, staring, unseeing.

"Andy! Can you hear me?" She tried to pull the cling film away, tried to tear at it with her fingers, poke holes into it, but it was layer upon layer, wrapped and wound tight, and her fingers were ineffectual.

Back to the kitchen, pulling out drawers looking for a knife, a screwdriver—something! Shit, shit—nothing. And then, the last drawer she came to, a set of stainless-steel cutlery. Back to the bedroom, to the box, using a blunt dinner knife to snag at the plastic. Then there was a hole she could pull at, make larger, and at last she could see him properly.

"*Andy!*"

Her hand inside the box, touching the skin of his face; he felt clammy. He needed air, he needed mouth-to-mouth—and there was no way she could get close enough to his mouth with the box in the way.

Yelling with frustration, back to the kitchen—scissors, there had to be a pair of scissors in here—all the time wondering about how long he'd been like this, if it was already too late to make a difference. *He was dead, he was dead. Too late.*

No. Lou pulled at the door of the dishwasher. Inside, clean and shiny, a basket full of cutlery and among them a black-handled sharp kitchen knife. *Yes.*

In the bedroom Lou knelt on the bed, sawing at the cling film at the side of the box, tearing the loose bits away, pulling at strands that just became stronger until she cut them free. Once she was down to the bare wood she pulled the cling film away, exposing the box. His face was gray-blue.

The knife was slipping out of her hand, and she saw there was blood everywhere. Where was it coming from? Had she cut Andy's neck somehow? She couldn't see a wound.

At last the lid of the box could be lifted and she took hold of a handful of Andy's damp, dark hair, lifting his head out of the box and pulling it away, throwing it off the bed.

"Breathe, damn it! Andy!"

As soon as she was certain he could get air, she started chest compressions, but his body bounced on the mattress, flailing underneath her clasped fingers. She had to get him off the bed. She took hold of the knife again, hacking at the black cords that secured his wrists to the bed. The first snapped quickly, and she moved to the other arm. By the time she was sawing at the cord tethering his right ankle to the bed, the blade was blunt. The cord frayed, then gave way. The last one took the longest and in the end she gave up, abandoned the knife, and pulled at his arm to drag him off the bed with one leg still tied.

He was so heavy and inert that at first she thought she would not be able to move him. Finally she dragged the corner of the bedspread and he came with it, slithered to the floor like a dead fish.

Now she could do it. His chest was slathered in blood, and it was only when she started the compressions with all her weight behind it that she realized it was her hand the blood was coming from. "Andy!" she shouted, as much to reassure herself that he was still there.

Was she imagining it, or was his skin a more normal color? And now she could hear steps on the gravel outside. "Get in here!" she roared. "I need help! Get in here now!"

The sound of boots on the broken glass in the kitchen. "In here!"

She didn't look round but she knew they were there, both from the sound and from the muttered "Jesus!"

She didn't want to stop, not for a second, until she knew Andy's heart was beating strongly and wasn't going to stop; didn't want to see their expressions as they took in the naked officer, the cords tied tightly around his wrists and ankles, one still attached to the corner of the bedstead.

And it was only when one of them said to her, "Stop, guv, let me take over now," and his colleague, who had been radioing for an ambulance, pulled her gently to one side, taking her hand and raising it, pressing tightly against her palm, that she saw through the tears that the cut to her hand was deep.

13:02

"I'm sorry about your hand," Andy Hamilton said.

He was sitting upright on a trolley in the back of the ambulance, wrapped in blankets that were barely enough to cover him. Two hairy shins faced in Lou's direction. She was on the jump seat the technicians used, her hand bound up in a great wad of bandage, holding it still as she'd been instructed.

"It's okay," she said.

The paramedics were about to cart them both off to hospital to be checked over, but Hamilton was recovering by the minute.

"How are you feeling?" she asked him.

He gave her a look. Stupid question, of course. She'd never seen him brought so low.

"What was it?" Lou asked.

"She must have drugged me. I think it was the sweetener tablet—I thought she'd put it in her cup."

"I didn't mean that. I meant, what was that bloody box for?"

"Oh, that. I read about them. It's called a smother box."

"Sounds charming. You into all of that sort of thing, then?"

"Not anymore."

Lou's phone was ringing. It was Sam.

"Ma'am. The nominal has stopped at an office block on London Road, just past the hospital. Lots of businesses in there, according to the sign. You want me to go in? I would have intercepted her outside but—"

"Don't worry, Sam. I don't want you to tackle her without backup. What's the building called?"

"Constantine House. It's the second turning left after the hospital. Opposite the entrance to Sainsbury's."

"Wait for me there. Don't move unless she does, right?"

The back doors of the ambulance opened and the paramedic came back in. "Let's get you both strapped in, then, shall we? Time to go to hospital."

But Lou was already clambering out.

"Lou," Andy called.

His use of her first name was what made her stop.

"Be careful," he said. "She—I think this is all just like fun and games to her. She doesn't give a shit."

Lou responded with a smile he probably didn't deserve. "I'll bear that in mind. Can I borrow your car?"

13:15

Hamilton's car was surprisingly clean and tidy. She'd had to pull the seat forward about three feet in order to reach the pedals, and it wasn't easy with a bandaged hand, but thankfully it was an automatic—gear changing would have been a challenge too far. Lou sped off in the direction of the one-way system through the town center, praying that the traffic would have cleared.

She had got as far as the one-way system when the sirens started. Two marked cars overtook her at the lights and a third turned into the main road from East Park Road, all of them going at top whack and heading in the direction of the hospital. If she'd been in a job car she could have turned on the lights and followed them, but Andy's people carrier was designed for safety, not for speed.

Swearing at the cars in front of her, she went as fast as she dared until finally she could see the hospital buildings on the left, the supermarket ahead. There were blue lights everywhere and police cars parked haphazardly on the road, another inside a small car park by a squat, square office building. She pulled into the car park.

Black-uniformed officers were gathered in a crowd in one corner of the car park, but they all looked relaxed and they were starting to disperse, heading back to their abandoned patrol cars.

Lou got out of the car and went over to them. Sam Hollands was holding open the door to one of the patrol cars as an officer built like a tank helped a blond woman into the backseat. Though handcuffed, she was clearly still trying to put up a bit of a fight.

"You sure you don't want to wait for the van?" the officer was saying to Sam.

"Not if it's in Newhall, Steve. It'll take too long."

"Get your hands off me!" the woman was yelling.

The gentle helping hand became a shove. "Keep that up and you'll end up on the floor again, and we don't want that, do we?"

"Ma'am," Sam said, seeing Lou approach. She had a graze on her cheek and dabbed a tissue at it. When she raised her hand, Lou could see a nasty-looking bite mark on her hand.

"Jesus, Sam, what the hell happened?"

Sam indicated the door of the office building. "It's a nursing agency," Sam said. "Turns out she was here to collect her payslip but there had been some mix-up with it. She came out just as I finished talking to you, and she was in a bit of a grumpy mood."

From the backseat of the car, a high-pitched shout. "You have no idea, *no idea* how much fucking trouble you lot are in! How dare you!"

"Fortunately I had my radio to hand," Sam carried on—as calmly as she would be a year or so later, reciting from her contemporaneous notes in the witness box: "As while attempting to arrest her she resisted and bit me, so during the assault I was able to call for emergency assistance. PC Steve Johnson here has been particularly helpful."

PC Johnson was still standing beside the car in case the occupant decided to kick off again.

"Good job we're handy for the hospital," Lou said. "As soon as we're done here you're going to get that wound cleaned up. You might need jabs."

"I'm assuming she hasn't got rabies," Sam said. She hadn't lost her sense of humor. "I'm up to date with my tetanus and hep C."

"You bit yourself, you crazy bitch!"

"That's enough," Johnson said. "You need to calm down now."

"Shut the fuck up!"

Lou looked down at the woman through the car window. Her face was red and contorted with rage, her blond hair messed.

"Would you stay there, a moment?" Lou asked Steve Johnson. "I'd like to have a quiet word with our suspect."

"Ma'am? You sure?"

Lou opened the front passenger door and climbed in, shutting it behind her. She turned in the seat and faced the woman, whose hands were cuffed awkwardly behind her. She looked like she was calming down, her skin returning to a more normal color. She was breathing hard, her eyes a cold, pale blue.

"You're Suzanne Martin?" Lou asked.

"Who the fuck are you?" she responded.

"My name is Detective Chief Inspector Louisa Smith, and before you get carted off to the nick and we start the long and arduous process of making sure you're safe and comfortable while we interview you, I wanted to tell you something."

"I know who you are," Suzanne said. "You're his boss, aren't you? Well, no wonder he has a problem with following simple instructions."

"I'm usually a very fair person," Lou said, her voice even. "But let me tell you that in this case what I'd really, really like to do is drive this car somewhere isolated with you inside it, and rip you apart with my bare hands for what you've done to my officers. I will do every-thing that's in my power to make sure we get you convicted and put in prison for a long, long time, and when that happens I will crack open a bottle of something and look forward to you getting everything you deserve while you're in there. Do you understand?"

Suzanne's lips were a thin, tight line.

Lou had expected some sort of a response but when none came she opened the car door and climbed out, shutting the door behind her. Sam was chatting with Steve Johnson and the other patrol officer who'd arrived in the car, a young woman who obviously knew Sam by the way they were laughing together.

"Are you two able to book her into custody?" Lou asked.

"I'll go with them," Sam said. "I made the arrest."

"Only if you go to the hospital straight afterwards," Lou said.

"I will, I promise. How's Andy?"

"He's going to be okay," Lou said. It would only be a matter of time before details of Andy's rescue would filter out—no doubt distorted into a far more amusing and humiliating version of the truth—but she would not be the one to start that particular ball rolling.

She watched as the car pulled out and turned back to Andy's fam-ily wagon, noticing for the first time the child seats in the back, the grubby-looking pink fluffy rabbit in the footwell. She picked it up and nestled it into the smaller of the two car seats, debating whether to strap it in and realizing that she wouldn't have the first clue how to do it.

Epilogue
Thursday 8 November 2012

09:56

Lou had been sitting outside DCI Neal Farrar's office for twenty-five minutes and it wasn't as though she didn't have other stuff to do. She looked at her watch—again—and was considering maybe coming back later just as the door opened and he beckoned her in.

"Neal," she said, shaking his hand. "I appreciate this. Thank you."

"How's the hand?" he asked.

"Twelve stitches. Pinches a bit, otherwise fine. Thanks for asking."

"I don't think there's much I can tell you, Lou, you know that."

"I still don't understand. He's my DI. He was completely pivotal to the investigation."

"The suspect's been charged, I understand?"

"Yes, she's been charged. The search team went back in there yesterday and found Polly's DNA. Not much of it. Flakes of blood on the hallway carpet. And they found what was left of Polly's phone in the dustbin. Smashed to pieces, even the SIM. And there's plenty on her laptop about her particular kink."

"Suffocating people?"

"They call it breathplay. Every possible way to almost kill someone by cutting off their air supply. Of course, she thought she could always bring them round again, thanks to her medical knowledge. Taryn Lewis told us that her father said Polly seemed to think Suzanne had killed people before, overseas. That might be why she felt the need to come back to the U.K. We think she met Polly while she was traveling, and came here to find her. We're looking into the time she spent traveling, now. She was working as a private nurse in Dubai just before she came back to the U.K.—in a bit of a hurry. I'm hoping I might get a trip in the sunshine out of it at least."

"Well, you know where to come if you need backup."

"Funny, you're about the fifteenth person who's said that."

"What about Fletcher-Norman?"

"He's still saying nothing to us about Suzanne. Maybe now she's in custody, he will feel more comfortable talking about her."

"Interesting case, isn't it? Have you ever come across someone like that before?" Farrar leaned back in his chair, swiveling gently from side to side.

"Never. Neal, she's unbelievable. She hasn't shown any sign of remorse, at all. She seems to find the whole thing slightly amusing. Scares the shit out of me, if I'm honest. Andy was lucky to get out of there alive."

"You do realize that Andy Hamilton's behavior all through this investigation was a major cause for concern, Lou? It needs to be looked at thoroughly, and while that happens he has to be suspended."

"It will have a positive outcome, though, won't it? Please tell me he's not going to lose his job over this. He's a good officer, even though he might come across like a right fuckwit sometimes."

He managed a smile. "I know. But there are plenty of officers out there who are good at their jobs without compromising matters with witnesses. It was unnecessary, wasn't it?"

Lou felt like telling him about it all, about the affair she'd had with him herself. How he'd lied to her. How when he'd turned up on the first day of Op Nettle, her heart had sunk because she didn't want to be anywhere near him. And so she didn't trust him—her own DI—didn't listen to him, didn't give him anything decent to work on. Therefore anything that had happened to him, his decision to take risks, go it alone—surely that had been her fault as much as his? And if he was suspended for a lapse of judgment, then surely she should be, too?

She stood up then and said her goodbyes. "You'll call me if there's anything you need? A statement? Anything?"

"We'll get round to that soon enough, don't you worry."

Lou found an empty office and used it to call Hamilton's mobile.

"Hello?"

"Andy, it's me. How are you?"

There was a long pause. "All right, I guess. How are you?"

"I'm not supposed to call you. I've just been to see Neal Farrar in Professional Standards."

"Ah. Was that a good idea?"

"I'm trying to help, you big twat."

"Thanks. Appreciate it."

"Don't know what good it will do, though."

"Look, Lou. Everything works out for the best, right? It's going to be a pain in the backside but you know what? I'm at home, spending time with Karen and the kids. She's not stupid, she knows full well that my job's on the line."

"Have you told her what happened?"

"Some of it. It wasn't easy, put it that way. But for the time being, strange as it sounds, we're getting on all right. It's like I—oh, I don't know—like I forgot that I like being with them. No, I *love* being with them."

"That's good, Andy, that's good to hear."

"You take care of yourself, Lou?"

"I will. I'll see you soon. Need you on the team."

He laughed then. "No you don't. I'm your worst nightmare, remember?"

"You're everyone's worst nightmare."

She disconnected the call and looked out of the window at the former custody block across the other side of the car park. The decorators had moved in, which meant it was only a matter of time before Computer Crime moved in. Brian had been remanded; his lover was still in the custody suite at Briarstone nick, trying to talk her way out of a murder charge and yet running out of things to say now that they had some hard evidence against her.

Lou looked at her watch. She was going to fit in a visit to see Flora in the hospital, take Sam with her. Somehow she felt there was a whole lot that Flora had left unsaid, and now Lou was more than ready to listen.

Appendix

When people hear that my previous job was as a police intelligence analyst, I'm often met with a blank look, and this may be partly because of the absence of analysts in police dramas in film and in crime fiction. And yet the role is an important one that can have a significant effect on the success of an investigation.

After seven years of working for Kent Police, I am still painfully aware of the limits of my expertise. Here's the thing—the police force operates on a "need to know" basis. If you don't need to know something, then you won't hear about it. Working on a particular case, you will have access only to the intelligence that directly applies to your job, even if the investigation isn't particularly sensitive. This has nothing to do with parochialism—the data are secured by legislation, including the Data Protection Act, which means that nosing around and showing an interest in something that doesn't concern you is not only frowned upon, it is actually illegal. My knowledge of the way things work is based on my experience and what other people are able to share with me.

An easy way to describe the analyst's role is that it seeks to answer the big question "What if . . . ?" Intelligence analysts work within various departments in the police organization (and other organizations, but that's another story). Some analysts work in neighborhood policing teams, looking for patterns in what they call "volume" crime (car thefts, burglaries, and criminal damage, for example). Their work includes geographical analysis (for example, "hot spot" mapping) and temporal analysis—showing where and when crimes are statistically most likely to occur. A smaller number of analysts work in more specialized fields, particularly in serious crime. There are analysts working within the fraud and financial investigation departments; analysts who deal specifically with organized crime; and analysts who work in public protection, providing profiles of sex offenders and seeking to minimize the risk to the most vulnerable people in our society. And there are analysts working in professional standards, who provide support to corruption cases, too.

The analytical role that always seemed the most interesting to me is that of the major crime analyst. The principles are the same—looking for patterns and details that someone else may have missed, providing an easy-to-read, at-a-glance guide to whatever it is that the police need to know—but the investigation is often developing quickly, with an urgent need to get to the truth before further crimes are committed.

Phone analysis—or, to use a more recent and more accurate description, communications data analysis (for these days contact with others takes many forms)—is often a crucial part of the investigation: data are supplied, under strict protocols, by service providers, and it is often simply a spreadsheet of numbers. Historically, police officers received little to no training in interpreting these data, despite the fact that the evidence they can yield may prove vital to an investigation. In major crime incidents such as murder, rape, and armed robbery, the early hours and days of an investigation are the most important, and so the quicker the data can be interpreted, the quicker an arrest might be made.

As well as communications data, the analyst has at his or her disposal various specialized software programs to create a visual interpretation of events and relationships between nominals involved in the investigation. This may include a timeline of events, which is useful to keep track of what happened when (and to prove when a witness statement can't possibly be accurate), and various network or association charts, to highlight the links between people, places, and events.

Examples of both timelines and association charts for Op Nettle follow later in this appendix.

Often charts will expand over the course of the investigation, with the analyst printing out wall-size copies (we sometimes have access to big plotter printers, otherwise we spend ages sticking sheets of Xerox paper together) so that investigators can catch up on recent developments in the case as well as spot potential new leads or opportunities.

If the phone analysis reveals something particularly interesting— for example, demonstrating links between phones—this can also be displayed visually and interpreted further by the software. This is often used to show which phones are in use by criminal associates, weeding out less relevant numbers—takeout shops, girlfriends, family members, and chat lines. Another way charts might be used is in relation to cellsite data—and one such chart is included here.

When I first started to write crime fiction, it was important to me to try to get as much procedural accuracy as possible into my stories—a very difficult balancing act, trying to find that tipping point between the excitement of an unfolding plot and the tedium of paperwork and legal bureaucracy. Usually crime fiction tends to tip the scales in favor of drama and suspense, not only because even the most assiduous research cannot compare to years of experience in the unique working environment of law enforcement, but also because reading about "real life" police work would mostly be quite dull.

It's difficult to explain how it's possible to get excited by a spreadsheet, but believe me, it is. Spotting the beauty of a pattern in pages of numbers, or noticing that one particular contact between two phones that really shouldn't have any connection, yet they do—that's something I hope the charts that follow will convey.

It's exciting to me, anyway. The ability to assist an investigation, believing that you may hold the crucial bit of information that will unravel a case and bring a serious offender to justice, is intensely rewarding. I hope *Under a Silent Moon* will give you an insight into the role of an intelligence analyst. I have tried to keep the events surrounding the investigation into Polly's murder as accurate as I can. The world of policing in the U.K. is constantly changing, and at a faster pace more recently with even more pressure on resources and staff. Aspects of police procedure have changed even in the time it's taken to edit this story, and will likely have changed further by the time you read it. Keeping things accurate isn't easy. In the interests of plot and suspense, I have also taken some small liberties. I hope you will forgive me for that.

ELIZABETH HAYNES

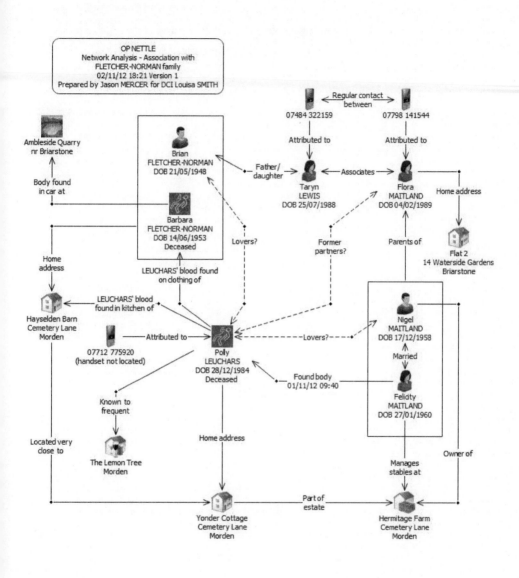

OP NETTLE
Network Analysis - Association with
FLETCHER-NORMAN family
02/11/12 18:21 Version 1
Prepared by Jason MERCER for DCI Louisa SMITH

Ambleside Quarry
nr Briarstone

Body found
in car at

Brian
FLETCHER-NORMAN
DOB 21/05/1948

Father/
daughter

Regular contact
between
07484 322159   07798 141544

Attributed to   Attributed to

Taryn
LEWIS
DOB 25/07/1988

Associates

Flora
MAITLAND
DOB 04/02/1989

Home address

Barbara
FLETCHER-NORMAN
DOB 14/06/1953
Deceased

Lovers?

Former
partners?

Parents of

Flat 2
14 Waterside Gardens
Briarstone

LEUCHARS' blood found
on clothing of

Home
address

LEUCHARS' blood
found in kitchen of

Hayselden Barn
Cemetery Lane
Morden

07712 775920
(handset not located)

Attributed to

Polly
LEUCHARS
DOB 28/12/1984
Deceased

Lovers?

Nigel
MAITLAND
DOB 17/12/1958

Married

Known to
frequent

Found body
01/11/12 09:40

Felicity
MAITLAND
DOB 27/01/1960

Located very
close to

The Lemon Tree
Morden

Home address

Manages
stables at

Owner of

Yonder Cottage
Cemetery Lane
Morden

Part of
estate

Hermitage Farm
Cemetery Lane
Morden

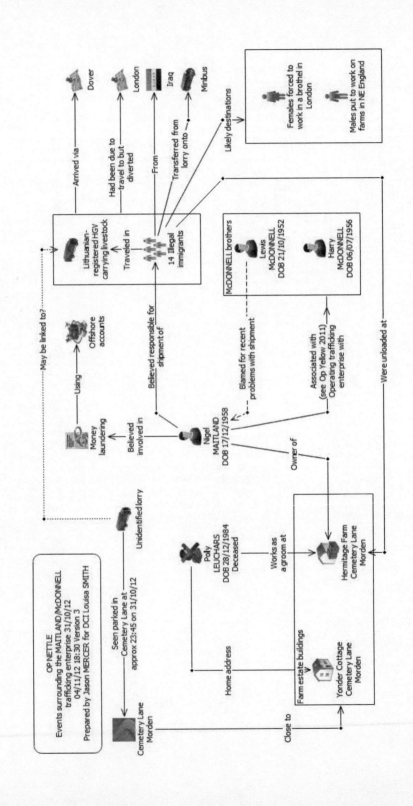

OP NETTLE
Events surrounding the MAITLAND/McDONNELL
trafficking enterprise 31/10/12
04/11/12 18:30 Version 3
Prepared by Jason MERCER for DCI Louisa SMITH

Cemetery Lane
Morden

Seen parked in
Cemetery Lane at
approx 23:45 on 31/10/12

Unidentified lorry

Close to

Farm estate buildings

Yonder Cottage
Cemetery Lane
Morden

Home address

Poly
LEUCHARS
DOB 28/12/1984
Deceased

Works as
a groom at

Hermitage Farm
Cemetery Lane
Morden

Owner of

Were unloaded at

Nigel
MAITLAND
DOB 17/12/1958

Believed
involved in

Money
laundering

Using

Offshore
accounts

Associated with
(see Op Yellow 2011)
Operating trafficking
enterprise with

Blamed for recent
problems with shipment

May be linked to?

McDONNELL brothers

Lewis
McDONNELL
DOB 21/10/1952

Harry
McDONNELL
DOB 06/07/1956

Believed responsible for
shipment of

Lithuanian-
registered HGV
carrying livestock

Traveled in

14 Illegal
immigrants

Arrived via

Dover

Had been due to
travel to but
diverted

London

From

Iraq

Transferred from
lorry onto

Minibus

Likely destinations

Females forced to
work in a brothel in
London

Males put to work on
farms in NE England

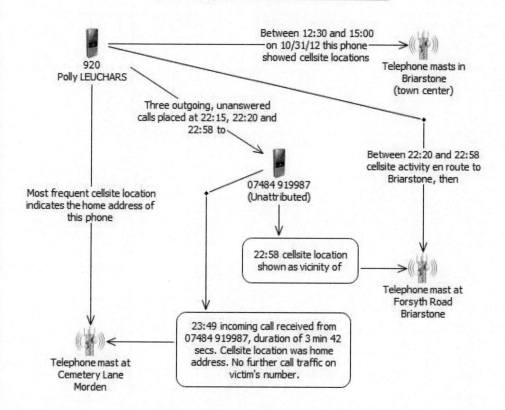

OP NETTLE
Preliminary Telephone Analysis - Cellsite
02/11/12 18:20 Version 1
Prepared by Jason MERCER for DCI Louisa SMITH

920
Polly LEUCHARS

Between 12:30 and 15:00
on 10/31/12 this phone
showed cellsite locations

Telephone masts in
Briarstone
(town center)

Three outgoing, unanswered
calls placed at 22:15, 22:20 and
22:58 to

Between 22:20 and 22:58
cellsite activity en route to
Briarstone, then

Most frequent cellsite location
indicates the home address of
this phone

07484 919987
(Unattributed)

22:58 cellsite location
shown as vicinity of

Telephone mast at
Forsyth Road
Briarstone

Telephone mast at
Cemetery Lane
Morden

23:49 incoming call received from
07484 919987, duration of 3 min 42
secs. Cellsite location was home
address. No further call traffic on
victim's number.

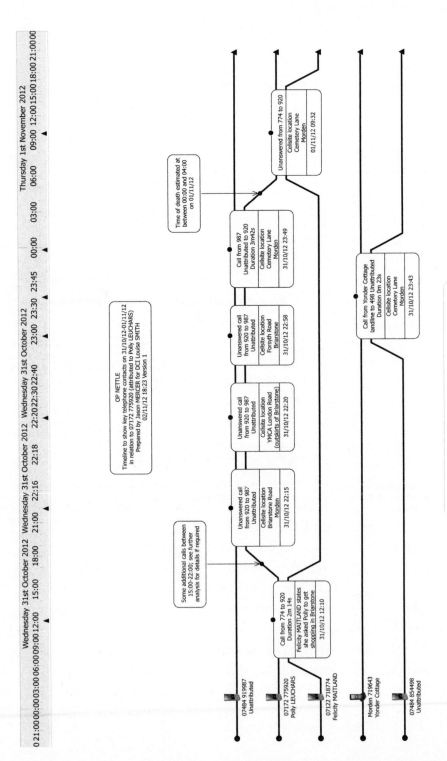

OP NETTLE
Timeline to show key telephone contacts on 31/10/12–01/11/12
in relation to 07172 775920 (attributed to Polly LEUCHARS)
Prepared by Jason MERCER for DCI Louisa SMITH
02/11/12 18:23 Version 1

Wednesday 31st October 2012 Wednesday 31st October 2012 Wednesday 31st October 2012 Thursday 1st November 2012

21:00 00:00 03:00 06:00 09:00 12:00 15:00 18:00 21:00 22:00 22:30 22:40 22:16 22:18 23:00 23:30 23:45 00:00 03:00 06:00 09:00 12:00 15:00 18:00 21:00 00:00

Some additional calls between
15:00–22:00; see further
analysis for details if required

Time of death estimated at
between 00:00 and 04:00
on 01/11/12

Call from 774 to 920
Duration 2m 14s

Felicity MAITLAND states
she asked Polly to get
shopping in Briarstone

31/10/12 12:10

**Unanswered call
from 920 to 987**
Unattributed

Cellsite location
Briarstone Road
Morden

31/10/12 22:15

**Unanswered call
from 920 to 987**
Unattributed

Cellsite location
YMCA London Road
(outskirts of Briarstone)

31/10/12 22:20

**Unanswered call
from 920 to 987**
Unattributed

Cellsite location
Forsyth Road
Briarstone

31/10/12 22:58

**Call from 987
Unattributed to 920**
Duration 3m42s

Cellsite location
Cemetery Lane
Morden

31/10/12 23:49

Unanswered from 774 to 920

Cellsite location
Cemetery Lane
Morden

01/11/12 09:32

**Call from Yonder Cottage
landline to 498 Unattributed**
Duration 0m 23s

Cellsite location
Cemetery Lane
Morden

31/10/12 23:43

07484 919987
Unattributed

07172 775920
Polly LEUCHARS

07122 718774
Felicity MAITLAND

Morden 719643
Yonder Cottage

07484 854498
Unattributed

Acknowledgments

I want to thank the brilliant team at Sphere, particularly Catherine Burke for her patience and for having faith in me when I didn't believe in myself. Lucy Icke and Thalia Proctor have also made this book so much better thanks to their genius ideas and creative input—thank you all so much! Thank you, too, to my agents, Annette Green and David Smith, who have helped me develop as a writer, and for calming me down and keeping me sane when the excitement got a bit much. I also want to thank my brilliant editor, Jennifer Barth, and the entire team at Harper in the States, especially Cindy Achar, Mark Ferguson, Heather Drucker, Kathy Schneider, Leah Wasielewski, and David Watson. I am so grateful for your hard work, your professionalism and dedication—and it's been a privilege to work with you all on this book. I hope you're as proud of the results as I am.

The first draft of *Under a Silent Moon* was written during November 2006 as part of the annual National Novel Writing Month (www .nanowrimo.org) challenge, and thanks are due to the wonderful people behind the website, without whom this book undoubtedly would not exist at all.

To my fellow NaNoWriMo participants, and Jacqueline Bateman in particular, who kept me going with write-ins both real and virtual, thank you. I assure you, it's your turn next. Lillian George helped me greatly with one particular scene, and provided support when I began to doubt whether this book could ever be completed—I'm very grateful, Lillian.

Thank you to Karen Aslett, Samantha Bowles, and Suze Dando for allowing me to use their names and for not minding how they were used. As well as lending me her name, and tirelessly listening to me wittering on about my plot, Sam had a tremendous influence on how this story developed, and many of the twists and turns are entirely thanks to her. I hope she approves of how it turned out.

Special thanks to the people who shared their expertise on various matters—and please be assured that any mistakes are mine, not theirs. To Lisa Cutts, Gina Haynes, Janice Maciver, Alan Bennett, Katie Totterdell, Alan Bennett, and Hugo Benziger, who advised on various aspects of police procedure; Nicola Samson, who put me straight on equestrian matters; Floss Wilks, for help with Fire and Rescue; Jess Adair, who helped me with Taryn's job; and Andy Kelly and Caroline Luxford-Noyes, for help with medical matters, thank you all so very much.

Sarah M'Grady, Lisa Cutts, and Mitch Humphrys all helped me enormously by reading through complete drafts of this book and making sure that I kept some degree of accuracy. Thank you!

Tricia Brassington, Jeannine Taylor, Shelagh Murry (who introduced me to NaNoWriMo in 2005 and therefore got me here in the first place), Heather Mitchell, Judy Gascho-Jutzi, and Cat Hummel all helped me to try and get Jason to speak and behave like a true Canadian. The decision to make him Canadian in the first place was all thanks to Cat—I really hope I did a good job with him.

During the editing process I decided to change the name of one of my main characters, and I turned to Facebook to help me; so I'd like to thank Chris Gage, Johanna Malin, Barb Stricsek, Lindsay Healy, Natalie Tamplin, Kate Matrunola, Sharon M. Godfrey, Jody Conklin, Jo Bober, and Becky Allatt, who all suggested that "Barbara" would be the best name for her.

I want to express my gratitude to the staff at i2 (IBM) in Cambridge, who generously gave up their time to help me produce fictional Analyst's Notebook charts for this book. John Gresty, Ron Fitch, and Steve

Dalzell looked after me and made sure I knew what I was doing with the software; Julian Midwinter, Patrick Miller, and Stephanie Juergens-Joerger worked hard to help me get the permission I needed to use the charts in the book. Most of all, I want to thank Christian McQuillan, who was the one who answered the phone to me that day and must surely have regretted it. Without doubt this book would have been a very different one without him, and I am enormously grateful for his tenacity, patience, and warmth.

As always, I'm very thankful for the support and love of my wonderful family, and especially my boys David and Alex, who put up with me. I love you lots.

About the Author

Elizabeth Haynes is a police intelligence analyst, a civilian role that involves determining patterns in offending and criminal behavior. She is the author of three previous novels: *Human Remains, Dark Tide,* and *Into the Darkest Corner,* which was selected as Amazon UK's Best Book of 2011 and is in development with Revolution Films. She lives in a village near Maidstone, Kent, with her husband and son.

CASTLES, BATTLES, & BOMBS

Also by Jurgen Brauer

Economic Issues of Disarmament: Contributions from Peace Economics and Peace Science. With Manas Chatterji. London: Macmillan and New York: New York University Press, 1993.

Public Economics III: Public Choice, Political Economy, Peace and War. With Ronald Friesen and Edward Tower. Chapel Hill, NC: Eno River Press, 1995.

Economics of Conflict and Peace. With William Gissy. Burlington, VT: Avebury, 1997.

The Economics of Regional Security: NATO, the Mediterranean, and Southern Africa. With Keith Hartley. Amsterdam: Harwood, 2000.

Arming the South: The Economics of Military Expenditure, Arms Production, and Arms Trade in Developing Countries. With J. Paul Dunne. New York: Palgrave, 2002.

Economics of Peace and Security. With Lucy L. Webster and James K. Galbraith. A volume in the *Encyclopedia of Life Support Systems.* Developed under the auspices of the United Nations Educational, Scientific, and Cultural Organization (UNESCO). Oxford, UK: EOLSS Publishers, 2003 (http://www.eolss.net).

Arms Trade and Economic Development: Theory, Policy, and Cases in Arms Trade Offsets. With J. Paul Dunne. London: Routledge, 2004.

Also by Hubert van Tuyll

Feeding the Bear: American Aid to the Soviet Union, 1941–1945. Westport, CT: Greenwood Press, 1989.

America's Strategic Future: A Blueprint for National Survival in the New Millennium. Westport, CT: Greenwood Press, 1998.

The Netherlands and World War I: Diplomacy, Espionage, and Survival. Boston, MA: Brill Academic Publishers, 2001.

JURGEN BRAUER

and

HUBERT VAN TUYLL

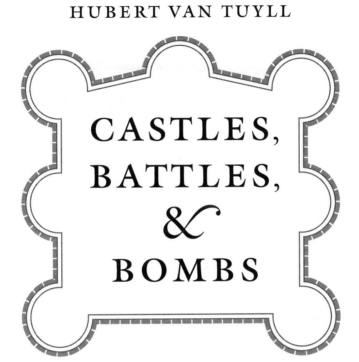

CASTLES,

BATTLES,

&

BOMBS

HOW ECONOMICS EXPLAINS

MILITARY HISTORY

THE UNIVERSITY OF CHICAGO PRESS

Chicago and London

Jurgen Brauer is professor of economics at Augusta State University.
Hubert van Tuyll is professor of history at Augusta State University.

The University of Chicago Press, Chicago 60637
The University of Chicago Press, Ltd., London
© 2008 by The University of Chicago
All rights reserved. Published 2008
Printed in the United States of America
17 16 15 14 13 12 11 10 09 08   1 2 3 4 5
ISBN-13: 978-0-226-07163-3 (cloth)
ISBN-10: 0-226-07163-4   (cloth)

Library of Congress Cataloging-in-Publication Data
Brauer, Jurgen, 1957–
Castles, battles, and bombs : how economics explains
military history / Jurgen Brauer and Hubert van Tuyll.
p. cm.
Includes bibliographical references and index.
ISBN-13: 978-0-226-07163-3 (cloth : alk. paper)
ISBN-10: 0-226-07163-4 (cloth : alk. paper)
1. War—Economic aspects—History. 2. Military
history. I. Van Tuyll, Hubert P. II. Title.
HB195.B69 2008
355.02'73—dc22
2007031667

To Leon
—J B

and to Laura
—H V T

CONTENTS

FIGURES AND TABLES

FIGURES

TABLES

PREFACE

Many readers will pick up this book for its military history, not for its economics. They may well be tempted to skip straight to a particular history of interest to them: the cost of castle building in the High Middle Ages, the nature and role of the *condottieri*, or private military contractors, of the Italian city-states in the Renaissance, generals' battle-related decision making in the Enlightenment years, "information warfare" in the American Civil War, the strategic bombing of Germany in World War II, or France's decision to develop atomic weaponry during the early Cold War years. To accommodate such readers, we have written these chapters in a reasonably self-contained and self-explanatory fashion, but an eventual reading of the economics chapter (chapter 1) should not be avoided. If first you must succumb to your appetite for history, then read the economics as soon thereafter as you dare — you may find it a surprisingly delectable dessert.

Castles, Battles, and Bombs is our attempt to write military history from the viewpoint of economic theory. By way of illustration, we study six cases. To provide scope, they span the past thousand years, the second millennium AD, that is. Five cases concern Europe, and one North America. We should have liked to expand coverage, to go farther afield and further back in time, but for a variety of reasons this seemed too ambitious. Even the cases we have chosen might strike some readers as just off the mark. For example, when one considers the Cold War period (1945–1991), what leaps to mind is the conflict between the former Soviet Union and the United States, not how France came to acquire its atomic arsenal. But what makes the case so fascinating, not just for France but for history, is that France's entry into the nuclear age changed the dynamics of the superpower clash. Before France, the United Kingdom had already acquired an atomic weapons capability, but it — then as now — was too closely aligned with the United States to be considered a fully independent player on the world stage. In contrast, France's aspiration to recover *grandeur* — then as now — threw the already dangerous nuclear game into confusion. Instead of a one-on-one Bobby Fischer versus Boris Spassky–type chess match, a third player moved pieces across the board, irking the Americans while offering no solace to the Soviets. With a multitude of states clamoring today to build, expand, and wield atomic arsenals of their own, a reexamination of what spirit animated the French in the 1950s and 1960s seems not tangential at all. What captures the economist's interest in this is the simple observation that conventional, nonnuclear forces were costing France, and everybody else, a pretty penny. To get on with the business of daily living, might France's reason to build its *force de frappe* have simply been that it would be cheaper to substitute atomic for conventional forces and recapture, if not global then European, stature in the bargain? Chapter 7 addresses this very question.

Stepping back in time, much history has been written on the Age of the World Wars (1914–1945). There is even some economic history of these calamities.[1] Much of this addresses the "economics of war," items such as the financing of war, the material resources required, acquired, and consumed, the economic impact and consequences at home and abroad, and the conversion of economies from civilian to military pursuits, in a word just the sort of issues one might expect economists competently to handle. But economics can reach further, into the operational territory of the very conduct of war. By way of illustration, we pick, in chapter 6, one dramatic instance, moreover one that would change the very conception of modern war: the strategic bombing of Germany in World War II. The press the effort received, certainly within the armed forces, was responsible for undertaking similar efforts in virtually every U.S.-led war since. Without question, the thousand-bomber raids flown over German cities were spectacular applications of brute force, but were they efficacious? That war planners might have done well to respect the economic idea of diminishing returns for the effort introduces a note of caution. Any student studying into the wee hours of the night knows that, although the effort may help to pass an upcoming exam, merely putting in more hours will not commensurately increase the exam score. As the saying goes, what counts are not the hours one puts in but what one puts in the hours. The same holds for bombing: merely throwing more bombers at Berlin might win the war but perhaps only at increasing and excruciating cost to Allied forces. Had the economic notion of diminishing returns been fully appreciated, the Allies might have pursued technological innovation in the European air war with even more urgency than in fact they did. They also might have saved countless lives, for no branch of the armed services suffered more losses, in proportion to its members, than did the air crews, and no conflagration was more searing than the firestorms the bombers seeded. If fight we must, one wonders what other simple economic concepts might have lessened loss of life.

The choice of the American Civil War as chapter 5's case study to illuminate the Age of Revolution (1789–1914) is dictated by the most important revolution of all: the industrial revolution. While the French Revolution revolutionized warfare, industrialization was not yet sufficiently advanced to much affect its conduct and outcome. In contrast, the American Civil War was the first major war fought in an industrial context. This brought, for example, new technology and, more significantly, mass production to the battlefield. In terms of information flows, three developments of the age were particularly notable. These were the telegraph, the railroad, and the newspaper. No one today needs to be convinced of the relevance of the introduction of electronic communication, which is what the telegraph represented. But because people could travel farther and faster than before, the railroad also moved information. And the newspaper, a product of improved printing and greater literacy, was used as a tool by both sides as well, as a source of information and as a way of circulating disinformation. Marrying aspects of the economics of information to the role of information in warfare is a relatively novel enterprise, certainly for the case of the American Civil War.

In military history the period 1618–1815 is sometimes referred to as the Age of Battle. This governed choosing a case closely tied to some aspect of battle. The feature we chose to examine in chapter 4 looks at commanders' decision making, namely, the decision to offer or decline battle, especially as decision making is a prominent feature of the economic analysis of behavior. The taking of this decision was a markedly prominent affair during the entire period and affected every significant campaign. Recognizing that battle was not a random event but flowed from a much deliberated choice, virtually every "great captain" of the age considered the decision to offer battle as requiring important, perhaps the most important, attention. Once battle was joined, the set of feasible remaining choices narrowed drastically, and generals' control of the situation could rapidly deteriorate. This was especially true of long battles when the opposing armies might degenerate into brawling, homicidal mobs. Battle offered the greatest possible reward — victory — but it also imposed the ultimate price: death to the soldier and loss of one's army to the enemy general. Better to offer battle with much forethought.

The employment of tens of thousands of private military contractors in the current wars in Afghanistan and Iraq has brought some public attention to the issue of how to supplement a state's "official" armed forces. The issue is not new to experts in the field. The wars in the former Yugoslavia in the

1990s already made much use of private military and private security companies, as did various states and factions in the numerous African wars in the same decade. Romantic notions still swirl around the "mercenaries" of the famed French Foreign Legion, and American readers at least will have heard about the role of "the Hessians" in the Revolutionary War of secession from Great Britain. Indeed, once one comes to think of it, purely public forces, fully staffed by conscripting a state's young male subjects, are an anomaly in history. In spite of the derisive "mercenary" and "soldier of fortune" labels, voluntary supply and demand in the military labor market have always been lively, and it is surprising that relatively little has been written about this market from an economic perspective. In one legendary instance, for example, historians generally ascribe the decline in the widespread employment of military contractors in the Italian Renaissance (1300–1600) — the condottieri so famously maligned by Machiavelli — to changing political fortunes of their employers and to certain developments in military technology. These were important changes indeed, but why not also consider, as we do in chapter 3, the nature of the very contracts (*condotte*) after whom the contractors, the condottieri, are named? The resurgence of private military contractors today demonstrates that this is a hugely important aspect of the trade to study. Perhaps the market for force can be organized very differently than entrenched habits of thought and practice suggest.[2]

Among the more obvious potential cases for the study of military behavior in the High Middle Ages (1000–1300) are the construction and use of castles, campaigns of conquest, the evolution of weaponry, war planning, the training of the individual knight, the development of the medieval army, and battle tactics. Of these, the castle towers above all. Its construction, defense, and besiegement dominated war in this era, and the increasingly positive view which historians now have of the medieval army only increases the castle's significance. Reliance on fortification seemed natural when we thought that the armies of the day were mere rabbles. But that armies turn out to be far better organized and led than previously believed makes the reliance on castles all the more interesting. The most important changes in weaponry were those which made assaults on castles possible. While battles mattered, army commanders more often than not avoided fighting, concentrating more on maneuvers designed to approach or defend castles. Yet even Europe's best knight, mounted on its best horse, carrying the best lance, and possessed of the best available armor, could not in person assault Europe's worst castle. Chapter 2, on the castle, thus complements the resurgence of historical interest in medieval armies. As we will see, in spite of the enormous amount spent on castles — on occasion, a king would lavish a whole year's revenue on a single castle — it was money well spent. Unexpectedly, a bit of economics might tell us just why this was so.

We do not presume that readers are familiar with economics and therefore set out, in chapter 1, to explain some of its principles. Curiously, no agreement exists on just what are the principles of economics, but no economist would dispute the six we discuss: first, the idea that in order to do one thing one must generally sacrifice the opportunity of doing another thing at the same time; second, the notion that incentives affect behavior; third, that decisions are made by comparing the extra benefits to be had against the extra costs incurred; fourth, that unequal information creates power favoring one party over another; fifth, the principle that, beyond some point, further applications of an input result in ever smaller yields of additional output; and sixth, the idea that people will substitute a relatively cheaper for a relatively more expensive item if the items are deemed comparable. (Apples and oranges *can* be compared, if all one wants is a piece of fruit.) These principles are (almost) self-evident, but their subtleties and implications are not, and it is part of our purpose to illustrate how these principles played out in the episodes of military history we have selected for review in this book.

In spite of significant advances in historiography since the 1960s, historical scholarship lacks generally accepted theoretical foundations. By what criteria does one select, order, and render the facts of history, and what events exactly would a theory of history predict, and predict in a way that is empirically testable and open to refutation? Historians in the United States are especially skeptical of theory. Referring to Hans-Georg Gadamer and Wilhelm Dilthey, Bruce Mazlish writes that "in general . . . historians, suspicious of theory from on high, go about their business while ignoring such arcane thinkers."[3] In this respect, military historians are no different. Even so, one way to illuminate history is to supply theory from other fields of study, such as sociology, psychology, political science, or indeed economics, or even geography, climatology, and other natural sciences, as, for instance, two recent and immensely popular books by Jared Diamond have done.[4] In these and other academic disciplines theory is more developed than it is in the realm of history. With the help of these fields of study, history might be viewed as a series of case studies in applied theory. Although the record is not bad, economics itself is not of course a body of impeccably successful theory. We ask the reader to relax and have some fun. Even if one harbors misgivings about economics, one may nonetheless enjoy what can be done with it.[5]

We should state clearly that while the book is written with the general-interest reader foremost in mind, each of the substantive chapters nonetheless makes a genuine contribution to the development of scholarly knowledge. For example, regarding the chapter on the condottieri, historical scholarship focuses on the complex politics and developing military technology of the time, to the neglect of the labor contracts after whom the condottieri are named. Drawing attention to these contracts, albeit from an economic viewpoint, marks a new contribution to that literature. Likewise, the chapter on Germany in World War II makes its own scholarly offering to the debate on the efficacy of strategic bombing that still engages historians today. And as much as has been written about the American Civil War — books alone number in the thousands — it is surprising how seldom that literature examines, as we do, the role of information in that war. Consequently, we ask the general-interest reader to overlook the copious chapter notes intended mostly for the scholar, just as we ask the scholar to bear with us when for the general reader's benefit we lay out a topic or period more broadly than the scholar might ordinarily find appropriate.

How representative are our six cases of the larger enterprise of infusing military history with economics? We do not yet know. We do know that by selecting six economic principles, rather than just one or two, and applying them to six distinct historical epochs stretched across one thousand years of history, a time period that is ambitious to cover, we have spread the dragnet widely. In our view, the results if not representative are at least encouraging: economics would seem to offer a fruitful way to (re)examine military history per se.

For comments on various portions of the book we thank Professors Jeremy Black, Mark Fissel, Jay Pilzer, Wendy Turner — historians all — and economists at the Conference on Defense and Peace Economics, hosted at Rutgers University, Newark, NJ, May 2001 and those at the Fifth Annual Conference on Defense and Peace Economics, Middlesex University Business School, London, June 2001. We further thank anonymous internal and external reviewers at the University of Chicago Press, its then-editor J. Alex Schwartz, its current editor David Pervin, and all their colleagues at the Press. We also thank Mr. Matthias Spoerle, Mr. Sertac Kargi, Mr. Nicholas Anglewicz, Mr. Milos Nikolic, and the Inter-Library Loan service personnel at Augusta State University for excellent research assistance. Capt. Joseph Guido provided highly useful comments on an early draft of the entire manuscript. For assistance with chapter 3 we thank Ms. Nadja A. Weber-Guido, Professor Kristin Casaletto, and Professor Duncan Robertson (translations) as well as Professors Stephan Selzer and William Caferro (correspondence). We also thank Debra van Tuyll (illustrations). The usual disclaimer applies: any remaining errors are ours.

A special thank you is due to Professors Peter Hall and Stefan Markowski and to all of their colleagues at the University of New South Wales campus at the Australian Defence Force Academy in Canberra, Australia. They provided one of us with a most hospitable, stimulating, and productive environment during a visiting professorship there in 2005 that substantially advanced the completion of this book.

Finally, various prepublication readers asked why we did not include a chapter on the current United States wars in Afghanistan and, especially, Iraq. Perhaps the most succinct answer is that, in contrast to the cases we use, the final data set does not yet exist. Yet if the point of economics is not just to explain but also to predict, does not the premise of our project—the injection of theory into history—demand that we be able to forecast the chronicles of the future? Whereas the psychohistorians of Isaac Asimov's science fiction achieved this feat, it would as yet be asking too much of the enterprise as others, from Marx to Tolstoy, have found out before us.[6] Let us first see whether theory, economic or otherwise, makes a useful contribution to explaining the past before we try our hand at the future again. Meanwhile, suffice it to say that while there is much to note about the economic aspects of the ongoing U.S. wars—from the economics of terrorism to the role of failed states, the rise of nonconventional forces, the formation of alliances, and the massive use of private military companies—our plans for this book were already well laid when the World Trade Center's twin towers fell in 2001. We nonetheless conclude the book, in chapter 8, with sections on the economics of terrorism, the economics of military manpower, and the increasing use by governments of private military and security companies. It may be seen, we believe, that economics well applies not only to military history but to contemporary military engagements.

ONE

Economics

Germany did not mean to launch the twentieth century and, with it, the remainder of history. In 1914, however, one of the world's most famous war plans, the Schlieffen Plan, impelled Germany to turn a developing east European squabble into the greatest, most encompassing, and costliest war civilization had ever known, a war that only later would be called a world war, for that is what it became. As the war years wore on, the slaughter was so massive in scale, and lives so appallingly sacrificed to new-fangled instruments of war such as poison gas, submarines, and machine guns, that at the time it was referred to simply and definitively as the Great War. For those who lived through it, worse horrors could not be imagined. This had to be the war of wars, the last war, the war to end all wars. On many a European battlefield, the environmental scars of that war may still be seen today. Because of its utterly pervasive effects — the still-unresolved Israeli-Palestinian conflict and the current wars in Afghanistan and Iraq are among them — most historians date the beginning of the twentieth century with the commencement of World War I.

Germany had a plan for the war. Deciding to execute it meant invading France and Belgium, which in turn could bring Britain into the war. The plan called for Germany to throw seven-eighths of its army westward, most of it sweeping through Belgium to encircle the French armies, thereby defeating France in six weeks. Then, the victorious forces would be shipped east to face the slowly mobilizing Russians. The plan was breathtakingly bold, simple to the point of genius — and risky. Its attempt and subsequent failure dramatically reshaped the world, and therefore some regard its implementation as the single most important operation in modern military history.

Almost a century later, the Schlieffen Plan still generates a lot of ink, scholarly and otherwise. Plenty of room for analysis remains, but as is so often the case of controversy in military history, and historical debate in general, many of the arguments are akin to treading water. For example, General Helmuth von Moltke, the leader of the invasion, was criticized even during the war for his failure to carry out the plan precisely as intended. The debate about Moltke still continues, with the pros and cons not much changed.

In this book, we use ideas from economics to help illuminate decision making in war. Moltke and his fellow generals might have appreciated this. The German General Staff was renowned for its methodical study of warfare, which explains Germany's astonishing success at waging (if not winning) war. Had the staff's "hard-thinking, hard-working"[1] body of officers taken on the task of applying a set of principles from the social sciences to the conduct of war, they would no doubt have produced an excellent, multivolume compendium of their findings.[2] They certainly would have found no difficulty applying economic principles to the invasion of 1914. Consider, for example, what Germany gave up by committing itself to a single war plan, which necessarily aimed its resources in a single direction. Germany could not save its primary ally, Austria. The plan was predicated on the assumption that a quick victory over France would ensure the defeat of the enemy alliance. This did not happen, and Austria suffered grievous defeats in the opening months of the war. It was not conquered, but it never fully recovered from the early disasters either. With the war, the Austro-Hungarian Empire expired in 1918. Similarly, Germany, in spending its resources on a large army, could not build a navy as big as Britain's — even though to many a German, Britain was becoming the true global enemy. Nor would German resources suffice to invade Russia, an alternative deliberately rejected by Schlieffen. None of this means that German decision makers were wrong. It simply meant that by choosing one alternative, they had to forego others. To economists, this is known as the principle of opportunity cost: taking one action costs one the opportunity to undertake another. (In chapter 2, we apply this principle to the case of castle-building in the High Middle Ages.)

Executing the Schlieffen Plan involved terrible potential costs. Germany was going to war with two, and possibly three, of its great power neighbors. There is no need here to delve into the question of who had responsibility for the war or whether Germany deliberately sought the war: what is clear is that the Berlin government did not make any attempt whatsoever to prevent it. Yet German decision makers were not reckless. They did not ignore the potential costs, at least those that were knowable. In weighing the potential costs and benefits of their actions, two considerations influenced their calculations. First, "war" seemed a cheaper option than "not war." Many German leaders believed that war was inevitable, so that entering the conflict was "free" from that perspective — the costs (such as risk of defeat, loss of life, and money spent) were going to be incurred anyway. Also, given that war was inevitable, sooner was better than later. Russia was weak but its situation was rapidly improving. To the German leadership, if war came soon, the benefits would outweigh the risks and costs; wait longer, and this would be reversed. Second, adding the French into the war did not raise Germany's costs either. Most among the German leadership believed that France would inevitably fight to help its ally, Russia. This assumption meant that there was no choice whether to add France as an enemy, but only whether to strike France first. Thus the only costs involved concerned the short-term military expenditure involved in launching the invasion. Even if one might question the accuracy of their calculations, on both points the Germans were in effect thinking about the principle of the expected incremental costs and benefits of their actions. (In chapter 4, we use this principle to examine how military leaders in the Age of Battle decided on whether to offer or decline battle.)

The decision to first take on France was by itself sensible enough as France was militarily a more powerful enemy than Russia. Before Schlieffen, Germany had planned the next war in precisely the opposite direction. German forces would attack Russia while maintaining a defense against France. This approach would leave France unmolested, however, while Russia's size would make the infliction of a decisive defeat impossible to achieve quickly. However, the shift from Russia to France as primary target involved two important choices. First, Germany would have to continue to rely on land power, not sea power. This meant that Germany could not compete effectively with Britain at sea. The British enemy would have to be fought by defeating its allies in Europe. Second, for the Schlieffen Plan to work, it had to be carried out fast. Every day of delay would give the enemy time to adjust and would interfere with the necessarily massive and complicated movement of men and matériel. This would have fateful consequences, because the need for speed forced Moltke to demand quick decisions, blocking the German government from considering more fully thought-through alternatives. Time would allow for diplomacy as well as for different military moves, but speed gave a better chance of a successful invasion. Stripped down to bare bones, one may say that Germany's leadership engaged in a series of substitutions: defeat of France and Russia was a substitute for a German assault on Britain, land power to carry this out was a substitute for naval power, and speed was substituted for time. (The principle of substitution is employed when in chapter 7 we revisit France's decision to develop its nuclear weapons arsenal, the force de frappe.)

The unprecedented size of the German invasion of 1914 created many problems. The advantages of having more troops are not absolute. For example, more soldiers imply the requirement of bigger supply lines and the creation of concomitant traffic jams. Likewise, terrain may nullify an attacker's numerical advantage. The Schlieffen Plan had called for a massive right wing to sweep through Belgium while a weak left wing maintained a defensive position in Alsace and Lorraine. Moltke had changed this somewhat, allowing himself to be persuaded by the German generals on the left wing to reinforce them and to allow them to go on the attack. This was done — and foiled by the French. Addition upon addition of German troops to the left wing provided fewer and fewer commensurate military benefits. Economists know this phenomenon well, under the forbidding label of diminishing marginal returns. (And we apply the principle of diminishing marginal returns to the case of the strategic bombing of Germany in World War II in chapter 6.)

As is true for America's involvement in Middle Eastern wars today, and as has been true for all warriors in the past, one reason why Germany launched a war based on assumptions was that certain factual information was either lacking or inaccurate. On the one hand, Germany assumed that France would attack in case of a German-Russian war, but there is evidence now that this may not have happened. Certainly the Russian government did not consult with its French ally in any way that suggests that Russia was expecting unthinking French participation. On the other hand, many German authorities believed that Britain would not enter the war — and were stunned when German troops encountered the British Expeditionary Force in Belgium. The British had in fact made fairly clear that they would intervene, but the German government chose to disbelieve this: in a sense Germany "had" the information, yet because of an information processing problem "did not have" it. In addition, the Belgians were not expected to fight at all. But fight they did, resulting in political embarrassment and causing Germany military problems. In contrast, all of Germany's western adversaries correctly believed that the Belgians would fight. These are examples of asymmetric information or, more precisely, examples of hidden characteristics about one's opponent, characteristics not revealed until battle is joined and swords are crossed.

The asymmetry may not just be about whether certain facts are known or not, or even how they are interpreted. Neither side knew for sure what kind of war it faced. It is doubtful the war would have happened if they had! The asymmetry may concern expectations rather than facts. For example, the general expectation in Germany was of a short war, especially because of the presumed superiority of the offense over the defense. Yet the reverse turned out to be the case, and every major combatant suffered the consequences. The successful execution of the Schlieffen Plan depended on quick, decisive offensives for victory in short order but instead Germany found itself mired in an interminable slogging match that benefitted no one but doomed Germany. To quote Emperor Wilhelm II, "now we bleed to death." (We apply the hidden characteristics aspect of the principle of asymmetric information in chapter 5 to the case of the American Civil War.)

There is another aspect to asymmetric information. Many students of World War I have been struck by the speed and apparent carelessness with which European governments jumped into the fray. This insouciance existed at the popular level as well and may explain why the armies of 1914 found it relatively easy to motivate their rank and file soldiers. No army suffered significant problems from disobedience or shirking. This cannot be explained by postulating superior discipline or professionalism as the majority of soldiers were draftees or reservists, many of the latter commanded by reserve officers as well. Patriotism and perhaps a prevailing, somewhat "rosy" vision of warfare explain why the leaders did not, at least then, have to worry, second-guess, or even guard against their subordinates' actions. But exceptions occurred. One, at the very end of the Schlieffen Plan advance on France, just may have cost Germany the war. The German 1st Army of Alexander von Kluck had been instructed to follow in echelon behind its neighbor, the 2nd Army, but Kluck, without informing headquarters, chose to continue his advance at breakneck pace, eventually costing Germany the Battle of the Marne and all the misfortune that followed therefrom. This is an example of a principal-agent problem. Kluck was the "agent," instructed by his superiors, the "principals," to undertake a certain action. Unbeknownst to them — asymmetric information — he disregarded the instruction. He engaged in a hidden action, hidden, at least, until it was too late. Thus ended the Schlieffen Plan. (The hidden action aspect of the principle of asymmetric information is taken up in chapter 3 with the case of the employment of private military contractors in the Italian Renaissance.)

The Schlieffen Plan encapsulates the six principles of economics that this book employs to examine various episodes in military history, stretching over one thousand years, the second millennium AD in fact. In a way, this book is the outcome of what has been called "economic imperialism," the extension of economic theory to noneconomic disciplines.[3] Just as economics has been "invaded" by insights from other fields of study, economic thinking in turn has been applied to fields as diverse as law, sociology, health care, biology, political science, human resource management, and military strategy.[4] Explicit economic reasoning has been applied to history, certainly economic history, but rarely to military history as a field.[5] Procedurally, as mentioned, we select a number of economic principles and apply them to illustrative cases of military history. But our larger purpose, by means of these illustrations, is to demonstrate that economics can usefully illuminate military history and to show that new insights can be gained by the application of a well developed theory to a field that generally lacks theoretical rigor.

The basic argument is simple enough. Planning and prosecuting war requires choices. But the provenance of economics, at least of the neoclassical branch of economics, is the analysis of decision making. Hence history, in this case military history, is amenable to economic analysis. We thus contribute to a revamping of the method of analysis in military history in which principles of economics, or principles of other disciplines, serve as guidelines with which to enrich historical analysis. Not that historians have not availed themselves of knowledge and insight readily available from other fields of study and applied it to their own; but to read and write history as seen from outside the field of history is a different task.[6] To have recourse to another discipline differs from being imbued by it. The facts of history will remain the same, but their selection, ordering, and interpretation change.

This chapter is a primer on economics and economic theory. Readers familiar with economics are encouraged to skip ahead to the subsequent chapters. Other readers are welcome to tarry or, should they feel the urge to read the history first, to return to this chapter at another time. This chapter is not a requirement to understand and enjoy those that follow, but they may be understood and enjoyed more deeply if the present chapter is read as well at some time.

We begin by sketching out the development of economic science; next we discuss the principles we have chosen to employ in this book; we conclude by describing how these principles are mingled with military history.

ECONOMICS

Economics has been defined in various ways. However defined, economics, like other disciplines, ultimately seeks to uncover an agreed-upon set of fundamental commonalities or regularities that underlie the multiplicity of observed behaviors and events. Not unlike biologists who work to understand genes and the ways in which they combine to give expression to life, economists seek to learn the vocabulary and understand the grammar by which economic life speaks. To this end, principles are proposed, tests conducted, laws promulgated, and theories constructed.

Principles, Laws, and Theories

A principle, says the dictionary, is a "fundamental truth, law, doctrine, or motivating force, upon which others are based." It is an elementary idea or, as a hypothesis, the idea of an elementary idea that must be put to a test. Some hypotheses ("God exists") cannot be put to an empirical test at all, or at least not to a generally agreed-upon empirical test. Testing ideas is difficult in fields that tend to be nonexperimental in nature, fields such as astronomy, meteorology, sociology, and economics.[7] To convert theoretical musings to an empirically testable statement is not a straightforward affair, and a specialized branch of mathematical statistics — econometrics — has sprung up that is devoted to dealing with the difficulty of testing hypotheses developed by economic theory. Moreover, even to develop a set of data to which to apply a statistical test is not a straightforward exercise.

Despite these difficulties work is done, and debate ensues. Students are trained, testing is independently repeated and reported, colleagues are won over (or skeptics die out), and the principle at hand is gradually refined to specify the exact conditions under which it is said to apply. If all goes well the principle matures to become a law, "a sequence of events in nature or in human activities that has been observed to occur with unvarying uniformity under the same conditions." An assembly of such laws may be combined to constitute a theory, "a systematic statement of principles involved," "a formulation of apparent relationships or underlying principles of certain observed phenomena which has been verified to some degree."[8] Ideally, our theories would explain past, and predict future, behavior and events. In a world of uncertainty, we want them to be reliable guides as to what was, is, and will be. Theories are structures of thought, alive in the minds of their users. There is now evidence that theories get codified as behavioral routines, hard-wired into brains and central nervous systems ("lions eat zebras; zebras smell lions; zebras run"). Emotions may be little more than codified rational behavior.[9] Codified rational behavior is not necessarily contemporaneously rational: what may have been rational in the past may not be rational today, but we continue to act on it. Without contradicting theory, observed behavior may thus deviate from that postulated by theory.[10] Even so, theories are not always internally consistent, and rarely do they completely explain all observed behavior and events. (For example, the Standard Model in physics struggles to unify general relativity with quantum physics.) Consequently, theories meet constant challenge and debate, and from time to time they need to be amended, or even overthrown altogether.[11]

The principles of economics that are said to occur with lawlike regularity and that aggregate into a theory of (neoclassical) economics then are best viewed as guidelines of where to look and what to expect. The modifier — neoclassical — suggests a particular theory within the economics profession. There are other economic theories.[12] For the most part, they pertain to the field of macroeconomics, which studies the measurement, theory, and policy regarding topics such as inflation, unemployment, sustainable economic growth, and how to smooth the ups and downs of business cycles. In contrast, microeconomics focuses on understanding individuals' motives that guide their behavior and then aggregates these across many individuals into observable large-scale outcomes.[13] For example, individual behaviors in the financial markets combine to help determine bond prices and interest rates, which, in turn, affect the economy at large. Likewise, microeconomics studies how individuals contribute to collective decisions, such as members within a family, employees within a firm, or politicians within a congress or political assembly.

Neoclassical Economics

Neoclassical microeconomics, from the classical foundation given by Adam Smith to the marginalist revolution provided by Alfred Marshall to the modern formulation initiated by Paul Samuelson, is sometimes referred to as "pure economics," to distinguish it from the more messy, less tractable "political economy."[14] Pure economics — at least in its highly stylized, indeed cartoon version of modern-day economics textbooks — postulates a set of behavioral principles by which a rational human being, the infamous *homo oeconomicus*, goes about his or her decision making. Individual decisions bring about collective consequences. The study of these decisions and the consequences they entail is at the heart of neoclassical economic analysis.

Early neoclassical economics — again, in its stylized version — progressed by making a number of assumptions that would lighten the economist's analytic workload. For example, the models used to explain observed behavior generally are ahistoric. The analysis is static rather than dynamic. How an economic agent moves from one point in time to another is not explored. Time does not exist. Neither does space, as the early models do not explicitly consider the significance of distance, topography, or climate on decision making. Similarly, in championing the analysis of production and mutually beneficial but competitive market exchange, pure economics assumes the absence of conflict and appropriation, surely a drastic narrowing of the scope of the analysis. Further, the models assume that economic agents possess perfect information about themselves, about each other, about product prices and qualities, and about every relevant piece of information that would be important in coming to a rational decision about costs incurred to be weighed against benefits received. Indeed, rational decision making itself is assumed, even as the reasoning skills required of decision makers may lie far beyond their intellectual powers. The models further assume the presence of well functioning institutions such as well defined property rights and the frictionless enforcement of such rights. They assume that when buyer and seller engage in trade, they do so without affecting anybody else who is not party to the deal. They assume, that is, that spillover or side effects on other people's well-being do not exist. The list of assumptions goes on.

Provocatively, one may say that this cartoon version of pure economics constructs and studies situations in which perfectly rational economic agents trade in a friction-free, spaceless, and timeless world. It is then also a perfectly useless world—or so proponents of classical political economy would argue. For if everything of interest is assumed away, then what is left to analyze? Nonetheless, even political economists acknowledge that the principles of pure economics would drive the economic system if only the existing imperfections could be removed, not by assuming them away but by proper government regulation and intervention in the marketplace. In contrast, neoclassical economists argue that what is proper is not regulation and intervention but the constructing of more advanced models that relax the restrictive assumptions of the cartoon models; after all, not only can private markets fail to deliver, but so can government. Thus, neoclassical economics hopes to gradually subsume its critics. And indeed, there now exists a school of thought, called "new institutional economics," whose purpose it is to bring analytic rigor to old-style political economy.[15]

Improvements

New institutional economics is not the only school that has improved upon the cartoon model of pure economics. It is instructive to study the economics Nobel Prize awards. First awarded in 1969, the prize is frequently awarded to those whose work has loosened the constraining corset of assumptions (see the appendix to this chapter). Of the fifty-eight recipients (as of December 2006), sixteen received the prize for empirical or methodological work; nine for work in macroeconomics; five for work in international economics and finance; five for work in financial economics; and twenty-three for work in microeconomics.[16] The prizes to Mirrlees and Vickrey (1996) and to Akerlof, Spence, and Stiglitz (2001), for instance, were awarded for their work on asymmetries in market information. Herbert Simon (1978) was honored for his work on "bounded rationality," the exploration of the consequences of our limited rational capacity. The press release announcing Simon's prize reads, in part:

> economists in the 1930s began to look at the structure of companies and at the decision-making process in an entirely new way. Simon's work was of the utmost importance for this new line of development. In his epoch-making book, *Administrative Behavior* (1947), and in a number of subsequent works, he described the company as an adaptive system of physical, personal and social components that are held together by a network of intercommunications and by the willingness of its members to cooperate and to strive towards a common goal. What is new in Simon's ideas is, most of all, that he rejects the assumption made in the classic theory of the firm of an omniscient, rational, profit-maximizing entrepreneur. He replaces this entrepreneur by a number of cooperating decision-makers, whose capacities for rational action are limited, both by a lack of knowledge about the total consequences of their decisions, and by personal and social ties.[17]

Similarly, Daniel Kahneman (2002), a psychologist at Princeton University, received the prize for work on understanding consumers' purchasing behavior, which, just as firms' decision making, is not quite as rational as the cartoon models would have it. Ronald Coase was recognized for a double achievement. As he puts it in his 1991 Nobel lecture:

> The view of the pricing system as a co-ordinating mechanism was clearly right but there were aspects of the argument which troubled me . . . Competition . . . acting through a system of prices would do all the co-ordination necessary. And yet we had a factor of production, management, whose function was to co-ordinate. Why was it needed if the pricing system provided all the co-ordination necessary?[18]

Who needs firms if rational, fully informed economic actors can instantaneously (timelessly) and costlessly (friction-free) issue orders for some amount of sisal to be transported to a weaver who forwards the resulting product to an assembler who has received pieces of processed lumber to produce a hammock to be shipped to an end-user by separately contracted shippers? (And all this in a one-dimensional, spaceless world.) In the real world, the costs of arranging these transactions (sensibly called "transaction costs") are so overwhelming that no one person would ever come to enjoy repose in his or her hammock. Hence the need for managers and firms. They economize on transaction costs and take a cut of the resulting savings as their reward.

The other part of the work for which Coase was honored concerned the inclusion of spillover effects (or "externalities") into the supply and demand apparatus of pure economics. A railroad and a locomotive producer privately contract as buyer and seller. But when the locomotive is put to use, it belches nitrous oxides into the air that, transported by the prevailing winds, rain down elsewhere as acid rain, kill trees, acidify mountain lakes, and damage tourist areas hundreds of miles away, quite possibly in another country. A private deal between two parties thus affects a third, and that third party is not compensated for the damage done. The third party is compelled to bear a cost that affects its operations. Clearly, this is economics but the cartoon model does not recognize such side effects. Coase remedied this shortcoming, which, unlike his transaction cost idea, is now standard, even in elementary economics textbooks.

The larger point of the discussion here is twofold. First, the cartoon model is limited because its assumptions limit its applicability to the variety of real-world behaviors and events we would like to understand. These limitations are gradually overcome as theorists relax the assumptions; the flower of economics then blooms more fully. Second, however, is the recognition that within the simple models of economics there are embedded some fundamental principles that continue to hold true, and perhaps especially so, in the fully blossomed versions of economic models. Never mind time, space, and rationality: more fundamental than even these are a set of underlying principles. In the following sections, we discuss six of these — opportunity cost, expected marginal costs and benefits, substitution, diminishing returns, and the matter of incomplete or asymmetric information (which comes in two flavors). The operation of each of these is matched with a case from military history later in the book. There is no universal agreement on what the principles of neoclassical economics are, but few economists would dispute that the ones we have chosen would be among them.

PRINCIPLE I: OPPORTUNITY COST

The cliché has it that we live in a world of limited resources and unlimited wants. Many point out that humanity need only reduce its wanton craving for a materialist life-style for earth's limited material resources to stretch much further. As regards economic science this is ill-informed on a number of counts, not the least of which is that economics deals with nonmaterial as well as material wants, for instance, wants for leisure time to spend with one's family, wants for fellowship with friends, wants for solitary or communal spirituality, and wants for beauty in nature and in artifacts. These wants face resource constraints. One in particular is time. In any 24-hour day, one's wish for companionship may clash with one's wish for solitude. One has to choose which one to indulge at any given time. One's wish for two spouses may clash with one's wish for social respectability in one society or, in another, with one's inability to provide for them. One's wish to study theology may clash with one's need to work for worldly rewards to secure physical survival. Even multibillionaires cannot do everything they wish to do. Even Bill Gates and Paul Allen, the fabulously rich cofounders of Microsoft Corporation, have to choose from among the multitude of wishes they harbor.

Choosing, and pursuing, any one want necessarily entails not choosing, not pursuing, one's other wants. For everything one chooses to get, there are other things one chooses to give up. These other things are of value, and one incurs a cost by foregoing the pleasure of indulging in them. The one thing that one does choose costs the opportunity to pursue other things. Every choice one makes entails an opportunity cost — the cost of not pursuing the opportunity of doing something else. It stands to reason that the things we give up are less valued than the thing we choose. The things we give up are, nonetheless, of value to us, only not as much as the things we do choose.

Students easily understand this fundamental principle of economics: attending lectures implies not goofing off (which also has its value); studying for an exam or putting the finishing touches to a term paper implies foregoing yet another wild party (which also has its value, at least to students); spending hours at library research or spending hours in the laboratory imply not spending hours at one's part-time job (which also has its value). The principle of opportunity cost, at its simplest, means nothing more than the mundane realization that trade-offs exist and choices must be made. What of it? Why would that be so important? It is important because economics makes a prediction: it is that of the multitude of valuable things from which they must choose, people tend to choose the one thing that is most valuable to them, given the conditions prevailing at the time the choice is made. They choose the one thing that, if not pursued, would carry the greatest sacrifice, the highest opportunity cost.

Would economics then not predict hedonistic behavior — all students always goof off? Not at all. As Alfred Marshall himself explains in a useful example, the law of gravitation explains why objects tend to attract each other, given a set of conditions (known as the *ceteris paribus*, "all else being equal," clause). These are specified in exacting detail by the scientist but not in colloquial conversation. Thus, a piece of chalk thrown up into the air, instead of "attracting" earth, smacks back down to the floor not because the law of mutual attraction (gravitation) is wrong but because one of the footnotes regarding the law of gravitation has much to say about the relative mass of the two mutually attractive objects in question. Similarly, a helium-filled balloon — to use Marshall's own example — does not smack down to the floor at all; without violating the law of gravitation it instead smacks up into the ceiling! Likewise, in an unconstrained — unconditioned — world, students might be expected to goof off always but in a less fantastic world even students realize that some study does have its uses, worth foregoing short-term pleasures. A sailboat in calm seas tends to stay upright but when tossed about by wind and waves it does not. The physical laws by which the sailboat tends to stay upright are not revoked by wind and waves. Wind and waves are merely the conditions within which other laws of physics acting on the sailboat — such as that of inertial stability — operate. Theories are not necessarily wrong just because we do not observe predicted behavior. Instead, we need to carefully isolate and enumerate the set of conditions under which the observed behavior or event occurred. In some fields of study this is more involved than in others. For this reason, Marshall thinks of physics as a "simple" science and of economics as a "complex" science, but a science nonetheless.

To use limited resources in the face of unlimited wants necessarily implies constrained optimization, the maximizing of value constrained by the conditions at the time a choice is made. At any point in time, applying scarce resources to any one purpose is costly because the same resources cannot be used simultaneously for another purpose. Eisenhower's famous statement is an example of recognizing opportunity costs:

> every gun that is made, every warship launched, every rocket fired signifies, in the final sense, a theft from those who hunger and are not fed, those who are cold and are not clothed. This world in arms is not spending money alone. It is spending the sinew of its laborers, the genius of its scientists, the hopes of its children.

Arms are not necessarily the wrong thing to spend dollars on. Eisenhower's statement is nonetheless true: a trillion dollars spent on a ballistic missile defense shield is a trillion dollars not spent on alternative uses.[19] The example is useful because it throws into sharp relief the question of whose opportunity cost we are to consider. Who makes the decision? Who does the choosing? One of the constraints under which public, rather than private, choices are made is that it is usually not feasible to poll all members of society as to the opportunity cost of weaponry. We would, moreover, expect to obtain a wide variety of individual valuations. How should and would we compare them? Do we simply add them up and compare that value to the values arrived at for the various alternatives? But who enumerates the alternatives? These are not only difficult questions; they are genuine questions. They illustrate that opportunity cost is associated with specific decision makers; they illustrate that it may be in certain people's interest to become decision makers; they illustrate that other people may contest one's right to or appropriation of decision-making power. And what happens when the conditions under which decisions are made change? One of the conditions of decision making is the decision maker him or herself. If the decision maker changes, so does the valuation. Mom makes different choices than Dad does. The Republican party chooses differently than the Democratic party. Merely recognizing that there are alternatives from among which to choose may change one's valuation. "Am I not destroying my enemies when I make friends of them?" asks Abraham Lincoln.

We learn that the principle of opportunity cost touches on a host of rather more fundamental philosophical nerves. Humdrum questions concerning mere money with which the popular mind ordinarily and wrongly associates the field of economics are but a small part of it. Economics, we learn, is strongly bound up with questions of freedom such as who has the right to choose from among which alternatives. We also learn, as economist Paul Heyne points out, that opportunity cost is a concept tied to action, to decisions, to choices, not to things.[20] A baseball "costs" ten dollars, say. But, no! What the baseball "costs" is not the ten dollars but whatever else the ten dollars would have bought now (current alternative consumption) or in the future (deferred consumption). Money is merely a means of transmission between two possible actions. Even more important, one of the alternatives is not to buy anything at all but to donate the money to a charitable cause so that the recipients can make decisions of their own.

We learn that economics is not a material science at all; it is not physics or engineering. Instead, it is a science of decision making, concerning material and immaterial matters. It is a science of decision making under conditions that are frequently ill-specified, nebulous, and uncertain: shall I marry you, or someone else? The focus on decision making and opportunity cost can lead to surprising answers to innocuous questions. To use one of Heyne's examples: regarding intercity travel, we know empirically that poor people tend to take buses and rich people tend to take airplanes. Why? The "obvious" answer is that the empirical regularity is observed because poor people do not have the money to pay for air travel, and bus travel is cheaper. An alternative answer lies in the observation that a $400/hour lawyer traveling from New York to Los Angeles by bus becomes a rather more expensive lawyer! The lawyer's opportunity cost of time spent traveling by bus is immense. Much better (cheaper) for the client to pay the lawyer to take the airplane. Poor people's time tends not to be valued as highly, not even by themselves.

Careful attention to opportunity cost stimulates us to think, and think again. Here is another example: why are divorce rates so high in modern culture? Are high divorce rates a sign of decadence and moral decline, as some would have it? Is our social fabric really tearing apart? Or is it a matter of thinking with care about the opportunity cost (especially for women) of staying married? A few hundred years ago (and in some societies even today), a woman's alternatives to being married to a man were few and unpalatable: they included joining a nunnery, becoming a spinster to live at home with parents, and social disgrace in case one's natural instinct led to out-of-wedlock childbearing. Sequential partnering was possible but only if the first spouse died and one could "honorably" marry a second time. Women had few options to obtain an education to earn a livelihood independent of their natural or acquired family. The alternatives were bleak, of little value, and not much was given up by getting—and staying—married. But the conditions under which the marriage choice must be exercised have changed. Today, the opportunity cost of getting—and staying—married is much higher as women give up much higher-valued opportunities. To a woman, the value of being married to a man has not increased nearly as much (if at all) as have the values of her alternatives. Men are getting relatively cheaper, as the value of what must be sacrificed by getting and staying married rises. It follows that men are more easily dispensed with, and also more easily reacquired.[21]

If nothing else, we learn that economics, here in the form of the principle of opportunity cost, rearranges the way we view and interpret behavior and events. And this is what we hope to accomplish in chapter 2, our chapter on fortresses, castles, and siege warfare during the High Middle Ages (AD 1000–1300). Just why would kings build insanely expensive castles, castles so expensive that just one of them could swallow a whole year's worth of kingly revenue to erect, let alone to maintain? One answer may be that, despite the expense, it was the most valuable among the available, conceivable, and feasible alternatives at the time. Or so the economist would predict.

PRINCIPLE II: EXPECTED MARGINAL COSTS AND BENEFITS

If one already owns a stable of fifteen race horses, what does one give up by foregoing the sixteenth? The usefulness of each additional race horse declines, given that one already has the others. The more one already has, the smaller the sacrifice of what one is to forgo. We can say that we become bored by having the sixteenth horse, or we can say that we have become satiated with the first fifteen. When one is newly wedded, to forgo even one minute with one's new spouse is costly indeed. But after twenty years, giving up a minute (or an hour, or a week, or — indeed — the spouse!)[22] may not seem so costly anymore.

The essence of the marginalist revolution in economics is that "no matter where you go, there you are."[23] What counts, given the accumulated satiation — the benefits and costs of one's past actions — is the anticipated benefit and cost of one's next action. What counts is to evaluate the next step one takes, not the totality of all steps one took to get to where one is. One loves one's spouse of twenty years much more than one loves football, but what matters, say the marginalists, is whether one spends the next three hours with him or her or at the football game. One loves the spouse more than one loves football but, at the margin (the next three hours), one loves football more than one loves the spouse. Love grows old, not cold. It does not matter, say the marginalists, that Bill Gates already has earned billions of dollars in the past. What matters is whether selling the next copy of the Windows operating system software brings in more revenue than it costs to produce and sell it. If so, his earnings will increase and that copy should be produced and sold. Having already eaten half a dozen slices of pizza, one cannot really derive much additional benefit from eating the next, the seventh, slice as well. It profits one little. Moreover, one would need to pay yet another five dollars for it, and the five dollars represent other goods and services (including saving the dollars for future use) one would need to forego.[24]

This marginalist view of life may seem an uncommonly crass, and crude, point of view to take but it does have its insights. The view was brought to full bloom by Alfred Marshall, whom we encountered before. The title page of his *Principles of Economics* textbook bears the motto *natura non facit saltum* ("nature does not leap") — this was prior to Bohr and Heisenberg — and he explains that catastrophic events such as earthquakes and floods are those requiring advanced study, to be undertaken after one has studied the generally smooth, gradual, and slowly evolving changes in nature.[25] Similarly, in economics we first study the "ordinary business of life," reserving for later study those phenomena that are "spasmodic, infrequent, and difficult of observation."[26] Nature does not leap. It proceeds gradually, one step at a time. Life happens at the edge, at the margin. Contemplating the benefit to oneself of one's next action, and calculating what one may need to give up, involves decision making concerning the future. Since the future is uncertain, decision making involves expected marginal benefits to be weighed against expected marginal costs, and the decision rule is straightforward: if the expected incremental benefit of an action outweighs its expected additional cost, then do engage in that action, and vice versa. If the expected additional benefit of watching a three-hour football game exceeds the expected cost of not spending those three hours with one's spouse of twenty years, then, the rule advises, go ahead and watch the game.

Decision making is decision making subject to degrees of uncertainty. What if the game is boring and one has overestimated the expected benefit? What if one misjudged one's spouse and one underestimated the expected cost? Life is an "experience good," an economist would say. We learn as we proceed. Early calls in life will frequently turn out to involve misjudgments, and we lose rather than profit. Over time, we learn to minimize the number of our mistakes; we make better decisions; we win more often than we lose. We grow more cautious, we become cleverer, we collect better information about costs and benefits to be expected. Economists do not deny that people make mistakes but they generally do deny that any one person will make the same mistake over and over again. One might eat a rotten apple but one is not likely to eat a second rotten apple. One will not ordinarily buy another novel of an author whose first novel one could not stand, and one will become more judicious about watching football games when one's spouse objects.

How does one form expectations of benefits and costs in the first place? Obviously, information is critical, and we address this in another section. For now, consider the troika of factors that an elementary economics textbook would list: preferences, resources, and prices. At first blush, prices of various goods and services are easy enough to establish. A piece of chewing gum goes for fifty cents; tuition, room, and board at a private college goes for $40,000 a year; and a ride to the space station can be had for a mere $20 million. In practice, we face at least two difficulties: first, many prices are negotiable and, second, many prices are nonmonetary. Granted, at the check-out counter of the local Wal-Mart, one is unlikely to succeed negotiating the price of a pack of chewing gum. Instead, one will either pay the posted price or not undertake the purchase at all. But one will negotiate the purchase price of a new car. And by applying for a variety of scholarships, one effectively negotiates the price of attending this or that college.

The final price that one is willing and able to pay for any good or service one desires has a lot to do with one's valuation of the expected benefit. So long as the benefit exceeds the final price one pays, one's net benefit is positive. Put differently, one's cost/benefit ratio is less than one where cost refers not to the cost of provision but to the cost of acquisition, to the price one paid. That price can be nonmonetary, and it certainly can include secondary costs. For instance, whatever the market price of a copy of Microsoft's bundle of word processing and other office software, the cost of acquisition may include a "switching cost" of moving from the current software with which one is familiar to a piece of software with which one is not familiar. A low market price by itself may not suffice to induce one to buy something. This is a general observation that applies not only to output markets (markets for finished products) but also to input markets (markets for the inputs firms use to produce goods and services). For example, crucial to the operation of labor markets is the cost of hiring and training one's work force as well as other nonwage costs such as employers' social security contributions. Costing requires a careful look at the full cost of acquisition. To make matters even more complex, further costs include the costs of contracting, contract fulfillment, and contract supervision and monitoring, that is, transaction in addition to transformation (production) costs.[27] There is some risk of contract failure, of someone reneging on contract terms, and the plain fact that many contracts specify obligations to be fulfilled in the future. But since the future is uncertain, legitimate differences may arise as to how a contract is to be interpreted. Dispute resolution may be needed, and that is costly as well. It is so easy to write that all a good decision needs is to figure the difference between expected benefits and costs. How is a military commander to calculate the risk of troop desertion? How is he to calculate the benefit of attacking a particular enemy position?

A second factor in the cost/benefit calculus concerns available resources. This includes current earned income, savings from past earned income, credit lines, and grants. Just as in the case of prices that can be monetary or nonmonetary, economists treat these resource categories generically, not literally. For example, in a military manpower context we might think of "savings" as the stock of troops, of "current income" as the regular flow of new recruits, of "credit lines" as additional troops such as army reserves we might be able to tap, and of "grants" as troops allies contribute. Past unspent income (savings) can be augmented by military training, an "interest" payment that shows up, say, in higher combat readiness and performance. Current income can decline through attrition and desertion. And so on. It is thus not so clear what exactly one's resources are. They can be magnified by alliances, which entail their own risks and costs, and they can be diminished by withdrawal from an alliance. They can be raised by complementary inputs that increase productivity, such as an increasing capital/labor ratio, or lowered by inappropriately adjusting a military's "tooth-to-tail" ratio (the ratio of front-line combat soldiers to back-office support staff).

The cost/benefit calculation begins to look formidably, even forbiddingly, complex. Yet surely it is preferable to do one's best calculation rather than to act by default? Not necessarily. Like the postman who delivers "time sensitive" junk mail, many decisions have to be taken under time constraints. At times, decisions need to be made instinctively, come what may. Preparation and training can improve one's instinct. They become institutionalized routines when the cost of information processing to conduct cost/benefit calculations becomes too high.[28] In simulations, one role-plays under controlled conditions before having to act in real-world events. But training drains the very resources training is meant to enhance. Quickly one enters a circular argument where real-world decision making is best prepared for by simulation exercises that are costly to conduct and drain resources, wherefore more resources are required to prepare for some actual, but uncertain, future event.

The third factor — "preferences" or "tastes" — is another catch-all term. It pertains to one's likes and dislikes, to fashions and fads, to wants and to needs. Preferences are an economist's black box. What a purchaser likes is not subject to dispute: *de gustibus non est disputandum,* as Chicago economists George Stigler and Gary Becker entitled their famous 1977 essay. This does not mean (or does not necessarily mean), as they point out, that tastes will be fickle, capricious, wildly fluctuating, and unruly. To the contrary, they propose that tastes are quite stable. What changes is not one's taste but the prices one faces and the available resources with which to satisfy one's taste. As a consequence, observed behavior can change even when — despite appearances — the underlying preferences or tastes have not. The argument is cleverly constructed, but the underlying insight is simple. Suppose for instance that one likes "good" music. One's appreciation of good music can be enhanced quantitatively by spending much time listening and qualitatively by studying music. In consequence, one is building up a stock of knowledge, music knowledge. Knowledge is capital. As capital accumulation increases, time spent listening to good music is more efficiently (enjoyably) utilized. The cost/benefit ratio of listening falls as the numerator, the cost, drops. If income and the prices of other goods and services are unchanged, a lower cost of music appreciation — on account of one's built-up music appreciation capital — will naturally induce one to listen to more good music. A self-reinforcing virtuous cycle is generated. The observed behavior is that one spends more time listening to good music — or reading good economics — but the explanation is not, Professors Stigler and Becker emphasize, that one's taste for a certain type of music has changed but rather that the underlying relative price of music acquisition has changed. (Of course with opposite signs a self-reinforcing vicious cycle, a harmful addiction, can be generated whereby people increasingly listen to "bad" music.)

Nonetheless, Harvard's late John Kenneth Galbraith argued in his celebrated book *The Affluent Society* (1958) that the consumer is not entirely sovereign. The consumer's supposedly sovereign preferences are in fact manipulated and shaped by powerful interests, both private and public.[29] Preference formation and decisions as to what, and how, and how much we value things has become an active area of research for public policy, marketing, psychology, economics, sociology, and other fields of study. Beyond the elementary textbook, this can be a fiendishly difficult subject matter: how, for instance, does one value the existence of whale sharks, redwood trees, avant garde art, or the survival of Papua New Guinean highland cultures? What benefit does one assign? How does one convert each of these into monetary equivalents, so that one can compare the value of whale sharks to the other items on the list of unlimited wants? If we were to survey the public, and asked how much money it would be willing and able to pay to ensure the sustainable survival of whale sharks, how would we ascertain whether it offered a considered and truthful reply?

There is no need here to enter into the mysteries of the literature on preference elicitation, revelation, and economic valuation. Suffice it to wonder how a military commander might arrive at valuations of expected marginal benefits and costs of various possible courses of action to make a determined, rational decision on a course of action to take. And suffice it to note that, in military and nonmilitary contexts alike, decisions are rarely made in isolation. Thus, a ruler may decide to engage in war, but his commander may decide not to. The ruler may replace the commander, but soldiers may decide to desert. In chapter 4, we illustrate the operation of the principle of expected marginal benefits and costs by examining battles, maneuvers, and commanders of the Enlightenment centuries (the seventeenth and eighteenth centuries), concluding with a consideration of Napoleonic warfare. As we shall see, even as complexity triumphed, there is no question that commanders carried out expected marginal cost/benefit calculations of one sort or another.

PRINCIPLE III: SUBSTITUTION

We can travel either one of two routes now. We can begin to home in on the economics of information and contracting or further explore the economics of (opportunity) cost and benefit. We will stick with the latter for the next two sections (substitution and diminishing returns), then take up the former in the remaining two sections (information and contracts), giving us our total of six principles of economic analysis.

The principle of substitution says that if two goods yield comparable benefits users will eventually drift toward usage of the good with the relatively lower price. (Of course this price is understood to reflect the full opportunity cost.) Alternatively, the principle may be restated as predicting that users of a good or service with comparable cost will eventually drift toward usage of the one offering higher benefits. More simply: if the benefit is fixed, people reach for the lower-cost item; if the cost is fixed, people reach for the higher-benefit item.

For illustration we may once again go from the silly and simple to the realistic and complex. Economists differentiate between substitution in production and substitution in consumption. An example for the former is a bakery manager wracked by indecision over whether to use white-shelled eggs or brown-shelled eggs for baking goodies. As there is no usage difference between the two—neither for the baker, nor for the ultimate consumer—the bakery will obviously choose the cheaper eggs regardless of the color of the shell. More realistically, a firm needs to decide how to ship its products. For intercontinental shipments it may choose between air freight and a containerized cargo ship; for transcontinental shipment it may choose from among air, rail, road, inland waterways, and various combinations of these. The benefit may be defined simply as product delivery or, a bit more realistically, as product delivery subject to a time constraint. The firm may further choose between developing and using in-house transportation capacities (having its own fleet) and contracting out or again a combination of these. Shipping becomes a matter of optimizing more or less complex logistics where the objective is on-time delivery and the constraints include production, warehouse, and customer locations, various capacity limits, shipping options, and of course prices. The number of variables to be considered can be very large. Mathematically, anytime one of the many variables changes, the optimal solution to the shipment problem may change as well. No wonder that shipping decisions in real-world companies require high-level skill sets among employees, especially in mathematics and computing. While no one would deny the complexity of logistics in military affairs,[30] the same complexity in business affairs is not equally appreciated, perhaps because it appears less often to the public eye. It stems, at any rate, from possibilities of substitution.

Substitution possibilities come in degrees. We speak of perfect substitution in the case of the white eggs and the brown eggs. The coefficient of substitution equals one. Substitution in the classroom is possible, but not perfect.

Professor Brauer, the economist, may substitute for Professor van Tuyll, the historian, but the former is not nearly as good at teaching history as is his esteemed colleague. Whereas this is not usually a problem that arises in the college classroom it is much more of a problem in the nation's elementary, middle, and high schools where, each morning, thousands of frantic phone calls are made to find a "substitute" teacher for a biology or math or English class. The production of education suffers. In the extreme, the coefficient of substitution is zero. Neither white nor brown eggs can be substituted for the flour, a million-dollar carpet-weaving machine cannot be substituted to serve as the truck that transports the carpet, and even though either Tiger Woods or Anika Sorenstam can be employed to hawk golf balls and golf clubs, neither will model for the other sex the latest in fashionable golf clothing. Substitution is a matter of degree.[31]

The possibility of substitution can induce fierce struggles, full of cunning, passion, and intrigue. Girls can choose from and substitute among a selection of boys, and boys from among a selection of girls. Marriage is a social device to limit substitution possibilities for a higher social purpose (the unimpeded rearing of children). In the medical field, hospital administrators substitute relatively cheap registered nurses for more expensive medical doctors. As nurses become expensive in turn, hospitals substitute bedside technology for nurses. Meanwhile, health maintenance organizations serve as institutionalized providers of medical second-opinions and can force substitution of one treatment plan for another. Pharmaceutical companies weigh in and offer substitute, drug-based treatment to reduce severity of illness and to speed up time of recuperation. Much of this takes place in an environment of skewed incentives and asymmetric information (on which much more in later sections).

The possibility of substitution goes to the essence of competition. It is not surprising that providers go to great lengths to stifle, limit, and restrict competition. Keeping out competition is tantamount to reducing the coefficient of substitution to zero, and there are many ways of keeping out the competition. A good many of these ways are illegal — for instance, for competitors to join in a collusive cartel — but many are entirely legal, for example, a merger or acquisition approved by the antitrust division of the U.S. Department of Justice (or their equivalents in other lands). Other ways involve intervention in the legislative process with various forms of lobbying to, for example, restrict imports of competing products from abroad. A favorite tool here is to claim special risks to the health and safety of U.S. consumers from imported goods such as unpasteurized French cheeses. An example more closely related to the subject matter of this book is that various industries have trotted out a national security argument to obtain protection from import competition. Among the more notorious cases is that of the U.S. wool and mohair industry, which from 1954 to 1994 received a yearly subsidy, the sum total of which came to billions of taxpayer dollars. If not keeping the competition out, it certainly kept plenty of sheep and goat herders in.[32]

Substitution in production is massive and pervasive. So is its flip side, substitution in consumption. As a user of mohair, one would rather have the option to choose between U.S. mohair and, say, Australian mohair. If there are in fact no discernible quality differences (as is often the case in commodity markets such as for metals and agricultural products), so that the benefit to the user is identical, then the user would be expected to go for the cheaper option. To rig the cost/benefit ratio, attempts are made to influence users' preferences, hence the "Buy American" campaign that if nothing else is at least more friendly than the "no foreign cars on this labor union parking lot allowed" campaign. One surmises that the proudly strutting union fellows buy nothing but made-in-America fly-fishing reel, wear only made-in-America plaid flannel shirts, and slog about in made-in-America john-boats only. In reality, they behave as all consumers do: substitute, and save a dollar — they do use Yamaha outboard engines after all.[33]

There are still other forms of substitution. An important one carries the fancy label "intertemporal substitution." The classic economics textbook example is that between consumption today and consumption tomorrow. Subtract one's tax obligations from one's earned income and one can do only one of two things with the net income: consume it or save it. It is immediately obvious that saving is just another word for deferred consumption.[34] Misers and inveterate savers prepare for a rainy day, or early retirement, and, at any rate, future consumption. In contrast, those who live it up as if there were no tomorrow, even to the extent of going into debt, pull future consumption forward in time. Substitution over time is common practice. Substitution over time applies also to nonmundane topics and nonmodern societies. When certain ancient societies offered blood sacrifice, they substituted one life for the expected benefit of those remaining behind, alive. When martyrs die for their cause, they substitute present earthly life for an expected future life in heaven.

Incentives play a great role in inducing substitution. This also goes for intertemporal substitution. Delaying childbirth from one's twenties to one's thirties or forties implies substitution decisions, however hazily made, between education and the early career years with parenthood and the later career years. It is no accident that more highly educated people tend to delay childbearing. The opportunity cost of having children early is to sacrifice (to some degree) advanced education and getting a good start in one's career. In the case of the monetary consumption-or-saving decision, interest rates play a crucial incentive role. Even dirt-poor people can be induced to save if the interest rate is high enough. As before, Marshall's ceteris paribus clause applies. A high interest rate by itself may not induce people to forego current consumption. After all, future consumption beckons only those who have good reason to believe that there will be a future. If one is living with AIDS in southern Africa, one's time-horizon is short, and one will discount the far-off future heavily. Likewise, if one is living in a region constantly torn by civil strife, it is entirely rational not to save for a future that one does not expect to come. Good economic decision making has little to do with literacy or numeracy. "Peasant-economics" works because economics revolves around available sets of incentives and options from among which to choose. Poor, desperate populations of peasants understand incentives and options just as well as do rich, spoilt, bratty children in suburban America, as indeed does every living creature.

We illustrate the operation of the principle of substitution in military history in chapter 7 with a look at France's substitution of strategic nuclear forces for its increasingly expensive conventional armed forces.

PRINCIPLE IV: DIMINISHING MARGINAL RETURNS

Combined with the ceteris paribus clause, the notion of the marginal leads straight to the notion of diminishing returns. If nothing in the world has changed except that one is now eating a second plate at the all-you-can-eat diner, one will experience a diminishing sense of satisfaction as one compares the enjoyment of the first to that of the second plate (because one is already somewhat satiated from having eaten the heap of food on the first plate). Granted, some may be so hungry that the second plate feels as good as the first. The principle of diminishing marginal returns merely claims that eventually a sense of satiation sets in, if not by the second then perhaps by the third or the fourth helping, commonly expressed as "oh, boy, am I stuffed!" As before, the principle applies both to production and to consumption, and it applies to noneconomic areas as well. If nothing in the world changes except that students spend extra hours studying for final exams, they will at first add mightily to their knowledge base but, sadly, eventually each extra hour will result in fewer and fewer additions to their production of knowledge. If nothing in the world changes except that one spends extra hours in the gym, one will at first add mightily to one's muscle mass but, sadly, eventually each extra hour in the gym results in fewer and fewer additions to muscle mass. One is "topping-out." And if nothing in the world changes except that we open borders to

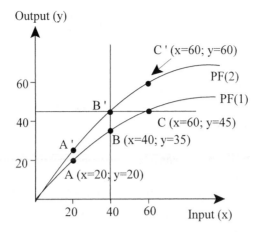

Figure 1.1. Production functions

immigrants, the economy will grow (because more people work and contribute to domestic production) but, sadly, eventually the economy will grow at declining rates as ever more people need to share the same capital stock.

These examples share the characteristic that more of a thing is not necessarily desirable. As professors, we regularly hear of students who work hard instead of smart. Yet, as noted before, what counts is not the hours one puts in but what one puts into the hours. Smart studying refers to the underlying "technology" by which studying is done. Figure 1.1 illustrates the point. It is a two-dimensional graph, and so we can depict changes in only two variables, one the "cause," the other the "effect." For now, we hold all other things in the world unchanged (Marshall's ceteris paribus condition). Along the horizontal or x-axis, we measure the effort that students exert in terms of number of minutes of study (input). On the vertical or y-axis, we measure the result, students' success or failure, in terms of points earned (output). Of course some students study little and still receive good grades while others study much but nonetheless receive poor grades, so that there will be no perfect one-to-one correspondence between minutes studied and points earned. Instead we display the average tendency, culled from thousands of (hypothetical) data points, with the line marked PF(1), where PF stands for "production function." This line suggests that a student studying twenty minutes on average receives twenty points (point A in the figure), a student studying forty minutes on average scores thirty-five points (point B), and a student studying sixty minutes on average earns forty-five points (point C). Of course, at the point of origin no study earns zero points![35] Thus, the first twenty minutes of study result in twenty points, the next twenty minutes in an additional fifteen points (for a total of thirty-five), and the next twenty minutes in another ten points (for a total of forty-five). Each additional set of twenty minutes of study results in a higher overall point-total, but at a decreasing rate. This is a visualization of the concept of diminishing marginal returns.[36]

To do better, students can work smarter. For example, they can take and conscientiously rewrite class notes regularly throughout the term, they can form study groups, they can complete assigned homework and unassigned problems, they can pester the professor with questions, and they can rid their study environment of distractions. In a word, they can change the "technology" of study. Technically, this means that Marshall's ceteris paribus condition has been violated. One of the many variables previously held unchanged now has changed. We display the effect in our two-dimensional figure as a shift from PF(1) to PF(2). Students with better technology (A′ versus A; B′ versus B; and C′ versus C) obtain more points, on average, than students with poor technology, that is, poor study habits. Indeed, the way figure 1.1 is drawn, the student at point B′ (at forty minutes of study) obtains the same exam score, on average, as the student at point C (at sixty minutes of study). Put differently, a student at B can choose between adding a technology to arrive at B′ or an extra twenty minutes of study time to arrive at C, either case yielding the same higher score. Alternatively, the student can add both and end up at point C′. An empirical point to bear in mind is that observation of the exam score does not tell us how the student did it. We need to observe the inputs as well. To consider how the student chooses study times and study technology we need to know, in accordance with our earlier discussion, the "prices" students face and the "resources" available to them. For example, if a student is shy, the "price" of joining a study group is high.

Similarly, a firm that adds more labor to its existing but unchanging capital stock, shop-floor layout, and work processes will initially obtain more production but at eventually declining rates. First, specialization improves output per employee (productivity increases) and lowers the cost per unit produced; then, crowding sets in, reduces productivity, and increases costs. If the firm is not careful, too many workers working the same machine will get in each others' way and output falls. Put one, two, and three people on a shrimp boat and the catch improves. Put one, two, and three-hundred people on the boat, and it'll sink (with a catch of zero). The heart of the matter is to shift the production function upward by working smart, not hard. The trick lies in judiciously adding technology to one's pursuits. But what about the student who would add not merely one study innovation, but two, or who would remove not one, but two distractions? Say in addition to eliminating a distraction the student joins a study group. And what about the firm that would add one, then another one, and then a third innovation? (Visually, we would display this as further shifts in the production function.) It stands to reason that here, too, there are natural limits one runs into. Coping with one new technology at a time is quite possible. Coping with three, five, or ten new technologies involves learning, coordination, and management costs that may well sink the student (or the shrimp boat). There are limits to "economies of scale." General Motors becomes Giant Motors — too big and complex for its own good.

A folksy example for lovers of American football lies in the fact that the average weight of linemen has increased from around one hundred and eighty pounds in the 1920s to nearly three hundred pounds in the 2000s. Concurrently, their sheer strength and speed has increased as well. A lineman of 2008 would truly strike horror in the ranks of the linemen of 1928! But speed, strength, and size are gradually acquired attributes as nutrition and physical and mental training (physiology and game film) have improved. But a four-hundred-pound lineman will be nearly as useless today as he would have been in 1928. Too big and too slow, he would literally embody diseconomies of scale. Yet given another eighty years of (we hesitate to write this) "technological progress," and he may well fit on the line by the year 2088.

The key to productivity then is technology, generously interpreted as changes in variables otherwise held constant. Because of the operation of the principle of diminishing marginal returns, economic theory predicts that we should observe an intrinsic drive among competitors to go from a difference of degrees (more input of the same kind, with diminishing returns) to a difference in levels (a switch to inputs of a different kind, with rising returns), that is, of technological and strategic innovation. This would apply to warfare as well. Throwing more men into battle will surely increase the carnage but not necessarily procure victory: "Gentlemen, that was magnificent; but it is not war," commented General Pierre Bosquet on one such slaughter, the Charge of the Light Brigade in the Crimean War.[37] In chapter 6, we illustrate the operation of the principle of diminishing marginal returns with a renewed look at the strategic bombing of Germany in World War II. We find that strategic bombing did yield diminishing returns, an economics lesson that military decision makers may have yet to fully appreciate as even recent strategic bombing campaigns illustrate.[38]

PRINCIPLE V: ASYMMETRIC INFORMATION AND HIDDEN CHARACTERISTICS

Information is so important that some physicists and computer scientists describe the entire universe solely in terms of its information content.[39]

Information plays a crucial role in life. Every breath we take depends on physiological information: a rise in carbon dioxide in our bodies beyond a critical level produces a signal that stimulates our respiratory system to expel used and to inhale fresh air. Information also plays a crucial role in the economic take on life. Information problems can be grouped into two general classes: those involving hidden characteristics, dealt with in this section, and those involving hidden actions, dealt with in the following section. To appreciate the first, consider this charming story told by textbook authors Michael Katz and Harvey Rosen.[40] Many years ago, one of them (they do not reveal who) took a train ride in what then was Yugoslavia. Along the way, a merchant boarded the train and offered to sell a pure-gold bracelet for $50. The potential customer voiced doubt about the bracelet's gold content, and so

> the merchant bit into the bracelet and held a match to it to prove that it was pure gold. Not seeing the point of either of these gestures, the author again expressed his skepticism. The seller responded by offering *two* bracelets for a *total* of $50. "Too much," he was told. So he threw in a gold ring and offered the package for $40. "But are they really gold?" he was asked. "Yes, pure gold," and to prove his sincerity the merchant offered two bracelets and two rings for a total of $5. "No, thank you," said your wily author, "at that price they couldn't possibly be real gold."

The seller and the buyer faced asymmetric information. In particular, the seller knew something about the goods that the buyer did not. The bracelets and rings are said to have had a hidden characteristic about them, namely, whether they truly were made of pure gold. One might have thought that the buyer would not easily be able to ascertain the seller's truth claim, but in this case the potential buyer found a "wily" way to elicit that information at zero cost. In other instances, it is the buyer who possesses information that is hidden, information that the seller needs to elicit. The standard example concerns the purchase of health insurance. One is likely to know much better than the insurance company whether one is healthy or ill, and the very fact that one wishes to buy insurance may be suspect. Thus, the insurance company needs to elicit information about one's health status (the hidden characteristic). Moreover, it needs to elicit truthful information.

It is important to emphasize that the hidden characteristic problem is an information problem that occurs before an action is taken (before the bracelet is bought, or before the insurance policy is signed), that is, before an irrevocable commitment is made.[41] The side with the superior information possesses potential market power and that, in turn, leads to two problems. First, market power can be exploited in that the side with superior information obtains a better deal than otherwise would have been possible (the bracelet is traded at $50). Second, the fear of being subject to market power (exploitation) will stifle the market and lead to a reduced amount of trading (the bracelet, even if it were of pure gold, is not sold). We see that the development of truth-revelation mechanisms becomes a crucial aspect of the operation of markets. Unfortunately, while truth-revelation is at times costless, as in the case of asking clever questions about the "gold" bracelet, in other cases eliciting true information about hidden characteristics is costly.

Here is an example that straddles the border between the costly and the costless, namely, the invention of a truth-revelation mechanism that is *less* costly than a widely used alternative. It concerns the case of eliciting truthful information from bidders at auctions. In the standard, ascending-bid auction one's incentive is never to reveal the full amount at which one values an item. Instead the incentive is merely to top the next bidder. Let us say that one participates at one's favorite annual charity auction. One fancies an item there and values it at $250. The auction begins at $50. The bidding seesaws back and forth. If the auction price reaches beyond $250, one's silence reveals one's true valuation and one is out of the running. But if the auction stops at $175 one has saved, by not telling the full truth, $75. One also made the charity $75 poorer than it could have been. Shame on the bidder? Or shame on the auctioneer for using a poorly designed auction mechanism? One alternative is to use a sealed-bid auction, in which each bidder submits an envelope with a single bid. The highest bid is accepted. But even here the incentive is not to tell the truth. If one believes that the next highest sealed bid will be $174, then one will bid $175 to win — and save $75 relative to one's true valuation of $250. Once more it is in one's interest to bid just above what one believes the next bidder's envelope contains.

The key to the difficulty is that auctions that link one's bid to someone else's bid encourage strategic bidding instead of truth-telling. To get one to reveal the truth, the link between oneself and other bidders must be cut. Instead, a link must be created between the bidder and the item. In 1961, William Vickrey of Columbia University (and corecipient of the 1996 economics Nobel Prize) came up with a cunning solution — the second-price auction — in which the highest bidder wins but pays the second-highest bidder's bid. Suppose the item on the auction block is worth $250 to one bidder and $230 to another. The first submits a secret bid of $250, the other fellow submits a secret bid of $230. When all bids are revealed (opened), the first wins the item but pays only $230. This works because if one continues to hide the truth and submits a bid of only $175 one loses out to the person bidding $230. From this, we learn three lessons. First, dishonesty does not pay (one does not get the item). Second, honesty does pay (one does get the item). And third, the truth-revelation mechanism does not work perfectly — after all, the charity gets only $230, even though the winning bidder valued the item at $250.[42]

Signaling and screening are other ways to deal with hidden characteristics. A signal is an observable factor taken as a proxy to reveal information about the hidden characteristic.[43] The uninformed party uses the signal (the proxy) to screen the informed party. For example, if one requests fare quotes today to fly from Chicago to Honolulu tomorrow, one is issuing a signal about the urgency of one's travel plans. The intensity of the urge is a hidden characteristic but the call today about flights tomorrow is a good proxy. Airlines' fare schedules reflect this by generally charging higher fares for short-notice buyers and low fares for those booking weeks in advance or who otherwise signal that their travel has an optional quality to it. Weekend travelers, for example, are more likely to be tourists who might as well fly to other destinations on other airlines. (It must be said, though, that airlines have become infamously good at reading signals to extract value even from their vacation customers.)

Signaling and screening explain why one should definitely dress down when shopping for a car and definitely dress up when shopping for a job! Wearing dumpy clothes to the car lot and fine clothes to the job interview is, however, a signaling strategy easily imitated by all. The signal is there but it is overlain by "white noise" and cannot be used effectively to screen. Car salesmen are trained not only to look one over but to elicit further information: what does one do for a living, where does one work, and where does one live? Does one need financing? Does one have another car to trade-in? And, hey, why not sign the deal right now, today? Verbal and nonverbal information elicited this way strengthens the signal-to-noise ratio and determines the initial "discount" off the sticker price. Similarly, at the job interview, the fact that (almost) everyone wears a nice suit does not allow firms to sort applicants. Hence the demand for and supply of additional signals or pieces of information: solid grades on one's high school or college transcript, a well-done résumé, good, credible reference letters, and personal networking, vetting, and vouching all help to separate the future star employee from the merely mediocre one.

Signaling and screening help overcome information problems, at a cost. The costs can be substantial (e.g., getting quotes from a variety of car dealers; job résumé and interview preparation). In fact, the costs can be so substantial that otherwise desirable trades do not take place at all. Even worse, in a number of markets we observe utterly undesirable effects. Called adverse selection, the most famous case in economics is George Akerlof's "lemon" model of 1970 (work for which he shared in the 2001 Nobel Prize). Simply put, only the seller of a used car knows whether the car is reliable or a "lemon" (reliability being a hidden characteristic). Knowing that they are at an informational disadvantage, prudent buyers offer low prices. But low prices discourage sellers of high-quality used cars from participation in the market. This is an instance of adverse selection: only sellers of low-quality used cars—the lemons—remain in the market. Akerlof extends the adverse selection idea to explain features of certain other markets. In health insurance markets, it is the sick, not the healthy, that apply in disproportionate numbers for insurance coverage. But those that apply are not those the insurance company wishes to cover. In credit markets in developing countries—Akerlof discusses India—deficiencies in credit-risk information lead to a disproportionate number of applicants that do in fact pose high credit risk; hence the success of microbanking, which is community-based and can tap into community-based knowledge of an applicant's creditworthiness. (This resulted in the 2006 Nobel Peace Prize being awarded and shared between the economist founder of one such bank, Muhammad Yunus, and the bank, the Grameen Bank in Bangladesh.) Akerlof's model also explains apparent discrimination in employment markets. When a job applicant's abilities are difficult to observe a priori, proxies may be used that might be individually undeserved but serve as a "good *statistic* for the applicant's social background, quality of schooling, and general job capabilities."[44]

Readers may find it difficult to believe that discrimination can occur "statistically," as an unintended consequence of search costs rather than as an intended consequence of prejudice. (Scholars do not deny that personal discrimination occurs, only that statistical discrimination is a credible, alternative or at least complementary explanation.) But statistical discrimination, the use of information about average characteristics of a group to predict an individual's abilities or behavior, has been experimentally confirmed. Donna Anderson and Michael Haupert report on an ingenious classroom experiment that demonstrates both the economic inefficiency of discrimination on personal characteristics such as gender and race (characteristics that are obviously not hidden) while also demonstrating that statistical discrimination nonetheless can take place as a result of search costs (costs to uncover hidden characteristics).[45] The experimentally confirmed logic is that running the risk of not hiring a productive worker from a group that on average is believed to be relatively unproductive and hiring an unproductive worker from a group that on average is believed to be relatively productive may be cheaper than incurring more intensive, and therefore more expensive, search costs to ferret out the hidden characteristic. Even if there is no discriminatory intent, the problem of finding low-cost means of signaling and screening can lead to adverse (discriminatory) selection.

Solutions to the problem obviously revolve around lowering search costs (better signals, better screens). Credit companies rely on local, personal, or community knowledge of the applicant to get a sense of credit-worthiness. They also employ computerized, formulaic approaches such as credit-risk scores to assess whether an applicant is a good or bad credit risk. Employers increasingly use computerized application procedures, at least as a first screen. Another option of dealing with the problem is risk-sharing. Insurance companies do this to some degree by requiring waiting periods, co-payments, and by offering group plans in which both the healthy and the ill are insured. Still, all attempts to elicit information on hidden characteristics incur a cost, whether shared or not. Clearly, some well deserving individuals will be denied service on account of remaining uncertainty and inability to furnish the information needed and this, in part, explains why having no record can be worse than having a mediocre record. This is an unfortunate consequence of hidden characteristics and information problems that cannot feasibly be overcome.

Another option is mandated truth-revelation. For instance, disclosure and reporting requirements mandated by government in the financial, credit, health, housing, employment, agricultural, and other markets provides buyers and sellers with higher-quality information. Nowadays it is easy to compare banks' interest rates for various kinds of loan and saving instruments or to engage in a rudimentary assessment of a product's claimed medicinal value (because of vetting by the U.S. Food and Drug Administration, which is anything but rudimentary). Mandates of this kind are costly, to be sure, but typically broaden market participation by bringing in those who otherwise might prudently have stayed out of the market. The attraction of broadening the market can be so strong that parties agree to voluntarily disclose information they otherwise might not have disclosed. In the military and political context, confidence-building measures are an example — we disclose if you disclose — a theme of obvious relevance to this book.

Finally, expectations are a form of information that influences behavior. For example, on 10 December 2002, the *Wall Street Journal* carried a brief story on how a flare-up of civil unrest in the Ivory Coast on the west coast of Africa was reflected in the cocoa futures market. (In a futures market prices are negotiated today for product delivery in the future. This differs from spot-markets in which prices are negotiated today for immediate product delivery.) "Rebels in the west of the country," reported the *Journal,* "claimed the seizure of the town of Blolequin and said they aimed to capture San Pedro port, a major export point for cocoa."[46] The fear that disrupted supplies will raise tomorrow's spot price induces buyers to demand more futures-contracts at today's futures prices. But this very demand drives up futures prices. Thus, an expectation about the future, based on more or less accurate information from a war-torn society, drives current behavior. Another source of information is clandestinely or illegally obtained information. However obtained, it is, nonetheless, information—and people act on it: insider trading and industrial espionage does have its place in financial and business history. Likewise, the isolation, humiliation, beating, and torture of prisoners do have their (uncivilized, immoral, and usually illegal) place in military history.

These sorts of examples suggest that the economics of information can be relevant to an understanding of military history. It can be read from the viewpoint of finding, inferring, coaxing, eliciting, trading, or even stealing information regarding one's putative opponent's hidden characteristics. Likewise, it can be read from the viewpoint of safeguarding information. In chapter 5, we illustrate this by examining pertinent episodes of the American Civil War (1861–1865). This, incidentally, is also the sole non-European case study in this book.

PRINCIPLE VI: HIDDEN ACTIONS AND INCENTIVE ALIGNMENTS

A second class of information problems—apart from hidden characteristics—is that of hidden actions. In contrast to hidden characteristics, which cause problems before an action is taken or a commitment made, a hidden action causes problems after an action or commitment is taken. Consider the following slew of examples. Suppose that one is in a legal scrap involving an employment contract dispute. One hires a lawyer and signs a contract for legal services (the action is taken). The lawyer happens to be a certain Dr. van Tuyll, who opines that to best make one's case an expert economist needs to be hired (who, unbeknownst to the client, happens to be his friend, a certain Dr. Brauer). Does one really need the economist working on the case? Or suppose that one experiences an ill-defined ache in the knee. The physician requests a $60 X-ray from a consultancy in which, unbeknownst to the patient, the doctor has a financial interest. Did one really need that X-ray? Suppose that one's car brakes squeak. The mechanic provides a $400 repair estimate. Could the squeaking have been fixed with a $40 alternative? Suppose that a professor assigns reading for next class, sixty-five dense pages of deadly-boring material. Will the good professor even remember the reading was assigned, let alone cover it in class? And suppose that shareholders elect a board of directors to supervise management. Will directors act in the shareholders' best interest or will they be co-opted by management for its own purposes?

What these examples share is that they belong to a class of problems known as principal-agent problems. The principal is the party giving an order or requesting a service (the patient, the client, the customer, the student, the shareholder); the agent is the party receiving the order or carrying out the service (the physician, the lawyer, the mechanic, the professor, the directors). Explicit and implicit contracts are contingent on the agent undertaking certain actions and the principal being able to observe these actions or their outcome. The problem is that it may not be feasible for the principal to observe what the agent does or does not do. How many clients observe how vigorously their lawyers work? How many customers check their car mechanic's honesty credentials? Only the agent knows, and can thereby exploit the situation. For example, corporate headquarters cannot observe how much work effort any one salesperson puts forth to ring up sales at any one of its hundreds of local retail stores. The principal (corporate headquarters) needs to find means of limiting the employee's moral hazard, the situation in which only the salesperson truly knows how much effort he or she put forth. Similarly, only the owner knows how diligent he or she is in preventing a fire or a burglary at home. In the absence of insurance, we would think that the owner would be rather more diligent. But with insurance, one might say, "oh, well; if something happens, I am covered," and let vigilance slide.

Resolution of the difficulty revolves around the writing of contracts that minimize moral hazard (opportunism), that make damage recoverable or impose a penalty for noncompliance, that enable better contract observation at low cost, that limit commitment by the potentially defrauded or damaged party or make that commitment revocable, that share risk-taking, or anything else that helps align the interests of the contracting parties. Insurance copayments are a device to shift some of the risk back to the purchaser of insurance so that medical services are accessed only in case of nontrivial health needs. Low base salaries combined with volume-based bonuses encourage sales effort. Sometimes customers can be made accomplices in firms' search for low-cost information. For example, pizza chain stores offer pizza delivery in thirty minutes or "it's free!" Here, customers tell the franchise owner whether pizza delivery is on time or not and thus provide low-cost observation of employee effort. Student evaluations feed back to merit pay increases and help keep professors' teaching efforts focused. An interesting example, not without relevance for the larger topic of the book, is supplied, once more, by textbook authors Katz and Rosen. In the nineteenth century the manufacture of explosives was a particularly dangerous occupation. They write that one way to reassure workers that appropriate manufacturing precautions had been taken — a hidden action, for how would workers know that appropriate precautions had in fact been taken? — was to locate the owner's family home, with its full complement of wife and children, right next to the plant![47]

This highlights the difference between hidden characteristics and hidden actions: the former is about information and information transmittal before a commitment is made, the latter is about incentives and incentive alignment after a commitment has been made. The former is about being truthful, the latter about acting truthfully. Failing the former, the point is to reveal truthful information about you; failing the latter, the point is to keep you honest so as to prevent shirking. If the contracted action itself (such as work effort) cannot be readily observed, a suitable proxy must be found that is highly correlated to the desired action. For example, say that one wants to escape alive and well from a surgeon's cutting table. A reasonably reliable proxy might be the surgeon's performance record for the sort of surgery one is about to undergo.[48] A problem arises when the proxy does not correlate well to the desired action. For instance, measuring professors' performance by the number of research papers they publish does not reveal information about their classroom performance. Thus, if the production of papers is observed and rewarded, one might expect professors to focus on publication instead of teaching.[49]

We mentioned at the outset that the principal-agent problem is but one class of hidden-action (or hidden-intention) problems. There are other difficulties, for example, that of dealing with teams of agents, that of reneging on contracts, or that of holding up contracts. To increase franchise value, the owner of a professional sports team obviously wants the team to do well. Contracts are written with each team member but only the team as a whole can win (or lose). To facilitate observation and to prevent free-riding on other team members' effort, absurd quantities of statistics are compiled and published for each player in each position. This is costly, even as it allows for endless trivia questions. In other cases, observation of individual team members is nearly impossible, for example, fighting effort on the battlefront, and the question arises of how to write a contract that properly motivates team members to give their best even as opportunities for shirking exist. Culture plays an important role, and not only because contesting contract fulfillment in a court of law can be exceedingly costly so that contracts therefore must be supplemented by relational ingredients. The role of culture is to bind agents so that they come to see themselves as a unit rather than as the individuals they are. Culture generates powerful social strictures, from approbation and elevation to disapproval and isolation, that confer benefits to or impose costs upon team members. A common culture simplifies communication (e.g., a common language, or a common babel of military acronyms); it reduces the cost of signaling and screening. Culture makes team members observe each other and directs each of them to comply with whatever the implied cultural contract is. Joint training, common cohort experiences, the creation of shared reference groups, the public recitation of a company's mission or one's country's national anthem all produce powerful psychological bonding. These are ways in which a cultural contract complements legal contracts. Problems may arise when a culture thus created goes awry: Nazism in Germany and the business accounting scandals in the United States in the late 1990s and early 2000s are not the only examples.

Depending on circumstance, reneging on a contract ranges from the merely annoying to the crushing. If Alice and Bob agree to meet for coffee, and Alice fails to show up, this is annoying but not particularly harmful (costly) to Bob. But if Alice and Bob agree to meet for coffee in Argentina, and Alice fails to show up, it is crushingly expensive for Bob to have gone there. Contracts, formal or informal, need to recognize exposure to risk, for example, by including penalty clauses or payment of risk premiums. For instance, it is usually difficult to observe and to assess exactly how much effort construction workers put into their jobs. The principal incurs the risk of delay of project completion. A penalty clause by which the contract value drops by 1 percent for each day beyond the deadline serves as a powerful inducement to the general contractor to get the job done on time. This helps to align incentives between principal (builder) and agent (contractor). But at times the agent is not responsible for the risk such as when bad weather delays construction. A cost-based contract encourages agent-shirking and the principal bears the entire risk. In contrast, a performance-based contract shifts the risk fully to the agent (the construction project will be done in 180 days or else penalties are imposed, regardless of any genuine mitigating circumstances beyond the agent's control). Ways need to be found to get around these extremes. A common form of risk-sharing involves the use of base payment plus bonus compensation. Thus, waiters receive base payment regardless of how many customers show up and bonus pay comes from customer tipping. If the base/bonus percentages are well designed, self-selection will take place. Inattentive, rude waiters will receive few tips and may not survive on base compensation alone. Before long they will sort themselves out of that particular labor market and look for something else to do. Other waiters, in contrast, will do well enough to continue in the job.

One problem in this setup is that there is no job progression. Waiting on tables is a dead-end job because it possesses only one level of hierarchy: waiting or not. In other firms, one may commonly find five, eight, and more levels of career advancement. Higher levels are occupied by fewer workers. Employees at the lower level compete (possibly in addition to outsiders) to progress to each higher level, at which there are fewer available spots. This amounts to a playoff tournament where those who are better able and/or willing to perform at the higher level are then also better rewarded. While this sort of self-selection encourages employees to provide observable signals about themselves at low cost to the employer, it faces at least two problems. First, "flat" organizations, while appealing in that a reduced number of decision-making layers helps an organization to be more nimble, also reduces the number of potential advancement slots and may induce valued team members to jump to another organization altogether. In this case, the organization's investment in the training and career grooming of team members is lost (e.g., military pilots who become commercial pilots). Second, influence costs can run rampant. A handy way to think of influence costs is to think of office politics and backbiting, that is, influence-seeking to strengthen one's own, or weaken one's putative adversary's future competitive position.

A holdup is a somewhat different situation. Suppose that Alice is a contract manufacturer who builds a specific plant to produce parts for Bob. Once the plant is built, Bob demands that Alice reduce the price of the parts she produces for him or else he is going to look for another parts manufacturer. In this scenario Alice is boxed in because she has already incurred irrecoverable, "sunk" costs in her plant and is inflexible to maneuver against Bob. The contractual commitment is unbalanced and involves more risk for one side than the other. She has to cave in or lose even more money (the value of her otherwise useless plant). Alice's problem here is the asset specificity of the plant. It is custom-built to produce parts for Bob. It has no other use and leaves Alice in an untenable position. There is a "fundamental transformation" in the relation, as Oliver Williamson calls it, once the relationship-specific investment is made.[50] This goes for business as for any other relation. Thus, marriage is a relationship-specific investment, subject to holdup that can quickly sour a marriage.[51] Relationship-driven asset specificity also explains why corporations invest in company-specific training programs but rarely in general education. Once the company-specific investment is made, the employee can use the knowledge gained at the company that provided the training but nowhere else.

In contrast, general education — a high school or college degree — is portable. Any employer who finances general education finds it highly valued by other employers, and the original employer would be left holding the bag. These examples show that asset specificity can be physical (the custom-built plant) or can take the form of human capital (employee training and education). It can also be tied to specific locations, for instance, a small retail shop moving into a mall next to an anchor tenant, a big department store. If the department store moves, walk-in traffic will drop and leave the small retailer scrambling. To reassure such retailers, mall owners need to write a long-term contract with the department store or in other ways compensate the small retailers for the risk of committing site-specific capital.

Solutions to minimize or prevent all these sorts of problems revolve around incentive alignment, that is, around the design of contracts. This, in turn, brings with it the arena of contract enforcement, which, itself, raises a multitude of problems. Contracts include, of course, the legal sort: a labor contract, a real estate contract, and so on. Less well appreciated is that habits, customs, and cultures all are forms of contract, albeit informal ones, that complement incomplete formal contracts. Indeed, something as innocuous as mutual trust is an excellent cost-reduction device, whether it applies to families, businesses, or nation-states. This book, for instance, is co-authored. Each author needs to trust the other to do his share of the thinking, researching, and writing. It is inconceivable to write this book on the basis of a completely specified formal contract. Negotiating and writing the contract would take as long as researching and writing the book itself.

Complete contracts make opportunistic behavior impossible. But in the real world, complete contracts are nearly impossible to write. Society seeks recourse to contract enforcement via culture or the courts. Some contracts cannot be complete for the simple reason that bounded rationality limits our understanding of contingencies that might legitimately occur but cannot be factored in at the time the contract is negotiated, written, and signed. Good will becomes important. Good will can be helped along by contracting parties holding each other hostage. For instance, if one co-author reneges on his part of co-writing this book, word might spread and damage one's academic credibility and reputation, both of which are highly valued assets among academics. In the business context, a "money-back" guarantee allows one to try a product without monetary risk. As for academics, so for firms: if a firm advertises high-quality products but sells shoddy ones, word of mouth will spread and hurt the firm's reputation and future prospects. To hold oneself hostage to one's own word can be good for business, hence the success of product branding: the image of product quality dictates that one must now deliver or face a potentially devastating customer backlash.

War is the collective pursuit of a dangerous activity. But the collective pursuit occurs person by person. Why do individuals participate in war, whether voluntary or conscripted? In battle, what makes the fighting unit stay together as a collective, even as the lives of the individuals are at stake? What are the hidden actions individual soldiers and commanders might wish to take advantage of? What are the observable, low-cost proxies that may serve as signaling and screening devices? How is the reward and punishment system structured? What sorts of formal and informal contracts govern the relation between and among the various players in the military? Promising loyal vassals land and peasants of their own is an incentive that induces effort on behalf of a king or lord. In contrast, failing to adequately equip and outfit troops constitutes a disincentive and makes them more likely to surrender or even to switch sides. Generous U.S. Army sign-on bonuses and college scholarships are needed to lure otherwise reluctant young people to sign up for service as even richer contracts and prospects in private sector employment turn their heads the other way. In a word, incentives and contracts matter greatly. In chapter 3, we illustrate the operation of the principle of hidden action, and many of its implications, by examining the rise and fall of mercenary armies in the Italian Renaissance (AD 1300–1500).

CONCLUSION: ECONOMICS — AND MILITARY HISTORY

We demonstrate in the remainder of the book that military history can be probed fruitfully through the lens of economic principles such as the ones delineated in this chapter. Our analysis of military history may be viewed as a matrix that takes two dimensions (table 1.1). Along the rows we place our set of six economic principles; along the columns we divide military events into requisite inputs — manpower, logistics, and technology — and, separately, into the planning and operations stages. At any given time, the first three are fixed, and planning and operations must proceed with what is at hand. This defines the short run. In the long run, manpower, logistics, and technology are variable and affect the planning and operation of future campaigns.

We use the following periodization: the High Middle Ages (1000–1300); the Renaissance (1300–1600); the Age of Battle (1618–1815); the Age of Revolution (1789–1914); the Age of the World Wars (1914–1945); and the Cold War (1945–1991). For each period, we select a single episode from military history, a case. For example, for the Age of the World Wars we examine the case of the

Table 1.1: A matrix on the economics of military history

	Manpower	Logistics	Technology	Planning	Operations
Opportunity cost		1000–1300 High Middle Ages: Medieval castles and siege warfare			
Expected marginal costs/benefits				1618–1815 Age of Battle: To offer or decline battle?	
Substitution	1945–1991 Cold War: *force de frappe*		1945–1991 Cold War: *force de frappe*		
Diminishing marginal returns		1914–1945: Age of World Wars: Strategic bombing of Germany in World War II			
Asymmetric information (overcoming) hidden characteristics				1789–1914 Age of Revolution: The American Civil War and information asymmetries	
Asymmetric information (overcoming) hidden action	1300–1600 Renaissance: The *condottieri* in Italian city-states				

Allies' strategic bombing of Germany in World War II. Our primary goal is to elucidate the application of the principle of diminishing marginal returns and to keep things manageable we focus on logistics and technology rather than on manpower or planning and operations (although all of these, of course, overlap). We have arranged the six cases so that each economics principle and each military component is covered in some way.

Regarding the Age of the World Wars, other cases might well be examined, such as the Pacific Theater in World War II (say, the economic story of the Burma Road) or the battlefields in World War I (from Gallipoli to Flanders) or, indeed, the interwar period, say, regarding the munitions industry. The same goes for the other periods for each of which numerous other cases might have been chosen instead of the ones we picked. For example, for the High Middle Ages one could have examined the campaigns of conquest, the evolution of weaponry, the training of knights, the development of the medieval army, or battle tactics instead of the case of the medieval castle. As explained in the preface, we have two notions in mind. One is to deal with slightly "offbeat" cases. Instead of the superpower rivalry we look at France's *force de frappe*, instead of dealing with the development of permanent armies in the late Renaissance we examine the transitional *condottieri* period, and instead of picking a battle from the Age of Battles we examine the puzzling truth of why so few battles were in fact fought. The other notion is that we did not wish to become bogged down in a single period. To illustrate the potential reach of economic analysis, we instead chose to cover a whole millennium.

There is an important refinement that needs mention here. Within each case, we actually apply each of our six principles to each of the five military categories, for a total of thirty entries in the matrix. The result is that even as we discuss, for example, the bombing of Germany primarily from the viewpoint of diminishing marginal returns, we also discuss the other principles, for instance, capital-labor substitution, opportunity costs of technology, and the role of information in air war planning. Each of our six cases makes one main point — and twenty-nine smaller ones (see p. 79 for an example of a completely filled-in matrix), although the details will probably not make sense until one has read the corresponding chapter.

In chapter 8, we carry the application of economics from military history to contemporary military events by venturing into the economics of terrorism, military manpower, and present-day private military and security companies. A considerable and long-standing body of economic literature exists for the first two of these topics but since the terror attacks in the United States on 11 September 2001 and the consequent wars in Afghanistan and Iraq, both have received renewed scholarly attention. The chapter reviews selected aspects of the literature, if only to provide an inkling that economics can speak to contemporary events as well as historic ones. The body of economics literature on the third topic, contemporary private military and security companies, is very slim. Nonetheless, it illuminates the opportunities for and limits to the use of these companies.

Readers may object to our project in at least two ways. First, that for the cases we have chosen we understand the historical material poorly and apply the economics to the wrong facts or that our history is correct but that the economic analysis is carried out wrongly. In either case, it should be straightforward to correct the factual or analytical record. But second, and more seriously, one may deny the very premise of our venture and say that we selected the illustrative cases to fit our views, that our cases are insufficiently representative of the sweep of years we cover, that our case selection is flawed, and that we therefore claim too much for the role of economic analysis in military history. Another selection of cases might show that economic principles have no bearing on the matter at hand at all. At least in principle, such a charge could stick. To state it clearly: we do not know just how representative (or not) our cases are. One of the problems is that it is not clear how one would go about selecting a statistically valid representative sample of cases from a thousand years of history. What we do know is that by selecting six economic principles, instead of just one or the other, and applying them to six distinct military events that historians regard as important, moreover events from six disparate epochs stretched across one thousand years of history, we have spread the net widely to catch representative cases. We concede, however, that only additional research on additional cases will show whether economics would seem to offer a fruitful way to (re)examine military history per se. Meanwhile, let us start with the cases we have assembled in this book.

APPENDIX

The Bank of Sweden Prize in Economic Sciences in Memory of Alfred Nobel

2007   Leonid Hurwicz, Eric Maskin, and Roger Myerson: "for having laid the foundations of mechanism design theory."

2006   Edmund Phelps: "for his analysis of intertemporal tradeoffs in macroeconomic policy."

2005   Robert Aumann and Thomas Schelling: "for having enhanced our understanding of conflict and cooperation through game-theory analysis."

2004   Finn E. Kydland and Edward C. Prescott: "for their contributions to dynamic macroeconomics: the time consistency of economic policy and the driving forces behind business cycles."

2003   Robert Engle and Clive Granger: *Engle:* "for methods of analyzing economic time series with time-varying volatility (ARCH)." *Granger:* "for methods of analyzing economic time series with common trends (cointegration)."

2002   Daniel Kahneman and Vernon L. Smith: *Kahneman:* "for having integrated insights from psychological research into economic science, especially concerning human judgment and decision-making under uncertainty." *Smith:* "for having established laboratory experiments as a tool in empirical economic analysis, especially in the study of alternative market mechanisms."

2001   George A. Akerlof, A. Michael Spence, and Joseph E. Stiglitz: "for their analyses of markets with asymmetric information."

2000   James J. Heckman and Daniel L. McFadden: *Heckman:* "for his development of theory and methods for analyzing selective samples." *McFadden:* "for his development of theory and methods for analyzing discrete choice."

1999   Robert A. Mundell: "for his analysis of monetary and fiscal policy under different exchange rate regimes and his analysis of optimum currency areas."

1998   Amartya Sen: "for his contributions to welfare economics."

1997   Robert C. Merton and Myron S. Scholes: "for a new method to determine the value of derivatives."

1996   James A. Mirrlees and William Vickrey: "for their fundamental contributions to the economic theory of incentives under asymmetric information."

1995   Robert E. Lucas Jr.: "for having developed and applied the hypothesis of rational expectations, and thereby having transformed macroeconomic analysis and deepened our understanding of economic policy."

1994   John C. Harsanyi, John F. Nash Jr., and Reinhard Selten: "for their pioneering analysis of equilibria in the theory of non-cooperative games."

1993   Robert W. Fogel and Douglass C. North: "for having renewed research in economic history by applying economic theory and quantitative methods in order to explain economic and institutional change."

1992   Gary S. Becker: "for having extended the domain of microeconomic analysis to a wide range of human behaviour and interaction, including nonmarket behaviour."

1991   Ronald H. Coase: "for his discovery and clarification of the significance of transaction costs and property rights for the institutional structure and functioning of the economy."

1990   Harry M. Markowitz, Merton H. Miller, and William F. Sharpe: "for their pioneering work in the theory of financial economics."

1989   Trygve Haavelmo: "for his clarification of the probability theory foundations of econometrics and his analyses of simultaneous economic structures."

1988   Maurice Allais: "for his pioneering contributions to the theory of markets and efficient utilization of resources."

1987   Robert M. Solow: "for his contributions to the theory of economic growth."

1986   James M. Buchanan Jr.: "for his development of the contractual and constitutional bases for the theory of economic and political decision-making."

1985   Franco Modigliani: "for his pioneering analyses of saving and of financial markets."

1984   Richard Stone: "for having made fundamental contributions to the development of systems of national accounts and hence greatly improved the basis for empirical economic analysis."

1983   Gerard Debreu: "for having incorporated new analytical methods into economic theory and for his rigorous reformulation of the theory of general equilibrium."

1982   George J. Stigler: "for his seminal studies of industrial structures, functioning of markets and causes and effects of public regulation."

1981   James Tobin: "for his analysis of financial markets and their relations to expenditure decisions, employment, production and prices."

1980   Lawrence R. Klein: "for the creation of econometric models and the application to the analysis of economic fluctuations and economic policies."

1979   Theodore W. Schultz and Sir Arthur Lewis: "for their pioneering research into economic development research with particular consideration of the problems of developing countries."

1978   Herbert A. Simon: "for his pioneering research into the decision-making process within economic organizations."

1977   Bertil Ohlin and James E. Meade: "for their pathbreaking contribution to the theory of international trade and international capital movements."

1976   Milton Friedman: "for his achievements in the fields of consumption analysis, monetary history and theory and for his demonstration of the complexity of stabilization policy."

1975   Leonid Vitaliyevich Kantorovich and Tjalling C. Koopmans: "for their contributions to the theory of optimum allocation of resources."

1974 Gunnar Myrdal and Friedrich August von Hayek: "for their pioneering work in the theory of money and economic fluctuations and for their penetrating analysis of the interdependence of economic, social and institutional phenomena."

1973 Wassily Leontief: "for the development of the input-output method and for its application to important economic problems."

1972 John R. Hicks and Kenneth J. Arrow: "for their pioneering contributions to general economic equilibrium theory and welfare theory."

1971 Simon Kuznets: "for his empirically founded interpretation of economic growth which has led to new and deepened insight into the economic and social structure and process of development."

1970 Paul A. Samuelson: "for the scientific work through which he has developed static and dynamic economic theory and actively contributed to raising the level of analysis in economic science."

1969 Ragnar Frisch and Jan Tinbergen: "for having developed and applied dynamic models for the analysis of economic processes."

Source: www.nobelprize.org (accessed 15 October 2007).

The High Middle Ages, 1000–1300

The Case of the Medieval Castle and the Opportunity Cost of Warfare

Historians may cringe, but the popular "castle and knight" image of the High Middle Ages does contain important elements of truth. Certainly, warfare was constant. To denizens of the twenty-first century, the scale of war a thousand years ago appears small, but the share of resources that was consumed by war was enormous. This consumption included not only the expenses of waging war but, almost invariably, the deliberate destruction of economic assets that accompanied invasions, and sometimes retreats as well. Power lay with substantial property owners.[1] In the absence of powerful centralized governments local rulers could and did make war for almost every reason imaginable. To be sure, tradition, chivalry, and (occasionally) law did place some limits on warfare, but it was almost impossible for any medieval ruler of substance to avoid fighting for his entire career.

Few were disposed to try. Trained from boyhood in the ways of war, even the less aggressive were rarely inclined to surrender territory or privileges just to avoid fighting. This did not mean that the decision to fight could be made casually or irrationally. As any economist will remind us, resources are always limited and placed on medieval rulers a far more stringent constraint than is the case today. A modern state possesses impressive tools to wage war such as a national tax system, conscription, and credit. None of these existed a thousand years ago. Rulers might tax, but neither economic reality, administrative capacity, nor tradition would allow collections anywhere near as extensive or methodical as today. Conscription was unknown. True, men could be ordered to wage war, but only for periods specified by tradition. And credit on a scale fit to serve an entire nation only began to appear late in the thirteenth century and was not, at any rate, a realistic option for lesser nobles. A king in 1008 was far more aware of the need to make choices than a president in 2008.

Decision making under constraints is the provenance of economics, and the decisions of medieval rulers regarding war form a fertile area for the study of the making of choices. Potentially, here we have a marvelous case for examining whether military history is amenable to economic analysis. The pithy popular image of the age — castles and knights — is actually helpful, even if the conjunctive and some of the details are wrong. For when it came to expenditure the ruler had but one stark choice: fortify or hire, that is, to build castles or recruit armies.

Although the medieval army was sometimes regarded as an almost irrelevant rabble among whom only the mounted knights truly mattered, recent scholarship has changed our view significantly. The dominance of the mounted knight in particular has been questioned. As we shall see, the armored man on horseback was of no use whatsoever attacking a castle.[2] Even with regard to the battlefield the picture has changed: "The notion that the medieval knight, his lance couched beneath his right arm, his shield and reins in his left hand, dominated military planning and strategy during this period is the stuff of epic poetry."[3] The medieval army was much more, and much more complicated, than the knightly armored cavalry alone. The cavalry's primacy has been exaggerated.[4] Some of these misunderstandings were exacerbated by the fact that, unlike their rulers, the commanders of the age offered battle infrequently. Medieval armed forces maneuvered, ravaged, and besieged more often than they fought each other in the open field. This was the result of a rather methodical and careful approach to military strategy but had the paradoxical effect of attributing poor qualities to the armies and the leaders of the day. The medieval army has been misunderstood and underestimated.

The same was not true of the costly and ubiquitous castles that dotted (and still dot) the landscape of Europe. The importance of the castle in European history, and not just military history, is impossible to overstate. The castle functioned as noble or royal residence, seat of government, defensive fortification, base of offensive operations, place of refuge, and tool of oppression. We know of no global calculation of the cost of castle building to European society as a whole, or even if such is possible. What we can do is consider the expenses that rulers poured into their construction, funds that then were unavailable for raising armies. The most powerful rulers could, of course, afford to build castles and raise armies, but funding one inevitably reduced funding for the other. The results were not trivial. Heavy spending on castles in some cases eliminated the opportunity for offensive warfare, the spender relying on the defensive strength of his fortifications to wear an enemy down. In extreme cases the spending bankrupted rulers. Yet the castle was not necessarily a bad investment. Seizing one by force was difficult, dangerous, and time-consuming, and even the introduction of gunpowder did not immediately render them obsolete.

Eventually, of course, gunpowder's effect was dramatic. Tall vertical walls became targets instead of obstacles. During the expulsion of the English from France after 1450, heavy artillery could topple walls "in a matter of hours." And the cost of fortifications designed to blunt cannon shot, such as the *trace italienne,* was "enormous. Only the wealthiest states and cities could afford the scores of cannon and the enormous labor of construction." All this took place, however, after the centuries studied here. In fact, well after; although the first gun was introduced in Europe in 1326, it was a century before guns overtook catapults in effectiveness.[5]

Gunpowder, however, only accelerated a trend well under way, namely, the centralization of government linked to the growing expense and scale of warfare. Paralleled by the growth of cities, monarchies steadily acquired power at the expense of the nobility. In Italy, for example, city-states retained their independence even past the Renaissance in some cases. Some German cities were not amalgamated into larger units until the time of Napoleon. The military result of the growth of cities in the Middle Ages is complex. Individual nobles could not besiege fortified towns but neither was aristocratic control over the countryside seriously threatened. Eventually, the small yielded to the great as the larger states accumulated capital, war expanded in scale and cost, and the great powers could "milk their economies" to pay for war.[6]

The period under examination, AD 1000–1300, is a reasonably well-defined period in military history. Warfare was different from preceding and succeeding periods. The period can safely be called the Age of the Castle. Stone fortifications became common. By the end of the thirteenth century development of the castle was essentially at an impasse. No major design advances were made in the fourteenth or fifteenth century.[7] Whether this was due to the changing nature of warfare or because design possibilities had been exhausted is beyond our scope here. Suffice it to restate that the typical ruler of the Middle Ages often chose to build castles despite thereby foregoing the only other pertinent military option—hiring an army. Choosing to build castles cost the opportunity to build armies.

Studying the economics of castles and warfare can also tell us a lot about the time. It is a truism to describe a period as "complex" or "controversial," but it is hard to think of one that deserves these terms more than the Middle Ages. Information is fragmentary and the numbers often literally do not add up. There was no well defined central government. Even the most popular term used to describe life—feudalism—creates arguments. Some historians refuse to use the word at all. Others disagree about what the "system" of that age really meant. Was it, for example, "government by contract" (as opposed to public law) or was it merely the legitimization of the power of violent groups who dominated the land and turned their raw power into tradition and principle that all had to obey? Those who have the capacity for organized violence, the argument goes, have the most rational self-interest to organize government. Among small groups peaceful agreement is more likely because everyone can see the benefits of collective security, but in larger entities the individual cannot see the benefits very clearly, just the cost, and may be less likely to agree voluntarily to pay for castles, weapons, and sundries.[8] If true, this argument could help explain the frequency of civil wars in the age.

The huge sums that medieval rulers spent on war (indeed, they seemed to spend on little else) mean that every aspect of war had major effects on economic trends, and vice versa. Improved taxation ("improved" from the ruler's perspective, of course) made military spending possible, and war required much of this sort of improvement. In the tenth or eleventh century a landholder might generate enough income to build a simple motte and bailey castle — consisting of an earthen mound, a circular wall or walls, and, in the center, a fortified tower as a final place for retreat — but revenues from estates could not keep pace with the growing costs of war. As landholdings of monarchs became less important, rulers became quite creative. The English kings exploited archaic land taxes, managed vacant bishoprics, pocketed profits from minting, collected every conceivable feudal due, taxed the laity for the crusades, and laid the foundation for the shift to universal taxation. This pattern — modernization of taxation due to war — can be seen in France and Spain as well. In France, the ordinary revenues grew from 86,000 to 400,000 *livres tournois* between 1180 and 1290, supplemented by a variety of special levies to fund wars and crusades. The Spanish monarchy achieved similar results, further stretching its money through devaluation. Monarchies grew in power as well as wealth. Only in the Holy Roman Empire did the pattern not occur, because the imperial "government" lacked the means to compel payment.[9]

Monarchs were thus able to acquire the funds for castles and armies and make war the province of the mighty alone. Ordinary nobles could not keep up. But it took time. Medieval European monarchs had few legal powers to tax and their organizations and institutions were too weak or disorganized to keep the flow of money steady. Payments in lieu of service were common, but these were so hard to keep track of that they disappeared in the fourteenth century. The creativity of royal treasurers was boundless, however. They chartered towns for a fee, took over church properties, used requisitions, paid for supplies with means other than cash, inflated the currency, borrowed money, and imposed public loans.[10] Yet it was never enough. Warfare consumed the treasures of state.

The chapter proceeds as follows. First we examine the concept of opportunity cost with respect to castle-based warfare. Next we present an accounting for the sheer number of castles, especially in relation to English kings. Then we assess the cost of castle building and show why, despite the truly enormous cost, the advantages outweighed the cost. Armies were not irrelevant but their cost was high and the advantages slight. Finally we point to where economic principles other than the principle of opportunity cost may be seen in the history of castle building.

OPPORTUNITY COST AND WARFARE

Opportunity cost is a fundamental principle of economics. This cost refers not to what one pays for a purchase, but rather to the highest-valued alternative purchase one could have made. For example, reading this chapter now implies foregoing the opportunity of doing something else with your time — such as reading something else, cooking, cleaning, working for money, enjoying one's family, or just savoring a quiet moment. Anything you do involves giving up the opportunity of doing something else. That is the opportunity cost.

The principle of opportunity cost is at once easy to understand and difficult to apply, in part because the values assigned to alternative courses of action vary from person to person. As regards war, opportunity cost can be applied at several levels. The level considered here involves spending decisions although relative scarcity of resources is not the whole story. In the twentieth century the capacity of governments to support war has increased immensely, but changing technology has made the choice process more difficult. First, decisions have had to be made about which weapon system to purchase. This has created controversy inside the military and outside. Different branches of the service compete for funds, and the competition does not always remain in-house. Major projects attract outside attention, and support may wax and wane. The United States' B-1 bomber, for example, was authorized by the Nixon-Ford administration, canceled by Carter, and then reauthorized by Reagan. Second, technological change generates ever increasing potential costs. Of course bigger projects have always cost more money, but now the capacities as well as the brute power of weapons have changed. The military airplane's capabilities and costs have risen so rapidly that a calculation once foretold the one-airplane air force, a machine so monstrously expensive as to swallow the whole of the procurement budget. Pursuing this avenue costs the opportunity to prosecute any realistic scenario of war.

Another level at which the principle of opportunity cost can be applied to warfare is in the arena of operations. A unit sent north cannot simultaneously go south. Reserves deployed to one zone to stop an attack are unavailable to stop one elsewhere. Military leaders attempt to avoid or at least mitigate this conundrum, for example, by deferring definitive deployment until the last possible moment. Eventually a choice is still made, of course, but battles are often won by one side keeping a strong reserve available until the decisive moment. Another way is to place the adversary in an untenable position, for instance, by maneuvering so that the enemy does not know which choice is going to be made, until it is too late. Improved mobility is also a way of moderating the opportunity cost problem as mobility further postpones the finality of the choice. But a choice must be made, and the next-best option must be given up. Thus, an opportunity cost always exists. The only question is just how valuable is the option given up. To be sure, opportunity costs can be low: slow moving, low quality forces can be "used up" without incurring high-valued foregone opportunities, at least from the perspective of the commanders, if not from that of the affected soldiers.

All this only scratches the analytical surface. Many other applications of the principle of opportunity cost to war can be considered. The very decision to go to war is perhaps the most important. The opportunity to fight different types of war should be considered,[11] as indeed the opportunity to choose nonwar options of waging, or resolving, conflict. Then there are the different opportunity costs for different "choosers" in a military system. For ruler, supreme commander, subordinate military leaders, and the rank and file, an aggressive — or any other — military strategy involves different opportunity costs. The potential complexity of the application of this seemingly simple principle is virtually limitless.

Even restricting the application of the principle of opportunity cost to just one facet, such as castle building in the High Middle Ages, involves many difficulties. Taxation, budgeting, and spending in the Middle Ages can only be described as haphazard, or at least they appear so because of the paucity of records.

> It would be very interesting to know the sums spent by medieval monarchs on fortifications in their countries. It is known that cities gave enormous sums for building walls and ramparts, and for digging moats. Unfortunately there is a total lack of information about costs for this period.[12]

This quotation, from a standard work on the military history of the age, reveals some frustration of the study of the period. Fortunately, progress has been made, and even as debate regarding the exact numbers will continue, a number of deductions can be made about the labor and capital cost necessary to construct medieval fortifications. About the overall cost there is little dispute. Medieval rulers had the greatest difficulties in paying for their wars, and powerful monarchs had no less trouble despite initially starting with more. "All were driven to desperate expedients to make ends meet." Worse, possession of more power and territory gave one more to defend. Castles and troops were both necessary, and this led to every conceivable way being devised to raise money. "Since the time of Cicero and Tacitus to the fifteenth century and beyond, authors often asserted that the tranquility of nations was impossible without armies, armies without soldiers' wages, or wages without tribute."[13]

The result of the search for funds has been described as "less a system of taxation than a system of plunder," and this was no metaphor. In England, for example, goods were sometimes seized from merchants and only released after "tax" was paid. And it was never enough. Despite the most vigorous tax collections England had ever known, Edward I (r. 1272–1307) constantly outran his financial resources. Between 1294 and 1297 wars with Scotland, France, and Wales required such heavy war levies that laity and clergy alike rebelled, leading to a major constitutional crisis. This was not the result of mere royal greed; bad policy is another matter. In Edward's last years, the Wardrobe, as the department that paid the army's bills was called, rarely had a thousand pounds at any given moment, while earlier in his reign it had been able to send its paymasters sums as large as £5,000 at once.[14]

Credit was no permanent solution. Since the twelfth century credit had been steadily expanding across Europe. Tempted, Edward I took two steps: he borrowed, usually from Italian bankers, and he did not repay them, at least not completely. His first bankers, the Riccardi, failed to collect some £18,924; the Frescobaldi firm was shorted some £25,000. It did little good. At his death, Edward I left a debt of some £200,000, almost four times the entire annual royal revenue. Justly, some of this could be attributed to the policies of a king who not only made war constantly but pursued policies almost guaranteed to lead to further wars. Unsurprisingly, periods of peace led to dramatic improvements in the condition of the treasury.[15] But there was more to the matter than the behavior of an overly, and overtly, aggressive king.[16] Far more interesting about Edward I is that, despite running repeated campaigns in France, Wales, and Scotland, he nevertheless chose to plow fortunes into the building of castles.

THE UBIQUITY OF CASTLES

Given the limits to tax collections, the calls on the purse for recruiting armies and waging campaigns, and the enormous cost of castle building, the number of castles in Europe is nothing but spectacular. Some authorities place the peak of castle building around the beginning of the millennium; others note the immense amount of construction in the twelfth and thirteenth centuries. The difference is partly a matter of archaeological interpretation because many left no surface trace other than the remnants of a mound. But no one who has studied them has come away unimpressed by the numbers involved. A recent survey of a 94-square-mile area (about 243 km²) of Normandy counted four stone castles and twenty-eight earth mounds, remnants of fortifications.[17]

It is important to appreciate that the castle was not merely the tool of a lord fearful of being attacked. Conquerors used them as well. Fulk Nerra (972-–1040), one of France's most famous conquerors and dynasty builders, may have constructed the nation's first stone castle at Langeais and built fortifications across his domain. William the Conqueror arrived in England in 1066 with a prefabricated wooden castle, and, after defeating the Saxons, sprinkled forts across his new land. As many as five hundred may have been built by the time of his death in 1087. The centrality of the castle in warfare can also be demonstrated by reference to the building of "countercastles," fortifications constructed by besiegers. This technique occurred at places as widely separated as England and Italy and was employed by William the Conqueror, among many others.[18]

In the Dark Ages, castles consisted of basic timber and earth construction. In the tenth century, there appeared the motte and bailey castle, a central fortified tower placed on an earthen mound surrounded by a circular wall or walls. Militarily useful, these castles were simple to build but were eclipsed by the arrival of the stone castle in the eleventh century, although one may have been built in France a century earlier.[19] Architects and masons now supervised building projects that lasted years and, occasionally, decades.

The result was a costly fortress, essentially impervious to the military machinery of the day. Rulers and nobles now had a residence that could protect them and serve as a base of operations. The political results were decidedly mixed. While kings invariably built castles and used them to tighten their grip on the countryside — "a good fortress was the medieval ruler's best friend" — they were not throwing up these structures randomly. "The defence systems which they designed, or which developed in the course of centuries are a remarkable expression of their military ideas." The downside was that this carpet of castles was a magnificent entity with which to resist central rule. Independent nobles as well as castellans, appointed to manage castles for the ruler, became increasingly powerful behind their stone walls. The effect on the countryside can well be imagined. Taxation for castle construction was heavy. Labor was sometimes conscripted for the building works. A castle's garrison could protect local villages, but it could also threaten them. William of Malmesbury wrote in 1140 that "there were many castles throughout England, each defending their neighborhood, but, more properly speaking, laying it waste." Small wonder that "to the medieval mind, the castle was the most intimidating force on earth next to the wrath of God, and with good reason."[20]

THE COST OF CASTLING

Building castles benefited rulers by intimidating enemies and friends, merchants and peasants, nobles and commoners, and especially taxpayers. To determine how much it cost rulers, we need to know how the cost of castling compared with the cost of recruiting an army. The cost lay mostly in direct labor cost, as most labor had to be paid. (In contrast, raw material cost does not seem to have been much of an issue.) In addition to this explicit outlay, there was also the opportunity cost of labor; for example, masons working on castles could not be employed elsewhere. The garrison cost of castles was not a major consideration as the number of soldiers needed to defend a well constructed castle was surprisingly small. The most important cost issue with garrisons was their reliability. An unreliable noble appointed as castellan now possessed a powerful tool with which to defy his mentor. As castellans often caused trouble, this was by no means a trivial issue, and rulers definitely considered it a significant matter.

The actual cash outlay for building substantial castles eventually exceeded the resources of many nobles and stretched those of even the most powerful kings. The English king Richard I, the "Lionheart" (r. 1189–1199), needed to construct a fortification that would protect Normandy from invasion and serve as a base for further operations at the expense of the French. In only two years, his laborers constructed Château Galliard, one of the twelfth century's most spectacular castles. The £11,500 spent there far exceeded the £7,000 he spent on all his other castles put together and was more than he spent fortifying an entire town like Dover. As his revenues for those two years amounted to about £39,500, Château Galliard cost him almost 30 percent of his income. In two of his ten years at the helm, his income was less than the cost of the château.[21]

Galliard was but one castle. The broader case can be seen in the works built by Edward I during his conquest of Wales. A powerful monarch who fought with success against the Welsh, Scots, and French, he enjoyed tremendous tax revenues by the standards of the age. It would not prove enough, although

Table 2. 1: Cost of castle building

Castle	Years building	Cost (£)
Aberystwyth	12	3,900
Beaumaris	3	9,000
Builth	5	1,700
Caernarfon	12	16–27,000
Conwy	13	15–19,000
Flint	9	7,000
Harlech	7	9–10,000
Rhuddlan	8	9,500
Total		71,100–87,100

Sources: Edwards, 1946, p. 63; Baumgartner, 1991, p. 119;
Morris, 2003, p. 118.

castle building alone did not break his bank. He launched major projects in Wales: Aberystwyth, Caernarfon, Conwy, Flint, Rhuddlan, Builth, Harlech, and Beaumaris. All but the last three were integrated with fortified towns. Considerable data survive about the total cost of these castles, although the numbers are conservative. The clerk in charge of each castle's budget did not pay every associated expense. For example, the substantial wages that workers were paid while traveling from home to the works were paid by each sending shire.[22] While this expense did not come out of the king's pocket, it certainly did come from the country's and thus counts as a cost of castle building.

Estimated costs for Edward I's Welsh castles are given in table 2.1. The variations in the total obtain because for some years only estimates can be made. Not only did repairs have to be made after Welsh attacks, castles were frequently modified years after the original building had begun. As noted, the calculations are conservative. But no authority places the cost of the Welsh castles under £80,000, and several place it closer to £100,000, "an outlay such as a modern government might devote to building a fleet of nuclear submarines."[23]

Edward I's annual income over twenty-five years ranged from less than £25,000 to over £100,000, with an average, including a variety of special taxes and parliamentary subsidies, of around £67,500. Unfortunately for Edward, not to mention the taxpayers, the fortifications outran his finances. Caernarfon, the most spectacular site, never was completely finished inside. "In Wales, Edward's great castle at Beaumaris remained unfinished, a striking witness to his financial problems." The castle's walls only reached half their intended height. The treasury could no longer pay the wages of the work crews at Beaumaris. Even heavy levies in Ireland could not make up the difference. As parliament's great magnates became unexcited about disgorging endless funds for war, a constitutional crisis resulted. No British monarch would ever attempt castle building on this scale again. Perhaps later rulers, or their advisors, were all too aware of the crisis that occurred in 1296–1297. Although not the sole cause, the magnificent walls of Wales perhaps were the single biggest factor:

> Now this financial crisis was not altogether of sudden growth: for although it had been hastened since 1294 by the coincidence of almost simultaneous wars with French and Welsh and Scots, it was largely the slow product of the costly enterprises of Edward's reign as a whole. Among those enterprises, none had more steadily devoured his treasure than his castle-building in Wales.[24]

The nobles' love of the king's masonry was doubtless tempered by their awareness that projects on this scale were no longer within their own grasp. A handful of nonroyals in England and on the Continent could afford big walls. Gilbert de Clare built the enormous castle at Caerphilly. In France, the counts of Champagne bought castles from financially strapped nobles. Of two hundred English baronies in the twelfth century, only 35 percent had castles, others making do with fortified houses. Between 1154 and 1214 the number of baronial castles actually fell, from 225 to 179, while royal fortresses more than doubled in number, from 45 to 93. In an age when royal income never fell below £10,000, only seven barons were earning more than £400, the average was about £200, and at least twenty had incomes of less than £20. An up-to-date castle at the end of the twelfth century cost about £1,000 although a basic stone castle could be built for £350.[25]

The nobles were at a disadvantage in the castle arms race with regard to both money and legal powers. The king had the greater ability to pay and also the greater ability to make people fulfill his wishes. The king could force a shire to cover significant military expense. The nobles were in a relatively poor position. While the king had begun in England, as elsewhere, as a primus inter pares, he was now very much primus. Yet as Edward discovered during the crisis of 1296–1297, he was definitely not free of fiscal constraints and hence remained somewhat dependent on the wishes of his nobles.

New weapons often increase the capability of the individual soldier, but this can be offset by growing development and construction (or manufacturing) costs. In this respect, the stone castle was fairly typical. The number of soldiers needed to defend it might be small, but the number of people needed to build it was quite large. In the days of the motte and bailey castle, the labor required for building a very basic fort was small. A hundred men working for a month could build a modest one, and if they labored about three months, a substantial mound could be constructed. The stone castle was another matter. The tower constructed at Langeais required about 83,000 "average work days"

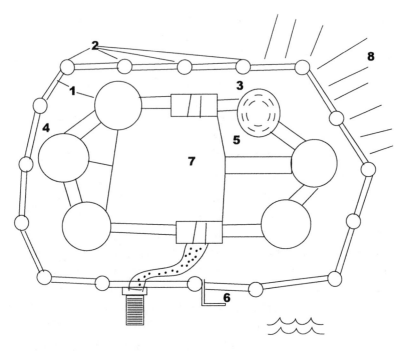

Figure 2.1. Edwardian castle design
This shows a "typical" Edwardian castle with some of the features that made it so expensive.
These included (1) multiple walls; (2) numerous towers; (3) concentric circles of masonry required to give strength to walls and towers; (4) the use of round, rather than square, towers;
(5) extensive interiors, as the castles were intended as royal residences; (6) water access; (7) multiple gate houses; and (8) difficult locations, such as hilltops. Additional architectural factors
in the high cost included size, height of walls, depth of foundations, and overall complexity.
Illustration by Debra van Tuyll.

to construct, ten times what a substantial motte and bailey needed. Langeais
was built in two seasons. If the workforce was able to labor six months each
year, there would have had to be some three hundred laborers continuously on
site. The labor of an additional 1,000 to 1,200 farmworkers would have been
needed to sustain the builders.[26]

 Edward I's castles required much more (fig. 2.1). None of his fortifications
were completed in less than five building seasons (six to seven months each),
and three took much longer. Many of the works were done at the same time.
After 1277, Builth, Aberystwyth, Flint, and Rhuddlan were being built at the
same time; after 1283, Conwy, Caernarfon, and Harlech were going up together. The number of workers at each castle varied enormously. At Builth
only a hundred might be present at any one time, but at Beaumaris the total

exceeded 3,000. In 1283–1284, about 4,000 men were employed at Conwy, Caernarfon, and Harlech, while 3,500 were hired in 1295 to work on Beaumaris and repair Caernarfon (which was damaged in an uprising). The population in Edward I's day was about three to four million people, so that the use of 4,000 workers was not a negligible number (an equivalent number of Americans today would be about 300,000). Workers had to be brought in from faraway shires. "In other words, we seem to be driven to the conclusion that the numbers of workmen employed by Edward I on his Welsh castles were sufficiently great to constitute a noticeable draught upon the total pool of mobile labour that was available in the England of his day."[27] That, of course, was the rub. With much of the population engaged in subsistence agriculture, the pool of labor on which to draw was not massive. Designers and masons were hired from the Continent. This reduced the labor drain in England (although at a financial cost) yet the castle-building program may, nevertheless, have absorbed a tenth of the national workforce. The impact was greater than army recruitment would have been. "The recruitment of men for the army may have had similar effects on occasion, but probably more serious was the call for skilled workmen to build the great Welsh castles, which must have had its effect on the building industry." While that conclusion cannot be accepted in its entirety — church construction may have contributed to a surplus of available stone masons — the burden was still huge. The true experts in the business, the architects and designers who knew the military ins and outs of castles, were greatly valued and greatly compensated, excepting the unfortunate architect of Ivry (France) who was put to death so that he could not reveal its secrets.[28]

Building a castle was only a first step. Castles had to be adapted, modified, improved, or even replaced if they became obsolete. Improvements in siege warfare required design changes. The square stone keep was sufficiently expensive that Norman castle-owners sought simply to reinforce their motte and bailey castles to hold costs down. Increasing costs of fortifications drove increases in military expenditure throughout the eleventh century. The crusaders further stimulated the process by bringing back innovations from the Middle East. The motte and bailey castles mutated from inexpensive palisaded hills to costly stone fortifications as powerful concentric walls replaced the palisade. The outer "curtain wall" became more sophisticated in the twelfth and thirteenth centuries as towers were added for flank fire. By the time castle building reached its peak toward the end of the thirteenth century, the two-wall system, with a "killing ground" in between, had become a standard design. This did nothing to constrain the continuing expansion of costs. There was increasingly no limit on how much could be spent, how many improvements made, and how many refinements introduced.[29]

Another cost, harder to calculate, was that the castle suffered from inherent weaknesses. No castle could hold out forever. Even Galliard, perhaps the most expensive castle of the twelfth century, fell to the French. No defense is impregnable. "The best that a besieged castle could hope for was to raise the price of victory to a point which the besiegers would be unwilling to pay."[30] That price could be exacted in various ways. Storming a castle was one of the most dangerous activities any medieval fighter could undertake because repelling such an attack was exactly what the stone walls were designed for. A besieging army often suffered more than the besieged from lack of shelter, the spread of disease, periodic food shortages, and the threat of a relief force appearing in the rear. Once feudal service requirements expired, the besieging troops would have to be paid, making long sieges unlikely.

Regarding pay and length of service, the castellan had two advantages. Garrisons tended to be small. Admittedly, their numbers, like those of armies, are hard to calculate because medieval chroniclers were notoriously bad with numbers. Nevertheless, it is rare to find evidence of large garrisons, and sometimes these were raided to flesh out field armies. A second advantage was that the soldiers in a surrounded keep could hardly leave, and no pleasant result could ensue from stopping fighting, unless the garrison in its entirety decided that its obligation to serve had expired, which occasionally did happen. Yet the maintenance of garrisons also presented many problems. Defending a castle was not a task for amateurs. Professionals had to be hired. Because many of these were essentially mercenaries, their loyalty was sometimes doubtful and mutiny was a serious risk (see chap. 3). Gatehouses were constructed to provide a safe place for the castellan to live and also to allow him to control entry and exit. But the loyalty of the castellan was also a problem for rulers. Moreover, the paid or "stipendiary" troops had to be convinced that their ultimate lord was loyal to them. If they were besieged and their lord made no effort to relieve them, they might surrender as they then "had no natural lord."[31]

Even if the cost of garrisoning castles were overcome, inherent weaknesses remained. A castle can do little to prevent an attacker from choosing his moment. "No matter how strong, an isolated castle was vulnerable . . . A network of castles supported by a field army was a very different proposition, but only a few kings could afford such a combination." Improved construction techniques could make the siege longer and more difficult, but not impossible. The early motte and bailey castle was highly vulnerable because the various parts of the defense could not support each other. That was solved by the more modern stone castles, but the impregnable fort was never built. Galliard was considered so, but it fell five years after its completion. Its fall illustrated a major conundrum for the builders. A well designed castle could deter an attack but not if its location was truly vital. Then the attacker would find a way. Any castle would eventually succumb to starvation.[32]

That a castle could be taken was perhaps no more significant than that a field army could be beaten. More significant to evaluating the opportunity cost of choosing a castle over an army is that a castle cannot maneuver. In fighting Edward I, the Welsh frequently bypassed the king's castles, attacking them only when they chose. In turn, Edward did not spend more than ten days besieging Welsh castles. The English did construct castles during the conquest of Ireland but these merely became targets for successful destruction raids by the Irish. Spreading castles over the countryside during a conquest sometimes created more resistance than it could contain.[33] The most expensive fortifications simply could not fulfill the strategic functions assigned them. Historian Michael Prestwich judged Edward I's castles to be "the most magnificent series of fortifications to be built in all of Medieval Europe," even as he questioned the wisdom of Edward's strategy regarding the resources required to maintain them.[34] If castles were stupendously expensive, ultimately vulnerable, and prevented the build-up of field armies (the main opportunity cost), why build them? The advantages must have been thought more than enough to offset these drawbacks.

THE ADVANTAGES OF CASTLES

Historiography of medieval warfare has dispelled the notion that commanders and rulers were simpletons. Medieval rulers were keenly aware of their choices and attending costs. Knowing the cost of castles, they continued to build them. Even when short of money, they continued to build them, risking confrontation with vassals and taxpayers over the bill. To leaders of the age, the benefit of permanent walls outweighed the cost.

This was based on a very important consideration: the multiplicity of goals met by building castles. The castle was anything but a stone ring within which to hide from conflict. The castle dominated the landscape, figuratively and literally.

The castle was also a storehouse for munitions, an advanced headquarters, an observation post in troubled areas, home of a lord, and a place where he could be secure from attacks by his enemies. Royal castles could in times of emergency act as havens for the king's field army, or supply the men to raise a new army if the field army was defeated. In the event of an invasion castles drew off large numbers of men from the invading force, which had to capture or at least contain the castles being left in the rear or the flanks to maintain supply and communication lines . . . [It was] not a place of refuge, but a centre of military power.[35]

This multiplicity of roles helps explain why castles were the "main bones of contention . . . and focal points" of struggles. As a center of government and war in a warlike age, the castle was a symbol. The great royal castles of Wales were more than Edward I's way of controlling the Welsh; they were a way of reminding the Welsh that he was there. Evidence suggests that Edward understood this perfectly well. External architecture was used as a means of impressing the people, such as at Caernarfon. Its expense was magnified by its unique construction: Edward intended its walls to look like Constantinople's.[36] Good locations were exploited without regard to expense, such as at Conwy, where the castle overlooks most of the town. In especially vulnerable locations, such as Beaumaris, on remote Anglesey, Edward's engineers incorporated every possible feature — double walls, moat, access to the ocean, a profusion of towers — that could add to its strength. Construction of Edward's castles frequently included huge round towers that were doubly advantageous because they were harder to assault and gave the castle an especially imposing visage. This method of building was expensive because for structural reasons the walls consisted of multiple layers of materials, as erosion and age now reveal. The appearance of the castles was more than a matter of aesthetics or ego. As is shown by the elaborate and complicated interiors, these buildings were also the residences of high officials — and sometimes the monarch himself. The castle was wasted expense if it were mere vanity, but sensible expenditure if viewed from the perspective of occupation politics.[37]

For the expansion-minded magnate the castle was the best, perhaps only, means of laying permanent claim to disputed, threatened, or rebellious land. "The great value of the castle was that it held down the land; without taking it there could be no secure mastery of the land that it dominated." Controlling territory required removing your rival's castles, as well as having your own castles there. This strategy can be seen in action in Germany, France, and Britain. In Germany, the Duke of Swabia advanced down the Rhine, building one castle after the other, using each one to subjugate the country before continuing to the next spot. Fulk Nerra laid the basis of the Angevin dynasty in France by building substantial castles across his territories, spacing them so that mounted forces could easily move from one to the other. Edward I's needs were slightly different from Fulk's as he had to contend with entire hostile populations but his techniques were, nevertheless, similar. Each Welsh castle was built no more than a day's march from its nearest neighbor, and they were also located where they could be easily supplied. Although the criticisms of the amounts spent seem just, the revolutionary spirit in Wales has led one author to conclude that a "policy of energetic castle-building was essential." Perhaps it is no accident that Edward kept Wales but lost Scotland, where he did not engage in much building. His strategy there has been described as "less impressive, consisting as it did of sending northwards large armies with the goal of bringing the Scots to battle."[38]

The Welsh were not the only medieval Europeans to look askance at the forbidding fortresses in their midst. The temptation to use the castle's advantage to abuse surrounding inhabitants was too great. According to the Anglo-Saxon Chronicle, early medieval castles were used to imprison and torture people who might have goods. The Normans were long thought to have gained supremacy in parts of the Mediterranean because of the supremacy of their mounted warriors, but it now appears that their most successful strategy was to take a castle and use it as a base from which to terrorize the surrounding district into submission. When Alfonso VI captured Toledo in 1085, he placed a garrison at Aledo, far to the south of his effective rule, where it functioned as "a thorn in Muslim flesh" until 1092.[39]

Normans, Anglo-Saxons, Anglo-Normans, and Spaniards were able to maintain castles for years among hostile peoples. A field army could hardly have done so. It might be a better instrument for short-term conquest, but permanent occupation was another matter. An army could rescue a besieged castle, but a castle could shelter a small army. In an age where capacity to stay in the field was limited, this gave the castle a crucial advantage. The historical literature is filled with examples of medieval commanders avoiding battles, and some never fought any at all. With a castle as a handy retreat, there was no need to fight unless victory was certain, in which case the adversary would not fight. Clausewitz's dictum that "no battle can take place unless by mutual consent" is unusually accurate for this age. Most invaders used a single line of advance and could easily be evaded. When Edward III (r. 1327–1377) invaded Scotland, the Scots either avoided battle or took up strong defensive positions the king was unwilling to assault. Even when multiple lines of advance made complete avoidance impossible, the weaker force could retreat into its castles and wait for the fighting season to end. Fulk Nerra avoided battle whenever possible. Even when it was not clear that the enemy was stronger, fighting from behind walls was tempting.[40]

Fighting from behind walls deterred direct assault, and this might tempt us to think of this kind of war as "low cost." It was not. The suffering among ordinary folk was magnified in two ways. Obviously a successful storming was followed by massive misdeeds. More often, it lengthened the war. According to J. F. Verbruggen, the lawyer and pamphleteer Pierre Dubois

> lamented that the enemies of Philip the Fair were unwilling to fight battles any more because the royal army was too strong, and castles and fortified towns made it impossible to finish a war quickly and successfully. Against such fortresses "your army of splendid knights usually has to fight out a lengthy siege."[41]

Longer wars spelled higher tax bills, more frequent military service, more raids, property seizures, burning of hovels and possessions, and the privations of being besieged, even if the result was not a storming or a subsequent slaughter. In fact, a type of conflict developed that was relatively low in direct military cost but devastating for the populace. Feuding, as it was called, involved plunder, looting, and devastation; in other words, warfare aimed directly at civilians. Absent a carelessly opened gate, the castle was immune to these attacks. It could, however, serve as a place to store the loot.[42]

Retreating behind walls might also imply that a cost of reliance on castles was the sacrificing of offensive strategy. Again, this was not quite true. Yes, castle spending inevitably meant less money for the field troops. But defending a castle was not quite the same as defensive warfare. A castle could have both offensive and defensive purposes, and very few castle builders thought solely in terms of defense. From the moment of their construction, castles "threatened neighbors, and . . . often served as bases for attack"; they "could menace enemies as well as protect friends." Rarely was the defense of a castle a passive operation. "The overriding thought in castle strategy was not passive defence but action and destruction." Moving across the drawbridge actually strengthened the "retreating" force. "Shutting oneself up in a castle was not an attempt to avoid conflict, but a manouevre to make the enemy fight at a disadvantage. . . . The defence had an enormous advantage. To an invader time would be vital." Depending on distance, essentially three cases existed in which the castle garrison threatened an enemy. First, sallies might be made against the immediate besiegers. Second, raids from the castle could threaten areas within a day's round trip or so. An example of this can be seen in the castle at Le Puiset, taken by Louis VI in 1111; no one dared to come within 8–10 miles of the walls. And third, the castle's troops could be launched on a major operation against a neighboring principality. It is no coincidence that the most offensive-minded leaders of the age often withdrew behind stone walls. The castle was not purely defensive.[43]

Raids and major operations could be contained by siege. A brief siege would be meaningless, as the castle's troops could return to their offensive ways as soon as it ended. To contain an aggressive prince, it follows that his garrisons had to be besieged to the point that they would surrender rather than face a worse experience. Siege warfare became the operational center of medieval warfare, not just to overcome the defense but to prevent the fortified enemy from engaging in offense. The castle became the geographic center of warfare. In civil wars the focus on castles was even greater than normal because there was more emphasis on establishing and maintaining control of territory. Even the English campaigns in Scotland revolved around castles. The English capture of Stirling (1304) ended resistance more effectively than the famous Battle of Falkirk (1298), and the English disaster at Bannockburn (1314) was a direct result of the need to relieve the garrison at Stirling. Robert Bruce attempted to make successful sieges more decisive by destroying captured castles but even such extreme "decastelization," practiced elsewhere as well, still depended on a successful siege to begin with.[44]

If we accept that siege was central to medieval warfare, why its lack of study until the 1990s, especially since the methods and conventions of siege warfare did not change very rapidly? A straightforward answer is that a generation of military historians preferred to emphasize medieval open-field battle. Historians were nearly as affected as people at large by the image of the heroic knight on horseback. The armored cavalry of the High Middle Ages can hardly be disregarded, of course, but it played no role in siege warfare. A knight could fight for or against a castle, but hardly while horsed.[45] He could climb ladders, fire weapons, pour boiling oil, or give orders to so do, but this fighting, while often more dangerous than the charge with lance and sword, would produce much less epic poetry. The horse in such operations was rarely a gallant, elegant steed, but rather the sturdy and ugly draft horse that pulled the battering rams and other heavy equipment. Sometimes that work was given to the even less glamorous ox.

Glamorous or not, medieval warfare required sieges. The only alternative was rapid raiding, so rapid that counterattacks by castle troops were irrelevant. This was unlikely as the most important points on the map were the most likely to be occupied by a castle. Sieges, while difficult and expensive, were inevitable.

The business of laying siege to a castle was a highly complex and costly affair and was not undertaken lightly. Frequently such sieges involved so many men and so much *materiel* that no other action could be undertaken by the army involved and once committed to a siege there arose the problems of guarding against an attack by a relieving force, maintaining adequate supplies of food and forage, and epidemic disease caused by the concentration of a large body of men in a small area for a long time.[46]

This seems to have been the case throughout the Middle Ages. Castles might be primitive, but taking them was often beyond "the incoherent and *ad hoc* armies of Western Europe." Even the simple motte and bailey castle was rarely captured. A documentary and archeological study of some one hundred and fifty such castles in Belgium has found scarce references or evidence of successful attacks. Only five are definitely known, although the baileys were sometimes burned, and one castle was captured by two knights and twenty peasants when the gate was left open.[47]

The single stone keep or *donjon* also posed extraordinary problems. The donjon of Coucy (built 1223–1230) was so strong that its barons defied royal commands for two centuries! That these castles were smaller than the motte and bailey variety was no balm for putative conquerors. "Long passive sieges were usually futile, because the small garrisons required to defend these keeps used up their vast stores very slowly and used little water." Even large castles, if properly designed, could be defended by small groups. Caernarfon survived two sieges (1403–1404) and inflicted three hundred casualties even though its garrison was down to twenty-eight men. In 1216 a substantial French army required fifteen days to capture a castle held by thirteen men; Harlech resisted the rebellion of 1294–1295 with a garrison of only twenty. The famous crusader castle Krak des Chevaliers, defended by a skeleton garrison, survived twelve assaults and was finally taken only by ruse in 1271. Château Galliard had more troops — one hundred and forty at the time of its surrender — and was only lost after a six-month siege, a five-week assault, an inadvertent failure to defend a window, which allowed the attackers in, and no serious relief attempt. For the attacker, the situation did not improve over time. "By 1300, the odds of a strong force successfully forcing a well-built and well-defended fortress were less than they had been three centuries earlier." Gunpowder changed things, of course, but seven seventeenth-century cannon could not reduce the twelfth-century keep at Rochester.[48]

The attacker faced severe costs. Money supplies sometimes succumbed before the defense did. Stephen (r. 1135–1154) spent £10,000 besieging Exeter

Castle, a sum five times his estimated annual income. Indeed, a successful siege could be financially disastrous. Henry III (r. 1216–1272) captured Kenilworth in 1266 through negotiation, "but the siege had been cripplingly expensive, absorbing the income of ten English counties." The personnel cost constituted the real culprit. On both sides specialists were needed. A long siege quickly raised expenses because feudal levies could only be required to serve for periods set by tradition and law, and once these were exhausted, they had to be paid. The cost of personnel — to ruler and soldier — was high. Estimates of the numbers needed for a successful storming range from 4:1 to 10:1, and this seems conservative in view of some castles' successful defense against odds of 50:1. For the soldier, the attack was extremely hazardous and even after a breach of the wall it was not always easy to get troops to assault, sometimes requiring leading nobles and rulers to lead from the front. This could easily backfire. In 1088 a king was leading an attack on a gate when a woman described as "female in sex but not in spirit" threw a millstone on his head, bringing his reign to a premature end.[49]

Consequently, the attackers often opted for the slow process. But time itself was a cost. The besieging army could do nothing else and decisive victory could prove elusive. Stephen attacked rebellious baronial castles one by one, capturing a number through starvation, but at his death much of his kingdom was still in rebel hands. Delays could result in failure and the collapse of morale.[50] To such psychological problems the garrison troops were vulnerable as well, but their mighty blocks of masonry were not. In a word, the nub of the problem was that the resources invested by an attacker were much greater than those of the defender.

> The disproportionate resources needed to take a castle in comparison to defending it, once it had been built of course, was one of the key reasons for the constant rebellions of the nobility that characterized medieval politics. The nobles often could defy their lords with impunity, at least in the short term, behind the wall of their castles."[51]

The result was an endurance contest that often ended without a decisive fight. No definitive numbers exist for successful versus unsuccessful sieges. That the failure rate was very high is undisputed; indeed, the majority of successes were the result of negotiation, not storming. William the Conqueror allegedly never failed to take a castle, but he did so mostly by agreement. Even after a three-year siege of a castle in Normandy, the famous duke offered terms because he "had been forced to recognize that taking the castle was too demanding in time and resources." And this medieval ruler, more than most of his contemporaries, was able to assemble and maintain the obvious alternative to the castle, a trained and reliable field army.[52]

Whether the castle could have survived much longer once gunpowder became prevalent is actually a moot point. Its very strength was a barrier to the growth of great national governments. Monarchs regarded private castles as an inherent threat. Legal and other measures were taken to eliminate them. In Britain, the Tudors were particularly effective in eliminating great noble castles as part of a well designed program to establish the state's monopoly on violence. In France, Louis XIII probably destroyed more castles than he built. This trend was actually a paean to the military virtues of the castle.

THE COST OF ARMIES

For most of the twentieth century the explanation for the domination of the castle over the army was couched in simple terms: no such thing as a true army existed in the High Middle Ages. The medieval army was portrayed as an undisciplined rabble, consisting of magnificent mounted knights who fought as individuals, a smattering of bowmen, and a ragtag band of peasants who carried supplies and performed miscellaneous jobs. Military history for the pre-1300s was seen as comparatively unimportant.[53]

The negative view of the medieval army survives to the present day:

> Medieval armies were notoriously motley agglomerations of knightly vassals, hired mercenaries, militia auxiliaries, and all manner of irregular contingents often hastily thrown together for a season's campaigns. This lack of uniformity, along with the usual fragmented chain of command in most medieval armies, reflected the considerable degree of control exercised by local lords and urban communities over their involvement in military matters.[54]

To be sure, there are grounds for this opinion. For example, the kings of England and France made do with a bodyguard and a military staff, and armies were raised for the occasion and paid off as quickly as possible. Yet there was a military staff, there was planning, and there was organization. The Middle Ages were not a primitive period where knowledge of war had disappeared. Half a century ago research began to show that "much military activity was planned and commanders did have some idea of what they intended to do." Armies, it turns out, were more than feudal arrays. They were usually well organized, and the infantry was important, albeit often overlooked because chroniclers did not write much about peasant soldiers. "Commanders, then as since, were quite capable of carefully weighing up the position and coming to sensible and practical decisions."[55] The field today tends toward the view that knights, heavy cavalry, isolated motte and bailey towers dominating a lawless countryside, small numbers of effectives, as well as a serious lack of training, discipline, and unit cohesion must be swept away as the dominant themes. Continuity from the later Roman empire through the Middle Ages is the proper focus. The medieval world was dominated by imperial military topography, antique military science, and the militarization of the vast majority of the able-bodied male population.[56]

If this shift in historical thinking is accurate, constructing a usable field army was possible. This is hardly to be doubted. Edward I, for example, had 30,000 men during one of his Scottish campaigns.[57] Despite the indubitable advantages of the castle, why did not more rulers build up their armies instead of endlessly raising their masonry walls?

Numerical data for the High Middle Ages is notoriously bad, but there is no evidence that large armies were anything other than aberrations. Armies had to be brought together through a combination of feudal obligation, persuasion, and hiring. Hirelings and vassals had to be gathered from far-flung lands. Of course there were exceptions. The Normans invaded England with about 14,000 men (1066). The crusaders deployed some 20,000 men at Hattin (1187).[58] Edward I deployed large armies for longer periods of time than his contemporaries. He was able to do this by enforcing feudal obligations — he was the last English monarch to enforce a general obligation of cavalry service — and spending fortunes on hiring troops. He hoped to crush his enemies by sheer weight of numbers. In 1277 and 1282, he invaded Wales with 15,000–17,000 men. In 1287 he fought there with 11,000–13,000 men, and in his last Welsh war (1293–1297) he had some 31,000 paid troops across the principality, although never assembled in one place. The largest armies he employed were in Scotland. During the first Scottish war, Edward commanded as many as 30,000 troops, and he may have had twice that many across the entire northern kingdom. His operations on the continent (1293–1297) involved fewer troops, probably 8,000–9,000. He did not find assembling these forces easy. The permanent core of his army — the household cavalry — waxed and waned with the royal finances, and by the end of his reign he could only afford a thousand riders.[59]

Edward I's massive campaigns were exceptional and occurred very late in the period we are studying. The small army was the norm. To understand why this was so we have to consider two rather separate aspects of the cost of an army: the actual expense of raising and maintaining armies and their limited utility, that is, the opportunity cost compared with that of the castle. In an age when credit was in its infancy and leaders had to consider with care what they could afford, any army meant a huge outlay. "Only the richest monarchs could afford to maintain a permanent fighting force greater than a few hundred soldiers." Raising cash for troops and supplies was a problem in a rural society. Land was the dominant form of wealth so that liquidity was very limited. Only in the later Middle Ages did economic growth make larger armies possible. Movement of supplies was also a financial problem, especially as bad roads slowed their transport. Nor was the problem completely economic; there was a political dimension as well.[60]

> Armies were collections of personal retinues centred on the following of the commander. The sheer cost of war meant that nobody could afford to maintain regular standing forces, and it is doubtful whether political circumstance would have permitted it if it had been possible. Richard I seems to have wanted a regular army of 300 knights supported by taxation, but this sank without a trace. Any such development would have struck at the influence of the great.[61]

Perhaps no medieval ruler squeezed more money out of his subjects than Edward I, who averaged more than £67,000 per year (not counting unrepaid loans). Yet even he outran his treasury. "The country had to be organized on a massive scale to provide the armies, materials and money that were required for the many campaigns." The first campaign in Wales (1277) cost a modest £20,000 to £25,000, but the bill for the second war (1282–1283) reached £150,000. War in Wales "consumed royal treasure at an alarming rate." The total cost of the French war (1293–1297) reached £750,000. The costs of the Scottish wars are more difficult to calculate, but each campaign probably cost about £40,000. Cash reserves were quickly exhausted and unpaid troops mutinied. The burden on the nation was immense. In 1294–1295 tax receipts exceed a tenth of all coinage in circulation in England. None of this deterred Edward, who set off in 1297 on an overseas campaign even though the country was on the edge of civil war.[62]

If we consider the data in table 2.2 and compare it to Edward's income for the affected years, his difficulty — or rather, the taxpayers' — becomes clear. He waged war for nineteen of his thirty-five years on the throne, and his entire estimated revenue for the war years is only slightly more than the campaign expenditures. But his problem was not that military expenditure often outran his revenue. The larger issue concerns the results. Edward I fought in three theaters of war, Wales, Scotland, and the Continent, and was ultimately successful in only one: Wales, where he engaged in substantial castle building.

It is difficult to escape the conclusion that raising armies proved of much more limited utility to medieval rulers than did castles. The cost of arming must take into account how well a system works. Before World War II, France invested a fortune building the Maginot Line. Had the line saved France from

Table 2.2: Edward I's campaign spending

War	Years	Estimated expenditure (£)	Estimated tax revenue (£)
Wales I	1277	22,000	31,000
Wales II	1282–1283	150,000	143,000
Wales III	1287	10,000	39,000
France	1293–1295	450,000	361,000
France/Scotland	1296–1297	380,000	220,000
Scotland I	1298–1305	320,000	514,000
Scotland II	1306–1307	80,000	146,000
Total		1,412,000	1,454,000

Sources: Expenditure: Prestwich, 1972, Keuper, 1994, Morris, 2003; revenues: Ramsey, 1925, vol. 2, pp. 87–89.

Note: The Revenues column includes parliamentary subsidies (in fact special taxes), which were granted occasionally. There were subsidies granted in 1295 and 1296 for which data is unfortunately missing and difficult to estimate. In 1294 a tax similar to the 1295 and 1296 grants had brought in some £86,000, but it is unlikely that the latter ones, coming so close one upon the other, could have brought in anywhere near that much. We have estimated the income therefrom in the neighborhood of £35,000 each. Regular revenue figures are unavailable for 1297 and 1301; we have averaged the results from the previous and following years to arrive at figures for these years.

Hitler, that spending would have looked more justifiable and its cost to France much lower. Likewise, Edward I's campaigns did not bring England final victory, although in the case of Scotland his sudden death may have had something to do with that. Medieval rulers shied away from raising and equipping large armies for an elementary reason: armies could not win wars. The reason is that during the medieval centuries, generals usually avoided battle unless they were so much stronger that victory was assured; but in such a situation the weaker opponent would avoid battle and retreat behind the walls!

The avoidance of battle was a staple of medieval warfare. Medieval commanders "offered very few pitched battles." Battles were "rare" even though "warfare was constant." During the Albigensian Crusade (1203–1226) in southern France, the crusaders fought the dissenters forty-nine times. Of these encounters only four were battles, the rest sieges. The bellicose and aggressive crusader Simon de Montfort sought battle but once. Richard Lionheart, as famous a warrior as any, fought three battles in his career, and only one in the west. Once described as the "the greatest conqueror since Charlemagne," Henry II (r. 1154–1189) fought a grand total of one battle. Philip II Augustus of France (r. 1180–1223) also fought one battle, which he had tried to avoid. The famous English victories at Crécy (1346) and Agincourt (1415) were less significant than the sieges that followed.[63]

Medieval commanders understood perfectly well that battle could bring an immediate, decisive result. During the siege of Tours in 1044 Geoffrey Martel, the leader of the attackers, was advised to abandon the assault and instead use all his troops against a relieving army, it being pointed out that once it was destroyed, Tours would inevitably fall. "Battles were without doubt the high-points of many campaigns." Nevertheless, battles remained the exception. Medieval commanders were necessarily risk-averse. This lesson was taught through the famous late Roman text *De re militari,* whose author, Vegetius, advised that a good general fights only when certain of victory. That circumstance was rare. Outnumbered opponents did not take the field. Not only could the loss of an army be a catastrophe, but replacing the loss was sometimes impossible and the death or capture of the leader could literally mean the end of the war. This was an age when rulers were expected to take the field, and did. The risk of battle casualties was not an abstract calculation made from a secure command bunker.[64]

Instead of battling each other in the open field, opposing forces mostly besieged each other. The siege was regarded as the decisive encounter. Most battlefield victories were indecisive, but the fall of a castle left the victor with a clear, tangible result. Battles were fought to raise or continue a siege. Occasionally, a relieving army even offered the besiegers the choice of whether to fight in the open or to raise the siege and withdraw.[65] Defending the castle was considered perfectly chivalrous and in no way an admission of a lack of courage. Even a defense that failed did not always spell disaster for the invaded land:

> In general, medieval defensive strategy was based on avoiding, rather than offering, battle. This was because the great number of castles and fortified towns allowed the defenders to shut themselves up and wait patiently to see what happened. Fortresses were nearly always strong enough to stand up to the attackers, whose siege engines were often inefficient. Putting them together on the spot wasted a lot of time, and they were often feeble or else were rendered ineffective by the defenders' countermeasures. As long as the fortresses themselves were in good condition and well provisioned, there was not much for a stout-hearted garrison to fear. The capture of a castle brought small advantage to an invader, who had to put into it a garrison who would be hard put to defend itself in a partly destroyed fortress. The defenders were nearer to sources of help and to their bases, and the invader was seldom strong enough to take all the fortresses in the area.[66]

By definition, an army is superior to a castle in the offense. After all, a castle cannot move. But to an extent that would not recur until 1914, when new technology would create a stalemate, this was an age when the defense was superior. In the eleventh to the thirteenth century, it was the refinement and superiority of existing technology that gave the defense the upper hand in any struggle. Siege engines could destroy a castle but not quickly and not cheaply. Battle was quicker but could result in disaster. As a consequence, the medieval army marched and maneuvered more than it fought in the field:

Medieval strategy displays great similarity to that of the sixteenth and seventeenth centuries, and more especially the eighteenth. Armies were small, and difficult to replace, therefore the leaders of the defence avoided battle, although it was one of the most effective means of gaining their ends. They often chose to manoeuvre, and the weaker of the contestants took refuge behind the defence of his many fortresses. This sort of strategy was dictated by social conditions, the equipment of the armies, and the state and number of fortifications. This created a certain balance between the fighting nations, and this balance was not easily upset unless new methods were used.[67]

Successful offensive campaigning took place mostly in those places where fortifications were the exception. This was certainly true for William the Conqueror's rapid march across England.[68]

It should not be thought that this type of warfare was better for the common man than big-battle, high-firepower fighting. To the contrary, the ubiquitous castles "decreased the attractions of battle and increased the need to ravage." This strategy was both preferred and reliable. The land rarely supplied all the needs of an army anyway, so even a moderately humane army (if there was such a thing) would have quickly consumed everything in its path. The fortifications designed to protect led to a style of warfare that culminated in the destruction of lives and livelihoods.[69]

A strategy of ravaging fit well with the nature of the medieval army. Infantry forces were poorly disciplined and prone to desertion. "The age of cavalry was really the age of bad infantry, and was a political, not a technological, phenomenon." Rulers would have preferred to field better infantry forces, but this was not easy to do. As mentioned, feudal service had certain drawbacks. The soldiers were responsible to their own lords, not the king. The lords themselves preferred serving over transmutation to pay, because in this way they retained more independence. Feudal service was limited. The length of English feudal service was only forty days. Edward I began paying troops, sometimes even before their feudal service was completed, in order to retain them and their loyalty.[70]

Relying on feudal levies at least saved money. We have already seen the cost of campaigning, which included the hiring of soldiers. The brevity of feudal service was compensated somewhat by the brevity of campaigns. Only when the crops were up was it feasible to campaign for any distance. For fighting closer to home a year-round army might have had advantages, but this was not possible. "There was never a royal standing army." The military equipment for a mounted soldier just before the millennium equaled in value some twenty oxen, "the plough-teams of at least ten peasant families." In an age when a master carpenter earned three pence per day and year's rental of an acre cost four pence, a knight could earn 24–48 pence per day, a mounted archer six per day, and even the lowliest foot soldier was paid two pence daily. Knights in debt might fight to keep both armor and horse, providing at least a few cheap armored warriors but beyond that, building a permanent army with its exorbitant expense and limited utility made little sense. This was especially true given that the army was seasonal while the castle walls stood the year round.[71]

Limited utility of the army does not imply zero opportunity costs in choosing walls over troops. Money spent on bricks could have been used paying men. And there were circumstances and situations in which possession of a field army was necessary because it could accomplish things that a castle could not. Portable forts aside, castles could not wage offensive war although they could serve as bases. Even on defense an army could fulfill a vital role though it might never offer battle. One reason is that the presence of a defender's army forced the invader to remain concentrated. A concentrated army could neither gather enough supplies nor destroy anything except the narrow corridor along which it advanced. Moreover, foraging and ravaging required an invader to spread out but detachments of foragers and ravagers could easily be ridden down by fast-moving companies of knights. A defending army by its mere existence could protect a swathe of land better than a castle could. Furthermore, despite habitual caution, when occasion arose, medieval commanders did offer battle. If an adversary moved with too few troops, strayed too far from his castles, or deployed carelessly, a quick strike could lead to decisive victory. Without an army no such quick strike could be made, and the enemy would be nearly invulnerable. The army was the supreme weapon wherever fortifications were sparse. Once governmental capacity to raise armies grew, rulers used it. By the end of the era under study, England was able to raise "huge" infantry forces. Nonetheless, for the High Middle Ages as a whole, the prudent ruler would be better served to place the greater weight of his resources on castles, supplemented by an army, rather than the other way around. Despite the colossal expense, the opportunity cost of castling (fewer or smaller armies) was smaller than the opportunity cost of armies (fewer or weaker castles).[72]

CASTLE BUILDING AND THE OTHER PRINCIPLES OF ECONOMICS

This chapter has emphasized the principle of opportunity cost in the telling of the story of the castle. But opportunity cost is far from being the only principle of economics. The story of the castle could as well have been told by emphasizing any other economics principle. If we wrote as extensive a chapter for each of our other five principles as we did for the opportunity cost principle, we would be justified to entitle this book "The Economics of Castles." Instead, we confine ourselves here to short discussions of where and how one may see the operation of these other principles in the case of the castle during the High Middle Ages. Full-fledged explorations of these additional principles are provided in the other chapters of this book in the context of different historical episodes.

The principle of comparing expected marginal cost with expected marginal benefit is closely related to the principle of opportunity cost. But whereas in the bulk of the chapter we discussed the totality of the castles versus armies decision, the marginal cost/benefit decision focuses on the additional action to be taken, for instance, the next castle to be built, in addition to those already in existence. To be sure, even the additional castle involves an opportunity cost of its own (an additional army, say), but, once built, that castle would offer many additional benefits at few additional costs. Garrisons required to hold a castle were relatively small, so that the initially high construction cost could be followed by limited expenditure (high start-up cost, small follow-on cost). A small garrison might have a rather limited impact on the military situation in the surrounding countryside, but the castle possessor would have the choice of placing more or fewer troops in the castle as desired. Without fortification a small military force is nearly useless, something that in the U.S. Army is known as a "Task Force Smith" situation, named after the pitifully small American expedition into Korea in 1950 that was completely defeated and overrun. Without fortification, a military force must either be capable of standing up to expected adversaries, or it must flee. With a castle, the small force has much more freedom of action. That additional benefit is hence bought at a small additional cost. The marginal benefit to marginal cost ratio was high. We examine this principle in depth in "The Age of Battle, 1618–1815" (chap. 4), where we examine commanders' decisions of whether to offer or decline battle.

Also related to the opportunity cost principle, as well as to the marginal cost/benefit principle, is the principle of diminishing marginal returns. Although a vast amount of research on sieges would have to be conducted to confirm this point empirically, at least conceptually the case of castle construction yields easily to diminishing returns analysis. Simply put, one hypothesis would be that ever larger castles yield ever smaller increments in military advantage. While doubling the size of a castle might more than double its military usefulness (increasing returns), tripling, quadrupling, and quintupling it might less than triple, quadruple, or quintuple its usefulness (decreasing returns). At some point — economic theory does not specify at which point — the benefits of a larger castle fail to be commensurate with the larger cost. Whereas the marginal cost/benefit principle focuses on individual decisions to be made one at a time (and at the time that they are made), the principle of diminishing marginal returns examines a series of actual or hypothetical decisions and states no more than that at some point a switchover from increasing to decreasing returns must result. If that were not so, castles would have grown to infinite size — an obvious impossibility. The trick is to figure when the switchover point has been reached.

A castle needs be of certain minimum size to fulfill its owner's requirements; it may have to house a royal court or provide barracks for a substantial military force. That the defense of a castle does not necessarily improve with size and expenditure is so for at least two bricks and mortar reasons. First, as its perimeter grows, so do the spots to be defended, and the ability of defenders to move from a secure to a threatened spot becomes more complicated. A larger garrison is required to counteract thinning forces. Second, larger castles often consisted of series of structures linked by walls, and the defenders of one structure — a tower, say — sometimes could not help defend the other. There was also a financial issue: in most cases, larger castles took longer to build. A castle under construction has limited military value until at least the keep or the curtain wall has been completed. Rather than being a deterrent, a castle under construction might invite attack. Scaling up the argument, it is obvious that populating the landscape from a sprinkling to a dotting to a drenching with castles will yield at first increasing, but eventually decreasing military advantages. How designers, advisors, and rulers decided how big each castle was to be, and how many of them to build in their realm, would go toward addressing the diminishing marginal returns principle. There is no presumption in economic theory that every ruler got things just right, but there is a presumption that following generations learn from predecessor generations; there is a presumption that people learn from the past, that they are in this sense "rational," although even the rational may, of course, fail. We examine the principle of diminishing marginal returns in detail in the case of the strategic bombing of Germany in World War II (chap. 6).

The operation of the principle of substitution may be seen in the use of castles as an instrument of occupation. Historically, conquerors have relied on several tools for controlling conquered peoples, including cooption of local elites or occupation by a large army. But newly made friends among the elite may turn out to be unreliable, and long-term occupation of hostile territory by one's own army is dicey. In the Middle Ages, fortifications afforded an alternative. Edward I, for example, could have spent his Welsh castle budget on occupation troops, but he chose not to. (In Scotland he did rely more on his armies but not for perpetual occupation.)

Nearly everything in economics, including the principle of substitution, is ultimately related to costs and benefits. If an item or action becomes more costly (less beneficial) and another becomes more beneficial (less costly), we would expect decision makers to explore alternatives and, as circumstances may permit, adopt them more or less rapidly. This applies not only to whether to use castles as alternative means of occupation but also to myriad other decisions, including which type of castle to build, where to place a castle relative to the available alternatives, which design to use, which materials to employ, and so on. The story of the castle may well be told on the basis of the principle of substitution. Instead, we examine this principle in depth with a different case, that of France's decision to construct a nuclear strike force, the *force de frappe,* and ask whether it was to be a substitute for its conventional armed forces in the Cold War confrontation with the then–Soviet Union (chap. 7).

Finally, consider the principle of information, or rather the principle of asymmetric information. It comes in two "flavors." At first blush, the principle might not seem applicable to the history of castle building as there is nothing secret about the location of a castle. A castle is the least stealthy weapon in the world. Yet, tactically, a form of asymmetric information called hidden characteristics favored the defenders. For example, during a siege the defenders could see the attackers much better than the attackers could see the defenders. It is noteworthy how often attackers were uncertain about the number of defenders. As noted in the main text, castles sometimes held out until only a handful of effectives manned the walls. The castle would have been stormed much sooner had this been known. Storming a castle by itself was a highly exposed activity as none of the attackers could be sure of exactly what would land on top of them. Not knowing the size of the defending garrison posed another problem, namely, that if it were large enough, midnight sallies could (and did) occur. Moreover, the defending troops had plenty of "cover." The attackers could construct some, but it was always makeshift. Thus, while a castle's existence was no secret, the military strength that it harbored could only be discovered the hard way, a clear case of hidden characteristics. We examine this aspect of the asymmetric information principle in the American Civil War of the early 1860s (chap. 5), our only non-European case in this book.

A second form of asymmetric information is that of hidden action. A hidden action is one that cannot feasibly be observed, at least not simultaneously to the action being taken. A king might expect a castellan to manage the countryside in the king's interest, but how was the king to ensure this? Informal contracts, such as culturally evolved mutual loyalty and obligation played a role, as did formal contracts, such as the granting of fiefs and ascendancy to nobility. The history of the Middle Ages is in fact so replete with emphasis on these roles (public law having played very little part) that it is sometimes forgotten that formal and informal obligations were often interpreted flexibly. No one who owed an obligation viewed it as completely unlimited, nor were they expected to. This applied not only to the relation between ruler and vassal or ruler and castellan but to any relation between a principal and his agent(s). For example, a garrison had to be paid and to be assured that it would be relieved if besieged, and it was the castellan's job to ensure that these contract terms would be met. If not, as noted, the men might decide that their obligation had been discharged and "walk off the job." In turn, once appointed, a castellan became a power in his own right. There was no simple solution concerning the maintenance of loyalty of one's castellans. With vassal lords the problem was even worse, and it was only when monarchies centralized and individual nobles became financially less able to fight their rulers that the problem lessened. We examine the hidden action aspect of asymmetric information at length in the next chapter with the case of the use of mercenary forces by city-states in the Italian Renaissance, about 1312–1494.

CONCLUSION

Opportunity cost is the cost of forgoing valuable alternatives; it is the value of what one cannot have or do when pursuing the option that one has chosen. Strictly speaking, the cost of purchasing castles includes the entire set of alternatives, not just the establishment of an army. Palaces could not be built, universities could not be endowed, and roads could not be improved. For the medieval ruler, these alternatives were somewhat hypothetical as war was his main occupation. The next highly valued alternative to the castle was the army. Dynastic and territorial survival depended on success with the sword. Even a pacific ruler had to protect himself or herself through the building of castles. Avoiding war meant preparing for war. The primary opportunity cost of choosing one form of military preparation (the castle) was the other form (the army).

A number of rulers, including the Anglo-Norman kings, could raise substantial armies, and their ability to do so grew in the thirteenth century. Yet an army represented such a huge investment that it could not ordinarily be risked in battle, a rather impractical constraint. Even merely keeping it over time meant that "support for horsemen had to be renewed on a regular basis, regardless of the strain that such an effort might place on the available resources, if one's military posture were to be maintained in a consistent manner." Thus, "the choice was not between building castles and sustaining large numbers of mounted troops on a regular basis; the latter was economically impossible." Castle building, despite the expense, emerged as "the most effective, indeed the most cost-effective, strategy."[73]

It is quite correct to focus on limited resources:

> War on a grand scale was extremely difficult in the Middle Ages, owing to the small size of medieval states, the scarcity of the knights and the resultant small forces. Medieval leaders had to overcome numerous obstacles when they went to war; they were well aware that even with careful planning it would be impossible to destroy the enemy army since defence was much more stronger than attack, and they therefore tended to limit their aims. In most cases medieval wars had limited aims.[74]

The lower cost of castle building is vitiated somewhat by its continuity. An army might require continuous infusions of cash, but so did a program of castle building. Nor was castle building a panacea. The Welsh castles have been described as "white elephants" because, although their presence did anchor English rule, their small garrisons could do nothing during rebellions but protect themselves. Eventually the very defensive strength of castles made them obsolete. Rather than engaging in long and costly sieges, armies fought away from the great forts and the importance of masonry began to decline in the fourteenth century.[75]

To some leaders, nonfinancial dangers of maintaining armies may have been the decisive consideration. In the eight and ninth centuries, the Carolingian rulers established feudalism in order to create armies, but as the empire disintegrated feudal warriors became rulers themselves. Ironically, the attempt to create an imperial army accelerated the empire's undoing. In contrast, medieval monarchs were reluctant to experiment. "Changes in methods of recruiting armies were . . . extremely dangerous politically for the monarch who carried them out."[76] Yet Edward I increased the size of his army, and there is no consensus on how much of this was the result of innovation and how much was the result of his usual way of avoiding choices: wild spending. Although the king "was very well aware of the importance" of having enough money, there was "no real budgeting . . . and without this it is inconceivable that any very careful consideration of the financial implications of policy could be made. There is no evidence of a proper balancing of probable expenditure against probable income." To keep the wars going, his Exchequer, on at least two occasions, did clamp down on other government expenditure. But this was more the bureaucracy's response to the king's demands than a result of a royal policy decision. "Even if realistic budgets had been produced, it is very unlikely that Edward would have allowed his plans to be altered substantially by such considerations: he was too obstinate a man."[77] The result of his failure to choose was a chain of unfinished castles and a neighborhood of unfinished wars.

The eleventh, twelfth, and thirteenth centuries were dominated by the castle, politically as well as militarily. The role of the castle and the decision making that emphasized castle construction is worth studying because it helps us understand both the absence and the appearance of modern centralized government.

> The edge that fortification provided also helps to explain why small states, especially cities, could be major players in European politics and why kings often appear not to have looked beyond their immediate domains, since there was always a nearby castle of a rebellious baron to be reduced. It can be argued that no other era of history saw fortification play as major a role in war and politics as the period from around 1000 to 1300.[78]

By the end of the age, however, "the great rulers . . . gained a monopoly in really large armies, and in the most expensive items of equipment." This was true of walls as well. No noble could compete with Edward I's construction.[79]

Even Edward could not escape an economic dilemma related to opportunity costs, however: sunk costs. Once spent, the money is not recoverable. It cannot be redirected, and the choice made is irrevocable. While this can be applied to many economic activities, it was a particular problem in the realm of castle building. Permanent fortifications do not move. The castles in Wales provided no security for English troops in Scotland. Except for prefabricated wooden versions, they could not be moved across the Channel to punish the French. While expenditure on an army had fewer lasting benefits, it generated a force with multiple applications. The problem was less significant for individual noble estates. That rulers were willing to incur huge sunk costs is yet another demonstration of the military value of castles in this era.

Fortification did not die away. Military fortification was still a major field of endeavor at the beginning of the twentieth century. It enjoyed a brief revival in France in the 1930s. Since then, conventional fortifications have lost favor, but the idea has never lost its fascination: "The last round in this phase may be a castle in the air in a practical sense. Space satellites are said to be the ultimate in military sophistication, and as such unassailable. So, of course, was Château Galliard."[80]

APPENDIX

A Matrix for the Medieval Castle

Principle	Manpower	Logistics	Technology	Planning	Operations
Opportunity cost	construction imposes heavy manpower cost	castles provide unparalleled protection for supplies	heavy cost of keeping up with construction developments	presence of fortifications somewhat increases options	armies tied down by castle-based strategy
Expected marginal costs/benefits	required garrison small	supply of builders difficult but supply of fort itself less so	investment in improved construction techniques yields better castles, greater deterrent	strategic location can deter attacker	castles and fortified towns provide bases for aggressive moves
Substitution	a wall has a multiplier effect	castles' limited needs make it easier to supply than invading force	advancements in construction make castle close to invulnerable by 14th century	a chain of castles may be more realistic than an occupation force	as a method of harassment, castle superior to raiding force (consider Alfonso VI)
Diminishing marginal returns	a castle designed for a bigger garrison is not necessarily more defensible	a larger garrison consumes more supplies and might be forced to surrender sooner	larger castles are not necessarily easier to defend; complexity sometimes interferes with defensibility	too many castles create problems, including reliability of defenders, protecting all, etc.	attacking all your adversaries' castles can create a stalemate (consider Stephen)
Asymmetric information (overcoming) hidden characteristics	existence of good fortification an excellent morale builder	attacker rarely in a good position to know exact strength of defense	during siege defenders can target attackers much better than vice versa	building of castle can have multiple purposes	ruler can send relief force at time of own choosing; besiegers can never be sure when this will occur
Asymmetric information (overcoming) hidden action	incentives necessary to maintain loyalty of garrison	successful designers given immense rewards	castle building requires top-notch masons and architects	knights who pleased monarch might become castellans	successfully constructed and defended castle awes, intimidates

——— T H R E E ———

The Renaissance, 1300–1600

The Case of the Condottieri and the Military Labor Market

Military contractors, or *condottieri*, and their men were not welcome anywhere. No one in Europe enjoyed the presence of these mercenary forces, and all were desperate to make them go away, fast and by whatever means. In a much repeated story, Catherine of Siena, a nun, famously beseeched one such contractor, John Hawkwood, with the uniquely compelling logic of her time: go join a crusade to harass the Muslim Turks for the good of Christendom.[1]

> I pray you sweetly for the sake of Jesus Christ, that since God and also our Holy Father have ordained for us to go against the infidels, you — who so delight in wars and battles — should no longer war against Christians, because that is an offense to God. Go and oppose them [the Turks] for it is a great cruelty that we who are Christians should persecute one another. From being the servant and soldier of the Devil, may you become a manly and true knight.[2]

The invocation fell on deaf ears. Hawkwood declined the proposition and resumed pillaging the Italian countryside. He had gotten there around 1360 with an assortment of experienced fighters who suffered unemployment when their erstwhile employers took a midterm break in the Hundred Years' War. The peace of Brétigny, concluded on 8 May 1360 and ratified in Calais on 24 October that year, released a "professional soldiery dependent for their livelihood on pay and other profits of war [and] those unable to find employ elsewhere joined up with others to form independent companies making war on their own account." These free companies "were to become the scourge of western Europe before the emergence of standing armies in the fifteenth century," and for a good portion of the population, "peace and war became indistinguishable."[3]

Stranded and in need of livelihood, they began to roam and ravage the French countryside. Some came to see the riches of the popes' residence in Avignon, a sumptuous court in southern France supplied by wealthy merchants from Italy. Pope "Innocent VI could have derived no pleasure from contemplating the vast encampment across the river, and he was quite prepared to pay an immense sum to the mercenaries to induce them to go away quietly. He also had to grant them a plenary indulgence," writes Geoffrey Trease, a prolific author, who adds that this "must indeed in this case have covered a multitude of sins."[4]

Thus induced, the more adventurous crossed the Alps or roamed along the Mediterranean coast to discover the origin of the French popes' riches for themselves — in Milan, Florence, Venice, Pisa, and other Italian cities.[5] There they met ready demand for their services. Italy in the 1300s and 1400s, as before and after, is a confusing affair.[6] Political power in Italy was split between the Guelph party, those favoring the Roman church and its designs on temporal power, and the Ghibelline party, those favoring the emperors of the Holy Roman Empire who saw themselves as protectors of the church and therefore intended to limit it to the exercise of spiritual power, though this split was frequently no more than a mask behind which to hide local rivalries.[7] Sicily and Naples were southern kingdoms, feudal in character, formerly part of the Holy Roman Empire, and recently contested by French, Spanish, and Hungarian interests, sometimes united as one kingdom, and sometimes split into two, and even three kingdoms (fig. 3.1).

Milan, located in the northwest of contemporary Italy, and firmly aligned with the imperial party, held sway over the Lombard region and jealously guarded its despotic independence. In addition to expanding its sphere of influence across northern Italy, Milan also pushed south, aided in part by Tuscan towns such as Pisa and Siena willing to use the Milanese threat to limit Florentine supremacy. Florence sent diplomatic missions to Venice, arguing that once Milan had acquired Lombardy and Tuscany, it surely would turn its ambition toward the East. But Venice was not much interested. To hold off encroachment from Milan, Florence built alliances with city-states located between itself and Venice. It also sought assistance from France and Bavaria to create additional fronts for Milan.[8] Clinging, with mixed success, to the ancient Roman vision of republican city-states, Florence generally based its foreign policy on anti-imperial and antityrannical precepts,[9] but the city aligned itself with whatever power was deemed necessary to retain its republican independence. On the whole, it exercised strong influence over the Tuscan lands surrounding it.[10]

Venice, well protected by its lagoon, was preoccupied with its eastern dominions and its seafaring ventures, not entering Italian mainland politics much until the 1420s, essentially to build a more secure bulwark against Milan

Figure 3.1. Italy, ca. 1494
Illustration by Hubert van Tuyll.

even while maintaining trade with it. It also thought that a Florence reduced by Milan might not altogether be a bad thing.[11] The resulting muddle led to a costly period of war among Florence, Venice, and Milan (and Naples and the Papal States) that lasted for more than two decades, not to be resolved until a three-year-long succession struggle over Milan, involving all the major powers, ensued. That struggle was won by Francesco Sforza, the preeminent condottiere of the time. A warlord had become lord.[12] He also proved himself a capable statesman, and in the spring and summer of 1454 a power-sharing arrangement among Milan, Venice, and Florence was worked out, to be joined in February 1455 by Naples and the Papal States as well. This five-power alliance and balance-of-power club would hold roughly to the end of the 1400s, the quattrocento.

Smaller powers — Bologna, Ferrara, Genoa, Lucca, Pisa, Perugia, Siena, and many others — existed in profusion, constantly fending off the larger powers.

Political identification of rural populations hinged not only on "which city's currency would prevail in the local market . . . [but on] the direction in which the inhabitants fled when war threatened." Meanwhile, the Papal States were a highly unstable amalgam of variously contested territories crossing central Italy in north-south direction from the Adriatic to the Tyrhennian Sea, dotted with a number of cities and regions of constantly changing political fortune. The church had got itself into trouble when, following Gregory XI's death, its cardinals on 8 April 1378 first elected the Italian Urban VI (r. 1378–1389), who was to reside in Rome, and then, disaffected by his performance, reversed course and also elected, on 20 September 1378, Clement VII (r. 1378–1394) of Geneva, who took residence in Avignon, a line that came to be known as the antipopes. The church had two (and briefly three) popes! This schism in the church was not overcome until 1417 with the election of Martin V (r. 1417–1431) and added greatly to the political and military distress in Italy. For the duration of the nearly forty-year split, the Roman popes were supported, on the whole, by England, central Europe of the Holy Roman Empire, and some powers in northern Italy while the Avignon line found support in France, Burgundy, Savoy, Naples, and Scotland.[13]

When the papacy was reunified, the Holy See, from the Latin *santa sedes,* or "holy seat," began to reassert regional territorial interests in Italy. Buffered from imperial-oriented "Ghibelline" Milan by nominally pope-friendly "Guelph" Florence, the Papal States issued demands and exerted pressure on Florence. Now, Florence felt encircled and came to bear the brunt of the burden of conflict as it tried to maintain its independence from a newly rapacious church in the south and Milanese ambitions from the north. The 1300s and 1400s certainly generated much work for military forces in Italy.[14]

We begin this chapter with an overview of some of the types of problems one may expect with regard to the labor contracts signed by the city-states and their mercenaries. These are then treated in more detail in the remainder of the chapter. Next we discuss issues of supply, demand, and recruitment; contracts and pay; contract enforcement issues; and the development of permanent armies in partial response to the difficulties the military labor contracts posed. Finally we examine ways in which the other principles of economics described in chapter 1 might apply to the condottieri period.

THE PRINCIPAL-AGENT PROBLEM

The *condotta* (plural *condotte*) was the contract signed between city leaders and the head of a company of mercenaries, the *condottiere* (plural *condottieri*). Hiring such a company presented a number of information-related obstacles of which the principal-agent problem is an example. The principal is the party requesting a service (the city-state), and the agent is the party contracted to perform it (the mercenary). Contract fulfillment requires that both parties perform the contracted action(s) and is therefore contingent on both parties being able to monitor and enforce contract provisions. One difficulty with this is that a city may not be able to observe at a feasible cost what the mercenary does or does not do. Only the mercenary knows, and he can thereby exploit the situation. Hence, the city will find it necessary to discover cost-effective ways of limiting the mercenary's moral hazard, the situation in which the mercenary is tempted not to put forth the contracted effort. Likewise, the mercenary needs to spot a way to limit the city's temptation to renege on the contract.[15]

Resolution of the principal-agent and other difficulties revolves around the writing, monitoring, and enforcing of contracts that reduce the number and severity of contract disputes, minimize opportunism, enable better observation (policing) at low cost, share risk-taking, and generally align incentives between principal and agent. The overall objective is to prevent shirking. If the contracted action cannot readily be observed, for instance, the effort that goes into the defense of a city and its surrounding countryside, an observable substitute must be found that is correlated to the desired action. While ostentatious display of an abundance of men, horses, and equipment may look impressive, it does not reliably signal a mercenary's ability and willingness to conduct battle and have his men — assets to be parlayed into future contracts — die in it. The condottiere faced a principal-agent problem of his own of course: how to raise, manage, and keep his soldiers, who, while securing their livelihood, could be expected to flock more readily to such leaders as would keep them out of harm's way. For purposes of collective bargaining, troops could and did engage in various forms of labor unrest, including mutiny (a form of labor strike).

The principal-agent problem is but one of a number of hidden action–related asymmetric information problems that cannot readily be observed and thereby pose a threat to contract fulfillment. Other such problems include the difficulties of dealing with teams of agents (when a city signs more than one mercenary company), of subcontracting (condottiere to his men), of contract holdup (holding out for more pay once the enemy stands before the city gates), or of altogether reneging on a contract when battle is near (desertion). If more than one agent is involved, the contract(s) must somehow provide incentives to avoid free-riding on other team members' effort, for instance, by the costly observation of each member's effort or by an incentive structure that encourages each to put forth his best effort while maintaining a cooperative and coordinated approach to campaigns and battles. Close observation of individual team members' fighting effort on the battlefront is impractical, and the question arises of just how to write a contract that properly motivates team members to put forth their best effort even as opportunities for shirking exist. One way to overcome this hurdle is to offer bonus payments as an incentive to perform as contracted, and this, along with a variety of other mechanisms, is in fact what the record shows took place. We see in this an example of how certain facts of history can be wedded to theory.

These few paragraphs already suggest why the mercenary period, at least in its specific Italian form, came to an end. In its bloom, the period lasted about two hundred years, the 1300s and 1400s. Eventually, mercenaries either were integrated into the cities that hired them or the cities redeveloped their own defensive forces (or, frequently, a combination of the two). Alongside various political and technological changes of the period, the incentive problems posed by mercenary contracts were too difficult to overcome effectively. A new way of organizing military force had to be found. It is surprising how much of the historical literature about condottieri is about power politics and military technology, rather than about the very contracts after whom the condottieri — the contractors — are named. If the condottieri period came to an end, should not one of the reasons be sought in the difficulty of designing and enforcing military labor contracts? This, at any rate, is the thesis explored in this chapter: that the contracts themselves are an important locus in which to find the seeds of their eventual demise.

DEMAND, SUPPLY, AND RECRUITMENT

Principal-agent problems are conditioned partly by opportunities that arise from movements in supply and demand. On the demand side, apart from the sheer frequency with which wars were fought in Italy, one prominent factor was that the external security situation outstripped the supply of troops that could legally and effectively be called upon. The forty-day levy, common in feudal Europe, was insufficient and raised numbers that were dwarfed by the size of mercenary bands. At its peak in 1353 the Great Company alone numbered 10,000 men. In contrast, cities and the surrounding countryside (the *contado*) were small. Even "by the middle of the sixteenth century, there were only ten cities in all of Europe with a population in excess of 60,000." Bubonic plague repeatedly ravaged communities throughout the 1300s to 1600s and depleted populations. Famine was frequent. Bribing a threatening band to simply go away could be cheaper than to engage in war with it.[16]

Nor were those who might be called to service necessarily willing to fight and die. An audacious subject might heed the feudal call to muster and appear with his bow and a single arrow![17] Uncertainties regarding feudal levies created ready demand for mercenary troops in the first place, and therefore for agents—leaders of mercenaries—to whom hiring and day-to-day management could be devolved. Most of Italy had left feudalism behind at any rate and relied on small-scale civic militias. These were not necessarily ineffective. To the contrary, there was

> a growing awareness that armored horsemen could be vulnerable even on their home ground: the well-watered, relatively open terrain of northwestern Europe. As early as the twelfth century, the cities of Flanders and northern Italy were beginning to produce foot soldiers able to defeat the best of the mounted chivalry. In 1176, it was the infantry of the Lombard League that broke the charge of Frederick Barbarossa's knights, then counter-attacked to drive the Germans from the field of Legnano. . . . At their best, however, the civic militias of urban Europe were part-time fighting men.[18]

Exceptions notwithstanding, the militias had in fact suffered some drastic defeats, and long-distance and long-duration military campaigns were not best left to civilians; moreover, Italy's city-states were doing well in business and had good reason, or so it seemed, not to set business aside to staff civic militias. The Italian regions of Lombardy and Tuscany were rather well off by contemporary standards. The forgone tax revenue to build a conscripted force or the tax revenue required to hire volunteers to create an indigenous professional army would have been high. Better to hire professional outsiders on an as-needed basis to look after the necessary defense of the realm.[19]

Another factor concerned internal security. In England, King Henry II engaged mercenaries "for the suppression of the great rebellion of 1171–4. . . . In some circumstances, particularly those of civil war, mercenaries might prove more loyal than English troops, [although] in general they were regarded as unreliable and untrustworthy." Suppression, or at least distrust, of one's own was widespread. There certainly were English and French precursors to Machiavelli. But especially in Italy, the intensity of discontent within the city-states, having lost the Roman republican ideal and recently been subjected by absolutist princes and a church bent on regaining temporal power, made princes keep weaponry and military affairs out of citizens' hands. The *signori* were not about to arm the *popolo* at large.[20]

Military skills and tactics also affected demand. Hastily raised, ill-trained feudal levies were not particularly skillful. In contrast, "the skill of mercenaries provided one strong motive for employing them. . . . Their use of the cross-bow may have been one significant element, but hardened expertise acquired over many campaigns was presumably what gave them their real advantage over less practised soldiers." German mercenaries in particular were sought af-ter because of the effective riding formation of their heavily armed knights and warhorses (*equis*). Lightly armed riders were usually Hungarians (using lighter, swifter horses, called *ronzini*), and foot soldiers were often Italians. Against massed hordes of heavily armored knights, an indigenous civic force stood no chance. In 1342, Florence's mercenaries outnumbered its citizen-soldiers at the ratio of 20 to 1. A wedge between professional, if foreign, and civic de-fense had opened. German *Ritter*, or knights, were high in demand and highly paid, at least until 1360.[21] Military tactics had changed, from reliance on the foot-soldier to the cavalry. This was very much "the age of the horse." In con-sequence, as we shall see, military labor contracts came to say as much about horses as about men—and with this contract disputes concerning horses arose that had to be addressed as contracts developed over time.[22]

Labor supply is defined in terms of those who are willing and able to make labor services available at the prevailing wage rate. Italy in particular reflected "good contracts and rich booty. . . . But there was also the question of the lack of opportunity elsewhere in Europe; economic recession and unemployment in Germany made Italy peculiarly attractive to German soldiers and these were the predominant race amongst Italy's mercenaries," at least until 1360. One reason was the opportunity for knightly combat—to gain honor—but an-other the opportunity for bonus pay: ransom and loot from Italy's riches. The knights generally came from nobility, in many cases second, third, and fourth sons, those unable to inherit landed wealth. In other cases, consolidation of power in Germany diminished landed wealth and forced knights to gain honor elsewhere, perhaps even to regain lost riches. Some nobles sold their landed wealth and other possessions to invest in warhorses and equipment, an indication of investment in war with the attendant hope of an adequate return. Selzer finds that by far the majority of German knights stayed for only one or two seasons whence their names disappear from the Italian record. As he can only rarely document continuation of the family in the German records, it would appear that they lost their investment in their Italian adventures. Like the theaters of New York or the studios of Hollywood, many waged a substan-tial bet, and few succeeded.[23]

While mercenary captains often were members of the small-time nobil-ity with aspirations for higher achievement and recognition, historian Wil-liam Caferro mentions additional forces: "Famine posed as much of a threat to the companies as it did to the commune. The companies lived off the land. . . . As companies moved through the countryside, they attracted to their numbers discontented and alienated elements of society." Another historian, Michael Mallett, adds that soldiering was an "escape from a situation of rural under-employment, or of urban social repression; the need to escape from justice or from creditors; the need to escape from a stifling family environment."[24]

Joining a company presented genuine economic opportunity, short run and long run. For instance, upon hearing rumors of an approaching band, one could sell land to the uninformed city, join the band, and receive the land back with a handsome cash bribe to boot. Others joined for the long run "to escape poverty and improve their fortunes." The city of Siena frequently banned, exiled, and condemned its citizens if they joined mercenary bands and offered rewards on their persons. But when in dire straits, Siena would offer its former citizens absolution, lift bans, issue amnesties, even hire and turn them against Siena's own unruly mercenary companies. While this spelled success, it also repopulated the city with unscrupulous folks.[25]

Recruiters were of at least four types. First, the mightier Italian powers operated something akin to a human resource department. Its messengers, ambassadors, or recruiters were permanently associated with Milan or Venice or other powers and carried out orders to hire a certain number of men and equipment. A second type are the condottieri themselves. After all, they knew the market well and could use their knowledge and connections to make an extra florin or ducat by serving as middlemen between demander and supplier. A third type is what today would be called a personnel agency, an independently operated business whose sole purpose it was to trade information on who wanted men and who was willing to hire out. Since it could be just as easy, or easier, to serve recruitment functions as a sideline to one's ordinary business, commercial traders and tavern owners make up a fourth category of recruiters. The traders already traversed the Alps on business, so why not relay information about the military labor market as well and earn a commission to boot? In contrast to these mobile information traders, tavern owners were stationary: the information came to them when condottieri, soldiers, traders, recruiters, and others stayed at their places of lodging. German ownership of Italian taverns is well documented in cities such as Bologna, Milan, Rome, and Venice.[26]

One might add a fifth type of recruiter: the church. Especially in 1350–1370 free companies of mercenaries threateningly romped through the countryside in France and Italy. In part to satisfy their obligation toward their subjects, in part to protect their own affairs and advance their own interests, the popes of the time issued bulls and ordered crusades and preached against the companies, the *routiers* as they were known in French. Conveniently, the church could sell plenary indulgences for sins committed and raise men, means, or both to fight the rebellious, heretic companies. Alas, this proved insufficient, even when the price of the forgiveness of sin was dramatically lowered, and the church itself began to hire the very companies it wished to fight.[27]

With one significant exception it is not entirely clear by what criteria recruiters and employers selected their hired men-at-arms. The exception concerns reputation effects. The successful and reputable condottiere, one on whose word one could rely to fulfill a given contract in letter and in spirit, could always count on being wooed for future contracts and campaigns. Much recruitment appears to have taken place via marriage, family, and social ties between Italian and German nobles of greater and lesser rank. For example, as the condottiere himself would need to do his own subcontracting, he would often seek recourse to his own regional social ties.[28] The primary recruiter would need to advance sometimes considerable sums to enable a condottiere to go about the subcontracting. Even with an advance payment, subcontracting could involve taking up large amounts of credit, mortgaging one's holdings and obtaining cosignatures as collateral for creditors. The financial risks were not insubstantial, and it stands to reason that the condottiere would contract with those whom he knew, the better to enforce the subcontract.

CONTRACTS AND PAY

In a lecture to the British Academy, Daniel Waley examines twenty Italian mercenary contracts that have been preserved in toto from the late thirteenth century. These include eleven from Bologna, five from Siena, one from Florence, two from Piedmont, and one from the March of Ancona, all issued between 1253 to 1301 (but fifteen after 1290). Virtually all have the following contract elements in common: the number of men to be hired; the type of force to be used (usually cavalry); the number of horses they must supply; the minimum or maximum value of the horses; the *mendum,* that is, compensation for horses if injured or killed; provisions regarding arms and other equipment; the length of the contract, normally either three or six months; a contract renewal option; payment for travel to the place of engagement; the rate of pay and the pay period, usually once every two months; the pay differentials among various grades of hired men, such as commander, cavalry, infantry, or crossbowmen; the division of prisoners, ransom, and booty; a clause to secure release if the hired men were themselves taken prisoner; bonus pay, for example, retention of booty, double pay for battle days; jurisdiction, default, and penalty clauses; dispute resolution within the hired band; a loyalty clause; and, in six of the eleven Bolognese contracts, a deposit of bond by the band to guarantee the men's behavior! Both sides would employ notaries to oversee contract negotiation and the terms to be agreed. As a matter of mutual control one Bolognese contract specified that the value of the men's horses had to be agreed by six representatives in all, and that the band could not be sent to service until an agreement was completed.[29]

The contracts were lengthy, one running on 4,000 words (equal to about eight pages of this book). Later contracts, those recorded for example by Ricotti and by Canestrini, run between 1,000 and 3,000 words. That the word count of contracts shortened in succeeding decades and that they became "formulaic" is explained in part by the hiring states' practice of developing extensive regulations regarding mercenaries to which the contracts referred.[30]

The earliest preserved English contracts date from around 1270. But in contrast to what has just been described for Italy, in the English contracts "no mention was made of any recompense for loss of horses, of arrangements for distribution of the spoils of war, or other details that would commonly feature in later contracts." Yet by the turn of the century, English contracts had become "elaborate," laying out details regarding food, clothing, horses, armor and equipment, wage rates, bonus pay for overseas service, and sundry other matters. During the 1300s, English contracts became "standardized." Further, as in Italy, so in England, subcontracts developed to cover captains and those serving under them. Again as in Italy, so in England, the initial contracts offered room for abuse, and gradually regular muster was introduced. This reflects the theme of this chapter: principal-agent relations are fraught with difficulty, and contracts must be designed and redesigned accordingly, with special emphasis placed on credible enforcement. In England, muster rolls were kept, among other reasons, to identify deserters.[31]

We also find examples of binding arbitration. In a contract between one Wolfhard von Veringen and the city of Florence, Wolfhard provides for breach of contract as follows:

> in all records and writings, estimates and accountings of people and horses, there must be involved one person on behalf of the community of Florence, one on behalf of the lord Francis in Padua, and two on behalf of count Wolfhard. If however among these four any disagreement should arise concerning said estimates, accounts or records, then the lord of Padua must appoint an

honorary mercenary soldier from Germany as a fifth, in order to resolve and decide such disagreements, and his decision must be respected by all parties from then on.[32]

In this instance, any necessary binding arbitration would appear to have favored the count, relying as it does on a fellow mercenary and countryman.

In the early 1300s, hiring men-at-arms entailed police as much as military functions, and mercenary forces were generally small, counting in the tens or dozens. Among other reasons, hiring outsiders served the cause of "freedom from any possible local attachment" (that is, graft and corruption) and was as sensible a policy as was the gradual relegation of the hiring of individuals, with all the complex and expensive administration this involved, to professionals, the constables. These later became condottieri, who would recruit, sign, command, and were responsible for all men under their leadership and with whom a single contract covering all their men could be concluded.[33] Beyond administrative cost, there was however a military problem to be solved. "Once in the field . . . individual fighters did not automatically sort themselves into the smoothly functioning combat teams required by medieval warfare [so that] from the employer's perspective, a sensible response to this situation was to hire already-formed bodies of men."[34]

The condotte were highly specific and varied hugely depending on the needs of buyers and sellers. The contracts could be short term or long term; they could be mere retaining fees leaving the contractor free to pursue other contracts simultaneously; they could set down offensive or defensive duties; they could stipulate a payment for *not* attacking, freeing the buyer to fend off lesser capable companies.[35] The contracts specified details such as the number and types of troops, their equipment, and inspections, the relation to other condottieri in rank and status would be clarified, whom to take orders from and give orders to, and what shares of loot and ransom money would be distributed how and to whom.

At the same time, military service contracts in the trecento and quattrocento are replete with standardized features central to which were simply the number of men and their equipment. To be hired were *Reiter,* mounted knights, and their organizational structure was regulated in the contract. The length of term, usually six months, was specified, at least until the last decades of the 1300s, after which longer terms became usual, certainly for the more prominent condottieri. Contracts routinely contained an options clause, exercisable by the employer, obligating the mercenary to serve another term. The employer would need to exercise the option within a specified number of days or weeks before the expiration of the current contract. Accordingly, we observe that certain mercenaries served the same master over a number of consecutive years. One Arnold von Hunwill, for instance, served Florence from July 1388 to August 1392 for fifty months in nine separate contracts. Hawkwood stuck with Florence for twenty years (1375 to 1394). Colleoni became one of Venice's primary condottieri by 1441 and remained so until his death in 1475.[36]

A loyalty clause would be part of the contract. The contracts also laid down when and where the mercenaries were to gather for muster, whether and if so how much of the time of transit would be considered part of the service to be rendered, when *solidus* (pay) would be paid, how much, in what installments, and under which conditions bonus pay would be due. The contracts would cover "the settlements of disputes, the fate of prisoners, reciprocal guarantees, [and] indemnities in case the contract was broken and its stipulations."[37] *Prestanza* would be paid, an advance payment to permit the mercenary leader to go about the hiring of underlings and to equip them. As mentioned, among the equipment, horses took supreme importance. They were a key requirement for battle as the technology of fourteenth- and fifteenth-century warfare favored use of cavalry forces. Consequently, horses were a soldier's greatest capital item, costing in Genoa in 1362, for instance, twice a knight's monthly wage and as much as half the annual pay for a three-man lance (consisting of a heavily armed man-at-arms, a lightly armed sergeant, and a page). "In the muster rolls the horses of a company were described as carefully as the men, indeed often with greater care." Particular care had to be taken to classify, brand (or otherwise mark), and register horses so that identification would be possible. This was to assist in the inevitable squabbles over compensation for injured, killed, or nonexistent horses. Compensation claims for lost horses had to be made within specified time limits. To prevent mercenary soldiers from drawing an income when not properly equipped for battle, Venice insisted that horses not only be replaced within ten days' time but that the skin of the horse be presented to Venetian inspectors to ensure that the horse was in fact dead. In war, attention was paid more to enemy horses than to enemy men, and horses made great booty. This caused problems for paymasters, city-states like Venice. They began to resist claims for compensation for lost horses and shifted responsibility to the mercenary company.[38]

In contrast to similar contract formulae known from England and Germany, the Italian system introduced certain modifications and differentiations to keep contracts flexible. One was the distinction between contracts *in modum stipendii* and those *in modum societatis*. The former were contracts with individual mercenaries paid a daily stipend, the latter with leaders of mercenary companies, which became increasingly common as the 1300s progressed, especially after 1360. It was recognized that in delegating recruitment to a condottiere, the benefit of administrative relief was to be weighed against the cost of dependency on that leader. "A military system based on extended and better managed contracts to experienced mercenaries became an obvious development."[39] In this regard, another refinement pertains to contract options (*condotta in aspetto*). The contract base period (the *firma*) could thus be extended. At times, the option was open-ended, and the condottiere would need to appear whenever called upon. This option would be handsomely rewarded with an advance payment of as much as half the value of the future contract. Likewise, contracts could and would contain clauses to refrain from turning against the present employer for a set period of time into the future, what today might be called a "noncompete" clause, whereby high-valued employees agree upfront not to join, upon contract termination, a directly competing firm for a set period of time.

The variety and changes in the contracts amply suggest that the parties were addressing disputes by writing their next contract differently. The number of disputes can certainly be lowered by increasing the number of contingencies covered in contracts. But this runs into the problem of bounded rationality, a concept that suggests that since knowledge and rationality are limited, contracts cannot capture all contingencies. Contracts can only reduce likely disputes; they cannot eliminate them. An example is provided by historian C. C. Bayley. He writes that it was established practice, incorporated into Florentine code in 1337, that conquered "lands, castles, and other immovables should fall to the share of the republic," whereas "harness, armour, and *mobilia* in general were claimed by the soldiery." But disputes arose, for example, "on the disposition of movables in castles taken from the enemy. The condottieri claimed all movables, wherever found, as their legitimate perquisite. The republic maintained that its proprietory right to a captured fortress included all movables found therein." In another example, Bayley writes that "the contract at short term, which enabled the city to drop incapable or lukewarm servants without undue delay, was naturally unpopular with the condottieri. They retaliated by slackening the tempo of their operations when their brief contract was approaching its term." Thus, despite standardized contract elements, in reality each contract appears to have been unique. In an 1851 collection of Italian contracts, Giuseppe Canestrini lists explicit and implicit contracts, simple and complex contracts, protectorate and honorific contracts, uncompensated and compensated contracts, and those based on recommendations and references; further, those based on an alliance between one state and a mercenary company, or of an alliance of several states among themselves with a mercenary company, and, finally, those based on an alliance among several states jointly with a condottiere.[40]

City-states published regulations that spelled out the expected behavior of the hired forces. Changes in these regulations tell us much about the failure of formal contracts, they tell us about informally expressed and expected behavior, and they tell us about enforcement problems. Historians have not yet fully pursued this promising avenue of research, even though Canestrini clearly pointed to the difficulties with contract enforcement. Why else would contracts have been so varied and variable if not for enforcement problems? Among the more well-known regulations pertaining to mercenaries were those of Florence in 1337 and detailed amendments made in 1363 and 1369 *stante i mali portamenti degli stipendiari* ("because of the ill deportment of the mercenaries"). Bayley adds that the problems were not all on the mercenaries' side, but also that there were "alarming abuses in the engagement and control of the stipendiaries by the responsible functionaries, the *ufficiali della condotta*."[41]

Such contract variety and depth required well-trained legal minds, on both sides, and mercenary companies did come with their own complement of lawyers. The condottiere, especially in the later years of our time period, headed a substantial business, requiring notable management skills, and to create and preserve reputation effects he needed to honor his portfolio of wide-ranging contractual obligations made with a multiplicity of partners that were frequently or even continually at each others' throats.[42] In particularly dicey situations, a condottiere might even feel compelled to make peace between employers to whom he was obligated rather than choose to make war for only one of them. In other situations, opposing condottieri might agree to persuade their respective employers to come to an arrangement. For instance, after a lengthy, involuntary residency in Florence, Pope Martin V returned to Rome on 30 September 1420. This had been made possible upon his promise to recognize and support the reign of Queen Joanna II of Naples, who held Rome at the time. But Martin reneged on his promise and recognized Louis of Anjou instead. Joanna turned to Alfonso of Aragon, who already held Sicily and claimed Naples. For helping Joanna, she might make him her heir. Being cautious, Joanna, however, engaged Braccio da Montone as well, whereas the Pope relied, in addition to Louis of Anjou, on Muzio Attendolo Sforza, financed by Medici bankers in Florence. Naples was divided between the opposing camps, and a stalemate developed. "Braccio and Sforza were largely the arbiters of the situation," especially the former who had "tempting offers to intervene in the struggle then proceeding between Venice and Milan." If the condottieri were frequently portrayed as faithless rascals, they would not appear to have differed unfavorably from their principals.[43]

A highly important development took place in the 1360s — the wholesale rewriting of contract formulas all across the major and minor Italian powers. Until that time virtually all contracts were written in terms of the basic combat unit, the *barbuta,* or Reiter (the helm or mounted knight). It is not entirely clear that the barbuta referred to is a single man, but it is clear that after the 1360s contracts were written in terms of the *lancea* (the lance) as the basic unit, and this lance definitely referred to a unit of three men, *cum duobus equis et uno roncino,* where the two equis referred to stout, armored warhorses to carry the armed knights to battle, and the ronzino was a gelding (or rouncey) to carry a page. The page would complement the knights to form the lance. In battle, he would hold all three horses at safe distance behind the battle line for, paradoxically, the key to the lance formation was that hundreds and thousands of mounted, paired knights would dismount, each pair jointly holding a single lance and, in close formation, like "human porcupines," march against an attacking mounted force. The two knights held the lance to absorb the shock of an oncoming mounted knight and would try to unsaddle him. On the flank would stand ready a phalanx of longbow or crossbow archers. The crossbow had a range of only about thirty yards, and reloading it took a long time. The longbow, in contrast, could be shot in rapid-fire fashion and well-aimed at two hundred yards distance. Its armor-piercing qualities became especially devastating not when aimed at the knights but when aimed at the horses. Once the oncoming force had been broken, the pages would rush their horses forward, to commence pursuit of the enemy. This tactic, attributed to the English at Crécy in 1346 and Poitiers in 1356, proved successful in Italy as well and necessitated a change in the basic accounting unit from barbuta to lancea. Contract praxis changed in Perugia in 1367, in the papal forces and in Venice in 1368, in Milan in 1370, in Modena probably in the same year, and in Florence in 1371. A Venetian contract with condottieri Gattamelata and Count Brandolini in 1434 "was on the usual and businesslike lines, reminiscent of the agreements Hawkwood had been signing with Florence half a century earlier." Despite variety, there was continuity.[44]

Certainly, much negotiating went on. Employer and condottiere kept tabs on each other's condition and exploited the information for their own purposes. For example, in 1425 Venice signed a condotta with Francesco Carmagnola (1390–1432). He had been exceedingly successful in Milanese service, so successful that Milan's ruler, the irascible Filippo Maria Visconti, thought him a threat to his own rule and issued orders to have him arrested. Carmagnola fled. Venice "knew his value. They knew also his difficult situation. For the moment there was no state of war, and they could afford to haggle." Carmagnola, in turn, knew that once war came, his bargaining position would naturally improve.[45]

Even if formal aspects remained constant, informal aspects of the contracts changed. For instance, in 1438 war between Milan and Venice, the latter allied with Florence, flared up once more. Niccolò Piccinino ran things for Milan; on the Venetian side stood as captain-general first Gattamelata, then Francesco Sforza, as well as Colleoni to assist them. Milan suffered a crushing defeat in 1440. Anxious to sue for peace, Milan's Filippo Maria Visconti made Sforza, by now forty years old, a striking proposal. He was to arrange for his employers, Venice and Florence, to make peace with Milan in exchange for which Sforza could have the Visconti's sixteen-year-old daughter, Bianca, plus the cities of Cremona and Pontremoli as Bianca's dowry. As Francesco Sforza and Bianca Maria Visconti had long laid eyes on each other, this proved a happy proposal indeed. And so the Peace of Cavriana was signed in 1441.[46]

The condotta, erstwhile a pedestrian if complex affair, had evolved to include much higher, if implicit, stakes. A movement from warlord to lord had definitely begun, and strategic marriage alliances among condottieri became important. One of Sforza's daughters was married off to Sigismondo Malatesta, a much despised condottiere in the Marches; a son was married off to a daughter of Niccolò Piccinino (Sforza's Milanese opponent); and another son was married to a daughter of the Este, a prominent political family in Ferrara. Military and political power began to intertwine.

If the mercenary system of the Italian Renaissance eventually came to an end, it was not for lack of political, legal, or requisite administrative sophistication. Instead it had very much to do with the difficulty of holding parties to contractual promises, with contract enforcement in a word.

Pay formed an important part of contracts, of course. Italy was by no means a high-wage paradise for German mercenaries in the 1300s, who, as we have seen, sold assets back home to equip themselves for the journey and adventure. This problem of inadequate return on investment was not restricted to German knights. Even John Hawkwood "found himself at the end of his life in constant financial difficulties and dependent for his income on annual payments from the government of Florence." The statistical evidence for Italy, across our two centuries of interest, suggests that on the whole pay was much below the earnings of even day-laborers in occupations such as construction. Many soldiers needed to be equipped even with basics such as footwear and a shirt, let alone arms. Because of the high probability of sickness, death, or desertion the value of this was subtracted from their pay, at rates as high as 25 percent of first pay. At times, soldiers were paid in kind, but the book value put on the items was invariably higher than the market value, so that soldiers again lost in the bargain. Soldiering was no pleasure. Mallett and Hale describe it "as a subsistence occupation."[47]

Monthly pay rates remained fairly constant at around the equivalent of nine florins from 1321 to 1368 in Pisa, Venice, and the Papal States before tapering off in nominal and real value. In Venice, rates fell during the first part of the fifteenth century, holding even thereafter. On occasion, foot soldiers were able to demand and receive cost-of-living adjustments when transferred to high-cost environments. It bears repeating that pay rates are not equal to pay received. Few pay records survive, but we do know of plenty of complaints. There were instances of "paying men in forged money, which seemed to circulate freely in the Veneto," and payment problems may well have stemmed from the "inability of Venice to produce the sums promised." Further, "in the second half of the [fifteenth] century troops were frequently months, or even years, in arrears with their pay." This was primarily a function of the difficulty of designing an effective treasury that would collect revenue from the provinces and channel it via Venice to its far-flung armies.[48]

Likewise things may be said for Francesco Sforza's troops in the first half of the 1400s. When cash was readily available at least part of the pay was paid in advance, a credit to be worked off; but when the cash flow was interrupted, actual pay dropped and the condottiere accumulated arrears. He had, however, to pay at least some absolute minimum in cash per soldier per month. When he was in exceptionally dire straits, this was sometimes accomplished via the communities that lodged his soldiers, to be repaid to the communities through reductions in their tax obligations. Lack of cash frequently led soldiers to pawn their equipment and horses in exchange for food and supplies, an undesirable circumstance for almost all concerned: soldiers without equipment are of no use to warlords; when necessary, condottieri then simply required citizens to supply equipment without recompense. This left local peasants holding the bag, put revenue pressure on communal leaders, and required of them to negotiate tax reductions with their overlords. Consequently, the tax revenue that the Sforzas were able to extract from their widespread possessions oscillated drastically over the years.[49]

Troops employed for a three-month-long war season had to be paid more (per month) than those employed on longer-term contracts, and troops had to be compensated for their moving expenses as well. Combined, certainty and stability resulted in a lower total wage bill and made for more loyal soldiers as the mercenary system gradually gave way to a permanent army. Indeed, the "highest rates tended to be paid by Florence whose army was always the least permanent and least well organised."[50]

If pay was generally low and insecure, why, then, soldier? In economic terms, it appears that the parties engaged in risk-sharing, taking the form of base pay plus bonus pay. The former did not make soldiering worthwhile, or perhaps barely so, and it might serve as a screening device for aptitude and effort. Bonus pay, in contrast, consisted of opportunities for plunder and ransom, and that is where a knight or a foot soldier might make a living and perhaps a fortune. Performance risk was therefore shared: incapable soldiers would not receive bonuses and screen themselves out of military duty, whereas capable soldiers might find soldiering worthwhile. As noted, evidence for German mercenaries shows that perhaps two-thirds of them stayed in Italy for but a season or two before returning home, evidently finding soldiering a hard lot.[51]

There are vivid accounts of kidnapping and ransoming of people and farm animals, which were a major capital item. While animals were captured and slaughtered for food, in not a few cases they were more valuable alive than dead, to be kidnapped and ransomed several times over.[52] In contrast, a prisoner's fate depended on his economic and social rank.

> Rank-and-file soldiers were usually released immediately by their captors after being stripped of their arms and horses; neither the companies nor the state had the facilities to keep them as prisoners, nor indeed was there any interest in setting up such facilities. In a mercenary system there was no concern with depriving the enemy of potential manpower, as this could always be recruited afresh; the damage was done by forcing him to re-equip and rehorse his troops. For the same reasons there was little point in killing or mutilating prisoners; such practices would only lead to reprisals and were rare except in particular circumstances when known deserters were involved, or specially trained men who would be hard to replace, like bombardiers and handgunmen. Men of any social standing were held for ransom.[53]

Contracts provided for danger premiums, bonus-pay incentives, and even pensions:

> An additional month's pay for storming a city was a well established custom and was indeed the very least that soldiers expected for exposing themselves to the particular dangers which storming and street fighting involved. Individual acts of bravery were often rewarded by cash payments . . . the first man over the

walls would be offered large cash rewards. The Venetians offered 300 ducats to the first man to enter Rovigo in the war of Ferrara, plus a pension for life if he was an ordinary soldier. In fact pensions for retiring or disabled soldiers were becoming increasingly common in the fifteenth century, particularly in the Venetian army where long service can be first noted.[54]

For Muzio Attendolo and for Francesco Sforza, loot, plunder, ransom for prisoners, and similar rewards of war frequently served as a substitute for regular pay, thus reducing the payroll expense for the successful warlord.[55] That this was not the usual outcome is illustrated by a squabble between Venice and Milan in the 1430s that involved a complaint about a

> contingent of Florentine infantry [that] had been sent to join the Venetian army in Lombardy. . . . they had come with no muster rolls, so that no meaningful inspection could be made of them; the Florentines had sent insufficient money to pay them and they were greatly deficient in arms. Manelmi commented graphically that the Florentines might as well have sent them straight to join the enemy, the Milanese, as to send them in this condition when they were bound to desert. Here in fact was the root of the whole problem of the infidelity of mercenary soldiers; an army that was properly and systematically controlled and paid would remain faithful and efficient, and most of the Italian states were beginning to realise this and act accordingly.[56]

In contrast to their underlings, the condottieri themselves could demand different terms, executive pay we might call it today, and frequently of huge proportions. In 1363 not long after John Hawkwood arrived on the Italian scene, his White Company was hired by Pisa (against Florence). The summer campaign proved uneventful and inconclusive, but he shrewdly realized that, if he left Pisa, the city would be unprotected with little chance to hire another company on short notice. He asked for, and received, 150,000 florins (FL) for the company for the next six months, free transit through Pisan lands, and unimpeded access to Pisa itself—"a riotous opportunity," as one historian remarks. Hawkwood also received a personal bodyguard of two constables, two pages for each constable, and the use of thirty-eight foot soldiers.[57] Even though contracts contained provisions for pay, enforcing them and collecting one's due were a different matter altogether. Once more, the overriding theme is that if mercenary companies were in time to die out, the reasons are not solely to be sought in the vagaries of Italian politics or changes in military technology but also in the difficulties posed by the enforcement of provisions in military labor contracts.

CONTROL AND CONTRACT EVOLUTION

Contracts work when they can be enforced. Across Europe, contracts were commonplace, and they contained standardized features, in Italy and elsewhere. What the condotte were to Italy, the *lettres de retenue* were to France. Among other details, they set down certain enforcement mechanisms. Philippe Contamine describes an ordinance of Charles V, dated 13 January 1374. Because of insufficiencies in prior contracts, the king specified in great detail how mustering was to take place and who would be held responsible if anything were amiss. In particular, the mercenary captains were held liable for their men and their men's behavior, both in transit to and from as well as during engagements. Moreover, "the captains were held responsible for damage caused by their troops." Hold a man who has a self-interested stake in the outcome responsible for that outcome and the cost of contract policing is reduced. In this manner at least part of contract policing was internalized.[58]

As in France, so in Italy. The Florentine amendments of 1363 and 1369 to the regulations of 1337 specified not only a more stringent inspection regime, with an attempt at an internal audit and control system to check abuses by Florentine officials, but also that the mercenary captain or one of his constables would have to pay a tax for each man or horse found insufficient and in need of replacement.[59] Regulations required that condottieri guarantee the private conduct of their charges. The problem would lie in the credible enforcement of such provisions. After all, the condottieri were armed and much in demand. Then as now, star players could dictate terms. Francesco Sforza, such was his military esteem, eventually managed to have all his forces excluded from muster. Nearly a century earlier, Pandolfo Malatesta, was given "absolute military control of field operations, unrestricted by the usual war council and civilian commissioners" of Florence. The condottieri, moreover, were capable men of business as well as of war. They well understood their paymasters' designs to wrest market control from them, and to protect their own interests they responded by forming associations of "confederated condottieri." They displayed foresight, for example by menacing, but not unduly so, a future employer's lands until a contract to their liking would be forthcoming. To split the companies, it would take the targeted city considerable financial resources to induce any one mercenary band to break ranks with its confederates.[60]

Apart from frequency and details of muster, areas of contract conflict involved the precise terms of loyalty and nonaggression clauses, the drafting and redrafting of double-pay clauses, the division of spoils, and the enforcement difficulties with requesting condottieri to turn over prisoners of war for ransom. Further enforcement difficulty arose with the *capitano della Guerra,* a city-state civilian official who nominally held supreme command over a condottiere and who was entitled to 10 percent of the spoils; over the duration of the contract (within a six-month contract the maximum obligatory time to be spent in warfare might be limited to only three months); over pay grades and types (e.g., full pay, *a soldo interno;* half pay, *a mezzo soldo;* lien on future services, *in aspetto;* nonaggression contracts, *condotta di garanzia*); over leave and discharge regulations (the *licenza*); and over other terms. By 1337, the Florentine code of contract regulations already "displayed the complex problems which emerged as condottieri were employed in steadily increasing numbers." A leading jurist of the age, Giovanni da Legnano, published *Tractatus de bello* in 1360, which deals expressly with the many practical problems of condotte.[61]

The evolution of the major phases in mercenary contracting in Italy appear to have been these six: first, multitudes of individual fighters are hired on individual contracts; second, in large part for reasons of administrative and military control, entire bands are hired with contracts concluded with the leader of the band, who, in turn, would subcontract with individual fighters; third, the bands themselves combined in the early and mid-1300s into companies with an internally elected leader; this gave them a certain degree of market power that lasted, roughly, from the 1350s to the end of the century. In these *societas societatum* decisions were made by a council composed of the leaders of its constituent bands, and city-states sought to influence these by selective bribing. A company could thereby somewhat be held in check because internal dissent could lead to break-up and consequent loss of market power.

Fourth, when the condottieri emerged — sole, undisputed, and usually Italian leaders — from about 1400 to about 1450, legal language changed as well. Instead of referring to *societas* — a group of independent leaders electing from among themselves a representative — contracts now referred to a single leader's *comitiva,* his "following." Contracts were fundamentally transformed.[62] A fifth contract phase emerged during the same time period in which the most prominent condottieri-warlords became lords, or else became willing, integrated citizen-employees of city-states. And in a sixth phase, after 1450, city-states become increasingly able to break mercenary companies into smaller units or hire unattached smaller groupings, such as *lanze spezzate* (free lances), to be subsumed under city-state military control and leadership. At the same time, independent lords became warlords in their own right to gain revenue to sustain their local courts (more on which later in the chapter).

What spelled the decline of the condottieri period was the limit placed on a condottiere's ability to move about in response to multiple offers and paymasters. Once the five-power coalition emerged in 1454 among Milan, Venice, Florence, the Papal States, and Naples, each effectively held a monopoly on power by offering long-term contracts to a few selected condottieri. The latter could not by threat of movement extract concessions anymore; they became subject to replacement and subjects of the power that hired them. For those who survived this market adjustment, the benefit was mutual. Even condottieri could tire of uncertainty, of the constant, distracting, and irksome musters, of the need to hunt a contract for the next season of war, the necessity of despoiling someone's countryside even in peace time, and of the general restlessness of life. Longer-term arrangements with states offering income, status, and continuity in exchange for loyal service became attractive. "Thus we see emerging in the greater continuity and permanence of military organisation, in the emphasis on discipline and fidelity to the state, in the development of hierarchical structures within long-serving companies, and in the implications for training and the improvement of skills, a substantial move towards professionalism." With loyalty and permanence, "very few *condottieri* were actually dismissed and therefore the traditional problem of demobilised companies holding the countryside to ransom did not arise" anymore. Contract incentives had become better aligned for mutual benefit.[63]

Yet if that is the case, why should the employing power still need to rely on hiring entire companies under a condottiere's leadership? It wouldn't. And so there then followed a gradual movement to hire not *ut societas* (as a company), but "in individual small bands, each of which entered into a separate *condotta* with the employing power."[64] The entire mercenary hiring process had now been reversed. Individuals seek certainty and permanence. As long as these were not forthcoming from an employing political entity but from a company, they signed on with the companies. But as military organization changed, and certainty and permanence were to be found with employing states rather than with employing companies, the soldiery gradually drifted toward the states.

Contract control or enforcement had to work both ways. The principal — king, pope, potentate, republic, or city — did not always pay up. In 1375, for example, Pope Gregory XI, known as an unreliable paymaster, stood up John Hawkwood, first delaying, then reneging on payment due, offering but two estates in the Romanga, and this only after Hawkwood took a newly minted cardinal hostage in Perugia on 1 January 1376. At the time, Hawkwood had been in the pope's service against Florence. Shrewdly, the Florentines exploited the pope's financial dissembling. They offered Hawkwood FL130,000 for a nonaggression pact, plus an annual stipend of FL1,200 for life. Indeed, they won over Hawkwood for good: for the remainder of his career he would remain loyal to Florence. Reliability proved to be its own contract enforcer. The shadow of the future — continuous employment — beckoned large.[65]

Yet the shadow of the future can, and did, work the other way around as well. The city-states would have representatives on campaign and on the battlefield to observe their hirelings. These were the *provveditori,* or civilian commissioners. For example, after a long, uneventful summer of mutual maneuvering, Florentine representatives in September 1325 pushed their condottiere, Raimondo di Cardona, and his 15,000 men to decisive battle against Castruccio Castracani and his men. "They had spent too much and received too little," they said, merely for Raimondo to settle in for the winter and take up campaigning next spring again. Florence lost the battle, but the episode shows that the city was able to push its condottiere to action, even against the hireling's better judgment. A like incident occurred in 1364, again involving Florence and Pisa. The Pisans had hired John Hawkwood and his English, German, and native Pisan troops and put them up against Florence's mostly German troops. One day an inconclusive battle took place at the gates of Florence. Hawkwood withdrew, and the night was spent celebrating four newly designated knights. Next day the men were weary, but "the English and German mercenaries returned to business, as demanded by the Pisan commissioners in their ranks." A city could also express its displeasure by reducing pay post facto. For instance, while on the payroll of Milan, its tyrant, Bernabò Visconti, grew impatient with John Hawkwood's lack of achievements. "Bernabò grumbled that he was not getting his money's worth, and thereupon decided to reduce his Captain General's pay."[66]

When contracts did not work well, either they or external circumstances were modified in an attempt to change the incentive structure. For example, an early biography of Hawkwood narrates that "mercenaries were not at all accustomed to save their earnings." To the contrary, the pleasures of Italy drove them into the hands of usurers who saw fit to take arms and horses in payment of debt. "This was a serious inconvenience to the republics," as disarmed mercenaries would more easily break contract than otherwise. In 1362, Florence went so far as to open a bank for mercenaries, capitalized with FL15,000 of public money, to extend loans to needy soldiers. Collateral was offered in the form of promises made by at least two superior officers per applicant. (It is not clear whether these officers were cosignatories to the loan.) Since the security — two high-ranking officers — could be difficult to obtain, thereby inducing needy soldiers to borrow elsewhere, laws were changed to prohibit lending to mercenaries, under penalty of loss of political rights.[67]

A key change came when the interests of a condottiere merged with the interests of a city-state, foreshadowing by a good 200 years Louis XIV's (1638–1715) perhaps apocryphal remark "l'État, c'est moi." So long as Italian condottieri were freely roaming from contract to contract, their interest lay in prolonged, or prolonging, conflict among their paymasters. Once they acquired landed wealth and cities of their own, their interest lay in reducing conflict to reduce the drain on tax revenue, at least on their own territories. Canestrini speaks of a noticeable *trasformazioni* (transformation) of the contracts offered to foreign as opposed to Italian condottieri.[68] The Italian condottieri were more privileged and, generally speaking, freer in their operations; they were treated as equals and looked upon as influential; they were included in all alliance or peace treaties, in all offensive or defensive treaties; in short, they had public rights as stipulated in the treaties.[69] Contracts were made, "quasi fra Stati e Stati"—as if from state to state—whereby one side supplied the money, the other the men. Gradually, interests were to be aligned, so that the principal-agent problem could be handled. One exceedingly convenient alignment, of course, was to eliminate the dichotomy between overlord and warlord, combining both roles in one person. The exemplar par excellence was to be Francesco Sforza, who took Milan and, with it, the dukeship. The warlord became lord and promptly arranged for a long-lasting peace among the remaining major powers in Italy. To use economist Mancur Olson's apropos phrase, the "roving bandit" had become the "stationary bandit," the pirate, a prince. Another convenient alignment, as mentioned, was to subsume rank-and-file soldiers under city-state authority. To be broken was the condottiere's power as middleman between fighting troops and employing states. What in the 1300s had been difficult to achieve—a company always insisted "on being engaged en bloc, in order to check efforts to split it into smaller units and thus to diminish its bargaining power"—had by the late 1400s become the fait accompli.[70]

THE DEVELOPMENT OF PERMANENT ARMIES

War was expensive, and war finance assumed great importance. The persistence of contracts implies that on average they were honored, and the commitments needed to be paid. This caused problems. For example, as mentioned previously, Pope John XXII (r. 1316–1334) used nearly two-thirds of his budget for Italian wars, and Innocent VI (r. 1352–1362) ran up a war bill of about 40 percent of the total budget. For the secular states, tax collection did not nearly suffice to finance the military outlay; proposals for new taxes caused uproar; and affected constituents lobbied to have the tax incidence shifted to others.

To raise funds, duty in militia service could be bought off. When the financial monster of military expense asked for yet more funds, the buy-off rate was raised. Cities started to tax the countryside more heavily. Assessments were levied, then raised, on subject cities. When all avenues of revenue raising were exhausted, Florence (and others) issued debt. "Even the dowries of Florentine girls were invested in public stock" (*monte delle doti*) and produced a rather more vested interest by the citizenry in the survival of the city.[71]

Florence's debt accumulated to around FL50,000 in 1300. A hundred years later, the debt amounted to FL3,000,000, and FL8,000,000 by 1450. This was "approximately equal to the total wealth of the Florentine populace." Interest on the debt was paid, often a hefty percentage, and the ability of Florence to pay the interest, let alone the principal — the *monte* — became not just a concern for individual lenders but for the entire community, since virtually all of its citizens were in hock to themselves. Florence took refuge in interest-bearing forced loans. Initially short term, these were soon converted to long-term obligations. But the interest rate on forced war bonds was below the return that Florentine merchants expected on investment in commercial ventures, and this "excited complaints that capital was being diverted from more profitable courses." To deal with that problem, "genial bookkeeping" raised the rate from 5 to 15 percent, higher than the 8 percent expected on land and the 10 to 15 percent from other commerce.[72]

Sometimes war itself could bring relief, such as when Florence went to war with the papacy in 1375, confiscated church property, and auctioned it off. The proceeds were used to pay interest and pay off debt. The financial burden of war led to a brief resurgence of reliance on the cheaper civic militia in the mid-1300s, at least in Florence, but the increasing distances involved in campaigns and warfare made the use of citizen militias impracticable; indeed, they proved quite ineffective.[73]

War is a negative-sum game: the sum of winnings is smaller than the sum of losses. For Renaissance Italy, military outlays were not just large; they were too large and burdensome. War was also economic war. Smaller communities, like Siena, fell by the economic wayside, and by the early 1400s even Milan "was within measurable distance of financial disaster." By the mid-fifteenth century Florence, more than once in dire financial straits, nearly collapsed as well. In addition to the principal-agent problem of contracts, the economics of war finance was quite unsustainable.[74]

Without doubt, great strain existed for troops to obtain promised rewards and for cities to receive promised military performance. Both sides had plenty of incentive to renege on contracts. But in a competitive environment consisting of many buyers and many sellers, cheating produces costly reputation effects, and both sides would be expected to evolve a more satisfactory way to ameliorate the principal-agent problem. The list of relief efforts includes better monitoring and supervision activities, changes in the payment and reward system, and the lengthening of contracts. Special problems were posed by demobilization and billeting issues and troubled efforts at alliance formation among the cities. Developments in military technology and associated needs in military labor skills also favored the eventual formation of standing armies. Not that we witness a wholesale "throwing out" of mercenaries, but the momentum shifted. Many still were mercenaries—placeless, foreign soldiers—but the mode of employment changed: still foreign in origin, many became settled.

Over time, all Italian states established recruiting offices and officers, the *collaterali,* one of whose main tasks it was to maintain records for mustering and inspection. This helped to identify and sort out deserters and to regularize pay—the lack of which was a major reason for desertion in the first place. Moving toward direct pay, rather than pay via the condottieri, helped to ensure that the men did in fact receive their due. Non-mercenary troops made up a rising proportion of total army size, so that by the sixteenth century even the remaining mercenary troops were paid directly. All in all, the "bargaining power of mercenaries was reduced by the growing permanence of armies." In the Milanese, Venetian, papal, and to a lesser extent the Neapolitan armies— but not Florence's— the ranks swelled "with growing numbers of professional soldiers who were not part of the *condotta* system." These came from stranded soldiers, members of the lanze spezzate, who were in wide usage by all Italian states by the mid-fifteenth century.[75]

> The name means broken lances and clearly the origins of such troops were individual cavalrymen who for various reasons had become detached from condottiere companies and their traditional lance formation, and had taken service directly with a state. . . . Some men presumably enrolled in *lanze spezzate* as a gesture of independence, but on the whole these troops were made up of deserters from other armies, and particularly of groups of soldiers whose condottiere had been killed. A standard way in which a state could retain the services of a good company whose commander had died, was to enrol them as *lanze spezzate,* appoint a new commander of its choice, and thus build up a nucleus of permanent cavalry.[76]

To treat payment problems by direct pay addressed not only undesirable peacetime troop behavior vis-à-vis the "local population on whom they were quartered or through whose lands they were marching" but also began to instill feelings of obligation and loyalty, even among the mercenary captains, toward the employing state. "The Venetians had a precocious awareness of this [type of] solution from early in the fifteenth century, and alongside the pattern of lengthening contracts and tightening administration, there grew up a complicated rewards system . . . designed not so much to encourage isolated acts of bravery as to turn fidelity and long service into norms." The reward system eventually extended from captains to troops to family members and often included "support of widows and bereaved children of soldiers . . . small pensions allotted to wounded, mutilated, retired and deceased soldiers of junior rank and their families . . . [or] a minor post conferred for life on a retired soldier."[77]

Early in the fifteenth century, the Venetians discovered the usefulness of employing permanent condottieri, six months in condotte (on contract) and six months in aspetto (on retainer) since there was hardly any fighting during the winter months and many troops were demobilized.[78] Lengthening contracts, peacetime service, and increasing fidelity of mercenary captains resulted in the "domestication of the condottieri." This is true not only of Venice but of other city-states as well. For example, although once driven out, "by 1378 Hawkwood had settled into . . . permanent employment with the Florentines. Although they allowed him on various occasions to work for others, he remained loyal to the Florentines until his death in 1394." Mallett comments that to see the gradual movement from condottiere to city-state command in the "better organized Italian states . . . as a deliberate attempt to reduce the mercenary element in Italian armies is probably misleading; the prime consideration was the retention of good troops . . . ," and the crux here was the furnishing of good contracts.[79]

Caferro's chronicle of the gradual transformation of free-roaming mercenary companies first into semipermanent, then permanent but locally bound forces conforms to contract-economic and game-theoretic expectation: repeated interaction in a competitive environment would foster the development of reputation effects, signaling of reliability, and an increase in contract certainty and stability. Both sides gain, and an institution of permanency evolves. Bueno de Mesquita provides a number of examples that show that not only the condottieri, with exceptions, sought longer-term contracts but that the employers were eager as well to sign experienced, reputable condottieri to lifelong contracts. Once a city found a warrior with whose services it was satisfied, why let him go over to the other side? The constant scrambling for leaders, troops, and equipment imposed uncertainty and expense that could be minimized by means of permanent condotte. So long, however, as the Italian countryside continued to offer rich pickings for an enterprising, or restless, soul, at least some of the condottieri would not (yet) bind themselves in perpetuity to any one paymaster. So it was that political control over military power remained spotty and would be obtained but gradually.[80]

A special problem, also overcome by the development of a permanent, standing army, was posed by demobilization. Once a city had raised thousands and tens of thousands of mercenaries, how could it rid itself of them? The best weapons were the florin and the ducat. With ample offers Florence split Hawkwood's company by hiring away his lieutenant, the German Hannekin Baumgarten (or Annechin Bongarden), and his men. Of the remainder, a portion elected a new mercenary captain, another German, by the name of Albert Sterz, so that out of thousands Hawkwood was left with but 800 men, and his mercenary company broke up.[81] For another example, consider Venice, which, in 1405, after its siege of Padua, issued instructions to its officials setting out

> various ways in which the difficulty could be tackled. One was to issue *condotte in aspetto* — i.e. promise a continuation of part-time payments if the companies would leave Venetian territory and remain on call elsewhere. Another was to take hostages from the companies which were to be demobilised and not give them their final pay until they had moved beyond the frontiers. A third form of coercion was to cut off supplies to them. Finally, and here was the real answer, the officials were instructed to rehire the best troops, and if necessary use them to drive out the inferior companies which were being demobilised.

While expedient for a particular situation at hand, none of these techniques were viable for the long term. Thus, "the problem of getting rid of soldiers at the end of their contracts was one of the factors which was pushing Italian states towards maintaining permanent armies in the early fifteenth century."[82]

A related factor concerned the billeting of mercenary troops. In the off season (again, war was seasonal), as well as in peacetime, armies were dispersed throughout the Venetian *terraferma,* the "firm land" or countryside, to find fodder for the horses and to distribute the burden across the civilian population. Troops were expected to pay rent. Some did, but some did not. Cities more heavily affected by billeting attempted to raise levies from surrounding areas not hosting soldiers, sometimes with success, sometimes without. At times, troops were able to extort bribes for *not* billeting in a particular location, moving on to a less fortunate place. The semipermanence of billeted troops led to military-civilian interactions and increased integration into the local communities. "Some of the companies were clearly sinking their roots deep into local life; soldiers bought property, . . . married local girls and even took up occupations within the local economy." Civilian and military economy became mutually interdependent.[83]

Fickle alliances among city-states also helped speed the process of developing permanent armies. For example, Siena frequently joined in defense leagues — in 1347, 1349, 1353, 1354, 1361, 1366, 1374, 1380, 1385, and 1389 — to hire mercenary forces jointly with other cities and to contribute indigenous forces as well. But insufficient commonality of objectives — and ulterior motives — conspired so that the leagues became objects of intrigue and collapsed easily. In the case of Siena, ultimate relief came with fiscal exhaustion. Siena and its contado formally passed into Milanese hands on 22 September 1389 and were incorporated into a growing Milanese empire against Florence. The era of consolidation among the city-states had begun.[84] This was achieved by 1454, with the Peace of Lodi, when Francesco Sforza (Milan), Cosimo de' Medici (Florence), Francesco Foscari (Venice), Nicolas V (Papal States), and Alfonso of Aragon (Naples) settled upon a balance of power that was to remain largely intact for the remainder of the century (fig. 3.1) — not altogether surprising as the year before (1453), the Turks took Constantinople in the East and threatened the whole of Christendom, and as the end of the English-French Hundred Years' War saw renewed French aspirations regarding the Italian peninsula. Italian powers saw a need to band together, and Italy became an idea in its own right.[85]

The gradual move from warlord to lord undermined the condottiere system as well, and with that the condottieri began "to formulate their own plans for their incorporation into the political and social life of Italy." The feudal link which once "equated service in arms with tenure of land" broke as the "frequency of war called for the professional soldier; and the professional soldier called for continuous employment."[86] But as the trecento and quattrocento wore on, the link between arms and land was reestablished:

> Lands granted to foreign Condottieri normally represented a pledge for debts that could not be paid. The bestowal of fiefs upon an Italian suggests something more — a reviving relation between military service and the ownership of land, the desire for a settled home and base. It furnished the state with a hold upon the allegiance of its military commander more concrete and more precious than the paper upon which the terms of his *condotta* were recorded. It pointed the way towards the further stabilization of a military career, which might draw the fangs of the mercenary system and make the Condottiere an instrument of policy rather than a menace to his employer.[87]

Thus, Francesco Sforza (1401–1466) is only the most famous condottiere who would come to rule a sizable realm himself. He was to become duke of Milan in 1450, culminating his warrior career with an enlightened, peaceful sixteen-year-long reign. In the 1300s, it was rare that a condottiere would be given real estate, a fortress perhaps, or a castle, or even a city to count toward his remuneration. At times this might be taken in lieu of pay, as in 1371 when Pope Gregory XI assigned two estates to John Hawkwood; at times this was a genuine reward for work well done, as in 1390 when Giangaleazzo Visconti (1352–1402) of Milan made one of his esteemed condottieri, Jacopo dal Verme, a citizen of Milan and Piacenza and awarded him several fiefs to boot.[88]

Gradually, the once rare land-grant became more common, but with much instability. A castle might be granted "for life" and then be revoked in a fit of pique. Filippo Maria Visconti (1392–1447), the despotic ruler of Milan, was notorious for this. For example, he gave the city of Piacenza, formerly dal Verme's, to his loyal mercenary stalwart Niccolò Piccinino. Or an estate might be awarded "in perpetuity," with heritable rights, and then be revoked — the Venetians did this to Colleoni's family upon his death in 1475. But the size and stability of the landed reward tended to grow. In addition, some warlords simply seized political power on their own. Thus, Biordo Michelotti, a Perugian, was the first of the "new-style condottieri who used their military power to make themselves dictators." He took Perugia in 1393 and ruled it until his assassination five years later. Not quite two decades further on, in 1416, a fellow Perugian, Braccio da Montane, likewise seized his hometown and, although not initially welcome, came to lead a respected rule until his death in 1424. Opportunities like these also arose when a political figure died. Such was the case with Giangaleazzo Visconti, the greatest of the Milanese dukes. Upon his death in 1402, his generals "began to grab territory in lieu of pay."[89]

Toward the end of our time period, we see in the figure of the widely respected humanist Duke Federigo da Montefeltro, of Urbino (1422–1482), a complete reversal in this trend. Revenue from his smallish realm could not finance the highly respected and well appointed court, and so Federigo took military commissions far and wide: a lord turned warlord. This was true for a number of the smaller Renaissance towns that became "dependent for much of [their] prosperity on the stipends of [their] mercenary captains."[90] Meanwhile, Alfonso of Aragon took an altogether different route, one that foreshadowed what was in store for the whole of Italy. To reduce dependence on fickle mercenary forces, the Spaniard, already ruler of the Kingdom of Sicily, created a civic militia system when, in 1442, he finally got to rule the Kingdom of Naples as well.[91] Some fifty years later, in 1494, the Florentines, having reestablished a

(short-lived) Roman republic following an uprising against Medici domination, also reestablished a civic militia. And in the year after the Medici regained
control of the city in 1512, Niccolò Machiavelli famously advocated in his little
book *The Prince*, dedicated to Florence's new prince, that he might retain the
civic militia. In this, too, Machiavelli merely accented a development already
well under way in England, France, Spain and, indeed, in Italy itself.[92]

Another set of developments toward the establishment of permanent and
predominantly locally staffed armed forces concerned evolving military technology and the need for higher and more differentiated skill levels among the
troops and support staff. For instance, despite Venice's many skirmishes, its
use of mercenaries in the 1400s tended to be sparse. It preferred to learn new
methods of warfare, for example, from Swiss pikemen and German handgun-
men, and to train locally available men in these new methods. Instead of reliance on constables drawn from mercenary infantry, Venice developed a scheme
of social recognition for local talent — some of whom obtained very high social
status and even became mounted when supervising infantry troops.[93]

In 1400, Venetian infantry forces were small as field fortifications were
minimal, and Venice controlled few towns in need of garrisons. Warfare was
dominated by cavalry movements. But during the course of the century, as
Venice extended its concerns and domain westward, garrisons and field fortifications assumed greater significance, and so did the need for associated skills in
engineering, design, and construction of large-scale defensive works, all quite
apart from permanently manning the finished works with *provisionati*. Warfare
slowed down, if not in frequency, then in conduct. Army size — infantry, cavalry, and militia — rose (it could number between ten and twenty thousand),
and centralized supervision and management became increasingly urgent.
"Professional paymasters, provisioners, quartermasters and transport officers
were soon in great demand. Most important of them all were the collaterali
who oversaw these new administrative structures."[94]

From "the point of view of the inclinations of the soldiers as well as the
intentions of the employing state," the development of a core of permanent
forces seemed eminently sensible.[95] Caferro concludes:

> It was not until the middle of the fifteenth century that marauding companies
> truly became a thing of the past. By then, the process of consolidation among
> Italian city-states, which had begun at the end of the fourteenth century, had
> reduced the political landscape of fifteenth-century Italy to five basic powers:
> Milan, Naples, Florence, the Papal States, and Venice. In this new alignment,
> condottieri were now firmly attached to the states they served.[96]

Well before Machiavelli deplored the use of mercenary captains and their troops and advocated the employment of civic militias, Venice had much progressed along the way to a standing, professional army. The reason was not so much fear of usurpation of power by mercenary captains — the Venetians always kept their condottieri at safe distance — but doubt about the adequacy of militia forces as well as the need for order.[97] Instead, the Venetians appreciated

> that they lived in an age of growing professionalism and technical sophistication, in which the amateur and the part-timer had little chance. . . . [They] were able to appreciate that strength in war and a reliance on citizen militias for that strength were contradictory aims in the circumstances and that the former was more important. In a city which made a fetish of republicanism like Florence the debate tended to be distorted as [the utility of mercenaries] had to be set against the fear of a military coup. But in Venice there was little of such fear both because of the natural security of the city and because the Venetians had the means to defend that city against any land army — their sea power.[98]

As historical periodization goes, the France of Charles VII (r. 1429–1461) is frequently selected as the symbolic turning point toward the formation of permanent, standing armies. "This decision, however, was not a response to the unreliability or inefficiency of mercenaries. It reflected instead a need to restore order in a country racked by a century of war, combined with a growing concern for concentrating power at state level . . . It also reflected acceptance of conventional European wisdom on the subject of hiring the best available men with the newest weapons and techniques, whatever their ethnic origins."[99] Not that mercenaries became superfluous; armies consisting of overwhelmingly national forces, and individuals fighting for national identities, did not fully emerge until the 1800s. Rather, force had to be organized differently, and in that new organization mercenary troops were retained while their leaders, the condottieri, were sacked.

But unlike the sentiment quoted in the preceding paragraph, our argument is not that a well ordered state needs a permanent military establishment, or that the condottieri were merely part of the transitional phase; rather, it is that in addition to developments in politics and military technology, the writing and enforcement of appropriate contracts with existing types of military force could or at any rate did not keep pace.

Selecting 1494 (the invasion of Italy by France's Charles VIII), or 1527 (the Sack of Rome), or even 1532 (publication of *The Prince*) as our cut-off date for the period under review is of course arbitrary. Despite appearances, dates frequently are symbolic. They are markers, milestones for the mind. (The atomic age began before Hiroshima.)[100] By 1494, the French already had successfully used siege artillery, indeed were considered the best in the world. For instance, on campaign in 1449, Charles VII's cannon "reduced some sixty English castles to submission." From stone to bronze to cast-iron shot, artillery was reduced in weight while increasing in firepower. This meant that heavy artillery could now be moved from theater to theater, and cannon now could demolish castle fortifications. In addition, gunpowder packed in barrels and placed and exploded in shafts dug horizontally underneath an elevated fortress, could collapse the structure from within. Warfare had changed. It made the free-roaming mounted knight anachronistic. Even so, siege trains demanded huge manpower and horsepower for transportation alone. By the mid-1550s, a full cannon still "weighed, with its carriage, over 8,000 pounds and was moved across country with great difficulty." But the role of the armored knight was reduced. Theater warfare became less mobile and more stationary. Indeed, instead of fleet horses, stocky draft animals were in demand.[101]

The latter part of the quattrocento also sees the introduction of the hand-held firearm, the arquebus. Warfare is transformed. Instead of close-quarter weapons — the swords, lances, crossbows, pikes, and halberds — weapons now are fired at range. The crossbow was fired from some (short) distance as well but it did not to the same degree possess the power of the firearm. Being heavy, the firearm initially was an encumbrance, but not for very long. Close encounter gave way to distanced encounter. Fighting and killing became less personal, valor a more questionable concept, and the profession of the chivalric, itinerant "knight in shining armor" mercenary more risky.[102]

The change was gradual.[103] Already "in 1448, at the battle of Caravaggio, Francesco Sforza had in his army so many *schioppeteri* [handgunners] they had great difficulty in seeing each other because of the smoke." In 1515, at Marignano, the Swiss, despite losing 20,000 men, held out against the French king's massed field guns (artillery cannon), arquebusiers, armored knights, and German *Landsknechte* pikemen until overrun by fresh Venetian forces that joined the fray on the battle's second day. But the age of the mercenary army hired for the occasion was largely over. The market for the free-lance general had declined. Tellingly, Italy's "last condottiere," Giovanni de' Medici, nominally defending Rome for Pope Clement VII but metaphorically perhaps defending all of Italy, died of a three-pound cannonball wound.[104] The inability of the city-states' mercenaries to defend Italy became clear. The Sack of Rome (1527) was at hand.[105]

There were additional changes. War, always gruesome, became vicious. No longer was the object one's display of chivalry and knights' honor, no longer was one content to capture opponents and hold them hostage for ransom. Instead, one came to conquer and to kill. Some foreign troops "were paid a ducat for every enemy head." The wars within Italy came to an end; those for Italy were about to start. Indeed, not just the "Sack of Rome," but the "Sack of Italy" was at hand. It was to be dominated by foreign powers until reunification in 1870, nearly three and a half centuries later. Meanwhile, back in the 1500s, permanent armies raised locally had become commonplace among the remaining variety of Italian states.[106]

CONDOTTIERI AND THE OTHER PRINCIPLES OF ECONOMICS

Throughout the chapter, we have touched implicitly on the other five principles of economics employed in this book. In this section, we make them explicit. The principle of opportunity cost arose on several occasions. In the manpower supply case, for instance, we noted the often slim alternative livelihood prospects many of the mercenary soldiers had in their home country: they had not much to lose by signing on with a condottiere. The principle also showed up in the shifting decisions to be made regarding the relative usefulness of infantry and cavalry, and in the eventual change after 1360 from the barbuta to the lancea formation.[107] In the planning arena, opportunity costs played a role when weighing the relative advantages and disadvantages of the use of civic militia as opposed to professional, if mercenary, forces, a topic one can surely explore at length. The principle of opportunity cost also was seen at work in the operations arena: battles were far from bloodless but this did not mean that a condottiere would sacrifice men, horses, and equipment thoughtlessly. While the men might be replaced, and while even horses and equipment might be replaced with a new employer's money, a major opportunity cost lay in the potential loss of reputation and therefore a rash condottiere's future income stream.

The opportunity cost principle is closely related to that of expected marginal costs and benefits. To say that a man's economic opportunities back home frequently were slim and that not much was lost by crossing the Alps to sign on with a mercenary company is to say that the expected benefit from that decision outweighed the expected cost. Adventure beckoned, even if the expectation would turn out to have been mistaken. In the realm of logistics, the principle shows up in decisions regarding the supply train. William Caferro writes with respect to Werner von Urslingen's Great Company, upon which later mercenary companies were modeled, that "the company drew to its service lawyers and notaries to deal with legal issues and make contracts (condotte), treasurers and bankers to handle money, priests and prostitutes to cater respectively to spiritual and carnal needs." Each company was an organism that would seek temporary attachment to other organisms, an "ambulant military state," as Bayley dubbed it, a "nomad military state," as Temple-Leader and Marcotti called it, a mobile state seeking affiliation with sessile ones.[108] The literature has yet to explore the details of just what it meant to move an entourage of thousands of armed men across the countryside. Decisions regarding spiritual and carnal needs surely were secondary to food for the men and fodder for the horses. Countless decisions would have had to be made daily and at various levels in the mercenary organization as to what to bring along and what to source locally.

Cost/benefit decisions also were made with respect to skilled men. Recall that while Venice built up indigenous forces, it relied, nonetheless, on importing foreign arms makers until locals could be trained in these skills. Another cost/benefit decision, usually more straightforward, concerned the length of the war season. Securing fodder for the horses meant seeking quarter for the winter. An audacious condottiere thus might launch a surprise attack to much effect. But the condottieri were a brotherhood with an unwritten but well understood honor code to uphold. That, too, involved decision making of a curious sort: campaign, win a battle, but lose face for dishonorable behavior?

The principle of substitution is easily noted. Shall a city substitute restive locals for armed foreigners? Shall it substitute one condottiere with another? Shall a condottiere billet in the countryside or shall he ravish the contado? We took note of the gradual substitution of cavalry for infantry forces in the 1300s but also that the reemergence of fortifications in the 1400s diminished the value of the cavalry and favored the infantrymen once again. As a side effect, the horse became less important and stocky draft animals more so, as one began to be substituted for the other. Substitution also is seen in the evolution of the payment system used. Initially paid via the company and its condottiere, this was eventually moved to direct pay for soldiers by the hiring city.

The principle of diminishing marginal returns would be worth exploring in relation to the question of company size. We know that mercenary forces started out in the dozens and hundreds but ended in the thousands and tens of thousands. They become larger, over time, but not all at once. This suggests that there must have been practical limits to their employment in any one campaign or battle — diminishing returns in other words — until the technology of leading large-scale forces into battle had caught up. The principle is easily seen at work in that ever larger number of foot soldiers with their limited effective reach would be of less use than a smaller but much more mobile cavalry. Diminishing returns also are seen with respect to armor. An ever more heavily armored horse and knight would bog down from sheer weight. Instead, some optimal compromise between armor and mobility had to be found. The principle of diminishing returns is also at work in Venice's attempt to construct fortifications westward. Nearer fortifications would yield higher returns than those farther and farther distant. Finally, the principle can also be seen as additions to manpower interact with terrain: additional men, horses, and equipment sent onto the plains would yield different returns than the same number of additional forces sent into the mountains, whether Alps or Apennines.

The focus of this chapter regards problems stemming from asymmetric information. The two types we discuss in this book and in this chapter relate to the need to get each of the contracting parties to reveal certain characteristics of importance to the other side (overcoming hidden characteristics) and the need to prevent each other from engaging in action harmful to the other side (overcoming hidden action). In the first rubric, the chapter repeatedly pointed to efforts by condottieri to build up reputational capital that would signal reliability. John Hawkwood was among the earliest warriors to build a "brand," for which he was handsomely rewarded, as was Venice on the employing side toward the end of our time period. Likewise, mustering and regular inspections were to ensure that the horses and equipment mercenary forces claimed to have did in fact measure up. The gradual evolution of sophisticated and centralized war administrations — on both sides — not only furthered mundane accounting purposes but also served to signal the parties about each other's intent and capacities. The same purpose was fulfilled by having the condottiere ride into battle himself. Understandably a city would be much more likely to contract with a fellow whose past battlefield actions and skills have been observed (revealed) than to contract with one who is unknown and merely talks a good game.

The hidden action problem was addressed in a wide variety of ways. For example, the common use of base and bonus pay served to ensure that men put forth requisite effort, as did the development of contract renewal options. Those who would not put forth visible effort would not receive bonus pay and not see the renewal option exercised. An action had to be revealed to be rewarded. In time, cities even send their own observers to the battlefield to keep tabs on their hired forces. This also held for horses lost in skirmish. After being subjected to false claims too often, cities came to specify in the contracts that soldiers had to present the branded and registered skin of their dead horse before being eligible for reimbursement or replacement monies.

Table 3.1: Foreigners in eighteenth-century armies

Country	Year	Foreign component (percentage)
Prussia	1713–40	34
	1743	66
	1768	56
	1786	50
Britain	1695	24
	1701	54
	1760s	38
	1778	32
France	1756–63	25
	1789	22
	Pre-revolution	33
Spain	1751	25
	1799	14

Source: Thomson, 2002, p. 29. Also see figure 4.6 (next chapter).

The matrix in the appendix summarizes examples encountered in this chapter for each economics principle and each military aspect (manpower, logistics, technology, planning and operation). As regards the chapter's main issue, there is no question that the economics of contracts played an extremely important role in the condottieri period of Renaissance Italy.

CONCLUSION

Mercenaries were used both before the 1300s and after the 1400s, but their use reached a fabled high point in Italy during these years. Why the employment of these forces eventually fell into disuse was the key question addressed in this chapter. Much of the literature emphasizes that the nature of warfare changed or that the nature of alliance-making among the city-states changed. For example, Janice Thomson writes:

> State rulers want power and wealth. To achieve those ends, they chose to exploit nonstate violence — a choice that produced the desired results. It also generated unintended consequences in the form of nonstate violent practices that states did not authorize, could not control, and themselves fell victim to. State preferences did not change; rulers' knowledge of the unintended consequences of their early attempts to realize those preferences did.[109]

What we suggest is that the economics of contracting usefully supplements and rounds out the explanations offered by military science (war making) and international relations theory (alliance making). Mercenary forces continued to be employed in very large numbers throughout Europe (table 3.1), but the contractual form of their employment changed. Instead of free companies, they were contractually and thus organizationally bound into the emerging standing armies of the continental forces.[110]

APPENDIX

A Matrix for the Condottieri Case

Principle	Manpower	Logistics	Technology	Planning	Operations
Opportunity cost	slim alternative livelihood prospects	mounted forces versus foot soldiers	1360 — barbute to lancea change	strength in war versus civil militia leads to professional armies	life or death
Expected marginal costs/benefits	adventure beckons	hauling varieties of gear in the supply train	Venice's import of foreign arms makers, Swiss pikemen, German handgunmen	winter versus summer campaigns (summer was war season)	honor code upheld
Substitution	restive locals versus hired foreigners	billeting versus ravishing the contado	fortress for cavalry; cavalry for infantry	direct pay for soldiers rather than via the condottieri	knights' horses versus draught animals for cannon
Diminishing marginal returns	armies become more sizeable — but to haul gear, not to do battle	use of foot soldiers; reduces effective distance	ever more heavily armored horse and knight	Venice builds fortifications westward, diminishing returns on long-distance campaign	manpower restricted by terrain; mountains versus plains
Asymmetric information (overcoming) hidden characteristics	efforts to build reputational capital	mustering and inspection to ensure equipment was up to specification	men must present horses for inspection	Centralized organization required information processing and resources	condottiere rides into battle himself
Asymmetric information (overcoming) hidden action	self-selection by means of base/bonus pay, indicated by length of service	contract specifies needed equipment; nothing else is paid for	present skin of dead horses	contracting with bonus payment	paymasters as observers on the battlefield

The Age of Battle, 1618–1815

The Case of Costs, Benefits, and the Decision to Offer Battle

In the Middle Ages battles between substantial armies were comparatively rare. The military landscape was dominated by sieges and skirmishes, with many engagements resulting from the former (see chap. 2). In the Renaissance this picture began to change as stronger governments, urban growth, and the introduction of gunpowder removed warfare from the private realm (chap. 3). By the seventeenth century war had become the prerogative of great dynasties that maneuvered and fought against each other with substantial and costly armies. For example, between the sixteenth and eighteenth centuries the French peacetime army grew by a factor of fifteen. The potential expense and difficulty of replacing these troops created legendary caution among many of the generals of the age, resulting in a "golden rule" that highly trained soldiers were too costly to be squandered.[1]

Nonetheless, "great" battles are common enough between 1618 and 1815 that these years of the Age of Enlightenment can also legitimately be called the Age of Battle. Caution on the battlefield thus should not be exaggerated. Commanders did seek battle when circumstances were favorable, and some of the most famous — the Swede Gustavus Adolphus, the Englishman Marlborough, and Prussia's Frederick the Great — were among the most aggressive generals in history.

With the French Revolution (1789) the prevailing studious avoidance of battle gave way to the doctrine of decisive battles. For two centuries, armies had marched, collided, fought, and broken apart. Weeks and months could pass before the next major collision. Almost every battle had been a one-day event. The Industrial Revolution, however, supplied the matériel and the managerial skill to make continuous warfare possible. This new pattern, emerging first with Napoleonic warfare, was clearly seen across the Atlantic in the later stages of the American Civil War (1861–1865; see chap. 5), and reached fulfillment in World War I (1914–1918). Generals in the Great War could choose when to launch offensives but "battle" now was continuous and never ending, with nary a chance to break away and make new choices. This was unfortunate for the soldier in World War I, for his general had been educated to uphold the examples of the great commanders of the past. Basil Liddell Hart was less kind, referring to his commanders' education as "a diet of theory, supplemented by scraps of history cooked to suit the prevailing taste; not on the experience contained in real history."[2]

It is not easy to develop a method for choosing battles and commanders for purposes of this chapter that can be justified from an empirical perspective. A comprehensive empirical study for the entire period would consume an entire book. Although the events and decisions we have chosen are certainly the ones that any military historian would expect to find, we recognize, nevertheless, that there is much work that remains to be done. The chapter proceeds as follows. First, we review the economic concept of expected marginal cost and marginal benefit as it applies to the decision to offer, or decline, battle. Next we examine certain episodes of the 1600s and 1700s. We reflect separately on the role and impact of Napoleon, whose actions, whether innovative or merely reflective of the French Revolution, could hardly be left out of any study of "battle" as a historical phenomenon. Finally, we briefly indicate how the remaining five principles of economics used in this book may be applied to the Age of Battle. Figure 4.1 identifies the locations of battles discussed in this chapter.

A debate rages over the extent to which the French Revolution was a break point in military history, but in this chapter we firmly take the position that it was. The French Revolution either introduced or represented the culmination of a vast expansion of national military power. The rise of the nation-state in the seventeenth and eighteenth centuries gave national leaders the resources for waging of war. It was not just a question of being able to afford supplies or having the legal power to compel military service. As economies grew in wealth and sophistication, the national ability to wage war burgeoned. Nationalism provided powerful emotional support for fighting. The French Revolution did not invent nationalism but harnessed it to great effect.

The financial and economic changes that allowed the modern state to support war efforts dovetailed with the introduction of gunpowder. In the 1400s the birth of national budgets coincided with the appearance of effective gunpowder weapons. This in turn required new types of fortifications that could stand up to cannon. Private warfare became financially impossible. Instead, the state combined two monopolies — military and taxation — and it could also borrow. National debts arose largely from borrowing for and during wars.

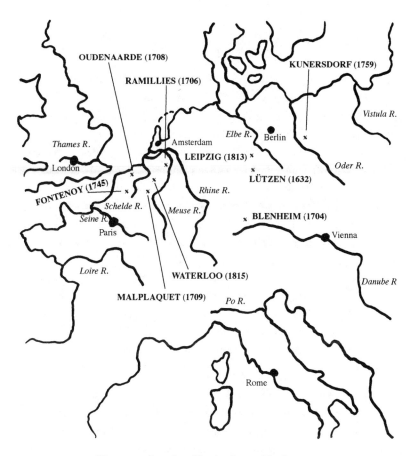

Figure 4.1. Location of battles discussed in chapter 4
Illustration by Hubert van Tuyll.

Taxation became broader and more innovative, and this in turn required in-creased surveillance of economic activity and also greater monetization.[3] In other words, taxes could not effectively be paid or collected in kind anymore and hence the role of cash became more important.

But there were many impediments to modernization. While feudalism be-came obsolete many of its traditions remained, including a wildly confusing array of special rights and privileges for nobles, the church, individual towns, the monarchy, and various provinces. The French Revolution swept all this away and created national military power on a new scale. It initiated the Age of Revolution (1789–1914), which is more fully covered in chapter 5 with the example of the American Civil War.

EXPECTED MARGINAL COSTS AND
BENEFITS OF BATTLE

Any movement which risks battle offers it as well. To analyze why and how commanders choose battle we turn to the economic principle of expected marginal costs and benefits, dealt with at length in chapter one but reiterated here with more specific attention paid to the decision to do battle.[4]

Because of the growing size of armies during the Age of Battle, peacetime and preparatory military expenses are already formidable. When war is declared or launched these rise even further. So the choice of whether to offer any particular battle does not involve the total but rather the expected additional costs and benefits that a battle engagement might bring. Is the spike in the expected extra cost justified by the expected additional benefit? War comprises a nearly infinite set of variables. If these could be computed with some certainty, the calculus to offer or to decline battle would be straightforward if complex. In reality, war's variables are compounded by considerable uncertainty about the expectations. This may explain why attempts to capture warfare in mathematical models, such as *Concept, Algorithm, Decision* and *Numbers, Predictions, and War,* have had at best mixed results.[5] The problem was well stated by Carl von Clausewitz:

> Since in this matter the diversity and the undetermined boundaries of all relationships bring a great number of quantities into consideration, since most of these quantities can only be estimated according to the laws of probability unless the true flash of genius discovers in a glance what is correct, a complexity of relationships and hindsights arises from which a judgement can no longer be drawn. In this sense, Bonaparte was quite right when he said that many of the decisions which confront a commander-in-chief would constitute problems in mathematical calculus not unworthy of a Newton and an Euler.[6]

Uncertainty is inherent in war because war is complex and changing and all decisions are made with imperfect information. Battlefield decision making is dynamic; according to Peter Thunholm it requires a series of decisions that are mutually dependent, the actions of the decision maker change the nature of the problem, and decisions must be made in real time, that is, immediately. (He might have added that the rapid pace of change in warfare places a high proportion of decisions out of phase with events.) As a result, the formal steps for command prescribed in modern warfare manuals often break down. The Swedish army, according to Thunholm, has a twenty-two-step process for making tactical decisions. Not surprisingly, a rather large gap appears between such elaborate models and the actions of officers dealing with the actual chaos and uncertainty of war.[7]

The economic concept of expected marginal (or additional) costs and benefits does not ignore the influence of personal psychology. Economic principles of behavior do not state that all people will analyze a given situation in exactly the same way. Economists merely say that all persons will weigh additional costs incurred as against additional benefits to be gained. They will simply do so in different ways and likely come to different conclusions and decisions based on these conclusions. Recall from chapter 1 the example of the seventh slice of pizza. To one of us (Brauer) the additional benefit gained from devouring the seventh slice, given that he already had six, might well be smaller than to the other one of us (van Tuyll). For Brauer that gain might not be justified by the dollar cost to be paid; but for van Tuyll the dollars put down for the seventh slice are a cost smaller than the benefit gained from acquiring and eating that slice. Van Tuyll's choice of the seventh slice is the result of his perception of the additional benefit as against the additional cost. The psychological or behavioral economics approach studies the perceptions, while the traditional economist merely notes that the action taken is a result of those perceptions.

How the individual evaluates and reacts to a specific situation (economic perspective) is the result of how that individual processes information related to that situation (psychological perspective). Individual idiosyncrasies can be magnified by the pressures of command, as noted by historian Barbara Tuchman: "It [is] said that senior command in battle is the only total human activity because it requires equal exercise of the physical, intellectual, and moral faculties at the same time. I tried to take this dictum apart (being by nature, or perhaps by profession, given to challenging all generalizations) and to think of rivals for the claim, but in fact no others will do. Generalship in combat does uniquely possess that distinction."[8] Under these pressures some fare better than others. The timid general magnifies potential costs, while an audacious counterpart focuses on the benefits. Some famous commanders invariably attacked as long as they had the physical capacity to do so. They did not ignore weighing costs and benefits of an impending action. But commanders such as Gustavus Adolphus, Frederick the Great, and Napoleon were predisposed to believe that attack was superior and that decisive victory was always possible. The benefits to be had simply loomed larger in their minds than in the minds of others. They considered the costs and benefits neither more nor less than say George B. McClellan, the American general whose calculations always led him away from the offensive (chap. 5). The three aggressive leaders' psychological frame of reference differed from McClellan's, but that just meant that their calculations led to different evaluations, conclusions, and actions based on these conclusions.

Evaluations regarding expected costs and benefits of impending battle inevitably vary from commander to commoner. For the soldiers, life on campaign was a struggle for food, shelter, and survival, their diaries filled with hellish accounts of battle in which only survival mattered. While the soldier may be hoping for nothing more than to survive and return home, this is hardly the typical general's view, and the ones most admired in popular history are often those marked by a willingness to expend others' life and blood.[9]

What is to be gained from giving battle that otherwise could not be gained, and against what cost? A perfectly reasonable response might be, "to destroy the enemy and win the war." Indeed, annihilation, or at least decisive victory, was often a goal, possibly, Russell F. Weigley suggested, the primary one:

> From Gustavus Adolphus to Napoleon, military strategy tended to be a quest for the destruction of the enemy army with the battle as the means to the rapid and efficacious accomplishment of that destruction. . . . The quest for decisive battle was the educated soldier's rationalist effort to make war cost-effective, the promptness of the decision through battle promising to prevent an inordinate drain upon the resources of the state. . . . [The] strategy of annihilation of the enemy through battle was a rational response to the difficulties of achieving the objects of policy through war.[10]

The calculation of expected costs and benefits of each additional engagement in battle then might be said to have had a rational goal: to lower the total cost of war. Even those who would disagree and instead focus on the indecisive nature of seventeenth- and eighteenth-century European warfare can accept the view that warfare that leaves the underlying issues unresolved is only superficially cheap.[11] We have here an argument that the most aggressive and bloody generals of the age, those seeking decisive outcomes, were trying to keep long-term costs down. Weigley writes:

> War between 1631 and 1815 revolved around grand-scale battles because, in that age more than any other, the economic, social and technological circumstances of war permitted the massing of tens of thousands of soldiers on a single field for the test of battle, while at the same time military strategists hoped by means of battle to secure decisions in war, and thereby to serve the objects for which men went to war, with a quickness and dispatch that would keep the costs of war reasonably proportionate to the purposes attained.[12]

He further observes that the "so-called period of limited war reverberates with a roll call of battles" and that war aims were not always limited; Louis XIV (1638–1715) sought hegemony in Europe, while the Seven Years' War was fought with the goal of destroying Prussia as a great power.[13]

If Weigley is right, the calculus of offering battle was fairly simple, with decisive results routinely sought. But Weigley himself notes that decisive results were rare and that costs rose "grotesquely." He adds: "If wars remained incapable of producing decisions at costs proportionate to their objects even then, consequently the whole history of war must be regarded as a history of almost unbroken futility." Rarely is an army completely destroyed in one battle, and even more rarely does that destruction lead to the end of the war. The generals of the age were intimately familiar with military history, they knew the costs and risks of throwing everything into an all-or-nothing attack, and in their writings and memoirs urged their fellow soldiers to be cautious. Weigley concedes that "Europeans of the eighteenth century were expected to wage war with moderation and within civilized limits" and that the officers of the day recognized that "indiscriminate violence was likely to prove strategically counterproductive." He is right to suggest that limited warfare did not mean avoidance of battle, but certainly many opportunities to fight were deliberately missed. "The strategic and tactical emphasis was on manoeuver and the avoidance of overmuch fighting — not on seeking out the enemy to destroy him." Daniel Defoe observed armies engaged "in dodging — or, as it is genteelly termed — observing one another, and then marching off into winter quarters." Fighting a battle for "no cogent reason" was known as *batailliren,* or fighting for its own sake." Cost, supply problems, and abhorrence of the barbarity of the Thirty Years' War all tended to limit war.[14]

But, if battles were rare, when they were joined, did generals' calculations solely aim at a decisive result? Not necessarily. Most generals did not want to fight until the army was in order. This was a very slow process and allowed the opponent time to prepare his position as well. Thus, a decisive result required extremely aggressive tactics, which risked very high costs, or it required a substantial numerical superiority, which did not come about often, or required clear intellectual supremacy of one general over another, which was also uncommon.

Offering battle, then, required a careful weighing — a calculation of sorts — of what was to be gained as against the cost to be incurred. As we have seen, total destruction was not and could not be the invariable goal of battle, and many have been fought for far more limited benefits. The physical benefit of substantial damage or even total destruction of enemy forces was certainly attempted but rarely achieved. Indeed, unless it faces massive desertion, even a "defeated" army can regroup. A more manifest physical objective of giving battle included to inflict unacceptable losses and attrition. In the American Revolutionary War, for example, Nathaniel Greene defeated the British army in the South even though he did not win a single battle. Ingeniously, he simply relied on the fact that every British regular shot down was an irreplaceable loss. Few generals claim attrition as their strategy in wartime, but it figures in the outcome of so many wars that it is probably more often deliberate than is admitted. Among tactical benefits of battle one may count "push back" — forcing an enemy to retreat can cost him a favorable position, good encampments with plenty of supplies, and other advantages; even a small advance can give the successful army a claim to success. To save, liberate, and gain territory procures at least temporary military advantage, which might compel the enemy into ill considered counterstrikes. Other tactical benefits of battle include to delay the enemy, to interrupt or gain information about his plans, methods, and timetables, or just to gain field experience, a practice once known as "blooding."[15]

Psychological benefits of offering battle included not only to possibly humiliate and demoralize the enemy, but to avoid an image of cowardice with respect to one's own. Even in the twentieth century the fear of being branded as a coward has influenced the behavior of military leaders in important situations (e.g., Midway, 1942). It has even been suggested that Germany's decision to go to war in 1914 was primarily due to emotional factors such as anger and frustration that magnified the German emperor's insecurity. Fighting for honor was not irrational because a person who would fight to preserve honor might be less likely to be attacked. Besides, loss of reputation might, in the short run, be too great a thing to lose.[16]

In the Age of Battle the relation between soldier and general was much more personal than today, and generals gained a more solid following among their troops by exposing themselves to enemy fire. To be seen to do one's duty — this applies mostly to commanders in secondary or subordinate positions — and to save one's honor also were important psychological benefits of battle. Honor matters to the military professional even today, but perhaps at no time more so than in the Age of Battle, which drew most of its generals from the aristocracy, a social class that placed at times ridiculous stress and emphasis on the importance of honor.

It should be noted that refusing to reach for any of these sorts of benefits implies a cost. Not inflicting unacceptable losses on the enemy can mean facing a stronger one down the road; not maneuvering for territorial position can mean to make one's work all the harder when battle is joined another day;

and not rallying one's troops psychologically can result in a weakened mental backbone when a truly decisive battle is at hand.

As mentioned, the key is not that war deals with innumerable variables whose expected values a commander was to weigh or calculate but that so many of these variables were, and are, beset with a considerable degree of uncertainty. Qualitative more so than quantitative assessments entered the cost/benefit calculus. Obviously, there would be ample room for divergent assessments but that assessments, or valuations, were made is indisputable. Indeed, as we now show in the next three sections, calculating for battle was a hallmark of the age.

THE 1600S: GUSTAVUS ADOLPHUS AND RAIMONDO DE MONTECUCCOLI

The evaluation of expected additional costs and benefits is conditioned by the circumstances of the times. The 1600s differed substantially from the 1700s, and these from the 1800s. This necessitates that we delineate at least some of the major aspects of the relevant military environments and how these changed over time. Superficially one might note a remarkable degree of continuity from the seventeenth to the nineteenth century. Given sufficient briefing, Swedish king Gustavus Adolphus (1594–1632) and French emperor Napoleon Bonaparte (1769–1821) could have commanded each other's army. Generalship did not change dramatically until the time of Napoleon, and even he was an avid student of past military leaders.

Within this era of apparent stability important transitions occurred, especially in the early seventeenth and early eighteenth centuries. Around the beginning of the seventeenth century, for instance, significant changes are noted in the conduct of war, the organization of armies, and hence the military objectives of generals. We need not delve too far into the controversial military revolution thesis, which attributes reshaping of government and major institutions to massive changes in warfare. For our purposes it is enough to observe that the ways of war were changing. Armies were growing, dynasties were acquiring resources for long-term conflict, the role of fortifications changed entirely, and as a result a new type of army was coming into being. Size was only one of its distinguishing features. Command at all levels was becoming more complex. Fighting came to be based on the art of maneuver. And the introduction of new weapons required more technical knowledge and more sophisticated tactics.

The new weaponry changed warfare in several ways. The armored knight was already obsolete (see chap. 3), perhaps due more to the (literal) collapse of the castle than to changes in battlefield technique. Partially armored, sword-bearing cavalrymen were still fighting in the nineteenth century, albeit in organized formations. But provided they were well protected by pikemen, arquebusiers—the first battlefield gunners—could make short work of a charging knight. Spanish innovators had developed a large square called the *tercio,* which combined pike and arquebus in a nearly impregnable formation. Yet weapon development during the seventeenth century doomed even this formation. When artillery appeared on the battlefield it simply turned large formations into large targets. Armies had to be disassembled into smaller, less vulnerable, and more maneuverable formations.

Paradoxically one of the more pronounced effects of the appearance of artillery on the battlefield was to increase the skill requirements of commanders. Artillery, infantry, and cavalry units had to be combined efficiently to achieve victory. The evolution of the arquebus into the more efficient musket made infantry units smaller than the tercio practical—but also required more of the officers. In turn, the presence of smaller infantry units created new opportunities for cavalry and required greater mobility and accuracy of the artillery, yet again increasing the burden on officers. The result was a class of professional officers. Instead of training for single armored combat, young aristocrats now joined the army and learned the art and science of war.

Walled estates were no longer the focus of combat. In the Middle Ages, warfare revolved around the castle. Battles often resulted from efforts to relieve sieges. The decline of the castle is usually attributed to gunpowder, and it is true that cannon did allow besiegers to conduct their work of destruction from a comparatively safe distance. But the role of fortifications in warfare did not disappear until the twentieth century—they continued to be built as recently as the 1930s—so guns alone do not completely explain the increasing irrelevance of the castle. To the contrary, the science of fortifications flourished in the Age of Battle partly in response to the threat of the gun. What killed the military role of the castle was money. Warfare could no longer be conducted by private individuals. The cost was too high. Only rulers of extensive domains could afford to fight. In our own age, the development of explosives has made warfare by individuals and small groups possible again, but in the Age of Battle warfare was the privilege of the great.

The scientific revolution affected warfare in two ways. In combination with money, science changed warfare from castle-based to army-based. The science of gunpowder weapons did make the traditional, vertical-walled castle obsolete, and its owners lacked the resources to replace their structures with large modern forts that could withstand cannon fire. The other effect takes us again to the realm of officer skills. As warfare became more scientific, so thinking about warfare became more scientific. Medieval commanders, to be sure, were far more methodical than they have often been portrayed. Even so, it is in the seventeenth century that one begins to see an increasing emphasis on observation, data-gathering, and evaluation of battles, on rationality and calculation in warfare, often from the pens of successful military commanders.

The changing political situation in the seventeenth century also affected the calculus of warfare. Most important, the modern nation-state was born. Today we take its existence and dominance for granted, but it represents only a small proportion of human history. A nation-state basically is what we call a "country" today. It contains a group that considers itself bound together by something greater than blood or tribal ties — the "nation" — and which now resides in a unified political entity — the "state." France, Spain, and England were the first major European nation-states. Monarchy played a somewhat ambivalent role. On the one hand, rulers such as Louis XIV in France deliberately and effectively moved France in the direction of being a nation-state. On the other hand, monarchs risked losing the traditional loyalty of their subjects and upending their relationship with the nobility. The nobles themselves were in an equally ambiguous position. While nobles in time became servants of the state — such as in Prussia, for example — this meant elevating their loyalty to the country over loyalty to their class.

Ultimately the nation-state would make unlimited claims on the loyalty and resources of its inhabitants and reject all forms of external restriction. The new system would not accept the meddling of the international church, the class ties of the nobles, or, later, the class ties of labor. It slowly replaced the complex and divided feudal system of the Middle Ages with its emphasis on individual relationships, contracts, privileges, and overlapping systems of authority. This was anything but an overnight change — for example, feudalism was more superseded than abolished, at least until the French Revolution — but with the Peace of Westphalia (1648) absolute state sovereignty was recognized as being part of international law. The Roman Church, Europe's most powerful transnational institution, protested, but to no avail.

These changes were not universally accepted and are not today. The rise of the European Union and the growing importance of international human rights principles demonstrate this. However, even in the seventeenth and eighteenth centuries there were attempts to limit the power of the nation-state. Proposals for international government emanated from the Enlightenment. The intellectuals of the latter movement saw themselves as much part of a civilization as of a country. Ruling multinational dynasties naturally struggled against the implications of the nation-state. Their efforts were largely, although not entirely, futile. The French Revolution represented a new climax of state power as nationalism, republicanism, and conscription combined to create a nearly unstoppable power.

The balance of power was also changing. The seventeenth century was bracketed by the decline of Spain and the rise of France, with a rather long, confused midcentury period during which there was no clear dominant power. Spain's power had been based on its tremendously able army and navy, its relatively efficient administration, the profits from colonization, the extent of its dynasty's holdings, and the lack of major adversaries. The dynastic ties began to unravel in the sixteenth century, the army was surpassed in quality and quantity by those of other nations, the navy failed to invade England in 1588, the finances of the state collapsed with two resulting bankruptcies, and France, England, and Holland all became formidable adversaries.

France replaced Spain as Europe's dominant power. This took some time, because in the mid-seventeenth century the monarchy had to contend with armed resistance from the nobility. By the time Louis XIV became France's ruler in 1661 he no longer had to deal with direct resistance. With the help of able ministers he more than quadrupled tax revenue, built a powerful navy, and expanded France into Europe's greatest land power as well. He very nearly absorbed Spain and Holland into his empire, and only two long and bitter wars between 1689 and 1714 checked his ambitions — the king realizing too late that his country's great power could still be overmatched by the combined power of others. No power in this age could conquer everything.

This had implications for the nature of warfare. Shifting alliances and political instability meant that the preservation of military power for future contingencies was at a premium. The tendency toward limited war was the product of realism, not pacifism or cowardice. Gambling everything on a single campaign or single battle, a masterstroke à la Napoleon, had no appeal to generals seeking to protect long-term interests amidst political-strategic near-chaos.

Finally, the changing military environment at the beginning of the seventeenth century also produced major reformers, notably the aforementioned Swede Gustavus Adolphus and Prince Maurits of Nassau of the Netherlands (1567–1625). Both addressed tactics, weapons, officer training, recruitment, and virtually every other area of military specialization. Both cause and effect, their reforms led to change but also responded to it. Both worked to integrate technological change and the opportunities created by political developments to establish better armies. In so doing they complicated the calculation process for commanders, and not accidentally. More flexible and better trained armies had more options and therefore posed more possibilities and dangers for adversaries to take into account.

This "environmental" review brings us squarely to the question of how the changes in warfare in the seventeenth century affected marginal cost/benefit calculations. Complexity in operations created complexity in calculations. Waging war by the early 1600s had indeed become more complicated. In the Middle Ages, the real skill in warfare was concentrated at the point of siege. But now field armies had developed into complicated articulated instruments utilizing large and small gunpowder weapons spread among all arms (cavalry, infantry, and artillery); this meant that commanders had much more to think about, both regarding their own possibilities, and those of the adversary. But there was an even greater problem that affected expectations about likely costs and benefits of engaging the next battle: the option of safe withdrawal was significantly reduced. A small medieval army could always fall back on its castle, provided it was not too far away. This was no longer a useful option. Armies were too big. The greater fortifications built in this age could provide a line of defense but not one as impenetrable as the medieval castle which, if properly designed, could furnish protection for some days at least without any effort beyond the raising of the drawbridge. The shift from siege to field warfare significantly raised the potential costs and benefits of offering battle. This new danger and opportunity was mitigated somewhat, but not eliminated, by the difficulties of pursuit after battle.

The risk of losing an army by engaging in battle had increased. An evaluation of that risk would involve an assessment of replacement cost. But as armies had much grown in size, so would the replacement cost. Offering battle and risk losing an army thus required a rather more serious evaluation of the potential battlefield situation. This was so not only for the somewhat mundane reason that paying a new cohort of soldiers, as in the past, with spoils of war became less practical when there simply were too many soldiers, but for the more practical problem that the expense of potentially replacing muskets for 30,000 or 60,000 troops was not trivial. Supply problems were so great that nations began to establish arsenals to stockpile materiél. Many maneuvers were conducted for no reason at all other than to protect or capture arsenals. Risking battle could be catastrophic if one's own arsenals were consequently endangered. Well-trained infantry could not be replaced overnight. The new methods of war meant that trained troops were more important than ever and their loss catastrophic.

Calculations also had to take into account long-term considerations.

Conflicts were increasingly between and among the dynasties that ruled the most powerful nation-states. Loyalties and alliances could shift quickly. In itself, this was not new. Medieval relations were also notoriously fungible. However, the loss of a castle as a near-impregnable base of operations did not necessarily invite ruin. In contrast, the only protection for the field army was the field army. It had to be kept basically intact not only to face the current enemy, but also the next. Here, the calculations of the general and his ruler diverged. The general had to conserve military strength, while the ruler had to conserve money. A ruler with a defeated army was endangered, but not as much as one with an empty treasury.

The interests of ruler and general could also diverge because of the rise of the new sovereign nation-state. In the Middle Ages a commander served a ruler. In the commencing modern age a commander obeys a ruler but serves the state. In the seventeenth century the transition between traditional monarchy and the ruler as servant of the state was still in an early stage. Nevertheless, the interests of the ruler and the entity he ruled were no longer the same thing. In most cases this was a distinction without a difference, especially as this was also the age of absolute monarchy. But a general concerned with the future of his country (we cannot speak of patriotism quite yet) might be reluctant to undertake actions that would be beneficial to the monarch but not to the nation.

Another potential cost of offering battle associated with the seventeenth century was loss of mobility. Mobility was much more important now. In the age of sieges armies existed mostly to attack or protect castles, and this often involved long stays in one place. Enemy armies would attempt to dislodge besieger or protector. Now field armies had to protect lands, arsenals, and cities while simultaneously threatening the enemy's. Battle threatened to deprive the army of the mobility to execute these multiple missions. Grappling with the enemy could turn into a lengthy series of fights and skirmishes as a result of close proximity. Of course this made eliminating enemy mobility a potential benefit of battle.

To analyze the actual mechanics of decision making in this century we examine the cases of two of the most famous military leaders and thinkers of the age, one of whom gained fame through both achievements and writings, while the other died in battle. The latter, Gustavus Adolphus, was a modernizer in an age when rulers routinely still took to the field, although not often with his aggressiveness. Gustavus Adolphus is a good example of a general who saw victory as the purpose of war and sought battle "eagerly."[17] In this respect he had more in common with Napoleon than with many other generals of the seventeenth century. He was fighting, however, in an extraordinarily bloody conflict, the Thirty Years' War (1618–1648; fig. 4.2).

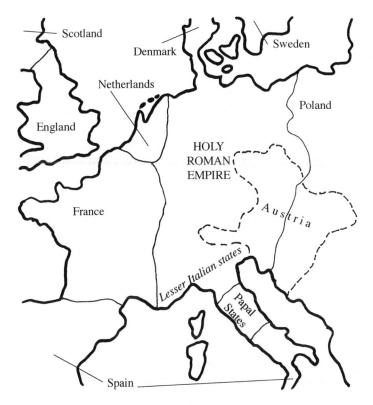

Figure 4.2. The Thirty Years' War
The Thirty Years' War (1618–1648) combined several conflicts. The ruler of Austria, who held the title of Holy Roman Emperor, attempted to gain effective control of the empire by allying with fellow Catholic princes against Protestant German princes. This gave the war its religious dimension. Spain pursued its rivalry with France and also attempted to reconquer the rebellious, mostly Protestant, Netherlands. Spain and Austria were natural allies because both were ruled by the Hapsburg family. Protestant Sweden and Denmark entered the war on the Protestant side. Austria, Spain, and the Catholic princes fought against (Catholic) France, Denmark, Sweden, and the Protestants; however, Spain's participation was intermittent, the princes' positions changed over time, and France, Denmark, and Sweden participated at different times. Spain fought the Dutch throughout this period. The Dutch received some support from England. Sweden also fought a separate war against Poland.
Illustration by Hubert van Tuyll.

The war had its genesis in both religion and politics — a formula for devastation. It began as a struggle for power within a huge territory known as the Holy Roman Empire, which roughly included Germany and a number of surrounding territories. In the Middle Ages, this empire had substance but by the seventeenth century, its ruler had very little power over the local princes who actually governed the people. The emperor decided to reassert his power, imposing a king on the imperial possession of Bohemia whom the local nobles — for both religious and political reasons — rejected. When the nobles chose their own ruler, the emperor invaded Bohemia. Because the Bohemian nobles were Protestant, some imperial princes of the same faith militarily supported them. In the first years of the war, the emperor tended to have the upper hand. In 1628–1629, however, the emperor overreached himself and began claiming powers that even princes who shared his Catholicism rejected. At this point the war became more international. Sweden intervened first, France entered later. Holland and England both participated as well.

The war was a disaster. The emperors were forced to give up their hopes of real power, and their title became an irrelevancy. Far more significant, however, was the effect on the common people. Harvests were disrupted, starvation set in, towns were repeatedly stormed and sacked, and if the population survived, it often had to flee. Magdeburg, for example, was sacked eleven times and saw its population fall from 30,000 to 5,000. Germany's population may have fallen by a third. Much of the suffering, however, was related to economic factors, not the immediate activities of the marauding armies. Severe economic problems were already plaguing Germany on the eve of war. Areas outside the tracks of war experienced problems almost as bad as those that endured invasion. The results were not short term either. The increasingly impoverished peasantry was forced to sell land to the great lords, financiers, and the state. Soldiers, while the perpetrators of much of this misery, were also its victims. Commanders routinely squandered large numbers of men: "The economics of war made it more expedient to use many unskilled men instead of fewer well-trained ones. And since little expense had been invested in training their men, the commanders were not reluctant to waste them in large numbers in bloody battles." By one estimate, the Thirty Years' War led to more battle deaths among the major powers than any conflict before World War I.[18]

This contrasts with a century and a half afterward, during which commanders had to husband highly trained troops. More interestingly, it contrasts with Gustavus Adolphus's situation; he could attack aggressively and risk huge losses (approaching 50 percent at Lützen), but he had a very highly trained army, which, despite Sweden's excellent recruitment system, was not easy to replenish. So why was he not more cautious — with his own person, and with his troops?

His aggressiveness was the result of rational calculation. His "persistence in seeking and fighting battles" resulted from the superiority of his enemy. The Holy Roman Empire's resources so far outstripped Gustavus Adolphus's own

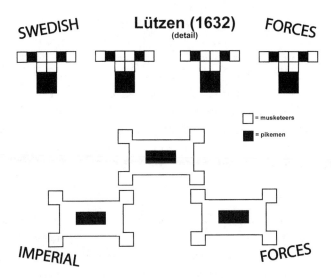

Figure 4.3. Battle of Lützen
This detail from the center of the battlefield at Lützen shows to good effect the innovative tactics of Gustavus Adolphus. The Swedish infantry units are smaller and more intricate than
their imperial counterparts, allowing the Swedes the tactical flexibility to defeat a larger, very
well-led army, albeit it at fantastic cost.
Illustration by Debra van Tuyll.

that he could not win a war of campaigns and maneuver but had to defeat his
enemy decisively in battle.[19] When the opportunity for battle presented itself,
if there were any reasonably clear possibility of victory, he attacked because the
additional benefit to be gained justified the risk of greater costs; the cost of not
ever offering battle was defeat. His aggressiveness was also a function of the
nature of the war. This was not merely a conflict over territory or the local balance of power. The Holy Roman Empire was attempting to assert its authority
over all Germany, which would have endangered Sweden's entire position.
More significantly, an imperial victory could threaten the existence of Prot-
estantism. Gustavus Adolphus, like his country, was Lutheran and therefore
greatly sympathetic toward the outgunned and outnumbered North-German
Lutherans. A compromise peace in this quasi-religious war seemed unlikely
unless the empire was decisively defeated.

This explains why Gustavus Adolphus chose to attack the imperial army
at Lützen on 16 November 1632, despite the risks and his opponent's slight
numerical superiority (fig. 4.3). Several things were going on that shifted the
cost/benefit analysis for engaging in battle in favor of attack. The imperial

army was gaining in strength. Swedish prestige in Germany was declining. His main ally was becoming doubtful. His communication lines were long, which made extended campaigns more difficult. And, of course, there were his "pugnacious instincts" and "warlike spirit." The latter assessment may be a bit exaggerated, because Gustavus could also avoid battle when circumstances were unfavorable. What stimulated his attack at Lützen was that the enemy had divided his forces, giving the Swede his best chance of victory. This constitutes a classic example of expected marginal cost/benefit analysis. All the other circumstances already existed, but the one additional item—a weakening in enemy numbers—led to the decision to attack. Gustavus calculated wrong, but he calculated![20]

The calculations of generals after the Thirty Years' War were significantly different. Like Gustavus, but unlike most of his contemporaries, they commanded highly trained and valuable soldiers. Unlike their predecessors, they did not face total war. The Thirty Years' War was the last fought for (ostensibly) religious reasons. In the absence of total war, there was little sense in risking everything in a single battle. The planning and thinking of war took on some of the scientific overtones of the early Enlightenment, with an emphasis on calculating the possible outcomes. "Assess your forces and compare them to those of the enemy the way a distinguished judge compares the arguments of the parties in a civil case." These words from imperial general Raimondo de Montecuccoli (1609–1680) suggest an increasing emphasis on objectivity, a much prized Enlightenment value. Calculation by soldiers was becoming more explicit. "If your army is strong and battle-hardened, and the enemy's is weak, recently raised, or softened by idleness, you should seek battle . . . if the enemy has the advantage in that area, avoid battles . . . and be content to prevent him from advancing." Note that Montecuccoli does not attempt to solve the offer-or-decline battle problem by recourse to simple numbers. Instead, he lists several factors (strength, experience, hardness), any one of which by implication could swing the decision. Like many of his contemporaries, he frequently ended up declining battle. He used the example of Roman general Fabius to justify withdrawal when at a disadvantage, advising his readers to "change the form of the war" and to "avoid risking the safety" of the country.[21]

Montecuccoli was not categorically counseling the avoidance of combat. To the contrary, he wrote, "give it where you have the advantage." He merely, and sensibly, also cautioned to "not let yourself be engaged at a disadvantage." Harking back to a very traditional style of fighting, he advised that "if you are much less strong than the enemy . . . you must abandon the countryside and withdraw into fortresses." Staying there forever was not a solution, however, and the great Italian general firmly stated: "To imagine that you can achieve great things without fighting is an illusion."[22]

In a word, battle had to be given when the circumstances were favorable, and they could only be considered favorable after careful calculation. Calculation must include both the physical and moral strength of one's own army and of the enemy's. A clear advantage in an important category could make the additional benefit of battle outweigh the additional cost. The calculation of relative strengths as suggested by Montecuccoli gives a general one means of estimating the costs of giving battle. Even without battle, certain costs are nonetheless incurred (supplies, desertion, losses from disease, etc.) and knowing relative strengths makes it possible to estimate, if roughly, how well the army is likely to come through the engagement. These expected costs must be weighed against the expected added benefits of giving battle, as opposed to benefits, if any, of not giving battle. The net effect of the added costs and added benefits of battle might be calculated as advantageous if one's own costs of battle plus loss of any strategic advantages were expected to be less than the enemy's costs of battle plus the strategic gains made by giving battle if successful.

This may strike a modern reader as crude but the overriding point is that Montecuccoli, like Gustavus, calculated with some deliberation whether to offer or to decline any given battle at hand. Here was a way to deal with capricious decision making, a way to arrive at monumentally important decisions in a more ordered, more methodical way than hitherto had been the case. It bears emphasizing once more not to confuse whether generals made the militarily correct decision regarding a particular battle — after all, once engaged, at least one general lost — with how the decision was arrived at. The point we make is only that battle in the Age of Battle had become too important for a general to fail to calculate the likely consequences beforehand.

THE 1700S: MARLBOROUGH, DE SAXE, AND FREDERICK THE GREAT

The eighteenth century is known as the peak of the Enlightenment period, and so it is not surprising that attempts not just to introduce and employ but to reduce warfare to a calculated and scientific enterprise peaked as well. Military writers emphasized the art of maneuver over the gains that could be made by means of battle. Yet the age was hardly free of battles. Several military leaders were nearly as aggressive as the battle-minded generals of the Napoleonic and Clausewitzian eras in the century to come. Charles XII (1682–1718), John Churchill, the Duke of Marlborough (1650–1722), and Frederick the Great (1712–1786) rarely shied away from battle—although the two latter leaders scarcely denied the role of calculation in seeking battle. The military differences between the seventeenth and eighteenth centuries were more evolutionary than revolutionary, however. Strategy, weapons, and tactics were refined and improved but not significantly changed.

The improvements had a paradoxical effect on warfare. Armies in 1750 were notably more effective weapons of war than were their predecessors of a century before, mainly because the art of maneuver and the science of gunfire had evolved. The troops required to do the job had to be trained intensively. Maurice de Saxe (1696–1750) concluded that not the larger but the better army had the advantage. Well-trained and reliable infantry formations could change position and direction under fire, move to parry threats, take advantage of sudden opportunities, and if worse came to worse, withdraw in reasonably good order to fight another day. An army that could do this was unlikely to be beaten by one that could not unless the odds were so great as to render skill irrelevant. Productivity had entered the fray. It was axiomatic among generals of this time that it took four years to train a really good infantry battalion. This made the investment in a good army very high even in peacetime and raised the replacement cost significantly.

The direct cost of war was also rising. (Already in the prior century, when warfare was becoming the sole prerogative of great kings, even they were financially strained by the expense of fighting. Louis XIV's treasury was nearly bankrupt after two major wars.) The rising expense was caused by several factors. The growth of armies meant an ever increasing payroll as regular payment of troops had become the norm. (All soldiers of the age expected some form of payment upon enlistment.) Larger armies required more guns. Almost invariably, these were manufactured in various royal and state factories, and this hardly lowered the cost of acquisition. Fortification of critical cities, arsenals, and likely invasion routes consumed fortunes. The officer corps, often bloated by the politically advantageous distribution of commissions, was also expensive. Some rulers preferred to rely on expendable foreigners rather than their own taxpaying farm lads. The tax revenue obtained from the latter would pay the cost of the former, with an offsetting effect on the state budget. If instead the farm lad were drafted, tax revenue would be lost twice, first the forgone tax revenue the young man would have produced, and second the tax revenue of some other citizen used to pay for the boy. Not only did this countermand the notion of emerging national armies, but it did not lower the cost of armies

Table 4.1: Monarchies' military expenditure (as percentage of total expenditure, by century)

15th	40
16th	27
17th	46
18th	54

Source: Ferguson, 2001, p. 41.

appreciably enough. The great kings of the century could borrow money, but, as the French rulers discovered, someone's willingness to lend it did not ensure the debtor's ability to pay it back.

While the cost of war kept rising in absolute terms, in relative terms the story is more muddled:

> A common error is to suppose that, over the long run, there has been a linear or exponential upward trend in the cost of war. In absolute terms, of course, the price of military hardware and the level of defence budgets have risen more or less inexorably since the beginning of written records. In relative terms, however, the patterns are more complicated. We need to relate military expenditure to the scale and frequency of war; to the size of armies in relation to total populations; to the destructiveness of military technology ("bangs per buck"); and above all to total economic output. Allowing for changes in population, technology, prices and output, the costs of war have in fact fluctuated quite widely throughout history. These fluctuations have been the driving force of financial innovation.[23]

In fact, the share of royal spending on warfare did rise, but not in a totally linear fashion (table 4.1). Individual wars, however, did become more expensive.

> The cost of a sixteenth-century war could be measured in millions of pounds; by the late-seventeenth century, it had risen to *tens* of millions of pounds; and at the close of the Napoleonic War the outgoings of the major combatants occasionally reached a hundred million pounds *a year.*[24]

The accuracy of this quotation can be seen in some actual numbers for Britain's wartime expenditures (table 4.2). Of course the rising costs were a burden. The growth of armies and navies could only be sustained by nurturing the economy. The ability "to maintain credit and to keep on raising supplies" explains why the English defeated the ostensibly more powerful French. The ability of the new nation-states to organize resources for the waging of war was a far greater change in the seventeenth and eighteenth centuries than technology, which did not change radically.[25]

Table 4.2: Cost of major British wars, 1689–1815 (millions of pounds, £)

Grand Alliance (1688–97)	49
Spanish Succession (1702–13)	94
Jenkins' Ear/Austrian Succession (1739–48)	96
Seven Years' War (1756–63)	161
American (1776–83)	236
Napoleonic Revolution (1793–1815)	1,658

Source: Kennedy, 1987, p. 81.

Neither did the balance of power change in the eighteenth century, which was somewhat more stable than during the chaotic seventeenth. Despite its humiliation in the Seven Years' War, France was the great power of the age. Prussia was born as a great state, Russia became a "player," while Austria declined somewhat and Spain sank into irrelevance. As before, these shifts were not radical and reflected evolutionary rather than revolutionary change. The great wars of the century (Great Northern, Spanish Succession, Austrian Succession, and Seven Years') were fought to change the balance of power in various ways, but the strategic picture changed with remarkable slowness. None of these conflicts quite reached the level of total war, although one came close.

This was the Seven Years' War (1756–1763), which is worth summarizing because of its extraordinarily global reach and complexity. When it "officially" began, two of the participants (Britain and France) had already been fighting an undeclared war for two years for control of North America (the French and Indian War). In 1756, France, Russia, and Austria, decided to end Prussia's existence as a great power. Frederick the Great, king of Prussia, had provoked this alliance by his earlier annexation of Silesia, previously an Austrian possession. The British joined Prussia, and not just because they were already fighting the French. Britain's ruling dynasty was German and still had a substantial German possession (Hanover). This turned out to be a clever decision, because Britain was the only clear winner. Britain defeated France in North America, India, and at sea. The French performance in Europe was poor. Prussia barely survived, and only because Russia suddenly withdrew from the war in 1762. But at least its status as a major power was secure, and its famous ruler avoided war for the remaining twenty-three years of his reign. Austria gained nothing.

To return to our analysis, how did the changes in war and strategy affect calculations regarding the costs and benefits of offering battle? The most significant change lay in the calculation of additional benefits. These became fewer as most conflicts now concerned boundaries and provinces rather than the core of states. In a total war, where a whole system or way of life is at stake, risking the lives of huge numbers of soldiers makes some sense. But when potential gains are fewer — literally marginal in the ordinary sense of the word — the acceptance of heavy losses is less rational. Not only were potential gains smaller, but potential losses loomed larger: the better-established powers now had more at stake should a campaign or battle end in defeat. This explains why some nations — not just individuals — behaved more conservatively. France in the War of the Spanish Succession and the trio of France, Austria, and Russia in the Seven Years' War had much to lose, which may also explain why the opponents in those conflicts behaved more aggressively. By the same token, the British in the War of Spanish Succession could afford to be more aggressive than their enemies or their Dutch allies because the British could lose their army and still not be invaded.

The rising total cost of war meant that the additional cost of battle rose as well. Risking battle meant risking costly formations. The more aggressive the general, the greater the potential loss: the cost sunk into an army that is put at risk. It is quite possible that generals even faced a problem of increasing marginal costs: the loss of twenty infantry battalions might be more than twice as bad as losing ten, if losing twenty crippled the army's entire operational capacity. Rising costs imposed some peculiar problems at the margin. For one thing, the monarchies of the age could not afford too many defeats. While public opinion had not the place it has today, abdication was often discussed after a serious military setback. A routed army lost not only the field of battle, but its weapons and its men. The former were often thrown away by running soldiers — cannon had to be abandoned anyway — and the running soldiers frequently deserted. Paradoxically, the latter problem inhibited pursuit as well, for it is difficult to chase the dispersed. Therefore, the possible benefit of totally defeating an enemy was effectively reduced in value: total defeat did not equal total destruction.

Not all rulers and generals seem to have appreciated the impact of rising cost. Marlborough's enormous losses undermined his alliance, his government, and finally, his position. Frederick the Great weakened himself almost fatally through his offensive approach. On his deathbed, Louis XIV famously counseled his successor that he had been too fond of war and that the people were overtaxed as a result. Of course, each of these rulers expected greater benefits from fighting their neighbors, which might have offset the greater marginal costs.

Even the more battle-minded recognized, however, that arsenals and other valuable strategic points had to be protected, and this was more important than battlefield victories. The risk of losing a vital town or arsenal was a potential cost that exceeded the benefit of defeating an enemy army because of one fairly straightforward consideration. The benefit of an additional battlefield victory was not always easy to foresee. A defeated enemy *might* disintegrate, or *might* be so badly defeated that he could not reappear, or *might* feel compelled to negotiate a peace treaty. In contrast, the loss of a vital town or arsenal *would* cost tax revenue, or *would* mean the loss of a weapons supply, or *would* sever the geographical connection with an ally or other significant town. The additional benefit was hazy, the additional cost all too clear. This should be kept in mind when criticisms are made of generals in this era for being overly cautious.

That criticism has never been leveled at Marlborough, who remains the most famous and controversial general of the early eighteenth century. Portrayals of Marlborough continue to change. He has been pictured as a daring general only frustrated by his cowardly Dutch allies, but more recently as a much more calculating individual who recognized that he was working with sensible Dutch allies. That he saw major battle as the key to victory is not in doubt. According to David Chandler, "from first to last he was the proponent of the major battle as the sole means to break an enemy's military power and thus his will to resist."[26] He actually spent much more time maneuvering and protecting or gaining fortresses than is usually recognized. Still, few generals of the century could add to their résumés four battles that are still famous today (Blenheim, Oudenaarde, Ramillies, Malplaquet).

Chandler may be right regarding Marlborough's proclivity toward major battle, but that does not immediately explain why he went over to the attack at particular points in time. One major consideration influencing his calculation was a very traditional military advantage: surprise. His attack at Blenheim (1704) violated one of the cardinal rules of the age in that his opponent was larger. Marlborough and his allies were expected to retreat. The Englishman wanted to attack, however, before the French received even more troops. So his adversaries expected the action to follow the maneuver-oriented chesslike moves of the age and instead found themselves under attack in a bloody battle that resulted in a total French defeat (fig. 4.4). Similarly, at Ramillies, Marlborough attacked once again when the French were expecting English passivity.[27]

What motivated Marlborough to break with the pattern of his time? Obviously his calculations of costs and benefits of offering battle were different from his contemporaries'. Expecting commensurately higher benefits, he was willing to risk higher costs. While governments discouraged "their generals from fighting on any but the most advantageous terms," of Marlborough's four major battles at best only one fit that requirement. He valued the probable

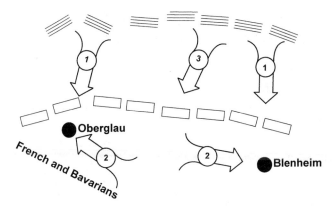

Figure 4.4. Battle of Blenheim
A classic eighteenth-century example of chesslike maneuvering, Blenheim represents the pin-
nacle of achievement of one of the age's most aggressive generals. Marlborough and Prince
Eugène of Savoy (1) attacked the villages of Oberglau and Blenheim (Blindheim). The French
(2) poured their reserves into the villages, weakening their center. Marlborough then launched
a massive attack on the center (3) , which led to a decisive victory.
Illustration by Debra van Tuyll.

additional benefits to be had much more highly. The Dutch, who tended to restrain Marlborough, wanted "to keep casualties and expenditures as low as possible" as they were trying to protect their national security. Certainly Malplaquet, where the Dutch began the day with eighty infantry battalions and ended with enough men for eighteen, reinforced their cautious views. Their casualties were "so heavy that the Dutch Army was never quite the same again: the vacant ranks could be replenished in time, but the memory of Malplaquet cast a long, dark shadow."[28]

Marlborough apparently did believe that decisive victories, even with risks, would be more likely to lead to a favorable result, for both allies. But why did he come to believe this? If he were a young officer on the make, rejection of the hidebound tactics of his ancestors might make sense; yet he was well past age fifty at the time of Blenheim, an old man for those days. There are at least two explanations. The first is that he sought decisive battle as a means of victory. Blenheim "altered the course of the war." After decades of maneuver artists, Marlborough had restored decisiveness in battle—all four were clear military victories—but not in war. This has led to the suggestion that Marlborough was in effect filtering his marginal cost/benefit calculations in a way that benefited his country and allies not at all: "One cannot escape the conclusion," write Windrow and Mason, "that throughout his career at command level he was constantly a victim of his own insatiable ambitions." Even so, Marlborough doubtlessly calculated his expected net advantages, and if accused of having done so through the filter of his perceptions, then that is exactly what any of us do and what the economic concept of marginal cost and benefit predicts us as doing.[29]

Maurice de Saxe took quite a different tack, his calculations of marginal costs and benefits more nearly reflecting the intellectual tenor of the age than Marlborough's: "I do not favor pitched battles, especially at the beginning of a war; and I am convinced that a skillful general can make war without being obliged to fight any." De Saxe's own writings as well his career show a high level of devotion to calculating the costs and benefits of military action. "I do not mean to say that when an opportunity occurs to crush the enemy that he should not be attacked, nor that advantage should not be taken of his mistakes. But I do mean that war can be made without leaving anything to chance." A casual reader of de Saxe's memoirs might take these comments as those of the theoretician, unaware that the French marshal was one of the most able soldiers of the age. He was particularly adept at using sieges to gain advantage. He advocated luring the enemy into a siege and waiting for him to be exhausted, and then attacking. His greatest victory, at Fontenoy (1745), shows how he could use a siege to bring about a battle, thereby combining archaic and modern warfare. He deliberately besieged a city only to draw the enemy into battle, and it worked. He changed the cost/benefit ratio by creating a favorable situation.[30]

Frederick the Great seemed to combine the attitudes of Marlborough and de Saxe. This may not have been accidental, as the king studied warfare and military history with a vengeance. He inherited one of the best trained armies in modern history and embarked on deliberate aggression to build Prussia into a significant state. He fought two wars totaling fifteen years, technically starting the second as well as the first, but spent the last twenty-three years of his reign in peaceful reflection, having only escaped destruction through good fortune.

Frederick never acknowledged whether near-disaster changed his ideas and calculations regarding the costs and benefits of offering battle. What can be said is that he offered often. During the Seven Years' War Frederick fought eleven battles, attacking nine times and clearly risking battle the other two (fig. 4.5). No calculations are needed to understand why this happened. While the costs of attacking were extremely high — Frederick's small and well-trained army suffered dreadful attrition — the benefits were great as well. The alternative, a defensive war of maneuver, would lead to the kingdom's being occupied

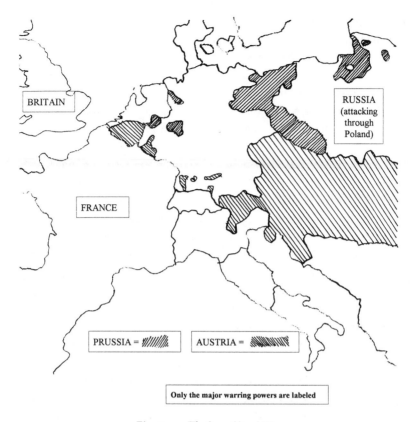

Figure 4.5. The Seven Years' War
The Seven Years' War (1756–1763) was a straightforward attempt by France, Russia, and Austria to curb the growth of militarily strong but geographically vulnerable Prussia — the latter nicknamed "a kingdom of borders." Britain was a natural ally of Prussia for two reasons. The British crown governed Hanover, which feared French expansion, and Britain had been at war with France since 1754 in North America (there known as the French and Indian War). Notwithstanding the great military ability of Prussia's King Frederick II, his country was on the eve of destruction when Russia's wayward Peter III withdrew from the war. Prussia survived, France was humiliated, and Britain became the world's dominant power.
Illustration by Hubert van Tuyll.

by the three great powers advancing on it. As for Gustavus Adolphus some years prior, the calculus was really straightforward.

Frederick's frame of mind influenced his calculations. When he invaded Bohemia in April of 1757, he intended "a decisive campaign ending with the destruction of the Austrian army and its ability to wage war." This represented a break with most of the past, and while it can be explained through his unfortunate geographical situation, he may have chosen this route even if he had not been surrounded. He claimed that "the Prussian Army always attacks" and stuck to that formula even when disasters occurred. Possibly his calculations were influenced by historical knowledge. The Enlightenment, of which he was very much an active part, stressed the search for knowledge as a tool for solving problems. Like a later German military thinker, Frederick's interest in winning a battle of annihilation was stimulated by his study of Cannae (216 BC).[31]

Why did Frederick's calculations add up to an attack order so much more often than his contemporaries? Certainly he was far more optimistic than de Saxe or Montecuccoli. Frederick saw no problem with numerical shortcomings. "If you are inferior in numbers, do not despair of winning." He suggested terrain, tricks, tactics, and other means to make up for numerical inferiority. To an extent this was necessity as the mother of Frederick's invention since under the rules of positional warfare of the age, he could never fight because Prussia was almost invariably outnumbered. This made it necessary for Frederick to choose the offensive under circumstances in which no one else would attack, Marlborough being dead. An additional consideration, however, was that he preferred short wars because long ones cost more and the troops deteriorated.[32]

As mentioned, Frederick did not explicitly acknowledge his narrow escape in his postwar writings. Had Russian empress Elizabeth not died in 1762 and left the throne to her wayward, pro-Frederick nephew Peter III, Prussia would have been a distant memory. However, Frederick's writings reveal that experience had given him a more nuanced approach to calculating the decision to give battle. "Never give battle if it does not serve some important purpose," he counseled. In fact, he suggested that the gap between marginal costs and benefits should be a large one: "War is decided only by battles, and it is not finished except by them. Thus they have to be fought, but it should be opportunely and with all the advantages on your side."[33]

This does not sound like the king who had attacked so often and sometimes in questionable situations. His thinking on calculations changed for at least four reasons. First, he explicitly recognized that there were things that could not be anticipated or controlled.[34] Second, the battlefield had been a painful taskmaster, in two ways. He had not always won. Of his eleven battles, three were defeats and a fourth could be rated that way. However, his experience with battles had left behind a worse ambiguity. The ten battles he fought between 1756 and 1760 had not prevented any of his three adversaries from continuing the war.[35] Third, his calculations were sometimes faulty, and he was hardly at an intellectual disadvantage compared to the average general. At Kunersdorf (1759), for example, he launched an utterly reckless attack on the Russians merely because he had an extremely low opinion of them (a mistake that seems to recur with some regularity). And fourth, he may have come to appreciate that there were other ways to wage war. Austrian field marshal Leopold J. M. von Daun (1705–1766) was much criticized later for his defensive strategy — but he was praised by Prussians, who were much frustrated by his strategy. Daun fought differently from Frederick and frustrated the intent behind the king's calculations. The Prussians, to their credit, realized this. Daun, who needed to preserve the Austrian army for political reasons as well as military ones, was not completely complimentary of the Prussian approach to war: "The king," he said, "has often fought without good cause. My opinion is that we should offer battle if we find that the benefit we derive from a victory is proportionately greater than the harm that would result from falling back or being defeated."[36]

Earlier we suggested that battle had become too important for a general to fail to calculate the likely consequences. What do we make of the apparent failures of Louis XIV and Frederick the Great, for example, to predict correctly? By themselves these failures do not compromise our contention that expected marginal costs and benefits determined the decision to offer battle. What we do see in both these cases is the complexity introduced into military calculations when rulers make decisions based on their national resources, not those of a particular army. Had Frederick been a general in the Prussian army, without control of the entire nation's resources, he might not have been nearly as reckless. Louis XIV was defeated not by waging costly battles, but rather by waging costly wars. His most famous adversary, Marlborough, was far more aggressive than the French king, who in any case did not command in battle. But although the centralized, resource-rich state of the French Revolution had not yet come into being, the impact of "infinite" resources on the decision to offer battle was already being felt.

NAPOLEONIC WARFARE

Because the Age of Battle (1618–1815) overlaps in our scheme with the Age of Revolution (1789–1914),[37] a few things need to be said about the latter and particularly the two and a half decades that they overlap. The long century, as the latter period is also called, contained an enormous number of changes in almost every aspect of life; some of these occurred late in the century, while others did not affect military establishments immediately. But there was enough change and ferment so that almost every major war in the century was decided in favor of the side that had militarily modernized the most. This was true of the wars of the French Revolution and most of the Napoleonic wars, as well as the Crimean, Austro-Prussian, and Franco-Prussian wars. (This effect was less visible in the American Civil War because the opposing armies were so similar and led by generals with identical military-educational backgrounds.) Calculation of additional costs and benefits generated by the prospect of an additional battle was complicated by the numerous changes that affected warfare, something eighteenth-century generals did not have to contend with nearly as much.

The French Revolution (1789–1815) affected all aspects of life and society and, therefore, war. The most famous event — the toppling of the monarchy — may well have been the least important, but it did finally clarify that the soldier served the state, not the person of a monarch. Although France would yet have two emperors and three kings after 1792, the idea of service to the state was firmly ingrained and became the norm in every other country as time went by. This also meant that each male citizen was deemed to owe duties to the state, including the duty of military service. The officer-soldier distinction was legally abolished as the aristocracy lost its exclusive right to hold military commissions. In many countries, however, noblemen continued to dominate the officer ranks until after World War I.

The effects of the French Revolution on armies were far reaching. National universal military duty, for all men irrespective of class, meant that the recruitment system was vastly changed. The state arrogated unto itself legal power to conscript forces that the absolute monarchs of the past had not had. The revolutionary armies began a pattern of vast growth. Smaller professional armies were replaced by larger forces with many conscripts. While the overall size of military establishments had been growing, now the size of individual armies — the number of soldiers who maneuvered and fought as a unit — grew as well (fig. 4.6).[38]

Far more than before, these new armies were "national" in character as almost their entire complement was drawn from inside the country. The means of motivation changed. Enlistment bonuses and harsh discipline did not disappear overnight but the concept of patriotism took root and became much more important. At first, desertion was less of a problem, although as the Napoleonic casualty rolls grew it became more common. Political motivation of the soldiers became a necessary practice, and the French even appointed "political officers" to complete this task.

The structure of armies also had to change. Napoleon divided his forces

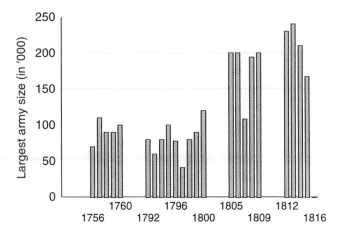

Figure 4.6. Size of field armies
Years discontinuous. The chart does not include the unusual situation at Leipzig (18 October 1813)
when three converging armies gave the allies 300,000 troops with which to oppose Napoleon.
Source: *Compiled from Dupuy and Dupuy, 1970.*

into self-contained units, called corps, and these sometimes fought battles independently of the rest of the army. This required that more commanders had to choose whether or not to offer battle. During Napoleon's last campaigns (1813–1815), his adversaries took advantage of this by attacking his subordinates acting independently, not Napoleon himself. The allies correctly calculated that this improved their chances of destroying the French.

The changing nature of the state also affected military practices. On the plus side (from the general's perspective) was that the postrevolutionary state could finance war on a much greater scale than before. Revolution meant centralization. The state no longer had to beg for money from its nobles. It no longer had to borrow in order to recruit young men to the colors. Both of these things could be accomplished by legal fiat. However, the new state existed in an era when there was great fear of revolution, at least until about 1850. War was now seen as a great destabilizer. Ironically, whereas resources were now more readily present to wage war, the political pressure was against doing so in the first half of the century.

The effects of the Industrial Revolution lie beyond the Age of Battles. True, it was underway, but its effects on warfare had barely begun. Modern economic history explains why. Early descriptions made it seem a quick and violent event, emphasizing its harmful sides. In reality the speed of change was modest. The word revolution has been called a "misnomer" in this context.

Nevertheless, the ways of production and distribution did change, eventually affecting all aspects of life. Modern industry arose. Mining, manufacturing, and construction became significant. Extensive use of powered machinery, new sources of energy, and the widespread use of materials not occurring naturally became the norm. The scale of enterprises grew as well.[39]

Eventually, it would have a profound effect on war. The telegraph created near-instant flows of information and meant that governments could control military decisions from afar.[40] The railroad revolutionized mobilization and logistics. Production made it possible to manufacture military goods on a scale that would have been unrecognizable to a seventeenth- or eighteenth-century general. War became industrialized. Entire industrial combines, such as Armstrong Whitworth, Blohm & Voss, Cammel Laird, Krupp, Thornycroft, and Vickers, were formed to "meet the needs" of the military establishments. The development of management techniques enabled powerful states to bring their wealth and populations to bear on the battlefield. Finally, the perhaps most immediate effect had to do with gunfire. The firepower and especially the range of weaponry changed faster than armies were willing or able to change tactics. However, all these took time to take effect. The formations and tactics of the 1860s and 1870s had far more in common with the military methods of the eighteenth century than with the twentieth.

How did these sweeping changes affect battlefield appraisal by commanders? Increasing resources in money, men, and matériel lowered the marginal cost of the all-out attack. Napoleon is supposed to have bragged about his annual income of soldiers. No eighteenth-century commander, even ones as aggressive as Frederick the Great or Marlborough, could have permitted himself such a view. (Whether or not Napoleon used those exact words, it certainly reflected his actual outlook.) The lowered-cost attitude dovetailed with the increasing emphasis on fighting the battle of annihilation. Carl von Clausewitz (1780–1831), in the long run the most influential interpreter of Napoleonic warfare, advocated this strategy. Eventually, the principle of annihilation became a strategic ideal, ignoring the relative rarity of its actual achievement in history and also ignoring Clausewitz's many qualifications on the subject. Having annihilation as a goal affected operations and grand strategy. The operational goal of total annihilation is most closely associated with the German plan to destroy France in six weeks in World War I (the Schlieffen Plan), but it was in fact adopted by most military establishments. Grand strategy moved in the direction of total war. Propaganda, of which Napoleon was an enthusiastic user (as seen by his founding of the army newspaper *Moniteur*), was developed as both a shield and a sword; the people at home were to be motivated, those of the enemy were to be demoralized. Economic warfare was not new, but Clausewitzian thought plus the economic realities of the industrial age made it a far more important weapon. (The economic realities included international trade and dependence on imported resources.) The First World War would bring all these together, with a dreadful result: annihilation without victory.

The doctrine of the battle of annihilation fit well with the French Revolution–era emphasis on total war.[41] Destruction, or avoiding same by the adversary, was well served by destroying his army. In total war the maneuvers of the eighteenth century seemed irrelevant. They yielded no decision, it seemed, and the huge armies of the new age could not remain in the field indefinitely because of supply problems. To be sure, the railroads would solve that problem, but they were also limiters; no army could afford to stray too far from its new, vital iron arteries, thereby further limiting wars of maneuver. At the same time, the battle of annihilation was made elusive by the growing cost of the frontal assault. The increasing range of weapons eventually made nonsense of the Napoleonic method of blasting through the center.

Changing politics also affected generals' calculations. Public opinion began to matter. This was shown most dramatically in the Crimean War, when military mismanagement led to the fall of a British government. Modern politics and modern media combined to give the public a role in military strategy. To an extent this meant that higher human marginal costs incurred by giving battle, while lowered by easier access to replacements, ultimately were raised by potential public opinion considerations. This manifested itself more in some conflicts than others. For example, generals in the American Civil War were quite sensitive to the political dimensions of their actions (see chap. 5). Another political dimension was the fear of revolution. This tended to discourage warfare, especially the high-cost kind, as destabilizing. But there was another, even more important element. The army had to be available to suppress uprisings. The loss of loyal regulars in battle could weaken the government's ability to survive internal dissent.[42] While most governments had been surprisingly successful in avoiding overthrow in the Revolution of 1848, in every case this can be linked to the solid support of the armies. War made revolution possible in two ways: it was an inherently destabilizing event, and it could cost a ruler the best tool to stop it.

Finally, generals had to consider the accelerated pace of war. Warfare and its accompanying diplomacy moved far more quickly in 1900 than in 1800. Armies, once deployed, still relied on the boot, but they could get to the battlefield much faster, their supplies could follow much faster, and the decisions that sent them there went much faster. Messengers still had a role, but the telegraph and train deprived soldiers and statesmen of the leisurely pace of decisions of the previous age. Troops could be redirected to meet new threats or take advantage of new opportunities much faster as well. This created yet another marginal cost of giving battle: soldiers, once committed, could not be easily redeployed. Three wars in one decade (the American Civil War, 1861–1865; the Austro-Prussian War, 1866; and the Franco-Prussian War, 1870–1871) showed generals trying to cope with the new calculus of war. Of course the Prussians did the best, perhaps inevitably given their inherent superiority in military affairs.[43]

Land warfare in the nineteenth century was Napoleonic. Generals attempted to emulate his tactics and strategies; army structures reflected his reorganizations. The most famous military writers of the century, Antoine Henri de Jomini (1779–1869) and Clausewitz, were both responding to the results of the Napoleonic age. Its military reforms and changes were not the product of one man. Many improvements came via pre-Napoleon revolutionary reforms, and even those made in the later Royal French army. His "genius lay in using everything better than anyone had before." But the effects of Napoleon's use of this reformed army were profound. Every modern state wishing to wage war after 1815 had to consider what had happened just before. Certainly generals of the age were mesmerized by the "golden age of generalship."[44]

How did Napoleon view the calculus of war? How did he decide when to offer battle? In general Napoleon always risked battle and never seemed to miss a chance to fight, at least as compared to the generals of the preceding century. His aggressive approach is perhaps the most famous thing about him, and many of his own maxims seem to support this view. According to memoirs dictated at St. Helena, he himself defined his method of waging battle as "on s'engage, et alors on voit" (one engages, and then one sees). While those dictates should be studied skeptically, this is one that recurs with some frequency. The Duke of Wellington (1769–1852) believed that "Napoleon's plan was always to try and give a great battle." His strategy, according to Wellington, was to assemble troops, deploy them, strike a great blow, and act afterward as circumstances allowed. His aggressiveness was legendary: "He won because he never stopped going after the enemy." Napoleon claimed to be singularly focused on the destruction of the enemy army: "There are in Europe many good generals, but they see too many things at once. I see only one thing, namely the enemy's main body. I try to crush it, confident that secondary matters will settle themselves."[45]

His seemingly unlimited aggressiveness has been attributed to his willingness to shed blood that was cheap. Certainly he had huge pools of manpower, and he had no qualms when it came to bloodshed. When he dispersed a hostile crowd in Paris in 1795, he fired at almost point-blank range to maximize the effect of his artillery to maim and kill as many people as possible.[46] The British strategist Basil Liddell Hart comments: "It is curious how the possession of a blank cheque in the bank of man-power has so analogous an effect in 1807–1814 and in 1914–1918. And curious, also, that in each case it was associated with the method of intense artillery bombardments. The explanation may be that lavish expenditure breeds extravagance, the mental antithesis of economy of force."[47] The costs were both short and long term. In the immediate term, Napoleonic attacks at the enemy strong point left the *attacker* so exhausted that pursuit became impossible. The Napoleonic era resulted in a dramatic drop in French population growth.[48]

This raises the question, just where was the calculation? It can be seen in two rather obvious things. First, Napoleon did not offer battle every day. He waited for the right opportunity or maneuvered to create that opportunity. During his many wars, Napoleon averaged about one day of battle for every fifty days of warfare. Second, during the Waterloo campaign he was every bit as aggressive as usual even though his supply of manpower was hardly what it had been. Louis XVIII had abolished conscription, and even Napoleon did not dare bring it back. He attacked, twice, for the same reason that he attacked so often in his career: he could not afford to give his enemies time to coalesce. The image of the careless shedder of blood is an oversimplification: "The lesson to be learned was that no generalisations could be derived about what Napoleon might do in any given situation."[49]

Napoleon was in fact a great believer in calculation, and his calculations of additional costs and benefits of an additional battle to be fought are quite easy to see in his career. He always intended to fight his opponent — no war of maneuver here — but his actual attack would take place when some circumstance or circumstances had changed to create a favorable situation. This usually meant having a numerical or firepower advantage at a critical place. He believed that the art of war consisted of the inferior army's having more force at the point of attack. "Military science consists first in accurately calculating the odds and then weighing up exactly, almost mathematically, the contribution of chance." Nor was this just a thought thrown up after the fact. In 1806, during the War of the Third Coalition, Napoleon claimed that "in war nothing is gained except through calculation." Later he went further and claimed that he had "the habit of thinking about what I ought to do four or five months in advance."[50]

It is interesting — and relevant — to note how differently some of Napoleon's interpreters treated his views on calculations. Clausewitz shared the view that many problems of generals were problems of mathematical calculation. Jomini, often accused of presenting too orderly and geometric a version of Napoleon's style of warfare, nevertheless notes the problem of collisions and unexpected battles. Clausewitz did not ignore chance, nor did Jomini propose reckless aggressiveness (if anything, he tended toward the opposite). While Napoleon had broken with his eighteenth-century predecessors on many points, he shared their desire to calculate before battle, and his careful choosing of circumstances reveals his attention to the marginal benefit (or cost) that might accompany fighting on any particular day. One can see this in his first famous campaign, Italy (1796–1797). He knew he had some basic advantages: his subordinates were competent and his enemies were inept. But that was not enough to provoke him to attack. He maneuvered until additional circumstances were such that he gained more advantages, thereby lowering his costs.[51]

By contrast Wellington seemed more cautious. Certainly his early view, while in India, that one should "dash at the first fellows that make their appearance" had been replaced by a more considered approach, carefully studying the terrain and watching the enemy. More than once he avoided pursuit because of the risks. As with Napoleon, the picture gets overly simplified. While Wellington was more careful with his troops and often fought on the defensive, he "would attack without hesitation, if he could do so with advantage." Napoleon even implied that Wellington had made a mistake by staying and fighting at Waterloo. As the preceding quote shows, Wellington, like Napoleon, was always looking for that additional advantage that would shift his cost/benefit ratio to a favorable point on the scale.[52]

THE AGE OF BATTLE AND THE OTHER PRINCIPLES OF ECONOMICS

The bulk of this chapter focuses on commanders from the beginning of the Thirty Years' War (1618) to the beginning of the French Revolution (1789), calculating expected costs incurred and benefits gained from the next contemplated battle. The database of battles spread over these nearly two centuries is so vast that it is of course easy to choose examples to prove one's point; but let any detractor choose an even simpler task: to show that the generals of the Age of Battle did not as a rule calculate the expected costs and benefits of the next battle to be undertaken!

As before, we use the remaining section of the chapter to briefly hint at how the other five principles of economics we use in this book may be applied to the main topic, the Age of Battle. Each of these principles, like that of expected marginal costs and benefits, can be expanded into a full chapter, even book, of its own. It requires no mental gymnastics to apply the economic principle of opportunity cost to warfare in this, or any other, time period. All phases of warfare require making choices because no military establishment truly ever has all the soldiers and matériel that it desires. Thus, for example, generals had to ponder which geographical point to target, and choosing one obviously meant abandoning another. This choice could perhaps be deferred, and certainly the enemy should be kept in doubt. Almost all successful generals in the Age of Battle did this. And in the Age of Revolution that followed, Napoleon did so right up to the end, even attempting to fool Wellington as to his exact intentions at Waterloo. In this he succeeded, even as this particular success was spoiled by his defeat.

A significant substitution in the Age of Battle involved the transitions in the type of soldier used. At the beginning of the seventeenth century the rewards for soldiering were irregular and unsystematic. Soldiers were recruited through a variety of mechanisms, including mercenary companies, but regular pay was not known. Gustavus Adolphus and Prince Maurits changed this and created the modern world's first professional, nation-state, standing armies. Regular pay dramatically improved discipline. Paid soldiers were bound more tightly to their commanders (especially those responsible for their financial situation) and put them under less pressure to help themselves at the expense of hapless civilians. The movements of armies are always destructive, but the newer paid and well disciplined armies were a lesser hazard to civilians than their predecessors. Then the French Revolution produced conscription, a system that gradually became accepted elsewhere. Now a mass of young recruits representative of the whole nation and (ideally) bound together by patriotism replaced the smaller paid, professional armies of the eighteenth century. Although there was and remains disagreement on this point, this system apparently worked well enough and is beginning to disappear only in our own age.

The economic principle of diminishing returns at first glance conflicts with a well-known military principle with which few would quarrel: concentration of force. If concentration is required because a smaller force cannot do the job at hand, superficially, diminishing returns do not seem to occur. But they do. In war, if two divisions are needed for a successful attack, increasing the attacking force from one to two is valuable because it produces the desired overall result. Yet diminishing returns still occur: the firepower of two eighteenth-century divisions would not double the effect of one such division. However, diminishing returns become much more serious if the force grows beyond the number needed to accomplish the mission. Too many troops in an attack get in each other's way, there may be too much crowding on the battle-field, formations may get entangled with each other, and confusion interferes with offensive effectiveness. In almost every battle there could be found units which never got into action, despite their officers' best efforts. Thus, concentration of force as a military principle is not at odds with the economic principle of diminishing returns to an ever larger application of resources.

Problems stemming from asymmetric information between principal (commander) and agent (soldier) had to be addressed and resolved. For example, a soldier may intend to desert his unit, an undesirable intent of action that until the moment the action is taken is effectively hidden from the commanding officer. The problem for the officer is how to uncover the intent, or how to prevent the action even if the intent remains hidden. This became particularly important as armies grew in size. By itself, desertion was not a new problem, but its impact now went beyond mere numbers. Infantrymen had evolved from mildly organized rabbles in the Middle Ages to the core of any army. The loss of such highly trained personnel had to be prevented by ingenious forms of contract. As pay in exchange for loyalty did not always suffice as a contractual device, one solution was to write contracts such so as to keep the troops in formations as much as possible. There were sound military reasons to fight in line and column, but it also meant that soldiers were rarely out of sight of one another and would supply highly effective internal policing. A deserter endangered his unit. In battle, soldiers could (and still can) legally shoot dead those who fled. Fighting desertion became particularly important when campaigns and wars dragged on longer than expected and the fortunes of war became misfortunes. Those were the very times that soldiers were the most needed, and the most likely time for them to flee. Keeping them together so that they could be watched (or watch each other) was essential. And even though it was often not enough, a public shooting of recaptured deserters undoubtedly served as a means of stimulating troops' loyalty, at least to each other.

Another aspect of asymmetric information concerns not principal and agent within the same party but that between opposing forces, especially the problem of uncovering, prior to battle, hidden characteristics of an enemy force. To deal with this, one development in the eighteenth century was that of war gaming. This did not provide information as such about the adversary but did create a systematic way of studying possible outcomes and thereby began to reveal potential hidden characteristics an enemy (or oneself!) might possess.

The Prussian army was particularly farsighted in developing this methodology. Peacetime maneuvers also became more important for the same reason and purpose, and also to train conscripts.

CONCLUSION

Why apply economic principles to the decision to offer and decline battle? The answer lies in the vastness of the military-historical landscape surveyed in this chapter. The Age of Battle lasted approximately two hundred years (and in fact we covered nearly three hundred). Major engagements can be numbered in the hundreds, and smaller ones in the thousands. The model of analysis we propose in this book gives birth to a type of study that would make it possible to understand better and to present a more meaningful comparison of the actions of generals across the ages. Generals from every part of this period could be analyzed according to a common standard, and our understanding of their times, and perhaps our own, would be enriched.

APPENDIX

A Matrix for the Battle Case

Principle	Manpower	Logistics	Technology	Planning	Operations
Opportunity cost	attack must consider both quantitative and qualitative losses	no attacks means long campaign which can consume more supplies	spending on fortifications reduces money for field forces, and vice versa	forces planned for one place cannot be used at another	once used, offensive power cannot be immediately reused
Expected marginal costs/benefits	short aggressive campaign might incur fewer casualties than long indecisive one	battle can conclude campaign before supplies run out	massing artillery can improve results over distributing cannon to all units	gains can be made if battle risked in area that is economically useful to occupy	benefit of risking battle increased if adversary is compelled to attack a strong defensive position
Substitution	conscripts instead of hired soldiers; hired soldiers instead of looting troops	trains instead of draft animals cost less because fodder for horses no longer needed	the bayonet for the pike; the former costs less because one no longer needed specialized pikemen	when ideal force is not "available" due to high costs others will have to do—cavalry instead of infantry, etc.	artillery bombardments sometimes used as alternative to infantry assault
Diminishing marginal returns	too many troops in an attack produces crowding and confusion	too many troops clog roads needed by supply convoys	massing more artillery than is necessary for a particular mission leads to waste of firepower, ammunition, etc.	concentrating all force on a single goal wasteful because more units than necessary may be employed	an excessive number of units participating in an operation may generate too much complexity
Asymmetric information (overcoming) hidden characteristics	low morale should be concealed, information about enemy morale can be critical	lack of ammunition must be carefully concealed	the telescope becomes a standard officer's tool	war gaming introduced by Prussia provides more accurate information about possible battle outcomes	concealment of part of force a standard technique (e.g., Rossbach, Leuthen, and Waterloo)
Asymmetric information (overcoming) hidden action	France's *levée en masse* creates obligations for citizenry, and harnesses patriotism	officers' economic situation related to purchase of supplies (more common in naval than land warfare)	private designers often develop new and better versions of existing weapons	introduction of regular pay for troops by Maurits and Gustavus Adolphus	troops in 17th and 18th centuries kept in tight formations to reduce danger of desertion

FIVE

The Age of Revolution, 1789–1914

The Case of the American Civil War and the Economics of Information Asymmetry

In chapter 1, we discussed the role of information in the marketplace. We distinguished, in particular, hidden characteristics and hidden action, the former due to information asymmetries before an action is taken, the latter to asymmetries that emerge after an action is taken. Market participants learn from mistakes, and in chapter 3 we saw that Italian city-states attempted to overcome hidden action problems stemming from contracts with condottieri. Elaborate contracts were written, inspections held, contracted payments deferred, performance benefits and bonuses offered, titles of nobility awarded, and so on and so forth, all for the purpose of prevailing over those who would renege on the military services contract. The theory of asymmetric information, at least the economic part of it, provides a rich tapestry by which to read history. In this chapter we examine elements of the hidden characteristics aspect of asymmetric information.

One note of caution must be issued at the outset, and that is not to confuse asymmetric information with asymmetric warfare! The latter deals with certain aspects of the conduct of war that can go far beyond its informational aspects. Even if war were symmetric, information asymmetries could still exist. This indeed was the case in the American Civil War, when forces were fairly equally arrayed in doctrine, equipment, leadership, and training, if not in numbers of men.

Military thinkers have woven the significance of information into every facet of warfare.[1] The use of information plays a central role in the thinking of Sun Tzu, and no particularly deep analysis of military history is required to discern the impact of asymmetric information on the outcomes of war. Indeed, it would be harder to achieve the reverse. The concept of hidden characteristics has special application to warfare. While both buyer and seller in the marketplace will generally seek to conceal certain information from each other, warriors would prefer to conceal all except those facts that might lead an adversary to give up — to leave the marketplace — or to take the wrong action. Correspondingly, the effort to gain information about the enemy's hidden characteristics is often massive. Yet no combatant can ever conceal everything about himself or know everything about the enemy.

Our focal point is an examination of problems posed by asymmetric information before an action is taken, before troops are called up, before supplies are moved, before a battle is engaged. If information is our monocle, the scene we watch is that of the American Civil War, 1861–1865. If both sides to a conflict had perfect information about each other with regard to every aspect pertinent to the conduct of battle and the whole of the war, there would be little need to fight.[2] Like animals, opponents might strut about, giving and reading signals by which to screen the opponent's strength — and decide whether to withdraw. In the parlance of information theory, a signal is an observable factor to serve as a proxy for an unobservable variable — strength — that can be revealed only in the action itself. Ordinarily signaling is cheaper than fighting, and so we observe, in man and beast alike, extraordinary development and displaying of signals, and, correspondingly, sophisticated abilities to read them. Reading signals results in the formation of expectations of benefits and costs, of thence adjusting tactics, and of revising strategies. Reading signals carries consequences, and both sides know this, the better to invest even more diligent effort into sending and reading signals. An information "arms race" may ensue.

On occasion, sender or recipient commits catastrophic errors. The aging alpha-male primate mistakes his young rival's challenge for a bluff, a fight ensues, the leader is replaced, and the regime is changed. Or, conversely, the young one was too self-assured, receives his beating, and must bide his time. Either way, the unobservable variable, strength, has now been revealed to an assembly of very observant bystanders, as any schoolchild knows. Cunning animals also know this and may not necessarily reveal the whole of their might in any given fight.[3]

The human animal is cunning. The very essence of human contest involves sending signals to mislead and deceive the opponent, just as it may involve, on occasion, sending true signals. May Day parades in Moscow during the reign of the Soviet empire quite literally involved the "strutting" of military men and their machines, the aim being to dissuade the United States and its allies from heedless attack. Similarly, the United States "strutted" underground nuclear explosions whose seismic waves could correctly be read in Moscow. This sending and receiving of correct signals secured the continued existence of life on earth. The inadequacy of signaling and screening, however, explains just why the Cuban missile crisis in 1962 resulted in so precarious a standoff. In private markets, mutual disclosure can increase confidence and increase the

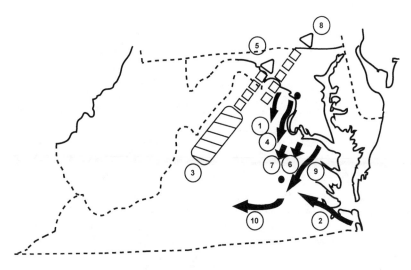

Figure 5.1. The War in the East
Legend (solid arrows depict Union): 1. First Bull Run; 2. Peninsula; 3. Jackson's Valley
Campaign; 4. Second Bull Run; 5. Antietam; 6. Fredericksburg; 7. Chancellorsville;
8. Gettysburg; 9. Grant's Advance; 10. Pursuit to Appomattox.
Illustration by Debra van Tuyll.

probability of a transaction, which is the reason why information disclosure is frequently mandated by legislation, for instance, regarding financial markets; likewise, prior to confrontation, confidence-building measures are aimed at conflict avoidance. But once the fight is joined, what is revealed and what is to remain hidden become strategic variables in their own right.

In this chapter we will discuss information and warfare in general terms before we turn to the American Civil War and examine specific eastern campaigns in that war (fig. 5.1). While no study of the military aspects of the Civil War can be considered complete without covering the western theater of war as well, limiting ourselves to the east provided several advantages. The eastern and western theaters usually operated with little connection to events in the other, especially in the Confederacy, where no large-scale east-west troop transfers took place before 1864. The combatants in the east were well balanced; the Union had the numerical advantage, while the Confederates could wage a strategically defensive war aided by Virginia's formidable geographical obstacles (fig. 5.2). This balance is well demonstrated by the inability of either army to gain a decisive victory—the Union going 1 for 6 on the offense, the Confederacy 0 for 2. In such circumstances the opponents naturally strove for every advantage, including the use of information. The first formal intelligence service in American history was born in this theater.

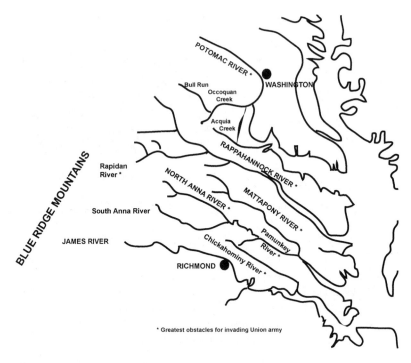

Figure 5.2. Virginia geography
The war in the east can only be understood in the context of the geography of Virginia. At-
tackers would need to conquer rough, wild, mountainous terrain and numerous rivers. The
geography thus heavily favored the defenders.
Illustration by Debra van Tuyll.

The campaigns in the east begin with First Bull Run (Manassas) in the summer of 1861, the first Union attempt to win a quick, decisive victory. There were many information "angles" to this battle, not the least being Lincoln's hope that a quick invasion would cause southern Unionists to rally to the flag. This did not happen, of course, and with the benefit of hindsight was unlikely. Even so, as the Union army did not even overrun northern Virginia, we can never be completely sure whether a more successful invasion might have quickened the end of the war. Certainly Union illusions about the fragility of the Confederacy were shattered by the Peninsula campaign (March to July 1862) and Second Bull Run (July/August 1862). Information deficits contributed substantially to the outcomes. The informational tide turned a bit thereafter. The Antietam campaign (September 1862) was a disaster for the Confederates because of an information deficit, while Union failures during the Fredericksburg (November/December 1862) and Chancellorsville (April/May 1863) campaigns were more attributable to Union command incompetence than information deficits. The Union victory at Gettysburg (June/July 1863), the greatest battle ever fought on North American soil, may have resulted from the Union's superior information (although superior numbers never hurt!).

Grant's massive and bloody campaign in Virginia (1864–1865) was different from its predecessors. Previous campaigns had consisted of advance, maneuvers, a great battle, and then one of the combatants would retreat to ponder the case. In Virginia, Grant's intention was to grab the Confederate army and hold it. Hence, a series of closely timed battles took place, at least one of which (Spotsylvania Court House, 8 to 21 May 1864) looked more like a World War I engagement than a traditional battle. It speaks well of Robert E. Lee, usually pictured as the more tradition-bound of the two main commanders, that he was able to wage this style of war as well as he did. For the last nine months of the war the armies would face each other at Petersburg, Virginia, fighting mostly from fixed positions. As will be seen, this had interesting results regarding the type of information that would be needed.

INFORMATION AND WARFARE

In commerce, differential information leads to advantages that can be exploited by the side with superior information to obtain a better than competitive price. In war, likewise, the primary role of information is to create differences to be exploited by the better informed side. Instrumentally, the role of information is as much to signal — verily or deceptively — as it is for it to be deciphered (to be screened). One difficulty is of telling when the opponent sends a correct signal and when not; another is to devise means by which to elicit information (a mock attack for instance to test responses). Some signals are sent inadvertently, by mistake, oversight, or loss. Some signals are come by clandestinely or are leaked deliberately. And some signals, intended for one's own side, are intercepted to the benefit — or consternation — of the other.

While the hidden characteristics aspect of the information principle is self-evident, the implications are many and subtle, as are the outcomes. What is the impact of information on behavior and action? How is information collected, processed, and used? Some agents act correctly based on limited information, and others are paralyzed into indecision by a flood of it, a situation not uncommon in the history of warfare. What kinds of information have the most impact? If there is asymmetric information, how important is it for one of the participants in the transaction to know about the asymmetry?

The economics of information should be of interest to the discipline of military history because of the unique role information plays in warfare, and not only because of the creation of information differentials by means of signaling and screening. This is so for several reasons. First, the need for information about one's own forces as well as the enemy's is virtually insatiable. West Point professor Dennis Hart Mahan (1802–1871), author of the first comprehensive American treatise on tactics and strategy, argued that "there are no more important duties which an officer may be called upon to perform than those of collecting and arranging the information upon which either the general or daily operations of a campaign must be based." Baron Antoine Henri de Jomini, the military theoretician whose interpretations of Napoleon influenced generations of American officers, believed that concealment of information should dictate operations: "Tactically, the offensive also possesses advantages, but they are less positive, since, the operations being upon a limited field, the party taking the initiative cannot conceal them from the enemy, who may detect his designs and by the aid of good reserves cause them to fail." Two of the United States Army's official principles of war relate to information. One regarding surprise reads: "Accomplish your purpose before the enemy can effectively react," and one regarding security states: "Never permit the enemy to acquire an unpredicted advantage."[4]

Second, not only is the need for information insatiable, but the information that is available in war often is inadequate, poor, unsatisfactory, and faulty. As suggested above, fighting — and indeed war — might not take place at all were there perfect information. Carl von Clausewitz noted that "many intelligence reports in war are contradictory, even more are false, and most are uncertain." The results of battle may be unclear even to its participants. The American Civil War is instructive in this regard. After the battles of Fredericksburg (1862) and Chancellorsville (1863) soldiers wrote home asking kinfolk whether they might have newspapers so that they would know who won. The enemy actively works to mislead, and, in contrast to much of the economic marketplace, there are no legal barriers to doing so. Knowing that generals on both sides read the other's newspapers, William T. Sherman recommended placing misleading accounts in the press. Apparently this was done, but Robert E. Lee, who constantly perused Northern newspapers, saw through some misleading published statements. To reciprocate, Confederate officers ran disinformation schemes against Union commander George B. McClellan. Later in the war, Jubal Early, knowing that the Yankees could decipher Rebel codes, deliberately sent deceptive messages.[5]

Third, commanders' knowledge concerning their own organization is of a far lower order than that of a business owner vis-à-vis his firm. The location, condition, morale, and equipment of an army unit could change in minutes, and reports to headquarters could be out of date by the time a commander finished reading—and even before he ever started reading. This uncertainty was exacerbated by conditions of scale, scope, and time of the era. To appreciate the commercial equivalents of changing location, condition, morale, and equipment status of any given army unit in battle, consider that few businesses of the time, if any, would have made use of tens of thousands of employees, as the armies did; few would have operated on as vast a geographical terrain as the Confederate and Union armies occupied; and few would have had to react within minutes, as officers were compelled to. In future wars, electronic communication would abate this problem somewhat, but not entirely.

Determining the role of information in commanders' decisions is difficult. During planning periods, when information uncertainty is the greatest, there may be a great many reports and memoranda, but battle orders were often verbal. Hence research depends on after-action reports and memoirs. Unfortunately, a general's postwar recollections may be a mixture of "what happened, what he believed happened, what he would like to have happened, what he wanted others to believe happened, [and] what he wanted others to believe that he believed happened." Even so, memoirs can be quite revealing. Ulysses S. Grant's memoirs, for example, reveal a surprising level of misunderstanding about Lee and his army in 1864, as we will have occasion to show in the pages that follow.[6]

NORTH, SOUTH, AND THE SEARCH FOR INFORMATION

Our choice for analyzing the economics of information fell on the case of the American Civil War for several reasons. First, none of our other cases examines the United States. It is the most quintessential "American" war, a substantial and lengthy conventional conflict without direct foreign participation. Second, the two sides' similarities were greater than their differences and made signaling and screening particularly important. Third, this war was the first major conflict anywhere in which the railroad and the telegraph played a significant role, for both directly affected the flow of, reliance on, and disruption of information. And fourth, the magnitude and significance of this war provide rich grounds to study it with the other principles of economics as well.

Civil War information gathering was often haphazard and inadequate.[7] Colorful stories about espionage frequently obscured the reality of the situation. While the senior generals were no doubt familiar with Mahan's dictum—nearly all had studied at West Point—their old professor had given no practical advice on how they should control the collection process or analyze the resulting information. Both sides invested considerable time and effort on intelligence even as large, formal staffs were unknown to Civil War generals, and commanders at times performed their own reconnaissance and intelligence work. The Confederacy began with certain advantages. Among these were that the Union had an organized government for spies to target[8] and that much of the fighting occurred in areas filled with Confederate sympathizers. To take advantage of these opportunities, the Confederacy spent four times as much as the Union on clandestine operations, and Lee's army kept a supply of greenbacks handy to pay scouts and spies.[9] The Rebels' greatest intelligence asset was Lee, who "outshone" his opponents in using intelligence to divine their intentions. Lee's "military success owed a great deal to his uncanny ability to size up an opponent and then act accordingly."[10]

In response to these Rebel advantages, the Union formed a Bureau of Military Information in 1863 that developed astonishingly accurate information.[11] At Appomattox it turned out that the bureau's chief, George H. Sharpe, knew more about the structure of the Army of Northern Virginia than did many Rebel officers. Lee tried to stem the flow of information by warning soldiers not to reveal their unit name, if captured. No wonder Lee was so concerned: at one point, the bureau managed to calculate the size of the Army of Northern Virginia within 2 percent of the actual number. The Bureau of Military Information, and Union forces generally, also benefited from one source not available to the Confederacy: runaway slaves.[12]

On the technology side of information gathering, the balloon seemed to offer a potentially spectacular perspective on the battlefield, but the expense (for the Confederacy) and the vulnerability to fire from rifled muskets (for the Union) caused its withdrawal by 1863. The telegraph had a far greater impact, both with regard to information transmission and espionage, although messages were sometimes delayed twenty-four to thirty-six hours, by which time the information might have lost its utility.[13] Even so, the telegraph's effect on information flow was revolutionary. The electronic information age had begun. Reports and orders could be sent instantly, but the effects went far beyond speed. A headquarters with a telegraph office could send messages far more frequently than if it were limited to the use of couriers. So long as the lines were intact, there were no limits on when messages went out. Yet messages and reports had to be brief, because during times of operations the networks were strained to the breaking point. Inevitably, generals and politicians became dependent on the telegraph. Lincoln, for example, was well known for haunting the War Department telegraph office to find out what the fate of his army was.

Dependence was an even more pronounced effect of the use of railroads, although more for logistical than informational reasons. Their effect on information flow was that large numbers of soldiers and civilians could move over much longer distances. This meant that information carried by word of mouth now moved across the country to a much greater extent than was true before.

An experiment with forward artillery observers was not repeated. Civil War gunners did not use indirect fire much and hence did not really need forward artillery observers. More useful were signal corps observation stations and scouts. The stations were originally intended for signaling but evolved toward two other functions: intercepting enemy messages and observing movements. The stations were placed on high ground and contained powerful telescopes. Both sides used some of their stations exclusively for observing the enemy. Confederate generals relied significantly on observations from the towers at First and Second Bull Run, Antietam, Fredericksburg, and the Wilderness. Armies fought vigorously for control of good observation station locations. But because the stations were immobile, a general wanting information about his enemy outside the stations' line of sight had to rely on scouts. The Confederates in Virginia used a very small body of scouts to penetrate Yankee terrain and even the rear of the enemy army. Occasionally, scouts captured enemy soldiers to bring back for interrogation. "Observers" were usually civilians, useful when one army was invading territory populated by enemy sympathizers. Their reliability, however, was always questionable.[14]

To speak of civilians as being involved in espionage is something of an anachronism because, by definition, almost all spies were civilians. Reliable or not, their information had to be used. Only in recent years, however, has there been systematic attention to the role of the civilian population as information-gatherers. The location of most of the fighting dictated that civilian spies were mostly in the Confederacy. The circle of Union sympathizers in Richmond is a well-known story. However, there were many active in other parts of the Confederacy. While some were paid spies in it for the money, others were drawn from the very large groups of dissenters throughout the south. The lack of attention to the civilian spies is related to the fact that the study of civilians in the war is a comparatively recent phenomenon. Since the mid-1990s major works have appeared on civilians in the war generally and in particular regions or states. Studies have also appeared on espionage, including examinations of women in general, and African American women in particular, as information gatherers. Spying by civilians helped the Union army overcome some of the inherent difficulty of almost always fighting in enemy territory—no small issue when one considers that the supposedly less competent Union army was never beaten on Northern land.[15]

Useful, too, was the cavalry. Lee considered his horsemen so valuable that he described his cavalry commander as "the eyes of the army" and said that "he never brought me a false piece of information." Spies were useful, especially if they occupied important positions. One Union spy, Samuel Ruth, was a railroad superintendent in Confederate Virginia and responsible for supplying Rebel armies. "Ruth supplied information on rail conditions, supply shipments, and troop strengths. His last contribution, in February 1865, was to transmit information north concerning a pending illegal tobacco-food trade, thereby preventing a large quantity of bacon reaching the starving Confederates." Ruth also slowed down the flow of supplies to Lee's Army of Northern Virginia. Chief of Staff Henry Halleck described Ruth as one of several Virginian agents as "worthy of [our] confidence," suggesting a long and fruitful relationship; otherwise Ruth would not have been known to someone as eminent as Halleck.[16]

The role of newspapers is nothing short of astonishing. Judging from their own reports and reminiscences, Civil War generals spent much of their time reading newspapers, the enemy's as often as their own. Grant recalled that newspapers went back and forth as easily as if it were peacetime. Lee once even correctly interpreted a lack of mention of a Confederate general in Northern papers to mean that Union intelligence had not yet picked up his unit's presence. Even Sherman, who blamed the press for Union problems at First Bull Run and Vicksburg, read the papers carefully for important information. The free flow of information (and misinformation) through the papers in the Civil War was used during World War I as a justification for the argument that "the case for some form of news control becomes a convincing one." (Many of the leaks appeared in Civil War newspapers because generals were attempting to build their careers through publicity.)[17]

The foregoing suggests the importance that American soldiers placed, for a variety of ends, on information. We now review some major war actions in the eastern theater of the American Civil War to learn the extent to which information helped determine battle-related decision making, and with what consequences.[18]

MAJOR EASTERN CAMPAIGNS THROUGH GETTYSBURG

Table 5.1 lists major campaigns and battles in the eastern theater of the war. Those up to Gettysburg are discussed in the remainder of this section. A

Table 5.1: Major eastern campaigns in the American Civil War

Campaign	When	USA	CSA	Significance
First Bull Run	6/61	McDowell	Beauregard, Johnston	CSA wins; no quick victory
Peninsula	4–8/62	McClellan	Johnston, Lee	Daring Union move fails due to McClellan's ineffectiveness
Valley	5–6/62	various	Jackson	Diverted Union forces from Peninsula campaign
Second Bull Run	8/62	Pope	Lee	Daring Confederate offensive succeeds
Antietam	9/62	McClellan	Lee	Union victory; leads to Emancipation Proclamation
Fredericksburg	12/62	Burnside	Lee	Union offensive fails
Chancellorsville	4–5/63	Hooker	Lee	Union offensive fails
Gettysburg	6–7/63	Meade	Lee	Confederacy's last offensive fails
Wilderness	5/64	Grant	Lee	Very costly Union victory
Spotsylvania	5/64	Grant	Lee	Very costly Union victory
North Anna	5/64	Grant	Lee	Complicated maneuvering; Lee withdrew
Cold Harbor	6/64	Grant	Lee	Very costly Union defeat
Petersburg siege	6/64–4/65	Grant	Lee	Long, complex campaign; Union unable to win rapid victory, but CSA loses mobility
Appomattox	4/65	Grant	Lee	Lee pursued and forced to surrender

Note: The USA and CSA columns list, respectively, the Union and Confederate commanders. The date column refers to month/s and year.

Reducing warfare to tabular exposition is difficult. The results of the major campaigns and battles do not always easily break down into victories and defeats. Grant's battles in Virginia led to Lee's withdrawal further southward, so by that measure they were victories. But the Union losses nearly undermined the entire war effort. Decisive victory was elusive. The most one-sided battles in this theater of war, Second Bull Run and Fredericksburg, were significantly caused by major blunders by the losers. Even Lee, the best general, could not destroy his enemy. Technology and terrain played their role, but so did information. Because of the shared military background of the opposing commanders, they knew each others' military conceptions and intentions fairly well.

separate section deals with General Grant's campaign in Virginia in 1864/5, after the tide of the war had turned.

First Bull Run

The Civil War began in earnest in the summer of 1861, when Irvin McDowell led the Union army toward Pierre Beauregard's Confederate army, encamped behind Bull Run, a small stream running west of the town of Centreville in northern Virginia. McDowell had 38,000 men but brought only 28,500 into battle at Bull Run. Beauregard initially had about 20,000 before, later on, reinforcements of another 15,000 men arrived under Joseph Johnston. McDowell and Beauregard each overestimated the other's initial troop strength by about 50 percent. McDowell mentally gave up the numerical advantage he held against Beauregard. Echoing Jomini, McDowell argued that an advance on Rebel positions would inform the enemy as to his intentions, his strength, and other militarily important matters.[19] He did not wish to reveal a hidden characteristic vis-à-vis the Confederate army. But the slowness that attended his misplaced, wrongly informed caution cost McDowell the chance of surprise. Meanwhile, to the northwest, a second, smaller Confederate army under Johnston guarded the Shenandoah Valley. McDowell assumed that Union troops in the valley would keep Johnston occupied. They did not. Johnston slipped away and joined Beauregard, with one brigade arriving by railroad, eliminating the Union's numerical advantage late in the afternoon of 21 July 1861. The battle that had been to the Union's advantage turned, and the Union Army suffered an embarrassing defeat.

McDowell had heard a rumor that Johnston had arrived the night before battle but either chose to disbelieve the report or decided to pursue his battle plan regardless; the official records do not reveal which. Beauregard, interestingly, was quite aware that McDowell did not know that Johnston had arrived yet; like McDowell, he did not have time to change his plans to avail himself of this advantage.[20]

On the tactical plane the Confederate army also obtained informational advantages. At two critical moments Confederate brigades used the terrain to conceal their actual, inferior numbers, and its Signal Corps reported McDowell's design — an attack on the Confederate left flank — in time for a countermove. The first is an example of maintaining a hidden characteristic of one's own, the other an example of discovering one of the opponent's. In all, First Bull Run demonstrates asymmetry of information. It prevented the Union's McDowell from attacking earlier and saved the Confederates' Beauregard from defeat, just as it ensured McDowell's defeat when Johnston joined the fray. The outcome was a decisive Rebel victory, so much so that President Lincoln relieved McDowell of his command and appointed George B. McClellan as his successor.[21]

The Peninsula Campaign

McClellan would seem a perfect choice when information in warfare is considered. He had observed the military use of the newly invented telegraph during the Crimean War, and as a railroad executive "he learnt more about the telegraph as a means of control and also about bulk supply over long distances."[22]

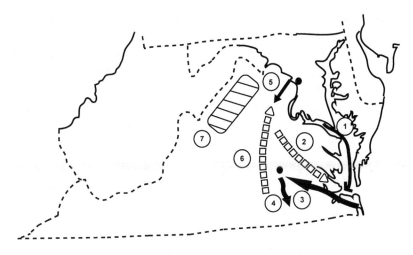

Figure 5.3. The Peninsula Campaign, Virginia, 1862
Legend: 1. (March/April) Union army moves to Yorktown Peninsula; 2. (April) Confederate
army moves to block Union advance; 3. (May) Union army advances to Richmond, heavy
fighting ensues; 4. (June/July) after heavy fighting, the Union army withdraws to the James
River; 5. (July/August) A second Union army advances south; 6. (July/August) Confederate
forces move north and defeat second Union army at Second Bull Run; 7. Area of Jackson's
Valley Campaign in March/April.
Illustration by Debra van Tuyll.

The Peninsula Campaign consisted of a series of battles fought between March and July 1862. After the first fight in history involving ironclad ships — in March, at Hampton Roads — the Union launched a seaborne invasion of Confederate Virginia in early April at Yorktown (fig. 5.3). The goal was to circumvent the great barriers that the many rivers flowing in an east-west direction off the Appalachians and the foothills into Chesapeake Bay posed to a land-based advance on Richmond, the Confederate capital. Initial success was complete, as was eventual failure. Rarely has the informational environment played as decisive a role in a campaign.

Like McDowell before him, Union commander McClellan was convinced from the outset that he was outnumbered by Confederate forces and hence advanced with excessive caution and slowness. His erroneous counting of the Confederate army then, as always thereafter, became legendary, and it has been described as "the one constant of his military character." When the Union army landed on the Yorktown peninsula, southeast of Richmond, McClellan grossly overestimated the strength of the local Confederate force. And when the main enemy army arrived, McClellan overestimated its size by more than twofold. By the time that he closed on Richmond, he estimated the Rebel army's strength at two hundred thousand, double his own and about two and half times its actual strength. Even when, late in the campaign, he conceded that part of the Confederate army had marched north to threaten Washington and confront another Union army (see Second Bull Run, below), he did not recognize his numerical advantage, even though both his military subordinates and his civilian superiors disbelieved his estimates.[23]

Their disbelief was logical — how could the smaller Confederacy have superior numbers everywhere? — but also a reaction against McClellan's endless pessimism. On 5 April 1862 he described the local enemy force as "large" and reported that Confederate deserters talked of daily reinforcements arriving. A day later he telegraphed Lincoln that "the enemy is strong in my front." Not until late May did he start to close in on Richmond. After a somewhat chaotic Confederate attack on 31 May 1862, McClellan reported that three of his corps had been "engaged against greatly superior numbers." He seemed optimistic on 2 June but still in guarded terms: "I do not fear for odds against me." By the end of June, he had withdrawn after heavy fighting and referred to "such great odds against us," of "contending at several points against superior numbers," and about being "attacked by greatly superior numbers in all directions on this side."[24]

McClellan found himself on the downside of a one-sided information asymmetry: the Confederacy knew his strength far better because Magruder, Lee, and Jackson worked diligently to deceive and mislead McClellan. Magruder, at one-to-six the hopelessly outnumbered commander at Yorktown, had his small columns march in circles with only one side visible to the Union and ordered his men to go into the woods at night and shout instructions to nonexistent brigades and divisions. Meanwhile, McClellan's own information security was porous. He complained about newspaper reports detailing his movements and positions and noted a specific instance in which a set of his orders was published a week later in the Baltimore *American*. "If any statement could afford more important information to the enemy I am unable to perceive it." But mostly he was deceived because he deceived himself. True, his intelligence chief, Major E. J. Allen (in reality, the famous detective Allan Pinkerton), supplied him with exaggerated estimates of enemy strength, but that was because Pinkerton was in awe of McClellan and only looked for information that supported McClellan's views. Nor did Pinkerton, who lacked a military background, understand the importance of timeliness in military information. This self-deception (or misperception) is visible in McClellan's views of Johnston, a close friend, and Lee, his former commander. McClellan was sure that Johnston would never invade the north, but Johnston in fact proposed that very thing to the Confederate government. When Lee took over the command from Johnston on 31 May 1862, McClellan was delighted, describing the new Rebel general as "*too* cautious & weak under grave responsibility . . . wanting in moral firmness when pressed by heavy responsibility & is likely to be timid & irresolute in action . . . Lee will never venture upon bold movement on a large scale." By contrast, Lee was willing to launch risky attacks on McClellan, not fearing counterstrikes. One of Lee's subordinates, James Longstreet, opined that McClellan would be slow to assault because he was a careful-minded military engineer. On both the material and personal levels, the Confederacy was better informed, appeared to know it, and pursued a daring course: dividing the already-outnumbered army and sending the bulk of it northward toward Washington while much of McClellan's army still sat south of Richmond.[25]

A clearer case of information-determined behavior can scarcely be imagined. McClellan relied on inaccurate, even fabricated, information to justify his lack of aggression. Preconceived notions influenced his views of the facts, such as they were. Prejudices and perceptions were part of the information available to him, and information can never be disentangled completely from the personality that processes it. Philosophers since Kant have understood that reality and perception cannot neatly be separated, but whether McClellan stood still because Pinkerton supplied him with erroneous numbers or because he already believed he was outnumbered does not now matter. The information of which McClellan was aware told him that he was outnumbered, and the result was lassitude and defeat. Why McClellan was so easily deceived, or deceived himself so easily, remains a matter of historical interest. If Lee sent signals, why did McClellan not install better screening devices to sort out signal from noise? There is no obvious reason to believe that improved screening would have been particularly costly to McClellan. In the event, the Confederate ruse led to an instance of adverse selection: the Union removed itself from a fight it thought it could not win. Lee prevailed because of a priceless piece of information — understanding his opponent's mindset. This caused him to pursue an aggressive campaign against McClellan, then to send much of his smaller army away, first for diversionary operations in the Shenandoah Valley, and then northward where a newly formed Union army under John Pope was preparing to come south. Lee's initial victory over McClellan was essentially informational. Lee had fewer troops, inflicted no serious defeats, and lost more soldiers. But he convinced McClellan that the Confederate strength was far greater than it was, and hence emerged the clear strategic winner.

Second Bull Run

McClellan's conviction of his numerical inferiority allowed the Rebel forces to shift northward, toward Washington. Lee first sent almost half his army and later followed with the remainder. Various units in the vicinity of Washington had been organized into a single army under a frontier Union soldier named John Pope. Pope began the campaign with bombastic overconfidence and suffered possibly the worst Union defeat of the war, largely due to lack and misuse of information. Not all of Pope's problems were of his own making. For example, telegrams he sent to his military superior were immediately sent to New York and published. Nor he was he completely insensitive to intelligence. He escaped Lee's first trap for him because of an intercepted letter.[26] But the bottom line of this campaign is that while both generals responded to available information, Pope had a tendency to forget or ignore facts, while Lee did not.

While Pope was generally aware by mid-July 1862 that Stonewall Jackson was approaching, his knowledge remained vague. Jackson, by contrast, "aggressively obtained intelligence as the foundation of his operational plans," defined what he needed, sought it, and responded decisively. Lee did no less. He instructed one subordinate to send his "most reliable & intelligent men" to observe McClellan's army to see if it was moving and soon correctly deduced that it would not, that in fact it would return by sea to Washington. Lee was well informed about Pope as well, deducing his intentions, using spies against him, and — just a week before the battle of Second Bull Run — capturing a set of Pope's orders.[27]

This was not a case of the Confederates' possessing perfect information — no such thing exists in warfare — but Lee's assessment of Pope's position was superior. In contrast, Pope's collection, analysis, and use of information were deficient. He did not ignore the information he had, but his actions, like McClellan's, were dictated by a false picture of the enemy in his mind. He was initially unaware of Jackson's advance and, later, of Lee's. He was misled by apparent Confederate withdrawals, which he interpreted as retreats, was confused by contradictory reports, conducted little reconnaissance, "failed to evaluate properly the information he received," and had a "persistent pattern of illogical reasoning." In the first phase of the battle, Jackson went around Pope's right. Pope did the right thing — he turned rightward and counterattacked — but he became so obsessed with his right that he completely forgot about the other half of the Confederate army, which attacked his exposed left with 28,000 men and crushed it. At the conclusion of the debacle Pope reported the enemy as "badly crippled" and suffering "at least double our own" losses.[28] But Pope had lost far more. And in a sense he had lost—forgotten—the information that he had, with fatal results. The Union lost nearly 14,000 men, as against the South's 8,350.

Antietam

All Union generals suffered from information asymmetry over which in many cases they had little control. Invading Virginia, they maneuvered in terrain inhabited by Confederate civilians and far more familiar to Confederate troops, among whom were many thousands of Virginians. This situation was reversed when Lee invaded the north. So long as he kept moving, the Union would not know where he was or was going. Union information would be out of date. But Lee would be foiled by one of the most famous information-related incidents of the war. During the invasion, a Union soldier discovered a copy of Lee's orders lying in a cornfield. Much postwar controversy ensued about who was responsible, but, for once, there was no question about the document's authenticity: a signature was recognized by a Union officer. McClellan now knew that Lee's army was divided and spread out. Nonetheless, he moved cautiously, allowing Lee to gather most of his army near Antietam Creek in time for the bloodiest day of the war, 17 September 1862, with more than twenty-six thousand casualties.[29]

It is largely a question of perspective which conclusions one draws about the extent to which McClellan was influenced by the possession of the lost orders. He did advance and offer battle, but did the slowness of this advance reflect limited informational influence? Probably not. He was cautious by nature, and he would not fight until he was sure that Lee was not aiming for Baltimore or Washington. Before his lucky break McClellan complained that his information came "from unreliable sources" and was "vague and conflicting" or "not fully reliable." He continued to overestimate the size of Lee's army but informed the president that he had "scouts and spies pushed forward in every direction, and shall soon be in possession of reliable and definite information." He began to sound more optimistic, telling one general that Lee would find it hard to escape. Once he received the lost orders ("the authenticity of which is unquestionable"), he knew what he needed to know—and also what he wanted to hear, as he continued to significantly overestimate the Confederate army.[30]

In his after-action report McClellan justified his moving "slowly and cautiously" due to "uncertainty as to the actual position, strength, and intentions of the enemy." On the eve of battle Lee just described McClellan's advancing as "more rapidly than convenient." The day after the battle he correctly described him as "indisposed to make an attack."[31] Once again, Lee's better understanding of McClellan had enabled him to survive, albeit barely, but McClellan's superior information had given the Union its first major battlefield victory.

Fredericksburg

Two months after Antietam, in November 1862, the fortunes of war were reversed. From an information standpoint, the appointment of Ambrose E. Burnside to Union command was a puzzle. As a corps commander at Antietam, Burnside had failed to reconnoiter the creek to his front, and his men had suffered heavily as a result. Initially, however, he managed to create some information asymmetry in his favor. As Burnside's army was in better shape, he had the initiative. He planned to move to Fredericksburg and there cross the Rappahannock River before Lee could move to stop him. Lee was very unsure at first about what Burnside was up to. He was quickly informed, particularly by his peripatetic cavalry, that the Union army was on the move. He later gave the cavalry credit for providing "early and valuable information of the movements of the enemy." Even if Lee believed that he was the best general on the field (and he was), he understood the difference between initiative and recklessness. On 15 November, Lee started moving troops to Fredericksburg, and four days later an entire corps headed for the city. By 20 November, he told Confederate president Jefferson Davis that Burnside was heading for the riverside city, but as late as 23 November he conceded that he was "as yet unable to discover what may be the plan of the enemy." Three days later Lee decided that the time to concentrate the entire army had arrived.[32]

When Burnside arrived at Fredericksburg he faced little opposition, but the expected pontoon bridges had not come. He could not cross. His informational advantage (knowing that he was going to Fredericksburg while Lee did not) started to disintegrate — but not completely, as the Rebels had not concentrated when the bridges finally arrived. Yet Burnside hesitated and, by the time his army made a heavily contested crossing, Lee was well ensconced above Fredericksburg. Burnside had deciphered Lee's hidden characteristic and kept Lee guessing for three weeks, but now Burnside sacrificed the advantage. He also sacrificed thousands of soldiers — his losses were almost thirteen thousand men — as their advance lacked any secrecy or surprise. Tactically, his advance on the Confederate position gave his opponents perfect information. Action reveals information, as Jomini had warned. The Confederates could see Burnside's strength and knew where he was going, and as fate would have it, the Northern troops were advancing over terrain where the Confederate artillery had pretested the range. Burnside later explained, "I . . . thought I discovered that [the enemy] did not anticipate the crossing of our whole force at Fredericksburg." In fact, Burnside attacked exactly where Lee wanted him to. The best that can be said is that Burnside slipped away almost unnoticed and Lee could not deduce what the unfortunate Yankee's next move would be. This was an asymmetry that Burnside was completely unable to exploit, however. Because of Fredericksburg and other failures, Burnside was relieved of his command and replaced in January 1863 by Maj. Gen. Joseph Hooker.[33]

Chancellorsville

Hooker, Burnside's successor, did better in preparing the informational battlefield — in a psychological sense perhaps too well because once he lost the informational advantage he became paralyzed and lost the initiative as well. Hooker paid a great deal of attention to prebattle information gathering. His establishment of the Bureau of Military Information gave him a regular flow of intelligence. He carefully studied information from deserters, contrabands, and regular citizens, as well as from balloon observation and newspapers (although that flow was sometimes cut off). He corresponded with Union officers commanding coastal enclaves in Virginia to deduce Confederate movements. He evaluated reports intelligently. When told that the enemy was evacuating Richmond, he responded astutely that this "will never be until he is compelled to."[34]

Like any competent general, Hooker worked to turn information to his advantage (or prevent disadvantage), and he succeeded. In the Chancellorsville campaign of April and May 1863, Lee did not have any idea where Hooker might cross the Rappahannock, and Lee's correspondence reveals no certainty about the Yankee general's intentions. Given Lee's track record, this has generated controversy about Lee's information-gathering skills in this time, including suggestions that there was no effective espionage and that Lee refused to believe accurate information sent him from Richmond. More recent research has suggested that he made better use of intelligence than Hooker, however. What Lee suffered from were effective federal disinformation and screening efforts. For example, knowing that the Rebels had figured out the Union flag codes, the federals provided Lee with false information about their destination.[35]

It seems clear that Hooker had a tremendous information advantage at first and acted accordingly. But once he crossed the Rappahannock River, he soon halted. The heavily wooded Wilderness area of Virginia where he now found himself was difficult terrain, and now that he was on the move his knowledge of Lee's positions and movements deteriorated. Hooker became increasingly tense, as is revealed by one response to a query from Lincoln about the situation: "I am not sufficiently advanced to give an opinion. We are busy. Will tell you all soon as I can, and have it satisfactory." This message reveals great uncertainty about his situation, including the status of his universe of information. It was not simply that he was busy. He found time to send a telegram complaining about highly confidential information appearing in two major newspapers.[36] Lee inferred quickly that Hooker would not advance further and launched a series of major counterattacks that gave the Yankee the false impression that he could only defend. Eventually a humiliating withdrawal resulted.

There is an interesting example during this campaign about how a general may act on the basis of correct information and yet do entirely the wrong thing (although through no fault of his own). While most of Hooker's army had advanced up the Rappahannock toward Chancellorsville, a Union corps under John Sedgwick had remained behind at Fredericksburg. A smaller Confederate force under Jubal Early occupied the heights above the city to prevent a Union advance. Early, who had roomed with Sedgwick as a cadet, believed that his old friend would be cautious and not attempt to assault the heights. Early was absolutely right; Sedgwick had no intention to attack except that, unbeknownst to Early, Sedgwick had received unequivocal orders to carry the Confederate positions. Obedient, he attacked, and with considerable difficulty drove Early off the heights. This disrupted Lee's plans and saved Hooker from worse.[37] But it could not save him from the public relations disaster of having gained the advantage of surprise, crossed the most formidable geographic obstacle on the road to Richmond, and then given the initiative. His behavior is explained by the principle of expected marginal cost and benefit (chap. 4) but the mental or emotional arithmetic that underlies this calculus was influenced by the information signaling and screening efforts both sides undertook. When Hooker was well supplied with information and enjoyed an information advantage, he took the initiative; when the advantage declined, he became hesitant. In spite of an almost two-to-one troop advantage for the Union, Chancellorsville ended with yet another Confederate victory, resulting in fourteen thousand Union and ten thousand Confederate casualties.

Gettysburg

During the Chancellorsville campaign both sides had enjoyed fairly good information, if at different times, first benefiting the Union, then the Confederacy. The situation during the ensuing Gettysburg campaign in June and July

1863 was almost exactly the reverse. Never was the Confederate army as poorly informed as it was during this effort, and Lee would blame his failure on this, at both tactical and strategic levels. As for the Union army, it went into the most titanic battle ever in North America under a new commanding general, George G. Meade, who, when the battle of Gettysburg commenced on 1 July 1863, had been in the saddle exactly two days.[38] That sudden replacement deprived Lee of one of his best information advantages: divining the intention of the adversary.

Lee's advance through Maryland into Pennsylvania occurred in a surprising vacuum of information. The Union initially lost track of Lee, and Lee (unusually) did not know where the enemy was either. An increasingly nervous Joseph Hooker, who followed Lee, was "uninformed" not because he received no facts but because he distrusted the ones he got. Lee's problems, however, were worse. By advancing north he had neither friendly civilians nor the strategically located signal stations he relied on in Virginia. He sent most of his cavalry on a separate operation and assumed that its silence meant that the enemy was not seriously threatening him yet. While tidbits of information trickled in, Lee lacked the cavalry to check and detail the reports. For example, on 24 June 1863 he speculated on whether Hooker had crossed the Potomac, but it was four days before a scout's report reached him on the matter. Lee and his cavalry commander were mutually ignorant of each other's locations as well. The latter could determine the former's movements only by reading Northern newspapers. Although the cavalryman (J. E. B. Stuart) suffered much posthumous Southern wrath over the episode, he had no urgent orders to obtain information. Thus, when Lee's troops collided with part of the Union army, Lee had no idea where the rest of the enemy force was. His corps commanders knew no more and did not know much about the terrain either. Lee admitted in 1868 that Gettysburg "commenced in the absence of correct intelligence."[39]

Lee's behavior at Gettysburg differed from his other campaigns. "Undoubtedly, Gettysburg was the lowest point of Lee's generalship. He was careless; his orders were vague; he suggested when he should have commanded; and he sacrificed the pick of his infantry in a foredoomed attempt to win a battle he had already lost." Lee did not maintain the initiative. The initial Confederate attack on 1 July was a product of chance and circumstance, not Lee's orders. His conduct of the battle lacked verve and imagination. All these behaviors can be linked to his informational situation. That does not prove other factors were irrelevant, but Lee's own words seem to support an information-related explanation. He emphasizes his lack of information throughout his final postbattle report. Even the most famous failure at Gettysburg — Pickett's Charge (3 July 1863) — he related to a shortage of artillery ammunition "which was unknown to me when the assault took place."[40]

Lee had faced and outwitted four Union generals, including the current commander, in thirteen months, and forced three retirements along the way (Pope, McClellan, and Burnside). His ability to divine his opponent's intentions was becoming legendary. On 28 June 1863, however, when George G. Meade was elevated to command, Lee, who knew of Meade, had no hard data on how Meade would behave. Lee respected Meade "both as a soldier and a person" and expected that the change was good for the Union — but not at that moment. He believed that the difficulties that would beset Meade taking command under such circumstances would nullify his greater abilities. "He was therefore rather satisfied than otherwise by the change." Although Lee regarded two of his own corps commanders with less favor than he regarded Meade, he figured that he faced a general who knew little about the current situation. To choose an aggressive stance made sense.[41]

Lee's analysis of Meade's problems made sense as well — up to a point. Meade was indeed in a difficult situation. When he was appointed he did not know his army's own plans (Hooker was notoriously secretive); he did not even have a decent topographic map of Pennsylvania, where the opposing armies were now moving; he acknowledged his unexpected appointment by noting his ignorance of Confederate movements; and just hours before the battle he was "without definite and positive information as to the whereabouts" of two of Lee's three corps. But Lee's analysis contained at least two problems. First, Meade's problems did not automatically translate into Lee's advantage. Meade still knew more about Lee's generalship than vice versa. Lee had won psychological victories over McClellan and Hooker — they had pulled back when it was not necessary. It was not a foregone conclusion that Meade's information problems would make him adopt the same option. Instead, Meade's problems might cause a tenacious defense to develop. After all, pulling away from Richmond was one thing, but what about a withdrawal that would expose Washington, not to mention other Northern cities? Second, the Army of the Potomac had an organized staff — Meade did not change it around — including a competent intelligence bureau. After two days of fighting, Union intelligence knew that Lee had only one fresh division left, and this convinced the Union corps commanders that the army should stay and fight. Meade correctly predicted where the final attack (Pickett's Charge) would happen.[42]

Lee made up for his information deficit with assumptions about Meade that turned out to be disastrous, and almost fatal. Meade, a cautious if tenacious general, carefully read incoming intelligence reports, especially information from friendly (and even "secesh," slang for secessionist) civilians, two of whom actually counted nearly eighty thousand Confederate soldiers as they marched through Hagerstown. Meade also disregarded some of the more exaggerated reports concerning army numbers. Even news of a Confederate general's attending Mass made it into Meade's reports. Just before battle he had a fairly accurate vision of where Lee's corps were and expected that "the battle will begin today." While he ultimately overestimated his enemy's strength, his 25 percent error looks modest compared to McClellan's calculations. Meade's information was far from perfect. He feared that Lee might go on the defensive, something Lee had never done. (Meade feared this because it would force him to attack under unfavorable circumstances.) And to be sure, one of Lee's corps commanders had urged just such a course. But Meade took no significant action based on this possibility. In contrast, Lee, who had shown again and again how much attention he paid to his adversary's intentions, lost this ability in the Gettysburg campaign since he knew neither what his enemy was doing nor, because of Meade's sudden promotion, what he was likely to do. Lee remained aggressive but did not maintain the initiative which, as we have suggested, probably came from his awareness of his informational disadvantage. When no low-cost signaling and screening options are available, one retreats or advances. Lee chose to advance. Under conditions of high uncertainty, the attending risk of failure was extraordinarily high.[43]

A contradictory view of Meade and his position (quality vs. ignorance) resulted in contradictory behavior by Lee (aggressive vs. lack of initiative). While we can understand Lee's behavior, connecting Meade's behavior to information is more difficult. His relative ignorance would have provoked caution, and his later career demonstrated that caution came naturally to him. His actions appear linked to information but one cannot say more. In the event, with some fifty-one thousand casualties, the three days of Gettysburg proved to be the bloodiest engagement of the entire Civil War.

GRANT IN VIRGINIA

In May 1864, not quite a year after Gettysburg, the new Union supreme commander, Ulysses S. Grant, launched a bloody six-week invasion of Virginia that culminated in a nine-month siege of Petersburg, a strategically located town south of Richmond, Virginia, then the Confederate capital (fig. 5.4). Petersburg fell on 2 April 1865. The entire campaign has remained controversial on

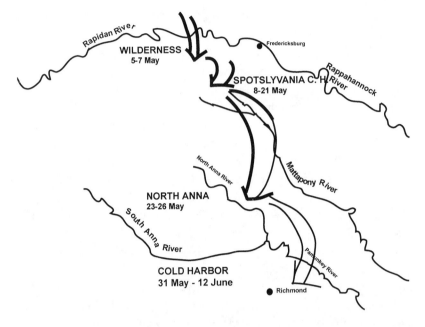

Figure 5.4. Grant's advance, 1864
Grant's advance in 1864 appeared to target Richmond, but in reality he was mainly interested in destroying Lee. He moved toward Richmond not to capture it but because he knew Lee would have to stand and fight. However, Grant underestimated how well Lee would do this. Illustration by Debra van Tuyll.

many levels, not least that of the use of information. Here we examine various way stations on what is known as Grant's Overland Campaign.

The Wilderness

Grant initially crossed the infamous Rappahannock River near Chancellorsville and entered the Wilderness, an area with poor visibility in which numerical superiority was of little importance. Grant did little to gather information about Lee, instead relying on general assumptions that were in no way accurate. When he heard that the Rebel flag station on Clark's Mountain was signaling his cavalry movements, he said that "this gives me just the information I wanted. It shows that Lee is drawing out of his position and is pushing to meet us."[44] So information did interest him, but his conclusion did not seem linked to the evidence. This was partly because, irritated with Lee's great reputation among Union officers, he discouraged their speculations about the Rebel's intentions.

Oh, I am heartily tired of hearing about what Lee is going to do. Some of you always seem to think he is suddenly going to turn a double somersault, and land in our rear and on both of our flanks at the same time. Go back to your command, and try to think what we are going to do ourselves, instead of what Lee is going to do.[45]

And so he did, instructing Meade that "if any opportunity presents itself for pitching into a part of Lee's army, do so." Two and a half hours of hesitation later, he ordered an attack — but not without consequences. The bitter fighting in the Wilderness, on 5–7 May 1864, exhausted both armies, although Grant cheered himself and Washington by reporting that "the loss of the enemy must exceed ours, but this is only a guess based upon the fact that they attacked and were repulsed so often." He described the Confederates as "very shaky . . . only kept up to the mark by the greatest exertions on the part of their officers, and by keeping them intrenched in every position they take." This was not true; the Union loss was more than half as much again as the Confederacy's. At the time, however, accurate casualty counts were hard to come by. The Wilderness was frustrating territory. Because cavalry movement was nearly impossible, neither army knew much about the other. It hampered Lee less, however. Lee had anticipated Grant's advance correctly and had moved to force battle there; the terrain nullified the Northern numerical advantage (about 102,000 against 61,000). The Union could have avoided this problem by moving quickly, but it did not. Lee, according to an aide, noted that Grant had "not profited by General Hooker's Wilderness experiences, and that he seemed inclined to throw away to some extent the immense advantage which his great superiority in numbers . . . gave him."[46]

There is a strange echo here in that Grant had suffered near-disaster at Shiloh (1862), where fighting in low-visibility, wooded terrain had nearly proved his undoing. Of course he had survived that experience, and that may have made him sanguine (or careless). Yet "Grant's experience at Shiloh, where he was taken by surprise due to poor intelligence, led him to vow that such would never happen to him again." Outwardly, he seemed superficial about his and the enemy's situation. "It is not yet demonstrated what the enemy will do, but the best of feeling prevails in this army, and [I] feel at present no apprehension for the result."[47] He had the information he thought he needed, and acted accordingly. He "knew" that he had superior numbers, that he could grind down Lee, and that his subordinates exaggerated Lee's abilities. He was right about the numbers, not quite right about the grinding, and wrong about Lee. However, Lee was weakening in numbers and health, and although Grant had no information about the latter, he knew the former even if he tended to exaggerate it. The Confederate general knew more, but his ability to act on this knowledge was declining, and the tide of the war turned.

Grant did demonstrate interest in using information more efficiently. On 9 May, as the combatants began to leave the carnage of the Wilderness battle, Grant instructed Meade to scout for major movements by Lee and, finding them, to attack Lee's left. This was a crude and simple process of asking for information and specifying the action to be taken on the basis of that information, without waiting for the supreme commander to think things over — while things were changing.[48]

Spotsylvania, the North Anna, and Cold Harbor

Lee was not infallible. In fact, neither Grant nor Lee was sure about the other's whereabouts until their armies, totaling 150,000 men, collided near Spotsylvania Court House. The collision would last two weeks, from 8 to 21 May 1864. Lee spent the day after the Wilderness battle visiting the line, "seeking to ascertain the probable designs of his adversary." He quickly discovered that he was wrong about the Union march route, however. Still, he remained better informed than Grant, who was relying exclusively on his (accurate) information about numerical supremacy — two to one — and (inaccurate) appraisals of the condition of Lee's army. As a result, he had sent most of his cavalry away, emulating Lee's approach to Gettysburg, so that he "experienced a significant decline in [his] ability to acquire intelligence." Lee made no such mistake, keeping two brigades of cavalry at hand. Grant's problems were worsened because his army's maps were so bad as to be nearly useless. This was all the stranger as operations in the area had been contemplated. Earlier, in August 1863, Meade had sent spies into the area.[49]

The result was another slogging, almost Great War–style battle with much blundering, mostly on the Union side. Relying on his superior numbers, Grant remained on the attack. Yet the initial attack was by a division commander who had to move "into position for a supposedly important attack with no knowledge of the position or strength of the enemy." Even Grant became aware that he was making mistakes and was missing opportunities because of his lack of information, conceding that he had recalled a corps that had (without realizing it) turned Lee's right. As a result, Grant's behavior became more flexible; he even attempted to set a trap for Lee by sending a corps to act as bait for a Confederate attack, that is, deliberately sending a signal that was intended to be screened wrongly. For the first time, information about Lee's behavior was beginning to influence Grant's actions. While suffering fewer losses — twelve thousand men, as against the Union's eighteen thousand — the Rebels did not leave Spotsylvania unscathed. Thus, the early fighting went the Union's way, something Lee blamed on inaccurate information. The overall outcome was inconclusive, and Grant continued on his overland campaign.[50]

In the wake of Spotsylvania, the Confederate army withdrew to the North Anna River, where the armies met 23–26 May 1864. Geographically, this was a difficult spot for the Union army to assault. Once again, the Union had neither maps nor guides as its long columns snaked through the Virginia countryside. Grant knew little about Lee's strength at this point, but Spotsylvania had given him information about the ability of the smaller Confederate army to defend itself behind fortifications (the lesson was expensive for his infantry, of course). He changed his behavior (briefly) and decided not to attack. The Rebels were well positioned for a counterattack but Lee was too ill to organize it. Strangely, Grant's information that his opponents were fewer in numbers never led him to appreciate why they fought behind fortifications. As he had earlier, he assumed that the Confederates' defensive position was a result of weakness in morale. "Lee's army is really whipped. The prisoners we now take show it, and the action of his army shows it unmistakably. A battle with them outside of intrenchments cannot be had. Our men feel that they have gained the *morale* over the enemy and attack with confidence. I may be mistaken, but I feel that our success over Lee's army is already insured." Grant appeared to believe a report that Lee was falling back toward Richmond.[51]

How had he come to these views that grossly overstated the problems of Lee's army, an army that still had eleven months of fighting left in it? Grant's information was not completely false. He preferred to see for himself what was going on, and he had seen plenty of bedraggled deserters. Yet deserters, or those captured easily, by definition are not the crème de la crème of an army. Large numbers of them are certainly a sign of weakness, even of impending collapse, but otherwise their accounts and views may mislead. What Grant inferred was useful and accurate, but it was incomplete. The information that Grant was relying on was Lee's unquestionable aggressiveness. He assumed (as did others) that no attack meant an inability to attack.[52] This perhaps explains his decision to throw his 108,000-man army at Confederate forces numbering only 62,000, fortified at Cold Harbor. Against a foe about to collapse, such an attack might have succeeded. Instead the battle, which lasted from 31 May to 12 June 1864, went Lee's way! At one point in the melee, the Union lost 7,000 men in a single hour, and it lost 13,000 overall. Grant reported that "on the 3rd of June we again assaulted the enemy's works in the hope of driving him from his position. In this attempt our loss was heavy, while that of the enemy, I have reason to believe, was comparatively light. It was the only general attack made from the Rapidan to the James which did not inflict upon the enemy losses to compensate for our own losses."[53] The last sentence is entirely wrong — the Rebel losses were always lower — although if sincere perhaps explains why Grant persisted with battering-ram tactics that nearly destroyed the Union. He may have known better: "I have always regretted that the last assault at Cold Harbor was ever made."[54] Lee's actions were also information-based, but his information was more accurate. Lee knew he was outnumbered and that defense would both protect his smaller army as well as take advantage of his adversary's aggressiveness. He was always prepared to return to the offensive but — except for Gettysburg — refused to do so blindly, for he also knew that one more defeat could be the end.

Petersburg and Appomattox

In the wake of the Cold Harbor fiasco, Grant's behavior changed. Predictable, straight-ahead assaults would not bring him victory. He would have to mislead Lee. He did. He managed a swing to the southeast, eventually reaching Petersburg, cutting Virginia off from most of the Confederacy. True information asymmetry existed, because Lee did not know where Grant was going until it was too late.

Grant helped create this uncertainty. He strengthened his trenches in front of Cold Harbor, and one of his corps demonstrated noisily just to the south, as if the Yankees were preparing a relatively minor repositioning. The rest of the army headed quickly across the rivers toward Petersburg. Further to the south, Pierre Beauregard sent warnings to Lee of the movement, but these were disregarded. At first, Lee had no information about the movement at all and accordingly stayed where he was. Eventually, he realized Grant was on the move but thought he might simply be moving to the same location east of Richmond where McClellan had been in 1862. By 14 June 1864, five days into Grant's maneuver, Lee began to think about Petersburg but still saw it as only a possible target. Having initially disregarded the information Beauregard had sent, two days later Lee had a much higher anxiety level, and he repeatedly requested additional information from Beauregard. Without cavalry — Lee had sent most of it to shadow Phil Sheridan's Union cavalry that was headed toward the Shenandoah Valley — he had no simple means for ascertaining the truth. On 16 June, Lee began to move southward, but slowly, unaware that some Union troops were already in a position to storm Petersburg. In this phase, asymmetry of information favored Grant, and Grant knew it. Grant had also improved the flow of information in the army. During the movement "all corps had been in constant contact during every engagement, every reconnaissance in force had had telegraphic connection with headquarters, and connections had been maintained while on the march [by stopping every half hour to an hour] to report changes." Yet even in these circumstances, the information situation saved the Confederacy: unaware of Petersburg's weakness, on 15 and 16 June different Union commands failed to storm the city.[55]

Still, the Union had changed the tide of war, for once in relatively bloodless fashion. Grant's awareness of Lee's limited resources allowed him to present Lee with more potential problems than the Confederate general could possibly deal with at once. The long siege of Petersburg that was to ensue — from mid-June 1864 to early April 1865 — meant that the Confederacy lost its freedom of action, which its aggressive commanders had used so often to create doubt in Union minds as to its strength and location. Signals emanating from Lee's camp could not hide his increasingly precarious position from Grant anymore. Consequently, Grant became more confident and behaved accordingly. For example, Lee had to suspend one attack because it had been signaled to the Union by numerous Rebel deserters. Union intelligence even monitored belated Confederate plans to enlist Blacks and undertook efforts to disrupt them. By the spring of 1865 Grant was certain that Lee could detach nothing of substance without the Union's knowing about it. There would be no more "valley campaigns."[56]

This was fortunate for Grant because, just as the Petersburg campaign was beginning, the Confederates nearly turned the tables. A corps under Jubal Early headed for the Shenandoah Valley, intending to threaten Washington. Grant did not know of the movement for twenty-two days, one of the worst intelligence failures of the year. Yet the Union, relying on its intelligence service, soon turned the situation to its advantage. Lee attempted to reinforce Early with a division. But when the division was marching toward the Shenandoah, Grant attacked. When it was ordered to march back to assist Lee, Union forces in the Shenandoah attacked. This game continued, with Union generals attacking based on superior information about the location and direction of movement of the division. The net result was that for several critical weeks a veteran division, instead of helping either Early or Lee in the fight, spent its time marching and countermarching across Virginia.[57]

During a siege the most important type of information concerns the weak points in the enemy lines, since it is rarely possible to man every inch solidly. Exposing such weaknesses might result in successful enemy attacks. With smaller numbers of men, this was a far greater problem for Lee. But the Union had its own share of problems, the most infamous being the "Battle of the Crater."

Union miners blew a 400,000-cubic-foot hole in the Confederate lines, but the chaotic advance that followed failed, and four thousand Union soldiers were killed.[58] Meanwhile, Confederate commanders benefited from their superior knowledge of the terrain. Yet these Rebel advantages became less and less consequential. The Union's growing numerical advantage made intelligence failures less important. Brawn overpowered brain. For example, while a Confederate intelligence coup in November 1864 foiled a Yankee attack, it yielded no lasting benefit to the South. Likewise, in March 1865, Grant was completely ignorant of a planned Confederate attack, but his front-line units quickly regrouped and the attack did not disrupt his plans in the slightest.[59] On the night of 1 April 1865 the defense of Petersburg collapsed, and the town was taken the next day, opening the way to Richmond. Lee surrendered seven days later, on 9 April 1865, at Appomattox Court House.

Grant and the Virginia Overland Campaign

It is easy to see how Grant was influenced by information, less so to analyze his relationship with it. He had the finest information-gathering organization in American history, the Bureau of Military Information, but at times seemed to operate with little interest in its findings. According to General Sherman, Grant "don't care a damn for what the enemy does out of his sight, but it scares me like hell!" To Grant, initiative was what mattered: "The art of war is simple enough. Find out where your enemy is. Get at him as soon as you can. Strike him as hard as you can and as often as you can, and keep moving on." Initiative shifted the burden of uncertainty to the enemy, thereby putting Jomini's dictum about offensives and secrecy on its head — itself of more than passing interest, as Jominian military thought dominated West Point. As noted earlier, at the beginning of the campaign in Virginia "Grant himself gave little thought to his opponent's intentions or possible responses."[60] Except for the "find the enemy" part, this shows a Grant little interested in information.

But there is another side as well. Grant took several important steps to improve his army's picture of the situation. He attempted to build a map database before his campaign began, but the geographical information he got was simply not very good. (In military operations, bad maps are indeed worse than no maps at all.) More significantly, Grant worked to improve the transmission of information, ensuring that it moved between those who collected and analyzed information and those who commanded in battle. He was also highly conscious of his own army's security, complaining (as did all his colleagues) about publication of information useful to the enemy. He certainly saw the importance of espionage. He personally visited his most important Richmond spy after the city fell. Rather than seeing Grant as less than interested in information, perhaps we should see him as refusing to let uncertainty become an excuse for inaction. Sometimes he was frustrated by circumstances. For instance, during a July battle for Harper's Ferry he was forced to issue orders based on inaccurate and out-of-date information resulting from breakdowns in the telegraph system.[61]

There is another reason why Grant's behavior is less contradictory than it seems. He actually did rely on information that trickled out of Lee's camp, but he often responded to it badly. For example, Grant believed that interrogations of deserters from Lee's army showed that Confederate morale was at rock bottom. Hence, he tried to pound what he thought was a disintegrating army into the ground — and instead suffered well over fifty thousand casualties in the first six weeks of the Virginia campaign, nearly double that of the (nondisintegrating) Confederates. Grant miscalculated so badly because in November 1863 he had had similar reports from deserters about the situation in Braxton Bragg's army facing him near Chattanooga, Tennessee, and they had turned out to be accurate.[62] Grant had nearly destroyed Bragg's army in the ensuing battle. Why were deserters' statements accurate in Tennessee but not in Virginia? By definition, deserters do not possess high morale. They reflect this attitude in their picture of their own army, for which they obviously have little love left. Deserting a truly "lost cause" may seem less dishonorable, at least in the deserter's mind. Grant understandably viewed Virginia deserters' statements through the same lens, missing important differences — including the fact that going from Bragg to Lee, he had moved from facing the Confederacy's least competent commander to its most competent. This is not a post hoc viewpoint but rather reflects the feelings of the rank and file.

Why was this not understood on the Union side? In fact, it was, but Grant was unwilling to trust his new army's staff. He was much like some modern corporate executive or university administrator for whom it is almost a point of pride to come in and ignore (or remove) the existing staff. Grant argued that the only eyes a general can trust are his own. So he personally engaged in information gathering and "readily swallowed stories that harmonized with his own preconceptions." The excellent Bureau of Military Information did not become part of Grant's headquarters until July 1864, nor did he "fully utilize its services during the campaign" until he was in front of Petersburg.[63]

Slowly the stubborn Yankee started to rely on his information gatherers; and if it was late for his dead men, it was good news for the rest. He came to rely on the Bureau of Military Information to such an extent that it has been described as "essential to Grant's cause." The organization's work "played a significant role in Lee's defeat." Grant also became much more perceptive about understanding Lee. He rightly rejected one statement from a Confederate officer because he thought Lee would be a fool to do what was alleged. He also deduced that Lee would maneuver to the bitter end to protect Richmond, while Lee did not fully grasp that the city was not Grant's primary target.[64]

Lee had some difficulty in gaining the measure of Grant, perhaps because the latter was a different man from his predecessors in Virginia. Not denigrating him, he said of Grant that he had "managed his affairs remarkably well," but Lee's initial prediction of a Union retreat to Fredericksburg after the Wilderness battle showed that his famed "uncanny ability to size up an opponent and then act accordingly" was not automatic. Confederate corps commander James Longstreet was closer to the mark when he said that Grant "will fight us every day and every hour till the end of this war." This opinion, expressed shortly after Grant's appointment, would definitely have been known to Lee. He and Longstreet were quite close. Nor would the aggressive, hard-fighting Lee have taken long to see that there were definite similarities between Grant's and his own thinking. Lee wanted to unite with the other main Southern army, and Grant feared exactly that. Grant and Lee each recognized that, sooner or later, the Union would want to envelop Petersburg and cut off Richmond; it was a question of when, not if. Both understood that Sherman's invasion of Georgia and the Carolinas spelled the defeat of the Confederacy.[65] When it came to the most important type of information — understanding the enemy — the Union and Confederate generals understood each other perhaps too well. They came from similar backgrounds, had been to the same military colleges, and had shared the same experiences afterward, fighting on the frontier and against Mexico. Perhaps one reason that the Civil War lasted so long, with neither side's armies able to destroy the other's until the very end, is that in some ways they were mirrors of each other and therefore had an incredible amount of information about each other. Unfortunately for the Confederacy, it was the smaller mirror.

THE AMERICAN CIVIL WAR AND THE OTHER PRINCIPLES OF ECONOMICS

In reviewing the American Civil War in relation to the other principles examined in our study, it becomes apparent that there is fertile ground for research. Some examples are suggested below and are summarized with the entries in the matrix appended to this chapter. These examples are not intended to be exhaustive. The following discussion merely suggests possible applications of some aspect of each principle to the American Civil War case.

Opportunity cost in military decision making involves the awareness that making one choice forecloses others. To an extent this was more significant for the Confederacy because of its inferiority in almost every material area of warfare. Two obvious operational aspects of Confederate warfare may be considered here. First, from the beginning the Confederacy tended to conduct offensive warfare, whether strategically (Antietam, Gettysburg, Kentucky, cavalry raids) or tactically (Confederate generals attacked throughout the entire war until their numbers became too few). This was not inevitable. There were a few senior officers, like Joseph Johnston, who favored a more Fabian, defensive war. The merits of offense versus defense for the Confederacy are still debated today.

Certain things are obvious about this choice, at least on a tactical level. Attacking meant concentration of force. Concentration of force meant that some areas would have to be left unguarded or but weakly covered. In 1862 the Confederacy lost New Orleans, its largest city, because it had garrisoned it with only three thousand troops. Attacking also exposed troops to high risks and high casualties. Of course, it should not be ignored that the Confederate armies, attack-minded though they were, finished the war with fewer casualties (but the reasons for this were complex). Invasion of enemy territory was risky (only one out of eight invasions in the eastern theater succeeded), and hurling troops at well-defended positions led to bloody repulses on both sides such as at Fredericksburg and Gettysburg. In addition, the offensive strategy in Virginia meant that transferring troops to the west was not feasible. A corps was sent in late 1863 with spectacular results, but it had to be recalled later. None of this is to prove that aggressiveness was bad policy, only that there were clear opportunity costs and that these were known to the decision makers.

A second example of one choice trading off against another was Lee's absolute commitment to the defense of Richmond, an attitude understood and exploited by Grant. Defending Richmond meant that Lee could not leave the state, meant that he could not advance northward in 1864, and meant that he could not join Johnston to the south (although he tried in the closing weeks of the war). Once more, this is not a critique of a choice taken, for the Confederacy probably could not have afforded the loss of its capital, but is an illustration of how we find economic principles at work in military history. Ideally, a choice should be made in awareness of the costs the choice imposes in terms of foregone opportunities. The option chosen may not be pleasant at all, but it does suggest that the options not chosen would have been more unpleasant still. At the least, a focus on opportunity cost will induce decision makers to enumerate and think with much care about feasible sets of alternatives from which to pick a particular course of action.

Military campaigns are not undertaken without an expectation of greater gain than loss (expected marginal costs and benefits), except where the commander is insane or where honor requires combat where no chance of success remains. (Even in the latter case, maintenance of honor may be considered a benefit; see chap. 2.) Here, we may again consider the aggressiveness exhibited by the Confederacy. The tactical offensive was risked by Confederate generals even though a casual analysis might suggest advantages for defensive warfare. Tactical defense, however, could not bring about a decisive result. From 1815 until well into World War I generals were influenced by the doctrine of the offensive. American generals of the Civil War were intellectually formed by their study of Napoleonic warfare, which was highly offensive. Confederate generals further attacked because the alternative meant the unchallenged occupation of part of their country by Union armies.

Specifically, in each major attack Confederate generals expected both strategic and tactical advantages greater than the costs to the secessionists' slim human and material resources. One example of this occurred during the planning for the Gettysburg campaign. In the spring of 1863 Lee and Stonewall Jackson discussed invading the north, the potential costs of which had already been made clear at Antietam (1862). Their thinking went beyond the usual considerations, however. They thought that an invasion of eastern Pennsylvania would disrupt the flow of anthracite coal to the north's great coastal cities and cripple their industries. The risks of fighting on Yankee soil would be counterbalanced by the damage done to Northern war production and logistics — the trains ran on coal, the Union armies were dependent on the trains, and so on. This was an especially important consideration as the Union had an overwhelming preponderance both in industry and railroads.

In warfare, substitution usually involves different types of forces or different weapons. The Civil War saw the introduction of a number of new weapons, often designed to achieve objectives with less blood and cost. During the war engineers, particularly from the navy, developed and brought into use longer-range guns. These were expensive and often heavy but on occasion achieved spectacular results. For example, the approaches to Savannah, Georgia, were defended by Fort Pulaski, a costly and expensive bastion. In 1862 Union commanders bombarded it with long-range rifled cannons and forced the fort into submission without having to make a single attempt to storm it. An operational type of substitution was to rely on deception to defend an area instead of sending masses of troops. Again in 1862, Confederates delaying McClellan's advance on Richmond used numerous deception methods, including some more akin to theater than battlefield. For example, we noted in the main text that during the defense of the Yorktown Peninsula, Confederate General Jeb Magruder sent men from his small force into the woods to shout commands to nonexistent battalions and regiments. He also had his men march in column through clearings visible to Union observers, then circle back out of sight and rejoin the back of the column so that from a distance it looked like a unit immensely larger than it actually was.[66]

Civil War generals had a peculiar problem in assessing what today we call diminishing marginal returns. In size, the Union and Confederate armies exceeded anything in American memory. European soldiers had the experience, and Americans had studied that to some extent, but the terrain and roads in North America were quite different. Nor had Europe yet experienced a major war in the railroad era. Awareness of diminishing returns took considerable time to develop. But it became evident in the use of both artillery and infantry that there were points beyond which increased numbers became less and less valuable. In the case of cannon, doubling the number of pieces in battle meant a doubling of the quantity of ammunition consumed, as well as doubling the road space needed to move the pieces (not to mention men and horses) but that did not mean double the number of enemy soldiers killed. Commanders would have needed to think with care whether — to achieve the overall objective — it would not have been better (marginal cost/benefit) to switch (substitution) the extra men, horses, and supplies to alternative uses (opportunity cost), a topic explored much more deeply in chapter 6.

In the case of infantry, Civil War generals sought to break the adversary through outflanking and the column attack, reflecting Jomini in the former, Napoleon in the latter. Infantry column assaults required numbers, but again, diminishing returns to additional effort did apply. In war-game theory, an attacking infantry column needs about a three-to-one advantage to succeed; two-to-one is considered feasible but very risky. A greater advantage, however, does not necessarily add as much as might be expected. A six-to-one attack is not twice as powerful as three-to-one. There are several reasons for this. The larger the formation, the more time it will take to prepare it, and this will delay the attack and give the enemy time to develop countermeasures (as at Fredericksburg). Also, more supplies are needed. Roads and paths become congested, and the congestion further delays the attack and makes last-minute changes more difficult. Finally, the more troops involved, the greater the problem of compression. As a column advances, the units in the rear will press into the units in front which are after all receiving fire. Two problems result. First, the front units lose their capacity to maneuver, and second, the front and rear units become intermingled, even entangled, and command and control disintegrates. The first happened at the Crater; the second, at Shiloh.

War is a fundamentally unhealthy activity, and certainly it was in the 1860s. To defend the homeland, many volunteered for duty, but many more needed to be coaxed by suitable contracts. Even this was not enough to augment the armies' numbers. In the end, both sides had resort to the draft, first enacted in the south in 1862, in the north a year later.[67] But a contract to fight — whether the contract is cultural (fighting for one's homeland), or formal, or both — gives rise to many of the asymmetric information-related principal-agent problems outlined in chapter 1 and examined at length in chapter 3, such as the possibility of reneging on the contract, contract holdup, contract enforcement, and contract structure to align incentives of commanding officers with those of the troops. The changing situation in regard to contracts is visible for instance in the experience of Lee's Army of Northern Virginia. For much of the war it maintained a remarkably high esprit de corps reflected in the immense popularity of its commander. To the common soldier, he was "Marse [Master] Robert" because of his enviable record of victory as well as his personality. As circumstances became more difficult and desertion rose (reneging on contract), more emphasis had to be placed on force — for example, punishment, even execution, of captured deserters — that is, on credible enforcement. Pressure to desert was exacerbated by soldiers' fears about the fates of their families as Sherman, Sheridan, and others marauded across the Confederate landscape. Remarkably, the Army of Northern Virginia remained a solid fighting force beyond the point where it had a chance to win. While punishment kept some men in line (even more true among Union soldiers due to the presence of many bounty-jumpers),[68] it seems that staying and fighting was more a function of unit cohesion, a cultural contract, than of the formal, for-pay, contract. This was, after all, an age when soldiers fought side by side by the tens of thousands, and the brotherhood forged under fire outlasted even the inevitability of defeat, a treasonous death thought worse than an honorable one.

CONCLUSION

This chapter, like the entire book, is an application of economic principles to military history. We cannot and do not claim to have proven that decision making is inextricably shaped by information, whether true or false. But it is noteworthy that not a single counterexample emerges. Two important considerations need to be kept in mind by those engaging in further study in this area. First is one of the economist's favorite concepts — ceteris paribus, all other things being equal. One aspect of war where things definitely are not equal concerns personality: no two generals were alike, and as discussed, no two reacted to information in the same way.[69] We finessed the issue by incorporating personality into the concept of information processing. Prejudices, preconceptions, and personal experience cause similarly situated commanders to read the same information differently. No fact exists independent of interpretation. For example, despite the possession of information that encourages aggressive behavior, cautious commanders react cautiously (e.g., McClellan before Antietam).

A second consideration, primarily of interest to those who study the American Civil War, concerns the exclusion of the western theater from our study. There are two ways in which further research on information aspects of the Civil War could make use of the west. First, the west may contain lessons and examples that could lead to entirely different conclusions from those reached for the eastern theater. The west was different. For example, maneuvers took place over much larger areas, commanders operated with less continual interference, and neither side was hampered by the need to defend a capital city. Second, the eastern and western theaters could be used for comparative study. For this chapter, we chose to center on the eastern theater. Because two armies fought over increasingly familiar terrain within a relatively constricted geographical area, ceteris paribus conditions more easily apply: every Union general had to cross the Rappahannock, for example.

It is too early to draw definitive conclusions regarding the other principles. Our brief coverage of them is illustrative and is intended to whet readers' appetite, not satisfy it. The thirty entries in the Civil War matrix appended to this chapter certainly suggest a number of hypotheses worth examining. By way of example, we spell out three hypotheses here. First, with regard to substitution and manpower, was Confederate use of slave labor an effective substitution strategy which prolonged the conflict (a "strict" draft that slaves could not escape)? Likewise, did the Union's "soft" draft — permitting draft escape by payment of commutation fees — prolong the conflict in that the fees were used to induce less able men to sign up for service? Second, regarding diminishing marginal returns and logistics, did the Army of the Potomac's enormous logistical tail reduce its effectiveness to the point of allowing its adversary to hold too much of the initiative during the war? (This applies, with opposite signs, to Lee at Gettysburg.) And third, with regard to diminishing marginal returns and planning, were both armies slow to learn the declining effectiveness of the head-on infantry assault, particularly against field fortifications? It would appear that mining the economic vein of American Civil War history might be a fruitful endeavor indeed.

APPENDIX

A Matrix for the American Civil War Case

Principle	Manpower	Logistics	Technology	Planning	Operations
Opportunity cost	failure to garrison New Orleans (concentration in field armies)	CSA delay in establishing quartermaster organization	CSA decides to build small fleet of ironclads; labor, iron, conventional vessels	offensive strategy in eastern theater	focus on defending Richmond, 1864
Expected marginal costs/benefits	redeploying ANV northward during Petersburg campaign	CSA attack on Pope's communications	discontinuance of balloons once they became vulnerable	Lee, Jackson, and Grant all believed offensive's inherent value greater than cost	Gettysburg: Lee and Jackson discussed advantage of interfering with Union coal shipments
Substitution	slave labor for Confederates	Union use of seaborne movements to avoid difficult or contested overland routes	building expensive long-range weapons (e.g., destruction of Ft. Pulaski)	cavalry raids where conventional invasions were not practical	reliance on screening and deception instead of large numbers; (e.g., Magruder at Yorktown)
Diminishing marginal returns	infantry column advance; numbers	Union armies' size increases railroad dependency, slows them down	size of artillery park; too many equals slower movement, add'l batteries each have lesser effect	increasing use of field fortifications as offensives fail to yield decisive results	multiple attacks by Grant in VA; successive waves less impact than first ones
Asymmetric information (overcoming) hidden characteristics	morale, both own and enemy's, a constant issue in dispatches	Vicksburg: Confederacy's attack on nonexisting Union supply line	construction of observation stations in VA; heavy fighting to protect them	establishment of Bureau of Military Information	Gettysburg: both commanders heavily influenced by lack of information
Asymmetric information (overcoming) hidden action	incentive alignment problem "solved" with drafts	Sutlers (private suppliers of basic needs); private incentive	USS Monitor and other innovations; speed gives inventor prestige and incentives; chance for more	units and commanders that failed were named in dispatches	Mott's attack at Spotsylvania; unreliable troops; many bounty soldiers

The Age of the World Wars, 1914–1945

The Case of Diminishing Marginal Returns to the Strategic Bombing of Germany in World War II

By remarking on "the morons volunteering to get hung up in the wire and shot in the stomach in the mud of Flanders," Air Chief Marshal Sir Arthur ("Bomber") Harris aptly captured the incomprehensible gore of trench warfare in World War I — the war to end all wars — and thereby commented on his infinite preference, in World War II, for aerial over ground combat.[1] War from the air, it seemed, had so much more to offer. Harris, upon assuming command of the Royal Air Force's (RAF) Bomber Command in February 1942, toed an unflinching line. Of the 755,531 tons of bombs the RAF was to drop on ten target categories in Germany in the sixty-six months from December 1939 to May 1945, fully 69 percent — some 523,615 tons — fell on cities, a target group euphemistically referred to as industrial areas. The first industrial-area ton, and the only one that month, fell in February 1940. In March and April there was a pause. In May, 154 tons fell, and 298 tons in June. The "phony war" had ended. The monthly bombing gradually increased to 2,384 tons by July 1941, then dropped to 486 in February 1942.[2]

In March 1942, within a month of Harris's assuming command, bombing levels on industrial areas ballooned to 3,241 tons. By May, Harris had organized the first-ever thousand-bomber fleet, to fly to Cologne on the night of 30–31 May. The 1,455 tons of bombs dropped that night[3] were more than half of the entire month's volume of 2,655 tons of bombs directed toward industrial areas. The city's loss was measured in acres, some 600 of them. Industrial area bombing peaked with 8,622 tons the next month, then dropped as German searchlight batteries, flak, and air defense fighters increasingly engaged in the fight and shot down unacceptable numbers of Harris's unescorted bombers.

Harris persisted. On the night of 24–25 July 1943, some 1,200 tons of incendiary bombs ignited a firestorm in Hamburg, and up to 40,000 civilians perished.[4] But Harris did not measure success in lives lost; he totted it up in square miles burned. The Hamburg raid amounted to only less than 10

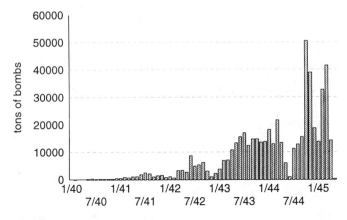

Figure 6.1. RAF bombing tonnage dropped on German industrial areas
Source: *Computed from USSBS, February 1947, Chart 6, pp. 49–91.*

percent of the month's total of 13,291 tons of industrial area bombing. From November 1943 through March 1944, while the Allies, including the bomber units, were to prepare for D-Day, Harris attacked Berlin several times, with little success. He blamed the Americans: "We can wreck Berlin from end to end if the [United States Army Air Force] will come into it . . . It will cost us 400–500 aircraft. It will cost Germany the war." In fact, from October 1943 to March 1944, Harris lost 1,128 bombers, and he nearly wrecked his command. He was rescued between April and September 1944, when Eisenhower, the Allies' supreme commander, took direct control of all Allied air forces to prepare for the Normandy landing and push to the Rhine. Harris's industrial area bombings fell from 21,656 tons in March to 13,395 tons in April, 5,971 tons in May, and a mere 855 tons in June. Following the successful Normandy landing on 6 June, Harris reverted to form, dropping 11,207 tons on industrial areas in July, 12,777 tons in August, and 15,518 tons in September. And when Eisenhower returned direct command, Harris dropped an astonishing 50,465 tons on industrial areas in October 1944 alone (fig. 6.1) and incinerated Berlin and Dresden, by then with American support, in February 1945 when the war had long since been won — on the ground.[5]

What held Harris to his unrelenting stance was his belief—not entirely incorrect until September 1944—that what is nowadays called the surgical mode of strategic bombing was militarily ineffective. Given the British experience in 1940 and 1941, prior to his assuming the leadership of RAF Bomber Command, he derided as "panacea-mongering" the Americans' insistence on picking out strategic targets and eliminating them with precision bombing. He had a point. When the United States joined the bombing fray in early 1943, the Americans frequently missed their assigned targets so outlandishly that the "bomber crews began making jokes about 'killing sheep' or conducting 'a major assault on German agriculture.'" Harris consequently preferred the sledgehammer to the scalpel.[6]

The theory of strategic bombing — in either mode, precision or area — had been straightforward and attractive. In the memorable, quaint language of the United States Strategic Bombing Survey (USSBS), "strategic bombing bears the same relationship to tactical bombing as does the cow to the pail of milk. To deny immediate aid and comfort to the enemy, tactical considerations dictate upsetting the bucket. To ensure eventual starvation, the strategic move is to kill the cow."[7] Consider the following two less original definitions:

> Strategic bombing . . . is aimed at the systematic destruction of those resources which will most weaken the enemy by denying him the materials or weapons he needs to prosecute the war.[8]

> Strategic bombing is best defined as the use of air power to strike at the very foundation of an enemy's war effort — the production of war material, the economy as a whole, or the morale of the civilian population — rather than as a direct attack on the enemy's army or navy. A strategic air campaign almost always requires the defeat of the enemy's air force, but not as an end in itself. While tactical air power uses aircraft to aid the advance of forces on the ground or on the surface of the ocean, usually in cooperation with those forces, strategic air power usually works in relative independence of armies and navies.[9]

In the hope that military efforts will be starved, strategic bombing, the first definition suggests, is about the bombing of essentially nonmilitary assets, that is, production sites. One shoots at the economic cow that would (re)fill the military's pail. The focus on the ultimate objective — the opponent's ability to prosecute the war — is operationally vague and is at any rate restricted to the physical inputs to war-making, the perceived potential bottlenecks or choke-points, neglecting human capital and institutional aspects.

The second definition helps to separate out strategic from tactical bombing and identifies three operational targets: (a) the opponent's actual arms production; (b) the enemy's economy as a whole that forms the supply chain to and from arms industry facilities; and (c) the morale of the adversary's civilian population. The reflection following the second definition also suggests, with the hindsight that the many failures of World War II strategic bombing permit, a certain logical sequence of events. Destroy, first, the opponent's ability to defend against air power; then, second, attack those targets inside the opponent's territory that support its war-making on the front, especially the supply chain; and third, wait until the enemy collapses from within. Interpreted thus, strategic bombing is to achieve certain war outcomes by itself, especially to avert the need for a land-based invasion of the opponent's territory, the capture of its capital, and the deposing of its leaders.[10]

Because "it lacked essentially everything except doctrine and will," the strategic bombing of Germany — or of any other state — was never carried out in any such pure form as extreme advocates of air power had hoped. The subsequent claim of many that strategic bombing was not meant to achieve victory all by itself is not only historically incorrect but suspect on logical grounds alone: in the absence of an integrated military strategy across service branches, if strategic bombing was not meant to achieve victory by itself — by attacking the enemy's war production, its economy, and the morale of its people — then what was it to achieve?[11] Consequently, one finds a good many historical narratives that essentially take the following position: yes, high hopes had been invested in strategic bombing; yes, strategic bombing did run into certain practical difficulties; but if nothing else, strategic bombing forced Nazi Germany into expending vast resources on air defenses that otherwise could have been poured into its front-line efforts; therefore, strategic bombing made a valuable, indeed indispensable contribution to winning the European war.[12]

Nearer to the truth is the exact opposite view: had the advocates of strategic bombing not been fitted with blinders, the Allies could have spent more resources, and could have spent them much earlier than they did, to develop long-range fighter-bombers to accompany their bomber fleet. In December 1943, when Brigadier General Ira C. Eaker was relieved of his command of the U.S. Eighth Air Force — and when "Bomber" Harris was losing aircraft by the hundreds and crews by the thousands — the Eighth's new commander, Jimmy Doolittle, noted a sign in his fighter commander's office. It read, "The first duty of the Eighth Air Force fighters is to bring bombers back alive." Doolittle had the sign replaced. It now read, "The first duty of the Eighth Air Force fighters is to destroy German fighters." And that was the crux of the matter: "bombing raids were less about bombing than about provoking the German fighters into aerial combat." Even more, the first duty was "to kill German fighter pilots." Virtually unanimous opinion, across all writers, now holds that ideal-type strategic bombing did not in fact begin until September 1944, after the power of the German air force, the defensive fighter aircraft of the Luftwaffe, had been broken, especially once the American P-51 (the "Mustang") aircraft, whose development Eaker had held up since June 1943, entered the scene.[13]

However, even though the topic cannot be skirted entirely, this chapter is not primarily about the opportunity cost of strategic bombing. It is about diminishing marginal returns to strategic bombing, such as it was, and makes a very specific, if technical point: to demonstrate that continuous increases in the tonnage of bombs dropped, when other inputs to the war effort remain unchanged, eventually yield declining increases in the destruction sought. In some cases we can even show that more bombing resulted in reduced destruction; not just increasingly smaller, diminishing returns but negative returns.[14]

First we introduce the notion of a strategic bombing production function that permits us to discuss more clearly the concepts of total and incrementally rising, declining, or negative returns to bombing. Next we discuss each of strategic bombing's three elements in turn: bombing to curtail the production of war matériel, bombing of the economy as a whole to undercut the supply chain, and bombing to sap the morale of the civilian population to induce it to revolt or commit acts of sabotage that would result in lowered industrial productivity. Finally we provide a summary assessment and show how the case of the strategic bombing of Germany in World War II generates numerous other examples and hypotheses regarding the manpower, logistics, technology, planning, and operations aspects of war when viewed in light of our six economic principles.

A STRATEGIC BOMBING PRODUCTION FUNCTION

In principle, bombing is open to economic theoretical and empirical analysis. One need merely relate a set of inputs to an output they are to produce. For example, one may write an equation, called a strategic bombing production function, $y_i = f(x_T; x_A, x_D, z)$, where y_i is the desired output and denotes the destruction of the defender's assets, x_T refers to the number of tons of bombs dropped, x_A is a vector (a set of factors) describing the attacker's input variables other than bomb tonnage, with expected positive coefficients (the higher the attack input, the higher the destruction), x_D is a vector describing the defender's input variables, with expected negative coefficients (the higher the defense input, the lower the destruction), and z is a vector that captures imponderables such as prevailing weather conditions.[15]

If one draws a hypothetical scatter plot of output of strategic bombing

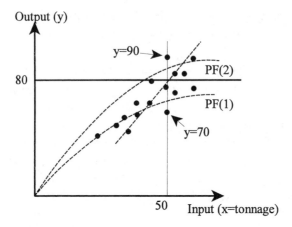

Figure 6.2. Strategic bombing production functions

(some measure of destruction) on a vertical axis against bombing tonnage on a horizontal axis, then it may at first appear that more bombing is associated with increased destruction (fig. 6.2). This is represented by an upward-sloping trend of the data points and a dotted straight line drawn through these points: the more bombing, the more destruction.

In economics, production theory says that an increasing tonnage of bombing is expected to lead to increases in destruction but it also predicts smaller and smaller increments in destruction so long as all the other required inputs, apart from the bombs themselves, are held at constant levels. More bombing is predicted to lead to decreasing gains in additional destruction per additional unit of bombing applied. This is the principle of diminishing marginal returns. Thus, for the data points gathered around the first production function — labeled PF(1) — the increases in destruction are increasing, but at a declining rate. If bombing tonnage were to increase ever further, the level of destruction achieved would peter out somewhere below the horizontal line drawn at y = 80. If this horizontal line is interpreted as the level of destruction needed to obtain victory — call it the victory threshold — then any amount of bomb tonnage alone will not secure victory.

What accounts for greater destruction, and eventual victory, is not more bombing per se but the greater application of other inputs alongside the bombing. Diminishing returns to increased tonnage along PF(1) can be countermanded only by increasing inputs other than bombing tonnage. In terms of the figure, the same tonnage of bombing (e.g., x = 50) can yield greater destruction only if for instance navigation technology is improved. With "old" technology, few bombers find their target and the destruction that bombing of x = 50 can accomplish is relatively low at y = 70; but with "new" technology, more bombers find their target and the destruction that bombing of x = 50 can accomplish is now relatively high at y = 90. Greater application of or improvements in inputs other than tonnage is depicted as an upward shift in the production function from PF(1) to PF(2). The victory threshold at y = 80 has now been crossed. Whereas tonnage alone would not have achieved victory along PF(1), tonnage combined with other bombing inputs can achieve victory.

With the possible exception of "Bomber" Harris, the Allies were well aware of the operation of this process. Harris essentially believed that PF(1) would at some point cross the victory threshold. Perhaps he believed that the threshold lay not at the equivalent of y = 80 but at some lower level so that it would be crossed by PF(1), or perhaps he believed that PF(1) had a higher trajectory, such as that of PF(2) in the figure. But other than to employ greater proportions of incendiary rather than explosive bombs, Harris was not, at any rate, a believer in technology although he could scarce avoid making use of the improvements the Allies put at his disposal such as radio navigation or four-engine bombers. Instead, he believed that the pure quantity of bombing tonnage would do the trick—hence his well-deserved nickname—and he incessantly complained about bombers being wrestled away from his command to protect ship convoys in the Atlantic or to prepare for D-Day. He was a single-minded believer in the idea that the brute number of tons of bombs dropped would suffice to secure victory, and rarely did he allow himself to express anything less than full confidence in his bombing program.[16]

In contrast to Harris, the British, the Americans, and the Germans fought a tug-of-war over pushing the production function either "up above" or pulling it "down below" the hypothetical victory threshold where each ton of bombs would have more (or less) destructive effect. The Allies worked as assiduously on navigation, targeting, code-breaking, fighter-escorts, pilot training, and myriad other complementary inputs to bombing tonnage as the Germans worked to negate any advantage that might spring from their opponents' efforts.

It is crucial to understand the following point. Virtually all of the strategic bombing debate that ensued during and after World War II is cast in terms of bombing's total destructive effect, of whether or not strategic bombing contributed decisively to Germany's collapse and war loss. In contrast, the aim here is to think about the incremental destructive effect of additional bombing tonnage applied, the marginal effect as economists refer to it. And there is some tantalizing evidence that we show later, suggesting that the marginal effects of bombing were in fact declining, just as production theory predicts.

Regrettably for economists and other mathematically-minded scholars, it is not possible to establish the coefficients of the strategic bombing production function. The reasons for this are at least fourfold. First, in spite of the availability of a large bombing data set, the number of usable observations is actually fairly small.[17] Take a best-case scenario and suppose output is defined as the destruction achieved as a result of bombing aircraft factories. Of the sixty-six months of strategic bombing (December 1939 to May 1945), there are only twenty-three months during which the United States Army Air Force (USAAF) bombed aircraft factories in Germany and twenty-six months of RAF bombing of such facilities. Allowing for an overlap of six months, the combined data set is of forty-three months of aircraft factory bombing by either force. This yields forty-three data points, barely enough from the point of view of statistical science to arrive at valid conclusions regarding the possible effects of strategic bombing on destruction of aircraft factories.

Second, statistically, these forty-three data points will have to be shared out among the very large number of relevant factors other than bombing tonnage — the factors responsible for the shift in the production function (as in fig. 6.2) — so that not enough data points are left over to identify the destructive returns to varying degrees of bombing tonnage per bombing technique. The list of bombing techniques, or bombing inputs other than tonnage, the x_A in the equation shown at the beginning of this discussion, is huge. Obvious inputs include the number of sorties flown, the number of bomber aircraft available, the fuel range of the bombers, the bomb load each bomber could carry, the type of bomb carried, and the explosive or incendiary charge of each bomb. Less obvious factors are the accuracy of the navigation system, the accuracy of the bomb-sighting equipment, the availability and range of escort fighters, the percentage of flights turned-around before reaching the designated target, and the flight training and experience of pilots, navigators, bombardiers, and gunners. Improvement in each input would be expected to result in a positive effect — better technique, more destruction — but there are not enough data points per technique to demonstrate this statistically.

Likewise, improvements in German air defenses (x_D), such as searchlights, flak, interceptor aircraft, and air defense strategies, would be expected to yield negative effects: better defenses, less destruction.[18] One may have as many relevant offensive and defensive inputs in the bombing formula as one has observations of destructive output (namely, forty-three) and therefore cannot statistically ascertain the effect of any one input while also controlling for the influence of the other inputs. Statistically, the results would not be reliable.

Third, the inputs other than tonnage were, of course, never constant. They changed so rapidly during the war that practically every mission flown consisted of a unique set of input values, so that the relevant sample size essentially equals one: each bombing run took place with a unique combination of inputs. On a subsequent bombing run, the number of tons of bombs may have been larger, and the destructive effect may have been correspondingly larger as well, but we could not tell statistically if the improvement in the destructive effect was due to the larger tonnage or to the effect of say better navigation or any other input changes. Statisticians sometimes overcome this sort of problem by aggregating data across fine gradations of inputs to gross gradations. For example, instead of detailing the data set by every type of navigational improvement that was invented, installed, and used, the navigation information can be assembled into two coarse groups: dead reckoning and assisted reckoning. This procedure is statistically acceptable so long as the less-detailed gradations do not gloss over differences that subject matter experts would find of fundamental importance to the issue at hand. Navigation — finding your target — definitely was of fundamental importance as to whether a bomb load dropped would bring about the desired damage. Contra "Bomber" Harris, the history of strategic bombing does not revolve around the tonnage of bombs dropped but around the means of "getting them there," and analysts now seem agreed that the single most important breakthrough in this regard was the destruction of the Luftwaffe's fighter wing and its pilots in the spring and summer of 1944. Thereafter, the strategic bombing fleet could get through. Strategic bombing had its greatest effect when it was unopposed! (And by the time it was unopposed, as from September 1944, the ground war had essentially been won.)

The fourth problem concerns the left-hand side, the y_i, in the formula, the "output" of bombing. The output is not, in fact, clearly defined. While we have plenty of bombing-tonnage and other input data, we are not in possession of unambiguous destruction data. For example, even though plenty of German aircraft factories were bombed (in Germany and in the occupied territories), they also were quickly repaired, rebuilt, or relocated so that the bombing at best delayed rather than destroyed aircraft production. This does not necessarily mean that the bombing was strategically useless — delays can be crucial — but it does mean that strictly statistical work cannot be carried out in the absence of well-defined output data.

Take another example. "Bomber" Harris succeeded in causing the world's first air-generated firestorm with his attacks on Hamburg. There were four night attacks in all: on 24/25 July 1943, 791 bombers flew on the city, on 27/28 July another 787 bombers came, on 29/30 July yet another 777 bombers appeared on the night sky, and a further wave of 740 bombers arrived on 2/3 August. In all, some 9,000 tons of bombs fell on the city. The Americans contributed over 250 daylight strikes as well. In all, between 35,000 to 50,000 civilians are thought to have died in the ensuing inferno. Murray and Millett write that "more than half of the city's living space, 75 percent of its electric works, 60 percent of its water system, and 90 percent of its gas works were destroyed," and industrial production fell 40 percent for large and 80 percent for small and medium-sized firms. Hewitt adds that "183 large and 4,113 small factories, 580 other industrial plants, 180,000 tons of shipping in the port, and 12 bridges [were destroyed in addition to] 24 hospitals, 58 churches, 277 schools, 76 civic buildings, 83 banks, 2,632 stores, and a zoo with many of its captive animals." It would appear that the "output" of bombing — destruction — has been well measured. And yet, Hewitt continues, "railyards and rail services were operating within hours. Electricity supply exceeded demand within nine days. Industrial production rose swiftly to preraid levels. Dehoused inhabitants were evacuated or relocated in the city within a short time." The German war machinery rolled on. When a boxer is knocked down and he gets up, what exactly is it that one's own energy expenditure of striking the blow has destroyed? Clearly, the opponent's cause is delayed, his energy is sapped, but if he does not stay down, the fight is not won.[19]

In sum, even though the effect of bombing is tractable in economic theory, data problems on the input as well as the output side of the strategic bombing production function prevent statistical analysis, at least of the inferential sort. Decidedly, this does not mean that we are without recourse to data, only that any inferences must be drawn even more cautiously than otherwise would be the case. In the next section, we examine the Allies' bombing of German war production assets; then we look at the bombing of the German supply chain and its civilian economy; and thereafter we take up the topic of area bombing. In each case, we need to distinguish between the total and incremental effects of the bombing. While we tell the story of the former, our particular interest is in the latter.

BOMBING GERMAN WAR PRODUCTION

Strategic bombing theory is quite specific: do not bomb the enemy but bomb his tools. Leave him with nothing but his bare knuckles, and he will see the folly of his ways. Mystique (and myth) of American frontier marksmanship and moral apprehension about indiscriminate terror bombing combined to create a school of thought that elevated precision bombing of an enemy's tools and tool-making capacity to a high form of the ethically fought war.[20] Do not so much fight your enemy as restrain him. Despite the savagery of what was to follow, not only in World War II in Germany but in Japan, Korea, Vietnam, the Persian Gulf War, and the Balkan wars in the 1990s, the uniquely American concern with precision did not come to fruition until, perhaps, and more than sixty years too late, the Iraq War.

Nonetheless, "strategic bombing was not on its face pointless or impossible," Stephen Budiansky reminds us, and he is echoed in this by many authors. Implementation hinged crucially on target identification and bomb delivery. The bomb delivery problem appeared to have been solved with the appearance of the Mark XV bombsight Carl L. Norden developed for the U.S. Navy in the early 1930s. In theory it cut the average bombing error to around 100 feet; it weighed just fifty pounds, and tests from 5,000 feet achieved a 50 percent hit rate on an anchored Navy cruiser, "a stunning improvement over previous accuracy rates." *Collier's* published, on 26 September 1942, an arresting cartoon showing a bombardier asking his navigator, "Was that address 106 Leipzigerstrasse, or 107?" Target identification was supplied by a subsidiary theory: the theory of the industrial web. This would highlight specific choke points, bottlenecks, and sundry critical nodes, war production taps that, once turned off by precision bombing, would paralyze the enemy into submission. It is useful to remember that the Great Depression had barely run its course at this time, and it appeared to confirm this theory of economic dominoes: find and take out the one card that would make the enemy's house of cards collapse upon itself.[21]

The theory would come to naught, not because it was wrong but because it assumed too much and because it was incomplete. It assumed too much, for example, in that even a perfectly functioning bombsight is utterly useless without navigation to get to the target. It is one thing to drop a test bomb on a tethered Navy cruiser when one flies in clear weather to a well-known, predetermined drop-off point; it is quite another thing to find one's way, unescorted and unguided, from an English air base across a cloudy Channel to a rainy

European continent, intercepted by searchlights, flak, and air defense fighters. It was not a matter of finding 106 or 107 Leipzigerstrasse, it was a matter of finding Leipzig — and finding it while one was still alive.

The theory also proved incomplete. As the Allies were to learn, the Germans proved adept at relocating and redistributing manufacturing sites, at stocking up supplies so that production flows would not be interrupted, at working extra shifts, at corralling slave and foreign workers, and at substituting one raw material for another. Although the Americans rarely wavered in the faith they put in precision bombing, it proved in practice much harder a task than they had made themselves believe.

To the utter amazement of the Allies, despite bombing of German aircraft factories, German aircraft production continuously increased during the war and reached its apex in 1944 with 39,807 aircraft produced. That year, the production high points were July, August, and September when, each month, more than 4,000 new aircraft rolled onto the tarmacs. But by 13 September, the Allies already stood on the Siegfried Line, and the Soviets pushed the Germans back home from the eastern front (to which Germany had committed three-quarters of its troop strength). It was the end game of the war, quite unlike what the champions of strategic bombing had promised.

If not aircraft production itself, perhaps the bombing at least reduced the German potential to produce aircraft. Might Germany have produced even more aircraft without the bombing? To answer that one would need to measure the German potential to produce aircraft (and arms, generally) rather than its actual aircraft (arms) production. The British did just that, only to find that Germany's arms production potential rose right through to the end of the war. An index of actual German armament production (fig. 6.3) set to equal 100 for January and February 1942 rose continuously and tripled to a level of 308 for the third quarter of 1944 (III/44) before falling off to 270 in IV/44, after which it continuously declined to the end of the war.[22] The British write that

the most careful study has failed to provide any evidence to support the major economic inferences derived during the war from the physical picture of destruction. Paradoxically, . . . war production, far from falling as a result of the levelling of the German cities, continued to mount until the second half of 1944, and its subsequent fall had little to do with the continued bombing of centres of population. It was in the military, not the economic spheres that our attacks had their major strategic effects.[23]

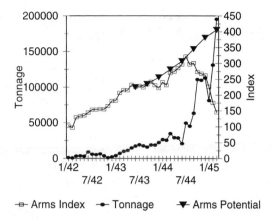

Figure 6.3. Monthly index of actual and potential German arms production, and tonnage of bombs dropped by combined strategic forces, 1942–1945
Sources: *USSBS, February 1947, p. 13 (tonnage), p. 113 (arms index), and BBSU, 1998, p. 91 (arms potential).*

And the Americans write:

> For [the early war] years the conclusion is inescapable that Germany's war pro
> duction was not limited by its war potential — by the resources at its disposal —
> but by demand; in other words, by the notions of the German war leaders of
> what was required to win.[24]

What the bombing may have achieved, in the view of both surveys' authors
and later analysts, was to hinder Germany from fulfilling its arms production
potential, which reached a high-level mark of 406 in the first quarter of 1945,
when the index for actual production had already fallen to 182. According to
the numbers, Germany's actual arms production fell only from the third quarter of 1944 (fig. 6.3). What is significant about this is that by that time — after
D-Day — the bombing of Germany was not strategic but tactical, to prepare
for the advance of Allied troops. It was, as we argue later on, not to coerce
Germany to surrender, but to ready it for conquest.[25]

By the time German arms production fell in the third quarter of 1944, only
30 percent of the total tonnage of bombs that the RAF and USAAF would
eventually drop on German territory had been expended.[26] That is, *after*
D-Day, *after* the invasion of Normandy, *after* the French-German border had
been reached, *after* the war on the ground had seen its decisive breakthrough,
70 percent of the bombs had yet to be dropped. The war had already been won

Table 6.1: Tonnage dropped on German aircraft production sites and German aircraft production, January 1941 to December 1944

Month/year	Tons dropped	Aircraft produced	Month/year	Tons dropped	Aircraft produced
1/41	1	633	1/43	0	1,525
2/41	44	871	2/43	4	2,004
3/41	61	1,174	3/43	0	2,166
4/41	35	1,129	4/43	631	2,100
5/41	0	1,037	5/43	211	2,196
6/41	4	1,040	6/43	652	2,316
7/41	22	1,054	7/43	1,301	2,475
8/41	2	1,021	8/43	620	2,337
9/41	17	987	9/43	658	2,214
10/41	0	957	10/43	862	2,349
11/41	0	895	11/43	347	2,111
12/41	0	978	12/43	851	1,734
1/42	40	1,018	1/44	2,356	2,445
2/42	8	906	2/44	4,888	2,015
3/42	0	1,400	3/44	3,954	2,672
4/42	215	1,321	4/44	9,296	3,034
5/42	269	1,315	5/44	5,165	3,248
6/42	316	1,282	6/44	2,477	3,626
7/42	0	1,360	7/44	5,597	4,219
8/42	19	1,345	8/44	7,567	4,007
9/42	173	1,310	9/44	1,444	4,103
10/42	250	1,444	10/44	1,385	3,586
11/42	295	1,307	11/44	547	3,697
12/42	129	1,548	12/44	200	3,155

Source: USSBS, February 1947.

and just needed to be seen through to its conclusion. While there might have been military reason to compress enemy forces into an ever smaller territory where increasing defense density also increases the likelihood of offensive hits, this cannot have been the purpose of strategic bombing if strategic is defined as undermining the enemy from within.

We turn now from the overall arms production picture to the marginal or incremental effects of strategic bombing to examine two specific cases, production in the aircraft industry both inside and outside of Germany (see table 6.1)[27] and production in the chemical industry (used, for example, for explosives production). Evidently, the largest number of aircraft produced occurred during the time period of the most intense bombardment of the industrial sites, in 1944. Without question, German aircraft production rose in spite of increased tonnage of bombing. How then can one assess damage to Germany's aircraft production effort? One approach is to take the highpoint of production, 4,219 aircraft in July 1944, and count, relative to this benchmark, the production shortfall in the other months to learn how this shortfall

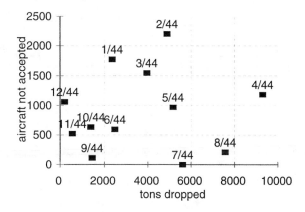

*Figure 6.4. German loss of aircraft production
January to December 1944, on account of tons of bombs dropped on aircraft production facilities located in or out of Germany.
Source: Computed from data in USSBS, February 1947.*

corresponds to bombing tonnage. In July 1944, the shortfall would therefore have been zero; in June 1944, it would be 4,219 minus 3,626 or 593 aircraft short, in May, 4,219 minus 3,248 or 971 aircraft short, and so on.

As neither bombing nor production was seriously ramped up until 1944, we will consider the numbers for that year only. Figure 6.4 presents the numbers visually. The vertical axis measures the hypothetical shortfall, that is, aircraft not accepted into service, relative to the July 1944 benchmark. The horizontal axis measures tons of bombs targeted on aircraft factories. If proponents of the strategic bombing theory were correct, we would expect to see the data trending upward: the more bombing, the greater the shortfall of aircraft not produced. And if the theory of diminishing marginal returns applies, we would expect to see that increasingly higher rates of bombing are associated with declining increases in aircraft not accepted into service. We would expect to see, in other words, something resembling the production function in figure 6.1, which first rises but then tapers off. The picture that we do see is considerably more muddled than theory. But prominently notable is that the four months with the highest bombing levels — April, May, July, and August 1944 — are not the months with the highest level of shortfalls, January through March 1944. Moreover, if one were to draw a line through the scatter plot, it evidently would be at first steeply upward-sloping but then bending and flattening out — exactly as the production function in figure 6.1 — before

Table 6.2: Tonnage dropped on German chemical industry and industry production index, January 1941 to December 1944

Month/year	Tons dropped	Production index shortfall
2/44	0	12.1
6/44	0	3.2
3/44	3	5.3
4/44	37	0
5/44	160	2.5
8/44	445	20.1
10/44	674	35.7
11/44	758	48.7
1/44	957	4.6
7/44	1,439	5.3
12/44	1,848	58.4
9/44	4,336	34.1

Source: USSBS, February 1947.

bending downward (which would signal negative returns). This evidence would at least not speak against the narrative point to which we alluded earlier, that Nazi Germany's main problem lay not in aircraft production but in pilot production.

A seemingly different, yet much the same, picture emerges with regard to production in the German chemical industry. Production reached a highpoint in April 1944, an index of 101.6, so that the hypothetical shortfall in production that month was zero. We use the April number as the benchmark and subtract from it the index numbers for the other months to calculate month-by-month industry shortfalls and display this against the bombing applied (see table 6.2). At first blush, one might disregard the data point for September 1944 as an outlier and view the number as evidence in favor of successful strategic bombing: more bombing, less production. But statisticians do not simply drop an outlying data point. They ask whether the data point has something important to tell us. And it does. It tells us that even though bombing in September with 4,336 tons was almost six and a half times as intensive as in October (674 tons), the curtailment of chemical industry production was about the same (to an index level of about 35). Moreover, when we examine the raw data in table 6.2, we note that bombing in the 1,000+ ton range reduced the production index to an average of 32.6, whereas production in the 400 to 800 ton range reduced it to 34.8, about the same "bang" for a considerably smaller "buck" of aircraft and crews sacrificed in the attacks.

Similar observations can be made for other types of war matériel. "The bottom line is," writes Werrell, "that the Germans had enough equipment:

they lacked fuel and numbers." Thus we turn to the bombing of the supply chain and the civilian economy. But before we do, it is worth reiterating an earlier remark: while we share many authors' skeptical look at the promise of strategic bombing per se, the specific point we make here concerns only the issue of diminishing marginal returns to strategic bombing. Even if the promise of strategic bombing had held true, it would still be the case that an increasing number of bombs dropped yielded, beyond some point, diminishing increases and even outright decreases. In the latter case, resources were squandered. Without any reduction in the specific destruction of aircraft factories, chemicals, and other war matériel the Allies sought, these superfluously applied resources in machines and manpower could have been brought to bear elsewhere in the war effort.[28]

BOMBING THE SUPPLY CHAIN AND THE CIVILIAN ECONOMY

Supply Chain Bombing

The Americans' air war plan, AWPD-1, principally cobbled together by four men in a mere nine days, from 4 to 12 August 1941, contains this famous passage, the mission statement:

> To wage a sustained air offensive against German military power, supplemented by air offensives against other regions under enemy control which contribute toward that power; to support a final offensive, if it becomes necessary to invade the continent; in addition, to conduct effective air operations in connection with Hemisphere Defense and a strategic defensive in the Far East.[29]

Even more bluntly, elsewhere in the document one reads: "If the air offensive is successful, a land offensive may not be necessary." The priority given to Germany and the nod to Hemisphere Defense and the Far East follow the overall pre–Pearl Harbor war plan, Rainbow 5. The air war plan could hardly deviate from this. But the conditional statements—"if it becomes necessary to invade the continent" and "if the air offensive is successful, a land offensive may not be necessary"—reflect both hubris and calculation, resulting from an unwarranted belief in air power based on "the American propensity to see war as an engineering science." The principal architects of America's air war plan calculated that by destroying "50 electric power plants, 15 marshalling yards, 15 bridges, 17 inland waterway facilities, and 27 petroleum and synthetic oil plants," that is, 124 electric, transportation, and oil targets in all, the German economy could be wrecked enough to make the Nazis sue for peace.[30]

To achieve this end, the air war planners realized that German air defenses would need to be overcome. Figuring that an air attrition war might be problematic, they went back to strategic bombing theory: bomb the places that make aircraft. And so they added thirty targets: eighteen aircraft factories, six aluminum plants, and six magnesium plants. George and Kuter had experience with peacetime bombing practice and added an inaccuracy factor to allow for wartime conditions.[31]

All told, AWPD-1 called for 6,860 bombers, in ten groups, for the German war theater alone. Adding in replacements for anticipated losses as well as escort fighters and support aircraft, let alone requirements for the other theaters of war, the sum total came to 63,467 aircraft and nearly 2.2 million men. Given industrial limitations in the Allied countries, it was thought that a suitable aerial armada to undertake an envisioned six-month-long onslaught on the German economy could not be fully assembled before April 1944.[32]

The engineers' formulas hinged on a logical flaw but, because they were ill-informed, also rested on bad assumptions entering the calculations. The logic proceeded like this: first, the objective is to destroy the key nodes of Nazi Germany's industrial web; second, to do that, one needs to get through the air defense system; and third, to do that, one needs to bomb the aircraft manufacturing facilities. This was circular reasoning: to bomb the factories, one needs to get through the air defenses; to get through the air defense, one bombs the factories. The problem was much more of a simultaneous than of a sequential nature. That aside, the planners assumed, as did virtually everyone at the time, that to sustain the war effort the German economy was operating at full capacity. After overrunning Poland, the low countries, France, and a good bit of Scandinavia, the Nazis had now taken on Soviet Russia (22 June 1941). How could the industrial system not be running at full capacity? As Eric Larrabee remarked: "Two myths coincided. Everyone knew that Germans are efficient and everyone knew that dictatorships are efficient: therefore, if Hitler says Germany is totally mobilized for war, Germany must be totally mobilized for war."[33] But unlike what was acknowledged to be required of the Allies to produce their 63,467 aircraft, the Nazis had hardly begun to flex the country's industrial muscle. Likewise, the AWPD-1 planners severely underestimated requirements for escort fighters, misjudged the severity of bad weather over Europe,[34] vastly erred in their estimate of bombing inaccuracy, and — like historians to this day — overlooked Germany's searchlight batteries and flak defenses, a vital, integrated component of the country's air defense system.[35]

Planning for an Allied invasion of the continent, eventually code-named Operation Overlord, had begun in earnest in January 1943 at the Casablanca conference. Charles Portal was selected to head up all Allied air forces, but for the duration of Overlord they were transferred to the command of Dwight Eisenhower, who, in December 1943, was appointed Supreme Commander, Allied Expeditionary Forces. A series of preparatory air strikes on the French and German railway system during March 1944 was intended to test what would happen to the German supply chain. For the Allies, the results were remarkably positive. As it turned out, Nazi Germany had built its air defenses primarily to protect the Reich, not to defend and hold any occupied territories. For example, Luftflotte Reich was expressly forbidden from pursuing Allied aircraft into France, a rule not revoked until a week after D-Day. French territory was the responsibility of Luftflotte 3, headquartered in Paris, which tended to be staffed by inexperienced controllers and equipped with outdated tools. Consequently, bombing runs on select French rail infrastructure could be flown at relatively low altitude with correspondingly increased bombing accuracy and very low casualty rates (both for Allied crews and civilians on the ground). This was very much in contrast to the results achieved over Germany. Loss rates in March, April, and May ran at 0.6, 0.5, and 2.1 percent, respectively, against non-German targets but at 4.5, 2.9, and 4.15 percent at German targets.[36]

These preparatory excursions were so successful that even "Bomber" Harris could not but admit: "I myself did not anticipate that we should be able to bomb the French railways with anything like the precision that was achieved." He boasted to his crews: "The U.S. air forces, who specialize in precision visual attacks by day, are in particular astonished at the results. You have in fact wiped their eyes for them at their own game."[37] Meanwhile, Harris's American counterpart, General Carl Spaatz, commander of U.S. strategic air forces in Europe, had been "no more eager than Sir Arthur to surrender strategic control of his heavy bombers to the requirements of a ground campaign." Like Harris, he sent bombers on their way to Berlin, for example, on 4 March 1944. A day later, he submitted to Eisenhower a plan to bomb German oil facilities, to stop the Germans not just in Normandy but on all fronts.[38] But Eisenhower stuck to what was called the Transportation Plan—the attack of fuels would come later. The goal was entirely tactical: stop German supplies and reinforcements from reaching Normandy. It was to support an invasion. The air war planners' "if it becomes necessary to invade the continent" had become necessary.

Werrell has argued that "when we discuss the accomplishments of strategic bombing, we are speaking of what occurred during the last months of the war," by which he meant after the summer of 1944.[39] In truth, the exact

Table 6.3: Effects of bomb tonnage dropped on German railroad and fuel industry, January 1944 to April 1945

Month/year	tons dropped	net tons-km not moved	tons dropped	aviation fuel not produced
1/44	367	1,007	0	134
2/44	735	1,774	0	85
3/44	955	0	0	38
4/44	4,003	381	201	9
5/44	7,823	532	2,459	0
6/44	1,955	477	10,877	38
7/44	3,685	709	11,425	164
8/44	2,149	681	12,066	252
9/44	17,615	3,159	8,145	238
10/44	25,221	4,162	12,241	381
11/44	23,554	5,719	32,542	416
12/44	61,392	6,377	11,290	411
1/45	43,644	8,787	8,516	428
2/45	55,391	11,687	18,608	464
3/45	61,007	12,587	24,973	490
4/45	31,253	14,187	7,458	544

Source: USSBS, February 1947.

opposite is the case: Harris and Spaatz had had their chances prior to that time. Eisenhower would not return direct command of strategic air forces to them until early September, and successful precision bombing for strategic purposes would have to wait another half century. Even then, as the events in Kosovo in 1999 and in Iraq since 2003 have made clear, taking out military assets of strategic value does not necessarily curtail an opponent's ability to commit atrocities against civilians. In Kosovo, the civilian slaughter was a major Serbian strategic objective and air power was not able to stop it; in Iraq, air power may have won the war but the fight continues.

The primary effect of the Transportation Plan bombing was that it diminished Germany's military abilities on the front lines. Disrupting land transportation, as we have seen, did not make Germany's arms production potential decline. It did not even affect actual arms production until after September 1944, because the factories had ample stocks of supplies to sustain production. Instead, the crucial point concerned the disruption of translating stocks into flows, the delivery of matériel and troops to the front. Clodfelter calls this effect of the attack on German land transportation "fortuitous rather than intentional." Surprisingly, military historians have paid scant attention to the role of land transportation, especially the German railroad system.[40]

As before, our main concern in this chapter is not with the total effects of bombing but with the marginal or incremental effects. Employing our earlier technique, we use the highpoint of net tons-kilometer moved by the

German railroad system, in March 1944, as our benchmark, calculating net tons-kilometer *not* moved as the destructive objective of the Allied campaign (table 6.3).

Apart from two outliers, one in December 1944, the other in April 1945, it would appear that the more bombing, the larger the desired effect. But with the beginning of 1945, the game was up. We therefore limit our attention only to the year 1944, as in the earlier examples of aircraft and chemicals production. Diminishing marginal returns to increasing loads of bombing of the railroad system are clearly apparent, especially from September to December. By January, February, and March 1945, the production function of bombing the railroads had shifted since the German defenses were by then destroyed, and again a diminishing marginal effect can be observed.

After the success of the Transportation Plan, Eisenhower next turned to Germany's fuel supplies. We have data on stocks of aviation gasoline, motor gasoline, and diesel fuel as well as data on bombing tonnage dropped on fuel plants (although not broken out by fuel type). To stop the Allied aerial onslaught, the crucial category for Nazi Germany was production of aviation fuel. Employing our previous technique one last time, table 6.3 again shows the effects. May 1944 was the highpoint of aviation fuel production (despite nearly 2,500 tons of bombs on fuel plants). Taking this as the benchmark, we measure aviation fuel *not* put into stock (not produced). From June to December 1944, the fuel industry was badly affected by bombing levels of about 8,000–12,000 tons of bombs per month. An extraordinary 32,500 tons of bombs in November did no more damage than either October's or December's bombing. Neither did the large bombings in February and March 1945.

In sum, we have shown two things: strategic bombing as envisioned—a force sufficient to win independent of the military's nonstrategic branches—did not win the European war. It had that chance before Operation Overlord. Thereafter, when Eisenhower used the strategic forces for tactical purposes and ground support operations, bombing became effective but with diminishing marginal returns.

Bombing the Civilian Economy

It appears that the German civilian economy did not suffer greatly from the bombing. To be sure, civilian consumer production and per capita consumption suffered but not because of bombing. Instead, production and consumption suffered because Germany's armed forces requisitioned so many "consumer" goods for their own use. Oxford University historian Richard Overy stresses that most of the reduction occurred from 1939 to 1942, that is, prior

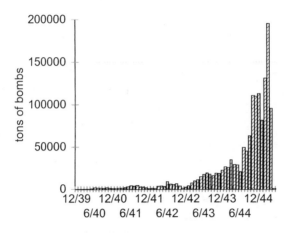

Figure 6.5. RAF/USAAF bombing of Germany, 1939–1945
Source: *USSBS, Statistical Appendix to Over-all Report (European War), February 1947,
Chart 6, pp. 49–91.*

to the time when Allied bombers actually got through to German territory
(fig. 6.5).[41]

War mobilization in Germany reached 13 million people, but the total
German civilian labor force fell by only 3.5 million people, from 39.4 to 35.9
million. Correspondingly, the greatest decline occurred in the male civilian labor force, which fell from 24.5 to 13.5 million. This decline of 9 million
men was nearly made up by 7.5 million foreigners and prisoners of war. The
average work week changed hardly at all (from 47.8 to 48.3 hours per week
between September 1939 and March 1944). Women's labor force participation changed negligibly from 14.6 to 14.9 million and could hardly have been
pushed higher. As regards capital, Germany had a comparatively high capi-
tal/labor ratio, and the vast majority of industrial work was carried out in
single shifts. Even of the crucial arms production facilities, only one-fifth to
one-quarter worked a second shift. Strategic bombing damaged or destroyed
a mere 6.5 percent of installed German machine tools. This was easily replaced.
Raw material stocks were ample, at least for about six months or so after the
start of the war. Thereafter, in addition to materials recycling and product
redesign, successful campaigns replenished supplies such as "chromium from
Bulgaria and Greece, nickel and molybdenum from Finland and Norway,
copper from Jugoslavia, Norway and Finland, manganese from Russia, mer-
cury from Italy and Spain, and bauxite from Hungary, France, Yugoslavia

and Italy." It was not until fall 1944 that raw material shortages began to affect civilian and armament production.[42]

In addition, Germany had large inventories of required materials so that temporary setbacks in raw material production did not noticeably affect production of finished civilian and war goods. Moreover, German industry was already geographically widely dispersed; remaining critical industries that were found to be too concentrated in too few locations were dispersed even further. At best, the strategic air war appeared to secure modest delays in further increases in German production, rather than securing decreases. A well-thought-out set of calculations shows that Germany's overall war production potential diminished on account of strategic bombing by a mere 2 percent or so, with the high point of a 3.8 percent reduction occurring in the second half of 1943, well before D-Day.[43]

Bombing the arms supply chain and the civilian economy did not bring about the desired strategic effects—making the enemy collapse from within. The land invasion was necessary.[44]

BOMBING GERMAN MORALE

It is improbable that any terrorization of the civil population which could be achieved by air attack could compel the Government of a great nation to surrender. . . . In our case we have seen the combative spirit of the people aroused, and not quelled, by the German raids. Nothing we have learned of the capacity of the German population to endure suffering justifies us in assuming that they could be cowed into submission by such methods, or, indeed, that they would not be rendered more desperately resolved by them.

So wrote Winston Churchill on 21 October 1917. We do not know why Churchill changed his mind—he may have done so as early as 1918—but nearly twenty-three years later, on 8 July 1940, he wrote: "We have no Continental army which can defeat the German military power . . . But there is one thing that will bring [Hitler] back and bring him down, and that is an absolutely devastating, exterminating attack by very heavy bombers from this country upon the Nazi homeland."[45] For Britain, the phony war had ended, and in May 1940 it threw its first serious load of bombs on German cities. In July, Bomber Command for the first time employed delayed-action bombs, and on the night of 12 August the first-time use of incendiary bombs followed, dropped on the cities of Bielefeld, Dessau, Frankfurt am Main, Halle, Hamburg, Kassel,

Koblenz, Köln (Cologne), Münster, Neustadt an der Weser, Osnabrück, and Weimar. Up until this time, the Nazis had focused on bombing British shipping. Now, the Luftwaffe responded by attacking the British Isles, indeed British cities. The "Battle of Britain" had begun, and so had "morale" bombing.

For the planners, morale bombing carried moral ambiguity with it. Koch writes "that very few of those responsible for initiating the policy of indiscriminate bombing from the air, or for carrying it out, seem to have felt any moral scruples about it at the time, or indeed to have paused to reflect upon the inevitable results and implications of what they were doing." If not immoral, bombing was certainly amoral: it was what the engineers had to do to win. *Morale bombing* was to become a euphemism, "the cosmetic word for massacre," made most famous by Kurt Vonnegut's *Slaughterhouse Five* (1969). But if the eventual outcome was immoral, that was not what had been planned at the beginning. To the contrary, the record is clear that for the American air war planners morale collapse was to be an incidental consequence of destroying the enemy's industrial web. Like Churchill in 1917, the U.S. air war plan AWPD-1, of August 1941, considered that "area bombing of cities may actually stiffen the resistance of the population, especially if the attacks are weak and sporadic." Moreover, the commander of U.S. strategic forces in Europe, Carl Spaatz, is clearly on the record, as are Ira Eaker, one-time commander of the Eighth Air Force, and other principal players such as Spaatz's bosses, General Arnold and General Eisenhower, that morale bombing, bombing of German cities, bombing of civilians was a no-go proposition.[46]

According to historian Ronald Schaffer the reason for this opposition to morale bombing was not that it was considered immoral but that—in the spirit of war as engineering—it was inefficient. In a detailed account of official histories, records, diaries, autobiographies, letters, and other sources, Schaffer finds that "none of the officers raised anything but pragmatic objections to morale bombing."[47] The pragmatic objections included that such bombing might actually strengthen resistance, that even if bombed, the population might not be able to take on the Nazis, that resources would be diverted from the more important aim of precision bombing of industrial-web targets, and that the Army Air Force's public image might be smeared back home, where there was moral opposition to bombing of civilians, leaving its postwar future in jeopardy.

As for the British, even "Bomber" Harris was not primarily interested in morale bombing. His particular peeve was that precision bombing manifestly did not work so that the only alternative that remained was indiscriminate area bombing. In this he took solace from the Butt report of August 1941, an account on the inefficacy of British precision bombing. The bombing was found to be pathetically inaccurate. For example, only 22 percent of pilots who even claimed to have hit their target got within five miles of it, let alone hit it. The remainder of the year would be no better. Henry Tizard, a scientific adviser to the British government, remarked in early 1942 that in the previous eight months fewer Germans were killed on the ground than Brits in the air. Thus Harris, in a curious leap of logic, concluded from the Butt report that the targets would not be industries, nor factories, nor morale per se. The targets would be cities. "The only way bombers could destroy *anything,*" writes Stephen Budiansky, "was to destroy *everything.*" Harris was helped, a mere week before his February 1942 appointment to lead Bomber Command, when the War Cabinet changed course and directed that the primary objective of a new air offensive be "focused on the morale of the enemy civil population and, in particular, of the industrial worker." This suited Harris well enough, and city bombing ensued, including the four firestorms in Hamburg, Kassel, Darmstadt, and Dresden that alone caused about half of the estimated 600,000 German aerial bombing civilian war deaths.[48]

When the German defenses had long been breached, in the winter and spring of 1945, "bombers were available in greater numbers than were required to eliminate the remaining important precision targets . . . [thus] they could be used against civilians with no loss of efficiency." Morale bombing slipped, Ronald Schaffer suggests, ever so gradually from pragmatic moralism to immoral practice.[49] But it was not indiscriminate, not uniformly random. To the contrary. It targeted of course cities rather than rural areas; it targeted factories and, with that, working-class neighborhoods rather than the well-off. It thus affected mothers, children, the old, the insane, the invalids, the infirm, and the immobile. The maelstrom of destruction consumed noncombatants and even Reich prisoners without regard to their actual participation in the war or support of the Hitler state. The war engineers' theory of strategic bombing had been put to the test, and the test had gone wrong. The British and, later, the Americans bombed because they could, and the Germans did not because they could not. The Allies had assembled a comprehensive long-range bomber fleet; the Nazis had not.[50]

In the event, neither in Britain nor in Germany did morale bombing have the hypothesized effects. The Germans were the first to learn this, in Guernica, prior to World War II. The Spanish Civil War, which would see Generalissimo Franco rise to a dictatorship that would not end until his death in 1975, became a welcome proving ground for those who would be titans a few years later. As participants or as observers, all the major players, save Japan, were involved to a greater or lesser degree: the Italians, the Germans, the Russians, the French, the British, and the Americans. The Luftwaffe, in particular, made a sport of putting its tactical and strategic air war doctrines to a real-war test. Despite warnings by the American military attaché that "the Flying Fortress died in Spain," his superiors would not heed the fundamental lessons the Germans learned: an air force must be a whole package of bombers, interceptors, and fighters, and an air force must be integrated into the ground war.[51] When Mussolini — another dictator — ordered his forces to bomb Barcelona, 16–18 March 1938, thousands were killed or wounded, yet Republican resistance to the Fascists rose. So found not only the British but also a Luftwaffe study.

Nearly a year earlier, on 26 April 1937, the German air force, for reasons of diplomatic deniability masked as the Condor Legion, had its own go at terror bombing. Pablo Picasso's *Guernica* became the icon of the massacre (three hundred civilians died in the attack) much as Kurt Vonnegut's *Slaughterhouse Five* years later would become an icon of the Dresden firestorm. There is no indication that Nazi Germany concluded in any way that terror bombing was the best way to conduct war.[52]

The early British bombings of Germany induced, at first, derision. The bombs were widely off the mark, doing little more than rattling the population in the few places where the bombs fell. The security service (the Staatssicherheitsdienst, or SD for short) had set up an ingenious reporting system that would routinely and scientifically sample popular opinion as to the bombings' effects and feed the reports back to the Nazi leadership. A seventeen-volume compilation of these reports was published in 1984. Koch, who examined these records in some detail for the May to September 1940 period, finds little more than reports of sleeplessness, nervousness, "some psychological and physiological wear and tear," but no effect on discipline or productivity. In contrast, the reports that made the round in Britain were gloating with the supposed success of morale bombing. They seemed rather misinformed.[53]

On the British side of the Channel, morale did not seem much dented by the fall 1940 Blitz on London either, nor would it be by later German attacks. For example, Solly Zuckerman, who was to be Britain's Chief Scientist for its postwar British Bombing Survey Unit (BBSU), the U.K.'s equivalent to the USSBS, found that the 1941 German attacks on Hull and Birmingham induced neither panic nor adverse effects on health and productivity, findings the BBSU would later confirm with regard to Germany: "In so far as the offensive against German towns was designed to break the morale of the German

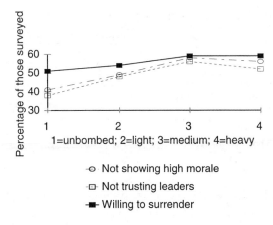

Figure 6.6. Diminishing returns of Allied strategic bombing on German people's morale
Source: *Constructed from USSBS, 30 September 1945, p. 96.*

civilian population, it clearly failed."[54] Moreover, with the power government confers, both sides' officials managed the information to their mutual, if internal, advantage. Morale bombing was to become a "public relations problem [of] managing information for the survivors."[55] The USSBS likewise would later write that although the bombing had measurable, serious effects on civilian morale as it had "appreciably affected the German will to resist," nonetheless, "depressed and discouraged workers were not necessarily unproductive workers."[56]

As before, what is of particular interest to us is not the total effect but the marginal effect: the effect of additional tons of bombs on an already adversely affected morale. It turns out that this is the clearest case for which diminishing returns to bombing (strategic or otherwise) can be shown. One can hardly do better than cite the USSBS conclusion verbatim:

> Continuous heavy bombing of the same communities did not produce decreases in morale *proportional* to the amount of bombing . . . These observations of the diminishing returns from heavy bombing point to the practical conclusion that the maximum *morale* effects of dropping a given tonnage of bombs on Germany would have been attained by lighter raids as widely distributed as possible, rather than by concentrated heavy bombing in limited areas.[57]

For example, the morale of those living in "towns subjected to the heaviest bombing was no worse than in towns of the same size receiving much lighter bomb loads."[58] Figure 6.6, constructed from data in USSBS, shows this diminishing effect.[59] The percentages on the vertical axis are stated in terms of the

Table 6.4: Home destruction and morale

	People showing low morale . . .	
	Cross-section Sample A	Cross-section Sample B
Cities with		
60–80% homes destroyed	55	53
49–59% homes destroyed	58	56
20–39% homes destroyed	59	59
1–19% homes destroyed	43	56
0% homes destroyed	—	41

Source: USSBS, September 1945, p. 96.

Allies' desired outcome: the percentage of people *not* showing high morale, of people *not* trusting leaders, and of people willing to surrender. All three variables show diminishing, indeed *negative,* returns as a function of increasing amounts of bombing. Heavy bombing was less effective in lowering morale than medium bombing. And in contrast to the strong wording of USSBS, even in the absence of any bombing whatsoever, 40–50 percent of the German population was demoralized. Light and medium bombing brought that percentage more surely to the 50 percent mark but not much beyond that,[60] reflective of a ceiling beyond which bombing simply could not reach. The marginal effect was diminishing and even negative, and the total effect was actually small: 59 percent of the unbombed showed "high morale," a percentage brought down by bombing to only 42 percent. Table 6.4 shows a similar diminishing returns effect with regard to home destruction and morale.

ASSESSING THE EFFECT OF STRATEGIC BOMBING

The concept of strategic bombing was first applied on a truly massive scale in World War II, especially in the European theater of operations. Naturally, it would take some time and experimentation to get things "right," to discover what the practical difficulties of such bombing might entail, of whether strategic bombing would be a viable, militarily useful concept or not. A learning curve would be expected. But it was also expected that the learning curve would lead to the expected result: an enemy collapse from within.[61] This was not to happen. The U.S. Air Force's own careful history—although written by independent historians—is quite correct in its assessment that up to late 1943 its forces were "inadequate" to bring about so drastic an outcome. By the end of 1943, "it had become apparent that an all-out attack on Nazi air power would be a necessary preliminary to any successful strategic bombardment campaign"—as Rainbow 5 had foretold. And so the first few months of

1944 were spent taking on the German Air Force. The result was that while "German fighter production was to increase rather than decrease during 1944 . . . production did not keep up with the planned schedule and for that failure the Big Week [in February 1944] and subsequent bomber attacks were largely responsible." In March 1944, however, Eisenhower took direct command of the strategic air forces for the tactical purpose of preparing and succeeding in the Normandy landing. Even as late as January 1945 as many of three-fourths of all United States Strategic Air Force missions were flown in support of the ground troop advance on Berlin. But by this time, the Nazis' game was long over. Ultimately, "victory was possible only through the combined efforts of the several arms of the associated powers and of the civilians behind those arms."[62]

Hewitt writes: "Most of the bombs, heavy bomber sorties, civilian deaths, and urban area destruction in Japan and Germany occurred not when these countries were at the peak of power or merely on the defensive, but after mid-1944 and especially in 1945 when they were on their knees." Of the 1,419,604 tons of bombs to fall on Germany, 1,016,157 fell between July 1944 and May 1945 — nearly 72 percent. Of that, much was directed in support of tactical operations on the ground; much of the remainder fell against towns and cities, after the occupied territories had been liberated, after Germany had dispersed its war production into the countryside, and after its supply routes to the front had been cut off. Following D-Day, strategic bombing cleared the brush for conquest. It did not coerce Germany's leaders, nor its civilians, to simply give up the fight.[63]

In Levine's view, this is too harsh a judgment. "The bombers were never expected to win the war alone or avert an invasion, and they received a far lower priority than would have been the case had this been planned." He also believes that the events of 1944 were due "primarily to the belated development of countermeasures to the Germans' radar and homing devices, and not, as is usually said, to the crippling of the German defenses by the loss of territory and gasoline." Indeed, "the efforts of the tactical and strategic air forces cannot be neatly separated. Up to D-Day the tactical forces played an important role in gaining air superiority, and in the final phase of the transportation campaign their efforts fused with those of [the United States Strategic Air Force] and [the Royal Air Force] Bomber Command." The USSBS adds: "During the war it was impossible to assess the real significance of this type of warfare . . . It was impossible . . . to know with certainty whether or not the effects of the air activity against the Reich justified the effort expended."[64] Despite these defenses and considerations, Levine himself concludes:

During this period [1943 and early 1944] . . . the strategic forces did not accomplish their explicit assigned aims, as set out in the Casablanca and combined bomber offensive directives. They made no important contribution to the winning of the Battle of the Atlantic and did not seriously impair German morale, reduce overall German war production, or stop the manufacture of any critical items.[65]

What, then, did the strategic forces achieve? Levine speaks for many with his view that the marginal effects, such as delaying, but not hindering, German weapons production, "would have justified strategic bombing even if it never accomplished a more positive aim. It is hard to see how any other use of Allied resources could have similarly affected the enemy in the same time period." This echoes USSBS's own account: "If strategic bombing did nothing but force the dispersal of the aircraft industry it would have paid its cost."[66]

This conclusion is illogical. The resources poured into the strategic bombing effort could have been applied elsewhere (e.g., more fighter-bombers for air-to-air combat and in tactical support) where, at worst, they also would have had little incremental effect. But in light of the eventual outcome, one must venture that more tactical air power would have made a declining but positive incremental contribution to breaking through the German defensive lines in France earlier than D-Day on 6 June 1944. An earlier invasion had, in fact, been planned but was not considered possible in light of resource constraints.

Another way to think about strategic forces — a way that perhaps reconciles the contrasting views — is to think of them not in isolation of other inputs but conjointly. Just as targeting technology helped shift the effectiveness of strategic bombing to a higher production function (fig. 6.2), so tactical air power may be seen as just a different technology. Once the "technology" of tactical air power had advanced, it shifted strategic bombing onto a higher production function and above the victory threshold — only that it then became conquest bombing rather than strategic bombing.

Although the data do not permit quantitative analysis in a statistical sense, it is quite clear that as envisioned by the air war planners strategic bombing did not have a significant impact on Germany's war production. Manufacture of weaponry did not fall, but actually rose in the last year of the war. Such effects as strategic bombing did have were due primarily to shift factors (e.g., improvements in the tactical air war) and displacement factors (e.g., German resources poured into air defense) rather than to increased amounts of bomb tonnage per se. The primary effect that strategic bombing brought was preparation for conquest.

In fairness to the Allied war effort, one must of course acknowledge that they suffered from severe information deficits during the war that made an assessment of the bombing's efficacy difficult. The larger point, though, is that one can well apply a concept in economic theory to the conduct of war. Historian Richard Overy repeatedly points to diminishing returns in the German war economy.[67] For example, in various essays he argues that from 1939 to early 1942, Germany poured increasingly more resources into its arms production machinery, but to declining effect. Only once it was realized that the war would be protracted did the Nazis shift conceptually from more production to more productivity in production, that is, a shift in the production function. This occurred most famously when Albert Speer was appointed armaments minister in February 1942. For example, with little increase in labor — moreover, much of it less productive forced labor — aircraft production nonetheless nearly quadrupled between 1941 and 1944.

STRATEGIC BOMBING AND THE OTHER PRINCIPLES OF ECONOMICS

The preceding sections elaborate how the principle of diminishing marginal returns may be applied to military operations in the case of the strategic bombing of Germany in World War II. This section indicates how the other economics principles used in this book may also be applied to the case.

Manpower and Other Resources

Albert Speer's ascension to direct Germany's arms production effort resulted in a massive streamlining of its efforts and in vastly more efficient outcomes. Arms manufacturing productivity surged as physical, human, and institutional resources were reallocated. The opportunity to forgo production the way Speer would organize it had become too costly. Germany could no longer afford a non-Speer production path, and resources were steered toward higher-valued usage.

An illustration with regard to the expected marginal cost/benefit principle is given by the reallocation of United States strategic air forces in 1942/43 from British bases to the North African theater. The early efforts of the British and American strategic bombing campaign against Germany soon ground to a halt as it was recognized that imprecision in targeting, frequent inclement weather (cloud cover), limited bomber-range, effective air defenses, and other factors much tempered the high hopes invested in strategic bombing. Shifting air force resources to the African theater would result in a higher differential of benefits and costs. The forces were used to fly missions to Italy (to prepare the invasion there), and beyond Italy to Romania and southeastern Europe, where they were used in an attempt to disrupt raw material supply routes to Germany.

The operation of the principle of substitution is illustrated by Germany's increasing use of foreign and slave labor as it drew its own men to the front lines. To economists, substitution is occasioned by relative price changes. If the use of one resource becomes too costly, people tend to switch to another, relatively cheaper resource provided it fulfills the same overall objective. To use a frivolous example, if the intake of vitamin C is the objective and oranges become more expensive, we would expect people to switch consumption toward grapefruit or blueberries or bell peppers. As the war wore on, the employment of German men in industry became more costly, measured as the forgone opportunity to use them on the front lines where they were more desperately needed. Foreign and slave labor, in spite of the attending addition of supervisory cost, became relatively "cheaper" and an economist could well have foretold this substitution.

Diminishing marginal returns are evident not only in the main theme of this chapter but in many related cases as well. For example, the aforementioned transfer of the USAAF Eighth Division from Britain to North Africa in 1942/43 to fly bombing runs on Italy and southeastern Europe would naturally result in diminishing returns the farther away flights strayed from base. The same anticipated advantage would take more resources to accomplish. But if more resources accomplish the same aim in one case as fewer resources in another, then diminishing returns are at work. This was well recognized by the decision makers who eventually re-relocated the Eighth to higher-valued uses — the western front.

The strategic bombing case also yields plenty of examples on the operation of the principle of (overcoming) asymmetric information before and after an action is taken. On the manpower front, for instance, bombing of Germany from 1940 to 1943 correctly signaled that the Allies did not (yet) have their bombing act together. The Allies revealed a previously hidden aspect of their air force, namely, its relative ineffectiveness. The principle of (overcoming) asymmetric information is also at work in the speed of personnel call-up and mobilization. Successful mobilization relies in part on government's ability to identify and draft men to fight war. It may be presumed that while people know where they are, government does not. Government is at an informational disadvantage. But part of Nazi Germany's evil genius was its detailed and efficient citizen registration system, a system that allowed massive mobilization in a short amount of time, mitigating the potential obstacle of asymmetric information.

On the flip side, that is, asymmetry after an action is taken, we have the example of successful enemy infiltration by spies. Once a person is a spy (has taken an action), how does one overcome the problem of hidden action (e.g., monitoring that the spy does not become a double-spy)? One must overcome asymmetries in information about intentions. One way to do this is by designing one-way gateways by which information flows only in the desired direction, that is, by placing spies in a position to collect and transmit information from target to home without putting them in a loop that would permit them also to transmit from home to target. A rereading of spy history would probably reveal a number of mechanisms by which the asymmetry problem was addressed, if perhaps not solved. Likewise, we would expect that successful double-agency revolves around the failure of overcoming the asymmetry problem.

A different example of overcoming hidden action asymmetry is given by an insidious form of bonding that leads people to police themselves. The authorities' problem is to avoid defection from the cause. If people disagree with the state, at least some of them will seek to shirk assigned responsibilities. To rein in, the state has to set up a costly monitoring system. Much better (cheaper) to create a "culture" in which people monitor each other and report to the authorities those thought to lack certain vigor and commitment to the state's cause.

Logistics

On the logistics front, the operation of the opportunity cost principle is evident in the switching of strategic air forces for tactical air support missions in preparation for and following D-Day in June 1944. To withhold the use of the strategic air assets would have involved a colossal cost, namely, the forgone opportunity to employ them tactically. The calculation of expected incremental costs and benefits were constantly pondered in bomb-targeting decisions. Examining the month-by-month bombing records, it is empirically evident — and so is the narrative record in the literature — how decision makers oscillated among target preferences as anticipated costs and benefits changed. Where to send the next wave of bombers? Shall we attack German rail stock or canals or bridges or fuel supplies or air fields or arms production sites? Which target of logistic value to Germany should be attacked next? Much of the decision making involved consideration and reconsideration of anticipated benefits to the Allied war effort and anticipated costs. The costs, crucially, involved not merely the potential loss of airplanes and crew but the opportunity to have used the same aircraft and crew to bomb another target that might have proven of greater value.

Not surprisingly, these benefits and costs were often falsely anticipated. The German railroad system proved resilient, for example, because it had so many unexpected (for the Allies) redundancies built in. Not infrequently, attacks on rail yards killed not Germans but foreign and slave workers, causing little substantive damage to Germany's war effort. To keep the trains, trucks, vessels, and aircraft moving — on all sides of the war effort — necessitated an information, communication, and signaling system of extraordinary breadth and depth. The very idea of strategic bombing was predicated on the notion that disrupting Germany's production and logistics would win the war. But once the fight was joined, the information needed to conduct such a war proved insufficient. Had this been more clearly understood from the outset, the strategic bombing effort might never have been made. Instead of acting on reliable information, the Allies frequently had to act on the basis of speculation. Toward the end, however, as Germany's declining capacity to fight the war was rapidly revealed, the situation reversed itself. Not unlike the case of the American Civil War (chap. 5), the Allies could be surer, prior to action, of what to expect. Likewise, German soldiers on the receiving end could be surer of their unhappy fate, and this prompted a serious break in the cultural compact between the Nazi state and its troops. Aerial bombardment and disruption now made it harder for officers to keep track of their underlings, to report them to the higher-ups, to punish the laggard, to pursue the deserter. Hidden action (the pursuit of the troops' real intentions) became more evident but there was not much the Nazis could do anymore. Units and fighting morale disintegrated. In the arena of logistics, things began to break down internally.

The principle of diminishing marginal returns is illustrated more narrowly than in the main sections of this chapter by examining the initial bombing runs into Germany. Only with the catastrophic failure of the bombing run on Schweinfurt in August 1943 did the Allies finally conclude that sending swarms of unescorted bomber planes to Germany territory was folly. German air defenses took down many a plane and crew. Packs of hundreds of bomber aircraft achieved little more than squadrons of smaller size did. This would not change until the introduction of the American P-47 Thunderbolt and P-51 Mustang aircraft.

Technology

Much has been made of the Allies' befuddlement over Germany's ability to keep producing, even increasing, its armament output. It turned out that Germany was able to disperse its research, development, and production centers widely and effectively. Nonetheless, despite its ability to adjust, dispersal increased communication and transportation costs. The presumption must be that Germany preferred not to disperse and incur the additional cost, subtracting resources it could and would have used to prosecute the war. The Allied effort imposed a however small opportunity cost on the German war effort. But dispersal also forced German managers, scientists, and engineers to be smarter, to make do in new circumstances, to be less visible, less easily tracked, more safely harbored from attack, and yet be equally or more productive than before. At least at first blush, it is not implausible to argue that bombing-induced dispersal assisted the German war effort. Better to know where your enemy is than to not know where he hides. Bombing-induced dispersal deprived the Allies of important information.[68]

The principle of substitution is well illustrated by Germany's technological effort to develop synthetic fuel sources for motor transport as natural oil and gas sources came under attack (cut offs from foreign trade and Allied attacks on German-occupied oil fields in southeast Europe, e.g., Romania). An example of incremental costs and benefits in the technology area is given by the Allies' development of add-on/drop-off fuel tanks to extend the range of their fighter fleet. One of the more fundamental problems the Allies encountered early on in the strategic air campaign was that their bombers could fly farther than their escort fighters. Fitting the fighters with add-on fuel tanks, to be dropped off when empty, allowed them to accompany the bomber fleets farther into German territory. The expected benefits are obvious. But the benefit was bought at a cost: fully loaded, the add-on fuel tanks slowed down Allied fighters, which then proved highly vulnerable to agile German air defense fighters, which merely needed to rise, shoot, and drop down for refueling.

The principle of diminishing marginal returns is illustrated by the curious case of the missing German pilots. As we have seen, it is well documented that almost to the very end of the war, Germany produced astonishingly large numbers of aircraft. What it did not have, or had only in declining numbers, were competent pilots to fly the aircraft. Once the United States did make the decision to design, build, and introduce the P-47 and P-51, the German Air Force finally encountered a formidable opponent in the air, so formidable that it overwhelmed the Luftwaffe. Survival rates dropped, and German pilots became scarce. Economically, aircraft and pilots are complementary goods. One requires the other. Building aircraft would not solve the problem, neither would fueling them. Without pilots, diminishing returns to more aircraft set in rather more rapidly.

Regarding the overcoming of hidden action problems, the development of the German arms industry serves as an example. Initially, much industry was private and worked on a cost-plus contract basis. The usual arms industry contracting problems that are much discussed today applied back then as well. How does the state know to what degree a privately contracted party honestly and conscientiously fulfills its contractual obligations? There are many ways to address this problem. The German state initially helped finance much of the construction of the industrial assets needed to rebuild its arms industry after World War I. The state engaged in risk-sharing, helped overcome market uncertainty, provided incentives to cooperate as well as incentives to discourage nonperformance (no contract renewal, for example). Eventually, the German state ever more closely tied the arms industry into the state apparatus itself; the industry effectively became nationalized, in deed if not always in name and legal terms.

Planning

Regarding war planning, the P-51 aircraft did not, of course, simply materialize in large numbers over German skies, but neither was the introduction of such a plane utterly unexpected. In anticipation, German officials strenuously argued for spending the necessary resources to further develop its air defense capabilities, but Hitler insisted on expending resources to develop bombers to push the offense. The opportunity cost of devoting resources to the production of bombers is to give up the opportunity to develop and produce fighter aircraft (and pilots) to accompany the bombers or to defend air space from Allied forces. Hitler's proved a fatal strategic mistake, with cascading consequences, and it was, in hindsight, one of the few clearly visible turning points in the war. Just as earlier in the war Allied failure to penetrate Germany's air space revealed information, it was now the other way around. The German Air Force revealed a crucial, if obvious, bit of information: its increasing inability to defend its aerial borders. This induced substitution by the Allies, who started to pour more resources into ever less-costly deeper bombing runs into Germany.

How different things were before the air war was won. The British Bombing Survey Unit illustrates particularly well how war planners labored over picking targets for the strategic air campaign and how various bombing phases developed in light of the available information and the anticipated likelihood of successful runs. Under conditions of uncertainty and setbacks, expected costs and benefits were debated back and forth until this or that commander spoke the final word and set the force on a new course, only to be corrected when the costs proved high and the benefits slim. The returns diminished to such an extent that Arthur Harris abandoned strategic bombing altogether and for the remainder of his career took to obsessively bombing German cities and towns. In return, the Americans gave up on him. There was no way, no tool, no incentive, by which to convince him to change his behavior and stop splitting the limited resources of the air force. The situation would not change until the creation of a combined RAF/USAAF force under American command. This helped to mitigate an incentive alignment problem between British and American forces.

Operations

Finally, we take a look at the operations side of the strategic bombing of Germany. The principle of opportunity cost has already been illustrated with the transfer of command over the Allied air forces to Eisenhower to prepare for the invasion of Normandy.[69] To forgo the use of strategic forces merely because they were so designated would have been an unforgivable misstep. The cost would have been great, quite possibly the failure of the invasion.

The incremental cost/benefit principle has also already been mentioned in regard to the operations phase of the war. The disastrous bombing run on Schweinfurt proved so enormous a miscalculation that it forced the reevaluation of the expected cost of bombing incursions into German territory: for the next several months almost no bombing runs took place at all. Some information can only be obtained in "real time" by the winning and losing of battles. But moral hazard exists in that the men ordering battle are not the men to die. Those who give orders must be subject to a set of incentives (the possibility of being relieved from duty, reassigned, court-martialed, etc.) that induces them to deploy resources under their command to best effect. The fighting men depend on it with their lives. Moral hazard is an aspect of information asymmetry: only the officer knows whether his men really need to be sent into this or that particular battle. As with King David, who covets Bathsheba and sends her husband Uriah, a general, to die in battle, what are a commander's real intentions when he gives orders? What benevolent or malevolent purposes are hidden beneath the veneer of his uniform, the impressive status his rank conveys to the underlings? To overcome this incentive alignment problem, hierarchies must provide for oversight and recourse. These may include appeal to higher authorities up the rank, but more effective is the simple requirement that commanding officers fight with their men. If the officer is to face death, he will think twice about being heedless; if he is truly mad, a mutiny may well be sanctioned upon inquiry. In World War II, rear-area officers were prone to go along on bombing missions. In addition, ineffective commanders were often fired, showing how the moral hazard problem can and has been addressed.

An example of substitution in the operations phase of strategic bombing was the switch of nighttime for daytime bombing of Germany and of area bombing for precision bombing. An important premise of strategic bombing had been that economic assets of importance to Germany's war effort could be snuffed out by precisely targeting and eliminating them with "surgical" strikes. But in the early 1940s, the scalpel failed for the many reasons previously mentioned: cloudy weather frequently obscured targets resulting in a high percentage of flights returning with bomb-loads intact (as in the Kosovo war of 1999), target acquisition was done by eye until the later development of technically assisted target-sighting, the nimble German Air Force shot down many a slow bomber unescorted by fighter aircraft, and often the bomber crews did not even make it to their assigned targets, losing their way over German territory on account of primitive navigational aids. In frustration, "Bomber" Harris switched from precision bombing to area bombing, from the scalpel to the sledgehammer, which made a bloody mess but without affecting the substance of the war. And for the same set of reasons, that is, the vulnerability of the bomber fleet during daytime runs, Allied commanders switched to nighttime bombing. Of course, this did nothing to facilitate target acquisition, nor the effectiveness of the bombing, and was reflected in the diminishing marginal returns to the morale of the affected bombed population and the relative lack of destruction of industrial assets.

An example of overcoming hidden actions is an early story in the history of electronic warfare. The British, in the spring of 1940, had picked up clues about a system called Knickebein (the Brits called it Headache, not inappropriate in light of the problems Knickebein was to cause). The system actually was used in commercial and military aviation as a blind-landing device. A transmitter would send out parallel "dash" and "dot" pulses. If an airplane was on target, an on-board receiver would merge the two pulses into a steady tone. Deviation to the right or left of target would result in dash-tones or dot-tones predominating and allow the pilot to correct course. A young British physicist realized that the Germans used the system in reverse — not to guide planes home but to guide them away, to preset targets. Thus, a plane flying into the beam might first fly into a dash-pulse (prepare to drop bombs) and shortly thereafter cross the dot-pulse (drop bombs). Once the Brits discovered how the Germans guided their bombers, the RAF overcame the previously hidden action, Headache, by developing a countermeasure suitably called Aspirins: develop transmitters that fake the Knickebein beam and confuse the German pilots.[70]

As with the other chapters in this book, the main idea in this section is not to fully develop the story of how one can see the operation of economic principles in the strategic air war on Germany in World War II. Rather, it is to provide enough background and flavor to provoke the hypothesis that a fuller account for each one of the items in this section would be worth an article or chapter or book in its own right, that infusing the telling of history with economics may be a productive endeavor.

CONCLUSION

Reconsider an early quote in this chapter: "Strategic bombing bears the same relationship to tactical bombing as does the cow to the pail of milk. To deny immediate aid and comfort to the enemy, tactical considerations dictate upsetting the bucket. To ensure eventual starvation, the strategic move is to kill the cow."[71]

The strategic bombing of Germany in World War II did not "kill the cow." But shooting at the bucket did upset the cow just often enough to stop giving milk or, if it did give milk, to stop it from filling the bucket. The bombing did so, however, with diminishing returns, and the resources expended might well have been used to help prosecute the war in other areas. If the first bullet emptied half the bucket, the second emptied only half of the remaining half, and the third half of the half of the half. While resource application triples from one to three bullets, the amount of additional milk spilled diminishes from one-half to one-quarter to one-eighth. Just how empty does the bucket need to be before the exercise becomes pointless? If the victory threshold lies at reducing the milk in the bucket to one-sixteenth of its full contents, then a fourth bullet becomes necessary despite the diminishing returns. Thus we have not argued that bombing was useless, only that diminishing returns can be seen to have occurred.

If the simile may be taken further, much of the practical difficulty with strategic bombing lies in issues such as figuring where the cow is, if the cow is a cow or a decoy, or breaking through the barn to get at the cow. Thus we have argued that the Allied effort was not strategic but tactical bombing. It was in fact not to kill the cow, as the strategic bombing theorists imagined, but to make a commotion and to shoot at the bucket, as the field commanders in practice attempted. Of course, even tactical bombing is subject to diminishing returns (shown with examples from German arms, aircraft, fuel, and chemical production, as well as railroad loadings), and the practical difficulties here lie with issues such as finding the right buckets to shoot at, taking square aim, being close enough to take square aim, doing so in daylight or appropriately illuminating the bucket for nighttime, overcoming countermeasures that shield the bucket, and so on. A final point, not much considered in the chapter but very important to the actual conduct of the war, is that Nazi Germany's expansionist drive asked perhaps too much of the cow and its bucket: they could not give and hold all the milk required.

APPENDIX A

A Matrix for the Strategic Bombing Case

Principle	Manpower	Logistics	Technology	Planning	Operations
Opportunity cost	Albert Speer takes over war planning and production	D-Day: use of strategic air force for tactical purposes	dispersion of German production facilities	Hitler's personal insistence on building bombers, not fighters	using strategic forces for tactical purposes (push to Berlin)
Expected marginal costs/benefits	U.S. strategic forces transferred to North Africa in 1942/43	target selection: bomb German rail, water, or fuel supplies?	Use of add-on/drop-off fuel tanks to extend escort fighter range	BBSU: switching phases of the strategic bombing plans	Schweinfurt did not work: marginal benefit overestimated; marginal cost underestimated
Substitution	use of foreign/slave workers to free up Germans for front-line duty	German railroad system had many redundancies	synthetic fuel plants built in Germany	defeat of Luftwaffe finally lowered cost of deep penetration bombing runs	Allies substitute night for day bombing; area for "precision" bombing
Diminishing marginal returns	the 8th running operations in SE Europe while being based in North Africa	Allied bombers had insufficient number of escort bombers	German air plane production: plenty of aircraft but not pilots	"Bomber" Harris gives up on precision bombing, starts area bombing	morale bombing
Asymmetric information (overcoming) hidden characteristics	massive but ineffective bomber fleets correctly signal Allied weakness, 1940–1943	in lieu of reliable info, Allies speculate about German supply chain strength	Hitler fails to perceive signals regarding the P-51 and similar new Allied technologies	failure of Luftwaffe in air war reveals hidden characteristic; changes air war planning	moral hazard for commanding officers to send men to battle
Asymmetric information (overcoming) hidden actions	Nazi "culture" to police manpower mobilization and effort	desertion of transport convoys in final war stage; enforcement of "contracts" impossible	German state engages in risk-sharing by financing the construction of German industrial assets	creation of combined strategic air command mitigates incentive alignment problem	Knickebein, Headache, and Aspirins

APPENDIX B

Percentage of Allied Bombing Tonnage by Target Class by Month

Period	Aircraft factories	Airfields, aerodromes	Oil, rubber, chemicals, explosives	Land transportation	V-weapons launching sites
Dec. 1939	0.00	100.00	0.00	0.00	0.00
Jan.–Dec. 1940	0.00	50.00	50.00	0.00	0.00
	0.00	50.00	0.00	0.00	0.00
	0.00	88.46	0.00	0.00	0.00
	0.00	93.14	0.98	5.88	0.00
	0.00	10.00	19.22	41.25	0.00
	2.67	13.53	23.66	22.89	0.00
	4.95	22.33	17.44	15.03	0.00
	12.45	14.73	22.79	6.67	0.00
	1.30	4.79	4.36	12.63	0.00
	0.92	11.52	15.09	8.87	0.00
	2.82	11.38	13.35	12.23	0.00
	1.25	4.07	5.79	7.72	0.00
Jan.–Dec. 1941	0.06	1.48	7.96	5.05	0.00
	1.91	2.65	6.73	6.78	0.00
	2.56	2.90	7.44	4.16	0.00
	1.14	2.53	3.15	4.58	0.00
	0.00	1.91	6.44	22.32	0.00
	0.07	2.22	0.18	36.99	0.00
	0.41	3.07	1.44	15.82	0.00
	0.03	2.90	0.14	30.88	0.00
	0.38	1.75	2.33	19.40	0.00
	0.00	2.70	0.00	19.10	0.00
	0.00	0.99	0.08	0.74	0.00
	0.00	0.45	2.21	0.00	0.00
Jan.–Dec. 1942	1.30	2.21	0.00	0.00	0.00
	0.53	1.86	0.00	0.20	0.00
	0.00	0.50	0.00	0.27	0.00
	3.73	0.64	0.00	2.08	0.00
	6.14	0.96	0.14	0.14	0.00
	2.67	1.03	0.10	0.09	0.00

Naval and water transportation	Miscellaneous manufacturing	Industrial areas	Military targets	All other targets	RAF not classified
0.00	0.00	0.00	0.00	0.00	0.00
0.00	0.00	0.00	0.00	0.00	0.00
0.00	0.00	50.00	0.00	0.00	0.00
11.54	0.00	0.00	0.00	0.00	0.00
0.00	0.00	0.00	0.00	0.00	0.00
0.00	0.00	24.53	5.00	0.00	0.00
2.06	6.64	15.33	2.88	1.18	9.16
12.61	7.60	5.49	3.14	0.24	11.16
3.72	8.37	8.89	3.93	6.61	11.83
56.28	2.23	3.66	2.23	3.66	8.88
30.19	5.10	7.83	2.21	5.02	13.25
21.91	6.06	8.19	6.54	4.26	13.24
19.52	3.55	18.74	3.71	1.93	33.72
16.27	0.65	25.18	1.54	0.59	41.21
24.63	0.26	33.45	0.74	1.87	20.98
32.27	4.71	25.84	0.80	0.38	18.95
34.93	6.99	32.23	1.17	0.49	12.80
26.19	1.47	26.39	0.70	1.47	13.12
16.93	1.23	32.05	1.89	0.96	7.46
19.39	3.24	44.50	0.35	2.37	9.40
10.36	5.00	34.86	0.98	1.10	13.75
23.10	8.16	23.21	1.59	0.40	19.67
20.44	0.90	31.41	6.54	0.14	18.78
14.54	0.18	37.37	0.05	0.05	46.02
32.07	0.00	21.07	0.00	0.03	44.17
44.55	0.00	32.84	0.10	0.00	19.01
27.83	0.00	32.21	0.00	0.00	37.38
7.04	12.97	68.00	0.00	0.71	10.50
17.63	7.33	58.45	0.26	0.56	9.31
7.47	4.77	60.68	0.09	0.53	19.09
1.95	0.01	72.97	0.03	0.34	20.81

(continued)

APPENDIX B

Continued

Period	Aircraft factories	Airfields, aerodromes	Oil, rubber, chemicals, explosives	Land transportation	V-weapons launching sites
	0.00	1.13	0.00	0.27	0.00
	0.22	1.19	0.01	0.51	0.00
	1.91	0.25	0.04	0.53	0.00
	3.37	1.28	4.18	3.86	0.00
	5.22	0.96	0.00	1.24	0.00
	2.80	1.21	0.00	5.12	0.00
Jan.–Dec. 1943	0.00	3.61	0.25	6.43	0.15
	0.03	0.81	0.19	1.63	0.00
	0.00	1.81	0.22	7.30	0.00
	3.05	5.02	0.00	3.26	0.00
	0.85	6.07	0.29	2.17	0.00
	2.28	5.39	1.60	4.18	0.00
	3.39	13.83	2.20	7.28	0.00
	1.47	8.64	6.13	15.11	0.00
	1.42	13.37	0.05	0.05	0.00
	2.73	7.43	0.94	14.57	0.00
	1.05	5.59	2.23	13.25	0.92
	2.18	7.93	3.31	13.53	3.37
Jan.–Dec. 1944	4.35	8.65	1.89	1.89	6.51
	9.59	9.66	0.25	8.88	2.95
	5.08	9.75	0.13	23.45	2.78
	9.02	10.07	1.44	39.57	4.28
	3.50	11.14	4.03	40.08	2.10
	1.28	10.26	9.52	28.02	7.16
	3.10	4.50	13.38	20.75	3.74
	3.94	11.66	14.86	17.45	1.17
	0.95	5.43	9.56	23.67	0.00
	0.91	2.42	9.89	22.95	0.00
	0.38	1.64	25.83	24.71	0.00
	0.14	3.07	11.04	51.28	0.01

Naval and water transportation	Miscellaneous manufacturing	Industrial areas	Military targets	All other targets	RAF not classified
10.34	0.02	49.79	0.07	0.13	38.25
1.62	0.09	61.78	0.59	0.07	33.91
1.48	0.07	68.42	0.03	0.13	27.14
1.93	0.08	50.47	0.00	0.07	34.76
11.05	0.09	28.74	0.00	0.00	52.71
5.42	2.06	55.73	0.26	1.41	25.99
24.24	1.45	42.40	1.56	3.30	16.61
39.04	0.47	49.65	0.35	1.24	6.60
15.80	15.36	39.92	0.54	2.44	16.62
10.60	3.75	52.73	1.91	2.88	16.81
15.88	2.68	55.14	2.34	6.38	8.21
6.53	0.24	55.35	10.43	4.33	9.67
3.41	1.29	48.18	1.21	6.84	12.38
2.46	6.82	38.62	1.92	5.05	13.76
3.32	3.46	35.83	3.79	5.51	12.93
5.50	1.88	49.73	1.51	5.54	10.17
6.22	2.86	49.76	2.86	4.94	10.33
5.95	3.51	47.10	3.57	4.32	5.23
4.30	1.75	40.71	2.61	6.73	7.11
3.43	2.83	32.18	7.34	11.12	11.77
2.44	2.63	37.50	2.89	6.43	6.93
1.97	2.02	17.98	4.07	3.59	6.00
2.79	1.11	9.69	15.30	3.91	6.35
2.16	0.49	11.26	13.20	10.11	6.53
1.33	2.36	28.68	7.07	7.94	7.15
2.95	1.17	21.51	12.01	5.09	8.20
1.32	4.90	12.22	28.55	3.15	10.25
0.93	7.68	33.93	11.97	2.97	6.35
0.22	0.47	27.89	8.45	4.25	6.16
1.47	2.31	15.44	4.37	5.90	4.96

(*continued*)

APPENDIX B

Continued

Period	Aircraft factories	Airfields, aerodromes	Oil, rubber, chemicals, explosives	Land transportation	V-weapons launching sites
Jan.–May 1945	0.00	3.61	0.25	6.43	0.15
	0.03	0.81	0.19	1.63	0.00
	0.00	1.81	0.22	7.30	0.00
	3.05	5.02	0.00	3.26	0.00
	0.41	6.18	6.14	35.53	0.16
Overall percentage for Jan. 1939 to May 1945	2.06	6.10	9.54	27.20	1.43

Source: Computed from USSBS, February 1947, chart 6.

Note: The last line in the table is the overall percentage per target class. For example, of the 2,770,237 tons of bombs dropped by USAAF and RAF, 2.06 percent were intended for aircraft factories.

Naval and water transportation	Miscellaneous manufacturing	Industrial areas	Military targets	All other targets	RAF not classified
1.61	1.39	16.89	2.82	5.19	5.90
1.56	1.19	21.33	3.59	5.54	7.66
5.10	4.23	19.94	3.89	4.68	7.18
7.63	0.90	11.20	15.43	5.44	10.97
1.31	0.00	18.78	10.05	0.08	43.66
3.90	2.53	24.95	8.36	5.24	8.70

SEVEN

The Age of the Cold War, 1945–1991

The Case of Capital-Labor Substitution and France's Force de Frappe

On 13 February 1960, a sixty-kiloton atomic explosion at Regane, Algeria, signaled the birth of France's nuclear force. It would become known as the *force de frappe,* or "strike force," although the French inventors of this term quickly regretted the name's aggressive implications and unsuccessfully attempted to substitute *force de dissuasion*. Dissuasion appealed to French military thinkers more than deterrence, the latter relying more on terror, the former including an appeal to reason.[1]

To most Frenchmen and to the larger world the name of the new creation seemed unimportant. Yet at Regane, France had changed forever the nature of the global nuclear confrontation. The bomb itself did not represent a scientific breakthrough. Although thrice the size of Hiroshima's, it was only 1/1,900th of the Soviet Union's most powerful hydrogen bomb. Nor was France even the first medium power to join the superpowers in the nuclear club, for Britain had set off its first bomb eight years earlier.[2] But France was the first country to break the superpower monopoly. For while the British force was linked to America's, France had opted for nuclear independence. It was not always so. While French officers and scientists had labored for many years on the project expecting it to be tied closely to NATO or the United States (which increasingly looked like the same thing to them), Charles de Gaulle, France's president (1958–1969), had opted for a separate course, and he now had the means to do so.

Regane's impact on the nuclear-strategic world was clouded by uncertainty about how to interpret France's achievement. By the 1960s, the superpowers were capable of destroying each other, and perhaps all life, with the strategic weapons they had developed, and how to use, or prevent the use of nuclear weapons had engaged brilliant thinkers in many countries. Mutual atomic warfare was and remains a subject of theory, untempered by experience. Although two bombs fell in August 1945, they struck a power that did not possess such weapons, whose allies had been destroyed, and which could not conceivably win the war even if it did continue to fight. This differed much from the nuclear-armed superpower situation in 1960. Volumes had been written about the two-power Cold War confrontation, but as far as nuclear weapons were concerned, it all remained speculative. French political scientist and strategist Raymond Aron conceded as much by asking, "Who can ever be absolutely sure of anything, in speculation of this sort?"[3]

The addition of a third force, a medium-sized power pursuing the nuclear option — independent of either Cold War side yet being associated with one — would complicate the picture even more. General de Gaulle, in 1960, had no compunctions about this, nor was there any reason to. But for strategists to make sense of France's intentions, and to correctly place her nuclear options into elegant if complex mathematical models, an understanding of her intentions was critical. Those who found the name of France's strategic doctrine unimportant were wrong. The linguistic subtlety of "deterrence" versus "dissuasion" did matter because when studying nuclear warfare doctrine, ideas, and the thought processes of potential adversaries, matter.

The force de frappe and the ideas behind it form the subject matter of this chapter. Mostly we are concerned with the economic principle of substitution. Did France purchase a nuclear force as a substitute for an existing or prospective alternative, most obviously conventional forces? The principle of substitution holds that if two goods yield comparable benefits users will drift, ceteris paribus, toward the good with the lower relative price.[4] In military terms, substitution might take place in several ways. For example, nuclear weapons (capital) might be acquired to substitute for conscripted military manpower (labor) if the price of capital is low relative to that of labor. This might be affected by the perceived cost, monetary or otherwise, including public reactions to casualties and conscription and by costs such as the forgone civilian contribution of conscripted forces.

It is important to emphasize relative costs. For example, even though he hardly possessed a surfeit of capital, Soviet premier Nikita Khrushchev built expensive strategic rocket forces partly because he wanted to reduce the even more expensive quantity of labor in the military. In a similar vein, the United States built coastal forts in the nineteenth century because this was less expensive than maintaining a powerful ocean-going fleet.[5] To answer the question whether the principle of substitution can be applied to the case of nuclear weapons requires an understanding of what is meant by the reference to comparable benefits. The outcomes of the alternatives being compared do not have to be identical. Nuclear weapons are so different — and so may be the benefits—from the conventional kind that they are difficult to compare. Although some officers and analysts persisted in seeing similarities until almost the time of Regane, for most the fundamental differences between nuclear and conventional weapons manifested themselves immediately after Hiroshima. Quite apart from the moral dimension of any use, even in operational terms such weapons are difficult to integrate into warfare or warfare gaming scenarios. For example, tactical nuclear weapons might invite a strategic response, giving them a characteristic not found in any conventional weapon.

Atomic weapons' capacity for instant and widespread destruction has no equal. A city, even an entire country, can be eliminated in a flash. French military strategist and nuclear force proponent André Beaufre considered the threat of nuclear war an entirely new level of conflict, "a new and overriding factor in the international balance and a form of armed contest at once possible and morally inadmissible." This moral dimension places special limitations on their use, limitations not found with conventional weapons. Indeed, author Robert Jervis criticized American nuclear strategists for "conventionalization," namely, "attributing to nuclear weapons a variety of uses for which conventional weapons have historically been appropriate." Because of the power ascribed to nuclear weapons, most models of their use assumed a single-move scenario, after which things are literally over. Paradoxically, unlike a multiple-move war of the conventional kind, single-move scenarios could be modeled mathematically, much as the final checkmate move in chess is easier to model than it is to model a complete chess game from the start.[6]

That a nuclear force can do things in wartime that conventional weapons cannot does not mean that there can be no substitution. Nuclear weapons may be different, but they can be substituted for conventional weapons—if raw power is the main criterion. Military expenditure allocations have to take place under a budget constraint, and the great power of the atomic bomb made it an enticing alternative to conventional forces: a cheap "lump" of undifferentiated great power as set against more graduated, and hence more flexible but also more expensive, smaller "lumps" of conventional power. Indeed, U.S. president Eisenhower's New Look strategy was based on this very idea, or to use the popular phrase of the time "more bang for the buck." The French saw the point, too. Charles Ailleret, a great advocate of strategic nuclearization, wrote in 1954 that "atomic weapons are . . . inexpensive weapons in contrast to classic weapons [and] constitute the criterion of a modern army." The presence of American nuclear deterrence drove down European conventional spending, and when President Kennedy shifted to a "flexible response" strategy it was rejected in Europe precisely because it required much more conventional force spending.[7]

Substitution was explicitly discussed by Pentagon planners as they attempted to modernize its budgeting and decision-making processes. Charles J. Hitch, an advisor to Secretary of Defense Robert McNamara, argued that "strategy and cost are as interdependent as the front and rear sights of a rifle" and that "tradeoffs or substitution possibilities . . . depend upon questions of cost and effectiveness, which in turn depend upon technology. . . . The choice of a particular military strategy or military objective cannot be divorced from the cost of achieving it." Hitch notes that there is nothing radical about this notion: President Truman in 1945 had stated that "strategy, program and budget are all aspects of the same basic decisions."[8]

In a broad sense, conventional and nuclear forces certainly may provide comparable benefits. Both are weapons of war, both are managed by military establishments although with different levels of control, possession of either may enhance real or perceived national security, both can destroy an enemy, and both provide deterrence although in greatly different degrees. Thus, the comparable benefit of atomic and conventional weaponry lies in that either can be used to prosecute or deter war, and the question of substituting one for the other naturally does arise. Yet nuclear weapons come with a unique set of benefits, unavailable to conventional arms. Beaufre refers to the "dissuasive or persuasive pressure" that atomic weapons exert.[9] The threat of their use, or further use, is greater than anything that conventional weapons can provide. Their power makes their political-diplomatic punch much greater than anything that could be achieved with the threat of use of conventional weapons. But every arm, not just the atomic one, features unique attributes even if they are comparatively minor. For instance, armies may substitute the firepower of armor and artillery for infantry or vice versa, but no one has ever attempted warfare with just one of these. Conventional war without air cover is inconceivable, but the airplane has not abolished the infantryman (chap. 6). And indeed no nuclear nation abandoned its conventional forces. Substitution is a matter of degree.

We begin this chapter by tracing the history of France's force de frappe, both before and after de Gaulle. The reasons used to justify the construction of the force are examined next, and then we probe its effect on France's conventional arms and argue that substitution of conventional by nuclear arms did in fact take place. We round out the chapter by suggesting how the other economic principles explored in this book (those other than the principle of substitution) might be applied to the case of the force de frappe.

HISTORY OF THE FORCE DE FRAPPE

A completely conventionally armed nation might be at the mercy of a nuclear opponent, but a nuclear nation might not be able to impress a nonnuclear, ruthless enemy. One of the early great nuclear theoreticians, Bernard Brodie, pointed out that governments had "never responded to the horrific implications of war in a uniform way" and that "great nations have very recently been ruled by men who were supremely indifferent to horror." The Napoleonic age notwithstanding, its strategic position had been in decline since the early eighteenth century, and France did not possess the indifference of which Brodie spoke. In 1945 it could look back upon a century of defeats, including disastrous ones in the Franco-Prussian War and World War II, and surviving World War I only because of Herculean efforts on the part of its allies. Security had been sought through alliances and massive fortifications (the Maginot Line), but these approaches had been found wanting. Atomic weapons promised a solution to quantitative inferiority. But the road to Regane was not short, nor simple. Recovering from World War II while fighting two significant wars, in Indochina and in Algeria, France possessed limited resources for atomic development, and nuclear decisions were made with some hesitation and lack of clarity, at least prior to de Gaulle's return in 1958. Consequently, from 1945 to 1960 France debated and prepared for its coming nuclear status; between 1960 and 1996 it was an operational nuclear power; and the post-1996 period has been called a "strategic pause" while the country reassesses its options.[10]

Origins

World War II had left France humiliated and divided. More than ever it was aware of its strategic vulnerability born of demographics and geography. To be sure, Germany was now in worse shape, but there was no reason to believe that that was to become an eternal circumstance, even as the totalitarian threat now had a Red face. Furthermore, France did not relish the possibility of domination by its Anglo-Saxon allies, a consideration that influences French foreign policy to this day. French leaders had not forgotten their exclusion from the major wartime conferences.[11] All of these considerations required that France be a major military power.

Acquiring a nuclear option was not the immediate answer. Because of the outbreak of the Indochina War, France could not afford to shrink its army and conventional forces were urgently needed to protect western Europe. A series of crises showed that French conventional power was deficient and that atomic weapons were needed to make up the difference. Under the circumstances, the question perhaps is not why France took the nuclear plunge but how it could have done otherwise.[12] France did have some advantages. The much-maligned Maginot Line demonstrated that the nation was willing to support major technological endeavors if they promised security. And France also had a first-rate history of nuclear chemistry and physics, symbolized by the Curies.

The Fourth Republic

While the Fourth Republic had the motives and some of the means to start a nuclear program, it did not have money or certainty.[13] France could not afford large military capital expenditure. The much-maligned Fourth spent its entire history waging unsuccessful overseas wars. "Indochina (1946–54) and Algeria (1954–58) were the cancer of the regime, a military running sore, which eventually proved terminal." One weakness led to another. Because operating costs prevented expenditure on military capital, France's army lagged behind those of its allies, and the country received subordinate roles in NATO. The lack of certainty in policy is equally understandable: the average French government between 1946 and 1958 lasted six months.[14]

This background has led to a remarkably confused history of the French decision to make "the bomb." No official decision was made until 11 April 1958, when Premier Felix Gaillard decided upon the manufacture of atomic bombs, but in reality the project had been underway for some time, though without a final decision from the top. "France drifted toward the possession of an atomic bomb without the project ever receiving official sanction at the cabinet level." Instead, and quite typically, planning and discussions proceeded among France's soldiers and powerful *fonctionnaires*. A foreign ministry official and member of the Atomic Energy Committee suggested that the bomb was "a sort of by-product of an officially peaceful effort."[15] "In the face of vacillation and indecisiveness by the government, and unawareness and abdication of responsibility by Parliament, policy issues were debated and resolved at another level, and the elaboration of a military atomic program was guided by a small group of persons from the CEA [Commissariat à l'Énergie Atomique], the military and the Government."[16] In fact, several sets of decision processes were going on, perhaps less confusing in reality than they appear in retrospect (which would, for once, reverse the historical tendency to impose clarity where none exists). Government could not issue a clear policy since the matter was, after all, a function of its foreign policy, which was in a state of perpetual flux due to the overseas wars. The situation on the ground was more responsible for the confusion than were the governments. Outwardly, however, things did look confused: "For it was not a single decision, a clear-cut long-range policy rationally planned and executed, but rather a series of events and decisions — or, perhaps, lack of decisions — which led to the Sahara test in 1960."[17]

It is more helpful to divide the republic's move toward the atomic bomb into two phases — the bureaucratic phase, and the political phase. During the former, from 1946 to 1954, there was little cabinet-level guidance in the military-nuclear sphere (although there was in the civil). In 1946, Colonel Charles Ailleret assembled an army group to study nuclear physics and its applications to military modernization. By 1949, the army's technical section contained a unit for the study of nuclear weapons. In 1950, discussions were held on the possibilities of atomic war. Ailleret became head of the Armes Spéciales section on 1 January 1952, assuring that his office would become a strong advocate for nuclear weapons.[18] While this may seem episodic and low-level, it was not. The senior generals were interested in what he was doing. Civil-nuclear expenditure was rising, and interest in military applications was substantial.

The political phase, from 1954 to 1958, was everything but smooth and driven by outside events, the more notable of which included Dien Bien Phu, the Suez crisis of 1956, and the 1958 proposed American testing moratorium. In 1954, the plight of part of the French army at Dien Bien Phu had led the French government to ask for American assistance, and the possible use of American nuclear weapons (Operation Vulture) was discussed extensively. Nineteen fifty-four is often viewed as the year that the "basic decision" for an independent nuclear force was reached, albeit secretly. Ailleret had gained an influential ally when an internal foreign service report concluded that "strategic leadership increasingly belongs to those powers possessing nuclear weapons." In December 1954, the issue was confronted by the cabinet for the first time. Premier Mendès-France chaired an interministerial committee that failed, however, to reach a consensus. But the premier was sympathetic, and the civilian Commissariat à l'Énergie Atomique (CEA) continued to study military options. Technically, neither Mendès-France nor his successor, Edgar Faure, made an official decision in favor of an atomic bomb program, but this may have been because France was not ready to build one and had nothing to gain by making an announcement. But the Faure government established the Bureau d'Études Générales, under General Albert Buchalet, to proceed secretly with military applications. For Ailleret, this represented for all intents and purposes an official decision to manufacture an atomic bomb, premierial demurrers notwithstanding. But here again reality, rather than policy, became the problem. The military's attention and resources became focused on the growing war in Algeria.[19]

In 1956, France, Britain, and Israel reoccupied the Sinai but were forced into a humiliating withdrawal in the face of Soviet threats and lack of American support. France concluded that a stark line existed between nuclear and nonnuclear powers, and apparently so did Israel. Defense Minister Bourgès-Manoury saw the question not as whether France would manufacture atomic weapons but whether she would have an effective national defense. Premier Guy Mollet agreed to convene a group of senior officers to discuss the matter. From the group, led by Chief of Staff Paul Ély, there emerged the idea that France could increase deterrence (or dissuasion) "by increasing the number of nuclear centers of decision in the Alliance, thus multiplying the uncertainty facing an enemy contemplating an attack." This reflected the view of Mollet (or perhaps vice versa), who saw the French force mainly as a potential backup for U.S. and U.K. weapons. Technically, Mollet did not decide to make a bomb, but he did favor building the capacity to make it. Arguably in 1956 this was a distinction without a difference, but politically useful for a Socialist premier. In 1956, Mollet ensured that France retained its military atomic rights relative to its relationship with EURATOM, the French Senate went on record as supporting nuclear weapons possession, the CEA and the Ministry of National Defense signed a formal agreement establishing a military program, and Ailleret was appointed as commander of the Commandement des Armes Spéciales to plan the tests. The Suez crisis may not have created the French bomb, but it certainly sped up the program.[20]

No major crisis triggered the final, official decision to detonate France's first atomic bomb. Felix Gaillard's official order of 11 April 1958 was influenced by a number of factors. The East-West balance appeared increasingly unfavorable, the Soviet Union appeared to be ahead in missile development, France's relationship with NATO was deteriorating, and SPUTNIK had visibly shaken America. The American proposal to end nuclear testing may also have added some urgency to the program. Secrecy was no longer necessary. The Bureau d'Études Générales now became the less euphemistic Direction des Applications Militaires. At the time of Gaillard's order, the Fourth Republic was only months away from extinction, but it had made the decision so often attributed to de Gaulle, and for some of the same reasons.[21]

As is often the case with new weapons and doctrines, the pressure for their development had come from the lower and middle levels of the military, not the top. Inevitably, this meant a lack of doctrinal clarity—not initially a bad thing as immediate consensus on doctrine could have stifled creative thinking.

Doctrinal issues were not resolved in this era, however. Would the French force be completely independent, or tied to NATO, or tied to someone else? Would it be purely strategic or tactical, a supplement to the conventional arms? Would the force be composed of land, sea, or air elements, or a combination thereof? What role could a small nuclear force play, politically or militarily? Would the French bomb merely act as a trigger to bring the U.S. deterrent into play?[22]

Creativity was not supplemented with thoroughness. French officials did little to consider the effectiveness, credibility, cost, or cost-effectiveness of the weapons, and there was little study of the use or credibility of a small or medium-sized nuclear force. Such study would have been highly theoretical, to be sure. The development of consensus on nuclear doctrine was also hampered by the army's development of a new conventional doctrine. One idea that gained some prominence was that there were now two types of war — guerilla war and large-scale war — and that the latter would be deterred by nuclear weapons. "For neither one would a large conventional force be needed, it was thought." While this conception had limited appeal to France's senior generals, certainly no Frenchman wanted to see the country's conventional forces becoming cannon fodder for NATO; yet this was a real possibility because France's most likely contribution would be infantrymen. The memory of World War I was strong.[23]

Various officers floated important ideas. Admiral Raoul Castex suggested as early as 1945 that a small power with a few nuclear weapons could deter a much stronger power. He thereby laid the foundation for "proportional deterrence," a concept under which a smaller nuclear power can deter a larger one by being able to threaten a cost that is greater than the value of the destruction of the smaller power. More significant was the influence of Ailleret, later chief of staff, and Pierre Gallois, a future general who would greatly influence Charles de Gaulle. Gallois's national influence began with a series of lectures given in 1956 to 1958, at the very end of the Fourth Republic.[24]

Ailleret's role, of course, began somewhat earlier. In 1949, he was asked to write a short history of armaments and realized that a device now existed that changed not only weaponry but potentially both tactics and strategy. Obliteration of the enemy, which once had been the hoped-for result of artillery and then of air power, was now possible. Nuclear weapons made reality of the theories of Giulio Douhet, the Italian apostle of strategic bombing in the 1920s. Nuclear weapons could shatter enemy resistance, which conventional strategic bombing had failed to do in Europe. For the first time, the enemy's military potential, even its very existence, could be threatened from a distance. Soon Ailleret began to question whether traditional battle was even possible in the nuclear era. Not surprisingly, the army clung to this possibility longer than Ailleret. For example, in its 1954 exercises, the army limited the available number of (hypothetical) atomic bombs and understated their effects. Ailleret's critiques of these unrealistic limits were not appreciated. But even figures more sympathetic saw the new bombs as useful only for strategic bombing.[25] Nuclear strategy coupled with traditional strategic air power doctrine threatened to substitute nuclear weapons for the conventional military establishment altogether. Yet Ailleret was not a lone wolf, and his career did not suffer. As the Fourth Republic searched for an innovative military solution to its problems, it reached out to pronuclear officers. Ailleret, Gallois, and others were ready and willing to act whenever the political establishment gave them the opportunity.

When this opportunity arose, the military and civilian bureaucracies had already mostly come around to supporting nuclear weapons development. Political movements on the left and the right were in favor, the latter to restore France's greatness, the former to avoid Cold War rigidity. The military's position was complicated. While military journals began advocating nuclear weapons in 1946, many military men were skeptical of the effect of atomic weapons on their services' effectiveness. Fear that the western alliance would be dominated by nuclear powers changed a few minds. CEA administrator-general Pierre Guillaumat, appointed in 1951, favored nuclear-military applications. The military mistrusted the CEA, however, regarding it as being too closely related to the communists, and imposed rigid security on its nuclear manufacturing site at Marcoule. Security was so tight that the engineer who had designed the control mechanisms was not permitted to see them because his father was a communist. Ironically, this was the time that American law forbade the sharing of nuclear secrets with France because of the presence of communists in the French government. Naturally this further increased Franco-American friction and the French desire for an independent deterrent — overcoming some military objectors.[26]

Military support for nuclear weapons increased in 1954, although it was not unanimous, as Mendès-France discovered. The valid fear that nuclear development would cut conventional spending was strong in an army that not only had many overseas commitments but was being defeated in Indochina. The military calculated that the bomb could be developed in five years, a very reasonable estimate as it turned out. But what may have turned the most uniformed heads were not the inherent problems exposed by Dien Bien Phu and Suez, but rather their international military implications. In neither case, for instance, had the American ally helped, and these two huge crises had only been two years apart. In addition, NATO increasingly based its strategy on nuclear weapons. Thus, to a growing group of officers, atomic weapons looked like the way out of France's strategic conundrums.[27]

De Gaulle Arrives

Charles de Gaulle did not launch France's nuclear program, as we have seen, but his role was crucial nonetheless. During eleven years as leader of France he was an unswerving advocate of the force de frappe. He understood its implications in military affairs, gave it a political foundation, and used it to achieve foreign, domestic, and military goals. By lending his massive prestige and fame to the atomic bomb he made it a symbol of French patriotism. He was also in a better position to face foreign opposition than his predecessors, and he gave the bomb program its form, as doctrine finally began to evolve. This did not begin until the political decision to proceed had been made.[28]

The influence of Ailleret remained steady (he eventually became chief of staff). De Gaulle's confidence in Ailleret can be seen in his appointment as commander in Algeria in 1961–1962, when France was negotiating peace while facing an army-based terrorist movement trying to stop independence. At least as influential was Pierre Marie Gallois, one of the first nuclear advocates to meet with de Gaulle, two years before the latter's return to power. Although the idea had come up earlier, Gallois was the father of proportional deterrence, a doctrine that began with the concept of "minimum deterrence." "When two nations are armed with nuclear weapons, even if they are unequally armed, the status quo is inevitable . . . Under certain conditions, a new form of equality can be established among nations. In questions of security and defense, there can no longer be strong nations and weak nations — at least in facing certain decisions."[29]

Traditional military notions of time and space were abolished by nuclear arms. Atomic weapons, Gallois believed, had leveled the relation between great and small, neutralized the power of mass armies, equalized demographics, contracted geographical distances, limited the benefits of large space, and — in a view clearly aimed at Russia — eliminated "General Winter." Proportional deterrence was more sophisticated, based on the concept of being able to do more damage than the enemy is willing to suffer for the sake of destroying the smaller power. In the case of the Soviet Union it was clear what could be targeted: the leadership. Stephen Cimbala comments that "this is precisely why a small nuclear force, if it can penetrate to its targets and those targets are highly valued intrinsically (as seats of government are), can be very menacing. In particular, with reference to the Soviet Union, the nuclear forces of Britain and France, small only in comparison to U.S. and Soviet forces, loom large in Kremlin planning."[30]

Gallois's proposals became increasingly radical—especially as he sought to substitute nuclear weapons for all arms, complete substitution—and this may have blunted his long-term influence. But he had laid the foundation. His views, especially those on proportional deterrence and the political ability to threaten with atomic weapons, appealed to André Beaufre, who after his retirement became one of France's most famous authors on strategy. Echoing Maurice de Saxe, Beaufre stressed violence as a means, not an end. "Cold War" was an entirely new form of war. A nuclear balance of power was actually more stable than a conventional one and also set limits to conventional war. Adversaries might fight conventionally but simultaneously engage in a psychological struggle with nuclear weapons. Beaufre stressed the differences between the conventional and the nuclear. Deterrence by a smaller power was possible but only in a purely defensive way. He endorsed minimum deterrence and was one of the few willing to put a number on the concept. Beaufre argued that equality between adversaries is reached if the weaker power could destroy at least 15 percent of the human and material resources of the greater enemy.[31]

De Gaulle did not demonstrate any predilection for theoretical arguments concerning doctrine, contenting himself with the larger issues and justifications (more on this later). His interest in nuclear arms long preceded even his meeting with Gallois. Moving swiftly on acceding to leadership, he declared that the nuclear force was "above all an instrument of policy, a means to an end, which is not so much security as independence, a diplomatic advantage that reinforces the status of this country and expands the role it may play." In 1959 de Gaulle told French officers in closed session that France must have a striking force, that its basis had to be nuclear weapons, and that it should be able to act anywhere on earth. Only in the most dire circumstances would they actually be used.[32]

The result of de Gaulle's stance was remarkable. On 7 January 1959, France embarked on a reorganization of its military establishment described as the most important since Napoleon. The military establishment was to consist of a nuclear strategic force, a homeland security force, and an intervention force. Nuclear weapons lay at the heart of this system, as "all other aspects of national defense served to complement it." Fifty single-bomb aircraft would form the first phase, to be followed by intermediate-range missiles and nuclear-armed submarines. Although planning for the Sahara test was well underway, de Gaulle's government moved quickly toward developing a more suitable site in Polynesia. The speed of these developments was astonishing, especially after the Fourth Republic's tendency to pass each major question to the next cabinet. Yet it is not conceivable that de Gaulle could have made these decisions on the spur of the moment. He accepted the concepts of minimum deterrence and proportional deterrence but demonstrated his respect for the shifting fortunes of war by not committing himself completely. He left France linked to NATO (although barely) so that France could benefit from a Soviet belief that an attack on France would bring NATO into the war. This hedging may have reflected his awareness that military doctrine, no matter how good, is a poor adversary for the frictions of war, and even of peace. Moreover, even de Gaulle could not prevent traditional interservice rivalries. According to Alexandre Sanguinetti, a powerful Gaullist, "as soon as the doctrine of nuclear dissuasion was adopted, the various branches engaged in a merciless struggle regarding now limited funds, in order to retain as much as possible of their traditional structures, presenting these, by ingenious arguments, as being integral parts of deterrence, thus as having the same priority." De Gaulle's concern was never with the abstractions of nuclear doctrine. In public, his officials seemed to share this view. The official military doctrines for the force de frappe "hardly developed in official statements beyond the most general propositions."[33]

The Evolution of the Force in the De Gaulle Era

It is commonly accepted that doctrine should determine weapons selection and that it should justify specific decisions made. Military doctrine was necessary to sort out the services' competing claims for deterrent roles (or, in the army's case, for tactical nuclear capacity). In some ways doctrine appeared quite stable. For example, the doctrine of proportional deterrence remained in force throughout the 1960s and not only gave the force more credibility but furnished justifications for its limited size. In the words of one analyst, the force was "alleged to be proportional in strategic capacity to France's political interests."[34]

A second relatively stable doctrine saw warfare with nuclear powers as inevitably going nuclear. Sanguinetti stated in 1964 that war against an atomic enemy would require "the total employment of nuclear weaponry when the stake of the struggle is our national territory and our people." This formulation—that nuclear weapons would be used, and only be used, to protect the national home—became known as "sanctuarization." Since the Soviet Union shared this belief in the inevitability of escalation, the threat of escalation was viewed by the French as the best deterrent (or dissuasion).[35]

But if war came and escalation was inevitable, what use were the conventional forces and did tactical weapons have a role to play? Here the consensus seemed to break down. Ailleret favored immediate strategic retaliation once a major conventional clash had occurred and was therefore willing to forego tactical nuclear weapons development. The regular army would be a trigger. He even considered placing the conventional forces in the wake of nuclear action. Others were less sure, believing that there should be a tactical nuclear "test" of the enemy before strategic weapons were fired. Ailleret also announced, in 1967, a far more controversial doctrine known as *tous azimuts*, the idea that the strategic force should be able to strike in all directions. The idea of a global strike force had been proposed in principle by de Gaulle in 1959 and in 1961, but Ailleret went further. He believed France needed global missiles to protect itself from threats everywhere and denounced reliance on alliances. De Gaulle confirmed the new doctrine in 1968, but it was never truly implemented.[36] His administration would soon unravel at any rate, and Ailleret (and his wife and daughter) were killed in an airplane accident on Réunion Island that to this day is surrounded by conspiracy theories, for no particularly good reason.

Although de Gaulle and Ailleret left an impressive force behind, difficulties remained. France and Britain were the only states to develop small versions of superpower arsenals, and France's enjoyed the advantages of independence. Rising expense, however, had forced curtailment of spending on the other sectors of the military establishment. The Mirage IV bomber force was on line by 1964, but nuclear missiles and nuclear-armed submarines had to wait for the next decade. De Gaulle's generals were forced to make subtle doctrinal adjustments. In 1958 the concept was *strike, intervene, survive,* while five years later it had shifted to *deter, intervene, defend,* which was more flexible and acknowledged the slower than expected development of the force.[37]

THE FORCE POST–DE GAULLE

De Gaulle's successor, Georges Pompidou (1969–1974), inherited a nuclear force that was behind schedule and conventional forces that were starved of resources. A solid Gaullist, he had fought for the nuclear force in parliament, but under his presidency the weapons' role in foreign policy declined. So did military spending as demand for more domestic services fed, in part, the May 1968 crisis, the massive Parisian student-worker demonstrations that had nearly toppled de Gaulle's government. One of the crisis's resulting casualties was Ailleret's tous azimuts policy. His successor as chief of staff, Michel Fourquet, dropped all references to it and instead proposed that French forces would "normally act in close coordination with the forces of our Allies." This shift away from tous azimuts was easy to make because others in the military thought that it warped spending, made national defense too elitist, and would only work, paradoxically, with strong alliances.[38]

Nuclear advocates consoled themselves with the thought that superpower arms reductions might strengthen France's relative power, but this hardly made up for their own problems. One of these was that "sanctuarization" actually made sense: the force was not credible as a deterrent to protect an ally, only to protect France. Moreover, how could France offer credible guarantees when its own force was based on doubts about American guarantees? How could France play a role in deterring threats to western Europe if the core of the force could not be used, even politically? Ailleret had suggested stationing the French army in western Germany to fight for the French border — but could a French army stop Soviet forces that had defeated American, British, and German forces? Something intermediate was needed, something that would permit graduated responses in a crisis. Fourquet developed the "test of enemy intentions," which might be made with conventional forces or with small or tactical nuclear strikes in the enemy rear. He was attempting to find a middle ground between the existing all-or-nothing approach and the American-inspired flexible-response strategy. The army would be more than a trip wire and provide government with additional time to decide about using atomic weapons. Simply abandoning Germany was not possible; such a policy might lead to a significantly rearmed, perhaps nuclear-armed, neighbor. Yet France could not afford a significantly enlarged conventional army either.[39]

Pompidou's successor, Valéry Giscard d'Estaing (1974–1981), came from the non-Gaullist right. This gave him a fairly free hand to rethink France's defense policies, and he took it. The wholesale substitution of nuclear for conventional strength, as advocated by Gallois in his later years, received little support. Viewing the reliance on nuclear weapons as excessive, Giscard instead merely upgraded them while ordering new tanks and combat aircraft. He was also notably closer to America, obtaining in return an explicit U.S. declaration of support for the force. At the same time, the government considered whether to offer "enlarged sanctuarization," that is, to extend French nuclear guarantees to European allies, but the feasibility of this was in doubt from the beginning.[40]

Tactical nuclear weapons got more attention. General Claude Vanbremeersch argued that France's Pluton tactical weapons would be useful only if they could be used before the United States used its atomic weapons; France could thus use them as a signal of its willingness to escalate to the strategic level to protect itself. The reactions were interesting. Giscard's approach was reasonably Atlanticist and likely to involve the French army in battles in central Germany. To stop these ominous trends, the French Socialist and Communist parties saw themselves compelled to endorse Gaullist policy — total nuclear independence — and to drop their historic opposition to the force de frappe. Traditional pronuclear Frenchmen, especially Gallois, accused Giscard of simultaneously neglecting the nuclear force and extending its mission. Yet Giscard's hesitation about purchasing a new generation of atomic weapons had a practical foundation in that nuclear targeting was becoming a more complicated issue. The Soviet Union's huge civil defense program led to thinking of targeting infrastructure of administrative control and certain economic and industrial assets, known as the "vital works" or "vital centers" doctrine. The concept was deliberately vague and hampered by the relatively modest size of France's force. Ultimately, flexible targeting was rejected, and the city-targeting strategy remained. But there were too many questions left unanswered to plunge unhesitatingly into any major military upgrading.[41]

François Mitterand, who was to follow Giscard, had run for president against Charles de Gaulle in 1965 and been a regular contender ever since. In 1981 he succeeded and became the Fifth Republic's first Socialist president. From an ideological perspective, a major shift in foreign policy, and hence military policy, might have been expected. There was none. To be sure, he made a few changes such as adding a rapid strike force, a separate headquarters for tactical nuclear weapons, and placing both classes of nuclear weapons and the strike force directly under his own presidential authority. The rapid strike force was intended to complement the nuclear force, giving the government a reinforced deterrent although its exact purpose remained somewhat ambiguous. Despite this conventional-arms expansion, the administration continued to believe that nuclear weapons provided better deterrence than the conventional kind. Still, Mitterand's tendencies led one observer to conclude that France's "nuclear priority," which had caused "underfunding of critical conventional military programs, is being deemphasized."[42]

And yet it is hard to see Mitterand's government as being atomically different from any of its predecessors. It favored the status quo, did not completely give up on American guarantees for Europe, but retained its own deterrent force. There was an "impressive continuity irrespective of president or government." Policy fell well within Gaullist norms, keeping the nuclear forces while starving the conventional ones. "The Gaullist model was maintained by all of de Gaulle's successors." During the last years of the Cold War the administration remained resolutely Gaullist in its thinking even when changing technology (such as antimissile systems) overtook doctrine. And because of the threat of proliferation that followed, even the fall of the Soviet bloc did not lead to significant nuclear policy changes. Gaullism was present also in the government's view of America. The force was and remained partly a substitute for overreliance on the United States. While Mitterand's government in some ways appeared close to the United States at certain times, mistrust, nonetheless, arose because the latter's Strategic Defense Initiative and the Reykjavik meeting made the American nuclear deterrent seem less certain — one of the very triggers of the founding of the force in the first place.[43]

France's most recent president, Jacques Chirac, is a lifelong Gaullist. The force he inherited was not trivial: larger than China's, twice as large as Britain's, and exceeded only by the much-shrunken American and Russian arsenals. Perhaps this explains why initially he appeared to retain the nuclear priority and dabbled with tous azimuts, indicating a willingness to extend coverage of the French nuclear umbrella, a seeming return to enlarged sanctuarization. Instead, he went the other way. The only real force remaining is the submarine one, which does have the advantage of global reach. But overall, according to Marc Theleri, "for the first time in forty years nuclear weapons lost their absolute privilege in the panoply of our weapons." France's test site in the Pacific has been shut down and two fissile material plants closed. No wonder Gallois became angry, accusing Chirac of abandoning independence. Perhaps that is an exaggeration, but if Theleri is correct then forty years of attempting to substitute an independent nuclear force for other means of maintaining national strength appear to be over.[44]

Although the nuclear program went through many changes, several trends are clear (see table 7.1). The army suffered the most from nuclearization. Even in the de Gaulle years, overall military expenditure shrank as a share of gross national product. But spending on atomic weapons soared even as public support shrank, and despite ambivalence about the primacy of nuclear weapons the number of nuclear warheads in the French arsenal grew steadily.

JUSTIFYING THE FORCE

As almost everything about nuclear warfare is theoretical, the question regarding substitution of conventional with atomic arms cannot be answered without examining the theories that formed the foundation for both the theory and practice, including theoretical practice, of France's nuclear force and strategy. Two questions in particular will have to be answered. First, did France shift its military and security spending from conventional toward nuclear weapons? And second, was the nuclear arsenal developed to fill similar aims as the conventional ones they appear to have replaced?

Table 7.1: French military characteristics, 1946–1995

Item	1946	1958	1969	1974	1981	1995
Army's share in individual service budgets (%)	73	52	40	42		
Army's share in equipment spending (%)		35	32	34		
Army's share in personnel (%)	68	74	57	57		
Military expenditure/GNP (%)	8	6	4	3	4	
Capital expenditure/military budget (%)		34	49	47		
Nuclear weapons/military expenditure (%)		9[a]	41			
Public support for having the *force* (%)	56	41	23[b]			74[c]
Number of tests			8[d]	7	12	5
Number of warheads, France			36	145	275	485
Number of warheads, U.K.		22	308	325	350	300
French military spending						
as % of U.K.:		96	113	107	102	141
as % of Germany:		169	87	74	100	117

Notes: a. 1960. b. 1967. c. 1993. d. 1968.
Sources: Martin, 1981, pp. 54, 58, 364–367, 370–371; Gordon, 1993, p. 36; Hecht, 1998, p. 243; Larkin, 1996, p. 229; Theleri, 1997, appendices; Chappat, 2003, p. 37; Stockholm International Peace Research Institute (various years); Norris and Arkin, 1997.

The most basic argument for nuclear weaponry was that France could not win conventionally: "It must be recognized that it is not possible for France to fight alone with a conventional force against the conventional forces of the U.S.S.R. That is the reason for which the government has decided to develop military atomic energy." Here was a weapon that acted as an equalizer, and against which defense was not practical.[45] Would it therefore become a substitute for conventional forces?

Grandeur

As with the bomb itself, French *grandeur* is so tied to the image of de Gaulle that it is easy to forget that he did not invent it either. The Fourth Republic was heavily motivated by the need to keep France in the first rank: nuclear technology would be a "second liberation" for the French; possessing the bomb might "reverse a deteriorating situation"; without atomic weapons France would be "a second rank power." These concerns had far more influence than any specific military-security reasoning.[46]

Specific military-security reasons did, however, play their role. For the Fourth Republic, the bomb was necessary but it was not intended to replace conventional forces. Nuclear weapons were essential but not exclusively so. The Fourth Republic did not aim to "nuclearize" the military. Its minister of defense in 1956 did say that "an army not having the atomic bomb will count for little," but he seems to suggest that the weapon was an extension of the existing army, not its successor. It cannot be denied that the French retained an interest in strong conventional forces because they did not wish to manifest any interest in fighting another catastrophic conventional war. Its conventional forces, therefore, had to be "strong enough to require that any Soviet attack be large enough to make plausible the threat of nuclear retaliation." Atomic weapons also made German conventional rearmament more palatable. And following the Suez fiasco, the maintenance of national power became an even stronger ideal. In the words of the journal *Carrefour,* "if France again wishes to intervene in international competition in an effective manner, her essential task is to establish her strategic and tactical nuclear potential so as to weigh in the balance of the destiny of the world." This had been given additional urgency in the public mind by the weakened credibility of the American deterrent and the decisions by Britain and America to reduce their troop strengths and rely more on atomic weapons. The Anglo-Saxons might be barbarians but on military matters could not simply be ignored.[47]

Yet the basic nuclear ideal of the Fourth Republic was different from de Gaulle's:

> The central importance of the force de frappe to the Gaullist conception of strategic threat cannot easily be exaggerated. It was intended to be responsive to internal and external strategic threats, both national and systemic, projected by the de Gaulle government. It was to be a tool of French diplomacy and *grandeur.* It was to foster internal cohesion and economic and social progress. It was, ultimately, a challenge to superpower rule. It was essential to the Gaullist critique of the instability and illegitimacy of the present international system. Its creation was not only evidence that France was a great power but proof that the nation-state was still a viable human agency, materially capable of defending its citizens and, therefore, morally competent to claim their final allegiance. With the stakes so high, there is little wonder that Gaullist France should have developed an elaborate rationale for the force de frappe, built on military, diplomatic, psychological, economic, technological, and scientific grounds.[48]

Opinions are divided on whether this was a major shift or merely a difference of scope and clarity. Gaullist policy has been described as one of "continuity" and his government as the "executor" of an existing policy; he is said to have added means and will to attitudes and ideas that already existed. Others have noted, however, that de Gaulle wanted to use the force de frappe to disentangle himself from alliances, whether with the United States or with NATO.[49] If the Gaullist rationale really was different, then the question of substitution will have to be examined differently; the Fourth and Fifth Republics may both have practiced substitution, but not necessarily for the same things.

The difference comes down to this. The Fourth Republic thought about atomic weapons in terms of the *defense* of France. Charles de Gaulle thought about atomic weapons in terms *of* France. De Gaulle intended, as the above quotation shows, to use the force to rebuild the country's stature and culture, both its standing and what it stood for. Grandeur had specific meanings to the general, referring to the country's status, independence, and self-esteem. De Gaulle's "entire conception of France was one based on French international stature." For France to survive—and he meant more than physical survival here—it had to be self-reliant. "Ah, yes, the weapon of independence! Independence is essential; so we must have the means to achieve it!" This meant independence from the western superpower, from the superpower conflict, and from the western alliance. To many, the atomic test at Regane represented the rebirth of France as a great power. This independence was viewed in political terms, and the emphasis was on avoiding war (and defeat), on creating a national sanctuary, and on regaining national credibility. The top leadership did not show much interest in the details of nuclear military doctrine; the notions used to defend the concept were mostly vague. One analyst sent de Gaulle a book on nuclear issues for which the general thanked him, but added that for him there was only one issue: "Will France remain France?"[50]

De Gaulle was not being impractical—he had more personal experience with great-power politics than any living Frenchman. The experience had not been good, and he had suffered acute humiliation as leader of the Free French. Perhaps this explains his goal (or obsession?) regarding France's strategic future. In a 1959 speech he made clear that the atomic bomb was intended to make France a world power once again. One of his ministers, Jacques Soustelle, called the bomb "an admission card among the truly Great Powers." This world-political view was based on the military reality of the destructiveness of the new weapon. Like Gallois, de Gaulle believed that the nature of military power had changed. "The field of deterrence is thus henceforth open to us." On the one hand, the balance of terror between the superpowers neutralized their power and created opportunities for midpowers, and on the other hand, "no independent nation can have a credible military defense without the ability to threaten nuclear war." There was an element of international security that only nuclear weapons could bring. De Gaulle's thinking was neither emotional nor irrational. He wanted to overcome the Cold War bipolarity's insensitivity to the interests of other states, especially France's of course. He was sufficiently practical to realize, when the bipolar order failed to crumble as he had anticipated, that his policy of independence had its limitations, and as a consequence he never fully abandoned his links with the United States or NATO.[51]

De Gaulle did, however, hope to strengthen his position in Europe — and here there was little to choose between Gaullists and others. De Gaulle intended to use atomic weapons to achieve this goal. As a midpower nuclear state France might be able to become the supreme strategic spokesman for Europe. This goal was based on the realistic awareness that France could not compete head-on with the superpowers. America's shift from massive retaliation to flexible response played to de Gaulle's advantage, for Europe could now become a battleground: denuclearization made Europe "safe" for conventional warfare again, with atomic warfare probably to follow. That was the paradox of reducing dependence on nuclear arms or reducing their numbers. No wonder that Gallois complained later that "everyone behaves as if, on this side of the iron curtain, it were to the free world's interest to disarm until war is again likely and, in all probability, will be lost."[52]

The prolific Gallois developed extensive justifications for nuclear warfare, but in the long run his influence declined. He tended to take strategic ideas to their logical, or illogical, conclusions. In later years he claimed that every country needed a nuclear deterrent, that alliances were useless, that the bomb made large and small powers equal, and that there was no need to increase conventional forces, which just made tempting targets and drained nuclear resources. Those who disagreed with him were either "idiots or they've been bought with U.S. dollars." He had made two important contributions, however: the insistence that nuclear weapons would be used only to defend the nation in a life-and-death struggle, which made the weapons more politically palatable, and the doctrine of proportional deterrence, which made them seem useful.[53]

Beaufre's contributions were more serviceable because they appeared more reasonable. He never completely rejected alliances. An admirer of the British strategist Basil Liddell Hart, he adapted the latter's "indirect approach" to the use of nuclear weapons, particularly their use to create superpower uncertainty by multiplying the number of independent centers of decision making. An independent force would become a help, not a hindrance, to allies. Justifiably he was called "by far the most creative and interesting French nuclear strategist" of the Gaullist era.[54]

Where generals like Gallois, Beaufre, and Ailleret may have played their most important role, however, was in justifying the new approach to its most important audience: the military. De Gaulle inherited a military establishment that was defeated, embittered, demoralized, and hostile. Elements within it participated in two coup attempts and a lengthy campaign to kill him. The armed forces had to be reorganized and streamlined and be made loyal to the state. Establishing the force and cutting many NATO ties gave the military new missions. Its political isolation and right-wing tendencies could be attacked. The nuclear force was "the means whereby the old dichotomy between permanent army and armed citizens, between right-wing and left-wing notions of defence could be superseded." Atomic weapons would "provide substitute satisfactions for the professional army corps," the gap between army and nation would be bridged, and the army would have its role back. "The defense of France must be French." It would not be the same army, however. There was going to be a break between the army of the past and the army of the future. The army would be modernized — and so would the country, in the latter case, it was hoped, through technological spinoffs.[55]

The pronuclear generals contributed to this debate in two very important ways. First, they acted as translators, selling the principles of nuclear armament to an officer corps that either did not understand or did not like the implications of the new weapon. Officers fresh from grueling campaigns in Indochina and Algeria might not see the relevance of the new weapon for military purposes, although focusing their attention on Dien Bien Phu and Suez probably helped. The possession of nuclear arms might improve the prestige of France in the world, but it would certainly improve the prestige of the military in France. Second, the generals understood the military-political linkages of nuclear weapons. In a sense the dichotomy between military force and nuclear force was unimportant because many nations had built up conventional forces to impress their neighbors; technology now required a new weapon, but the underlying principles still existed. If war is the continuation of policy by other means, nuclear weapons were merely the most efficient way of executing policy in periods of conflict between actual nonnuclear wars.

Justification Denied

Critics denounced the force as expensive, weak, useless, and damaging to the conventional forces. The cost argument was straightforward: a meaningful force was beyond France's means. The French military budget's share of gross national product fell under de Gaulle from 5.6 to 4.4 percent. The size of the military inevitably shrank in the wake of the Algerian war, so this did not automatically represent a decline in capability. However, the military had not upgraded its equipment in the 1950s precisely because of the expense of Indochina and Algeria. Nuclear development consumed 10 percent of scientific manpower, 60 percent of the electronics industry, and 70 percent of the aerospace industry. France's total military budget at the time of de Gaulle's appointment was only about 70 percent of Britain's. Military spending was barely twice what America spent on just flying the B-52s. The United States was spending as much on missiles in 1960 as France allocated for its entire national budget. Altogether too much money was spent on a small force while draining money from conventional forces and nonmilitary science. De Gaulle responded to the utility and cost questions laconically by noting resistance to heavy artillery before 1914 and to airplanes before 1939: the new and unfamiliar will be expensive.[56]

The utility of heavy artillery, and airplanes, had been solidly proven, if too late for some. But the utility argument was much less clear for the case of nuclear weapons. One study concluded that midrange powers simply cannot afford or benefit from a nuclear force. Credibility was questionable. "Few alternatives are so grim that the prospect of nuclear annihilation would be preferred." Raymond Aron questioned whether France could deter the Soviet Union if Britain and America could not. Despite certain political benefits, strategically the force was viewed as "of less value to France."[57]

In addition, two practical problems existed from the beginning. First, the force was weak. France and its nuclear force were devastatingly vulnerable to a first strike. Deterrence requires a second-strike capability. Otherwise, how can a first strike be deterred? Gallois was criticized for being too optimistic about the survivability of the conventional missiles as well as for overestimating the effects of a weak second strike and the impact of fallout on the aggressor. In a word, critics charged that at least some of the claimed benefits of substituting nuclear for conventional weapons did not withstand scrutiny. Proportional deterrence was rejected. Moderate critics accepted that possession of some nuclear weapons might bring advantages but rejected the more enthusiastic arguments for what they might do.[58]

The second problem was that the force was not just weak but that the nuclear capability gap between the superpowers and the rest of the world was growing. Even Gallois noted the problem, although as a justification for expansion. France's nuclear systems were threatened with obsolescence because of changes in superpower technology. France could not match the evolution in nuclear weaponry and delivery systems. Defensive systems made the situation worse. Soviet strategic defense might not stop an American attack — but stopping a French attack was a different matter. In the 1960s the only attack mode possible was through the Mirage IV aircraft, which could certainly be shot down. Unsurprisingly, France offered in 1981 to participate in arms control only if the superpowers agreed not to have defensive systems. Possessing atomic bombs was not the same thing as being equal (or proportional) to the superpowers. Weakness of the force made its eventual use a less credible choice.[59]

Confronted with brilliant and subtle but inevitably theoretical arguments on both sides, the French nation remained divided if not confused. There were other issues confronting the public as well. One was proliferation, which Gallois had described as a positive. Yet Jules Moch pointed out that proliferation might someday mean a Polaris submarine under a German commander, an argument that still had considerable resonance in 1963. Aron thought that a *conventional* force strong enough to stop all but a massive assault could also act as a deterrent. By the mid-1980s, just before the issue became moot, a consensus was developing that Aron was right and that the West would be better off if it were less nuclear-reliant. Divisions remained great, with clear popular majorities favoring nuclearization only in 1946 and 1960, although in de Gaulle's lifetime support for nuclear weapons certainly was much stronger in France than in Germany.[60]

The force and the concepts behind it have received their share of foreign endorsements. The French were able to develop a mini-triad, that is, a diverse nuclear force; de Gaulle's concerns had a "genuine strategic basis" and might indeed enable France to defend itself; the credibility of the American deterrent was indeed questionable, and American public support for intervention on behalf of allies was even more so.[61] The political dimension stressed by de Gaulle and the nuclear generals can be seen in 1960s American thinking:

> Military strategy can no longer be thought of, as it could for some countries in some eras, as the science of military victory. It is now equally, if not more, the art of coercion, of intimidation and deterrence. The instruments of war are more punitive than acquisitive. Military strategy, whether we like it or not, has become the diplomacy of violence.[62]

Gallois and Beaufre could hardly have said it better. In this same vein, NATO commander U.S. General Bernard Rogers said that the force made "the Soviet calculus of costs and risks of aggression much more complex." The Soviets may have thought so as well. Although they tended to belittle France's nuclear development, they also emphasized the certainty of reprisals — even going so far as to note that such reprisals would not necessarily include the United States. Such threats hardly support a perception of irrelevance.[63]

THE FORCE'S EFFECT ON FRANCE'S CONVENTIONAL ARMS

The officers who in the 1950s feared that nuclearization meant trouble for the conventional forces were right. The decline of French conventional forces cannot be attributed to nuclear weapons alone of course. Defense budgets, after all, are always limited, and the operational expense of two significant wars took a large toll as well. France's military expenditure was more than she could afford: almost one-tenth of GNP in 1958. But the nuclear force did impose limits on the conventional forces and contributed "to a difficult situation that would not soon disappear." Many of the soldiers opposed to de Gaulle's Algerian policy voted for socialist François Mitterand because he symbolized opposition to the force. France's conventional arms acquisition was not the only trouble. Henry Kissinger commented on the "amazing conclusion" that nuclear parity meant that conventional manpower forces should be cut, but he also suggested, as will we, that the interest in the nuclear deterrent was a function of the political impossibility of raising adequate regular forces.[64]

France's limited resources meant that the impact of nuclearization was bound to be quite significant. Raymond Aron had estimated that the nuclear deterrent would cost about 20 percent of the defense budget, and 40 percent of arms procurement, and that the second-generation deterrent would be even more costly. He described his own calculations as conservative, "yet even these low estimates jeopardize programs *regarded as minimal* in the area of conventional arms." Half or more of the program budgets of the first two programs were spent on nuclearization, and the share of actual spending was even higher. In all three programs that were generated during the de Gaulle era, nuclear spending exceeded what was planned. In 1965–1971, half of heavy weapons spending was on the nuclear force. Of the first program's 11.79 billion NF for modernization, 6.05 billion went for the force. Aron had indeed been conservative: by the later de Gaulle era nuclear expenses consumed half of all military equipment spending and a quarter of the total. Spending on conventional forces declined by 43 percent between 1962 and 1967.[65]

That drop might or might not be significant. In 1962 France officially made peace with the Algerians, so the need for conventional forces declined. But the decline does turn out to be important in three ways. First, France obviously could not, and did not, rely on a large conventional force for deterrent effect. Second, the conventional forces suffered numerous weaknesses. Between 1960 and 1969, military personnel fell by 470,000 people, with the lion's share (431,000) coming at the expense of the army, the one service with no direct force de frappe mission. Navy personnel fell by 9 percent, the air force's by 23 percent, and the army's by a gigantic 57 percent. In 1967, 1968, and 1972, the army's capital expenditure fell behind the much smaller navy's. By the 1970s the conventional forces were in a parlous state. German chancellor Helmut Schmidt told Giscard that what struck him "the most in the French situation was the state of weakness of her conventional defense." The army, which had been planned to have 4,000 modern combat vehicles, had 500, and 190 helicopters instead of 900. The air force and navy had significant problems as well but were at least exposed to technological modernization through their nuclear-linked programs. The army was not. The 1991 Gulf War revealed the poor condition of French forces. France's relatively modern Jaguars could not operate at night. Its best bombers could not go on conventional missions at all. So weak were the French forces that U.S. General Norman Schwarzkopf deliberately placed the French troops where they would not encounter the main body of Iraqi forces.[66]

The third way in which the conventional force decline was significant was in its failure to modernize. Gallois had accepted this "problem" for obvious reasons. Aron rightly worried whether even minimal modernization could be funded.[67] It could not. The 1960 budget, which included the first nuclear-weapons program of the de Gaulle era, provided for Algerian operations and development of the force. "This declaration makes clear that the third point intentionally omitted, the modernization of the conventional army, has nevertheless been sacrificed and abandoned, or at least neglected and compromised." In many areas, not only would France not acquire modern conventional arms, but it would not even develop them. "Our conventional army dates from a different time." The situation was worsened by the tightness of the existing budget.[68] Delivery of conventional equipment "fell far behind schedule." Worse, the cost of the nuclear forces during the second program were much higher than forecast, leading to a delay in the production of modern battle tanks and even to the cancellation of nuclear-powered submarine purchases. Five army divisions were to be modernized; only two were. By the mid-1960s there was vigorous debate over the force's impact on the conventional arms.[69]

Ailleret was not overly concerned by this state of affairs, noting that grand offensives and great amphibious landings were no longer possible anyway. His critics pointed out that in World War II no one had used poison gas, the doomsday weapon of the day, necessitating conventional forces, but Ailleret rejected the comparison, arguing that gas was useful primarily against unprotected troops engaged in static warfare, neither of which was the case in World War II. Alain Peyrefitte also defended the spending trends by maintaining that the nuclear costs were exaggerated. The big drain on defense spending was not the atomic bomb; it was the soldier, he said. A single armored division cost more than the fifty-bomber Mirage IV force. Nor could that division even attack the enemy heartland. He also pointed out that the draft, backbone of the conventional army, was bad for the national economy. The conventional forces accounted for four-fifths of the defense budget in the 1980s, by which time they had recovered somewhat. France's mass army system did start to change around 1965, but conscription remained the norm. It was not abolished until 2001.[70]

There was, however, a solution to the army's conundrum, albeit one not embraced with much enthusiasm by the Gaullists: tactical nuclear weapons. The firepower of the army would increase dramatically, and, like the air force and navy, it would be linked to the force de frappe. But in that formulation lies the basic problem of tactical nuclear weapons: What exactly are they? Are they conventional weapons, a smaller version of the strategic kind, or something sui generis? No one could know, because the use of tactical nuclear arms might depend on the reaction to their use: the applicant might rate them as tactical, the recipient as strategic. Would tactical nuclear weapons lead to escalation, and under what circumstances? They might cause an escalation, but that escalation might be inevitable anyway.[71]

When de Gaulle came to power, the superpowers at any rate already seemed to think of tactical nuclear weapons as conventional arms. As they hardly fit his conception of grandeur, de Gaulle was not particularly interested in tactical nuclear weapons, but his administration was not blind to their possibilities. By 1962 tactical nuclear weapons were integrated into army maneuvers, in theory, at any rate, for there were as yet no weapons.[72] At the time there was no particular urgency for developing them because the United States provided some. But these were withdrawn when de Gaulle pulled out of NATO's military command structure.

This placed all powers in a difficult position. While the Soviet position appeared strengthened, western military behavior became somewhat less predictable. The United States lost leverage over France, but the reverse was also true. For NATO, it meant that one of the four large European powers was politically affiliated but militarily separated — and in a crisis there was less certainty of France's support and cooperation. For France, it meant that questions about its military capacity could no longer be avoided by casual references to the NATO alliance. For Europe as a whole, the move was at best ambiguous. A reduction in American influence might be welcomed, but following the 1965/66 "Empty Chair Crisis" in which France had withdrawn from the European Council of Ministers and the European Commission, France appeared bent on undermining all its international ties. But de Gaulle's move was not irrational. While many reasons lay behind his move, for example, irritation with America and Britain, uncertainty about NATO and U.S. nuclear strategy, as well as appeal to France's tradition of grandeur, for our purposes his withdrawal certainly gave even more ammunition to those who favored developing the force further, including the addition of tactical weapons.

And so it happened: the decision was taken to develop tactical weapons independently. Pierre Messmer, military minister throughout de Gaulle's presidency, announced that the "distinction between nuclear and nonnuclear forces will become more and more artificial, for all our forces will progressively be equipped with nuclear armament." Neither the air force, itself a possible possessor of tactical weapons, nor the navy was happy about the prospect of army atomic bombs, and the army found itself in some difficulties fighting the two "strategic" services.[73]

Conventional wisdom was that the tactical weapon was another form of deterrent. It placed the deterrent in a local context, giving a local force its own deterrent power. Tactical nuclear weapons could deter both conventional and nuclear attack and thus be used to protect ground forces. The location of their use was problematic. France's European allies supported the use of tactical weapons, but not on their own soil. For instance, for France's first-generation Pluton tactical weapons to be effective, they would have to be deployed in Germany, but that would translate into early entry into a conflict, precisely what the French wanted to avoid. If deployed on French soil, the Plutons would have to be fired into allies' territory, for which their permission would be required. Ailleret, who had approved the development of the Pluton, had left the "how" and "where" questions somewhat obscure, perhaps not by accident.[74]

Ailleret was not impressed by the tactical-use concept, which he saw as an attempt to maintain the idea of traditional, conventional warfare. Its proponents assumed, he thought, that both sides in an exchange would agree to limit themselves to tactical weapons. As little as anyone knew about thresholds for strategic weapons, even less was understood about their smaller cousins. The temptation to use them as a counterweight to superior Warsaw Pact conventional forces was enormous. They could also make up for technical shortcomings due to the lack of modernization of the French conventional forces. But ultimately it was hard to think of a nuclear weapon as anything else, regardless of its smaller size. Tactical weapons could be fired as a symbolic act to warn the enemy of the defender's seriousness. No conventional artillery shell could have such an effect. Like Ailleret, de Gaulle realized this and was concerned that too many officers thought of tactical nuclear weapons as "super artillery." He even wrote an instruction emphasizing that nuclear weapons existed to deter war and that it was global politics rather than the European military balance that mattered. It was unusual for de Gaulle to descend to doctrinal levels, but in so doing he emphasized that, for him, tactical nuclear weapons were not going to be a substitute for conventional weakness.[75]

SUBSTITUTING NUCLEAR FOR CONVENTIONAL FORCES

This review of the history and rationale for the force de frappe demonstrates that some type of substitution did indeed occur. The limitations on resources were obvious. France's military expenditure entered an inevitable period of decline during the Gaullist era as the country ended sixteen years of counterinsurgency warfare and steered more resources toward economic development and social welfare. Political and economic reality demanded that defense spending stay below 5 percent of economic output, even as the shrinking military pie had to accommodate substantially expanding expenditure on the nuclear arm. The extent to which substitution took place is more problematical. De Gaulle expected that nuclear spending would stimulate French achievements in aerospace and technical industries.[76] There also remains the comparable benefits issue. In some ways nuclear weapons were substituted for the conventional kind but, if Gallois's logic is accepted, in other ways they filled an entirely different set of requirements.

Even the more moderate Beaufre saw a new era of political and military conflict in which nuclear weapons played a unique role. He also pointed out that French nuclear decision making was actually quite consistent with its own history. To ensure its security, France frequently looked toward a single great reform. He listed thirteen major changes, covering the years 1939 to 1963, and found that frequently a single overriding solution was applied; once it had been "the continuous front and the power of the defensive; today it is the nuclear weapon," he wrote. In the view of another author, psychologically, the bomb was not so different from the Maginot Line: "both are concerned with the protection of French boundaries from invaders."[77] But this reflects the viewpoint of the Fourth Republic more than that of de Gaulle, who, as we noted, saw France's independence more endangered than its territorial integrity. Those who would analyze nuclear for conventional arms substitution have to consider not only the different areas in which it took place but also its time dimension.

De Gaulle sought independence, refused subordination to America, searched for grandeur, believed in the primacy of the French nation-state, and stressed the importance of national defense. In analyzing the extent to which nuclear weapons were substituted for conventional weapons or other policies to achieve these goals we again have to consider whether nuclear or conventional weapons were suited for each or any of them. The issue is further complicated by the changing nature of military establishments. The mass infantry army was declining across the globe. The necessary expense of conventional equipment caused postwar armies to become smaller than their prewar predecessors. And armies no longer had to prepare for mass invasions. The existence of nuclear weapons had changed the role and boundaries of the conventional force whether or not it was coupled to atomic weapons. De Gaulle furthermore suggested that nuclear weapons were also a means of strengthening the established army. But was it, or was it merely that a completely denuclearized army was in an even weaker position — a form of "negative" substitution? Even the purpose of military establishments was in doubt. According to U.S. economist and strategist Thomas Schelling, nations no longer sought conventional victory but wanted to extract bargaining power from their capacity to inflict hurt. Was the nuclear weapon substituted here because of its greater power, or was the difference so great that it had to be considered as something completely different? Could comparable benefits exist at all?[78]

Substitution of Nuclear Weapons for Conventional Forces

Budget numbers are both useful and deceptive: useful because they show what was being bought and deceptive because the decisions may not reflect the results of deliberate substitution but instead those of the vagaries of service and national politics. Nevertheless, it is unquestioned that the size, funding, and modernization of France's conventional forces all suffered. France's regular troops were in no position to provide much grand-strategic support for national strategy. That was the bomb's task, obviously. But was the nuclear force purchasing substitution providing comparable benefit, or was it so different from conventional capacity, perhaps providing benefits that no conventional force could, that it can no longer be considered substitution? To answer this question, let us look at several areas and see where conventional and nuclear arms can be substitutes for one another (see table 7.2).

Both types, clearly, fall within the general national security category. France's national security spending had to accommodate operational expenses, equipment purchases, and nuclearization. The latter was funded at the expense of the former categories. Even under the Fourth Republic nuclear spending impinged on the conventional forces although this was masked somewhat by the huge operational budgets for Indochina and Algeria. From this perspective, substitution clearly took place, most notably between 1960 and 1974. This does not, however, address the question of comparable benefits of nuclear and conventional forces.

Table 7.2: Substitution and the force de frappe

Item substituted	Weak*							Strong*	
	1	2	3	4	5	6	7	8	9
Conventional: franc and numbers							7		
Conventional: national security									9
Conventional: deterrence					5				
Conventional: defense									9
Conventional: strike			3						
Conventional: psychology		2							
Conventional: foreign policy						6			
Foreign policy: relations to the U.S.				4					
Foreign policy: relation to NATO								8	
Foreign policy: per se	1								

Note: The items are rank-ordered ordinal, not cardinal numbers. For example, a "2" means "more than 1," not "twice as much as 1."

In the realm of deterrence comparability is more complicated. Can conventional forces deter? In theory, of course, they can, but not in the same way that nuclear weapons do. The amount of punishment that conventional forces can inflict is obviously much smaller. Strong conventional forces can threaten the attacker with defeat, or at least deny the chance of a quick victory; they threaten quagmire. Conventional forces can also threaten a counterattack, although this becomes less believable if only the original aggressor has nuclear arms. But the credibility of the nuclear deterrent threat is less than that of the conventional kind. Suppose that the Soviet Union threatened an invasion of the West, and assume France could threaten to throw either its conventional or its nuclear forces into the battle. How credible would France's implied threat be? Not very. The Soviet Union had already made it clear that any French nuclear strike would be met with instant annihilation. The power of France's nuclear weapons would be far greater than its conventional forces, but which would the government be more likely to use? The threat of which arm would most likely be believed? Despite the immense difference in kind and effect, conventional deterrence is not a chimera.

If this discussion is confusing, that is because it reflects the reality of French strategic thought at the time. France never fully resolved the relationship between conventional and nuclear deterrence. Most French strategists believed that conventional forces could not replace the nuclear kind but also that nuclear weapons avoided a costly conventional arms race. While all three services suffered from this argument, the army suffered the most. Gallois in particular favored minimal conventional forces. Conventional deterrence was less stable than nuclear deterrence, it was argued, and imposed less uncertainty on the aggressor. Conventional forces were also criticized for being impractical. The western alliance simply could not raise the soldiers projected as necessary. NATO's numbers could not match the Bloc's. Beaufre conceded, however, that a nuclear-deterrent stalemate would require larger conventional forces, which he thought might be organized in a militia system. De Gaulle, instead, apparently hoped to use Germans as his conventional deterrent troops.[79]

No simple answer emerges regarding comparable benefits and deterrence. French and foreign thinkers were, however, trying to work out the inherent problems of the nuclear-conventional relationship in a deterrence system, and therefore it is logical to conclude that substitution was taking place. This is buttressed by the concern over whether the threat of nuclear weapons was truly meaningful, given the many reservations about their use.[80] Perhaps this explains why no one, including France, sent all the regular troops home.

Substitution is perhaps clearer in the realm of defense, meaning actual success in combat. Both types of weapons can be used in wartime. There is a difference, presumably, between using nuclear weapons against an invading force and using them to devastate the enemy interior. With regard to guarding one's homeland, the above-mentioned numerical problems created a clear justification for obtaining nuclear weapons to make up for the size of the "communist hordes" that one's conventional forces could not reasonably withstand. In this case, substitution took place. But the reverse is the case when the different arms are compared regarding the ability to strike the enemy. Conventional forces can do that but at costs so immensely greater that comparability is brought into question. For example, the destruction of Tokyo and the killing there of more civilians than at Hiroshima was accomplished by a conventional force — but of 279 airplanes as compared with one at Hiroshima, and this with complete air superiority. The air fleet that destroyed Tokyo was small compared with the ones that could not disable Nazi Germany's cities (see chap. 6). With atomic weapons, air superiority was unnecessary. Only one bomber has to penetrate in order to destroy a city. Primitive missiles can cheaply carry atomic bombs. If fifteen Mirage IVs attacked Moscow with conventional weapons (a perfectly plausible number), the results would be derisory even if all of them got through; but if carrying atomic bombs, Soviet air defenses could have a 93 percent shoot-down rate and still lose most of the capital. The "bang for the buck" argument seemed incontrovertible. Even an outmoded bomber carrying an outmoded atomic bomb could inflict devastating damage. The costs of conventional forces that could strike by air or land and do that much damage appeared astronomical. Beaufre argued that advanced conventional arms have become so expensive that even medium powers cannot afford them in decisive quantities. A twenty-kiloton atomic bomb, he calculated, produced an explosive force equal to a salvo from four million 75-mm cannon. More prosaically, Pierre Messmer concluded that the expensive Pierrelatte gaseous diffusion plant cost less than the equipment of a mere two armored divisions.[81]

Raymond Aron was not convinced. To quote at length:

> The proponents keep insisting that a program of conventional arms would prove even more costly. This is true if the destructive power of nuclear arms is simply measured against that of conventional ones. No weapon can possibly compete with the H-bomb when it comes to killing millions of people at the lowest possible cost per person. To say that the conventional arms program advocated by our allies would be even more expensive is meaningless, because we would ourselves determine the size of allocations even if we agreed not to manufacture the atom bombs that no one asked us to acquire, since no one considers our deterrent a substantial contribution to common security. One may readily accept the fact, pointed out by M. Alain Peyrefitte, that an armored division costs three hundred billion old francs, or twice the cost of fifty Mirage IV bombers. But all this proves is that a modern army requires vast resources, which happens to be a truism. And since France cannot do without a minimum of conventional armed forces, the question arises whether a second-generation deterrent, given the finite limits of the national defense budget, is at all compatible with this indispensable minimum of army divisions, warships, and airplanes of all types. [82]

Aron advances two arguments. First, if nuclear weapons are so expensive as to force conventional arms below a minimum threshold, then nuclear arms may not be worth their expense. Second, the relevant cost comparison is not between nuclear weapons and all conventional forces but that between nuclear weapons and the cost beyond the minimum threshold of conventional forces, a marginal cost/benefit argument in other words. On either argument, the expense of nuclear weapons increases in relative terms.

Criticisms of France's failure to develop world-class nuclear or conventional forces, however, must take into account that the country could not afford either. Even a minimum acceptable conventional force *and* such a nuclear force might well exceed any realistic budget. The nuclear strike force, however, replaced two conventional options, conventional air attack and land invasion. Clearly, comparable benefits exist. The actual comparison is complicated by the difference in scale between conventional and nuclear munitions.

De Gaulle and many atomic activists also considered public morale. Of course, conventional military force can also be used to build public morale, but in the case of France this might not have been realistic. France's conventional forces had failed to defeat the Vietnamese, failed to defeat the Algerians, and — on three recent occasions — failed to defeat the Germans. Public support for the bomb was strong in 1946 and 1960, respectively, when memory of defeat and disaster at the hands of conventional forces were also strong. Substitution of modernized conventional forces for older ones in order to build morale was feasible in many countries, but probably not in France.

Finally, did substitution take place with regard to France's foreign policy? Before de Gaulle, the Fourth Republic thought nuclear weapons would prevent Dien Bien Phu and Suez-type situations, where France was too weak to avoid international humiliation. De Gaulle went further, wishing to ensure France's great-power status. Could this be achieved with conventional forces? Gaullists would say no, thereby denying comparable benefits; otherwise justification for the force would be undermined. Yet even a casual review of the international situation beginning with the 1950s shows that global power did not automatically flow from possession of nuclear weapons. A large, well-equipped conventional military could engage in any number of interventionist exercises, and the use of such a force might give a country more power and prestige than the possession of an atomic bomb of doubtful practical utility. Indeed, France showed plenty of willingness to get involved in foreign crises, although often stealthily via its intelligence arm. In contrast, simple possession of nuclear weapons draws far more attention than possession of a conventional army. While the merits of the case were argued, at least in the pertinent French decision makers' minds comparable foreign policy benefits did exist and substitution did take place.

Substitution of Nuclear Weapons for the United States

After World War II, the dependence of Western Europe on the United States was nearly absolute. National sovereignty existed courtesy of Washington, and France felt particularly uncomfortable. De Gaulle and others had suffered being ignored at the great conferences that decided the war and its aftermath. All independent European states depended on the American deterrent and American military force but had no control over when and whether the American umbrella could be relied upon. For France, in addition, Dien Bien Phu, Suez, and Algeria were defining moments. While Great Britain could tolerate following Washington's lead after 1956, for France that was temperamentally impossible. Certainty about the American deterrent diminished, and France's nuclear force became a substitute for a close (or at any rate closer) relation with Washington.

A closer relation with Washington would mean continued presence of American tactical nuclear weapons in France. The presence of American troops in France meant that an attack on France was an attack on America, increasing the likelihood of American retaliation in case of an attack. The hoped-for independence from the United States did not mean abandoning strategic relations with it. French strategists still counted on the American "umbrella" and realized full well that the role of the United States remained essential. In the words of Gaullist Michel Debré, "In the event of a crisis, we would have to rely on American support." The French force was a means of reinforcing the American one. In addition, the French could threaten to use their force as a "trigger"; for example, a French bombardment would cause a Soviet attack which would compel the United States to get involved, exactly the reason why Washington opposed the French plans. The U.S. government's opposition was effective and French progress slowed. Eventually the United States made a number of concessions, never acknowledged in the French sources.[83]

This reaction might be as much attitudinal as practical. De Gaulle noted American objections and commented that a monopoly always looks like the best system to the monopolist. Gallois went much further, as usual, writing that "the Anglo-Saxon world was loath to permit a Latin country, seen as unstable and even unpredictable, to possess weapons of mass destruction." Other Frenchmen were less vociferous, but, with the possible exception of Mitterand, there was no natural Atlanticist leaning in France. The United States' great power was and still is viewed as a menace. Thus, the arguments for independence, or lessened dependence, were strong. American credibility was declining. Even critics of the force as it developed conceded that it did bring benefits in regards to the Franco-American relationship.[84]

Did the two alternatives — an independent nuclear option or dependence on the United States — present comparable benefits? In terms of national security, the answer is yes. Each option provided some protection against a Soviet attack. Only the force, however, provided the additional benefit of the kind of French independence de Gaulle desired. At first, under the Fourth Republic, substitution took place only in one sense, the purely military one; later, under the Fifth, de Gaulle added the political one. The independence that France achieved, however, was not total; it was idiosyncratic for, despite not having the bomb, other European states were not subservient to America either.

Substitution of Nuclear Weapons for Alliances

France could not defend itself. In 1870 it was entirely overrun when on its own. In 1914 it survived only due to alliances, but at immense cost. In 1940

military alliances had failed to save the country. The Fourth Republic's government retained some faith in military alliances (the world wars had shown they
could be solid), but de Gaulle was doubtful (allies were unlikely to sacrifice
themselves in atomic war, and the costs of the world wars had been much too
high for France).

Few postwar international actions of France exceed in importance its 1966
withdrawal from NATO's military command structure. Pictured on occasion
as a fit of pique, the French action represented a neatly packaged act of substitution. The Mirage IV atomic bombers were finally ready. No one familiar with French military thought could have been overly surprised. Gallois
claimed that nuclear war had abolished traditional notions of military alliance.
In the past, joining a war could mean losing an expeditionary force; now it
might mean losing half one's population. Even the more moderate Aron believed that modern alliances should either become communities or dissolve.
Kissinger basically agreed and criticized the United States' handling of the
alliance. In a word, even prior to de Gaulle, NATO was in theoretical and
practical trouble among the French.[85]

French attitudes had been colored long before 1966. France held few command positions in NATO and received no support from the alliance outside Europe, and its contributions had been correspondingly small. De Gaulle's 1960
declaration that he wanted the right to veto nuclear weapons use by any NATO
member raised fundamental questions about the nature of the alliance. It was
also a tactical move to get better treatment for France, which he secretly hoped
would ease the cost of his own arms program. He failed and lost the American
tactical weapons — although, interestingly, they were secretly returned.[86]

All this did not decrease French mistrust of dependence on outsiders, which
had now been reinforced by Gallois's arguments about the impossibility of
one country extending its deterrent to another. This mistrust manifested itself
in many ways. It was extended to Britain, which had collapsed during the Suez
crisis. For some, it extended to Germany. Gallois, for example, believed Germany wished to denuclearize France. It even extended to the French Community (France's answer to the British Commonwealth); the former empire was
no longer seen as a source of strength. Overseas bases, once the sine qua non
of global military force, were no longer significant because it did not matter
from whence the force would be launched. Of course, an integrated military
command with all NATO nuclear forces included might have been an alternative — but was this feasible? The United States would never have given up
any degree of control over its weapons to any foreign nation. An all-European
arrangement might have been more palatable, but to de Gaulle only if it had

been under French domination.[87] So from the French perspective there was a choice to be made between a system of alliances that, according to Gallois, could not work and the force, with all its admitted shortcomings.

And yet the Gaullists never completely abandoned alliances. The general kept the door to NATO open, and even the strident Gallois conceded that, given the immense cost of indigenous nuclear arms development, there would have to be transnational approaches (which have indeed occurred). Gaullists flirted with the idea of the force's becoming the foundation for a European defense. Certainly France had every intention of retaining its close links with Germany, with its possession of nuclear arms providing a certain amount of leverage. But the tension between Europeanization and Gaullist nationalism was not resolved. The force, supposedly at the disposal of European security, was yet to remain under complete national control, the very sort of thing France despised about America.[88]

As different as military alliances and domestic nuclear weapons are from each other, in the de Gaulle era they were indeed alternatives. From the French perspective, they provided an important comparable benefit with regard to national security, but at different cost. Unsurprisingly, foreign critics saw the French action of 1966 as reducing collective security. It was viewed much like someone who drops out of an insurance plan to become self-insured and thereby undermines the viability of the insurance plan for those who remain in it.[89]

In 1966 American economists Mancur Olson and Richard Zeckhauser sought to analyze alliances by comparing the value that members place on them to how much they are willing to spend. An analysis of NATO spending revealed that large nations spent disproportionately much, because they valued the alliance more, although this tendency decreases in time of war. Their model does not, however, distinguish between collective and purely national benefits of alliance members' military spending. The authors do reach a conclusion that has important implications for our case. They demonstrate that an alliance does not become ineffective if the members cease to feel a community of interest, because they will spend more militarily to protect their own position, so that alliance forces will actually be larger.[90] This applies clearly to the French—who argued consistently that their behavior was more helpful than harmful to NATO.

Olson and Zeckhauser also address the free rider problem, where alliance members underspend but still get all the benefits of alliance membership. The authors argue that "the exclusion of those who do not share the cost of the good is impractical or impossible." Larger nations in alliances spend proportionately more — but this does not mean that the smaller ones should be punished for spending less. The spending patterns of the large and small nations are "solidly grounded in their national interests."[91] Nor is this a bad thing, as the French claimed:

> A final implication of our model is that alliances and international organizations, as presently organized, will not work efficiently, or according to any common conception of fairness, however complete the agreement and community of interest among the members. Though there is obviously a point beyond which dissension and divergent purposes will ruin any organization, it is also true that some differences of purpose may improve the working of an alliance, because they increase the private non-collective benefits from the national contributions to the alliance, and this alleviates the suboptimality and disproportionality. How much smaller would the military forces of the small members of NATO be if they did not have their private fears and quarrels? How much aid would the European nations give if they did not have private interests in the development of their past or present colonies? How much would the smaller nations contribute to the U.N. if it were not a forum for the expression of their purely national enmities and aspirations? The United States, at least, should perhaps not hope for too much unity in common ventures with other nations. It might prove extremely expensive.[92]

According to another pair of economists, Todd Sandler and Keith Hartley, nuclear weapons make free riding more likely because of collateral damage. A great power cannot permit the nuclear destruction of a weaker neighbor because neither blast nor fallout is a respecter of borders. "It is easier for the United States to turns its back on a NATO ally in Europe during a nuclear threat than for France, for example, to ignore pleas for protection from a nearby European ally, since in the latter case any collateral damage from an attack is apt to be greater." From a purely military perspective, the smaller country's needs might be met by spending nothing at all. As this does not happen, and the Olson and Zeckhauser "pure public good" model does not permit further analysis of free riding, an alternative has been proposed: the "joint product model." Defense spending meets multiple needs. Some of these needs are partly met through alliances. Benefits of actions by one individual state for another can be taken into account. This model has been shown to be the more meaningful.[93] It certainly explains France's relationship with its allies better. France's independent force undermined NATO in some ways but actually strengthened it in others (as the French always maintained). France's actions left Germany more vulnerable (uncertainty about instant French support in case of invasion) but protected it in others (an invader could not know at which point France decided it would be necessary to use nuclear weapons to keep an invader away).

Substitution of Nuclear Weapons for Foreign Policy

Earlier we asked whether the substitution of nuclear for conventional weapons took place regarding France's foreign policy: did the republic's choice of atomic bombs allow it to fulfill foreign policy goals that otherwise would or could have been fulfilled with large conventional forces? Now we ask a broader question: were the weapons themselves substituted for an entire foreign policy? Did France move from having a particular foreign policy to having a weapons system, which then became the *urbi et orbi* of foreign policy? On the one hand, the global strategy of Beaufre and Gallois did constitute the proverbial third rail of the Gaullist perspective. De Gaulle placed much of his reputation and strength on the table to get his force. But French foreign policy thinking was fairly consistent over time and did not change much with possession of the bomb. The bomb was merely a tool. Whether it was ever more than that depends on the extent to which the nuclear force justifications and doctrine were a true foreign policy in which substitution can be said to have occurred or if they were merely additional support for existing foreign policy in which case substitution did not occur.

THE FORCE DE FRAPPE AND THE OTHER PRINCIPLES OF ECONOMICS

The case of the force de frappe presents unusual challenges for the application of our economic principles. Whereas wartime actions come with a large quantity of operational decisions to study, with nuclear weaponry there only exist budgetary decisions as well as nuclear warfare theory, simulations, and peacetime maneuvers about which there is limited information accessible. As a result, there is a good deal of overlap among the examples used to illustrate the various principles.

OPPORTUNITY COST. The nuclear era obviously did not free decision makers from the problem of having to make choices. "We have not escaped the ancient necessity for choice arising out of the scarcity of available resources."[94] This affected France in many ways. For example, choosing nuclear weapons meant a degradation of France's conventional battle capacity. It is clear that de Gaulle was willing to accept this penalty, and his military background may have enabled him to impose this on the military. With no major remaining imperial commitments and protected to a certain extent by the German buffer between France and the Soviet bloc, de Gaulle was able to make this choice. Neverthe-less, the risks were high. In a crisis, the French government would have had no intermediate options, no flexible response. If France were attacked or invaded, annihilation or surrender would be the only military options.

EXPECTED MARGINAL COSTS AND BENEFITS. The concept of expected mar-ginal costs and benefits has been utilized as part of weapons choices for centu-ries, but this has only become explicit (and not necessarily more efficient) in relatively recent times. This modernization took place in the Pentagon in the 1960s. One of its protagonists wrote, "Cost-effectiveness analysis is completely neutral with respect to the unit cost of a weapon."[95] The analysis of marginal costs and benefits revolves strictly around the expected results achieved for each additional defense item (or defense dollar, or franc in this case), not the total monetary amount for each weapon system. (Otherwise the total bill would have rendered the system unacceptable.) The concept of expected marginal costs and benefits can be applied to nuclear targeting. Threatening enemy cit-ies and civilian populations would generate the greatest benefits per unit cost. The least proportion of the explosive force delivered would be "wasted," and the damage threatened by each additional missile would be substantial — up to a point.

DIMINISHING MARGINAL RETURNS. In nuclear warfare, diminishing returns is a well-known phenomenon with the bombs themselves. As bombs get big-ger, the proportion of explosive force that is wasted upward increases (hence the contemporary research emphasis on ground-penetrating nuclear muni-tions). The force demonstrated this principle in several interesting ways. On the one hand, proportional deterrence could not exist without diminishing returns. If diminishing returns did not exist, a larger nuclear force would au-tomatically be "better" than a smaller one. The whole point for Gallois and similar-minded people, however, was that the damage of an atomic bomb is so great that a potential aggressor has to consider the effect of *any* successful counterstrike. Beyond a certain point, the size of that counterstrike becomes irrelevant, as was realized by figures as diverse as Khrushchev and McNamara. The latter's conclusion that it was sufficient to be able to destroy a quarter of the Soviet population and half of its industrial capacity was influenced partly by "the fact of strongly diminishing returns at levels beyond these."[96] As a simple illustration consider that with a 50 percent kill ratio, one hundred attacking missiles would destroy fifty defending enemy missiles. It would then require four hundred missiles to destroy ninety-four enemy missiles, and five hundred missiles to assure destruction of ninety-seven! Increasing kills from ninety-four to ninety-seven requires another one hundred shots. This does not mean that the attack should never be made but that diminishing marginal returns, given the technology of the time, strongly affected nuclear targeting — and this actually benefited the French.

HIDDEN ACTION.   The principle of asymmetric information has two components, one of which is hidden action that the other party would like to be able to uncover. One way to do so is by offering incentives such that the opposing party voluntarily refrains from hidden, potentially harmful, action. In France, several ways were found for public and private agents, including military personnel, to reveal their support for the force. Although popular history grossly distorts the extent to which innovative officers have to struggle against hidebound military bureaucracy, this does of course happen. It is therefore remarkable how rapidly nuclear-minded officers such as Charles Ailleret rose to the top. Two things helped. First, the French army was searching for new methods, and even its conservative traditionalists were interested in the potential of the new weapon, thereby coaxing themselves "out of hiding." Second, the government apparently actively reached for such officers, especially in the de Gaulle era, and promoted them. De Gaulle had struggled with little success to modernize the French army's armed force and understood on a personal level that innovators have to be helped and protected. By institutionalizing this, he helped to overcome the hidden action problem and encouraged self-revelation. Nuclearizing the military was a way to motivate the innovators and move them from the back row to the front and give them an incentive to continue nuclearizing.

HIDDEN CHARACTERISTICS.   The hidden characteristics aspect of the principle of asymmetric information also has an application to the threat of nuclear warfare. To quote Gallois, "use belongs in the realm of the imaginary" and "the 'force' aspect of grand strategy includes only what you see."[97] Almost all nuclear strategy is based on the threat posed by the weapons, which means that the mindset of potential adversaries lies at the core of everything. For this reason information has to be given to the enemy, but not too much, and sometimes the enemy must be misled. Denying the enemy all information is counterproductive as that would undermine deterrence. Giving the enemy too much information is counterproductive as well because that can encourage a first strike or other undesirable behavior. As a result, control of information is very centralized (as is decision making). The role of asymmetry of information is particularly interesting. In nuclear warfare, or the threat thereof (the real function of the force), the ideal situation occurs when one's own government knows everything about the enemy's atomic force and its intentions, while the enemy only knows what one's own government wishes the other to know. But perhaps that is true of all warfare, suggesting that on this level at least nuclear weaponry is but one more item in the infinite arsenal of war.

CONCLUSION

After World War II France developed an independent nuclear force which peaked in importance under Charles de Gaulle but has lost some of its primacy since. France was motivated by its history of strategic decline, serious questions about its allies, the expense of conventional rearmament, fears about its infantry becoming NATO cannon fodder, but, above all, the need to restore greatness and grandeur.

French strategists argued that nuclear weapons abolished traditional battle and military notions of time and space and enabled a relatively small force to deter a much larger one. The most radical thinkers advocated abolition of the conventional forces. Moderates hoped to protect the homeland or utilize nuclear weapons to improve France's world, or at least European, position. De Gaulle also wished to create a completely new army. Doctrine, however, remained unclear and contradictory, and many issues remained unresolved. The picture was further clouded by the introduction of tactical nuclear weapons, about whose role no consensus existed.

Doctrinal haziness does complicate our analysis of whether substitution occurred but does not make it impossible. Our assessment is reflected in table 7.2. Budget choices were made. The nuclear force was substituted for conventional forces, particularly in terms of spending and numbers of personnel and maintenance of national security, and to some extent in the areas of deterrence and defense. The ability of conventional forces to launch strategic strikes at the enemy's heartland was perhaps only weakly substituted by the nuclear force, but nuclear weapons were used as substitutes for dependence on America and for alliances in general. Possession of nuclear weapons also allowed France to pursue cultural and general foreign policy objectives which conventional forces could not fulfill.

APPENDIX

A Matrix for the Force De Frappe Case

Principle	Manpower	Logistics	Technology	Planning	Operations
Opportunity cost	cost of scientific personnel unavailable for peaceful purposes	missile submarine development means reduction in sealift capacity	conventional battle technology degraded	emphasis on deterrence means absence of flexible response strategy	tous azimuts means a lack of concentration of force
Expected marginal costs/benefits	fewer conscripts better for the economy	'vital targets' may include logistical targets	aerospace industry	city targeting provides greatest deterrent effect	Regane: better to test outside homeland
Substitution	small number of technicians instead of large numbers of draftees	rockets and planes are better than overseas bases	more 'bang for the buck' (more 'frappe for the franc')	proportional deterrence makes up for limited force size	submarines replace more vulnerable delivery systems
Diminishing marginal returns	increasing number of infantrymen does not increase power	more weapons and people do not automatically strengthen strategic forces	larger bomb does not automatically increase effect	given proportional deterrence, no value to increasing force beyond country's value to aggressor	number of similar weapons crowded into homeland would become increasingly vulnerable to attack
Asymmetric information (overcoming) hidden characteristics	military morale issue used by de Gaulle	nuclear submarines have few requirements and hence deny enemy information on location, etc.	exact targets kept vague	all nuclear decision making concentrated with president	submarines are always on the move, keeping enemy uninformed
Asymmetric information (overcoming) hidden actions	scientific and technical education	aviation industry benefits (Gallois is advisor to Marcel Dassault)	military can exploit high public confidence in technology	innovative nuclear officers rewarded with promotions	successful tests help build public confidence

Economics and Military History in the Twenty-first Century

In our analysis we impose a framework of thought on ages in which the principles we discuss were not yet articulated, at least in a formal sense. Such is the role of science and scholarship. In particular, it is the claim of (neoclassical) economics that these are universal principles — laws of nature — operating in all time and space, applicable to all situations, ceteris paribus, regardless of whether event participants have identified and named the underlying cause. Information affects exchange always; substitution is to be found everywhere; decisions at the edge (on the margin) have been made in all times by all peoples; diminishing returns are a physical fact; and so on, irrespective of whether the actors involved "knew" this. Even one who is not cognizant of these forces still operates by them. Economic forces work just as gravity "works." No nonhuman animal "knows" about natural selection, yet that force has shaped the world. All are compelled to live within the constraints imposed, and the opportunities offered, by the laws of nature.

In each case taken up in this book, economic principles were found to be a useful tool by which to parse military history. Economics cannot explain everything, but the extent to which its principles illuminate certain behaviors and events suggests a fruitful avenue for military historians to impose structure on description. It stands to reason, then, that we apply these principles to other episodes or to invoke additional principles of economics to reread and rewrite more military history. We will not outline a second book here but consider two examples of what is possible. Since 1944, a huge literature has applied game theory to economics, biology, strategic studies, public health, and other fields.[1] But gaming is very much older than game theory, and it would probably be good sport to reread theoretical or applied war strategists of old in light of modern game theory. Which "games" did they know of and play, and which escaped them? How precisely did they understand the assumptions underlying specific games? In the absence of modern mathematical tools to help think through a particular game, how secure was the logic of their conclusions? What did the great military strategists of the past see that escaped their less fortunate counterparts? Indeed, might game theory reveal that certain prominent strategists might have been lucky rather than having been strategic?

We have said little in this book that would involve principles of public finance; we have touched on this in the case of Italy's condottieri and France's budgetary problems financing its force de frappe, for example, but we have not directly addressed principles of taxation and public expenditure. Nor have we dealt squarely with so-called public goods, even though defense is usually economists' prime textbook example of a public good—a good that, once produced for one, can yield benefits to additional users without additional cost and from whose value flow these additional beneficiaries cannot feasibly be excluded. For instance, if one cannot be excluded from enjoying watching the sun rise, one cannot be made to pay for the benefit thus received; likewise, if one cannot feasibly exclude Switzerland from the protection the NATO alliance offers to the core of Europe, one cannot make Switzerland pay for the protection thus received. Switzerland gets a free ride (or, at any rate, an easy ride, i.e., a disproportionately large benefit relative to the cost contribution made, for whatever contribution the country may choose to make). When exclusion can be instituted in a foolproof way, the benefit can be restricted exclusively to those who share in the cost of provision: the good becomes a "club good." Clubs can be joined, and benefits received, upon payment of a membership fee. Nonpayment results in exclusion: benefits can effectively be withheld from nonpayers. Military alliances are attempts to build defense clubs. Not just creations of modern nation-states, they reach far back in time and can be observed among nonhuman species as well. As any schoolchild knows, alliance politics can be complicated, and it might be of much interest to military historians to come to understand alliance stability and volatility from an economic point of view. What are the determinants of alliance formation and dissolution? Why were some alliances notoriously more fickle than others? How can alliance members protect themselves from a fall in membership rolls? Why can alliances not grow beyond a certain number of members? These and many other such questions can be tackled from an economic viewpoint.[2]

Apart from the limited number of principles of economics used, two main drawbacks of our work would need to be rectified in further work: five of our six cases come from western Europe, and one from North America, and all are from the second millennium AD. It would be instructive to expand the scope to other peoples, those of the Asia-Pacific region, of Central and South

America, of Africa, and of Central Asia and the Near and Middle East, and to include a few cases prior to AD 1000. In some areas few documents are available, but physical anthropologists, botanists, geologists, and others have found ways to let other records speak to us. These, too, a military historian might access and use to reconstruct history with economic principles of behavior in mind. Regarding the past, much exciting work lies yet before us.

Having been steeped in so much history throughout this book, one may wonder whether economics has useful things to say about contemporary military affairs. By way of example, we hint at how economic thinking may be applied to current issues of terrorism, military manpower, and the use of private military companies. We also comment briefly on a complex of topics regarding economics, historiography, and military history, and summarize the main arguments and findings of the book.

ECONOMICS OF TERRORISM

Terrorism is not a "9/11 and thereafter" phenomenon. As a form of violence, or threat of violence, to wring political concessions from fear, it has been around for ages. Although associated today with nonstate actors, the origin of the modern term *terrorism* stems from state terror, namely, that perpetrated by the revolutionary French regime, the Reign of Terror, from September 1793 to July 1794. This is not the place to review the convoluted antecedents and history of *la terreur*. Suffice it to say that it was akin to, although in degree and quantity certainly different from, Nazi Germany's internal security apparatus, Stalin's pogroms, Maoist excesses, Argentina's "dirty war," and South African apartheid in the twentieth century — pervasive and brutal repression by representatives of the state against internal dissent.

A response in kind by nonstate groups against the state is domestic terror. Antecedents include acts of terror perpetrated by anarchists in the late nineteenth century, but in the post–World War II era they are exemplified, for instance, in France, Germany, and Italy from the late 1960s through the 1980s, in Colombia during the past roughly fifty years, or in India for the past few decades as well. Violent internal dissent does not usually make for world news headlines. To attract those, terrorists plan for different, more spectacular, events. Perhaps the signature event of this sort was the hostage taking and killing of Israeli athletes by Palestinian terrorists during the 1972 Olympic Games held in Munich, Germany. Here, terrorism transcended nation-state boundaries. For illustration, this section focuses on transnational terrorism.[3]

Media, political, and fictional accounts of acts of terror invariably highlight the terrorist, the villain who controls the doings of his minions, the mastermind at whose bidding underlings lay down their lives.[4] One may recall names such as Andreas Baader and Ulrike Meinhof of Germany's Red Army Faction of the 1970s, the Venezuelan-born "Carlos the Jackal" (Ilich Ramírez Sánchez), who during the 1970s and 1980s committed terrorist acts across a number of continents; the Palestinian Abu Abbas, who was responsible for the killing of an American tourist, Leon Klinghoffer, on the hijacked Italian ship *Achille Lauro* in 1985; and the Kurd Abdullah Ocalan, whose group, the PKK, waged a terror campaign from the mid-1980s to the late 1990s in Turkey. One might also recall the names Shoko Asahara, the mastermind of Aum Shinrikyo's sarin-gas attack in Tokyo's subway system in 1995 and, of course, the Saudi Osama bin-Laden, responsible for the 11 September 2001 attack, and of the Jordanian Abu Musab al-Zarqawi, the prime suspect in the wave of beheadings and bombings in Iraq that followed the American war there in 2003.

Terror, in a word, has a face, or at least the affected public wants to see a face it can associate with specific acts of terror. But to focus on individuals is myopic. The primary objective is not to "take out" individuals but to undermine the organization within which they operate. Indeed, acts of terror "without a face" are more numerous than those "with a face." Few will recall any Basque terrorist's name, or that of any member of the IRA, or of Japan's Red Army, of Colombia's FARC, or of the countless, nameless Tamil suicide bombers in Sri Lanka, or of those setting off improvised explosive devices in Iraq. Basing counterterrorist policy on terrorists, rather than terrorism, would be like basing industrial policy on labor alone without also understanding the firms and industries within which labor works. What counts are not just the workers but their recruitment, their training, their productivity, and how they are financed and supported.

Economists analyze markets on the assumption that its participants — people and the groups they form — behave rationally. Thus, economists' fundamental proposition is that a terrorist organization — like all organizations — is a rational actor. This is to say that, given its beliefs, its members choose the where, the when, and the how of attacks subject to a set of constraints, which include the production costs it faces, and the labor, capital, institutional, and other resources available to the organization. The use of the term *rational* has been much misunderstood. Economists are not saying that the way terrorists come by their particular beliefs is rational. They are saying that the way they go about implementing their beliefs is rational. By analogy, economists are not saying that McDonald's Corporation is rational about its passionate belief of providing hamburgers to the world; they are saying, it is rational in the way it goes about doing so, that it is responding to changes, risks, and opportunities in the marketplace in a reasonably sensible and predictable way. Economists treat a terror organization the way they would treat any company or firm, except that what is being produced is not a good or a service but a bad or a disservice.[5]

Suppose we wish to examine the matter as if we were one of these producers. In that case, we are facing a problem of production under adverse business conditions, adverse because government will throw hindrances in our way. The organization needs to ask itself three questions: first, what hurdles can be erected to make business more difficult for the terror organization; second, how may it best respond to government action (the hurdles) if it does not wish to be pushed out of business; and, third, what can government learn from the difficulties it encounters in placing hurdles in the organization's way?

The hurdles come in two categories, namely, government actions that decrease the organization's revenue and actions that increase its cost (or both). Prior to 11 September 2001, governments focused predominantly on increasing costs. The U.S. government famously introduced the use of metal detector screening devices at airports in early 1973, doubled U.S. embassy security budgets in 1976, passed antiterrorist legislation in 1984, and undertook embassy fortification measures in 1985 and 1986. These were passive, defensive measures intended to raise the cost to terrorists of getting through to the intended target. Among active, offensive measures, the United States undertook a raid on Libya in 1986 following a bombing in the Berlin discotheque La Belle aimed at American armed forces personnel and, more recently, attacks on suspected terrorist facilities in Afghanistan, Sudan, and elsewhere. Serious efforts to intervene on the revenue side are much more recent.

From the viewpoint of a terror organization, the interventions are logically equivalent. By way of example, suppose that the current revenue and cost situation is such that a terror organization can carry out two terror attacks per time period. If revenue is constant but the cost per attack increases, then the organization may be able to carry out only one attack per unit of time. Conversely, if the average cost is constant but revenue declines, it also may be restricted to carry out only one attack. Either mode of intervention is conceptually equivalent to the imposition of a tax on the business of terror. Since the economic consequence of a tax on terror is the same for a terror organization — reduced output — it would appear that government has the luxury of choosing the cheaper intervention (either on the revenue side or the cost side).

Government must, however, consider two problems. First, it must consider its own expense in either reducing terror revenue streams or increasing terror production costs. This is important because to be effective, the reduction of the revenue stream requires virtually universal cooperation from other governments, and the cost of coordination among two hundred or so governments and international organizations can be very high indeed (as we address in more detail in a moment). In contrast, unilateral defensive measures may be cheaper.[6] Second, apart from the cost to government of imposing restrictions on terror organizations, government must also anticipate the reaction of the terror producers. For example, while it was relatively cheap to install metal detectors at airports, an unforeseen, and unintended, consequence was that terror organizations changed their product mix: they produced fewer skyjackings and more embassy bombings. Similarly, it has been shown that a program of embassy fortification induced terror organizations to shift toward more assassinations and terror threats.[7] In a word, in choosing the appropriate "terror tax," government must choose not the cheapest but the optimal option across the available product mix.

Whatever the resulting tax mode, terrorists can and must be expected to take tax evasion measures. These consist of finding new sources of revenue or ways to lower the average cost of attack, or both. Regrettably, this can be achieved in a disturbing variety of ways, as we now know from the empirical record. First, one way is to raise alternative revenue. We have learned in recent years that revenue comes from licit as well as illicit sources and is transferred by Western and non-Western means that are difficult to monitor and, even if monitored, may not be detected or not detected in time. Unlike regular money laundering where "clean" money results from a "dirty" action, such as an illegal narcotics transfer, terror can be organized as a "dirty" action that follows "clean" money (and is, not unreasonably, referred to as "reverse money-laundering").[8]

Second, another option for a terror organization is to change the place of production, that is, the location of attack, away from more fortified targets to less fortified targets or, what amounts to the same thing, from more fortified countries to less fortified countries, hence the recent large number of attacks, post-9/11, in developing nations such as Egypt, Indonesia, and Turkey. Of course, it does not help to bring potential victims, such as aid workers or journalists or private reconstruction contractors, closer to terrorist bases of operations. Instead of bringing terror to people, as in 9/11, we now bring people to terror—and lower the cost of attack. Third, a terror organization can wait for the tax effort or enforcement intensity to subside. It can wait until government vigilance declines; it can contribute to declining vigilance by changing the timing of attack. There is empirical evidence that terror attacks and counterterrorist action move in cycles whereby an attack is followed by intense counterterrorist measures, and these in turn are followed by a delay in a further round of attacks.

Fourth, terror organizations may be expected to improve the efficiency of their operations, which also lowers average costs. For example, economies of scale can be achieved by sharing fixed costs of planning across a greater terror effort for a given time period. Economies of scope can be achieved by sharing fixed costs across a larger set of products, that is, not more attacks but more types of attacks. Economies of agglomeration may be achieved when terror groups locate in close proximity to each other, and economies of learning can take place when a successful attack by one group signals to other groups what works. To some degree, all of these behaviors have been observed and may be anticipated in future, and all of these result in efficiency gains.

Fifth, terror organizations can and do change their product mix. Already mentioned was the product substitution from one attack mode to another, say from skyjackings to assassinations to hostage-taking events. In particular, there is empirical evidence that not only the mode of attack responds to the taxes placed on a particular mode of attack but the lethality or deadliness of the average attack has increased. This is, in part, because terror threats, which need not be followed through, have become less credible with the advent of more effective countermeasures, and terrorists appear to have responded to this by conducting fewer but more deadly attacks.[9] In a word, substitution can take place from bombings to assassinations, but it can also take place from bombings without casualties to bombings with casualties.

Sixth, terrorist organizations can and do innovate and offer new products or product targets; for example, in addition to common targets such as embassies, military compounds, and tourist spots, they can release nerve gas in subway tunnels, fly airplanes into buildings, conduct a large number of beheadings in public, and seize public schools or theaters, and we may expect more innovation of this sort especially as the government tax on terror compels terror groups to disperse and to lower their rate of communication and coordination.

Seventh, terror organizations further substitute by changing their risk-profile. Old-line terror organizations driving on left-wing ideology in the 1960s, 1970s, and 1980s were relatively risk-averse, in part because their finance base and labor pool were small and they could not be expected to put limited financial and human resources at high risk of confiscation or imprisonment. In the 1990s and 2000s, these groups have been replaced by terror groups with a more risk-loving profile, in part because their finance and labor pools are larger.

Eighth, we have spoken mostly of "a" terror organization or even "the" terror organization, but there is empirical evidence that suggests that terror activity clusters, that is, when one organization undertakes action and strains government responses, it becomes relatively cheaper for other terror organizations to carry out their own attacks at that time. The intent is to induce government force thinning, an attempt to diffuse a concentrated government response to one attack and inhibit government's ability to respond simultaneously to multiple attacks or threats of attacks.

The overriding message is that the effort to tax terror out of business calls forth resistance and that it breeds innovation, substitution, and efforts to increase productivity, all of which reflect at their foundation the operation of economic principles such as the principle of substitution: terror organizations substitute by changing the time of attack, by changing the mode of attack, by changing the capital-intensity of attack, by changing the lethality of attack, by changing the location of attack, and so on. And all of these are rational responses: a terror organization looks at its available resources, looks at the hurdles being put in its way, and then figures how best to achieve its objectives anyhow. The only thing that may be irrational is how a terror organization comes by its particular beliefs, but not how it goes about implementing them.

It is also interesting to note that terror organizations can compete with each other. The 9/11 attack in particular was so bold and commanded so great a response by the governments of the United States and its European allies as to drive up the cost of conducting terror strikes for smaller organizations such as the IRA in Northern Ireland and ETA in the Basque region in Spain.[10] In the past, especially in the 1970s, many terror organizations shared a common left-wing ideology, and their activities appeared to be loosely coordinated and cooperative in the sense that the actions of one group in one country would not adversely affect the survival of another group in another country (no "negative externalities," or spillover effects). A certain honor among thieves prevailed. But the new terror associated with so-called Islamic fundamentalism does not share an ideological commonality with the old terror groups and therefore does not particularly care about spillover effects that might drive the old terror organizations out of business.

What does any or all of this imply for government policy, and what are the prospects for successful counterterrorism?[11] Unfortunately, the prospects are not particularly good because it can be shown that governments tend to overinvest in defensive measures and underinvest in offensive measures. To see why, consider a set of asymmetries between terror organizations and their targets (table 8.1). These asymmetries provide a tactical advantage to terror

Table 8.1: Attributes of terror organizations and target governments

Terror organizations	Targeted governments
▶ **target poor**	▶ **target rich**
▶ weak relative to adversary	▶ strong relative to adversary
▶ **long-term time horizon**	▶ **short-term time horizon**
▶ **agreement on common enemies**	▶ **no agreement on common enemies**
▶ can be restrained or unrestrained in their response	▶ generally, must be restrained in their response
▶ non-hierarchical organization	▶ hierarchical organization
▶ **small size furthers common interest**	▶ **large size hampers common interest**
▶ **luck needed only once**	▶ **luck needed always**
▶ reasonably well-informed about government responses	▶ not well-informed about terrorist organizations

Source: Excerpt from Enders and Sandler, 2006, table 6.1, p. 144; emphases ours.

organizations, and it is within the scope of these (and other) asymmetries that government must choose between offensive and defensive measures. Offensive measures include actions such as infiltration, preemptive strikes, and retaliatory raids, mostly aimed at raising the production cost for terror organizations. Defensive policies include efforts such as preventive intelligence gathering, installation of technical barriers, target hardening, and new antiterror laws. The practical problem is that the properties of defensive measures are different from those of offensive measures. In particular, defensive measures, such as building a wall around one's home country, deflect terror attempts toward softer targets elsewhere and thereby impose a cost on other countries. But other countries can do the same thing and thereby impose a cost on the home country. This seems senseless, except when one considers that offensive measures usually require coordination among several governments, and here one runs into a free-rider problem. If, for instance, the United States were to take the lead in pursuing unilateral offensive action, essentially it would assume the full cost of doing so and, if successful, provide a benefit to other countries, countries that, once the threat is removed, or even while the threat is being removed, have no incentive to pay a share of the cost. And so the United States will engage in preemptive or retaliatory strikes only if the expected benefits to itself outweigh its costs, regardless of the benefits that may accrue to other countries. But if the benefits of offensive action are judged too small relative to the cost incurred, the United States will then prefer to engage in defensive action only. Other countries reason along similar lines, and so we can explain the empirical regularity with which countries tend to overinvest in defensive measures that require no international cooperation and underinvest in offensive measures that do require such cooperation. In a word, the international response to transnational terrorism is suboptimal.

With these asymmetries and the dynamic between offensive and defensive measures in mind, consider the following points regarding counterterrorism. First, counterterrorist action ought to be broad-based across all countries and agencies. This might be summarized as going after "everything, everywhere, all the time." But to pursue such a truly comprehensive program is extremely costly and unrealistic, as we are now finding out. The free-rider problem does exist. We thus arrive at the paradox that if counterterrorist action is to succeed it cannot be piecemeal and haphazard, and yet we know that it will be and is, in fact, piecemeal and haphazard.

Second, while governments struggle with international counterterrorist coordination, each one of them must beware of terrorist substitution and fortify likely substitute targets. If government proceeds in a stepwise defensive fashion, as it must for it cannot protect all potential targets simultaneously, it must endeavor to direct likely terrorist attacks toward those substitute targets whose net cost to society is the least — and it is by no means easy to determine just which those targets might be.[12]

Third, for a terror organization, a low-labor, high-tech attack may be equivalent to a high-labor, low-tech attack. This implies that going after the financing that funds hi-tech events will induce a terror organization to recruit more labor to switch to low-tech events. The organization will attempt to stay on the same "isoquant," that is, produce the same amount of damage but with a different combination of labor, capital, and other inputs, given its overall resource constraint. Again, for government it is important to go after "everything, everywhere, all the time" in order to make the overall resource constraint more biting, but that is exactly what governments by all accounts have not yet been able to achieve.

Fourth, one potential counterterrorist measure that has not received much attention is that before a person joins a terror organization — and even thereafter — that person has an option of choosing to participate in a terror action or a nonterror action. Governments' counterterror activities almost always are "sticks" to counter the terror choice, whereas the "carrots" of offering an incentive to choose a nonterror action are largely missing from the debate, for example, offering people alternative means of expressing dissent. This is a research and policy agenda that has not yet been sufficiently explored. We are better at creating obstacles than we are at crafting incentives that might induce people to choose alternative, nonviolent behavior.[13]

Fifth, in liberal democracies terror success thrives on the constitutional free-press guarantee. Relatively few attacks take place in countries where the media are state-controlled. There is empirical evidence of media congestion:

if there are too many terror events to be processed by the media, the political message is lost. One effect of this congestion is that we may expect more spectacular terror events, as terror groups compete for attention. The World Trade Center's twin towers (in 2001) were an example, as was the Beslan school attack in Chechnya (2004), as were the gruesome public beheadings in Iraq (2004) and the Madrid train (2004) and London subway attacks (2005). Terror attacks today are not just local or regional but truly global events, facilitated by inexpensive video and Internet technology. Regrettably, given the rules under which open societies function, it is unlikely that media attention to the personal drama and tragedy of terror will subside. So from that perspective also it is entirely logical to expect terror organizations to continue doing what they do.

Sixth, even if transnational terrorism is directed primarily against the United States (and over the past four decades for which we have data, about 40 percent of all transnational terror events involve U.S. targets), it cannot simply dispense with coalition-building, fortify its own borders, and deflect terrorists toward non-U.S. targets. The reason for this is that U.S. diplomatic, military, business, and tourist interests outside the United States can still be attacked. The same holds true for other countries, although in different degree. And that is a problem. The lower the probability of the home country's being the target of attack, the lower the incentive to contribute to joint counterterrorist measures such as intelligence collection and sharing, that is, the free-rider problem referred to earlier. A redeeming thought is that inasmuch as a stronger or wealthier country can deflect terror attacks to other countries, these other countries will have more of an incentive to cooperate. If a leader leads, a follower might follow because of the implicit threat of becoming a substitute target, and one can argue that this is exactly what happened immediately after 9/11 when the United States could issue credible threats against member states of the European Union which rather suddenly "found" numerous terrorist cells in Britain, France, Germany, Italy, and Spain they somehow did not know of beforehand. Unfortunately, unless the more motivated party makes counterterrorist resources available to less motivated countries, weak links will exist that terror organizations will seek to exploit. This plays into another one of the asymmetries mentioned before, which is that terror organizations are better informed about government than vice versa.

Using economists' language illustrates that there is no analytic difference between producers of goods and services and producers of bads and disservices. (Obviously, there is a moral difference.) This language has the advantage of permitting us to abstract from the problem of terror per se and to bring to bear the considerable experience that domestic governments and international organizations have in regulating domestic and transnational business. In all instances the regulatory intent is to direct business into sanctioned areas of activity. For example, health care, trade, or environmental policy drives on regulations designed to affect behavior. Firms' behavior is steered into desired directions under threat of adverse government action. It is useful to view terror-producing firms in a similar way but with the much more onerous "everything, everywhere, all the time" requirement if one wants to regulate these "firms" out of business altogether. This regulatory effort must be global without any loopholes, but, as indicated, that is not going to happen. In the end, we are stuck with approaches that are cobbled together and second-best. A demand-side or "carrot" approach that reduces the perceived demand for acts of terror would be a useful complement to the currently dominant supply-side or "stick" approach. Be that as it may, certainly in response to the 9/11 attack, the United States has decided to throw its considerable conventional armed forces into a "war against terror." This motivates us to more generally examine, in the next section, some economics of military manpower.

ECONOMICS OF MILITARY MANPOWER

Since the United States' 1973 switchover from a conscript army to an all-volunteer force, a relatively small band of economists has made substantial progress in comprehending the economics of military manpower. Although data availability has restricted empirical applications primarily to the United States, the advances in theoretical work underlying the empirical work are applicable to any country or statelike entity at any time in history. There is the initial decision any government has to make, namely, how much of its resources to expend on war-fighting capabilities.[14] This is not independent of its ability to tax, nor independent of the country's underlying economic strength. A second decision pertains to how many of its people to bring into the armed forces, both in absolute as well as in percentage terms. Of those brought in, a portion will be front line and another will be support personnel, the result of decisions (deliberate or implied) as to what the tooth-to-tail ratio should be. This ratio, in turn, depends at least in part on the quality of the manpower but also on the quantity and quality of the capital that military manpower works with. Put differently, the productivity of military manpower carries implications for the demand for military manpower. Further decisions relate to the optimal amount of training, to the optimal mix of manpower experience and quality, to the optimal mix of active and reserve forces, and to whether or not, and if so to what degree, to resort to voluntary versus conscripted military service or, indeed, to mercenary forces. For example, as compared to a volunteer force, which relies on self-monitoring to secure future promotions, a conscripted force will generally require a more costly set of performance monitoring, as would mercenary forces which raise special contract enforcement problems.

The vertical composition of the force will tend to be weighted toward entry-level positions when lateral entry is restricted, necessitating a bottom-heavy large base from which to promote via up-or-out rules. This, in turn, implies a comparatively large, and therefore costly, force. In such a system, junior-rank promotions are based on skill acquisition, but senior-rank promotions resemble a play-off or tournament contest in which many qualified contestants compete for a limited number of promotion slots. This can produce performance incentive problems that need to be addressed. Supply decisions depend of course not only on military planners but on the force members themselves. Thus, economists have examined enlistment and re-enlistment decision making. Here, factors such as forgone civilian opportunities, postmilitary civilian opportunities, pay scales, incentive bonuses, the structure of retirement vesting, education, housing, and medical benefits, community demographics, attitudes, values, and belief systems, and so forth play important roles, as do the tools, means, and incentives made available to recruiters.

The economic theory of military manpower examines a wide range of interesting and important issues, and it is clear from our examination of the market for mercenaries in Renaissance Italy (chap. 3) that these issues are not restricted to modern-day armed forces but that they carried important weight in times past as well. In what follows, we review some of the issues regarding conscription and the establishment of an all-volunteer force, which naturally leads to the topic of the modern-day use of private military companies. As for the case of the economics of terrorism, there is no claim here of completeness. To indicate the relevance of economics to contemporary issues in military affairs, it suffices to sample one or the other aspect of the various topics.

Conscription of (usually) men into a state's armed forces amounts to involuntary servitude.[15] There would be no need to compel people, under threat of punishment, to join up if enough volunteers of sufficient fighting spirit and quality stepped forward on their own. In the past, a call to arms was frequently answered by volunteers, often from abroad, as, for example, in the case of New Zealanders heeding mother Britain's imperial call to go fight in the (Second) Boer War in South Africa (1899–1902). But for the all-consuming large-scale conflicts of the nineteenth and twentieth centuries, reliance on volunteers was deemed inadequate. Conscription became the norm, certainly with the Napoleonic wars, and it is only with the end of the Cold War in 1991 that nontotalitarian states at least are shifting recruitment policy from conscription toward the raising of all-volunteer forces. For example, by late 2006, only eight of twenty-six NATO members still relied on conscripts. To appreciate why this shift has taken place, one needs to understand certain pros and cons of both conscripted and volunteer forces.

Conscription — involuntary service, whether in the armed forces or for "alternative," civilian purposes — imposes an unequal exchange. The recruit is coerced to surrender labor services in exchange for which he receives something (e.g., subsistence) he would not otherwise have taken. This contrasts starkly with the way economic relations ordinarily work. No one is compelled to purchase a five-dollar bag of apples at the grocery store. Instead, consumers can choose when, where, and how to expend their resources. And as employees, people can freely choose when, where, and to whom to hire out their capacity to work. The very fact that conscription amounts to an involuntary trade suggests that it is an unequal trade, and that is something economists tend to frown upon: limitations placed on the freedom of choice can generally be shown to be economically inefficient.

The unequal exchange may be viewed as an in-kind tax. But it is a triply curious tax. Inasmuch as conscripts earn less than volunteers, it reduces a state's budgetary cost of staffing its armed forces but only by deflecting some part of the overall (or opportunity) cost elsewhere, namely, to the conscripts or draftees. Moreover, unless conscription is universal, it affects not all young men but only that part of the relevant cohort of young men that does in fact end up being drafted. If, for example, 100,000 men are needed for service in the armed forces and the relevant age pool of youngsters consists of one million men, then each has a one-in-ten chance of being drafted. The draft is a lottery. Yet a tax liability determined and levied by lottery would not be deemed appropriate in any other area of taxation. The draft-tax also discriminates by age, gender, skill, and time. It is imposed by the old on the young, by females on males, by the unskilled on the skilled (who are prevented from parlaying skill into fortune in the private marketplace), and by the present on the future (as draftees must delay civilian education and training, a delay that lowers their future productivity and contribution to society). Empirical studies suggest that earnings of draftees lie below those of nondraftees: in Holland, for example, conscripts of the 1980s and early 1990s later earned 5 percent less, on average, than a comparable group of nonconscripts. For the United States, studies find much larger earnings disparities. The reason for this appears to lie in two factors: first, conscripts on average obtain less training and education, thereby harming their future average productivity and income and, second, even if equally trained or educated, the conscription period interrupts work-place experience and, through nonuse, depreciates human capital that then needs to be replenished before it can be used again. (In the postconscription era, it appears that there are no appreciable earnings differences in the United States between members of the all-volunteer force and workers in other jobs, probably precisely because the all-volunteer force needs to compete for talent in the private labor market.)

If the imposition of taxes causes efforts to evade them, the special inequities of the draft-tax cause special efforts at avoiding ("dodging") the draft. Two recent U.S. presidents, of draft age during the Vietnam War, did not serve in that war. In this regard, both faced heavy questioning during their respective presidential bids. South Africa during its years of apartheid lost many a capable youngster, unwilling to serve racist state policy, to emigration. Today, many Russian young men evade conscription through fake medical certificates, brib-ery, and simply not showing up at drafting stations.

Conscription even has undesirable military effects as artificially cheap military labor distorts the choice between labor and capital (i.e., weaponry). Governments overinvest in recruits paid below-market compensation and underinvest in equipment. Moreover, the operation of modern sophisticated high-tech equipment is perhaps not best left to one- or two-year recruits but to professionals, and empirical studies suggest that professionally staffed armies do show higher capital-to-labor ratios — more firepower per soldier — than conscript armies. (Although we do not know of any scholarly study to demonstrate why the United States now routs its opponents so easily on the traditional battlefield, we suspect it is attributable at least in part to its use of all-volunteer, professional forces.)

Some states make special efforts to draft the skilled among the young. In the Philippines, the draft effectively works only for college and university stu-dents while other groups mostly escape it. This gives the lie to the notion that conscription serves to pull a representative sample of society into service. In Turkey, all males are subject to conscription — short enough so that all must serve, that is, a draft lottery need not be used — with temporary deferment for those wishing to complete university education.[16] This has the undesir-able effect that just as graduates would convert school knowledge into labor market experience and expertise, they are pulled off the private labor market. Upon reentry months or years later, knowledge has depreciated and needs to be recouped before it can be put to good use. Given the findings for the United States referred to earlier, it is therefore likely that Turkey permanently lowers the productivity of its (male) citizens and thereby harms the entirety of its economy and standing in the world. Meanwhile, the common practice of purchasing exemption (commutation or buyout) from military service is well documented for a variety of states. In essence, draftees choose between paying an in-kind or an in-money tax. Those paying the former signal that they have no better option in the private labor market; those paying the latter signal that they do have better options in the private labor market. Buyout therefore recoups some of the productivity loss to society. In either case, however, the draft is an onerous tax imposed on a thin slice of the population: young males at about eighteen to twenty years of age.

There is no empirical evidence in support of the claims that conscripted forces fight less often, are more equally drawn from all segments of society, are subject to a higher degree of democratic control, and generally display an increased sense of civic duty than all-volunteer forces. Instead, what the empirical evidence shows is that conscripted armies are called to fight more often than all-volunteer forces and do not necessarily lack egalitarian representation in their composition (contrary to popular claims, those with higher social status are often overrepresented in conscripted forces) and that many democratic states with conscription frequently succumb to military coups.[17] As to civic duty, the argument that every citizen has a duty to serve the state is countermanded by reemphasizing that the draft tax falls on so few of a state's citizens. In contrast, an all-volunteer force that must hire its workers from the general labor market, and must pay accordingly, imposes an equivalent fiscal (i.e., money) tax burden on all taxpayers and therefore spreads the tax burden much more widely than a draft-tax does. The fulfillment of civic duty might thus be better sought in making all taxpayers pay the cost of an all-volunteer force than in deflecting the duty solely to draftees. It has therefore been argued that the very appeal, the political allure, of the draft "originates from its specific statutory incidence: its prime victims are young males."[18]

If conscription holds up so badly against an all-volunteer force, why was it so prominent until the end of the Cold War, and why is it that only in the post–Cold War world many NATO members have converted their recruitment system from conscription to the United States' model of an all-volunteer force? One explanation revolves around two points: the size of the needed force and its productivity. It can be shown that when the size of the needed force is large and the productivity differential between conscripts and volunteers is small, the economic cost to a state may be smaller under a conscription regime than under an all-volunteer force. The size argument relies on how the tax burden to society cumulates to a sum total. If the needed force is large, a volunteer system needs to offer rising military wages to attract more people away from their current civilian occupations so that the cost of staffing a volunteer force rises exponentially. In contrast, all conscripts are paid the same fixed wage so that its budgetary cost rises only linearly. Suppose, by way of example, that there are three people and that the first has a civilian job that pays $10 an hour, the second's job pays $15 an hour, and the third's pays $20 an hour. If the military has a single job opening, then — to attract a civilian — the military needs to pay at least $10.01 an hour to make it worthwhile for the first person to switch from a civilian to a military job. Now suppose that there is a need for a second job in the force. The military has to pay $15.01 an hour to attract the second civilian, but at that pay grade, the first person who is already in the military can resign and reapply for the higher-paid military job. In practice, then, both military jobs will need to pay $15.01 an hour. And if there are three military jobs, all three will have to pay $20.01, and so on. For one volunteer, the cost to the state is $10.01 an hour; for two it is 2 times $15.01 an hour for a total of $30.02 an hour; and for three volunteers, the cost is 3 times $20.01, or $60.03 an hour. Thus, the cost rises exponentially.

In contrast, under conscription if the state offers a pay package worth $15 an hour, each conscript is obliged to take the same package, for a total cost to the state of 3 times $15 or $45 an hour. From this it follows that a conscript force of size 1 is more expensive than a volunteer force ($15 against $10.01), a conscript force of size 2 is about equally expensive ($30 against $30.02), and a conscript force of 3 is cheaper than an all-volunteer force of size 3 ($45 against $60.03). Thus, the larger the force requirement, the more the budgetary advantage tilts toward the conscript force.

The advantage is mitigated by considerations of military productivity. A force not only costs money but is also supposed to do something; there is to be a benefit to society or to the hiring state. Clearly, a more costly force is, nonetheless, desirable if its productivity more than compensates for its higher cost. To be crass but to the point, if three conscripts costing $45 an hour can kill 45 enemies in an hour, then "productivity" is one dead enemy per dollar spent. But if two, more productive, volunteers, costing $30.01 an hour, can also kill 45 enemies in an hour, then "productivity" is about 1.5 dead enemies per dollar spent. For the hiring state, the more productive, volunteer force would then seem preferable to the conscript force.

For the United States, studies show, the all-volunteer force is more productive, at least inasmuch as one can measure this. For example, when comparing pre- and postconscription periods (pre- and post-1973, that is), force turnover rates dropped from 21 to 15 percent, reducing training costs. Average length of stay in the military increased from 4.7 to 6.5 years, resulting in more on-the-job experience, and the average age of members of the United States armed forces increased from 25 to 27.6 years, leading to a more mature force.[19] In civilian employment, lower turnover, longer stay, and more maturity all play into higher measurable productivity, and there is no reason to believe that this would not also be true of the military even if its defense output cannot readily be measured. But a variety of empirical studies that have examined individual and unit performance or readiness measures — stand-ins for defense output productivity — generally support the view that education and experience are the key variables that drive higher performance.

If one takes these two reasons — military labor cost and military productivity — and evaluates them for the pre– and post–Cold War eras, it is clear that demand for large-sized forces has declined since 1991, certainly in NATO Europe, tilting the cost advantage in favor of a volunteer force. Regarding productivity, too, to effectively employ ever more sophisticated weaponry requires a stabler, more mature, and longer-serving force — professionals, in a word — again giving the advantage to volunteer forces. This would appear to explain the observed shift from conscription to all-volunteer forces in NATO Europe in the post–Cold War years, a shift that still continues as several states have announced conversion of their recruitment system toward volunteers to take place in the next few years.

Decisions regarding enlistment and retention are major supply-side issues affecting the management of the all-volunteer force of the United States, especially in the wake of its large-scale involvement in Afghanistan and Iraq since 2001 and 2003, respectively. These issues have been compounded in that widespread media reporting regarding extended duty tours negatively affect both the initial enlistment decision and the reenlistment decision. Likewise, with the active-duty force drawdown in the wake of the end of the Cold War, from 2.1 million to 1.4 million members in 2005, the United States chose to rely on its reserve forces to provide surge capacity but now finds that reserves are stretched too far, again adversely affecting individuals' decisions to join. Part of the resulting tension can be addressed in the short run with improvements in pay, benefits, and entitlements, but it is unlikely that these offer long-term solutions. In this sense at least, one might advance for debate the thought that the armed forces of the United States have lost their capacity to stay in the field. Cries to "bring the troops home" stem not merely from the budgetary cost of the war efforts and the intractability of the urban conflicts in Baghdad and Kabul but also from the difficulty of keeping the pipeline of troops filled with qualified and fresh people. (It is worth noting in passing that the first Gulf War, from staging in August 1990 to completion in March 1991, involved some 400,000 U.S. troops without much effect on recruitment; but that war took but half a year to complete.)

Factors that affect the initial enlistment decision include one's "taste" for or perception of military as opposed to civilian life and the respective opportunities one foresees in either. The booming civilian labor market in the 1990s, as measured, for instance, by unusually low civilian unemployment rates, made it hard for the armed services to compete with the private sector. Civilian pay growth outpaced that of military pay growth. And as the pay differential between high school graduates and college graduates rose sharply in the 1990s, military recruiting faced strong competition from colleges for young people's attention. An additional factor is that the number of surviving veterans has been declining, leading to reduced word-of-mouth encouragement within families and communities to consider and sign up for military service. Changes in recruitment advertising, the number and incentive structure for recruiters, and a variety of other factors also adversely affected successful recruiting.

In the United States, the armed forces have been able to keep the pipeline filled, but at a cost. Extending duty tours and increasing reenlistment bonuses has kept people in the field, and higher first-time enlistment bonuses as well as lowering the average quality grade of incoming recruits have replenished troop strength.[20] But lengthy and repeat deployments take their toll on recruitment and retention, for both active-duty and reserve forces. Beyond these relatively short-term force management issues lie longer-term concerns such as how to deal with optimal career-lengths and problems caused by the current military health and retirement system. For example, a soldier's term of effective service on the front line will be shorter than that of a military procurement official back home. Why then treat both, as the current system does, to the same twenty-year vesting period before each becomes eligible for postcareer health and retirement benefits? The current system encourages the soldier to stay in for the full twenty years even when his most productive military years are already past, just as it encourages the procurement official not necessarily to continue to give his best once he has passed twenty years of service (as he is then vested and has nothing much to lose). One solution does not fit all. The private sector is rapidly changing from a system of defined benefits, wherein an employer promises today a set of benefits its employees are eligible to receive in future — regardless of future cost — to a system of defined contributions, wherein an employer makes contributions beyond wages or salary that its employees may use to purchase health insurance and retirement benefits on their own. This switch severs employer-based health and retirement services and makes the labor market more efficient as it encourages employees to seek the best possible match of their skill and experience set with available jobs while taking portable health and retirement benefits with them. The armed services might consider a move in that direction and, in the process, address other concerns in military compensation across the service branches and active-duty and reserve forces as well.

Economics plays an important role in force management, not only on the supply side, to which most of the preceding discussion was devoted, but also on the demand side. To pick just one issue, military manpower planners need to predict and smooth needed force levels through demand-peaks and troughs. While the United States has handled the force drawdown at the end of the Cold War well, it has not been equally successful handling the transition to the post-9/11 environment. The post–Cold War drawdown was accomplished in large part through Voluntary Separation Incentives (VSIs) and Selective Separation Bonuses (SSBs). These payments, as authorized by Congress, served to induce nonvested members of the armed forces (i.e., those with fewer than twenty years of service) to leave and forgo future benefits. The clever design and implementation of VSIs and SSBs not only achieved the desired force reductions virtually without any involuntary separations but also resulted in a balanced exit so that the remaining force continued to be of high quality. But when authorization to offer voluntary separation incentives expires, as it has, undesirable problems can result. For the sake of exposition suppose that vesting occurs after three years of service. Also suppose that there are three annual cohorts of size 100, 100, and 100 (in the first, second, and third year, respectively), for a total force strength of 300. As the third-year cohort becomes vested in retirement and other postservice benefits, 100 people drop out of the service, so that the corresponding first-year intake has to be 100 recruits if the force strength is to remain at 300. Now assume that demand changes so that the force requirement is only 250. The third-year cohort drops out, leaving 100 second-year people becoming the third-year cohort and 100 first-year people becoming the second-year cohort, so that only 50 recruits are taken in to form the first-year cohort. This changes the average age and experience (i.e., productivity) structure of the force. Eventually, the 50-member first-year cohort will become the second and then the third-year cohort. At that point, the most experienced members form the smallest cohort. If, instead, voluntary separation inducements were authorized, members of the original first and second-year cohorts could be induced to leave early, so that the new incoming cohort could be larger than 50 people. The scheme can be designed to keep the age, experience, and productivity structure fairly constant across all cohorts.

Topics in the supply and demand of military manpower constitute a rich and fascinating vein of applied economics. As for the case of the economics of terrorism, the foregoing pages have sampled some of the many issues without claim of completeness. Beyond conscription and volunteer forces lies another potential source of manpower: mercenaries, or employees of private military and security companies.

ECONOMICS OF PRIVATE MILITARY COMPANIES

Private military companies, or PMCs, have been in existence for hundreds of years. The discussion about the employment of condottieri and their men by city-states in the Italian Renaissance (ca. AD 1300–1500), is an extensive case study of PMCs, for that is what they were. PMCs have come to renewed prominence, especially after the end of the Cold War. Seemingly interminable civil wars in Africa and elsewhere led to some highly publicized cases of governments' hiring mercenary troops. Among these were companies such as Executive Outcomes, hired by Sierra Leone in West Africa, and Sandline, hired by Papua New Guinea in the South Pacific. Americans first became widely aware of the use of PMCs with their employment in the U.S.-led NATO war against Serbia in 1999 and certainly with their use by the tens of thousands in the ongoing wars in Afghanistan and Iraq. Because the tasks these companies fulfill go far beyond combat, experts separate private military companies (PMCs) from private security companies (PSCs). The distinction is not firm but, at least as a first cut, separates out those companies whose employees may see combat action or provide direct combat-related services from those who provide other services, even rather more mundane ones such as cooking, laundry, and housekeeping. Once among a prototypical soldier's duties, many such services have been contracted out to the private sector.[21]

In this section, we ask two questions. Taking the second question first — what is the best feasible governance structure by which to provide security? — one has to entertain the possibility that the answer might well be a private force rather than a public force, if only because the private provision of security, or at least of elements thereof, is now pervasive. In our discussion regarding conscripted and all-volunteer forces, we simply assumed that the public provision of security services is best. Yet the very existence of PMCs and PSCs suggests that there are alternatives. Before the second question about the organization of force can be asked, we must still pose the first question: what kind of good is security anyway? It makes little sense to ask what the best feasible governance structure is by which to supply security unless one has gained a feel for the sort of security one wishes to see supplied. Perhaps different types of security are best supplied by different governance structures.

It is not well appreciated that the private security sector is larger than the public one, both in the numbers of employees and in dollar terms. In the United States, most shopping malls hire private security guards, virtually every private college campus has its own public safety department (that, despite its name, is actually private), all big sport events come with security services on hand, businesses erect fences around manufacturing plants and patrol their premises twenty-four hours a day, hospitals employ guards, gas stations and retail stores use cameras to videotape customers (and employees), and private citizens wire their homes and yards with security cameras and alarm systems that are linked to private security firms, and some of them even go so far as to place the entire neighborhood inside a gated community. Even the manufacture of major conventional arms — armored personnel carriers, fighter aircraft, submarines, and the like — is done mostly by private companies, even if on the public dollar, and the all-volunteer army of course hires from the private labor market.

The private provision of security thus is a long-established fact. Why the unease, then, over the use of mercenary forces in war?[22] To explore the matter, we follow economists into making the important distinction between the public or private *provision* of a good and the public or private *character* of a good.[23] A good's (or service's) character is determined by two aspects, the degree to which it is rivalrous and the degree to which it is excludable. A rivalrous or high-rivalry good is one that yields benefits to only one or a very few users at a time. In contrast, a low-rivalry good can be enjoyed by several or many users simultaneously. A piece of cheesecake ordinarily satisfies only one person (high rivalry). But a cheesecake as a whole may satisfy an entire family (low rivalry). A good is excludable or shows high exclusion if people can be prevented from benefiting from the use of a good. Conversely, a good shows nonexclusion or low exclusion if it not feasible to prevent people from enjoying the good. A person can be excluded from enjoying a piece of the cheesecake if he or she does not pay the bakery that made it. The price of the cake serves as the exclusion mechanism. In contrast, once the cake is in the family refrigerator, for all practical purposes members of the family cannot be excluded from "sneaking" a piece.

The two extremes of rivalry and of exclusion can be arranged in tabular form, with examples to be discussed already filled in (fig. 8.1). In the domestic

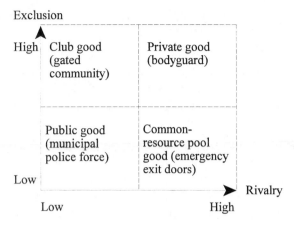

Figure 8.1. Goods space

security context, an example of a good with high exclusion and high rivalry, the upper right-hand corner of the table, would be a Hollywood celebrity or corporate chieftain hiring the services of a bodyguard. Economists refer to this as a private good, not because the provider is a private person or firm but because the character of service is that it applies to only one person at each moment in time (i.e., high rivalry) and because one can be excluded from protection if one does not pay the bodyguard for services rendered. Note that the president of the United States is surrounded by bodyguards employed by the U.S. government. Thus, bodyguarding can be either privately or publicly provided, but in either case it is a private good as regards its underlying character (high rivalry, high exclusion). Knowing this, an assassin might try to divert a bodyguard by first attacking an individual located close to the ultimately intended target. If, in negligence of duty, the bodyguard reacts to defend the decoy, the guard's service becomes "private" to the defended person, thereby providing the opening to the real target the assassin was seeking.

The gated community we spoke of earlier would be an example of a club good (the upper left-hand entry in the table). The neighbors jointly and simultaneously benefit (low rivalry), but those not living in the neighborhood are excluded (high exclusion). Another example is that of visitors to Disneyland. Once inside the compound, security services are available to all those who paid the price of admission. Those on the inside benefit simultaneously, while those on the outside are excluded. A municipal police force is an example of a public good (the lower left-hand entry in the table). Protection is afforded to all within the ambit of the police, and exclusion is not feasible. (No 911 telephone operator asks "Are you current on your city tax payments?" before dispatching help!)

Finally, a common-resource pool good, in the lower right-hand corner of the table, is characterized by high rivalry and low exclusion. Virtually anybody who wishes to benefit from the good can so benefit, but when too many people do so, the good's benefits are exhausted. A nonsecurity example is a congested highway. Any motorist can drive onto the highway and benefit from the higher average speed it normally affords. But too many motorists on the highway bring traffic to a halt. Congestion signals high rivalry for the good's benefits. In the security context, emergency exit doors fulfill the characteristics of a common-resource pool good: a number, or "pool," of doors serve as a common resource to all potential users, hence the term common-resource pool. Suppose that a fire breaks out in a discotheque, theater, hotel, hospital, or airplane. People rush to the emergency exit doors, but because it is not feasible to exclude anyone from doing so, they find that the doors, the common resource, are crowded. Only the strong and lucky may get out in time.

For all of our examples, note that the security good itself can be privately or publicly provided. Emergency exit doors in federal buildings are "publicly" provided; those at the city mall are "privately" provided. A local military base is a "publicly" provided gated community; but the neighborhood next to it provides the service "privately." The bodyguard can be paid from the "public" or the "private" purse, and even in the case of the municipal police force there is no particular reason that would hinder a municipality to contract with a private security service to fulfill police functions in the same way that municipalities contract with private waste haulers to empty trash bins.

The table has been constructed in a special way so that it may also be viewed as a figure (fig. 8.1). Thus, instead of polar low and high entries regarding rivalry and exclusion, one may think of the lowest low as zero rivalry and zero exclusion (a "pure public good") and of the highest high as 100 percent rivalry and 100 percent exclusion (a "pure private good"), and likewise for the other two goods. Low and high then are the endpoints of a range of degrees of rivalry and a range of degrees of exclusion. One advantage of converting the table to a figure with rivalry and exclusion axes is that this permits the easy incorporation of intermediate cases ("impure public goods," "impure private goods," and so on). For example, the fewer the passengers on the airplane, the more the case of airplane emergency exit doors moves along the horizontal axis from being a common-resource pool good toward being a public good: eight emergency doors for 300 passengers make for high rivalry during an emergency, but eight doors for eight passengers make for low rivalry. This ability of a good to move within the goods space is important for the discussion that follows.

The examples used in conjunction with figure 8.1 can be transferred from the domestic to the international arena. Private military or security companies hired by charitable organizations and aid agencies providing disaster relief or other humanitarian services in Africa or elsewhere may be viewed as the equivalent of bodyguards in the domestic arena. Warlords and their private armies that stake out specific territories as their fiefs likewise may be seen as providing a private good inasmuch as they provide security services for their members but not to anyone else. Ethnic, cultural, or language markers serve as exclusion devices, and rivalry is high.[24] As a particular warlord's army or a rebel band becomes increasingly successful and takes over more territory, it offers its services to more and more people: the high-rivalry good moves in the direction of becoming a low-rivalry good, even as high exclusion remains; the private good moves in the direction of becoming a club good. Eventually the warlord's army or rebel band may take over the whole of a state and convert to become the equivalent of a national armed force. Now, the club good moves to become a public good (low rivalry and low exclusion). In many cases, however, especially in states with poor political infrastructure, national armed forces effectively serve only part of a country's territory, for example, only the capital city. The armed forces are spread so thin that rivalry for protection sets in even as low exclusion formally still holds. The good thus moves to become a common-resource pool good. If the force is corrupted, it may metamorphose yet again, for example, into a palace guard (regime protection), in which case it is once more a private good (high rivalry, high exclusion; available only for the protected head of state and, effectively, to no one else besides).[25]

This "walk around goods space" suggests several things in answer to the first question: what kind of good is security anyway? First, different forms of security may be defined by different combinations of degrees of rivalry and exclusion. Some forms of security may be more amenable (or vulnerable) to movement in goods space than others. Security has become too complex a good to easily submit to a simple public versus private supply decision. Different aspects of security may, at different times, best be provided by different combinations of providers. Second, then, the boundaries among private, club, public, and common-resource pool security goods are fluid, and there may be something to be learned about the design of a good and the organization of its governance, public or private, that facilitates (or prevents) its desired (or undesired) movement in goods space. It has become clear, third, that the phrase "private military or security companies" does not refer only to the much publicized case of the U.S. government hiring private contractors for security-related service in Afghanistan or Iraq but also to the many examples used in the past few paragraphs, from drug gangs, rebel armies, and warlords to humanitarian aid agencies and oil and mining companies hiring security services to protect their operations. Along with health and education, security is a fundamental good without which societies cannot prosper. But how each specific security service should be provided, public or private or by a mixture thereof, first depends on the specific purpose a specific security good is to fulfill. It follows, fourth, that the main issue lies not, or not primarily, as is commonly believed, with *how* force is organized, public or private, but with how it is *organized,* that is, how it is internally and externally regulated, with its complement bookends of legitimization and control.[26] It is to these issues, embedded in the second question — what is the best feasible governance structure by which to provide security? — that we now turn.

The 2004 Abu Ghraib prison scandal — the abuse of Iraqi detainees by U.S. military, secret service, and private contractors — is a reminder that employees of public agencies and private contractors alike can misbehave. Even at the supranational level, the recent row over U.N. peacekeepers' involvement in the sexual exploitation of their charges testifies that suprapublic forces can misbehave as well. Other U.N. examples involve standing by and doing nothing (Dutch U.N. forces in the Srebrenica safe haven, in Bosnia-Herzegovina, in the mid-1990s) or knowingly refusing to come to the aid of those obviously in grave danger (Rwanda in 1994, Darfur in the 2000s, and myriad other examples). Conversely, employees of private military companies, while often burdened with the emotion-laden but ill-defined mercenary label, can behave quite properly and honorably and in several instances have demonstrably prevented the very sort of slaughter the United Nations and its member states frequently have not.[27] After all, as PMC executives have made clear, the prosperity of their companies crucially depends on their good image: building a brand that reliably delivers services of known quality drives the bottom line of PMCs as much as that of Google or Wal-Mart, the very sort of brand mage that the U.S. and the U.N. — post scandals — are trying to repair.

How force is culturally legitimated, by whose authority it is armed and paid, by whom it is supervised and controlled, and by whom it, or its employees, are called to account when things go awry are important issues best left to other experts.[28] The economic legitimization for the provision of a force, however, revolves around an efficiency criterion. For example, if free-riding can be avoided, it may be more efficient for a community to pool its resources to provide for the common defense than for each member of that community to do so individually. If the community as a whole can maintain control of the sheriff, things will likely be all right. Politically, the monopoly of force lies with the community (the principal) but functionally it lies with the sheriff (the agent). But even legitimated monopoly power can corrupt the officeholder, and mechanisms must be in place to prevent abuse and, prior to that, tools by which to assess the risk one takes in designing and assigning the provision of security to a public or private agency.

One way to think about efficiency is to conceive of armed force in terms of in-house versus outsourced production. Companies can perform accounting services in-house, or they can hire an accounting firm. Companies can build a human resources department in-house, or they can hire a personnel agency. Companies can manufacture components in-house, or they can contract out component manufacturing and only do the final assembly in-house. Likewise, households can decide who gets to mow the lawn or do the dishes, or they can hire a lawn-mowing or maid service. And so it is for any public agency. It can be provided with a budget and a direction by its political masters to operate its own waste-hauling department or to outsource the work to a private contractor. It can be asked to run a prison under its own agency or to outsource the task to a private contractor. It can run its own public schools or hire a private firm that runs schools for the public agency. And a public agency can be provided with a budget and a directive to either hire a public armed force or outsource the task, or parts thereof, to private military and security firms.

Economists refer to these sorts of decisions as make-or-buy decisions,[29] touched on in chapter 1. If the provision of a good is outsourced but the contracting out brings with it great risk, then it may not be efficient to outsource. Efficiency consists of at least two components. One concerns production cost or technical efficiency, as if things were purely a matter of dollars and cents; the other concerns agency cost (agency efficiency), the risk associated with either keeping things in-house or outsourcing them. If, for example, the risk is considered high that a private military company will turn on its employer, as happened repeatedly in the Italian Renaissance, then it is probably more efficient to hire an in-house force, a force consisting of one's own citizens, even if it is more costly in dollar terms. If the risk is thought high that private security companies might not properly account for monies spent or pad their bills or otherwise abuse the position that incomplete contracts or weak supervision may place them in, then it is probably more efficient to hire in-house forces. If there is high risk that private contractors will engage in actions illegal under the provisions of international law of war and that the sending state consequently stands to lose face among its state peers in the international community, then that risk may be high enough to make an in-house force preferable even if it were to cost more in terms of technical efficiency.

To explore this, the following paragraphs outline, first, Oliver Williamson's transaction cost theory of sovereign transactions and, second, Eric Fredland's application of this theory to the case of PMCs.[30] Fredland uses it to argue both the limits to the use of PMCs and the opportunities that account for their rise.

Economists like to study extreme cases, for they often reveal more clearly the factors that account for their existence. In this spirit, Oliver Williamson, a professor of business, of economics, and of law at the University of California, Berkeley, writes that "although almost no one recommends that [a state's] foreign affairs transaction be privatized, what is it about foreign affairs that makes this an 'obvious' candidate for governance by a public bureaucracy? Why is privatization comparatively unsuited?"[31] Change a few words to match this quote to our topic: although almost no one recommends that a state's defense transaction be privatized, what is it about defense that makes this an "obvious" candidate for governance by a public bureaucracy? Why is privatization comparatively unsuited?

Each mode of governance of an activity carries advantages and disadvantages relative to other modes of governance. All transactions and contracts that parties can engage in suffer from limits to rationality and foresight (see chap. 1). Contracts cannot be completely airtight and foresee all eventualities; incomplete contracts thus open the way to opportunistic behavior. But rational actors can foresee that they cannot foresee perfectly; and they can foresee that opportunities for opportunism arise when contracts are incomplete. Rational actors will therefore structure transactions and contracts so as to minimize the attendant risks, and this is factored into the design of the desired mode of governance. The higher the risk of abuse or failure, the more likely that a transaction will be made internal to an organization rather than to leave it to the market. For example, the owner of an asset is the more vulnerable to contract holdup the more highly specific is the asset he owns. In the extreme, the asset cannot be redeployed to any other application at all, resulting in complete dependence on those who may wish to hire it. Thus, if a firm commits to build a new slaughterhouse for a chicken-processor in a rural county then the expense cannot be recovered (a slaughterhouse cannot readily be relocated) and the firm becomes vulnerable to the chicken-processor's decisions. This risk can be foreseen, and the contract would need to include provisions for appropriate risk-sharing and safeguards before the plant is built. When risks such as these become sufficiently great, so that no contract can be written to include appropriate safeguards for all foreseeable risks, it may be best to carry out the transaction within an organization rather than to transact via the market. The slaughterhouse would be built by the chicken-processor and become part of the latter's overall operation. A potential market transaction becomes internal to the hierarchy of a single organization.

With regard to a government's foreign transactions, for example, its diplomatic relations with other sovereign states, Williamson argues that the risk of handing this function to a private firm via the market outweighs the additional administrative cost that internalizing this function to a government office or public bureau, such as the Department of State, implies. In particular he argues that it is important that diplomats and associated officials have "lower-powered incentives, more rules and regulations, and greater job security than are associated with a counterpart private bureau." Although these increase the cost, they are the cost of mitigating the hazards that arise when there are high-powered incentives, few rules, and little job security — as ordinarily would be the case for private actors. Imagine carrying out foreign policy, communicating U.S. policy to Iran or North Korea, for instance, if it relied on private diplomats who can be fired at will instead of for cause, make up policy on the spot, and respond primarily to monetary incentives and promotion opportunities! In particular, there is the hazard of "probity, . . . the loyalty and rectitude with which the foreign affairs transaction is discharged." Probity includes a vertical aspect with respect to the head of state who must be certain that the foreign affairs bureau or agency follows and properly communicates his official policy and that he, in turn, receives appropriate information from the agency about the diplomatic efforts of other states. It also includes a horizontal aspect with respect to counterpart agencies in other states who must be certain of the authority vested in the bureau by its head of state, must be sure of the competence, expertise, and professionalism of its staff, and must be able to count on the bureau's larger mission beyond the immediacy of policy promulgated by the current head of state. In addition, probity refers to internal aspects of the agency, for example, the very absence of high-powered incentives that would give rise to "unwanted enterprise and zeal" in the pursuit of promotion or other rewards.[32]

Laying out his case much more elaborately and elegantly than we have done in our summary here, Williamson arrives at the well-reasoned conclusion that "as compared with alternative feasible forms (all of which are flawed), the public bureaucracy is the most efficient mode of organizing sovereign transactions." The key lies in the criterion of "remediableness": can the apparent inefficiency of the public bureau be remedied by moving the transaction to a private bureau? If not, then "recourse to public bureaucracy for those transactions for which it is comparatively well-suited is properly regarded as an efficient result."[33]

Eric Fredland, an economics professor at the U.S. Naval Academy, applies Williamson's argument to another sovereign transaction in the foreign policy realm, namely, that of transferring defense or security functions to PMCs and PSCs. It seems clear enough that war-making contracts with private companies can fall prey to a number of contractual hazards. One is uncertainty. For instance, the government of Papua New Guinea (PNG) contracted with Sandline, a for-profit organization that needs to satisfy its shareholders, to "conduct offensive operations in Bougainville in conjunction with PNG defence forces to render the [Bougainville Revolutionary Army] militarily ineffective and repossess the Panguna mine." The contract contained this clause: "The achievement of the primary objective cannot be deemed to be a performance measure for the sake of this agreement if it can be demonstrated that for valid reasons it cannot be achieved within the timescale and with the level of contracted resources provided."[34] Contract fulfillment, Fredland comments, depends on effort, not results, an example of incomplete contracting reminiscent of some condottieri (see chap. 3).

Williamson's probity hazard also applies to PMCs such as Sandline in the Papua New Guinea case. Recall that probity is defined as "the loyalty and rectitude with which the [defense] transaction is discharged." But apart from reputation effects that may hold in check a contractor such as Sandline, its loyalty is to the size of its paycheck. Moreover, an organization's reputation depends on the behavior of its employees. If soldiers misbehave they are subject to significant penalties; if employees of a PMC operating on foreign soil misbehave, they are, at worst, subject to being fired from the job. Thus, opportunistic behavior of PMC employees is more likely to occur than among soldiers. To forestall this, the PMC must offer very good terms so as to entice employees into good behavior on the threat of losing lucrative employment. This seems to be borne out in practice. For example, in 2006, DynCorp, a PMC providing security services in Afghanistan on behalf of the U.S. government, paid starting salaries of $100,000 a year to its American expatriate employees. That same year, the average annual pay, all inclusive, of U.S. military personnel was $85,553, and U.S. Special Forces earned annualized incomes of between $25,000 and $120,000.[35] Another hazard is that in fighting on behalf of a client, PMCs risk their physical, human, and other assets. The incentive structure therefore points to the avoidance of battle while prolonging the conflict, again much like what we found to be the case for city-condottieri relations in Renaissance Italy.

If hazards of outsourcing defense and security functions are high, what then accounts for the successful emergence of PMCs and PSCs? One argument is that public active-duty forces, whether conscripted or volunteer, are expensive. Like electricity-generating plants, they need to be large enough to meet even improbable contingencies, or else "the lights go out." Electric utilities deal with demand surges by building economies-of-scale base-generation capacity that supplies most of the need and top this off with expensive peak-load generation capacity that kicks in on an as-needed basis. Militaries, certainly that of the United States, avail themselves of this concept by having a large active-duty force supplemented with a large reserve force. Reserve forces are expensive. They need up-to-date equipment, they must train regularly, they need to be paid, retained, and provided with benefits beyond the paycheck. The advantage of ideal-type footloose PMCs and PSCs is that they can be hired at will, fully equipped, trained, and ready to go. This may save the hiring state some costs, but at the sort of contractual risks described earlier.[36]

In many states, national armed forces regularly pose the threat of military coups to civilian state leadership, for instance, in Thailand in 2006. Here the probity hazard is not with respect to the contracting out of defense and security functions but with the difficulty of keeping the national armed force's "loyalty and rectitude" to the state intact. If a state's leadership is distrustful of its own national armed force, it may find it useful to keep the size of the force small and rely on the hiring of PMCs and PSCs, should the need arise, either for truly national defense or for regime protection purposes. In terms of goods space, it is not clear whether the services provided by PMCs and PSCs then are public or private goods. They may be both.

If Papua New Guinea and others have imported private military contractors, other states have exported such forces. To the exporting state this can provide certain advantages. Soldiers of fortune roaming about abroad are less likely to cause trouble at home; casualties that private contractors may incur are not usually as politically sensitive as casualties incurred by a state's official defense force; if the importing country pays up, the exporting country does not even have to foot the bill for sending forces abroad; and the exporting country may be able to carry out foreign policy objectives while officially maintaining a hands-off policy. This last point has raised concerns in the United States and Britain in particular: If private contractors carry out foreign policy, how transparent and accountable are they to democratic control? Are private contractors used to carry out foreign policy without legislative supervision? Consequently much has been written about the ethics, economics, and proper regulation of PMCs and PSCs.

Fredland makes the good point that to the importing state it may not matter much whether the exporting state provides public or private forces. For example, during the first Gulf war in 1991 and during the U.N.-sanctioned Somali operation in 1993, the United States government sent mostly public forces.[37] But in the 1990s wars in the former Yugoslavia and in the 2000s wars in Afghanistan and Iraq, the United States sent, along with public forces, large contingents of private contractors to provide various combat- and noncombat-related services. Similarly, although frequently at loggerheads with each other, Bangladesh, India, and Pakistan are regularly among the top providers of U.N. peacekeepers: they export nominally public forces for their own "private," state-specific ends (e.g., to keep troops well exercised in the art of war) to whichever state the United Nations Security Council determines has an import need. But the contractual hazards for the importing state are great. For example, whether private, public, or suprapublic (i.e., United Nations) forces, or a mixture thereof, all are subject to breach of contract and sudden withdrawal, for example, the United States' and hence United Nations' withdrawal from Somalia in the mid-1990s.

Transaction cost economics teaches that whether any given transaction is carried out between independent agents in markets, or placed within organizations (private or public), or conducted in hybrid form depends not merely on criteria of technical efficiency (cost in the traditional, narrow sense) but on agency efficiency, in particular on the risks or hazards that attend to any transaction. Hazards stem from factors such as uncertainty, asset specificity, the frequency of the transaction,[38] and, in the sovereign transactions category, on probity. The degree of uncertainty, asset specificity, frequency, and the specifics of probity have changed to permit some PMCs and PSCs to flourish. As in all newly emerging markets, business pioneers will experiment and risk investors' capital to search for viable, sustainable business models. In some business environments, the combined hazard value will favor private contractors over public or suprapublic forces; in others, it won't. In addition, the increasing fluidity of exactly what the security good is that public or private forces provide (public, private, club, or common-resource pool goods) and who can best provide it also opens up opportunities for the generally nimble private sector to carve out profitable business niches.

The market for privately provided security services is in flux. Players must deal with much uncertainty. For example, Sierra Leone, in West Africa, suffered from an atrocious civil war lasting from 1991 to 2000, the sort that ordinarily reaches the United Nations Security Council (UNSC) but may not result in action that might prevent the slaughter of thousands of people. The involvement of Executive Outcomes, hired by Sierra Leone's military regime in 1995, quickly stopped the war, and democratic elections were held in 1996. Executive Outcomes left the country by January 1997. But in May 1997, the newly elected president, Ahmad Tejan Kabbah, was overthrown in a coup by Johnny Paul Koroma. As the UNSC offered at first no more than a declaration condemning the coup and banned arms supplies to the country, Kabbah then hired Sandline, a British firm—some say with the connivance of the British government—to illegally import arms and attempt to mount a countercoup to stop the renewed violence. Under pressure from the international community, the contract was apparently breached by Kabbah, following which the war resumed. Eventually, a West African peacekeeping consortium, sanctioned by the U.N. and led by Nigeria, sent thousands of suprapublic peacekeeping troops to Sierra Leone. (Kabbah was reinstated in March 1998.) This force was ultimately supplemented by U.N. peacekeeping troops as well. The war did not end until 2000, after heavy intervention by about 1,000 public British forces. President Kabbah declared the war over in 2002, but U.N. troops did not withdraw until 2006. At its peak, the U.N. force numbered 17,500 people, whereas Executive Outcomes in 1995/96 is said to have used no more than 150–200 people when it stopped the violence.[39] Use of the company was quick, inexpensive, and effective. Arguably, it saved thousands of people life and limb. The hazard tradeoffs clearly worked in favor of a private military company and in disfavor of public ones: Sierra Leone's forces themselves were in disarray and international forces did not come at all. Perhaps the certainty of being eclipsed by private contractors encouraged the United Nations and its member states to provide supranational forces, reducing the uncertainty of international behavior that Sierra Leone had suffered up to that time. The balance of the expected hazard tradeoff changed, for President Kabbah if not for the country, in favor of the use of international public forces.

Thinking about goods space (the changing nature and diversity of the security good) and contract hazard (agency efficiency) puts much needed nuance into the ongoing discussion of public versus private forces. These ideas may prove valuable for disentangling when and how best to use private contractors to complement or substitute for public or suprapublic forces, depending on the precise intended purpose of the security good at hand.

ECONOMICS, HISTORIOGRAPHY, AND MILITARY HISTORY

University of Chicago historian Peter Novick wrote in 1988 that "the level of concern with epistemological issues within the American historical profession had never been high — compared either with other American academic disciplines or with historical communities abroad," and he cites Michael Kammen, another prominent historian, who in 1986 spoke of the "'utter indifference' of the overwhelming majority of American historians to issues of epistemology or philosophy of history." Novick adds: "The matter-of-fact, antitheoretical and antiphilosophical objectivist empiricism which had always been the dominant stance of American historians continued to be enormously powerful." For illustration Novick refers to Otto Pflanze, who, when he stepped down in 1985 as editor of the prestigious *American Historical Review*, "warned historians that while models and theories had their uses, they had a dangerous 'seductive power,' which could divert historians from their prime obligation to come as close as humanly possible to reporting the past 'wie es eigentlich gewesen [ist],'" that is, reporting the past "as it really was."[40]

Historians of a theoretical inclination do not see much improvement since. Referring to postmodern approaches for instance, Willie Thompson writes that "most historical journals ignore them, much to the indignation of certain postmodernist historians, and the majority of historians continue along their incorrigibly *empirical* pathways, leaving convinced postmodernist historians in a somewhat isolated separation." David Hackett Fischer, another distinguished historian, nearly touches on theory when he writes about the emphasis on the role of historical contingency and that books in a series he edits will "offer a way forward, beyond the 'old political history' and the 'new social and cultural history' by reuniting process and event." That, however, is as explicit as he is willing or able to get.[41]

What is true for the study of history at large holds even more so for military history in particular. Theory and military history have an uneasy relation, at least as far as traditional military historians are concerned. One problem is military history's perhaps overly close link to the armed services and government agencies. Current and former members of the armed forces understandably take an intense interest in unit histories, battle accounts, and campaign chronicles; their superiors are interested in history serving the goal of "lessons learned" to be applied to the next clash of arms; and politicians and civilian overseers still order up massive official histories of this or that war engagement. Ironically, the academy feeds this tendency by marginalizing military history. A danger is that military history becomes appropriated, becomes the military's history rather than military history, a history that seeks to understand the military in the context of nonviolent antecedents that somehow give rise to organized violence and preparation therefor. Not always welcomed by traditional military historians, the so-called New Military History school tends to be much informed by gender, race, and cultural studies and by postmodern, postcolonial theory. In recent years, this seems slowly to have been broadened to fields with a more established record of theory. Economics, however, is still largely absent.[42]

History need not lack theory, nor need theory be thrown out when writing popular history. Still, theory in history is often brought to it from the outside, sometimes with dramatic consequences. For example, since the cliometrics revolution of the 1960s, economic history has been infused with economic theory to such an extent "that few departments of history now have economic historians at all; in effect, the new economic historians extinguished the other side," writes Claudia Goldin, a renowned economic historian at Harvard University.[43] What we have done in this book is to infuse economic theory into the study of military, not economic, history and have done so, we hope, without further endangering the already imperiled status of military historians in the few history departments that still house them.

Economics has been applied before to particular episodes in military history, and even to larger topics, as, for example, Fritz Redlich's monumental work on German military entrepreneurship from 1350 to 1800, as well as to current military affairs, such as mobilization during World War II and on economic aspects of nuclear war. Also, a sizeable literature exists on certain themes, for example the relation of war financing to the fiscal formation of states, and even to the wholesale rise and fall of nations, although much of this is by historians rather than by economists.[44]

Over the years, a surprisingly large number of exceedingly prominent economists, holding exceedingly divergent economic views, have written on war and peace, often in book-length treatments.[45] But our claim is not merely that a particular event, period, topic, or theme might be usefully illuminated by recourse to economic principles but that the entire field of military history would so benefit. We do not aim to present a grand theory of history based on economics, only how military history can be infused with economic reasoning and that from this new insights can be gained. By way of illustration, our aim has thus been to revisit six select cases in military history, spanning the past millennium. Although not obvious from the completed book, when the authors first met to discuss the project, the economist did ask the historian to simply name and list important military episodes, events, or characteristic features of the six time periods we considered. We selected six cases and then decided which principle of economics to apply to which episode before actually sitting down to research and write the respective chapters. Other authors have looked at specific aspects of military history from an economic viewpoint but none, we believe, have attempted to apply a variety of economic principles to the entire sweep of a millennium's worth of military history as we have.

CONCLUSION

The principle of opportunity cost helps explain the medieval preference for castle building. Despite the immense expense, the cost of a single siege could match or exceed that of building a castle. Of the three reasons for the limited emergence of field armies in the Middle Ages (cost, supply, tradition), two are economic in nature. In particular, the cost of raising, fielding, and maintaining a field army would have been even more stupendous than that of dotting the landscape with castles.

Strictly speaking, the opportunity cost of castles includes the entire set of potential alternative uses of the resources employed, not just the establishment of an army. But for the medieval ruler, alternatives such as building palaces, laying roads, or endowing universities were hypothetical, for war was his main occupation. Thus, practically speaking, the primary opportunity cost of choosing one form of military preparation (the castle) was the other form (the army). Some rulers could, of course, raise sizable armies, but doing so represented such a huge investment that the army could not ordinarily be risked in battle. Even just keeping it operational implied an ongoing cost that far exceeded the ongoing cost of maintaining a castle. Castle building, despite the enormous expense, emerged as the most cost-effective strategy.

It is true that the very strength of castles could be turned against their builders if they were taken by opposing forces or a rebellious castellan, but then, as many a ruler found out, armies could turn as well. Medieval monarchs became reluctant to experiment with armies, and the eleventh, twelfth, and thirteenth centuries were to be dominated by the castle, politically as well as militarily. For a time, it was the most highly valued among the militarily viable alternatives considered by the rulers of the age.

The principle of asymmetric information comes in two flavors, one emphasizing hidden characteristics, traits to be uncovered before a contract is signed, the other highlighting hidden actions, undesirable or harmful conduct by one of the contracting parties that cannot feasibly be monitored by the other. It is primarily with the latter that the chapter on mercenary captains in the Italian Renaissance was concerned, and attention was paid to how contracts evolved, if not to prevent then at least to lower the cost of discovery of hidden actions. Contracts had to be designed to align incentives so that both sides would be better off not trying to cheat on each other.

One way to accomplish this is by providing proper incentives for both sides to internalize contract policing. For example, the prospect of contract renewal for the next war season can encourage a condottiere to put forth necessary effort in the current war season. Similarly, the prospect of retaining a worthy warrior and his men for the next season would encourage a city-state to act honorably, that is, to pay up as agreed, in this season. The branding and registration of horses and equipment served a similar purpose, as did muster rolls, namely, to identify and sort the reliable men from the deserters. Of course, honorable men can disagree, and many are the instances in which an eminent condottiere, his contract suitably fulfilled, chose to switch employers or, vice versa, an employer chose to hire another's army. It was an active market after all, with many demanders and more suppliers, a market, moreover, that outlasted the lifespan of any one participant. Men died, of natural causes or otherwise, and young ones needed to learn the ropes, including the intricacies of contracting. Likewise, city-states appeared, disappeared, and reappeared, at times under republican, at times under despotic rule, under the sway of this or of that power. In this political flux, one constant was the need to hire and keep military men under contract. Naturally, the craft of contracting evolved.

It is surprising how much of the historical literature about condottieri is about power politics and military technology rather than about the contracts after whom the condottieri, or contractors, are named. If the condottieri period came to an end, one of the reasons ought to be sought in the difficulty of designing and enforcing military labor contracts. With the rise of permanent armies, capable military leaders were of course still very much in demand, but the role of the independent, roving military contractor had given way to the still powerful but ultimately state-dependent employee. Market power had permanently shifted from the contractors to the city-states.

Many well-known commanders have claimed that their decision to offer or decline battle stemmed from rational calculations of costs and benefits. Inasmuch as such decisions always concern the next battle, rather than past ones, these are "marginal" decisions. Decisions at the margin are those taken at the frontier of where one is. At the frontier of time, a marginal decision refers therefore to the next time period, the immediate future; it refers to a decision concerning the next battle, the impending battle. By necessity, the future is unknown and thus all such decisions involve uncertainty. It follows that the decision of offer battle involves expected additional costs to be incurred — in addition to those already incurred up to that point — to be weighed against expected additional benefits to be gained — in addition to benefits already obtained. It further follows that expectations will be disappointed, for in all cases where both opposing commanders opted for battle at least one, and possibly both, must have miscalculated. Still, even miscalculation is calculation.

Few are the commanders, in any time period, who would have rashly ignored either the cost about to be paid or the benefit about to be garnered. But the Age of Battle is distinguished by the particularly deliberate, rational, calculating way in which its most famous commanders went about the decision making. The age was, after all, coincident with the Enlightenment years and a resurgent belief in enumeration, accounting, measurement, calculation, and science. The age was just preceded by or concurrent with the lives of Copernicus, Galileo, Kepler, Newton, Leibniz, and Pascal — astronomers and mathematicians all, men who relied on observation, computation, and consequent deduction of general laws of nature. It cannot be a surprise that men of science would be followed by men of a science of war who would aspire to base war on calculation.

This does not deny the role of intuition or psychological makeup. No commander has perfect information and when 60 or 80 or 90 percent of the information was in, the remainder was not. Information, by its nature, is always outdated. Even with a theoretical 100 percent of information available, the underlying formulas to press interpretation from information could still be wrong. When modern meteorologists predict a 10 percent chance of rain, it can still rain. The improbable is not impossible. Too many are the variables and vicissitudes of weather, and so it is with war. Nonetheless, what distinguished the commanders in this time period was their belief that more information and calculation is generally better than less. Mistakes and adverse outcomes did not reflect intellectual shortcomings, merely the imperfections of their science.

The answer to the paradox of why the Age of Battle saw battle so rarely is that the prospective loss of one's army was too horrific a cost, too big a wager. More than at any prior time, to lose a battle often did mean to lose the war. Hence, the incessant, unremitting maneuvering for advantage characterizes the age more than battle did. This happened to be the outcome of the military conditions of the time, but the idea of calculation became firmly entrenched in future generations of generals.

In the chapter on the American Civil War, we returned to the principle of asymmetric information but focused on its hidden characteristic aspect rather than the hidden action aspect. In war, one wishes to hide certain of one's own characteristics as eagerly as one wishes to uncover them about one's opponent. Information, famed military historian John Keegan reminds us depends on "five fundamental stages," namely, acquisition, delivery, acceptance, interpretation, and implementation.[46] During the course of the chapter, we met them all: substantial and innovative efforts at acquisition of information, delivery thereof (not excluding ingenious ruses to deliver misleading information), acceptance, or compelling belief, of that information by those in the command chain, proper interpretation of what usually were only pieces of the overall puzzle, and implementation of an action to be taken on account of the information collected.

But more than that we emphasized not just that information was crucial or that there are stages to it but just how deliberate were the efforts to create or undo information asymmetries so as to obtain tactical and strategic advantages. The age cannot be blamed for the absence of modern tools such as completely computerized topographic maps that can be displayed real-time on rugged, solar-powered laptops, GPS-based force location analysis, and instantaneous communications among multiple parties (human and machine). No age has the future available for its use, but each invents its own novel means of collecting, dispersing, and using information. For the American Civil War the telegraph, the railroad, the newspapers, even the balloon, and the creation of the Bureau of Military Information count among these.

In the end, they proved to be too novel, experimental, unreliable, or easily disrupted, and in at least two respects the information war came down to a strangely human, even personal, side. First, the information advantage lay with those who would defend their home terrain. The information technologies of the time generally did not succeed in balancing the information advantage locals had, even when the attacking force greatly outnumbered the defenders.[47] Second, all of this war's generals had studied the same curriculum under the same professors at the same military academies—no asymmetry here—but somehow Robert E. Lee was to emerge as the primus inter pares. His unique strength lay in his superior assessment and anticipation of his opponents' likely train of thought. The Union had the overwhelming advantage in men and matériel but did not know where to put them to best effect and proved as timid as the Confederates proved clever. The end came when the "asymmetry of minds" evened. Grant's mental resources may not have exceeded Lee's, but he created two informational advantages. First, he relied on his superior intelligence organization. By trapping Lee in Petersburg, Grant cost the Rebel his ability to create uncertainty in Union minds through maneuver. But, second, perhaps it was just as important that Grant remained in command so much longer than his predecessors that he had more time to learn his opponent's mind.

Strategic bombing does not appear to have had a significant adverse effect on Germany's war production. Production of weaponry did not fall; in fact, it rose throughout and even into the last year of the war. Such effects as strategic bombing did have were due primarily to shift factors (e.g., improvements in the tactical air war) and displacement factors (e.g., German resources poured into air defense) rather than to increased amounts of bomb tonnage dropped on German industrial and population centers, and its chief effect was preparation for conquest, not military coercion to surrender. In fairness, it must be acknowledged that the Allied war effort suffered from severe information deficits during the war that made an assessment of the bombing's efficacy rather more difficult.

The emphasis of the chapter was not, however, on the overall or total effect of strategic bombing. It was on the marginal or incremental effect, the effect of additional tons of bombs. Examining such data as are available, we find evidence to show that larger bombing efforts did result in declining increases to the desired destructive outcome, as economic theory predicts, sometimes even in negative returns (e.g., the morale bombing data show that ever larger amounts of bombing strengthened rather than diminished the morale of the attacked populations). That an abstract theory of production should find an application to the very real, bloody world of warfare may surprise. Yet for the casualties, on all sides, it would have been best had it been possible for the lesson of theory to be heard and heeded and the war been brought to an earlier end.

The application of the principle of substitution to the acquisition of nuclear weapons by France during the early Cold War years depends on whether one wishes to focus on the bombs' incredible firepower as opposed to conventional weapons — their "use value" — or on their diplomatic and political value. Substitution is easier to establish in the former case than the latter. The French force de frappe was a substitute for both ground and air power. The decline in French conventional strength cannot be explained as a result of a shrinking colonial empire because France historically maintained virtually separate colonial and metropolitan armies, and the latter's size was not linked to colonial problems. The Soviet threat should have caused it to grow, but the army shrank and the atomic bomb was obtained instead. A clearer case of substitution is difficult to imagine.

Doctrinal haziness does complicate the analysis of whether substitution occurred but does not make it impossible. Certainly, budget choices were made and nuclear force was substituted for conventional forces, especially in terms of expenditure and numbers of personnel and maintenance of national security, and to some extent in the areas of deterrence and defense. Atomic weapons were also used as substitutes for dependence on America, and on alliances more generally. Further, possession of atomic weapons allowed France to pursue certain diplomatic, foreign policy, and even domestic policy objectives, for example, grandeur, which conventional forces could not possibly fulfill. Nuclear strategy coupled with traditional strategic air power doctrine even threatened to substitute nuclear force for the conventional military establishment altogether. Although events did not go quite this far, the animated discussion in France about just how far the military reach of the atom could and should be stretched is prima facie evidence that substitution possibilities were closely considered.

Economic thinking helps illuminate not just military history but contemporary military affairs as well. By way of example, we observed transnational terrorism from the angle of opportunities for substituting one time, venue, or form of terror for another (e.g., from hostage taking to bomb threats). Clearly, the principle of substitution is relevant and must inform counterterrorism policy. Following the terror attack of 11 September 2001, the United States responded by launching two large-scale wars, in Afghanistan and in Iraq. This brought us to a discussion of military manpower, in particular of the economic costs and benefits of conscription as compared with all-volunteer active-duty and reserve forces. Whereas the decisions to go to war were mostly couched in political terms, the practicalities of managing war provide many opportunities for applied economic thinking.

We also reviewed the reemergence, from the 1990s, of private military and security companies. In terms of goods space and contract hazard, we find that the monopoly of force, since Napoleon largely vested in official, public, state-sanctioned and funded forces, may be on the way to breaking down in the twenty-first century. Many defense and security tasks do not serve exclusively public good functions anymore; instead many such tasks now more nearly resemble private, club, or common-resource pool goods — and the boundaries are fluid — and may be better supplied by private providers. Moreover, in filling new niches in goods space, tradeoffs in contract hazards, that is, uncertainty, asset specificity, frequency, and probity, assume new forms such that the exclusive provision of all defense and security services by exclusively public forces may not necessarily result in economically efficient solutions.

The still young field of defense and peace economics has already made many contributions to the understanding of alliance formation and dissolution, arms races, arms production, arms trade, military manpower, procurement, nuclear strategy, disarmament, conflict management and resolution, terrorism and nonconventional conflict, and other topics relevant to security. This book shows that economics deals well with the past and present and, we hope, with the analysis of future conflict, military, defense, peace, and security affairs as well.

NOTES

PREFACE

1. See, e.g., Broadberry and Harrison, 2005, and Harrison, 1998, and the literature cited therein.

2. In recent years, a huge literature has sprung up regarding the privatization of modern warfare. See, e.g., Bryden and Caparini, 2006, and Alexandra, Caparini, and Baker, forthcoming, and the literature cited therein.

3. Mazlish, 2003, p. 13. This may reflect national culture as well as the orientation of a scholarly discipline. Alexis de Tocqueville noted in 1835 that "in no country in the civilized world is less attention paid to philosophy than in the United States" (de Tocqueville, 1984, p. 143).

4. Diamond, 1997, 2005; also see Bryson's, 2003, popular science account and his frequent attempts to put human history within the constraints of what the physical world permits.

5. In chapter 8, we speak directly to some issues of economics, historiography, and military history, issues that for now we like to defer.

6. The first book of what came to be Asimov's Foundation trilogy features a character, the mathematician Hari Seldon, who creates psychohistory, a science that would predict future events. In real life, psychohistory is, in fact, an academic subdiscipline within psychology.

CHAPTER ONE

1. Tuchman, 1962, p. 10.

2. It might have made for tiresome reading, though: Alfred von Schlieffen himself, before he wrote his eponymous plan, had devoted two volumes to a single famous Roman battle.

3. On economic imperialism, see, e.g., Radnitzky and Bernholz, 1987; Lazear, 1999.

4. See, e.g, Posner and Parisi, 1997, Becker, 1976, Fuchs, 1975, and Schelling, 1960, 1966. Economics, in turn, has been influenced prominently by mathematicians but also, for example, by psychology and neuroscience.

5. An impressive effort is that by the sociologist Charles Tilly, 1990, especially as contrasted to the literature cited therein in chap. 1. For economic history, see, e.g., Crafts, 1987, North, 1990, Goldin, 1995, Temin, 2006, and literature cited therein. See chapter 8 for a fuller discussion.

6. An example is Dixon, 1976. Norman Dixon was an experimental psychologist at the University of London. His book *On the Psychology of Military Incompetence* was guided by explicit psychological theory, an effort impressive enough to still warrant, in 2004(!), a formal book review by one Capt. Adrian Choong in *Pointer, the Journal of the Singapore Armed Forces,* vol. 30, no. 2. Dixon's effort — and, we hope, ours — is very different from ad hoc theorizing, as for instance in Cohen and Gooch's *Military Misfortune: The Anatomy of Failure in War,* 1990 (and reissued in 2006). Not that Cohen and Gooch's work is without interest. To the contrary. It provides an appropriate critique of Dixon's, and others', work and moves the spotlight to organizational rather than personal failure, but in the end the effort is too shallow: all failures are classified into failures of learning (from the past), failures to anticipate (the future), and failures to adapt (to the present). Unlike Dixon's work, this carries no predictive power and therefore offers few potential levers of intervention.

7. Experiments may be difficult to design and conduct, but it is not necessarily impossible to carry them out. In 2002, the Bank of Sweden Prize in Economic Sciences in Memory of Alfred Nobel (the Economics Nobel Prize, in short) was awarded to Daniel Kahneman and to Vernon Smith for work involving experimental testing of economic ideas. Kahneman is a psychologist, Smith an economist. Some experiments are designed; others are not. For example, it would be deemed unethical to experimentally deprive people of half their income to learn how their purchasing and saving behavior changes. But if people happen to become unemployed, one can study how the attending income-loss affects consumption and saving behavior. This is called a "natural" experiment.

8. All quotes are taken from Neufeldt, 1997.

9. Dolan, 2002. Also see Haidt, 2007, and Niedenthal, 2007.

10. For example, a large percentage of children living in cities exhibit fear of lions — that's the emotion codified into aversive behavior — even as the probability of being killed by one (which they have never seen) is far exceeded by the probability of being killed by automobile traffic or neighborhood gunfire (which many children have witnessed).

11. See Kuhn, 1962, and the ensuing debate over the structure of scientific work and the sociology of science. In this regard, we find Mayr, 1997, chap. 3, of special interest.

12. Especially noteworthy is Heilbroner's 1999 [1953] book. Its opening paragraph (p. 13) reads as follows: "This is a book about a handful of men with a curious claim to fame. By all the rules of schoolboy history books, they were nonentities: they commanded no armies, sent no men to their deaths, ruled no empires, took little part in history-making decisions. A few of them achieved renown, but none was ever a national hero; a few were roundly abused, but none was ever quite a national villain. Yet what they did was more decisive for history than many acts of statesmen who basked in brighter glory, often more profoundly disturbing than the shuttling of armies back and forth across frontiers, more powerful for good and bad than the edicts of kings and legislatures. It was this: they shaped and swayed men's minds."

13. A particular delight to read on this is Schelling, 1978.

14. Smith, 1976 [1776]; Marshall, 1961 [1890]; Samuelson, 1947. There exists a bit of terminological confusion. Originally, political economy was used to describe the economics of human societies, as distinct from the economy of nature. The first sentence of Marshall's Principles defines "Political economy or economics [as the] study of mankind in the ordinary business of life." Further on — in a useful discussion on economic methodology, and one that all stripes of economists and their detractors should reread — Marshall refers to "pure," as distinct from "applied," economics (Marshall, 1961 [1920], p. 37, n. 2). Nowa-

days, it appears that Marshall's "pure" and "applied" economics have been lumped together into "neoclassical" economics, to be juxtaposed to "political economy" that somehow takes noneconomic aspects of human life into account. Meanwhile, the economy of nature has been almost forgotten, although the newly emerging fields of bioeconomics and neuroeconomics may yet resurrect it. A very ambitious effort in that regard — coming from biology itself — is Geerat Vermeij's *Nature: An Economic History,* 2004.

15. See, e.g., the symposium in *American Economic Review,* vol. 88, no. 2 (May 1998), pp. 72–84. Certainly much more may be said on classical, neoclassical, the "old" institutional, and the "new" institutional economics. But this would lead us far astray into a very different kind of book. Regarding new institutionalist economics, particularly for the historical context taken up in this book, suffice it to point, especially, to North, 1990, and perhaps to Greif, 2000, who discusses some theory and historical examples of how individuals recognize opportunities for mutually beneficial exchange and must build institutions to deal with the problem of credibly committing to contractual obligations that arise from desired trade.

16. One may dispute the ordering. Some would put financial economics into the microeconomics category. Some would take, say, Kenneth Arrow's work and describe it as methodological rather than microeconomic in nature. But whichever way one classifies, few would disagree that the majority of prizes has been awarded in the category that examines individual motives and behaviors, i.e., microeconomics.

17. See http://www.nobel.se/economics/laureates/1978/press.html Press release of 16 October 1978 [accessed 14 November 2002].

18. Coase, 1994, p. 7.

19. The trillion dollar estimate regarding the U.S. missile shield program is taken from Kaufman, 2003.

20. Heyne, Boettke, Prychitko, 2003, p. 66.

21. Men, of course, have always easily "dispensed" with their wives by carrying on affairs, generally without ill consequence for the men. Nowadays, this increasingly carries the risk not only of marriage dissolution (divorce) but of net asset division. On the one hand, this carries consequences, for instance, for the evolution of marriage-contract law (e.g., the rise of prenuptial agreements). On the other hand, in the secondary marriage market (the "market" for second, and further, marriages) these men are more likely to meet divorced women who bring in net assets from their own previous marriages, so that the net asset status per couple may not change much. This is not the place to carry the discussion any further, but it does indicate just how quickly the consideration of the economic principle of opportunity cost leads one into a fantastic landscape of thought, and one that well matches empirically observed behavior and events. A symposium of papers on the economics of marriage, family, and households may be found in the spring 2007 issue of the *Journal of Economic Perspectives,* vol. 21, no. 2. For a sociological view on economic aspects of intimacy, see Zelizer, 2005.

22. This sentiment is captured in the bumper-sticker joke: "My wife said 'fishing — or me'. I chose fishing." (We have also seen the sticker with the gender assignment reversed.)

23. Quoted from Buchholz, 1989, p. 141. To some this has a Yogi Berra ring to it, to others one of Buddhist truth. Either way, economics is in good company.

24. Satiation levels depreciate with time. If one has not seen one's spouse for the past three weeks, one's satiation level may be supposed to be "low." In that case, one might rather spend the next three hours with the spouse than with the football game. But if satiation

levels are "high," it stands to reason that one might seek to fill the next time period with satisfaction derived from a different source.

25. The motto *natura non facit saltum* first appeared in the textbook's fifth edition of 1907 and was retained through Marshall's last, in 1920. Bohr first broached the notion of energy quanta in 1913, and Heisenberg's famous quantum mechanics paper was published in 1925. Marshall was not, at any rate, suggesting the absence of "leaps," or discontinuous effects in nature, or in political economy, only that the smooth, continuous parts be studied first.

26. Marshall, 1961 [1920], p. xiii.

27. North, 1990.

28. This is one of the key points of North's, 1990, new institutional economics. Also see the aforementioned Dolan, 2002, on the brain's hard-wiring of behavioral routines, thus "institutionalizing" them.

29. Actually, Stigler and Becker, 1977, directly respond to Galbraith, 1958, by arguing that consumers exhibit stable tastes for commodities such as "style" or "social distinction." The specific goods with which one acquires style or distinction commodities are logically subject to fads and fashions since, in order to be distinctly stylish, one has to differentiate oneself from other people. A fad is created. It is then in the interest of firms to foster the differentiation by advertisement to sell products to consumers who wish to be seen as distinct. Consumers compete with each other. Only the means by which the competition takes place change, but the underlying taste (for style or distinction commodities) is stable. It is a nice theory, one that comes up with new interpretations of observed behavior, and one that does not contradict Galbraith's point at all. Galbraith did not argue that firms change tastes, but that firms mold desires with which people seek to satisfy their wants.

30. The classic work on military logistics is van Creveld, 2004 [1977].

31. And this, precisely, is one of the conclusions in chapter 7, on whether or not, and if so, to what degree, France substituted its atomic force de frappe for its conventional armed forces.

32. Interestingly, although not surprisingly, 90 percent of U.S. mohair production occurs within a 150-miles radius of San Angelo, Texas (the seat of the Mohair Council of America). For details, see http://www.mohairusa.com/index.html [accessed 4 December 2002]. For those interested in the story, a United States Senate debate in 1993 is a good starting point (see http://www.senate.gov/~rpc/rva/1031/1031288.htm). Defenders of the wool and mohair subsidy explicitly mention the national security rationale, namely, to sustain an industry that could provide raw materials for the clothing of U.S. soldiers, even as its clothing has long since migrated to the use of synthetic fibers.

33. A "john-boat" is a narrow and long (12 to 22 foot) boat. Originally made of rough cut green oak and hemlock planks, gaps between the planks would be closed by the use of tar and hemp rope and by natural swelling as the raw wood absorbed water.

The story of the Yamaha outboard engine is interesting in itself. First manufactured in Japan in 1960, the first overseas production plant was opened in France in 1988. Of course, the same happened with Yamaha motorcycles and Yamaha golf carts. In December 1999, for instance, Yamaha started motorcycle production in Vietnam. Yamaha golf carts are produced in the state of Georgia in the United States. Attempts to keep imports out leads importers to come in, in the end still providing choices — possibilities for substitution — to users. We learn once more how crass it is to think of economics merely in terms of money or material things. Instead, economics is deeply entwined with fundamental issues of philosophy, here the issue of freedom of choice.

34. As ever, economists think of consumption creatively. For example, a bequest of one's accumulated savings to one's children is a form of consumption, for what one "consumes" is foreseeing the enjoyment the children will have. Even if one does not buy this argument, one must agree that the children surely can do only one of two things with their inheritance: consume or save. It follows that all saving is (deferred) consumption.

35. At a minimum, one has to "study" the syllabus to know on which day to show up for the exam. As professors, we assure the reader that the number of students failing to show up because they did not know the exam day — or those urgently emailing the professor about the exam date, since emailing is cheaper than looking up the date, time, and place on the syllabus, another example of substitution that professors had better not accommodate — is not trifling.

36. It is entirely possible that even more study leads not only to diminishing but to decreasing returns such as when students pull an "all-nighter," oversleep, and fail to show up for the exam. Again, as professors — and parents! — we know all too much about this.

37. When the same number of men fight with sufficiently different technologies, the better equipped side is likely to win. Similarly, when the same technology is employed by armies of sufficiently different size, the larger force is likely to win. And when equal-sized armies with equal technologies fight, the better trained, led, and motivated force is likely to prevail. Rotte and Schmidt, 2003, quantified battles from 1600 to 1973 to analyze empirical determinants of success. Focusing on material and nonmaterial factors of battlefield success, they found that numerical superiority has retained its crucial role for battlefield performance throughout history. In general, human elements of warfare, such as leadership, morale, and surprise, have continued to be important determinants of battle outcome despite technological progress in weapons. The most likely reason is that battle technology is imitated as it spreads whereas leadership and morale depend strongly on whether things are worth fighting for.

38. To instantly forestall at least one possible misunderstanding: diminishing returns to bombing does not mean that any and all bombing is militarily useless; instead, it means precisely what it says: that the additional returns to additional bombing diminish.

39. See, e.g., Stonier, 1990.

40. Katz and Rosen, 1991, p. 595.

41. Since we have used so many marriage-related examples already, we might as well add one more. Marriage, before it became so easy to dissolve in contemporary societies, was very nearly an irrevocable commitment. This placed a higher burden on the prospective partners, and their parents and families, to elicit information about each other prior to marriage than would be true today. The bride's parents would generally seek information about the groom's likely earning-power and capacity to build assets; the groom's parents would be concerned about the likely respectability, childbearing, childrearing, and householder abilities of the bride.

42. This example is based on Sandler, 2001, pp. 112–13.

43. The medical community commonly uses the phrase "signs and symptoms." Signs are things outside observers can notice (does the skin feel hot or cold; does the patient sweat or is the skin dry; is the pulse rapid or shallow?); symptoms are things only the patient or victim can describe (I feel hot; I feel weak; I feel such-and-such pain in such-and-such a place). Economics uses the word "signal" in exactly the same way: an outside assessment of a hidden quality that only the other party can reveal or confirm.

44. Akerlof, 1984 [1970], p. 14.

45. Anderson and Haupert, 1999.

46. *Wall Street Journal,* Tuesday, 10 December 2002, p. C11.

47. Katz and Rosen, 1991, p. 626. Another example: the passenger airline industry (airlines and airplane manufacturers) is discussing the introduction of fully automated, pilotless passenger aircraft. This is technically feasible and would lower the cost of flying. But passengers would be happier to have a pilot risk his or her life as well; the economic function of the pilot is to serve as a (voluntary) "hostage." Similarly, troops are oddly reassured when their commanders and generals fight alongside them as we will have occasion to mention later in the book.

48. To obtain customers (patients), we would expect that it is in the surgeon's interest to collect and release this sort of data for independent assessment except that it can be even more profitable for surgeons to collectively refuse to collect and release such data. Sadly, hitherto this has been the preferred stance and record of the medical profession.

49. The attempt to rectify this problem can lead to second-generation problems. For example, in the name of the fashionable notion of "accountability" in public education, efforts are made to measure teaching performance. But what is measured and counted is not necessarily what one would wish to measure and count. The incentive system is skewed and can change behavior in undesired ways. For instance, instead of providing education, which cannot be measured well, teachers begin to "teach to the standardized test," the results of which can be measured.

50. Williamson, 1985. The entire section draws heavily on Besanko, Dranove, and Shanley, 1996, especially chaps. 3 and 16.

51. At least in the past, this was more of a problem for women whose marriage commitment tended to be less revocable than that made by men.

CHAPTER TWO

1. France, 1999, p. 2.

2. Bachrach, 1994, p. 121.

3. Bachrach, 2002, p. XII:54. (This is a collection of Bachrach articles. The publisher did not repaginate, so XII:54 refers to article or chapter 12, p. 54.)

4. Curry, 1998, p. 82.

5. All quotes in this paragraph from McNeill, 1982, pp. 83, 90. The trace italienne developed in the fifteenth and sixteenth centuries to counter cannon fire. It combined low walls, the use of earth, and many angles to enable defenders to fire in many directions.

6. Tilly, 1990, p. 190.

7. Wise, 1976, p. 134.

8. Olson, 1993, pp. 567–68.

9. For example, the English kings' landholdings actually declined after 1086. See Ormrod, 1999b, pp. 21–30; Henneman, 1999, pp. 103–5; Isenman, 1999, pp. 243–52, 254; Ladero Quesada, 1999, pp. 177, 179.

10. Webber and Wildavsky, 1986, pp. 174–75, 180, 183–205.

11. Nicolle, 1999, passim.

12. Verbruggen, 1997, p. 320.

13. France, 1999, pp. 2, 132; Molho, 1995, p. 97.

14. Harriss, 1975, pp. 7, 49, 57; Prestwich, 1972, pp. 218–19, 247–61. For those who care about such matters, let us note that Edward is misportrayed in the film *Braveheart.*

15. Biddick, 1990, pp. 7–8; Prestwich, 1972, pp. 207, 211; Buck, 1983, p. 172; Ramsay, 1925, vol. 2, p. 89. Also see Ormrod, 1999a, p. 178.

16. Edward I's successor, Edward II (r. 1307–1327), at one point waged a short continental war — the War of St. Sardos (1324–1325) — at a cost of some £65,000. Although this was much less than had been expected, it almost equaled the entire holding of gold, silver, and relics in the treasury (see Buck, 1983, pp. 170–71). And Edward III, to continue the line, bankrupted prominent Italian-based, multinational trading houses, the Bardi's and Peruzzi's, when overextended credit lines were not paid up (Cameron and Neal, 2003, p. 66).

17. Donnelly and Diehl, 1998, p. 17; Bradbury, 1992, p. 67; France, 2001, p. 456.

18. Bradbury, 1992, pp. 60, 63, 301–2; Baumgartner, 1991, pp. 112–13; Gillingham, 1999, p. 73; Rogers, 1997, p. 95.

19. Baumgartner, 1991, pp. 111–14; France, 2001, p. 456.

20. Verbruggen, 1997, p. 321, 350; Bradbury, 1992, p. 53; Donnelly and Diehl, 1998, p. 19, 28–29.

21. France, 1999, p. 87; Bradbury, 1992, pp. 69, 131; Gillingham, 1984, p. 90; Hooper and Bennett, 1996, p. 54; Ramsay, 1925, vol. 1, p. 227.

22. Edwards, 1946, pp. 16–17.

23. Keuper, 1994, p. 161; also see Edwards, 1946, pp. 62, 65. The cost of each has also been compared with a Concorde aircraft: Jeffreys, 1973, p. 15.

24. Ramsay, 1925, vol. 2, pp. 86, 88–89; France, 1999, p. 132; Edwards, 1946, pp. 64–65; Morris, 2003, pp. 136–41.

25. France, 1999, pp. 83, 85–86.

26. Calculations based on France, 1999, p. 83, and Bachrach, 2002, pp. 12:46–53.

27. Edwards, 1946, pp. 19, 21–52; 54–61.

28. Warner, 1968, p. 155; Prestwich, 1972, p. 44; Jeffreys, 1973, p. 14; Bradbury, 1992, p. 68.

29. Warner, 1968, p. 2; Jones, 1999, pp. 165, 172; Baumgartner, 1991, pp. 115–16; Gillingham, 1999, p. 69; Wise, 1976, pp. 136, 139–43, 146.

30. Warner, 1968, p. 4.

31. Bradbury, 1992, pp. 74 (quoting surrendering stipendiaries), 75; Wise, 1976, pp. 145, 148; Bachrach, 2002, p. 13.

32. France, 1999, p. 95; Wise, 1976, p. 139.

33. Prestwich, 1996a, p. 282. This was true for instance during the efforts of Henry IV and Henry V to conquer Saxony; Gillingham, 1999, pp. 73–76.

34. Quoted in Housley, 1999, p. 120.

35. Wise, 1976, pp. 134–35.

36. Gillingham, 1999, p. 70; Hooper and Bennett, 1996, p. 70.

37. The assessment expressed in this paragraph is based on a personal visit made and photographs taken by one of the co-authors to the castle's mentioned in the text.

38. France, 1999, p. 103; Gillingham, 1999, p. 81; Bachrach, 2002, pp. 7:549, 11:541–42, 560; Bradbury, 1992, p. 62; Morris, 2003, pp. 110–13; Keuper, 1994, p. 160; Housley, 1999, p. 120.

39. Bradbury, 1992, p. 70; Gillingham, 1999, pp. 64, 81.

40. Von Clausewitz, 1908, p. 154; Verbruggen, 1997, p. 327; Bachrach, 2002, p. 11:541; Marvin, 2001, p. 382.

41. Verbruggen, 1997, p. 306.

42. Volckart, 2004, p. 288.

43. Bachrach, 2002, p. 11:534; France, 1999, pp. 77–78, 105; Warner, 1968, p. 2; Jones, 1999, p. 164.

44. Bradbury, 1992, p. 72; Prestwich, 1996a, pp. 281–82.

45. Bachrach, 1994, pp. 119–21, 123, 125.

46. Wise, 1976, p. 161.

47. France, 2001, p. 457; De Meulemeester and Matthys, 2001, pp. 44–46, 50.

48. Baumgartner, 1991, pp. 114, 115, 117, 118, 120, 121; Warner, 1968, pp. 138, 156; Bradbury, 1992, pp. 133, 144.

49. Warner, 1968, p. 94; Ramsay, 1925, vol. 1, pp. 62–63; France, 1999, p. 104; Gillingham, 1984, p. 91; Gravett, 1990, p. 17. Bachrach, 1994, p. 132; Warner, 1968, p. 12; Gillingham, 1999, p. 79; Bradbury, 1992, p. 72.

50. Baumgartner, 1991, p. 120; Bradbury, 1992, p. 72.

51. Baumgartner, 1991, p. 123.

52. Bradbury, 1992, pp. 61, 63–64.

53. France, 2001, p. 441.

54. Corfis and Wolfe, 1995, p. 12.

55. France, 1999, p. 132; Curry, 1998, p. 83; Bradbury, 1992, pp. 271–73, 276–77; Bachrach, 1994, p. 126 (quoting Bradbury).

56. Bachrach, 1994, p. 133. The term "effectives" refers to fighters on duty and available for service at a given moment. Invariably, this number is smaller than total strength.

57. Housley, 1999, p. 126.

58. France, 1999, pp. 5, 6, 12–13.

59. Prestwich, 1972, pp. 48, 52, 91–93, 95; Morris, 2003, p. 104. See also Dupuy and Dupuy, 1993.

60. Donnelly and Diehl, 1998, p. 48; France, 1999, pp. 2–3, 32–37.

61. France, 1999, p. 230.

62. Prestwich, 1972, p. 13; Morris, 2003, p. 109; Keuper, 1994, p. 142; Prestwich, 1972, pp. 166, 172–73, 175–76, 195, 203, 205. We figure £150,000 per year for the French wars and about £40,000 per year for the wars in Scotland.

63. Verbruggen, 1997, p. 328; Morillo, 1999, p. 46; Marvin, 2001, pp. 373, 374, 393; Gillingham, 1984, p. 81; Prestwich, 1996a, p. 281.

64. Verbruggen, 1997, p. 280; Prestwich, 1996a, p. 11; Donnelly and Diehl, 1998, p. 49; Gillingham, 1984, p. 82; Bradbury, 1992, p. 71; McGlynn, 1994, p. 29; Gillingham, 1999, pp. 78–79. These are themes we find repeated in many respects in chapter 4 for the years 1618–1815.

65. Gillingham, 1984, p. 83; Rogers, 1997, p. 5; Bradbury, 1992, p. 71.

66. Verbruggen, 1997, pp. 329–30.

67. Verbruggen, 1997, p. 348.

68. Gravett, 1990, p. 3; see also Bachrach, 2002, pp. 11:558–59, and Gillingham, 1984, p. 90.

69. France, 1999, p. 84; Gillingham, 1984, p. 84; see Harari, 2000, pp. 297–98, 307–8, 310.

70. Prestwich, 1972, p. 95; Morillo, 1999, p. 58; Prestwich, 1972, pp. 61, 70; Prestwich, 1996a, p. 7; Keuper, 1994, p. 143.

71. See France, 1999, p. 10; Curry, 1998, p. 88 (quoting Stephen Morillo); White, 1967, p. 29; Donnelly and Diehl, 1998, p. 49; FitzNigel, 1983, p. 111.

72. Gillingham, 1984, p. 85; Housley, 1999, p. 113; Gillingham, 1999, pp. 70, 76. "Huge" quoted from France, 1999, p. 67. Numbers, even approximate, apparently are not available.

73. Morillo, 1999, p. 55; Prestwich, 1996a, p. 9; France, 1999, p. 8; Bachrach, 2002, pp. 12:53–54.

74. Verbruggen, 1997, p. 319.

75. Wise, 1976, pp. 73, 149–50.

76. Verbruggen, 1997, p. 348.

77. All quotes from Prestwich, 1972, pp. 204–5.

78. Baumgartner, 1991, p. 123.

79. Bradbury, 1992, p. 128.

80. Warner, 1968, p. 204. In early 2007, China used antisatellite technology to destroy one of its own satellites. This caused an international stir as it was now demonstrated that even castles in the sky are no longer unassailable.

CHAPTER THREE

1. John Hawkwood, an Englishman, ranks among the most chronicled condottieri. For a fictional first-person account of Hawkwood's career in Italy, see Angellotti, 1911. In a similar vein, see Westcott's, 1962, historical novel on Colleoni.

2. Deiss, 1967, pp. 128–29. Contamine, 1984, pp. 292–96, has assembled some interesting materials on medieval pacifism. Some of these reflect Catherine's sentiment that Christian should not battle Christian.

3. Fowler, 2001, p. ix; Villalon, 2003, p. 313. Waley speaks of the "threatening spectre of peace," (1975, p. 349), although in the context of Italy of the late 1200s.

4. Trease, 1971, p. 52; also see Deiss, 1967, p. 115.

5. Others were induced by Charles the Wise and the new pope, Urban V (r. 1362–1370), to cross the Pyrenees to fight Pedro the Cruel on the Iberian peninsula. This, too, served to lower the French reservoir of free companies, at least for a few years. On this Iberian episode, see, e.g., Villalon, 2003.

6. Excellent background pieces on the politics of the Italian Renaissance in the 1300s and 1400s (the trecento and quattrocento) are Baron, 1953a and 1953b, Ilardi, 1959, and Bayley, 1961. This is a most turbulent period of Italian history during which the papal court moved in 1309 to Avignon, France, and back to Rome by 1378, and much of the warfare revolved around power struggles between England and France (the Hundred Years' War), between French popes and Italian lords regarding the temporal powers of the Roman church in central Italy and beyond, among the Italian city-states themselves, and between the Emperors of the (German) Holy Roman Empire and virtually everyone else. On the background of the French popes and their relation to mercenaries, 1356–1378, see, e.g., Housley, 1982. The relation between Italian towns and the countryside (contado) is explored, e.g., in Epstein, 1993. On the crushing cost of war in this period, see, e.g., Becker, 1966, but also Partner, 1999, Hocquet, 1999, and Capra, 1999. On the city-states, see, e.g., Waley, 1988.

7. "Contemporary terminology for the Empire varied greatly over the centuries. The term Roman Empire was used in 1034 to denote the lands under Conrad II, and Holy Empire in 1157. The use of the term Roman Emperor to refer to Northern European rulers started earlier with Otto II (r. 973–983). Emperors from Charlemagne (d. 814) to Otto I, the Great (r. 962–973), had simply used the phrase Imperator Augustus ("August Emperor"). The precise term Holy Roman Empire dates from 1254; the full expression Holy Roman Empire of the German Nation (German: Heiliges Römisches Reich deutscher Nation) appears in 1512, after several variations in the late 15th century" (http://en.wikipedia .org/wiki/Holy_Roman_Empire; accessed 27 September 2004).

8. Ilardi even describes Florence as "francophile" (1959, p. 130).

9. Baron, 1953a, p. 271.

10. On Florence's internal politics, see, e.g., Bayley, 1961, chap. 2, and Molho, 1968. On the Florentine domination of Pisa in the fifteenth century, see, e.g., Mallett, 1968.

11. Among other beliefs, it was thought that a Florence ransacked might result in a welcome wave of highly skilled immigrants to Venice (Baron, 1953b, p. 560). A similar thing had happened a hundred years before in the Florentine sacking of Lucca on 14 June 1314. Hundreds of artisans in silk manufacture and trade wandered off to settle in Florence (Deiss, 1967, pp. 90–91).

12. One of the earliest warlords-turned-lords was Castruccio Castracani, who was to rule Lucca from 1316 to 1328. For a book-length study of Castracani, see Green, 1986. We cannot explore here the warlord-turns-lord theme from Olson's theoretical perspective of how "roving bandits" become "stationary bandits," but to do so would be, we suspect, a luscious intellectual enterprise. See Olson, 1993. Similarly, as will be seen, there is much in this chapter to which Olson and Zeckhauser's, 1966, economic theory of alliances can be applied. Again, we have to take our pick and in this chapter stick fairly narrowly to selected aspects of the economics of contracts.

13. Lane, 1999, p. 130. Studies on the smaller Italian powers are fascinating in their own right. For one example, see, e.g., Caferro, 1998, on Siena. On Rome in 1378, see Trexler, 1967. In the literature, the Papal States are also referred to as the States of the Church or sometimes only in the singular, the Papal State.

14. On continuous French ambitions for the whole of the peninsula and on imperial, Aragonese, Florentine, Venetian, Genoese, Milanese, and other interests, see Ilardi, 1959. Drees has this comment regarding the evolution of Italian city-states: "Northern Italians had freed themselves from the authority of the Holy Roman Emperor as early as the twelfth century and had established a patchwork of independent city-states across the Po valley and down through Tuscany and the Romagna. Many of these states created communal forms of government — actually, oligarchies of prominent citizens — that styled themselves 'republics' and rotated important offices and assembly seats among members of the most influential families in town. Eventually some of the communal governments proved unable to control the various family factions competing for power in the city-states and so gave way first to invited *podestà* judges from other cities and then to *signoria* governments run by a single individual or family. Thus by the middle of the fifteenth century Milan was under the control first of the Visconti and then the Sforza dukes, Florence was ruled by the Medici, and various smaller towns such as Ferrara, Mantua, and Urbino were governed by the Este, Gonzaga, and Montefeltro families, respectively"; Drees, 2001, p. x. The formation of city-states and, later, national states, is a fascinating topic in its own right that, once more, we cannot pursue in this chapter.

15. While we will have much to say in this chapter on contracts with various of the Italian city-states, the emphasis is placed on the nature and role of contracts in general rather than, say, on differences in mercenary contracts concluded with the Florentine republic as opposed to contracts concluded with despotic rulers of Florence.

16. For levies, see, e.g., Dupuy and Dupuy, 1993, pp. 362–63; Prestwich, 1996b, p. 132; and others. Also see chapter 2. For mercenary force size, see Caferro, 1998, p. 87. For population, see Parker, 1976, p. 208. In the 1340s, London, England's largest city, had a population of but 75,000 (Cantor, 2002, p. 63). Rome, once a thriving metropolis of two million people, had shrunk to 20,000 or fewer people by 1328 (Deiss, 1967, p. 105). See Caferro, 1994, for detailed calculations for the case of Siena. The go-away money could take other forms. For instance, Braccio da Montone, a Perugian aristocrat and condottiere of consider-

able skill and influence at one time sold Bologna its "freedom"—for 82,000 florin—from his employer, the pope, who had just been deposed and held captive by his own church. Braccio used the funds to attempt to capture his own home town; he eventually managed to do that and was a reasonably popular master (Trease, 1971, pp. 211, 214).

17. Prestwich, 1996b, p. 135; more elaborate in Prestwich, 1996a, p. 73.

18. Showalter, 1993, p. 411.

19. Contamine, 1984, pp. 157–58; Bayley, 1961, p. 3; Selzer, 2001, p. 24; Trease, 1971, p. 22.

20. Prestwich, 1996b, p. 141; Contamine, 1984, pp. 156, 158; Machiavelli, 1980, p. 75. In this, the signori echoed a growing sentiment in France. "There is if I may dare say so, no greater folly for a prince, who wishes to hold his lordship freely and in peace, than to give the common people permission to arm themselves"; Christine de Pizan, cited in Contamine, 1984, p. 156.

21. Dupuy and Dupuy, 1993, pp. 362–63; Prestwich, 1996b, p. 140; Becker, 1966, p. 7; Selzer, 2001, pp. 25–27. If any Italians qualified for a position as a *barbute* (the equivalent of a German Ritter), he would also be compensated at a higher rate; Selzer, 2001, p. 43. Apparently, there was discrimination only by military skill. For the use of Ritter and barbute, see n. 36.

22. From the 1350s to 1450s, the role of the infantry declined as that of cavalry increased. Thereafter, the introduction of firearms led to a revival of the infantry; see Contamine, 1984, pp. 126, 132–33.

23. Mallett, 1974, p. 27. It is not in fact known what the proportional distribution of German knights was across the European warfare scene. Although Germans were not unknown among those fighting in the French countryside, they were rare. Of about ninety mercenary leaders identified by Fowler (2001, appendix B), only five appear to be of German origin. What is clear is that substantial numbers engaged in Italy. Between 1313 and 1360, about half of all mercenary leaders in Italy were of German origin. Catalans had left Italy by 1313, the French had mostly left by 1343, not to resurface in great numbers until 1375, the English appear primarily between 1360 and 1369, Hungarians appear in the late 1340s but in militarily somewhat subordinate position, and Italians became prominent only with the beginning 1400s; see Selzer, 2001, pp. 39–45.

In fact, Selzer finds a preponderance of Swabian knights in the Italian wars, as many as half or more of all Germans. Compared with Germans residing elsewhere in the Reich, their access route to Italy was reasonably short. In addition, the population density of nobility in Swabia was higher than elsewhere and located at considerable distance to their kings' courts. Density meant more economic pressure as landed property was divided among many and supplied incentive to look for riches abroad; distance meant that it was easier to escape the king's service and set out on one's own, especially since the culture of the time demanded of nobles to engage in the knightly occupation of war. Even among those who took to warfare in Prussia, a large number came from Swabia. It also appears that Swabian nobles, for whatever reason, fathered larger numbers of sons than nobles elsewhere. All these factors combined to create a considerable "push" factor to move a good number of knights southward across the Alps.

24. Caferro, 1998, p. 27; Mallett, 1974, p. 226.

25. Caferro, 1998, pp. 27–29.

26. Selzer, 2001, pp. 77–96. In the latter years of this period a good number of the condottieri were noblemen and rulers with landed estates to maintain. Instead of serving as

middlemen, they hunted for contracts for their own account. To finance his court and reign, Federigo da Montefeltro of Urbino was particularly well-known to search out condotte far and wide during his military career which spanned more than thirty years. See, e.g., Trease, 1971, chap. 20; also Lauts and Hertzner, 2001.

27. On this whole topic, see Housley, 1982. That the church paid dearly is evidenced by its ballooning debt; see, e.g., Partner, 1999. Incidentally, *routiers* gave us the verb "to rout," an opposing team, for example.

28. Bueno de Mesquita, 1946, p. 223; Showalter, 1993, p. 427. "Subcontracting," a suitable term used, for example, by Trease, 1971, p. 61, with reference to Hawkwood.

29. Waley, 1975, pp. 338–42, 344.

30. Waley, 1975, p. 343, n. 1. See Ricotti, 1844, and Canestrini, 1851.

31. All quotes and information in this paragraph from Prestwich, 1996a, pp. 88–96.

32. Selzer, 2001, p. 396.

33. Waley, 1975, p. 347; also stressed by Prestwich, 1996a, p. 91, for England around 1300.

34. Showalter, 1993, p. 418. He adds that on the employees' side, "groups of warriors were often better able than isolated individuals to make more profitable arrangements for themselves"—collective bargaining, in a word.

35. For example, in exchange for 130,000 gold florins, payable over four months, John Hawkwood in the summer of 1375 agreed not to attack Florence for the next five years (Trease, 1971, p. 88). This was lucrative, and he struck similar "nonaggression pacts" that summer with Siena, Arezzo, Pisa, and Lucca for a further FL95,000 (p. 90).

36. Early in the 1300s, the knight or helm (*Reiter* or *Ritter* in German, *barbute* in Italian) was a heavily armored individual fighter. The *banneret* was a higher military rank, commanding perhaps ten to twelve knights. Several bannerets were supervised by a marshal, and several of these, if the company was large enough, were led by a condottiere, the contractor. Toward the end of the century, this military organization gave way to the *lancea* (or lance, in English), a three-man formation consisting of a heavily armed knight, a less heavily armed attendant, and a page boy. Note that Fowler's (2001) description differs from Selzer's (2001), probably because "like most things in medieval times," the meaning of certain terms was not standardized across the entirety of the continent and like terms could mean different things; Redlich, 1964, p. 8. Also see Deiss, 1967, p. 18. On Hawkwood and Colleoni, see, e.g., Trease, 1971.

37. Transit time meant transit costs. Contracts had to provide for this, and they did, on the order of two or three weeks, with first pay offered perhaps at halfway. (Interestingly, contracts also provided for vacation time.) Travel usually took place in small groups and is documented in Geleitbriefe, letters requesting travel permission through some lord's territory. But having a group of armed men travel through might be expected to result in certain damages, and to guard against this possibility a high-ranking member of the group might be held in hospitable ransom until the other men had passed without incident; see Selzer, 2001, p. 95. Contamine, 1984, p. 100.

38. Selzer, 2001, table 11, p. 314, based on a sample of 15 knights. Mallett and Hale, 1984, p. 138–139.

Italy during the fifteenth century suffered from repeated shortages of horses. Breeding took place in Germany and Hungary, also in Spain, and to some extent in Gonzaga, but not much in the Venetian terraferma. "That the shortage was severe is indicated by the price of horses which normally cost at least 30 florins—or the equivalent of an infantryman's wages for a year—and could cost up to 150 or 200 florins"; Mallett, 1974, p. 141. "The capture of warhorses was considered as valuable a booty as that of armour or even jewels"; Contamine, 1984, p. 131. It was therefore not custom to target and kill horses but exceptions did occur. In 1424, for instance, Michele Attendolo engaged Braccio da Montone in a vicious battle during which Attendolo ordered his men to go after Braccio's horses; Trease, 1971, p. 229.

39. Mallett, 1999, p. 219.

40. Simon, 1997; also see chapter 1; Bayley, 1961, p. 13–14; Canestrini, 1851, p. lviii: "le condotte reali e le condotte apparenti, le condotte semplici e le condotte miste, le condotte di protettorato, le condotte di onorificenza, le condotte di gratificazione, le condotte di compenso, di raccomandigia, di alleanza d'uno Stato col condottiero, di alleanza di più Stati tra loro per la condotta d'una Compagnia; e infine la condotta o puittosto alleanza di più stati col condottiero."

41. Canestrini, 1851, p. lix; Bayley, 1961, p. 9.

42. It is not clear from the literature exactly what the material importance of reputation effects might have been. It is clear that ample complaints and threats to reputation existed. For example, in a letter one Jescho Lamberger complains about one Michael Strangello: "you did not satisfy [fulfill your agreement with] us according to the promises made by your own mouth, so that we everywhere and in every way demand what is due to us, and we will denounce and make complaint about you, and declare that you were bound by these promises, for if by your grace you do not satisfy us according to your letter that we have, we will have to show it to princes, barons, soldiers and cities, and we will send our letter to your brother Karl [Charles], the emperor of the Romans, for you have not fulfilled your letters or your promises" (approximate translation from Latin; original in Selzer, 2001, pp. 399ff.).

43. This situation reflects no more than the usual complexity of the time. Trease, 1971, pp. 219–22.

44. Trease, 1971, pp. 57–58, 268; Cantor, 2002, p. 35; Selzer, 2001, p. 57. Up to this time, the early 1360s, the heavily armed, mounted German Reiter dominated the Italian warfare scene. The military innovation that literally unseated the Reiter was brought to Italy by mercenaries in search of employment with the break in the Franco-English Hundred Years' War described earlier. The Germans did not adjust well to this change and disappear from the Italian record shortly thereafter; Selzer, 2001. A side effect of the changed tactic was that the dismounted knight would need to wear less, and lighter, armor, and so would his horse—ensconced as it was behind the battle line. This made the English lighter, more flexible, and more mobile, allowing longer or quicker marches; Trease, 1971, pp. 60–64.

45. Trease, 1971, pp. 244, 247. War between Milan and Venice resumed soon enough, but the loss was Carmagnola's. The Venetians, observing Carmagnola's battlefield lethargy, thought he might be a double-agent. Luring him to Venice, they put him on trial, then tortured and executed him; Trease, 1971, pp. 257–58.

46. Trease, 1971, p. 272.

47. This paragraph is based on Selzer, 2001, pp. 269–300. See also Postan, 1964, p. 45. Not that the difficulties were limited to Italy: one Gilbert Talbot, an Englishman, "had run up huge debts and was sitting in debtor's jail in London. His debts were the result of a lifetime of unprofitable military campaigning in France and Spain" in the 1300s; Cantor, 2002, p. 133. A similar, generally dire assessment appears to apply to Welsh and English knights of the Hundred Years' War period at large; Postan, 1964, p. 44. See also Mallett and Hale, 1984, pp. 496, 500, and appendix. On labor conditions in Florence ca. 1400, see de Roover, 1968.

48. Selzer, 2001, table 8, p. 237; Mallett and Hale, 1984, p. 126; Blastenbrei, 1987, p. 251; Waley, 1968, p. 85 (for 1288 already); all quotes from Mallett and Hale, 1984, p. 127.

49. Blastenbrei, 1987, pp. 208–20, 258–59.

50. Mallett, 1974, pp. 136–37. In the 1300s and 1400s the war season lasted roughly from June to September, sometimes starting earlier or lasting longer, hence the prevalence of three- to six-month contracts. According to Blastenbrei (1987, pp. 270–71), the reason for the winter pause had less to do with the men than with their horses, the warriors' primary assets. During winter, it was difficult to find fresh fodder and this necessitated withdrawal to winter quarters.

51. Selzer, 2001, p. 185. Today's militaries, for whom war is rare, receive much base pay (readiness pay) and little bonus pay. But in high-frequency conflict areas, for example, in Africa, there are reports of limited base pay (because of depleted state treasuries) and more frequent "bonus" pay (the opportunity to plunder, extort, and rape).

52. Caferro, 1998, pp. 66–67.

53. Mallett and Hale, 1984, p. 143. Similar in Blastenbrei, 1987, for the Sforzas in the early to mid-1400s.

54. Mallett, 1974, p. 138.

55. Blastenbrei, 1987, e.g., pp. 226, 230.

56. Mallett, 1974, p. 130.

57. Deiss, 1967, pp. 117–18. For the interesting background and Florence's view of the event, especially its condottiere Pandolfo Malatesta's success in wrangling money from the city for little action, see Bayley, 1961, pp. 27–34. An extract of the contract is in Canestrini, 1851, pp. 57–60.

58. Contamine, 1984, pp. 153–54. There seems no one superior place in this chapter to insert a note pointing to Avner Greif's work on the economics of contract evolution in the medieval period. While our work is restricted specifically to the military labor market, Greif deals with markets and impersonal exchange at large. See, e.g., Greif, 2006, and literature cited therein, including his own work.

59. Bayley, 1961, pp. 9–10. "Ad ogni scambio di uomini o di cavalli, il capitano o conestabile doveva pagare una tassa proporzionata"; Canestrini, 1851, p. lx.

60. Bayley, 1961, p. 11 (the particular passage of that contract is in Canestrini, 1851, p, 150), pp. 26–27, 29 n. 91, 38, 42.

61. Bayley, 1961, p. 15; for a discussion, see Bayley, 1961, pp. 45–49. In one instance, a battle at Maclodia on 11 October 1427, condottiere Carmagnola, fighting for Venice, took 10,000 prisoners. Included were Carlo Malatesta, Francesco Sforza, and Niccolò Piccinino, exceedingly prominent condottieri fighting for the Milanese side. That evening, it appears, all four shared a rousing good time of camaraderie. Next day, Carmagnola released his prisoners — all 10,000 — without ransom. Only the Milanese captain-general, Malatesta, was handed over to Venetian authorities. In the end, they released him, too, without ransom; Trease, 1971, pp. 252–53.

62. Bayley, 1961, pp. 51–53.

63. Mallett, 2003, pp. 74, 78. One way to understand this is to suppose that free-agency in modern professional sports were eliminated. A few dominant teams would emerge and hold each other "in check," and given the lack of exercisable demand, players' salaries would drop — the model of contemporary American collegiate sports, in other words.

64. Bayley, 1961, p. 43. He speaks of 1366 which demonstrates that the six contract phases we identified were overlapping.

65. Trease, 1971, pp. 87–90. Florentine largesse did not end there: Hawkwood's tax debt was forgiven in November 1390 after conveniently just having won a major Florentine campaign in Bologna. A few months later, in April 1391, Hawkwood was made a Florentine citizen, tax-exempt for all future, a right heritable to all male heirs (he was to have only one), received a FL2,000 grant in addition to his usual income, his wife was offered, in the event, a widow's pension of FL1,000, and his three daughters would receive a state-paid dowry of FL2,000 each as well; Trease, 1971, pp. 94, 143. He moved to Florence in 1381, and his family followed the next year. He died there in 1394. Incidentally, Hawkwood was the first foreign condottiere to hold land in Italy.

66. Nicolle, 1983, p. 16; Deiss, 1967, p. 102, 119, 126. At the time, there existed at least two legal notions of the term tyrant, "tyrannus ex parte exercitii, who had some legal title to rule, but performed morally reprehensible or illegal acts [and] tyrannus ex defectu tituli . . . a de facto ruler, good or bad, who had no hereditary title, was not vicar for pope or emperor, and was not created signore or given a life office by the commune's representatives"; Black, 1970, p. 248. Bernabò Visconti was of the first type.

67. Temple-Leader and Marcotti, 1889, pp. 42–43.

68. Canestrini, 1851, p. lxxix.

69. "I Condottieri italiani sono più priviligiati, più liberi, in generale, nelle loro operazioni: vengono trattati da eguali, e riguardati come potenze, ed inclusi in tutti i trattati d'alleanza o pace, in tutte le leghe offensive e defensive: godono, in somma, del diritto pubblico stipulato nei trattati"; Canestrini, 1851, p. lxxx.

70. Olson, 1993. Also see McGuire and Olson, 1996, and Wintrobe, 1998; Bayley, 1961, p. 22, n. 66.

71. Selzer, 2001, p. 32; also see Partner, 1999; Becker, 1966, p. 38. Among the very numerous works dealing with war finance, in addition to those cited in this section, see Capra, 1999, Hocquet, 1999, and Partner, 1999, as well as Ferguson, 2001, and the literature cited therein.

72. Becker, 1966, pp. 9, 30; Bayley, 1961, pp. 18, 26. Presumably, the FL8 million refers to the Florentine nondebt wealth.

73. Becker, 1966, p. 18; Bayley, 1961, pp. 15–16, 34–36.

74. Bayley, 1961, pp. 74, 82–110. Similarly, Baron, 1953a, p. 286.

75. Mallett, 1974, pp. 109, 114, 133–36.

76. Mallett, 1974, p. 112. The modern term "free-lancers" derives from the *lanze spezzate*.

77. Mallett and Hale, 1984, pp. 185–86, 195. Another method is to integrate foreigners. We have not come across detailed accounts of this with regard to Renaissance Italy but elsewhere in the literature examples exist. For instance, until their dissolution in 1826, the Janissaries were the Ottoman armies' increasingly elite infantry. Founded in the fourteenth century, they were the children of conquered peoples. Legally the Sultan's slaves, they were taken to Turkey to be raised, educated, and trained there in the Turkish language and the art of soldiery (Ottoman Chronicle in Chaliand, 1994, pp. 455–56). There was tradition in this: the Koranic prohibition of Muslim fighting Muslim made the use of slave-soldiers convenient. The sultans used a clever incentive scheme to assure and retain the loyalty of Janissaries ("new troops") and their parent populations as well as to reduce chances of rebellion. Taking a fifth of all male children deprived the conquered population of significant numbers of their own. Moreover, it would make the conquered more hesitant to fight against their own. Further, Janissaries could look forward to preferential treatment in war in terms of

assured food rations (Busbecq in Chaliand, 1994, p. 458) and to decent opportunities for promotion to and standing in government — just as the Turkish Mamelukes in Egypt a few centuries before — and, finally, Janissary conversion to Islam would assure that their own children were exempt from military service. Baumgartner writes that "the number of known defectors from their ranks is extraordinarily low" (1991, p. 153). There should be no illusion about their numbers, though; until 1500 they did not number more than 4,000 in all.

78. In Venice, the peacetime army tended to be half of the wartime army. Condottieri do not appear to have had any problem expanding the units under their control. Supply was responsive to demand (see Mallett and Hale, 1984, chap. 2), and the question arises how a doubled army could be raised as quickly as the record suggests. We have not noted suggestions in the literature that address this question.

79. Mallett, 1974, pp. 109–10; Caferro, 1998, p. 13; Mallett, 1999, p. 223.

80. Caferro, 1998, chap. 1; Bueno de Mesquita, 1946. See North, 1990, on the nature and role of institutions as reducing transaction costs among contracting parties, of which dealing with the cost of high levels of uncertainty is one.

81. Trease, 1971, pp. 71–72. Ironically, Baumgarten and Sterz later formed a new company, the Company of the Star, to be hired by Siena against Florence; Trease, 1971, p. 72. More ironically still, Siena suffered at least thirty-seven mercenary raids between 1342 and 1399; Caferro, 1998, p. xvi. Siena itself would decline from economic exhaustion, to be absorbed (for awhile) by Milan, and would lose against Florence in Renaissance prominence.

82. Mallett, 1974, pp. 143–44.

83. See, e.g., Deiss, 1967, p. 51, and many other sources; Mallett and Hale, 1984, pp. 132–33, 135, 197.

84. Caferro, 1998, pp. 99–101, 166, 173; eventually, after the death of Giangaleazzo Visconti, Siena became independent again. A happier alliance outcome occurred in 1495, by which time Italy had transformed into an oligopoly of a handful of city-states. In 1494, France's Charles VIII moved nearly unimpeded with 28,000 men along the Italian west coast onto Naples. He took the city and declared himself king of Naples. The deposed king, Alfonso, fled to Sicily from where he sought help from his cousin, Ferdinand of Aragon, Spanish ruler of southern Italy, who obliged. Frightened, Charles turned home by early 1495 with half his army. But Milan, Venice, and the Papal States (and Austria) had formed an alliance and engaged him in battle, certainly not bloodless, with 15,000 mostly mercenary troops. That July at Fornovo 3,300 Italian troops lost their lives, and Charles his Italian possession, which was as short-lived as his own life (1470–1498; r. 1483–1498); see Baumgartner, 1991, pp. 174–75. Nonetheless, Caferro, 1996, concludes that "the depredations of the mercenary companies may have contributed significantly to the process by which smaller states were swallowed up by larger ones in the late fourteenth and early fifteenth century, a process that drastically altered the political landscape of Italy and ultimately helped set the stage for the establishment of the five great Renaissance states a half-century later" (p. 9 of Internet printout).

85. Trease, 1971, p. 295; Ilardi, 1959, p. 130. The Peace of Lodi held, with few exceptions, for about twenty years.

86. Bueno de Mesquita, 1946, p. 232. Blanshei, 1979, refers to the warlord-lord as the "condottiere-prince" (p. 613).

87. Bueno de Mesquita, 1946, pp. 220, 229.

88. Trease, 1971, pp. 87–90, 133–35.

89. Bueno de Mesquita, 1946, p. 231; "Who but a fool would expect generosity from

the Venetians," asks Trease as he recounts the episode of revoking Colleoni's estate (1971, p. 300); Trease, 1971, pp. 158, 184. On "tyranny" versus "dictatorship" in the Perugian context, see Black, 1970, esp. pp. 248, 275, 281.

90. Blanshei, 1979, p. 618.

91. Alfonso ruled Naples until his death in 1458. Thus, for a time, he reunited the two Kingdoms of the Sicilies (see Trease, 1971, p. 266). On Naples and Sicily see the useful time line at www.kessler-web.co.uk/History/KingListsEurope/ItalySicily.htm [accessed 8 June 2005].

92. Contamine, 1984, pp. 165–72. Niccolò Machiavelli, son of a prominent Florentine lawyer, entered public service in 1494. This included substantial diplomatic service both in Italy and at foreign courts. His career lasted until 1512, when the Medici's returned to power. The year thereafter, 1513, *The Prince* was circulated. Dedicating the book to Florence's new prince, Lorenzo II de' Medici, Machiavelli argues against mercenary forces and in favor of the use of civic militias. Far better, he counseled, to earn the confidence and respect of one's people and to rely on them rather than to rely on those whose vested interests lie elsewhere. Bueno de Mesquita (1946) is among the first to question the most common interpretation of Niccolò Machiavelli's *The Prince*. To this day, that work is frequently read to mean that "whatever is expedient to do is necessary to do," a Renaissance example of utilitarian realpolitik (http://en.wikipedia.org/wiki/Niccolo_Machiavelli; accessed on 17 September 2004). Thus, "political institutions . . . determine the character of military organization." But for Bueno de Mesquita, Machiavelli merely "presents the other side of the medal, the fatal consequences for any political organization of inadequate military institutions" (both quotes, p. 219).

93. Mallett and Hale, 1984, pp. 80–81; Trease, 1971, p. 331. There was one exception. Those skilled in manufacturing and in the use of artillery tended, by far, to come from beyond Venice, mostly from across the Alps. "These highly prized non-Italian experts were able to command high wages"; Mallett and Hale, 1984, p. 84. "With the growing availability of suitably trained Italians in the later years of the century, average salaries came down; but in the first decade of the sixteenth century the demand for gunners was such that their rewards were once more steadily rising"; Mallett and Hale, 1984, p. 84.

94. Mallett and Hale, 1984, p. 75, and chap. 2; Contamine, 1984, p. 172; Nicolle, 1983, p. 16 (*provisionati,* from the troops' regular wage, the *provisione*).

95. Mallett and Hale, 1984, p. 66.

96. Caferro,1998, p. 14.

97. War proved too costly in terms of order, certainty, and prosperity, in Italy as elsewhere. "England in a time of civil war was an attractive target to such men [mercenaries], and their expulsion was an important element in the restoration of order in the 1150s" (Prestwich, 1996a, p. 148). Likewise, it is said that the beginning of permanent armies under France's Charles VII was more related to the (re)establishment of order than to any other single factor (Showalter, 1993, p. 423).

98. Mallett and Hale, 1984, p. 202.

99. Showalter, 1993, p. 423; similarly, Mallett, 1999, p. 216.

100. On that history, the history of the atomic bomb, see especially Richard Rhodes' acclaimed works, 1988 [1986] and 1995.

101. Contamine, 1984, p. 149; Pepper and Adams, 1986, pp. 8, 11; Deiss, 1967, pp. 26–27 (as might be imagined, this led to changes in castle design, itself a fascinating topic to trace over the centuries); Trease, 1971, pp. 330–31.

102. Deiss, 1967, p. 25.

103. Black, 1996, pp. 48–50, provides a sense of the gradual change in military technology for the Italian Wars period, 1494–1559, during which gunpowder replaced earlier weapons but also forced attendant changes in tactics, fortification, finance, and the organization of force.

104. Contamine, 1984, p. 135; Trease, 1971, pp. 327, 332, 340; Deiss, 1967, pp. 284–86. Giovanni, born of a de' Medici and Sforza union, became known as Giovanni delle Bande Nere (Giovanni of the Black Band) and was the only de' Medici ever to become a condottiere.

105. Deiss, 1967, pp. 28, 30: "The ruin of Italy is now caused by nothing else but through her having relied for many years on mercenary arms. These did indeed help certain individuals to power, and appeared courageous when matched against each other; but when the foreigner [King Charles of France] came, they showed their worthlessness." Thus, Machiavelli argues for the unification of Italy under a civic militia system. Trease, 1971, p. 340. For an impressive description of the sack, see Connor, 2004, pp. 107–13.

106. Nicolle, 1983, p. 20; Trease, 1971, pp. 332–33. Italy did not become a unified kingdom until 17 March 1861. Rome, until then under papal rule, was added on 20 September 1870. For comparison, German unification, under Bismarck, occurred in 1871.

107. See, e.g., Selzer, 2001, p. 56.

108. Caferro, 1998, p. 4; Bayley, 1961, p. 22, referring to Fra Moriale's outfit (or Fra Monreale's in Bayley's rendition). Temple-Leader and Marcotti, 1889, p. 44, refer to the companies as "Nomad Military States: they elected their captain or freely accepted him if entering a company already formed; the captain had great power, but it was limited by the council of constables and marshals, while in the most important decisions the cavaliers or caporali were called into the deliberations."

109. Thomson, 2002, p. 20.

110. A similar fate was suffered by other nonstate purveyors of violence, such as privateers and mercantile companies. They faced a choice either of incorporation into the state-sanctioned and state-run apparatus in which rested authorization, ownership, and control of and over the use of violence, or outright elimination by being banned and outlawed. See Thomson, 2002; also see Singer, 2003, and Brauer, 1999.

CHAPTER FOUR

1. Lynn, 1999, p. 50; Liddell Hart, 1967, p. 93.

2. Liddell Hart, 1976 [1934], p. 48.

3. Tilly, 1990, pp. 74–76, 87, 89.

4. Synonyms for the term "marginal" are extra, additional, or incremental cost or benefit, that is, cost and benefit of an impending action in addition to those already incurred and received as a result of previous actions.

5. Druzhinin, Kontorov, and Shtemenko, 1973; Dupuy, 1979.

6. As quoted in Milward, 1977, p. 18.

7. Thunholm, 2005, pp. 43–44, 47.

8. Tuchman, 1981, p. 177.

9. For a Napoleonic example, see Walter, 1993. The aphorism "You cannot make an omelette without breaking eggs" is attributed to Frederick the Great.

10. Weigley, 2004, pp. 536–37.

11. Fuller, 1970, vol. 2, p. 36 (citing the views of Guibert); see also Weigley, 2004, p. 73.

12. Weigley, 2004, p. xii.

13. Weigley, 2004, p. 537.

14. Weigley, 2004, pp. xii–xiii, 195, 542; Montgomery, 1968, p. 322; Baumgartner, 1991, p. 297; Duffy, 2000, p. 398; Fuller, 1970, vol. 2, p. 36.

15. Unplanned attrition battles can occur, for example, as the result of a failed offensive. "Possession of the battlefield seems to be a generally accepted criterion of victory in the battle"; Helmbold, 1971, pp. 1–2.

16. Offer, 1995, pp. 217–20, 223–25.

17. Baumgartner, 1991, p. 253. He was killed at Lützen (1632), a blow to Swedish political and military fortunes, and presenting a paradox in the calculation of marginal costs and benefits for one might expect a ruler who is present on the field to be more cautious, as he is sharing the same risks as his soldiers. But not in this king's case, who died leading a cavalry charge.

18. Kamen, 1968, pp. 45–48, 54; Baumgartner, 1991, p. 249; Tilly, 1990, pp. 165–66.

19. Weigley, 2004, pp. 18–19.

20. Weigley, 2004, p. 31; Fuller, 1970, vol. 1, p. 489.

21. Raimondo de Montecuccoli, as quoted in Chaliand, 1994, pp. 566–67.

22. Montecuccoli, in Chaliand, 1994, p. 567–568.

23. Ferguson, 2001, p. 25.

24. Kennedy, 1987, p. 77.

25. Kennedy, 1987, pp. 75–76.

26. Quoted in Lynn, 1999, p. 273, n. 10.

27. Roskolenko, 1974, p. 58 (Edward Creasy); Lynn, 1999, p. 304.

28. Chandler, 1973, pp. 65, 322; Weir, 1993, p. 95; Weigley, 2004, p. 97.

29. Lynn, 1999, p. 294; Weigley, 2004, p. 103; Windrow and Mason, 1991, p. 188.

30. Maurice de Saxe, in Chaliand, 1994, pp. 588, 594; Browning, 1995, pp. 207–9.

31. Luvaas, 1966, p. 37; Pois and Langer, 2004, p. 15; Laffin, 1995, p. 141. The reference is to Alfred von Schlieffen, author of Germany's concept for World War I (see chap. 1).

32. Frederick the Great, in Chaliand, 1994, p. 606; Fuller, 1970, vol. 1, pp. 556–67.

33. Luvaas, 1966, p. 139; Frederick the Great, in Chaliand, 1994, p. 608.

34. Frederick the Great, in Chaliand, 1994, p. 608.

35. The eleventh battle, Burkersdorf, was fought in 1762. At that point Russia had withdrawn, as had Sweden, so that war had completely changed in character.

36. Pois and Langer, 2004, p. 18; Duffy, 2000, pp. 378, 398, 422–24.

37. Here we adopt the chronology used by many historians who treat the nineteenth century as running from 1789 (beginning of the French Revolution) to 1914 (outbreak of World War I). Some texts start this century in 1815 but this requires treating the age of the French Revolution (1789–1815) as a completely separate unit tied to neither century.

38. Dupuy and Dupuy, 1970, pp. 668–93, 744–69.

39. Cameron and Neal, 2003, pp. 161, 163–64.

40. One drawback was that this initially led to "micro-management" of maneuver and battle decisions. For the case of Marconi's invention of wireless telegraphy, i.e., the radio, and its enthusiastic use by land-based superiors to intrude on commanders' decision making powers at sea, see, for example van der Vat, 2001, pp. 34–35. "Exasperated seagoing commanders were wont to remark that if Nelson had been reachable by wireless, he would never have won at Trafalgar" (p. 34).

41. The term "total war" is sometimes used as a reference to the amount of firepower

used in or destruction resulting from a particular war. Actually, total war means a conflict in which the survival of one or more of the systems involved is at stake. Such a war generally becomes extremely destructive, hence the confusion over the term.

42. Consider, for example, a case from a later period, the fall of Tsar Nicholas II (1868–1918) in 1917. He had deployed his most loyal troops to the front and left his capital in the hands of troops of unknown political reliability.

43. In the Civil War the Americans were compelled to move large numbers of troops from east to west after the Confederate victory at Chickamauga (1863). In the other two campaigns, Moltke ordered the Prussian armies to maneuver according to certain strategic directions, but even he could not prevent commanders from "marching to the sound of the guns," which as often as not resulted in costly frontal attacks.

44. Connelly, 1987, p. 3; Uffindel, 2003, p. xxxi.

45. Connelly, 1987, pp. 1, 221; Neillands, 2003, p. 99; Roberts, 2001, p. 151; Connelly, 1987, p. 48; Uffindel, 2003, p. 172.

46. Connelly, 1987, p. 21.

47. Liddell Hart, 1967, p. 127.

48. Liddell Hart, 1967, 1967, p. 117; Marc Raeff, in his introduction to Walter, 1993, p. xv.

49. Keegan, 1976, pp. 121, 122; Roberts, 2001, p. 150 (referring to Wellington's views).

50. Napoleon Bonaparte, as excerpted in Chaliand, 1994, pp. 647–48; Wasson, 1998, p. 22; Connelly, 1987, p. 8.

51. Carl von Clausewitz, as excerpted in Chaliand, 1994, p. 715; Antoine Henri de Jomini, as excerpted in Chaliand, 1994, p. 739; Connelly, 1987, p. 31.

52. Keegan, 1987, pp. 145, 152, 154; Paget, 1990, p. 97; Neillands, 2003, p. 146. Roskolenko, 1974, p. 86. His calculating nature can be seen by his 1813–1814 attack on the French frontier along the Pyrenees. He did this only to force France to keep 200,000 men there for defense; another marginal benefit, calculated for the benefit of the overall campaign, not just his own part of it. See Adrian Liddell Hart, as excerpted in Chaliand, 1994, p. 644.

CHAPTER FIVE

1. We do not delve here into the technical distinctions between "information" and "intelligence."

2. A somewhat different analysis would be required in the case of deterrence, because there avoiding battle (the "transaction") rather than victory in the field is the actual goal of both sides.

3. See, e.g., primate expert Frans B. M. de Waal, 1982, 1989.

4. Mahan, 1853; Feis, 2002, p. 3; Quoted in Chaliand, 1994, p. 741; United States Army, 2001.

5. Quoted in Feis, 2002, p. 4; Sutherland, 1998, pp. 69, 183; Randall, 1918, pp. 311–12; Bartholomees, 1998, pp. 120, 255.

6. Lynn and Jay, 1985, p. 9; Long, 1952, pp. 391ff. Most of General Robert E. Lee's battle orders were verbal, and many of his written 1864/65 battle reports were burned. See Dowdey, 1961, p. xii.

7. See Fishel, 1964; Bartholomees, 1998, p. 248, writes: "The Confederacy had an eighteenth-century intelligence apparatus unsuited to the semimodern war it fought." Its Intelligence Office had very limited functions. For a contrasting view see Gaddy, 1975, pp. 20–27.

8. Bartholomees, 1998, pp. 4–8, 12, 248–249, 252; Markle, 2000, pp. xvii, 2.

9. Tidwell, 1991, pp. 219–31; Bartholomees, 1998, p. 251. United States dollars — green-backs — were valuable in themselves as they could have been used for other purposes, but especially so as the Rebel currency faded. Few authentic records of the clandestine efforts survive; see Canan, 1964, pp. 34–51.

10. Bartholomees, 1998, p. 256; Trudeau, 1989, p. 26.

11. Joseph Hooker established the Bureau before Chancellorsville. See Sutherland, 1998, p. 101. While we know, post facto, of the Bureau of Military Information's effectiveness, much of its activity was not recorded. See Elley, 1992, p. 9.

12. Feis, 2002, pp. 11–15, 196–99, 264; Feis, 2002, pp. 196–98. Markle, 2000, p. 5; Markle (pp. 11–15), claims an error of only 0.25 percent. According to the *Military Encyclopedia,* Lee had 60,000 men at Chancellorsville. An error of 0.25 percent would then equate to 150 men.

13. Bartholomees, 1998, p. 252. Discontinuance: Markle, 2000, p. 33. See also Truby, 1971, pp. 64–71; Robinson, 1986, pp. 5–17. Elley, 1992, p. 12. It appears that movable (as opposed to tethered) balloons relayed information after landing.

14. Morgan, 1959–60, pp. 209–12; Elley, 1992, p. 13; Bartholomees, 1998, pp. 116–18, 250. See, e.g., Hancock to Butterfield, 25 June 1853, Scott, 1880, series I, vol. 45, p. 309.

15. See, e.g., Dyer, 1999; See Baggett, 2003; Marten, 2003; Cashin, 2002; Leisch, 1994; Berkey, 2003; Stith, 2004; Mangus, 1994; Axelrod, 1992; Leonard, 1999; McDevitt, 2003.

16. McWhiney, 1998, p. 43; Elley, 1992, pp. 17–18. For information on spies, see Davis, 1994; Stuart, 1981; Bakeless, 1971, 1975; Sabine, 1973; and Weinert, 1965. Ruth's career is further described in Johnston, 1955, and Stuart, 1963. Halleck's comment can be found in Halleck to Sheridan, 23 April 1865, Scott, 1880, vol. 97, p. 307.

17. Long, 1952, p. 373; Bartholomees, 1998, p. 249; Guback, 1959, pp. 171–76; Markle, 2000, pp. 7–11; Randall, 1918, pp. 303, 309.

18. For those unfamiliar with the American Civil War, the conflict was divided into two fairly distinct theaters by the Appalachian mountain range. Movements of forces between the two theaters were comparatively uncommon. For manageability we have chosen to limit our study to the eastern theater, where intensive, large-scale war was ensured by the close proximity of the two national capitals, Washington, DC, for the Union, and Richmond, VA, for the Confederacy.

19. McDowell believed that Beauregard had about 35,000 men when in fact Beauregard had only 20,000, before reinforcement came. Likewise, based on newspaper reports, Beauregard thought that McDowell had about 55,000 men when in fact he faced only 38,000 men and of which only 28,500 were brought to battle. See McDowell to Army HQ, 24 June 1861, in Scott, 1880, series I, vol. 2, p. 720; and Beauregard to CSA HQ, 14 October 1861, in Scott, 1880, series I, vol. 2, p. 486; McDowell to Army HQ, 24 June 1861, in Scott, 1880, series I, vol. 2, p. 720.

20. McDowell to Army HQ, 24 June 1861, in Scott, 1880, series I, vol. 2, p. 720; Mc-Dowell to Army HQ, 20 July 1861, in Scott, 1880, series I, vol. 2, p. 308. Had McDowell known of Johnston's approach, his own actions would unquestionably have been different. McDowell to Army HQ, 21 July 1861, in Scott, 1880, series I, vol. 2, p. 316. Neither general could change plans to take advantage of changing information: McDowell could not be-cause he was engaged before he was certain Johnston's reinforcements were present, and Beauregard could not change plans either because McDowell arrived and attacked first (see McDonald, 2000, pp. 17–19).

21. McDonald, 2000, pp. 43–44, 84–85; Bartholomees, 1998, pp. 113–16. It was this battle, incidentally, that earned southern officer Thomas J. Jackson his nom de guerre "Stonewall" Jackson.

22. Keegan, 2003, p. 83.

23. Sears, 1992, pp. 38, 61, 96, 98–100, 162; McClellan to Lincoln, 20 July 1862, in Scott, 1880, series I, vol. 11, part 3 (1884), p. 328.

24. McClellan to Lincoln, 5 and 6 April 1862; McClellan to Stanton, 26 and 27 June 1862, in Scott, 1880, series I, vol. 11, part 3, pp. 71, 73–74, 257, 264, 266; and McClellan to Stanton, 1 and 2 June 1862, in Scott, 1880, series I, vol. 11, part 1 (1884), pp. 749–50.

25. Sears, 1992, pp. 33, 37–45, 47, 57, 153–54, 182–83, 195; McClellan to Stanton, 27 May and 5 June 1862, in Scott, 1880, series I, vol. 11, part 3, pp. 194, 214; Markle, 2000, pp. 5, 6; see also Fishel, 1988. Luckily for McClellan's personal reputation, those statements were never publicly known during his lifetime. As for Lee, he already knew that McClellan was hesitant and took advantage of that.

26. Randall, 1918, p. 306; Long, 1952, p. 187.

27. Pope to McClellan, 19 and 20 July, in Scott, 1880, series I, vol. 11, part 3, pp. 327, 329; and Stith, 2004, pp. iii, viii–ix; Lee to D. H. Hill, 13 August 1862; reply, 14 August 1862; Lee to Davis, 25 July 1862, in Dowdey, 1961, pp. 227, 237, 251–52; Lee to CSA HQ, 18 April and 8 June, 1863, in Scott, 1880, series I, vol. 12, part 2 (1885), pp. 176, 555; Hennessy, 1993, pp. 30–31.

28. Hennessy, 1993, pp 60, 108, 311, 322, 469, 470; Pope to McClellan, 17 July 1862, in Scott, 1880, series I, vol. 11, part 3, p. 325; Pope to Halleck, 22, 24, and 30 August 1862; Pope to Army HQ, 3 September 1862, in Scott, 1880, series I, vol. 12, part 2, pp. 17, 59, 64, 78; Pope to McDowell, 28 August 1862, in Scott, 1880, series I, vol. 12, part 1 (1885), p. 196.

29. Jones, 1966; Bridges, 1958; Dowdey, 1961, p. 289. The campaign and McClellan's failure to act more aggressively has fascinated many since, and similar situations were used in simulations at West Point for many years thereafter. Interestingly, the students have tended to act cautiously; see Reardon, 1999, pp. 290–91, 294.

30. McClellan to Governor Curtin, 8 and 10 September 1862; McClellan to Halleck, 9 September 1862 (twice); McClellan to FitzJohn Porter, 9 September 1862; McClellan to Lincoln, 10 and 12 September 1862, in Scott, 1880, series I, vol. 19, part 2 (1887), pp. 24, 216, 218–19, 221, 233, 272; McClellan to Halleck, 13 September 1862 (twice), in Scott, 1880, series I, vol. 19, part 2, p. 282.

31. McClellan to Halleck, 15 October 1862, in Scott, 1880, series I, vol. 19, part 1 (1887), p. 26; Lee to Davis, 16 and 20 September 1862, in Scott, 1880, series I, vol. 19, part 1, pp. 140, 142.

32. Reardon, 1999, pp. 302, 305; Quotes in this paragraph from Lee to CSA HQ, 10 April 1863; Lee to Davis, 19 November 1862; Lee to Jackson, 23 and 26 November 1862; all in Scott, 1880, series I, vol. 21 (1888), pp. 550, 556, 1020, 1027, 1033; Lee to George W. Randolph, 17 November 1862; Lee to Davis, 20 November 1862, in Dowdey, 1961, pp. 337–38, 341.

33. Sutherland, 1998, pp. 38, 46, 72–73; Burnside to Halleck, 17 December 1862, in Scott, 1880, series I, vol. 21, p. 66; Lee to James A. Seddon, 16 December 1862 (twice); Lee to CSA HQ, 19 December 1862; in Scott, 1880, series I, vol. 21, pp. 548, 1064, 1068.

34. Hooker to Stanton, 25 February and 2 April 1863; Hooker to Army HQ, 25 February 1863; Hooker to Lincoln, 11 April 1863; Hooker to John J. Peck and reply, 13 April 1863; all in Scott, 1880, series I, vol. 25, part 2 (1889), pp. 99–100, 187, 199–200, 207.

35. See Dowdey, 1961, pp. 421–45; Markle, 2000, p. 3; Sutherland, 1998, pp. 125, 129, 133; Luvaas, 1990.

36. Hooker to Lincoln, 27 April 1863, in Scott, 1880, series I, vol. 25, part 2, p. 263; Hooker to Stanton, 27 April 1863, in Scott, 1880, series I, vol. 25, part 2, pp. 269–70.

37. Sutherland, 1998, pp. 147, 165–67; Lee's report on Chancellorsville, 21 September 1863, in Scott, 1880, series I, vol. 25, part 1 (1889), p. 800.

38. As Lee moved north into Union territory, Hooker was forced to follow him instead of carrying out a planned attack on Richmond. Hooker resigned on 28 June 1863 as commanding officer of the Union's Army of the Potomac, to be replaced by George B. Meade.

39. Dowdey, 1961, p. 478; also see Luvaas, 1990; Bartholomees, 1998, p. 256; Nolan, 1999, pp. 13–14, 17, 18; Lee to Davis, 4 and 31 July, in Scott, 1880, series I, vol. 27, part 2 (1889), pp. 298, 306–7; Gallagher, 1999a, p. 32; Gallagher, 1999b, p. 114.

40. Esposito, 1972, page facing map 99; Battle Report on Gettysburg Campaign, in Dowdey, 1961, pp. 574, 580.

41. Dowdey, 1961, p. 478; Long, 1952, p. 274; Gallagher, 1999b, p. 119; Bicheno, 2001, p. 37.

42. Bicheno, 2001, pp. 36, 192; Meade to Halleck, 28 June 1863; Meade to Couch, 30 June 1863, in Scott, 1880, series I, vol. 27, part 1, pp. 61–62, 68; Sauers, 1999, pp. 235, 238. Markle, 2000, pp. 11–15.

43. Meade to Halleck, 1 July 1863, first message, in Scott, 1880, series I, vol. 27, part 1, p. 71; Meade to Halleck, 28 and 29 June and 1 July (twice) 1863; Meade's final report on Gettysburg, 1 October 1863, in Scott, 1880, series I, vol. 27, part 1, pp. 65, 67, 70–72, 113; Gallagher, 1999b, p. 118; see, e.g., Lee to Davis, 31 July 1863, in Scott, 1880, series I, vol. 27, part 2, p. 305.

According to Nolan, 1999, Lee wavered on the first day; he experienced "conservative instincts" (p. 22) and told his local commander that he did not want a general engagement. But within hours Lee had changed his mind and allowed the attacks to go forward (p. 23). Elsewhere, Nolan (1999, p. 13) charges that Lee exaggerated his lack of knowledge somewhat.

44. Long, 1952, pp. 391ff.; Elley, 1992, p. 28.

45. Trudeau, 1989, p. 113.

46. Trudeau, 1989, pp. 26, 42, 45, 49; Grant to Halleck, 7 May 1864, in Scott, 1880, series I, vol. 36, part 1 (1891), p. 2. In fact, Grant lost 18,400 men as against 11,400 for Lee; Grant to Halleck, 11 May 1864, in Scott, 1880, series I, vol. 36, part 1, p. 3; McWhiney, 1998, p. 45.

47. Elley, 1992, p. 5; Grant to Halleck, 8 May 1864, in Scott, 1880, series I, vol. 36, part 1, p. 2.

48. Elley, 1992, p. 29.

49. Elley, 1992, p. 29; Trudeau, 1989, pp. 120, 130; Matter, 1998, pp. 33, 37 (prior quotes also taken from Matter); Henderson, 1987, p. 13.

50. Matter, 1998, p. 48; Long, 1952, pp. 418–19; Trudeau, 1989, p. 197; Gallagher, 1998, p. 7.

51. Grant to Halleck, 26 May 1864, in Scott, 1880, vol. 36, part 1, p. 9; Long, 1952, pp. 429–30; Grant to Halleck, 24 May 1864, in Scott, 1880, vol. 36, part 1, p. 9.

52. Trudeau, 1989, p. 245.

53. Grant to Army HQ, 22 July 1865, in Scott, 1880, vol. 36, part 1, p. 22.

54. Trudeau, 1989, p. 298.

55. Lee was perhaps guessing that this was only a raid; Trudeau, 1989, pp. 309, 311; Elley, 1992, pp. 10–11; Horn, 1993, p. 56; Greene, 2000, pp. 7–8.

56. Grant to Army HQ, 22 July 1865, in Scott, 1880, series I, vol. 36, p. 12; Feis, 2002, pp. 254, 260–61. In 1862 Union plans had been disrupted by a brilliant campaign in the Shenandoah Valley led by Thomas "Stonewall" Jackson.

57. Feis, 2002, pp. 221–25, 232, 242–49; see also Feis, 1993.

58. See, e.g., Greene, 2000, p. 266; Horn, 1993, pp. 108–19. Ambrose E. Burnside had already been relieved of his command of the Army of the Potomac after his role in Fredericksburg, 1863. But he retained command of a corps and was responsible for the Battle of the Crater disaster. After the war, he became governor of Rhode Island.

59. Horn, 1993, pp. 79, 189–95; Greene, 2000, pp. 156–61, 179.

60. Feis, 2002, pp. 10, 205, 209, 267, 268; McWhiney, 1998, p. 23.

61. Elley, 1992, pp. 12, 18–19;

62. Feis, 2002, p. 211.

63. Reardon, 1999, p. 295; Feis, 2002, pp. 200, 235.

64. Feis, 1997, p. ii; Elley, 1992, p. 35; Long, 1952, p. 539; Horn, 1993, p. 246.

65. Trudeau, 1989, pp. 26, 166; Greene, 2000, pp. 149–50, 153.

66. McClellan's division commanders were not entirely taken in by these ruses — but McClellan was!

67. The idea of a volunteer force faded quickly as the Civil War failed to come to an early end. The number of volunteers dried up. The Militia Act of 1862 compelled states to furnish troops to the Union. This soon proved ineffective, and enlistment bonuses ("bounties") went from $50 at the beginning of the war toward $1,000 at the end (this, when average incomes were around $500 a year). When even the bonuses did not bring in sufficient numbers of men, Congress passed four drafts, in the summer of 1863, the spring and fall of 1864, and the spring of 1865. Of more than three-quarters of a million men (777,000) whose draft numbers were called, only 46,000 were drafted, and another 160,000 furnished substitutes or had their draft commuted by payment of a "commutation fee." The other 571,000 did not report (161,000), were discharged upon reporting (94,000), or exempted after reporting (316,000). (The numbers, obviously, are rounded.) The draft legislation included provisions to legally avoid service (e.g., by paying the commutation fee). This attracted bounty-brokers who matched draftees with means with nondraftees without means. Draft insurance societies also arose, a means whereby potential draftees would pay a premium into a mutual fund; when drafted, the fund would pay the commutation fee. On this, see, for example, http://www.academy.umd.edu/publications/NationalService/citizen_soldier .htm [accessed 28 October 2003]. For print literature on the draft, see, e.g., Shannon, 1965, Murdock, 1980, Geary, 1991, and Phisterer, 1996.

68. Some soldiers would enlist, collect the bounty (i.e., sign-on bonus), then disappear and enlist again elsewhere, hence "bounty-jumpers." Often these were men joining the service on behalf of someone else (one could hire replacements in those days). Interestingly, those who accepted bounty, even if they did not "jump," were not considered the best soldiers.

69. See, e.g., Rotte and Schmidt, 2003.

CHAPTER SIX

1. Quoted in Budiansky, 2004, p. 330. One gruesome description of trench fighting in World War I is Keegan, 1999. One of the tragic ironies of the air war in World War II was

its own goriness; the U.S. strategic air forces would lose over 8,000 bombers, nearly 4,000 fighters, 29,000 dead, and 44,000 wounded. The RAF also lost over 8,000 bombers and suffered 64,000 casualties, including 47,000 dead. See Budiansky, 2004, p. 330; Werrell, 1986, p. 708 and sources cited there.

2. United States Strategic Bombing Survey (USSBS), February 1947, Chart 6, pp. 49–91. The phony war was a period of relative military inactivity from September 1939 to May 1940, the time between Germany's invasion of Poland and the commencement of serious hostilities among European powers. Germans called it Sitzkrieg (pun on Blitzkrieg), the Brits the Bore War (pun on the Boer War).

3. Murray and Millett, 2000, p. 310.

4. Rhodes, 1988, p. 474, mentions "at least 45,000 . . . the majority of them old people, women and children."

5. Budiansky, 2004, pp. 316–17; Murray and Millett, 2000, pp. 320–21; quoted from Budiansky, 2004, p. 317; Murray and Millett, 2000, p. 321; Schaffer, 1980, p. 331. The official Royal Canadian Air Force history describes Harris's "fixation on Berlin" as "his insolent failure to do what he was told"; Greenhous et al., 1994, vol. III, p. 770.

6. Budiansky, 2004, p. 316; Werrell, 1986, p. 705.

7. USSBS, January 1947, p. 5.

8. USSBS, January 1947, p. 2, pt. 2.

9. Levine, 1992, p. 1.

10. Innumerable sources make the point that an ideally executed form of strategic bombing could vanquish an enemy all by itself. One useful recent comprehensive history of air power is Budiansky, 2004. The development of strategic bombing theory by the Americans, as well as the first warning that it might not work as advertised, is described there on pp. 176–80.

11. Werrell, 1986, p. 704; See, e.g., Levine, 1992, p. 192; Smith, 1976, passim (in a curiously defensive piece comparing World War II and the American bombing of Vietnam). For a detailed working up of American strategic bombing history prior to Pearl Harbor, see, e.g., Clodfelter, 1994. Like many others, this work also includes reference to Giulio Douhet (1869–1930), the Italian original air power theorist.

To be clear: It is incorrect to claim that air power advocates did not believe the war could be won by strategic bombing alone. They most certainly, and mistakenly, believed that. What is historically correct is that, although not opposed per se to the use of strategic bombing, General George Marshall and other Allied leaders in World War II, like Pershing in World War I, did not accept air power advocates' claim that strategic bombing could win the war "independent" — an oft-used phrase — of the Army and Navy (see, e.g., Clodfelter, 1994, pp. 90, 95). Or, as Lord Kitchener of the United Kingdom observed: "We have to make war as we must and not as we would like to" (cited in Webster and Frankland, 1961, vol. 1, p. 17). What is also historically correct is that the Americans' principal pre–Pearl Harbor war plan — Rainbow 5 — "cast all strategic air operations in the form of a preliminary to the invasion, not as a substitute for it" (Jacobs, 1986, p. 133). Air power advocates therefore were constantly jostling between idealist belief in the efficacy of strategic bombing theory and the practical limitations their superiors set down.

12. So, e.g., Fuller, 1961, p. 286, and Murray and Millett, 2000, p. 332. Recognizing and acknowledging the pronounced lack of success until mid-1944, Werrell, 1986, p. 707, argues that "when we discuss the accomplishments of strategic bombing, we are speaking of what occurred during the last months of the war." Even with this restriction on the

pertinent time-frame he concludes that "strategic bombing did not achieve the goals that some sought . . . the war proved the prewar air prophets wrong" (p. 712). In an analysis based on concepts borrowed from cognitive psychology, Biddle, 2002, shows that British and American airmen were quite wedded to the notion that strategic bombing would bring about political capitulation, even if they neglected to ask exactly how this was to be achieved. Biddle also expresses skepticism about the success of strategic bombing. On the struggle between representatives of the U.S. Navy and the U.S. Army Air Force regarding the writing of the relevant reports on the Pacific theater of the USSBS, see, e.g., Gentile, 2000. Both sides correctly foresaw the huge influence the final reports would have on the future U.S. force structure. Similarly, Budiansky, 2004, pp. 340–41, on the attempt to ensure that the American public and its politicians would come to see atomic weapons as part of the U.S. strategic forces. So, too, Schaffer, 1980, and Jacobs, 1986.

13. Budiansky, 2004, pp. 325–26. Werrell points out, correctly, that the P-51 (the "Mustang") long-range bomber escort fighter is somewhat overrated in historical accounts. It flew its first mission only on 5 December 1943 (Werrell, 1986, p. 706) so that in the crucial air war months of January to April 1944, the P-47 ("Thunderbolt") predominated in the Allies' arsenal. The P-47 had been designed as an interceptor and began service as a short-range escort fighter. Pilots found its most valuable, and what would prove to be decisive, role as a fighter-bomber "by accident." On account of its great speed and superior maneuverability, it could effectively engage air defense fighters and evade anti-air fire from the ground; its air-cooled engine could sustain damage more easily than other aircraft; and its 2,430 hp engine was strong enough to also carry a 2,500 ton bomb load (for the story, see Budiansky, 2004, p. 297).

14. A related issue is discussed in chapter 7 on France's *force de frappe:* what is the destructive contribution of a second atomic bomb?

15. Although z may have been considered a random term in a war-fighting operational sense, it is not an error term in the statistical sense.

16. Murray and Millett, 2000, p. 307. His staff actually called him "Butch," short for "the Butcher"; Rhodes, 1988, p. 470.

As an example of an exception, Harris allowed that the incredibly costly raids on Berlin, which resulted in the loss of hundreds of aircraft and thousands of crews for minimal gain, "did not appear to be an overwhelming success" (quoted in Budiansky, 2004, p. 317; see also Murray and Millett, 2000, p. 322).

17. The United States Strategic Bombing Survey (USSBS, February 1947) was a massive effort involving over 1,000 people whose purpose it was to evaluate the strategic bombing effort. More than 200 reports were produced concerning the European war, and a further 109 reports on the war in the Pacific. U.S. personnel were moving along with U.S. troops into liberated territories and then into Germany so as to secure original documents and interview factory managers, officials, and Nazi leaders upon capture. The British also produced a report, the British Bombing Survey Unit (BBSU, 1998). First published in 1947, it is of much smaller scale, often making use of data derived from the USSBS. Monthly bombing data are available from December 1939 to May 1945. An example is provided in Appendix B of this chapter. The data are classified by tonnage dropped, by country or region on which the bombs were dropped (Germany; France; Italy and Sicily; Austria, Hungary, the Balkans, and "all other countries"), by who dropped the bombs (the RAF or the USAAF), and by target class. The ten target classes were: (1) aircraft factories; (2) airfields/aerodromes; (3) oil, rubber, chemicals, and explosives; (4) land transportation (mainly rolling stock, rail-

road yards, and bridges); (5) V-weapon launching sites; (6) naval and water transportation (e.g., canals, bridges); (7) miscellaneous manufacturing (armaments, tanks, motor vehicles, machinery and equipment, bearings, electrical products, optical and precision instruments, steel, light metals, radio and radar, and "manufacturing not identified"); (8) industrial areas (i.e., towns and cities); (9) military targets; and (10) and all other targets. A further class is "RAF not classified." This refers to tonnage dropped by RAF forces where the location is known (e.g., Germany, France, Italy, etc.) but the target class is unknown (this amounted to a total of about 241,000 tons of bombs).

18. For a book-length treatment on German flak, for example, see Westermann, 2001. A brief account of the Kammhuber line of searchlights, radar, and night fighters is in Murray and Millett, 2000, pp. 314–15.

19. Quoted material from Murray and Millett, 2000, p. 311; Hewitt, 1983, p. 272.

This is perhaps why Harris never seemed to care much about anything other than throwing still more punches at German cities. He might have done better, as the Allies urged, to think about how and where and when to throw them, not just how many punches to throw.

20. Budiansky, 2004, pp. 171, 177. We take up the issue of morale bombing in a later section. On the specific topic of American ethics and morale bombing, see Schaffer, 1980. His argument is that the Americans engaged in pragmatic moralism. An alternative interpretation would be that the air war leaders all grew up in a uniquely American culture of moralism cum pragmatism: they preferred to act morally and dragged out precision bombing — even when it evidently did not work — to uphold their moralism. The real question is why they succumbed to the temptation of morale bombing as late as 1944, by which time the war had essentially been won.

21. Budiansky, 2004, pp. 175, 282, 286 (cartoon reproduction). Others, for example, Fuller, 1961, p. 281: "Hypothetical though it [a rapid end brought about by strategic bombing] was, there is nothing unstrategic about it."

22. British Bombing Survey Unit (BBSU), 1998, table 25, p. 91.

23. British Bombing Survey Unit (BBSU), 1998, p. 69.

24. USSBS, 30 September 1945, p. 31. So also Milward, 1965, esp. chap. 1. The view that Germany was under misapprehension of what was required to win the war is disputed most prominently by Richard J. Overy (e.g., 1994). Whereas the USSBS argued that a Blitzkrieg military strategy was accompanied by a Blitzkrieg economy caught off guard when lightning war turned into protracted war, Overy argues that Hitler planned for Germany's economy to support a major, protracted war to commence around the mid-1940s but was caught off guard when war started early. Overy's evidence is strong but does not affect our argument about diminishing marginal returns to bombing.

25. Pape, 1996, p. 279. Canada, which supplied substantial numbers to the British, as did other members of the Commonwealth, takes in its official history of the Royal Canadian Air Force an intermediate, almost apologetic, position that nonetheless comes to the same conclusion: "the effect of the damage inflicted on the German war effort by Bomber Command . . . was certainly substantial, particularly in the degree to which the strategic bomber offensive became a virtual second front before D-Day and before the Americans were heavily involved. However, in the pre-nuclear era, airpower alone could not strike a decisive blow, and postwar analysis showed clearly that the damage inflicted on the German war economy was never as great as hoped (and believed) at the time" (Greenhous et al., 1994, p. 527).

26. This can be calculated from USSBS, February 1947, pp. 49–91.

27. We also have bombing tonnage numbers for January to May 1945 but not corresponding numbers for aircraft produced. The figures in the table refer to the combined RAF and USAAF bombing of aircraft factories. The overall tonnage dropped was 57,041, of which the RAF contributed 6,024 and USAAF the remaining 51,017.

28. Werrell, 1986, p. 712. In fairness we must of course acknowledge that it took the considerable postwar USSBS data collection effort to permit us to reach this conclusion. During the war accurate intelligence on destruction achieved was notoriously difficult to come by.

29. The quoted passage is from "AWPD-1: Munitions Requirements of the Army Air Forces," as quoted by Clodfelter, 1994, p. 90. The men in General Arnold's recently formed Air War Plans Division were Harold Lee George, the division leader, as well as Haywood S. Hansell, Laurence S. Kuter, and Kenneth N. Walker. The men all had been instructors in the 1930s at the Air Force Tactical School in Alabama, where Kuter "resurrected" strategic bombing from its World War I antecedents (Clodfelter, 1994, p. 83). Arnold himself had become chief of the Army Air Forces in June, when the former Air Corps was renamed.

30. See Clodfelter, 1994, pp. 91, 94, 97 (Barry Watts). Few writers on the strategic bombing topic place it within the overall strategic context. Jacobs, 1986, is a useful corrective to this shortcoming.

31. George: Clodfelter, 1994, p. 92; Kuter: Budiansky, 2004, pp. 179–80.

32. Details from Clodfelter, 1994, pp. 91–94. In the event, AWPD-1 turned out to be remarkably prescient, even if for the wrong reasons. While the proposed attacks on electric power stations, for example, never took place because it was coal, not electricity per se, that powered industry, by coincidence the envisioned numbers were not far off target: 80,000 machines, 2.4 million men, and, as regards Germany, an eight-month pounding from the air, from September 1944 to April 1945. See Mierzejewski, 1988; Clodfelter, 1994, p. 99.

33. Quoted in Clodfelter, 1994, p. 96. Milward, 1977, chap. 1, has a good discussion on the Blitzkrieg concept which avoids the need for full mobilization of economic resources. "Too often [Blitzkrieg] has been used merely in its tactical sense of a quick knock-out blow delivered against the enemy's forces from a position of strength. But the concept was strategical as well as tactical" (p. 7) in that it allowed Hitler not to transform Germany into a total-war economy and therefore be able to deliver guns for the army and butter for the people. Milward goes through a sizeable list of other advantages this sort of strategy entails, including that of fighting short, limited-objective wars, making economic planning for long, drawn-out wars unnecessary. As mentioned, Overy, 1994, disputes the point and argues that Hitler did plan for a long war, only that it started before the economy was ready to sustain it.

34. Which hindered precision bombing but also hindered German interceptor efforts, a point made repeatedly in Greenhous et al., 1994.

35. This shortcoming has been rectified only recently by Westermann, 2001. He estimates that between July 1942 and April 1945 flak destroyed more than 40 percent of the roughly 3,600 aircraft Bomber Command lost on night sorties while the Luftwaffe destroyed the remainder. For the duration of the entire European war, USAAF lost 5,400 aircraft to flak, and only 4,300 to the Luftwaffe (p. 286). Further aircraft were damaged beyond repair. Many of the damaged aircraft became "stragglers," easy Luftwaffe targets (and credited to the fighters rather than to flak). Moreover, flak forced aircraft to higher altitudes, drastically increasing bombing inaccuracy (p. 289). Westermann's book is crucial reading on the topic. Even so, in terms of Nazi ideology about warfare a focus on air defenses early on would have been almost unthinkable (although there are counterexamples — Todt's organization,

Atlantic Wall, etc.). Still, as late as 1945, Carl Spaatz complained that he could not completely suppress the Luftwaffe.

36. As a deceptive measure Operation Fortitude included air strikes on railway systems away from the intended Normandy landing sites, hence the attacks in Germany; Greenhous et al., 1994, p. 793. See Greenhous et al., 1994, pp. 796–808 on German air defense responsibilities, resource allocations, and achievements, p. 803, table 8.

37. As quoted in Greenhous et al., 1994, pp. 795, 805–6.

38. Greenhous et al., 1994, pp. 790–91.

39. Werrell, 1986, p. 707.

40. Clodfelter, 1994, p. 99. Clodfelter is one of the few who have taken note of Mierzejewski's discussion of the bombing of the Reichsbahn as from September 1944 (Mierzejewski, 1988). Budiansky, 2004, p. 302 adds: "After the war, the U.S. Strategic Bombing Survey would cite the Transportation Plan among the accomplishments of the strategic-bomber offensive. Assigning credit for military successes is always a tricky business, but giving credit for a success to a command that not only did not accomplish it but indeed opposed it as the wrong objective carried out by the wrong force against the wrong targets using the wrong strategy and the wrong tactics — this was taking credit to the extreme."

41. Cox, 1998; Overy, 1994.

42 Overy, 1994; USSBS, 31 October 1945, p. 10 (both spellings of Yugoslavia in original). Of course, one should not assume there was a one-to-one correspondence between the productivity of native and slave labor.

43. BBSU, 1998, table 27, p. 96.

44. The land invasion was necessary in the sense that strategic bombing alone did not get the job done. Many historians point out that, given Soviet Russia's pressure in the east, the western Allies' land invasion may not have been strictly necessary to defeat Germany but was equally calculated to hold off a Soviet run on central and western Europe.

45. As quoted in Koch, 1991, pp. 119, 134, and Fuller, 1961, p. 281; Koch, 1991, p. 120. Churchill does not appear to have been troubled morally by issuing terror. In 1919 he wrote: "I do not understand this squeamishness about the use of gas. We have definitely adopted the position at the Peace Conference of arguing in favour of the retention of gas as a permanent method of warfare. It is sheer affectation to lacerate a man with the poisonous fragment of a bursting shell and to boggle at making his eyes water by means of lachrymatory gas. I am strongly in favour of using poisoned gas against uncivilised tribes. The moral effect should be so good that the loss of life should be reduced to a minimum. It is not necessary to use only the most deadly gasses: gasses can be used which cause great inconvenience and would spread a lively terror and yet would leave no serious permanent effects on most of those affected." War Office Departmental Minute, 12 May 1919, Churchill Papers 16/16, Churchill Archives Centre, Cambridge. See http://en.wikipedia.org/wiki/Winston _Churchill_Quotes [accessed 22 July 2004]. Evidently, Churchill's views evolved eventually to include the acceptance of quite serious effects of terror bombing as well.

46. Koch, 1991, p. 141; Terraine, 1985, p. 677; Clodfelter, 1994, pp. 84, 91; see, e.g., Schaffer, 1980, p. 318. Koch goes on to acknowledge that "it may well be unreasonable, having regard to the circumstances, to expect them to have acted otherwise." Vonnegut was a prisoner of war held in a Dresden slaughterhouse during the firestorm attack; Rhodes, 1988, p. 593.

47. Schaffer, 1980, p. 323. Spaatz even said so directly: "It wasn't for religious or moral reasons that I didn't go along with urban area bombing" (p. 325).

48. Budiansky, 2004, pp. 282, as quoted 283, 285. They were Hamburg (July 1943), Kassel (October 1943), Darmstadt (September 1944), and Dresden (February 1945). See Hewitt, 1983, pp. 263, 265.

49. Schaffer, 1980, p. 330. These are our phrases but clearly Schaffer's intent. For a uniquely German perspective on the fire bombing, see Friedrich, 2002, a book not wholly appreciated overseas. The book caused international opprobrium: why would Germans, having done so much to kill others with little compunction, revolt at being killed? This is disingenuous. All victims have the right to speak, and similarly gruesomely descriptive books by English-language authors should not be deemed morally superior for having been written by the eventual victors in the war.

50. Hewitt, 1983. This was not necessarily true in 1940 for the "Battle of Britain" (see Budiansky, 2004, pp. 221, 242) but was certainly true by 1944. But see Koch, 1991, pp. 139–40.

51. As quoted in Budiansky, 2004, p. 206. The significance of this comment goes back to British Prime Minister Stanley Baldwin, who remarked on 10 November 1932 that "the bomber always gets through" (as quoted in Terraine, 1985, p. 13). In 1935, Boeing had just developed the B-17 — dubbed the Flying Fortress for its enormous size — and the Army ordered the first batch in January 1936; on the B-17, see, e.g., Budiansky, 2004, pp. 180–83. But witnessing the air fights over Spain, the attaché wrote a mere year later, in February 1937, that "the Flying Fortress died in Spain."

52. Koch, 1991, p. 122; Budiansky, 2004, p. 211. On the Spanish Civil War, Barcelona, and Guernica, see Budiansky, 2004, pp. 200–214.

53. Koch, 1991; quote from p. 133.

54. Budiansky, 2004, p. 284; BBSU, 1998, p. 79.

55. Budiansky, 2004, p. 244; quote from Hewitt, 1983, p. 279. The morale effect frequently went the other way around: there were considerable, debilitating morale, indeed psychiatric, effects on the bomber crews; for details, see, e.g., Greenhous et al., 1994, and Westermann, 2001.

56. USSBS, 30 September 1945, pp. 95, 97.

57. USSBS, May 1947, p. 1.

58. USSBS, 30 September 1945, p. 96.

59. The data for fig. 6.6 are: percentage of people showing "high morale" in heavily bombed towns (30,000t): 44; in medium bombed towns (6100t): 42; in light bombed towns (500t): 51; and in unbombed towns: 59; percentage of people "trusting leaders" in heavily bombed towns: 48; in medium bombed towns: 48; in light bombed towns: 52; and in unbombed towns: 62; percentage of people "willing to surrender" in heavily bombed towns: 59; in medium bombed towns: 59; in light bombed towns: 54; and in unbombed towns: 51. Source: USSBS, 30 September 1945, p. 96.

60. A point also made by Pape, 1996, p. 272, n. 48.

61. Craven and Cate, 1983 [1948], vol. 2, pp. viii–ix: "In the [European Theater of Operations], during the period covered in this volume, AAF units were engaged exclusively in strategic bombardment as that term was conventionally defined in American doctrine. Their aim was not to aid immediately a ground army; there were no Allied armies on western European soil, and the concept of the bomber offensive as a sort of second front to relieve pressure on the Red Army was an argument after the fact rather than an initiating move. The true mission of the Eighth Air Force was to weaken Germany by hitting directly

at its war potential—industrial, military, and moral—although this required the previous destruction of German air power." This from the U.S. air force's own official history.

62. Craven and Cate, 1983 [1948], vol. 2, p. ix, 1983 [1951], vol. 3, pp. xi–xii, xvi, 1983 [1947], vol. 1, p. xix.

63. Hewitt, 1983, p. 279; calculated from USSBS, February 1947, chart 6. Pape suggests that the Germans feared a Soviet invasion more than invasion by the western Allies and hence fought "to buy time to permit soldiers and civilians to flee the advancing Red Army" (1996, p. 302). This is not entirely convincing as in that case Germany could simply have surrendered on the western front while maintaining an eastern front until the western Allies had completed its invasion all the way to the Polish border.

64. Levine, 1992, pp. 189, 190, 192; USSBS, January 1947, p. 2, pt. 3.

65. Levine, 1992, p. 193.

66. Levine, 1992, p. 193; USSBS, January 1947, p. 7, pt. 10.

67. Overy, 1994 (a collection of 11 of his essays).

68. See Milward, 1977, especially the chapter "war, technology and economic change." He argues that the main "spin-off" of military efforts on the postwar civilian economies of all the major powers may well not have lain in successfully commercialized products but in managerial know-how of performing under duress.

69. Incidentally, in today's high-technology war environment, military assets are often so specific that they cannot easily be swapped to alternative duties. An Eisenhower today would be stymied, although he might have found other ways to get around constraints of the moment.

70. For details, see Budiansky, 2004, pp. 242–51.

71. USSBS, January 1947, p. 5.

CHAPTER SEVEN

1. Kohl, 1971, pp. 45–46; Anthérieu et al., 1963, pp. 252–53; Larkin, 1996, p. 27, n. 17.

2. On the history of atomic and hydrogen weapons, see the incomparable works by Rhodes, 1988 [1986], 1995.

3. Aron, 1965, p. 106.

4. The ceteris paribus clause is crucial because it conditions the application of the principle of substitution (see chap. 1). The principle states that if all other things that influence decision making were to remain unchanged, then given alternatives yielding comparable benefits users will tend to drift toward selecting the alternative with the least relative price to be paid. Of course, things do not stay constant, certainly not in world military politics, and this complicates the analysis.

5. See Baer, 1993, chap. 1.

6. Beaufre, 1966, p. 30; see Cimbala, 1989, pp. 33–34; Enthoven and Smith, 1971, pp. 211–12, 216.

7. Scheinman, 1965, p. 109; Cimbala, 1989, pp. 43, 46. Also see Sandler and Hartley, 1999. Tongue in cheek, the American "bang for the buck" became for the Soviets, Brits, and French, respectively, "rubble for the ruble," "pounding for the pound," and "frappe for the franc."

8. Hitch, 1966a, p. 116; Hitch, 1966b, p. 126; Hitch and McKean, 1967, p. 3.

9. Beaufre, 1966, p. 32.

10. See Chaliand, 1994, p. 992; Theleri, 1997, p. 9.

11. Nussio, 1996, p. 8.

12. Browder, 1964, p. 134; Scheinman, 1965, p. 216.

13. The Fourth Republic: 1946–1958. France was under its fourth republican constitution, which featured a relatively weak parliamentary government. In contrast, constitutional changes resulting in the Fifth Republic created a powerful presidency in France.

14. Howorth and Chilton, 1984, p. 4; Waites, 1984, p. 38.

15. Holmquist, 1969, p. 12; Scheinman, 1965, p. 94.

16. Scheinman, 1965, p. 95.

17. Wohlstetter et al., 1976, pp. 44–45.

18. Ailleret, 1962, pp. 11, 35, 57–59, 65.

19. Nussio, 1996, pp. 10–11; Buchan, 1966, p. 9; Rynning, 2002, p. 36; Scheinman, 1965, pp. 112–20, 124; Ailleret, 1962, p. 9; Browder, 1964, pp. 35–36.

20. Scheinman, 1965, p. 168; Kohl, 1971, p. 44; foreword by Pierre Gallois in Rynning, 2002, p. xv; Scheinman, 1965, pp. 166, 168–69, 173, 182; Regnault, 2003, p. 1226.

21. Scheinman, 1965, pp. 116–17, 186–87; Regnault, 2003, p. 1229.

22. Waites, 1984, p. 39.

23. Scheinman, 1965, p. 219; Holmquist, 1969, p. 20; Nussio, 1996, pp. 11–12.

24. Rynning, 2002, p. 44; Kohl, 1971, p. 46.

25. Ailleret, 1962, pp. 36–37, 60–63, 198.

26. Cerny, 1984, p. 49; Browder, 1964, pp. 6, 108; Holmquist, 1996, p. 7; Scheinman, 1965, pp. 96–97, 100–101; Hecht, 1996, pp. 490–91; Nussio, 1996, p. 11.

27. Holmquist, 1996, p. 11; Scheinman, 1965, pp. 97–99, 106, 218; Browder, 1964, pp. 6, 103.

28. Howorth and Chilton, 1984, pp. 7–8.

29. Menard, 1967, p. 228; Cimbala, 1998, pp. 186–87; Wohlstetter et al., 1976, p. 116. Ironically, Gallois' meeting with De Gaulle had been encouraged by the Allied supreme commander, U.S. General Lauris Norstad; see Rynning, 2002, pp. 43–44.

30. Anthérieu et al., 1963, pp. 44, 116; Cimbala, 1988a, p. 127.

31. Kolodziej, 1967, pp. 417–20, 422–23, 426–27.

32. See Regnault, 2003, p. 1227; Kolodziej, 1967, p. 450; Browder, 1964, p. 71. It is not clear whether Regnault is quoting de Gaulle or one of his followers.

33. Martin, 1981, pp. 39–40, 45–46; Morse, 1973, pp. 154–55; Browder, 1964, p. 49; Regnault, 2003, pp. 1224–25; Cimbala, 1998, p. 187; ; Zoppo, 1964, p. 126.

34. Kolodziej, 1974, p. 102. See also Ifestos, 1988, p. 276; Gordon, 1993, p. 57.

35. Martin, 1981, p. 42; Holmquist, 1969, p. 83; Yost, 1986, pp. 153–54.

36. Yost, 1986, pp. 133–34; Rynning, 2002, pp. 26–27, 34–34, 55; Kohl, 1971, pp. 158–59; Gordon, 1993, p. 63.

37. Beeton, 1966, pp. 32–33; Gordon, 1993, p. 40; Morse, 1973, pp. 155–56.

38. Anthérieu, 1963, pp. 27–33; Kolodziej, 1974, pp. 141–42, 147–48, 152; Kohl, 1971, p. 160; Morse, 1973, p. 156.

39. Kolodziej, 1971, p. 466; Wohlstetter, 1987, p. 11; Ifestos, 1988, p. 277; Gordon, 1993, pp. 66–68; Howorth and Chilton, 1984, pp. 10–11; Cimbala, 1988a, p. 250.

40. Gordon, 1993, pp. 84–85, 104; Howorth, 1996, p. 33; Ifestos, 1988, pp. 279, 287–92; Gordon, 1993, pp. 92–93; Martin, 1981, pp. 25–27.

41. Yost, 1986, pp. 131–33, 135–36, 141–43, 152–53; Howorth and Chilton, 1984, p. 11; Gordon, 1993, p. 103; Gallois in Rynning, 2002, pp. xxii–xxiii.

42. Chilton, 1984, pp. 155–56; Waites, 1984, p. 42; Ifestos, 1988, pp. 292–93; Cimbala, 1987, p. 181; Gordon, 1993, p. 181.

43. Ifestos, 1988, pp. 275, 297–98; Gordon, 1993, pp. 137–38, 163; Howorth and Chilton, 1984, p. 11; Wohlstetter, 1987, pp. 12–13; Larkin, 1996, pp. 27–28.

44. Nussio, 1996, pp. 46, 57; Larkin, 1996, p. 26; "Pour la première fois, depuis quarante ans, les armes nucléaires perdent le privilège absolue dans la panoplie de nos armes"; Theleri, 1997, pp. 385–86; Gallois in Rynning, 2002, pp. xv, xxv.

45. "Il faut reconnaître qu'il n'est pas possible à la France de lutter seul avec une armée classique contre les armées classiques de l'U.R.S.S. C'est la raison pour laquelle le gouvernement a décidé de développer l'énergie atomique militaire"; Dollfus, 1960, pp. 70–71; Chaliand, 1994, pp. 995–96.

46. Scheinman, 1965, pp. 116, 191; Hecht, 1998, p. 201; Browder, 1964, pp. 15, 37.

47. Browder, 1964, pp. 17, 20, 25; Martin, 1981, p. 38; Chaliand, 1994, p. 1052; Gordon, 1993, pp. 38–39; Scheinman, 1965, pp. 171, 188–90. The passage quoted in the text is Scheinman's translation.

48. Kolodziej, 1974, pp. 96–97.

49. Scheinman, 1965, pp. 192–95; Gordon, 1993, pp. 4–5; Kohl, 1971, p. 47; Martin, 1981, p. 23.

50. Browder, 1964, pp. ii–iii; Morse, 1973, p. 17; Gallois in Rynning, 2002, p. xiv; Kohl, 1971, p. 157; Hecht, 1998, p. 209; Howorth and Chilton, 1984, p. 12; Kohl, 1971, p. 150.

51. Browder, 1964, p. 47; Scheinman, 1965, pp. 192–95; Morse, 1973, pp. 149–51; Kolodziej, 1971, p. 457; Zoppo, 1964, p. 114; Kolodziej, 1974, p. 45; Waites, 1984, p. 40; Morse, 1973, pp. 92–95; de Carmoy, 1969, p. 433.

52. Ifestos, 1988, p. 276; Browder, 1964, pp. 65–66; Haftendorn, 1996, p. 5; Howorth and Chilton, 1984, p. 8; Gallois, 1961, p. 169.

53. Gordon, 1993, p. 58; Aron, 1965, p. 122; Gordon, 1993, p. 58; Kohl, 1971, pp. 152–53.

54. Gordon, 1993, p. 62; Chaliand, 1994, pp. 1025–26; Kohl, 1971, pp. 155–57.

55. Morse, 1973, p. 153; Howorth and Chilton, 1984, p. 5; Gordon, 1993, pp. 42–43; Kolodziej, 1974, pp. 104–5; Anthérieu et al., 1963, pp. 9–10; Menard, 1967, pp. 229–32.

56. Morse, 1973, p. 33; Dollfus, 1960, pp. 27–29, 35, 55; Anthérieu et al., 1963, pp. 21–23, 34–39; Gordon, 1993, p. 40; Moch, 1963, p. 41.

57. Wohlstetter et al., 1976, pp. 116–42 passim, 149; Aron, 1965, p. 106; Holmquist, 1969, p. 1.

58. Wohlstetter, 1959, pp. 213, 217, 228–29, n. 9; Halperin, 1966 [1963], p. 120; Morse, 1973, p. 194; Aron, 1965, pp. 114–19; Club Jean Moulin, 1963, p. 60. Also see Aron, 1965, pp. 119, 257.

59. Chaliand, 1994, pp. 1065–66; Ifestos, 1988, pp. 284–86; Cimbala, 1988a, p. 126; Cimbala, 1988b, p. 46; Yost, 1987, p. 144; Martin, 1987, p. 47; Wohlstetter et al., 1976, pp. 39, 118.

60. Moch, 1963, p. 264; Aron, 1965, p. 108; Freedman, 1986, p. 778; Hecht, 1998, pp. 243–44; Ifestos, 1988, pp. 281–84; Morse, 1973, p. 195.

61. Chilton, 1984, p. 135; Doran, 1973, pp. 257, 261–63; Chaliand, 1994, p. 1045.

62. Schelling, 1966, p. 34.

63. Quoted in Nussio, 1996, p. 24; Wolfe, 1965, pp. v–vii.

64. Dollfus, 1960, pp. 100–101; Gordon, 1993, p. 38; d'Abzac-Epezy, 1990, pp. 250–51; Chaliand, 1994, p. 1046.

65. Aron, 1965, pp. 115, 116, n. 12; Martin, 1981, pp. 68–69; Cerny, 1984, p. 56, 59; Dollfus, 1960, p. 70; Gordon, 1993, p. 36. The Nouveau Franc (NF) was introduced on 1 January 1960 and abolished when France joined the Euro system. The five-year program budgets do not cover all capital expenses. The first covered 38 percent, the second about 69 percent of capital expenses. See Martin, 1981, p. 67.

66. Rynning, 2002, p. 52; Martin, 1981, pp. 72, 75–78, 366–67; Chicken, 1996, p. 94; Fysh, 1996, p. 184; Gordon, 1993, pp. 180, 194; Gallois in Rynning, 2002, p. xxiv.

67. See Gallois in Rynning, 2002, p. xvii; Aron, 1965, p. 114.

68. "Cette declaration laissait entendre que le troisième point volontairement omis, le rééquipement classique de l'armeé, était sinon sacrifié et abandonné, du moins négligé et compromise"; "Notre armée classique date d'un autre âge"; both quotes from Dollfus, 1960, pp. 69, 71, 83–84.

69. Gordon, 1993, pp. 37–38; Morse, 1973, p. 183; Browder, 1964, p. 54. It is not clear why France decided it had to develop its own main battle tank, the AMX-30. The United States, the United Kingdom, and Germany had developed excellent machines. If the nuclear force was so important, and the budget was so tight, the development costs of the AMX-30 benefited the French Army not at all — those costs could have gone into purchasing more tanks from foreign sources (or build them under license) or other conventional equipment.

70. Ailleret, 1962, p. 199–202; Anthérieu et al., 1963, pp. 253–58; Chilton, 1984, p. 154; Martin, 1981, pp. 5–6; Chicken, 1996, p. 96.

71. Moch, 1963, p. 33; Kolodziej, 1967, p. 432; Carver, 1986, p. 782.

72. Freedman, 1986, p. 747; Browder, 1964, pp. 100–101.

73. Nussio, 1996, pp. 22–23; de Carmoy, 1969, p. 426; Martin, 1981, pp. 41, 46–48.

74. Beaufre, 1974, pp. 18, 68–69; Chaliand, 1994, pp. 1051, 1062, quoting General Lucien Poirier; Holmquist, 1969, pp. 62–63; Martin, 1981, pp. 42–43; Kohl, 1971, pp. 160–62.

75. Ailleret, 1962, pp. 200–201; see Yost, 1987, p. 127; Kolodziej, 1967, p. 432; Chilton, 1984, p. 137; Halperin, 1966, pp. 58–59; Rynning, 2002, p. 56.

76. Morse, 1973, pp. 180–83; the efficiency of this approach was questioned. See Aron, 1965, pp. 112–13.

77. Beaufre, 1966, pp. 125–26; Holmquist, 1969, p. 30.

78. Gordon, 1993, p. 3; See Beaufre, 1966, pp. 127–28, 138; Browder, 1964, pp. 97–98; Schelling, 1966, chap. 1.

79. Rynning, 2002, pp. 17, 26; Larkin, 1996, pp. 28–29; Anthérieu et al., 1963, pp. 51–53; Beaufre, 1974, pp. 17–18; Cimbala, 1988b, p. 76; Betts, 1985, p. 154; Carver, 1986, p. 781; Dollfus, 1960, pp. 13, 51; Gallois, 1961, p. 168; Beaufre, 1966, pp. 128, 130; Holmquist, 1969, p. 28.

80. Freedman, 1986, p. 740; Carver, 1986, p. 783.

81. Aron, 1965, p. 2; Chaliand, 1994, pp. 996, 999, 1005; see the scenario in Browder, 1964, p. 130; Beaufre, 1974, pp. 44, 70; Browder, 1964, p. 91.

82. Aron, 1965, pp. 113–14.

83. Dollfus, 1960, p. 21; Ifestos, 1988, p. 278; Gordon, 1993, pp. 59–61; Haftendorn, 1996, p. 3; Kolodziej, 1974, pp. 76–82.

84. Anthérieu et al., 1963, pp. 16–17; Gallois in Rynning, 2002, p. xvi; Howorth and Chilton, 1984, p. 6; Waites, 1984, p. 42; Martin, 1981, pp. 24–25; see Holmquist, 1969, p. 48; see Browder, 1964, p. 139; Anthérieu et al., 1963, pp. 15–16; Cimbala, 1998, p. 13; Doran, 1973, p. 258; Aron, 1965, p. 110.

85. Haftendorn, 1996, 3; Anthérieu et al., 1963, pp. 48, 61–63; Holmquist, 1969, p. 40; Holmquist, 1969, p. 40; Kissinger, 1969, p. 202.

86. Browder, 1964, pp. 41–43; Kolodziej, 1974, pp. 84–85; Gordon, 1993, pp. 23–29; Zoppo, 1964, p. 122; Rynning, 2002, p. 55.

87. Larkin, 1996, p. 304; Browder, 1964, p. 101; Chaliand, 1994, p. 997. The Fourth Republic had launched a proposal for a European Defense Community, but it was ultimately rejected by the French National Assembly.

88. Dollfus, 1960, p. 41; Gallois, 1961, p. 205; Gordon, 1993, pp. 44–45, 78; Ifestos, 1988, p. 277; Kolodziej, 1967, p. 21. De Gaulle's critics charged, at any rate, not that the alliance system would not work but that the idea that France could provide for its own defense was unworkable.

89. This is a fundamental issue with all goods and services provided collectively. Economists refer to these as public goods, goods that yield simultaneous benefits to multiple users and from whose benefits none of the users can feasibly be excluded once they are provided. In the case of France, it knew well that NATO would not simply leave it in a lurch in case of attack. French territory was valuable not just to the French, but to NATO as well. Hence France could afford to play "hardball," withdraw from NATO's military command structure, and pursue grandeur at little foreign-policy or military cost. It could extract the concession of greater French independence without quite risking a NATO collapse, figuring that other NATO members such as Norway, say, could never be as bold as France. To them, NATO was a lifeline, and countries such as Poland served as a warning of what might happen without it. Viewing France's nuclear-weapons decisions from the public goods point of view would make for another interesting chapter, but we will leave that for another time.

90. Olson and Zeckhauser, 1966, pp. 268–70, 272.

91. Olson and Zeckhauser, 1966, pp. 273, 278.

92. Olson and Zeckhauser, 1966, p. 279.

93. Sandler and Hartley, 1999, pp. 18, 29–30; Sandler and Hartley, 1999, pp. 30–31; Sandler and Harltey, 1999, pp. 33–37.

94. Enthoven, 1966, p. 135.

95. Hitch, 1966b, p. 124.

96. Enthoven and Smith, 1971, p. 175; Hitch, 1966b, pp. 125–26.

97. Chaliand, 1994, p. 1067.

CHAPTER EIGHT

1. The original work on game theory is von Neumann and Morgenstern, 1944.

2. The original public goods work is Samuelson, 1954, 1955. We pick up the topic later on in this chapter. The classic reference to alliance work is Olson and Zeckhauser, 1966. On primates, see, e.g., de Waal, 1982. The application to NATO, for instance, is examined in Sandler and Hartley, 1999.

3. The economic literature on the topic is large. Handy overviews are provided, for example, by Frey, 2004, Frey, Luechinger, and Stutzer, 2004, Sandler and Enders, 2004, Enders and Sandler, 2006, Brück, 2007, and Llussa and Tavares, 2007. Even though transnational terror captures the world's media headlines, it should not be overlooked that the victims of domestic terror exceed those of transnational terror by several orders of magnitude.

4. This section is based on presentations given by coauthor J. Brauer in October 2004 at the NATO Defense College in Rome, Italy, and in April 2006 at the University of North Carolina, Asheville. They are based, in part, on the sources given in note 3.

5. As John Keegan, the eminent military historian, says in his *History of Warfare*, "even the pirate needs capital to start in business" (1994, p. 64).

If terrorists supply a disservice to the market, one may wonder who is the demander. This need not be a conundrum as the situation may be compared with planting and tending a vegetable garden at home where the producer is also the consumer. Rather than producing for somebody else's satisfaction, one produces for one's own satisfaction of needs. In either case—whether there is terror production for an external market or for an internal market—we may conceive of the existence of a "market for terror," where the objective of government actors is to disrupt trade in this market, much as we wish to disrupt trade in international narcotics, prostitution, small arms, and other criminal activities.

6. Disturbingly, one cheap measure is to "collude" with terror organizations, an implicit arrangement by which a terror organization will not be pursued domestically so long as attacks take place elsewhere. See Lee, 1988, and Brauer, 2002.

7. Enders and Sandler, 1993. Threats are costly as precautionary measures must be taken. Moreover, the mere threat of attack can lead to substantial redirection of tourism and of direct foreign investment.

8. See, e.g., Center for International Security Policy, 2003.

9. Enders and Sandler, 2006, fig. 3.2, p. 61 and fig. 3.6, p. 66.

10. Both groups then pledged to renounce terror, although ETA meanwhile appears to have reneged on its pledge.

11. See Sandler and Hartley, 1995, 1999; Enders and Sandler, 1993, 2000, 2006.

12. Efforts by the United States and Western allies to train counterparts in developing nations raise the relative cost of attack there and may be expected to lead to more attacks in the developed countries that are rendering the assistance.

13. This is a point made especially forcefully by Frey, 2004.

14. This and the next paragraph draw on an excellent review article by John Warner and Beth Asch, 1995, who themselves have been major contributors to our knowledge of the economics of military manpower.

15. The following pages much rely on the excellent review articles by Poutvaara and Wagener, 2007, Simon and Warner, 2007, and Asch, Hosek, and Warner, 2007.

16. For some aspects of conscription in Turkey see Yildirim and Erdinc, 2007.

17. It also appears to be the case that sending conscript forces into battle potentially riles the population of the sending state more than when all-volunteer forces are sent. France in Algeria and the United States in Vietnam are examples of this.

18. Poutvaara and Wagener, 2007, p. 11.

19. The specific numbers are from Asch, Hosek, and Warner, 2007. A related argument has been made according to which larger countries with correspondingly larger bureaucracies will have lower average cost of conscripting a force. If it costs, say, $100 million to set up a conscription system, then a state conscripting 100,000 people per year will have a lower average cost of doing so than a state conscripting only 10,000 of its young men. The prediction follows that, all else being equal, large states are more likely to conscript than small states. Likewise, if one state's bureaucracy is relatively efficient, it is more likely to conscript because of the lower cost per conscript. For example, if it costs one state $100 million to conscript 100,000 men but it costs another state $200 million to conscript the same number, then the former is more likely to use conscription than the latter. The empirical evidence on this line of reasoning is mixed.

20. The decline in average recruit quality varies by service—Army, Navy, Air Force, and Marine Corps—and in 2006 had fallen to the level prevalent in the mid-1980s. This should

not surprise: the smaller the needed force, the more selective it can afford to be, and vice versa.

21. Two recent volumes of papers that, in turn, review much of the antecedent literature, are Bryden and Caparini, 2006 and Alexandra, Caparini, and Baker, forthcoming.

22. Inasmuch as all are paid (the age of unpaid volunteers long since having passed), all soldiers are mercenaries. So, the issue cannot lie with the overt economics of the matter, or even with whether the hirelings are foreigners. The United States presently employs some 30,000 active-duty and 11,000 reserve "green-card" troops culled from over 200 countries (*Economist,* 3 February 2007, p. 34). Rather, the source of the unease is found in concerns regarding legitimacy, transparency, and accountability of forces, whether private or public. It lies with whether states are surrendering their monopoly on force to private actors. This is the issue addressed in this section.

23. The discussion borrows from Brauer, 1999, and Brauer and Roux, 1999.

24. We are not speaking of rivalry in the conventional usage of the term, as in "rival" drug gangs in Brazil or "rival" warlord groups in Afghanistan or Somalia. We are speaking of it in the economic sense: if a group is large enough to provide protection to 10 people in a population of a 100, then there is rivalry among the 100 for which of them will be the 10 who are protected. The more nonrival the good, the more of the 100 people will be covered by the protection umbrella.

25. To drive the point home, here is another set of examples. Television sets are private goods (high rivalry, high exclusion). Ordinarily produced by private firms, TV sets surely could be produced in some government-run factory as well. An over-the-air broadcast signal, however, is a public good (low rivalry — many people can receive the signal at the same time — and no one who has a TV set can feasibly be excluded from receiving the signal). The signal can be produced (sent) either by a public or a private provider. Thus, commercial TV stations are private providers of a public good, but Britain's famous BBC is a public provider of a public good. Cable TV is an example of a club good: only those paying the cable company's access fee can view the channels (high exclusion but once inside the "club," there is no rivalry). Finally, the electromagnetic spectrum over which an over-the-air TV (or radio or cell phone) signal is sent is a common-resource pool good. No one can feasibly be excluded from making use of the spectrum (low exclusion), but if several providers do so on the same frequency, interference may result (high rivalry).

26. Brauer, forthcoming.

27. See, e.g., Shearer, 1998.

28. See, e.g., Wulf, 2005, and the literature cited therein.

29. The discussion borrows from Fredland, 2004. Also see Fredland and Kendry, 1999. Brauer, 2007, separates economic efficiency from the organization of force. Here, following Williamson, 1999, p. 321, we fold the latter into the former, expanding the domain of "efficiency analysis."

30. Williamson, 1999; Fredland, 2004. For literature on and an exposition of transaction cost economics, see Williamson, 1985.

31. Williamson, 1999, pp. 307–8.

32. Williamson, 1999, pp. 318, 322, 325.

33. Williamson, 1999, pp. 321, 340.

34. Both quotes as reported in Fredland, 2004, p. 211.

35. Giustozzi, 2007, p. 31.

36. The risk is not all on the side of the state. In the case of Papua New Guinea and Sandline, it was the state that broke the contract; see Fredland, 2004, p. 213.

37. The Gulf War effort was so amply reimbursed, mostly by Saudi Arabia, that the U.S. trade balance turned positive. It was vastly negative both before and after 1991.

38. A one-off exchange is more hazardous than a repeat transaction. Thus, a late-night TV "special" is more likely to result in dissatisfied customers as the seller wants to complete just a single transaction with the buyer, whereas Coca-Cola wants to continue to sell soft drinks. The prospect of future transactions with the same customer has Coca-Cola concerned about its reputation and the quality of its brand.

39. See http://www.fas.org/irp/world/para/excutive_outcomes.htm (accessed 17 June 2007).

40. Novick, 1988, pp. 593, 594.

41. Thompson, 2004, p. 1; Fischer, 2002, p. xiii. A more current example, an exchange by UCLA diplomatic historian Marc Trachtenberg with various professors of international relations on the role and nature of international relations theory in diplomatic history may be found in *Historically Speaking,* vol. 8, no. 2 (November/December 2006), pp. 11–21. Economics, like virtually every academic discipline, has its own internal quarrels as well. Reacting to the dominance of the neoclassical school of economics, for instance, the perhaps not inappropriately named Post-Autistic Economics Network, started in 2000 and featuring its own online journal (see www.paecon.net), has found some resonance among economists, although this may reflect discontent with the status quo more than that it signals approval of the alternative.

42. For a useful essay on military history in the European and American molds and on the new military history, see Paret, 1992.

43. Goldin, 1995, p. 206.

44. For examples, see Conybeare, Murdoch, and Sandler, 1994; Redlich, 1964/65; Steiner, 1942; Hitch and McKean, 1967; Bonney, 1999; Ferguson, 2001; Olson, 1982; Kennedy, 1987.

45. Covering the past 200-odd years, here is one sample of elite economists that have written on conflict, war, and peace: Kenneth Arrow, Kenneth Boulding, F. Y. Edgeworth, John Kenneth Galbraith, Jack Hirshleifer, Michael Intriligator, Lawrence Klein, Wassily Leontief, V. I. Lenin, Friedrich List, Karl Marx, Oskar Morgenstern, Mancur Olson, Vilfredo Pareto, A. C. Pigou, David Ricardo, Lionel Robbins, Joseph Schumpeter, Werner Sombart, Thomas Schelling, Adam Smith, Jan Tinbergen, Thorstein Veblen, and Knut Wicksell. For a review, see Coulomb, 2004.

46. Keegan, 2003, pp. 3–4.

47. Keegan, 2003, pp. 87–91, has an interesting discussion on cartography, or rather the relative lack thereof, as it pertains to the American Civil War. "Positively bad maps of the [Shenandoah] Valley would lead [the] Northern enemies into serious error" (p. 91).

REFERENCES

Ailleret, Charles. 1962. *L'Aventure atomique française.* Paris: Grasset.

Akerlof, George A. 1984 [1970]. "The Market for 'Lemons': Quality Uncertainty and the Market Mechanism." *Quarterly Journal of Economics,* vol. 84 (August), pp. 488–500. Reprinted in George A. Akerlof, *An Economic Theorist's Book of Tales* (Cambridge: Cambridge University Press, 1984).

Alexandra, Andrew, Marina Caparini, and Deane-Peter Baker, eds. Forthcoming. *Private Military Companies: Ethics, Theory, and Practice.* London: Routledge.

Anderson, Donna M., and Michael J. Haupert. 1999. "Employment and Statistical Discrimination: A Hands-on Experiment." *Journal of Economics* (MVEA), vol. 25, no. 1, pp. 85–102.

Angellotti, Marion Polk. 1911. *Sir John Hawkwood.* New York: R. F. Fenno and Co.

Anthérieu, Étienne, et al., eds. 1963. *Pour ou contre la force de frappe?* Paris: John Didier.

Aron, Raymond. 1965. *The Great Debate: Theories of Nuclear Strategy.* Translated by Ernst Pawel. Garden City, NY: Doubleday.

Asch, Beth J., James R. Hosek, and John T. Warner. 2007. "New Economics of Manpower in the Post–Cold War Era," in Todd Sandler and Keith Hartley, eds., *Handbook of Defense Economics,* vol. 2. Amsterdam: Elsevier.

Axelrod, Alan. 1992. *The War Between the Spies: A History of Espionage during the American Civil War.* New York: Atlantic Monthly Press, 1992.

Bachrach, Bernard S. 1994. "Medieval Siege Warfare: A Reconnaissance." *Journal of Military History,* vol. 58 (January), pp. 119–133.

———. 2002. *Warfare and Military Organization in Pre-Crusade Europe.* Aldershot, UK: Ashgate.

Baer, George W. 1993. *One Hundred Years of Sea Power: The U.S. Navy, 1890–1990.* Stanford, CA: Stanford University Press.

Baggett, James Alex. 2003. *The Scalawags: Southern Dissenters in the Civil War and Reconstruction.* Baton Rouge: Louisiana State University Press.

Bakeless, John. 1975. "Lincoln's Private Eye." *Civil War Times Illustrated,* vol. 14, no. 6, pp. 22–30.

———. 1971. "Catching Harry Gilmor." *Civil War Times Illustrated,* vol. 10, no. 1, pp. 34–40.

Baron, Hans. 1953a. "A Struggle for Liberty in the Renaissance: Florence, Venice, and Milan in the Early Quattrocento: Part One." *American Historical Review,* vol. 58, no. 2 (January), pp. 265–289.

———. 1953b. "A Struggle for Liberty in the Renaissance: Florence, Venice, and Milan in the Early Quattrocento: Part Two." *American Historical Review,* vol. 58, no. 3 (April), pp. 544–570.

Bartholomees, J. Boone. 1998. *Buff Facings and Gilt Buttons: Staff and Headquarters Operations in the Army of Northern Virginia, 1861–1865.* Columbia, SC: University of South Carolina Press.

Baumgartner, Frederic J. 1991. *From Spear to Flintlock: A History of War in Europe and the Middle East to the French Revolution.* New York: Praeger.

Bayley, C. C. 1961. *War and Society in Renaissance Florence: The* De Militia *of Leonardo Bruni.* Toronto: University of Toronto Press.

Beaufre, André. 1966. *Deterrence and Strategy.* Translated by R. H. Barry. New York: Praeger.

———. 1974. *Strategy for Tomorrow.* New York: Crane Russak and Stanford Research Institute.

Becker, Gary. 1976. *The Economic Approach to Human Behavior.* Chicago: University of Chicago Press.

Becker, Marvin B. 1966. "Economic Change and the Emerging Florentine Territorial State." *Studies in the Renaissance,* vol. 13, pp. 7–39.

Beeton, Leonard. 1966. "Capabilities of Non-Nuclear Powers," pp. 13–38, in A. Buchan, ed., *A World of Nuclear Powers?* Englewood Cliffs, NJ: Prentice-Hall.

Berkey, Jonathan M. 2003. "War in the Borderland: The Civilians' Civil War in Virginia's Lower Shenandoah Valley." Ph.D. diss., Pennsylvania State University.

Besanko, David, David Dranove, and Mark Shanley. 1996. *Economics of Strategy.* New York: John Wiley.

Betts, Richard K. 1985. "Conventional Deterrence: Predictive Uncertainty and Policy Confidence." *World Politics,* vol. 37, no. 2 (January), pp. 153–179.

Bicheno, Hugh. 2001. *Gettysburg.* London: Cassell.

Biddick, Kathleen. 1990. "People and Things: Power in Early English Development." *Comparative Studies in Society and History,* vol. 32 (January), pp. 3–23.

Biddle, Tami Davis. 2002. *Rhetoric and Reality in Air Warfare: The Evolution of British and American Ideas about Strategic Bombing, 1914–1945.* Princeton, NJ: Princeton University Press.

Black, C. F. 1970. "The Baglioni as Tyrants of Perugia, 1488–1540." *English Historical Review,* vol. 85, no. 335 (April), pp. 245–281.

Black, Jeremy. 1996. *The Cambridge Illustrated Atlas of Warfare: Renaissance to Revolution, 1492–1792.* Cambridge: Cambridge University Press.

Blanshei, Sarah R. 1979. "Population, Wealth, and Patronage in Medieval and Renaissance Perugia." *Journal of Interdisciplinary History,* vol. 9, no. 4 (Spring), pp. 597–619.

Blastenbrei, Peter. 1987. *Die Sforza und ihr Heer: Studien zur Struktur-, Wirtschafts- und Sozialgeschichte des Söldnerwesens in der italienischen Frührenaissance.* Heidelberg: Carl Winter Universitätsverlag.

Bonney, Richard, ed. 1999. *The Rise of the Fiscal State in Europe, c. 1200–1815.* Oxford: Oxford University Press.

Bradbury, Jim. 1992. *The Medieval Siege.* Woodbridge, UK: Boydell Press.

Brauer, Jurgen. 1999. "An Economic Perspective on Mercenaries, Military Companies, and the Privatisation of Force." *Cambridge Review of International Affairs,* vol. 13, no. 1 (Autumn/Winter), pp. 130–146.

——. 2002. "On the Economics of Terrorism." *Phi Kappa Phi Forum*, vol. 82, no. 2, pp. 38–41.

——. 2007. "Arms Industries, Arms Trade, and Developing Countries," in Todd Sandler and Keith Hartley, eds., *Handbook of Defense Economics*, vol. 2. Amsterdam: Elsevier.

——. Forthcoming. "Private Military Companies: Markets, Ethics, Economics," in Andrew Alexandra, Marina Caparini, and Deane-Peter Baker, eds., *Private Military Companies: Ethics, Theory, and Practice*. London: Routledge.

—— and André Roux. 1999. "La paix comme bien public international: Une application préliminaire à Afrique australe." *Pax Economica: Revue economique de la paix*, vol. 1, no. 2 (Automne), pp. 3–24. Reprinted in *Annuaire français de relations internationales*, vol. 4 (2003), pp. 742–756.

Bridges, Hal. 1958. "A Lee Letter on the 'Lost Dispatch' and Maryland Campaign of 1862." *Virginia Magazine of History and Biography*, no. 2, pp. 161–168.

British Bombing Survey Unit. 1998. *The Strategic Air War against Germany, 1939–1945: Report of the British Bombing Survey Unit*. With forewords by Michael Beetham and John W. Huston and introductory material by Sebastian Cox. London: Frank Cass Publishers.

Broadberry, Stephen, and Mark Harrison, eds. 2005. *The Economics of World War I*. Cambridge: Cambridge University Press.

Browder, John Morgan. 1964. "The *Force de Frappe*: Its Evolution and Objectives." M.A. thesis, University of Virginia.

Browning, Reed. 1995 [1993]. *The War of the Austrian Succession*. New York: St Martin's Griffin.

Brück, Tilman, ed. 2007. *The Economic Analysis of Terrorism*. London: Routledge.

Bryden, Alan, and Marina Caparini, eds. 2006. *Private Actors and Security Governance*. Vienna and Berlin: LitVerlag.

Bryson, Bill. 2003. *A Short History of Nearly Everything*. New York: Broadway Books.

Buchan, Alastair. 1966. "Introduction," pp. 1–11, in A. Buchan, ed., *A World of Nuclear Powers?* Englewood Cliffs, NJ: Prentice-Hall.

Buchholz, Todd G. 1989. *New Ideas from Dead Economists: An Introduction to Modern Economic Thought*. New York: New American Library.

Buck, Mark. 1983. *Politics, Finance, and the Church in the Reign of Edward II: Walter Stapeldon, Treasurer of England*. Cambridge: Cambridge University Press.

Budiansky, Stephen. 2004. *Air Power: The Men, Machines, and Ideas That Revolutionized War, from Kitty Hawk and Gulf War II*. New York: Viking.

Bueno de Mesquita, D. M. 1946. "Some Condottieri of the Trecento and Their Relations with Political Authority." *Proceedings of the British Academy*, vol. 32, pp. 219–241.

Caferro, William. 1994. "Mercenaries and Military Expenditure: The Costs of Undeclared Warfare in Fourteenth Century Siena." *Journal of European Economic History*, vol. 23, pp. 219–247.

——. 1996. "Italy and the Companies of Adventure in the Fourteenth Century." *Historian*, vol. 58, no. 4 (Summer), pp. 794–801. [Internet version, accessed 10 January 2002.]

——. 1998. *Mercenary Companies and the Decline of Siena*. Baltimore, MD: Johns Hopkins University Press.

Cameron, Rondo, and Larry Neal. 2003. *A Concise Economic History of the World: From Paleolithic Times to the Present*. 4th ed. New York: Oxford University Press.

Canan, Howard V. 1964. "Confederate Military Intelligence." *Maryland Historical Magazine*, vol. 59, no. 10, pp. 34–51.

Canestrini, Giuseppe. 1851. "Documenti per servire alla storia milizia italiana dal xiii secolo al xvi raccolti negli archivj della toscana e preceduti da un discorso di Giuseppe Canestrini." *Archivio Storico Italiano,* ser. 1, vol. 15 (the entire volume).

Cantor, Norman F. 2002 [2001]. *In the Wake of the Plague: The Black Death and the World It Made.* New York: HarperCollins Perennial.

Capra, Carlo. 1999. "The Italian States in the Early Modern Period," pp. 417–442, in Richard Bonney, ed., *The Rise of the Fiscal State in Europe, c. 1200–1815.* Oxford: Oxford University Press.

Carver, Michael. 1986. "Conventional Warfare in the Nuclear Age," pp. 779–814, in Peter Paret, ed., *Makers of Modern Strategy: From Machiavelli to the Nuclear Age.* Princeton, NJ: Princeton University Press.

Cashin, Joan E. 2002. *The War Was You and Me: Civilians in the American Civil War.* Princeton, NJ: Princeton University Press,

Center for International Security Policy. 2003. *Proceedings: Swiss EAPC/PfP Workshop on Combating the Financing of Terrorism.* Swiss Federal Department of Foreign Affairs, Centre for International Security Policy: Geneva, 27–28 November 2003.

Cerny, Philip G. 1984. "Gaullism, Nuclear Weapons and the State," pp. 46–74, in J. Howorth and P. Chilton, eds., *Defence and Dissent in Contemporary France.* New York: St. Martin's.

Chaliand, Gerard, ed. 1994. *The Art of War in World History: From Antiquity to the Nuclear Age.* Berkeley and Los Angeles, CA: University of California Press.

Chandler, David. 1973. *Marlborough as Military Commander.* New York: Scribner's.

Chappat, Richard. 2003. *La dimension budgetaire: Les resources consacrées à la défense européene.* Paris: Ecole des hautes études en sciences sociales.

Chicken, Paule. 1996. "Conscription Revisited," pp. 93–103, in Tony Chafer and Brian Jenkins, eds., *France: From the Cold War to the New World Order.* New York: St. Martin's.

Chilton, Patricia. 1984. "French Nuclear Weapons," pp. 135–169, in J. Howorth and P. Chilton, eds., *Defence and Dissent in Contemporary France.* New York: St. Martin's.

Cimbala, Stephen J. 1987. *Nuclear War and Nuclear Strategy: Unfinished Business.* Westport, CT: Greenwood.

———. 1988a. *Nuclear Strategizing: Deterrence and Reality.* Westport, CT: Praeger.

———. 1988b. *Rethinking Nuclear Strategy.* Wilmington, DE: Scholarly Resources.

———. 1989. *Strategic Impasse: Offense, Defense, and Deterrence Theory and Practice.* Westport, CT: Greenwood.

———. 1998. *The Past and Future of Nuclear Deterrence.* Westport, CT: Praeger.

Clodfelter, Mark. 1994. "Pinpointing Devastation: American Air Campaign Planning before Pearl Habor." *Journal of Military History,* vol. 58, no. 1 (January), pp. 75–101.

Club Jean Moulin. 1963. *La Force de Frappe et le citoyen.* Paris: Editions du Seuil.

Coase, Ronald H. 1994. "The Institutional Structure of Production," pp. 3–14, in Ronald H. Coase, *Essays on Economics and Economists.* Chicago: University of Chicago Press.

Cohen, Eliot, and John Gooch. 1990. *Military Misfortunes: The Anatomy of Failure in War.* New York: Free Press.

Connelly, Owen. 1987. *Blundering to Glory: Napoleon's Military Campaigns.* Wilmington, DE: Scholarly Resources.

Connor, James A. 2004. *Kepler's Witch.* New York: HarperCollins.

Contamine, Philippe. 1984. *War in the Middle Ages.* Oxford, U.K.: Blackwell.

Conybeare, John A. C., James C. Murdoch, and Todd Sandler. 1994. "Alternative

Collective-Goods Models of Military Alliances: Theory and Empirics." *Economic Inquiry,* vol. 32, no. 4 (October), pp. 525–542.

Corfis, Ivy A., and Michael Wolfe, eds. 1995. *The Medieval City under Siege.* Woodbridge, UK: Boydell, 1995.

Coulomb, Fanny. 2004. *Economic Theories of Peace and War.* London: Routledge.

Cox, Sebastian. 1998. "The Overall *Report* in Retrospect," pp. xxiii–xli, in British Bombing Survey Unit, *The Strategic Air War against Germany, 1939–1945: Report of the British Bombing Survey Unit.* With forewords by Michael Beetham and John W. Huston and introductory material by Sebastian Cox. London: Frank Cass Publishers.

Crafts, N. F. R. 1987. "Cliometrics, 1971–1986: A Survey." *Journal of Applied Econometrics,* vol. 2, pp. 171–192.

Craven, Wesley Frank, and James Lea Cate, eds. 1983 [1947–1958]. *The Army Air Forces in World War II.* 7 vols., 1947–1958. New imprint by the Office of Air Force History. Washington, DC: U.S. Government Printing Office.

Curry, Anne. 1998. "Medieval Warfare: England and Her Continental Neighbors, Eleventh to the Fourteenth Century (Review Article)." *Journal of Medieval History,* vol. 24 (March), pp. 81–102.

D'Abzac-Epezy, Claude. 1990. "La société militaire, de l'ingérence a l'ignorance," pp. 245–256, in Jean-Pierre Rioux, ed., *La Guerre d'Algerie et les Français.* Paris: Fayard.

Davis, Robert Scott, Jr. 1994. "The Curious Civil War Career of James George Brown, Spy." *Prologue,* vol. 26, no. 1, pp. 7–31.

De Carmoy, Guy. 1969. "The Last Year of De Gaulle's Foreign Policy." *International Affairs,* vol. 45 (July), pp. 424–435.

Deiss, Joseph Jay. 1967. *Captains of Fortune: Profiles of Six Italian Condottieri.* New York: Thomas Y. Crowell Co.

De Meulemeester, Johnny, and André Matthys. 2001. "Castles at War: Some Reflections Based on Excavations of Motte and Bailey Castles in Belgium," pp. 44–50, in Witold Swietoslawski, ed., *Warfare in the Middle Ages.* Lodz: Institute for Archaeology and Ethnology of the Polish Academy of Sciences.

De Roover, Raymond. 1968. "Labour Conditions in Florence around 1400: Theory, Policy and Reality," pp. 277–313, in Nicolai Rubinstein, ed., *Florentine Studies: Politics and Society in Renaissance Florence.* London: Faber and Faber.

De Tocqueville, Alexis. 1984 [1956]. *Democracy in America.* New York: Mentor.

De Waal, Frans B. M. 1982. *Chimpanzee Politics: Power and Sex among Apes.* New York: Harper and Row.

———. 1989. *Peacemaking among Primates.* Cambridge, MA: Harvard University Press.

Diamond, Jared. 1997. *Guns, Germs, and Steel: The Fates of Human Societies.* New York: Norton.

———. 2005. *Collapse: How Societies Choose to Fail or Succeed.* New York: Viking.

Dixon, Norman. 1976. *On the Psychology of Military Incompetence.* New York: Basic Books.

Dolan, R. J. 2002. "Emotion, Cognition, and Behavior." *Science,* vol. 298, no. 5596 (8 November 2002), pp. 1191–1194.

Dollfus, Daniel. 1960. *La force de frappe.* Paris: René Julliard.

Donnelly, Mark P., and Daniel Diehl. 1998. *Siege: Castles at War.* Dallas: Taylor.

Doran, Charles F. 1973. "A Theory of Bounded Deterrence." *Journal of Conflict Resolution,* vol. 17 (June), pp. 243–269.

Dowdey, Clifford, ed. 1961. *The Wartime Papers of R. E. Lee.* Boston: Little, Brown.

Drees, Clayton J. 2001. "Introduction," pp. vii–xiv, in Clayton J. Drees, ed., *The Late Medieval Age of Crisis and Renewal, 1300–1500: A Biographical Dictionary.* Westport, CT: Greenwood Press.

Druzhinin, V. V., D. S. Kontorov, and S. M. Shtemenko. 1973 [1972]. *Concept, Algorithm, Decision.* Washington, DC: Joint Publications Research Service and Moscow: Voenizdat.

Duffy, Christopher. 2000. *Instrument of War.* Rosemont, IL: Emperor's Press.

Dupuy, R. Ernest, and Trevor N. Dupuy. 1970. *The Harper Encyclopedia of Military History: From 3500 BC to the Present.* Rev. ed. New York: Harper and Row.

———. 1993. *The Harper Encyclopedia of Military History: From 3500 BC to the Present.* 4th ed. New York: HarperCollins Publishers.

Dupuy, T. N. 1979. *Numbers, Predictions, and War: Using History to Evaluate Combat Factors and Predict the Outcome of Battles.* Indianapolis: Bobbs-Merrill.

Dyer, Thomas G. 1999. *Secret Yankees: The Union Circle in Confederate Atlanta.* Baltimore: Johns Hopkins University Press.

Edwards, J. Goronwy. 1946. "Edward I's Castle-Building in Wales." *Proceedings of the British Academy,* vol. 32, pp. 15–81.

Elley, Ben L. 1992. *Grant's Final Campaign: Intelligence and Communications Support.* Fort Leavenworth, KY: School of Advanced Military Studies.

Enders, Walter, and Todd Sandler. 1993. "The Effectiveness of Antiterrorism Policies: A Vector-Autoregression-Intervention Analysis." *American Political Science Review,* vol. 87, no. 4, pp. 829–844.

———. 2000. "Is Transnational Terrorism Becoming More Threatening?" *Journal of Conflict Resolution,* vol. 44, no. 3, pp. 307–332.

———. 2006. *The Political Economy of Terrorism.* Cambridge, UK: Cambridge University Press.

Enthoven, Alain C. 1966. "Choosing Strategies and Selecting Weapon Systems," pp. 133–148, in Samuel A. Tucker, ed., *A Modern Design for Defense Decision: A McNamara-Hitch-Enthoven Anthology.* Washington, DC: Industrial College of the Armed Forces.

——— and K. Wayne Smith. 1971. *How Much Is Enough? Shaping the Defense Program, 1961–1969.* New York: Harper and Row.

Epstein, S. R. 1993. "Town and Country: Economy and Institutions in Late Medieval Italy." *Economic History Review,* n.s., vol. 46, no. 3 (August), pp. 453–477.

Esposito, Vincent J., ed. 1972 [1959]. *West Point Atlas of American Wars,* vol. 1, 1689–1900. New York: Praeger.

Feis, William B. 1993. "Neutralizing the Valley: The Role of Military Intelligence in the Defeat of Jubal Early's Army of the Valley, 1864–1865." *Civil War History,* vol. 39, no. 3, pp. 199–215.

———. 1997. "Finding the Enemy: The Role of Military Intelligence in the Campaigns of Ulysses S. Grant, 1861–1865." Ph.D. diss., Ohio State University.

———. 2002. *Grant's Secret Service: The Intelligence War from Belmont to Appomattox.* Lincoln, NE: University of Nebraska Press.

Ferguson, Niall. 2001. *The Cash Nexus: Money and Power in the Modern World, 1700–2000.* New York: Basic Books.

Fischer, David Hacker. 2002. "Editor's Note," pp. xiii–xiv, in James M. McPherson, *Crossroads of Freedom: Antietam.* New York: Oxford University Press.

Fishel, Edwin C. 1964. "The Mythology of Civil War Intelligence." *Civil War History,* vol. 10, no. 4, pp. 344–367.

———. 1988. "Pinkerton and McClellan: Who Deceived Whom?" *Civil War History,* vol. 34, no. 2, pp. 115–142.

FitzNigel, Richard. 1983. *Dialogus de Scaccario — The Course of the Exchequer.* Translated and edited by Charles Johnson. Oxford: Clarendon Press.

Fowler, Kenneth A. 2001. *Medieval Mercenaries,* vol. 1: *The Great Companies.* Oxford, UK: Blackwell.

France, John. 1999. *Western Warfare in the Age of the Crusades, 1000–1300.* Ithaca, NY: Cornell University Press.

———. 2001. "Recent Writing on Medieval Warfare: From the Fall of Rome to c. 1300." *Journal of Military History,* vol. 65 (April), pp. 441–473.

Fredland, Eric. 2004. "Outsourcing Military Force: A Transactions Cost Perspective on the Role of Military Companies." *Defense and Peace Economics,* vol. 15, no. 3, pp. 205–219.

—— and Adrian Kendry. 1999. "The Privatisation of Military Force: Economic Virtues, Vices, and Government Responsibility." *Cambridge Review of International Affairs,* vol. 13, no. 1 (Autum–Winter), pp. 147–164.

Freedman, Lawrence. 1986. "The First Two Generations of Nuclear Strategists," pp. 735–778, in Peter Paret, ed., *Makers of Modern Strategy: From Machiavelli to the Nuclear Age.* Princeton, NJ: Princeton University Press.

Frey, Bruno S. 2004. *Dealing with Terrorism: Stick or Carrot?* Cheltenham, UK: Elgar.

———, Simon Luechinger, and Alois Stutzer. 2004. "Calculating Tragedy: Assessing the Costs of Terrorism." Working paper. University of Zurich.

Friedrich, Jörg. 2002. *Der Brand: Deutschland im Bombenkrieg 1940–1945.* München: Propyläen Verlag, Ullstein Heyne List GmbH.

Fuchs, Victor. 1975. *Who Shall Live? Health, Economics, and Social Choice.* New York: Basic Books.

Fuller, J. F. C. 1961. *The Conduct of War: 1789–1961.* New Brunswick, NJ: Rutgers University Press.

———. 1970. *The Decisive Battles of the Western World.* 2 vols. Edited by John Terraine. London: Paladin.

Fysh, Peter. 1996. "Gaullism and the New World Order," pp. 181–192, in Tony Chafer and Brian Jenkins, eds., *France: From the Cold War to the New World Order.* New York: St. Martin's.

Gaddy, David W. 1975. "Gray Cloaks and Daggers." *Civil War Times,* vol. 4, pp. 20–27.

Galbraith, John K. 1958. *The Affluent Society.* Boston: Houghton Mifflin.

Gallagher, Gary W. 1998. "I Have to Make the Best of What I Have: Robert E. Lee at Spotsylvania," pp. 5–28, in Gary W. Gallagher, ed., *The Spotsylvania Campaign.* Chapel Hill, NC: University of North Carolina Press.

———. 1999a. "Confederate Corps Leadership on the First Day at Gettysburg: Hill and Ewell in a Difficult Debut," pp. 25–43, in Gary W. Gallagher, ed., *Three Days at Gettysburg: Essays on Confederate and Union Leadership.* Kent, OH: Kent State University Press.

———. 1999b. "'If the Enemy Is There, We Must Attack Him': R. E. Lee and the Second Day at Gettysburg," pp. 109–129, in Gary W. Gallagher, ed., *Three Days at Gettysburg: Essays on Confederate and Union Leadership.* Kent, OH: Kent State University Press.

Gallois, Pierre. 1961. *The Balance of Terror: Strategy for the Nuclear Age.* Translated by Richard Howard. Boston: Houghton Mifflin.

Geary, James W. 1991. *We Need Men: The Union Draft in the Civil War.* DeKalb, IL: Northern Illinois University Press.

Gentile, Gian P. 2000. "Shaping the Past Battlefield, 'For the Future': The United States Strategic Bombing Survey's Evaluation of the American Air War against Japan." *Journal of Military History,* vol. 64 (October), pp. 1085–1112.

Gillingham, John. 1984. "Richard I and the Science of War in the Middle Ages," pp. 78–91, in John Gillingham and J. C. Holt, eds., *War and Government in the Middle Ages: Essays in Honour of J. O. Prestwich.* Woodbridge, Suffolk, UK: Boydell Press.

———. 1999. "An Age of Expansion, c. 1020–1204," pp. 59–88, in Maurice Keen, ed., *Medieval Warfare: A History.* Oxford: Oxford University Press.

Giustozzi, Antonio. 2007. "The Privatizing of War and Security in Afghanistan: Future or Dead End?" *Economics of Peace and Security Journal,* vol. 2, no. 1, pp. 30–34.

Goldin, Claudia. 1995. "Cliometrics and the Nobel." *Journal of Economic Perspectives,* vol. 9, no. 2 (Spring), pp. 191–208.

Gordon, Philip H. 1993. *A Certain Idea of France: French Security Policy and the Gaullist Legacy.* Princeton, NJ: Princeton University Press.

Gravett, Richard. 1990. *Medieval Siege Warfare.* London: Osprey.

Green, Louis. 1986. *Castruccio Castracani: A Study on the Origins and Character of a Fourteenth-Century Italian Despotism.* Oxford: Clarendon Press.

Greene, A. Wilson. 2000. *Breaking the Backbone of the Rebellion: The Final Battles of the Petersburg Campaign.* Mason City, IA: Savas.

Greenhous, Brereton, Stephen J. Harris, William C. Johnston, and William G. P. Rawling. 1994. *The Crucible of War, 1939–1945: The Official History of the Royal Canadian Air Force,* vol. 3. Toronto: University of Toronto Press.

Greif, Avner. 2000. "The Fundamental Problem of Exchange: A Research Agenda in Historical Institutional Analysis." *European Review of Economic History,* vol. 4, no. 3, pp. 251–284.

———. 2006. "The Birth of Impersonal Exchange: The Community Responsibility System and Impartial Justice." *Journal of Economic Perspectives,* vol. 20, no. 2, pp. 221–236.

Guback. Thomas H. 1959. "General Sherman's War on the Press." *Journalism Quarterly,* vol. 36, no. 2, pp. 171–176.

Haftendorn, Helga. 1996. *NATO and the Nuclear Revolution: A Crisis of Credibility, 1966–1967.* Oxford: Clarendon Press.

Haidt, Jonathan. 2007. "The New Synthesis in Moral Psychology." *Science,* vol. 316 (18 May), pp. 998–1002.

Halperin, Morton H. 1966 [1963]. *Limited War in the Nuclear Age.* New York: John Wiley and Sons.

Harari, Yuval Noah. 2000. "Strategy and Supply in Fourteenth-Century Western European Invasion Campaigns." *Journal of Military History,* vol. 64 (April), pp. 297–333.

Harrison, Mark, ed. 1998. *The Economics of World War II: Six Great Powers in International Comparison.* Cambridge: Cambridge University Press.

Harriss, G. L. 1975. *King, Parliament, and Public Finance in Medieval England to 1369.* London: Clarendon Press.

Hecht, Gabrielle. 1996. "Rebels and Pioneers: Technocratic Ideologies and Social Identities in the French Nuclear Workplace, 1955–69." *Social Studies of Science,* vol. 26 (August), pp. 483–530.

———. 1998. *The Radiance of France: Nuclear Power and National Identity after World War II.* Cambridge, MA: Massachusetts Institute of Technology Press.

Heilbroner, Robert L. 1999 [1953]. *The Worldly Philosophers.* 7th ed. New York: Touchstone.

Helmbold, Robert L. 1971. *Decision in Battle: Breakpoint Hypotheses and Engagement Termination Data*. Santa Monica, CA: RAND.

Henderson, William D. 1987. *The Road to Bristoe Station: Campaigning with Lee and Meade, August 1–October 20, 1863*. Lynchburg, VA: H. E. Howard.

Henneman, John Bell, Jr. 1999. "France in the Middle Ages," pp. 101–122, in Richard Bonney, ed., *The Rise of the Fiscal State in Europe, c. 1200–1815*. Oxford: Oxford University Press.

Hennessy, John. 1993. *Return to Bull Run: The Campaign and Battle of Second Manassas*. New York: Simon and Schuster.

Hewitt, Kenneth. 1983. "Place Annihilation: Area Bombing and the Fate of Urban Places." *Annals of the Association of American Geographers*, vol. 73, no. 2 (June), pp. 257–284.

Heyne, Paul, Peter Boettke, and David Prychitko. 2003. *The Economic Way of Thinking*. 10th ed. Upper Saddle River, NJ: Prentice Hall.

Hitch, Charles J. 1966a. "Prospect and Retrospect," pp. 106–117, in Samuel A. Tucker, ed., *A Modern Design for Defense Decision: A McNamara-Hitch-Enthoven Anthology*. Washington, DC: Industrial College of the Armed Forces.

———. 1966b. "Cost Effectiveness," pp. 121–132, in Samuel A. Tucker, ed., *A Modern Design for Defense Decision: A McNamara-Hitch-Enthoven Anthology*. Washington, DC: Industrial College of the Armed Forces.

——— and Roland N. McKean. 1967. *The Economics of Defense in the Nuclear Age*. Cambridge, MA: Harvard University Press.

Hocquet, Jean-Claude. 1999. "Venice," pp. 381–415, in Richard Bonney, ed., *The Rise of the Fiscal State in Europe, c. 1200–1815*. Oxford: Oxford University Press.

Holmquist, Richard C. 1969. "A Political and Strategic Evaluation of the French 'Force de Frappe.'" M.A. thesis, George Washington University.

Hooper, Nicholas, and Matthew Bennett. 1996. *The Cambridge Atlas of Warfare: The Middle Ages, 786–1487*. Cambridge: Cambridge University Press.

Horn, John. 1993. *The Petersburg Campaign: June 1864–April 1865*. Conshocken, PA: Combined Books.

Housley, Norman. 1982. "The Mercenary Companies, the Papacy, and the Crusades, 1356–1378." *Traditio* [New York], vol. 38, pp. 253–280. Reprinted as chapter 15 in Norman Housley, *Crusading and Warfare in Medieval and Renaissance Europe* (Burlington, VT: Ashgate, 2001).

———. 1999. "European Warfare, c. 1200–1320," pp. 113–135, in Maurice Keen, ed., *Medieval Warfare: A History*. Oxford: Oxford University Press.

Howorth, Jolyon. 1996. "France and European Security 1944–94: Re-reading the Gaullist 'Consensus,'" pp. 17–38, in Tony Chafer and Brian Jenkins, eds., *France: From the Cold War to the New World Order*. New York: St. Martin's.

——— and Patricia Chilton. 1984. "Introduction: Defence, Dissent, and French Political Culture," pp. 1–23, in J. Howorth and P. Chilton, eds., *Defence and Dissent in Contemporary France*. New York: St. Martin's.

Ifestos, Panayotis. 1988. *Nuclear Strategy and European Security Dilemmas: Towards an Autonomous European Defence System?* Aldershot, UK: Avebury.

Ilardi, Vincent. 1959. "The Italian League, Francesco Sforza, and Charles VII (1454–1461)." *Studies in the Renaissance*, vol. 6, pp. 129–166.

Isenman, Eberhard. 1999. "The Holy Roman Empire in the Middle Ages," pp. 243–280, in Richard Bonney, ed., *The Rise of the Fiscal State in Europe, c. 1200–1815*. Oxford: Oxford University Press.

Jacobs, W. A. 1986. "Strategic Bombing and American National Strategy, 1941–1943." *Military Affairs,* vol. 50, no. 3 (July), pp. 133–139.

Jeffreys, Steven. 1973. *A Medieval Siege.* Hove, UK: Wayland.

Johnston II, Angus J. 1955. "Disloyalty on Confederate Railroads in Virginia." *Virginia Magazine of History and Biography,* vol. 63 (October), pp. 410–426.

Jones, Richard L. C. 1999. "Fortifications and Sieges in Western Europe, c. 800–1450," pp. 163–185, in Maurice Keen, ed., *Medieval Warfare: A History.* Oxford: Oxford University Press.

Jones, Wilbur D., Jr. 1966. "Who Lost the Lost Orders? Stonewall Jackson, His Courier, and Special Orders No. 191." *Civil War Regiments,* vol. 5, no. 3, pp. 1–26.

Kamen, Henry. 1968. "The Economic and Social Consequences of the Thirty Years' War." *Past and Present,* vol. 39 (April), pp. 44–61.

Katz, Michael L., and Harvey S. Rosen. 1991. *Microeconomics.* Homewood, IL: Irwin.

Kaufman, Richard F., ed. 2003. *The Full Costs of Ballistic Missile Defense.* Economists Allied for Arms Reduction (ECAAR) and Center for Arms Control and Non-Proliferation (CACNP). Pearl River, NY and Washington, DC: ECAAR/CACNP.

Keegan, John. 1976. *The Face of Battle.* New York: Viking.

———. 1987. *The Mask of Command.* Harmondsworth, UK: Penguin.

———. 1994 [1993]. *A History of Warfare.* New York: Vintage Books.

———. 1999. *The First World War.* New York: Knopf.

———. 2003. *Intelligence in War: Knowledge of the Enemy from Napoleon to Al-Qaeda.* London: Hutchinson.

Kennedy, Paul. 1987. *The Rise and Fall of the Great Powers: Economic Change and Military Conflict from 1500 to 2000.* New York: Random House.

Keuper, Richard W. 1994. "The Welsh Wars," pp. 142–176, in Larry Neal, ed., *War Finance,* vol. 1, *From Antiquity to Artillery.* Aldershot, UK, and Brookfield, VT: Elgar.

Kissinger, Henry A. 1969. *Nuclear Weapons and Foreign Policy.* New York: Norton.

Koch, H. W. 1991. "The Strategic Air Offensive against Germany: The Early Phase, May–September 1940." *Historical Journal,* vol. 34, no. 1 (March), pp. 117–141.

Kohl, Wilfrid L. 1971. *French Nuclear Diplomacy.* Princeton, NJ: Princeton University Press.

Kolodziej, Edward A. 1967. "French Strategy Emergent: General André Beaufre: A Critique." *World Politics,* vol. 19 (April), pp. 417–442.

———. 1971. "Revolt and Revisionism in the Gaullist Global Vision: An Analysis of French Strategic Policy." *Journal of Politics,* vol. 33 (May), pp. 448–477.

———. 1974. *French International Policy under de Gaulle and Pompidou.* Ithaca, NY: Cornell University Press.

Kuhn, Thomas S. 1962. *The Structure of Scientific Revolutions.* Chicago: University of Chicago Press.

Ladero Quesada, Miguel Angel. 1999. "Castile in the Middle Ages," pp. 177–199, in Richard Bonney, ed., *The Rise of the Fiscal State in Europe, c. 1200–1815.* Oxford: Oxford University Press.

Laffin, John. 1995 [1966]. *High Command: The Genius of Generalship from Antiquity to Alamein.* New York: Barnes and Noble.

Lane, Steven G. 1999. "Rural Populations and the Experience of Warfare in Medieval Lombardy: The Case of Pavia," pp. 127–134, in Donald J. Kagay and L. J. Andrew Villalon, eds., *The Circle of War in the Middle Ages: Essays on Medieval Military and Naval History.* Woodbridge, Suffolk, UK: Boydell Press.

Larkin, Bruce D. 1996. *Nuclear Designs: Great Britain, France, and China in the Global Governance of Nuclear Arms.* New Brunswick, NJ: Transaction.

Lauts, Jan, and Irmlind Luise Herzner. 2001. *Federico de Montefeltro, Herzog von Urbino: Kriegsherr, Friedensfürst und Förderer der Künste.* München: Deutscher Kunstverlag.

Lazear, Edward. 1999. "Economic Imperialism." NBER Working Paper #7300. Cambridge, MA: National Bureau of Economic Research (NBER).

Lee, Dwight R. 1988. "Free Riding and Paid Riding in the Fight against Terrorism." *American Economic Review,* vol. 78, no. 2, pp. 22–26.

Leisch, Juanita. 1994. *An Introduction to Civil War Civilians.* Gettysburg: Thomas Publications.

Leonard, Elizabeth D. 1999. *All the Daring of the Soldier: Women of the Civil War Armies.* New York: W. W. Norton.

Levine, Alan J. 1992. *The Strategic Bombing of Germany, 1940–1945.* Westport, CT: Praeger.

———. 1967. *Strategy.* 2nd rev. ed. New York: Praeger.

Liddell Hart, B. H. 1976 [1934]. *History of the First World War.* London: Pan Books.

Llussa, Fernanda, and Jose Tavares. 2007. "The Economics of Terrorism: A Synopsis." *Economics of Peace and Security Journal,* vol. 2, no. 1, pp. 62–70.

Long, E. B., ed. 1952. *Personal Memoirs of U. S. Grant.* Cleveland and New York: World Publishing Company.

Luvaas, Jay. 1990. "The Role of Intelligence in the Chancellorsville Campaign, April–May, 1863." *Intelligence and National Security,* vol. 5, no. 2, pp. 99–115.

———, ed. 1966. *Frederick the Great on the Art of War.* New York: Free Press.

Lynn, John A. 1999. *The Wars of Louis XIV, 1667–1714.* New York: Addison Wesley Longman.

Lynn, Jonathan, and Antony Jay, eds. 1985 [1981]. *The Complete Yes Minister: The Diaries of a Cabinet Minister by The Right Hon. James Hacker MP.* London: British Broadcasting Corporation.

Machiavelli, Niccolò. 1980. *The Prince.* Based on revised translation by Luigi Ricci, 1935. Introduction by Christian Gauss. New York: Mentor Edition, New American Library.

Mahan, Dennis Hart. 1853. *An Elementary Treatise on Advanced-guard, Out-post, and Detachment Service of Troops, and the Manner of Posting and Handling Them in Presence of an Enemy.* New York: J. Wiley.

Mallett, Michael. 1968. "Pisa and Florence in the Fifteenth Century: Aspects of the Period of the First Florentine Domination," pp. 403–441, in Nicolai Rubeinstein, ed., *Florentine Studies: Politics and Society in Renaissance Florence.* London: Faber and Faber.

———. 1974. *Mercenaries and Their Masters: Warfare in Renaissance Italy.* Totowa, NJ: Rowman and Littlefield.

———. 1999. "Mercenaries," pp. 209–229, in Maurice Keen, ed., *Medieval Warfare: A History.* Oxford, UK: Oxford University Press.

———. 2003. "Condottieri and Captains in Renaissance Italy," pp. 67–88, in D. J. B. Trim, ed., *The Chivalric Ethos and the Development of Military Professionalism.* Leiden: Brill.

——— and J. R. Hale. 1984. *The Military Organization of a Renaissance State: Venice c. 1400 to 1617.* Cambridge: Cambridge University Press.

Mangus, Michael Stuart. 1994. "'The Debatable Land': Soldiers and Civilians in Civil War Virginia." M.A. thesis, Ohio State University.

Markle, Donald E. 2000 [1994]. *Spies and Spymasters of the Civil War.* New York: Hippocrene Books.

Marshall, Alfred. 1961 [1890, 1920]. *Principles of Economics.* 9th (variorum) edition with annotation by C. W. Guillebaud. 2 vols. London: Macmillan. (The 1890 edition is the first, the 1920 the eighth; the 9th [variorum] edition is an annotated edition of Marshall's 8th.)

Marten, James Alan. 2003. *Civil War America: Voices from the Home Front*. Santa Barbara, CA: ABC-CLIO.

Martin, Lawrence. 1987. "European Perspectives on Strategic Defense: Then and Now," pp. 37–50, in Fred S. Hoffman, Albert Wohlstetter, and David S. Yost, eds., *Swords and Shields: NATO, the USSR, and New Choices for Long-Range Offense and Defense*. Lexington, MA: Lexington Books.

Martin, Michel L. 1981. *Warriors to Managers: The French Military Establishment since 1945*. Chapel Hill, NC: University of North Carolina Press.

Marvin, Laurence W. 2001. "War in the South: A First Look at Siege Warfare in the Albigensian Crusade, 1209–1218." *War in History*, vol. 8 (November), pp. 373–395.

Matter, William D. 1998. "The Federal High Command at Spotsylvania," pp. 29–60, in Gary W. Gallagher, ed., *The Spotsylvania Campaign*. Chapel Hill, NC: University of North Carolina Press.

Mayr, Ernst. 1997. *This Is Biology*. Cambridge, MA: Belknap Press.

Mazlish, Bruce. 2003. "Empiricism and History." *Historically Speaking*, vol. 4 (February), pp. 12–14.

McDevitt, Theresa. 2003. "African American Women and Espionage in the Civil War." *Social Education*, vol. 67 (no. 5), pp. 254–260.

McDonald, JoAnna. 2000. *"We Shall Meet Again": The First Battle of Manassas (Bull Run), July 18–21, 1861*. Athens, NY: Oxford University Press, 2000 (also Shippensburg, PA: White Mane, 1999).

McGlynn, Sean. 1994. "The Myths of Medieval Warfare." *History Today*, vol. 44 (January), pp. 28–34.

McGuire, Martin C., and Mancur Olson. 1996. "The Economics of Autocracy and Majority Rule: The Invisible Hand and the Use of Force." *Journal of Economic Literature*, vol. 34, no. 1 (March), pp. 72–96.

McNeill, William H. 1982. *The Pursuit of Power: Technology, Armed Force, and Society since A.D. 1000*. Chicago: University of Chicago Press.

McWhiney, Grady. 1998. *Battle in the Wilderness: Grant Meets Lee*. Abilene, TX: McWhiney Foundation Press.

Menard, Orville D. 1967. *The Army and the Fifth Republic*. Lincoln, NE: University of Nebraska Press.

Mierzejewski, Alfred C. 1988. *The Collapse of the German War Economy, 1944–1945: Allied Air Power and the German National Railway*. Chapel Hill, NC: University of North Carolina Press.

Milward, Alan S. 1965. *The German Economy at War*. London: Athlone Press.

——. 1977. *War, Economy and Society, 1939–1945*. Berkeley, CA: University of California Press.

Moch, Jules. 1963. *Non à la force de frappe*. Paris: Robert Laffont.

Molho, Anthony. 1968. "The Florentine Oligarchy and the Balie of the Late Trecento." *Speculum*, vol. 43, no. 1 (January), pp. 23–51.

——. 1995. "The State and Public Finance: A Hypothesis Based on the History of Late Medieval Florence." *Journal of Modern History*, vol. 67/Supplement (December), pp. 97–135.

Montgomery, Bernard L. 1968. *A History of Warfare*. Cleveland: World.

Morgan, Prentice G . 1959–60. "The Forward Observer." *Military Affairs,* vol. 23, no. 4 (Winter), pp. 209–212.

Morillo, Stephen. 1999. "The 'Age of Cavalry' Revisited," pp. 45–58, in Donald J. Kagay and L. J. Andrew Villalon, eds., *The Circle of War in the Middle Ages: Essays on Medieval Military and Naval History.* Woodbridge, Suffolk, and Rochester, NY: Boydell and Brewer.

Morris, Marc. 2003. *Castle: A History of the Buildings That Shaped Medieval Britain.* London: Macmillan.

Morse, Edward L. 1973. *Foreign Policy and Interdependence in Gaullist France.* Princeton, NJ: Princeton University Press.

Murdock, Eugene C. 1980 [1971]. *One Million Men: The Civil War Draft in the North.* Westport, CT: Greenwood Press.

Murray, Williamson, and Allan R. Millett. 2000. *A War to Be Won: Fighting the Second World War.* Cambridge, MA: Belknap Press.

Neillands, Robin. 2003 [1994]. *Wellington and Napoleon: Clash of Arms, 1807–1815.* Barnsley, UK: Pen and Sword.

Neufeldt, Victoria. 1997. *Webster's New World College Dictionary,* 3rd ed. New York: Macmillan.

Nicolle, David. 1983. *Italian Medieval Armies, 1300–1500.* London: Osprey.

———. 1999. "Medieval Warfare: The Unfriendly Interface." *Journal of Military History,* vol. 63 (July), pp. 579–599.

Niedenthal, Paula. 2007. "Embodying Emotion." *Science,* vol. 316 (18 May), pp. 1002–5.

Nolan. Alan T. 1999. "R. E. Lee and July 1 at Gettysburg," pp. 3–24, in Gary W. Gallagher, ed., *Three Days at Gettysburg: Essays on Confederate and Union Leadership.* Kent, OH: Kent State University Press.

Norris, Robert S., and William M. Arkin. 1997. "Global Nuclear Stockpiles, 1945–1997." *Bulletin of the Atomic Scientists* 53 (November/December).

North, Douglass. 1990. *Institutions, Institutional Change, and Economic Performance.* New York: Cambridge University Press.

Novick, Peter. 1988. *That Noble Dream: The 'Objectivity Question' and the American Historical Profession.* Cambridge: Cambridge University Press.

Nussio, Ricky J. 1996. "A New *Force de Frappe:* Changing French Nuclear Policy." MA thesis, Troy State University at Fort Bragg.

Offer, Avner. 1995. "Going to War in 1914: A Matter of Honor?" *Politics and Society,* vol. 23 (June), pp. 213–241.

Olson, Mancur. 1982. *The Rise and Decline of Nations: Economic Growth, Stagflation, and Social Rigidities.* New Haven: Yale University Press.

———. 1993. "Dictatorship, Democracy, and Development." *American Political Science Review,* vol. 87, no. 3 (September), pp. 567–576.

——— and Richard Zeckhauser. 1966. "An Economic Theory of Alliances." *Review of Economics and Statistics,* vol. 48, no. 3, pp. 266–279.

Ormrod, W. M. 1999a. "Finance and Trade under Richard II," pp. 155–186, in Anthony Goodman and James Gillespie, eds., *Richard II: The Art of Kingship.* Oxford: Clarendon Press.

———. 1999b. "England in the Middle Ages," pp. 19–52, in Richard Bonney, ed., *The Rise of the Fiscal State in Europe, c. 1200–1815.* Oxford: Oxford University Press.

Overy, Richard J. 1994. *War and Economy in the Third Reich.* Oxford: Oxford University Press. Reprinted by Clarendon Press, Oxford, 2002.

Paget, Julian. 1990. *Wellington's Peninsular War: Battles and Battlefields*. London: Leo Cooper.

Pape, Robert A. 1996. *Bombing to Win: Airpower and Coercion in War*. Ithaca, NY: Cornell University Press.

Paret, Peter. 1992. "The History of War and the New Military History," pp. 209–226, in Peter Paret, *Understanding War: Essays on Clausewitz and the History of Military Power*. Princeton, NJ: Princeton University Press.

Parker, Geoffrey. 1976. "The 'Military Revolution,' 1560–1660—a Myth?" *Journal of Modern History*, vol. 48 (June), pp. 195–214.

Partner, Peter. 1999. "The Papacy and the Papal States," pp. 359–380, in Richard Bonney, ed., *The Rise of the Fiscal State in Europe, c. 1200–1815*. Oxford: Oxford University Press.

Pepper, Simon, and Nicholas Adams. 1986. *Firearms and Fortifications: Military Architecture and Siege Warfare in Sixteenth-Century Siena*. Chicago: University of Chicago Press.

Phisterer, Frederick. 1996 [1883]. *Campaigns of the Civil War*. Supplementary Volume. *Statistical Record of the Armies of the United States*. Carlisle, PA: John Kallmann Publishers.

Pois, Robert, and Philip Langer. 2004. *Command Failure in War: Psychology and Leadership*. Bloomington, IN: Indiana University Press.

Posner, Richard, and Francesco Parisi, eds. 1997. *Law and Economics*. 3 vols. International Library of Critical Writings in Economics. Cheltenham, UK: Elgar Reference Collection.

Postan, M. M. 1964. "The Costs of the Hundred Years' War." *Past and Present*, vol. 27 (April), pp. 34–53.

Poutvaara, P., and A. Wagener. 2007. "Conscription: Economic Costs and Political Allure." *Economics of Peace and Security Journal*, vol. 2, no. 1, pp. 6–15.

Prestwich, Michael. 1972. *War, Politics and Finance under Edward I*. Totowa, NJ: Rowman and Littlefield.

——. 1996a. *Armies and Warfare in the Middle Ages: The English Experience*. New Haven, CT: Yale University Press.

——. 1996b. "Money and Mercenaries in English Medieval Armies," pp. 129–150, in Alfred Haverkamp and Hanna Vollrath, eds., *England and Germany in the High Middle Ages*. Oxford: Oxford University Press.

Radnitzky, Gerard, and Peter Bernholz, eds. 1987. *Economic Imperialism: The Economic Approach Applied Outside the Field of Economics*. New York: Paragon House Publishers.

Ramsay, James H. 1925. *A History of the Revenues of the Kings of England 1066–1399*. 2 vols. Oxford: Clarendon Press.

Randall, James G. 1918. "The Newspaper Problem in Its Bearing upon Military Secrecy during the Civil War." *American Historical Review*, vol. 23 (January), pp. 303–323.

Reardon, Carol. 1999. "From Antietam to the Argonne: The Maryland Campaign's Lessons for Future Leaders of the American Expeditionary Force," pp. 289–312, in Gary W. Gallagher, ed., *The Antietam Campaign*. Chapel Hill, NC: University of North Carolina Press.

Redlich, Fritz. 1964, 1965. *The German Military Enterpriser and His Work Force: A Study in European Economic and Social History*. Vierteljahreszeitschrift für Sozial- und Wirtschaftsgeschichte. 2 vols. Beiheft 47 (1964) and Beiheft 48 (1965). Wiesbaden: Steiner Verlag.

Regnault, Jean-Marc. 2003. "France's Search for Nuclear Test Sites, 1957–1963." *Journal of Military History*, vol. 67 (October), pp. 1223–1248.

Rhodes, Richard. 1988 [1986]. *The Making of the Atomic Bomb*. New York: Touchstone.

——. 1995. *Dark Sun: The Making of the Hydrogen Bomb*. New York: Simon and Schuster.

Ricotti, Ercole. 1844. *Storia delle compagnie di ventura in Italia.* 4 vols. Turin.

Roberts, Andrew. 2001. *Napoleon and Wellington.* London: Weidenfeld and Nicolson.

Robinson, June. 1986. "The United States Balloon Corps in Action in Northern Virginia during the Civil War." *Arlington Historical Magazine,* vol. 8, no. 2, pp. 5–17.

Rogers, R. 1997 [1992]. *Latin Siege Warfare in the Twelfth Century.* Oxford: Clarendon Press.

Roskolenko, Harry, ed., 1974. *Great Battles and Their Great Generals.* Chicago: Playboy Press.

Rotte, Ralph, and Christoph M. Schmidt. 2003. "On the Production of Victory: Empirical Determinants of Battlefield Success in Modern War." *Defence and Peace Economics,* vol. 14, no. 3 (June), pp. 175–192.

Rynning, Sten. 2002. *Changing Military Doctrine: Presidents and Military Power in Fifth Republic France, 1958–2000.* Westport, CT: Praeger.

Sabine, David B. 1973. "Pinkerton's 'Operative': Timothy Webster." *Civil War Times Illustrated,* vol. 12, no. 5, pp. 32–38.

Samuelson, Paul A. 1947. *Foundations of Economic Analysis.* Cambridge, MA: Harvard University Press.

———. 1954. "The Pure Theory of Public Expenditure." *Review of Economics and Statistics,* vol. 36, pp. 387–389.

———. 1955. "A Diagrammatic Exposition of a Theory of Public Expenditure." *Review of Economics and Statistics,* vol. 37, pp. 350–356.

Sandler, Todd. 2001. *Economic Concepts for the Social Sciences.* Cambridge: Cambridge University Press.

——— and Walter Enders. 2004. "An Economic Perspective on Transnational Terrorism." *European Journal of Political Economy,* vol. 20, pp. 301–316.

——— and Keith Hartley. 1995. *The Economics of Defense.* Cambridge: Cambridge University Press.

———. 1999. *The Political Economy of NATO.* Cambridge: Cambridge University Press.

Sauers, Richard A. 1999. "'Rarely Has More Skill, Vigor or Wisdom Been Shown': George B. Meade on July 3 at Gettysburg," pp. 231–244, in Gary W. Gallagher, ed., *Three Days at Gettysburg: Essays on Confederate and Union Leadership.* Kent, OH: Kent State University Press.

Schaffer, Ronald. 1980. "American Military Ethics in World War II: The Bombing of German Civilians." *Journal of American History,* vol. 67, no. 2 (September), pp. 318–334.

Scheinman, Lawrence. 1965. *Atomic Energy Policy in France under the Fourth Republic.* Princeton, NJ: Princeton University Press.

Schelling, Thomas. 1960. *The Strategy of Conflict.* Cambridge, MA: Harvard University Press.

———. 1966. *Arms and Influence.* New Haven, CT: Yale University Press.

———. 1978. *Micromotives and Macrobehavior.* New York: W. W. Norton.

Scott, Robert N., ed. 1880. *The War of the Rebellion: A Compilation of the Official Records of the Union and Confederate Armies.* United States War Department. Washington, DC: Government Printing Office. [CD-ROM version. Zionsville, IN: Guild Press of Indiana, 1997–2000.]

Sears, Stephen W. 1992. *To the Gates of Richmond: The Peninsula Campaign.* New York: Ticknor and Fields.

Selzer, Stephan. 2001. *Deutsche Söldner im Italien des Trecento.* Tübingen: Max Niemeyer Verlag.

Shannon, Fred Albert. 1965. *The Organization and Administration of the Union Army, 1861–1865.* Glouchester, MA: Peter Smith.

Shearer, D. 1998. *Private Armies and Military Intervention.* Adelphi Paper 316. International Institute for Strategic Studies. Oxford: Oxford University Press.

Showalter, Dennis E. 1993. "Caste, Skill, and Training: The Evolution of Cohesion in European Armies from the Middle Ages to the Sixteenth Century." *Journal of Military History,* vol. 57, no. 3 (July), pp. 407–430.

Simon, Curtis J., and John T. Warner. 2007. "Managing the All-Volunteer Force in a Time of War." *Economics of Peace and Security Journal,* vol. 2, no. 1, pp. 20–29.

Simon, Herbert A. 1997. *Models of Bounded Rationality,* vol. 3. Cambridge, MA: MIT Press. Vol. 1 was published in 1982; vol. 2 in 1984; both also from MIT Press.

Singer, Peter W. 2003. *Corporate Warriors: The Rise of the Privatized Military Industry.* Ithaca, NY: Cornell University Press.

Smith, Adam. 1976. [1776]. *An Inquiry into the Nature and Causes of the Wealth of Nations.* Edited by Edwin Cannan. Chicago: University of Chicago Press.

Smith, Melden E. 1977. "The Strategic Bombing Debate: The Second World War and Vietnam." *Journal of Contemporary History,* vol. 12, no. 1 (January), pp. 175–191.

Steiner, George A., ed. 1942. *Economic Problems of War.* New York: John Wiley and Sons.

Stigler, George, and Gary Becker. 1977. "De Gustibus Non Est Disputandem." *American Economic Review,* vol. 67, no. 2 (March), pp. 76–90.

Stith, Shawn. 2004. "Foundation for Victory: Operations and Intelligence Harmoniously Combine in Jackson's Shenandoah Campaign." MA thesis, Naval Postgraduate School.

Stockholm International Peace Research Institute (SIPRI). Various years. *Yearbook.* Oxford: Oxford University Press.

Stonier, Tom. 1990. *Information and the Internal Structure of the Universe: An Exploration into Information Physics.* New York: Springer-Verlag.

Stuart, Meriwether. 1963. "Samuel Ruth and General R. E. Lee: Disloyalty and the Line of Supply to Fredericksburg, 1862–1863." *Virginia Magazine of History and Biography,* vol. 71 (January), pp. 35–109.

——. 1981. "Of Spies and Borrowed Name: The Identity of Union Operatives in Richmond Known as 'The Phillipses' Discovered." *Virginia Magazine of History and Biography,* vol. 89, no. 3, pp. 308–327.

Sutherland, Daniel E. 1998. *Fredericksburg and Chancellorsville: The Dare Mark Campaign.* Lincoln, NE: University of Nebraska Press.

Temin, Peter. 2006. "The Economy of the Early Roman Empire." *Journal of Economic Perspectives,* vol. 20, no. 1, pp. 133–151.

Temple-Leader, John, and Guiseppe Marcotti. 1889. *Sir John Hawkwood (D'Acuto): Story of a Condottiere.* Translated from the Italian by Leader Scott. London: T. Fisher Unwin.

Terraine, John. 1985. *The Right of the Line: The Royal Air Force in the European War 1939–1945.* London: Hodder and Stoughton.

Theleri, Marc. 1997. *Initiation à la force de frappe française: 1945–2010.* Paris: Éditions Stock.

Thompson, Willie. 2004. *Postmodernism and History.* New York: Palgrave Macmillan.

Thomson, Janice E. 2002. *Mercenaries, Pirates, and Sovereigns: State-Building and Extraterritorial Violence in Early Modern Europe.* Princeton, NJ: Princeton University Press.

Thunholm, Peter. 2005. "Planning under Time Pressure: An Attempt Toward a Prescriptive Model of Military Tactical Decision Making," pp. 43–56, in Henry Montgomery,

Raanan Lipshitz, and Berndt Brehmer, eds., *How Professionals Make Decisions.* Mahwah, NJ: Lawrence Erlbaum.

Tidwell, William A. 1991. "Confederate Expenditures for the Secret Service." *Civil War History,* vol. 37, no. 3, pp. 219–231.

Tilly, Charles. 1990. *Coercion, Capital, and European States, AD 990–1990.* Cambridge, MA: Blackwell.

Trease, Geoffrey. 1971. *The Condottieri: Soldiers of Fortune.* New York: Holt, Rinehart, and Winston.

Trexler, Richard C. 1967. "Rome on the Eve of the Great Schism." *Speculum,* vol. 42, no. 3 (July), pp. 489–509.

Truby, David J. 1971. "War in the Clouds: Balloons in the Civil War." *Mankind,* vol. 2, no. 11, pp. 64–71.

Trudeau, Noah Andre. 1989. *Bloody Roads South: The Wilderness to Cold Harbor, May–June 1864.* Boston: Little, Brown.

Tuchman, Barbara W. 1962. *The Guns of August.* New York: Macmillan.

——. 1981. *Practicing History: Selected Essays.* New York: Knopf.

Uffindel, Andrew. 2003. *Great Generals of the Napoleonic Wars and Their Battles, 1805–1815.* Staplehurst, Kent, UK: Spellmount.

United States Army. 2001. "Army Field Manual FM 3-0, Military Operations." Washington, DC: Department of the Army.

United States Strategic Bombing Survey (USSBS). 30 September 1945. *Over-all Report (European War).* Washington, DC: USSBS.

——. 31 October 1945. *The Effects of Strategic Bombing on the German War Economy.* Washington, DC: USSBS.

——. January 1947. *Aircraft Division Industry Report.* 2nd ed. Washington, DC: USSBS.

——. February 1947. *Statistical Appendix to Over-all Report (European War).* Washington, DC: USSBS.

——. May 1947. *The Effects of Strategic Bombing on German Morale,* vol. 1. Washington, DC: USSBS.

Van Creveld, Martin. 2004 [1977]. *Supplying War: Logistics from Wallenstein to Patton.* Cambridge: Cambridge University Press.

Van der Vat, Dan. 2001. *Standard of Power: The Royal Navy in the Twentieth Century.* London: Pimlico.

Verbruggen, J. F. 1997 [1954]. *The Art of Warfare in Western Europe during the Middle Ages: From the Eighth Century to 1340.* Woodbridge, Suffolk, UK, and Rochester, NY: Boydell and Brewer.

Vermeij, Geerat. 2004. *Nature: An Economic History.* Princeton, NJ: Princeton University Press.

Villalon, L. J. Andrew. 2003. "'Seeking Castles in Spain': Sir Hugh Calveley and the Free Companies' Intervention in Iberian Warfare (1366–1369)," pp. 305–328, in Donald J. Kagay and L. J. Andrew Villalon, eds., *Crusaders, Condottieri, and Cannon: Medieval Warfare in Societies around the Mediterrean.* Leiden, Netherlands: Brill.

Volckart, Oliver. 2004. "The Economics of Feuding in Late Medieval Germany." *Explorations in Economic History,* vol. 41, no. 3, pp. 282–300.

Von Clausewitz, Carl. 1908. *On War.* London: Kegan Paul.

Von Neumann, John, and Oskar Morgenstern. 1944. *Theory of Games and Economic Behavior.* Princeton, NJ: Princeton University Press.

Waites, Neville. 1984. "Defence Policy: The Historical Context," pp. 27–45, in J. Howorth and P. Chilton, eds., *Defence and Dissent in Contemporary France*. New York: St. Martin's.

Waley, Daniel. 1968. "The Army of the Florentine Republic from the Twelfth to the Fourteenth Century," pp. 70–108, in Nicolai Rubinstein, ed., *Florentine Studies: Politics and Society in Renaissance Florence*. London: Faber and Faber.

———. 1975. *Condotte and Condottieri in the Thirteenth Century*. Italian Lecture. London: British Academy.

———. 1988. *The Italian City-Republics*. 3rd ed. London: Longman.

Walter, Jakob. 1993 [1991]. *The Diary of a Napoleonic Foot Soldier*. Edited by Marc Raeff. New York: Penguin.

Warner, John T., and Beth J. Asch. 1995. "The Economics of Military Manpower," pp. 347–397, in Keith Hartley and Todd Sandler, eds., *Handbook of Defense Economics*, vol. 1. Amsterdam: Elsevier.

Warner, Philip. 1968. *Sieges in the Middle Ages*. London: G. Bell and Sons.

Wasson, James N. 1998. *Innovator or Imitator: Napoleon's Operational Concepts and the Legacies of Bourcet and Guibert*. Ft. Leavenworth, KS: Command and General Staff College.

Webber, Carolyn, and Aaron Wildavsky. 1986. *A History of Taxation and Expenditure in the Western World*. New York: Simon and Schuster.

Webster, Sir Charles, and Noble Frankland. 1961. *The Strategic Air Offensive against Germany, 1939–1945*. 5 vols. London: Her Majesty's Stationary Office (HMSO).

Weigley, Russell F. 2004 [1991]. *The Age of Battles: The Quest for Decisive Warfare from Breitenfeld to Waterloo*. Bloomington, IN: Indiana University Press.

Weinert, Richard P. 1965. "Federal Spies in Richmond." *Civil War Times Illustrated*, vol. 3, no. 10, pp. 28–34.

Weir, William. 1993. *Fatal Victories*. Hamden, CT: Archon.

Werrell, Kenneth P. 1986. "The Strategic Bombing of Germany in World War II: Costs and Accomplishments." *Journal of American History*, vol. 73, no. 3 (December), pp. 702–713.

Westcott, Jan. 1962. *Condottiere*. New York: Random House.

Westermann, Edward B. 2001. *Flak: German Anti-aircraft Defenses, 1914–1945*. Lawrence, KS: University Press of Kansas.

White, Lynn. 1967 [1962]. *Medieval Technology and Social Change*. London: Oxford University Press.

Williamson, Oliver E. 1985. *The Economic Institutions of Capitalism*. New York: Free Press.

———. 1999. "Public and Private Bureaucracies: A Transaction Cost Economics Perspective." *Journal of Law, Economics, and Organization*, vol. 15, no. 1, pp. 306–342.

Windrow, Martin, and Francis K. Mason. 1991 [1975]. *A Concise Dictionary of Military Biography*. New York: John Wiley.

Wintrobe, Ronald. 1998. *The Political Economy of Dictatorship*. Cambridge, UK: Cambridge University Press, 1998.

Wise, Terence. 1976. *Medieval Warfare*. New York: Hastings House.

Wohlstetter, Albert. 1959. "The Delicate Balance of Terror." *Foreign Affairs*, vol. 37 (January), pp. 211–234.

———. 1987. "The Political and Military Aims of Offense and Defense Innovation," pp. 3–36, in Fred S. Hoffman, Albert Wohlstetter, and David S. Yost, eds., *Swords and Shields:*

NATO, the USSR, and New Choices for Long-Range Offense and Defense. Lexington, MA: Lexington Books.

—— et al. 1976. *Moving Toward Life in a Nuclear Armed Crowd?* Los Angeles, CA: Pan Heuristics.

Wolfe, Thomas W. 1965. "Soviet Commentary on the French 'Force de Frappe.'" Memorandum prepared for the Assistant Secretary of Defense for International Security Affairs. Santa Monica, CA: RAND.

Wulf, Herbert. 2005. *Internationalizing and Privatizing War and Peace.* New York: Palgrave Macmillan.

Yildirim, J., and B. Erdinc. 2007. "Conscription in Turkey." *Economics of Peace and Security Journal,* vol. 2, no. 1, pp. 16–19.

Yost, David S. 1986. "French Nuclear Targeting," pp. 127–56, in Desmond Ball and Jeffrey Richardson, eds., *Strategic Nuclear Targeting.* Ithaca, NY: Cornell University Press.

——. 1987. "Strategic Defense in Soviet Doctrine and Force Posture," pp. 123–157, in Fred S. Hoffman, Albert Wohlstetter, and David S. Yost, eds., *Swords and Shields: NATO, the USSR, and New Choices for Long-Range Offense and Defense.* Lexington, MA: Lexington Books.

Zelizer, Viviana. 2005. *The Purchase of Intimacy.* Princeton, NJ: Princeton University Press.

Zoppo, Ciro. 1964. "France as a Nuclear Power," pp. 113–156, in R. N. Rosecrance, ed., *The Dispersion of Nuclear Weapons: Strategy and Politics.* New York and London: Columbia University Press.

INDEX

Page numbers in italics refer to illustrations.

6/13/08